CW01085307

Sex and Cycling

A tour of Yorkshire, with a bit of sex,
and an excursion to Vienna

Stephen Holden

authorHOUSE®

AuthorHouse™ UK
1663 Liberty Drive
Bloomington, IN 47403 USA
www.authorhouse.co.uk
Phone: UK TFN: 0800 0148641 (Toll Free inside the UK)
UK Local: (02) 0369 56322 (+44 20 3695 6322 from outside the UK)

Published by AuthorHouse 02/08/2024

ISBN: 979-8-8230-8609-7 (sc)
ISBN: 979-8-8230-8610-3 (e)

Library of Congress Control Number: 2024901210

Print information available on the last page.

This book is printed on acid-free paper.

CONTENTS

Part 2: "Oh Boy!"

Part 3: "Butterflies"

Part 4: "Son And Lover"

Part 5: "Salt"

Part 6: "Maybe, Baby .... Well, Alright!"

SYNOPSIS

Leela Drake, a 16 years old schoolgirl, begins a friendship and some years later a love affair with an 18 years' old A-level student, Edmund Rice. He is already in a relationship with a woman, Dorothy, somewhat older and more mature than he, but for a short while he retains his attachment to both of them. He is restrained in his sexual desire for the young girl as he feels she needs to mature more before she makes the "ultimate" commitment of physical love. It also becomes clear that while the backgrounds of Edmund and Leela are middle-class in terms of income, their parents have very different styles of life, and different perceptions of their relationship.

They are parted when Edmund is called up to do his two-years National Service, which takes place in Austria, and so he sees little of Leela while he is away. He has a comparatively interesting time in the Army, and in some ways reluctantly decides to return to civilian life. For her, the waiting is romantic and magnifies her desire and love for him. He too finds his feelings for her have not diminished. Soon after his return they make love for the first time.

It soon becomes clear that Leela and Edmund also have views of their affair which are widely apart. Edmund, who likes to picture himself as an idealist, believes in the seriousness and permanency of anything of worth. Leela feels that the moment is just that - and cannot be captured again, however deeply she or Edmund felt at that moment. She is fiercely passionate and sensual, and lives her love through her sexual love as much as in any other way. Edmund is just as physically involved with her, but wants more than merely the experience they have at the moments of intercourse. This incompatibility is heightened when Leela discovers she is pregnant, and eventually the couple decide to end their intimacy. Their baby, a boy, is born and Edmund takes much interest in him and spends time looking after him. He is fascinated by having his own child, although he still hankers after some greater, wider experience and plans to go abroad again. Their families are affected by their affair, but in a great variety of ways, reflecting their differing outlook on life and morality.

This Book 1 ends with the marriage of Leela's brother, John.

THE PLACES AND CHARACTERS

WELLAWNBURY is a prosperous market town and tourist centre in the area of the North Yorkshire Moors. It is quite near to the sea.

PARK LEAT is the house of the Drakes: Leela, her parents, brother John and sister Pauline. See below.

DRAKES	RICES
William b.1908 & Sarah b.1910	Oscar b. 1918 & Vivian b. 1920
John b. 1929	Edmund b. 1938
Leela b. 1940	Marsha b. 1947
Pauline b. 1949	Timothy b. 1949

OTHER CHARACTERS INCLUDE:

Jeremy (Jerry) Jones a Welsh Draughtsman. Edmund's friend and colleague at his work place, a Council Planning Office in Wellawnbury. Kitty Hopeness - Leela's best friend, and colleague at Barclays Bank in Wellawnbury.

Part 1

“UNCHAINED MELODY”

CHAPTER ONE

Saturday morning, 9 a.m., April, 1956

"Catching you, Nip!", exclaimed one youngster, in breathless triumph.

"Not a hope!" rejoined another.

Two young boys, about 11 or 12, were having a private race on their bikes and circled round near to Edmund, as youngsters tend to do, and as he looked across the car park, he was aware of one head, blurred with speed, followed by another.

For Edmund, it was like the persistent oscillation of a pendulum, this to-and-fro across his vision, on that crisp, bright spring morning in the Co-op car park in Wellawnbury. Edmund Rice breathed the fresh morning air and smiled to himself. He was 18 years old, and studying at the local Boys' Grammar School for 'A' level Technical Drawing, Art and Geography. He was quite tall, and attractive to the girls: blond with grey-blue eyes and aloof enough to always appear interesting.

Glancing down as he sat astride the cross-bar of his own bike, he noticed the two machines of the two young boys were almost identical, seemingly, except for the colour. One was bright blue, the other purple. Both had derailleur gears, and both bikes were, he guessed, just a few days old. Some yards further off, and by the low wall, were the parents of the two boys, clucking with anxious pleasure towards their offspring.

Edmund was waiting, with the other members of the cycle club, for the late-comers to get there, so they could set off on their Saturday trip. George Bartram, Secretary of the club, in profile looking like an alert but friendly ferret, and surrounded by a dozen or so cyclists ready to venture forth, looked towards him and shouted:

"You two stop riding round like two mad things! You'll make young Edmund dizzy!"

And they did stop, immediately, and took their pose, together, nudging and prodding, and giggling, astride, like

Edmund (their secret hero), and near to him. Edmund smiled at them as George walked towards them, having left his bike propped up against the wall some yards away.

"Edmund, I think we'll go. There're twelve of us now. Supposed to be another two coming. Girls from the Old Oak Grammar School. Probably too cold for them I suppose!"

Edmund nodded towards the car park entrance as George finished speaking, as he saw two girls on cycles arriving, one dark and pony-tailed, the other fair, with hair in two bobs, either side of her head, looking eager and fresh, mused Edmund, a little like a young Doris Day.

"Ah! Welcome girls!", and George scurried over to them, shaking their hands and introducing himself. He turned to the main group and raised his voice:

"OK everyone! We are now ready to go. I will lead, David will take the rear, and Edmund - can you stay roughly in the middle to try to keep us together? Please remember - road care and courtesy is our watch word! And if you're struggling, don't suffer in silence! Signal to David, or Edmund or me like this.", and he waved his right hand in slowing down mode, "then stop as soon as it's safe, and you will be attended to. For the rest of the group, unless it's an emergency, just carry on. Nothing to be gained by all of us stopping if one of us needs a breather! If you haven't read the plan for today, I'll remind you that we're going to make our first stop at Blackstone Abbey, a distance of about 10 miles, and have some refreshment and a look round. We'll then return via Hartstone Vale, a further 8 miles, and imbibe the beautiful river Eden from Pike Bridge, and have lunch. Has anyone not got their lunch? Good! We'll be able to get snacks and tea at all our stops, I imagine. We will take the Wolburgh road back here, about 6 miles. It will be a 24 mile round trip, so if any of you have any second thoughts, please indicate now. Excellent! It's really not too bad anyway, just three steepish climbs, and if you need to, stop as indicated and someone will walk with you if necessary. You will not be abandoned!"

He'd finished, and beamed at everyone, looking very pleased with himself. Everyone had turned up this morning, and he was looking forward to the trip.

David, George's son and a fanatical cyclist, waved the

group to follow his father out of the car park and into the main road, but they had to wait as a blinkered horse hauled the morning's milk trailer back to the depot.

A cycle-friendly car stopped to let them out, as they snaked, some uncertainly, others swerving slightly, following the leader down the road. It was tricky to be sure everyone negotiated safely the staggered vehicles on that Saturday morning road, bare legs and coloured shirts flagging their progress. Almost all the bikes had one or two water bottles spiked with plastic drinking straws, on the front of their handlebars. At the town centre traffic island, with enjoyed and exaggerated alertness by George Bartram as he looked back at the group - shouting to the youngsters to "look out for that car"! The group wobbled in an ungainly string around the island, and then into the open road, where they could see the black and white sign declaring "Burley 6 miles, Blackstone Abbey 10 miles ".

They made their first stop with few events - chains leaving sprockets the only significant interference on the planned course. There was the fatigue of cycling up steep hills, and the ecstatic relief of freewheeling down.

Flushed-faces, panting breath, red legs and bulging veins were there, in the leading group, where the older boys and George set the pace. It was not only these usual things that Edmund loved about these cycling jaunts, and even the smell of the tarmac, although subdued in the cool spring air, was a perfume to his senses.

After some time, he knew they were approaching the Abbey, and he could see, some distance ahead, the leaders turn into the Abbey park gates. George looked around, and indicated in a great and histrionic flourish to "turn right here".

They all gathered at the massive ruin which was the gate house, and after a quick check by George, they propped their machines in the small grassy courtyard bearing the notice "CYCLES".

Inside the gate house there was a permanent exhibition with plans, maps and descriptions through the whole experience of this holy place, to its sacking and looting by Henry VIII.

Edmund was engrossed in some of this great history, written on documents secured inside a glass-topped table in the centre of the building, set level on the otherwise very roughly cobbled floor. He felt the cool breeze blowing through this crumbling edifice set goose pimples on his arm, and looked up to see those old columns, perhaps being seen as they had been seen over 400 years ago, he mused. He returned to the narrative, but in a few moments he became aware of someone nearby. He looked around to see a girl silhouetted in one of the doorways, through which the bright sunlight streamed only to be swallowed up by the cold dark space.

"Is it interesting?", the girl asked.

"Oh! I suppose so. I'm reading it, anyway." He recognised her as one of the cyclists, the dark-haired grammar school girl.

"Instead of enjoying the beautiful sunshine!" she laughed.

"I can do that too!", he said, laughing and walking quickly towards her, ushered her through the doorway. As he emerged, he involuntarily squinted to avoid the blinding sunlight. They walked together, in silence, down the narrow pathway which led to the main Abbey ruins. A large dragonfly escorted them, darting effortlessly in every direction in turn, till he tired of the game, and disappeared into the bushes.

"It's the first time I've seen you on one of our trips", said Edmund, glancing down towards her.

"And it's the first time I've seen you!", she laughed, almost defiantly, ignoring an invitation for refreshment.

"I'm Edmund, what's your name?"

"Leela"

"Unusual name! How did you come to be called 'Leela'?"

"It was Dad's idea. A friend of his from Poland had named his daughter Leela, and she died at the age of 3 of smallpox. I'm not sure I like being named after a dead girl, but I'm now just about used to it."

"It isn't such a bad name.", said Edmund, lying chivalrously.

"Don't bother being kind about it! I've resented it for most of my life. Now I'm resigned to it. In fact I almost like it! Like a mole on the face, it's become a beauty spot!"

"Do you find the cycling tiring?"

"No, no, not at all. I cycle a great deal anyway. This day I wanted to get Kitty out with me. She's looking for a boyfriend at the moment, and she seems to have run out of availables at the local dances!"

"There aren't many free ones here, today, with us.", he said.

"She seems to have latched onto someone already. That's why I left her and came to see what you were doing."

"Oh!"

"Don't worry, Edmund. I'm not looking for a boyfriend. I've just finished with one and I'm in purdah now. You're safe. Kitty's found one, and I'm not looking. So you can relax."

"How do you know I'm not looking for a girlfriend?", he asked quietly.

"I can tell. I know I'm not bad looking, and I can see that you're more interested in my cycling ability than me."

"You're very direct", he said, stopping by a gate and looking out into an area of stones, where several people were picking their way, peering down, whispering to each other.

"Take me out tonight, Edmund. To the Carlton. It's not your scene, I suppose, but I'll pay if you like and I'll teach you how to bop."

"What? Well, I suppose ... but why?"

"See over there", and Leela was pointing a long, thin finger to the distance, where a dancing Doris Day was hand-in-hand with a beaming, glowingly proud young male member of the cycle club.

"She'll be OK for a week at least, and she'll take him to the dance tonight. So will you take me?"

"Yes. And... er... I'll promise to take more interest in you!"

Kitty and her new boy friend had seen Leela and Edmund, and were running towards them laughing and screaming gleefully like little children.

"Leela" gasped Kitty, "this is Gerald!"

"Kitty!" exclaimed Leela, "and this is Edmund!"

"Yes I know. He's the one who copes with stragglers. None today, though. We all kept up! Gerald, let's go to the other bit", and she pointed over to another area of ruins.

They ran off, and Edmund now looked closely at his

companion. Whilst he found her daunting in manner, her face was soft and, he thought, lovely. Her skin was dark, and her eyes and hair were almost black. She was slim, and walked quickly, swinging her hips as she did so.

"Hold this!" she commanded, and he took a large hair grip from her proffered hand. She tied her hair, and was looking down the path, and he was looking down on her, and he now experienced something quite unique for him. He almost audibly gasped at his feeling of desire for her, quickly doused by guilt, confusion and later, torment. Yet he couldn't deny it. Her eyes flashed at some target in the distance, and she kept with clenched teeth a hairpin as she tugged and threw her hair into place.

"OK!" she said, smiling up at him, and took the hair grip, and slotted it into the back of her hair.

"Do I look alright?", she asked, with the unexpected uncertainty of a little girl.

"Wonderful", he said, involuntarily, but truthfully, and she blushed brightly, and smiled, and tugged at his forearm to follow her down the pathway.

Later he remembered that pathway walk. He

remembered walking through shafts of sunlight clouded with dusty pollen, the jumping swirls which are the love-dance of midges, the bright stones shining through deep red clay where they walked.

"I think Gerald has a girlfriend", he said suddenly as they came to the open space.

"As usually happens", replied Leela "and I suppose we'll get that story soon today unless Gerald is a rat."

"Not at all. He's a good bloke, I believe", said Edmund "well, the Carlton idea seems superfluous, I suppose?"

"Yes, forget it."

He nodded, and shrugged his shoulders; in some ways sorry to miss the bop lesson. As they were talking they picked their way through the stones and broken columns for a little time until Edmund heard George calling to him:

"Better be off now, Edmund! Collect who you can from this area!", as he drew a circle with his arm to indicate the open area. Edmund nodded and seeing two of the cycle party, made towards them, and called for them to get back to the cycles. Seemingly from the air, Kitty bobbed up, smiling, but obviously crestfallen:

"He has a girl. And he won't go out with me!", she said with mock jocularity.

Head down, with Leela's arm around her waist, the two girls walked slowly back to the Abbey entrance, whilst Edmund, peering around massive broken stone screens, checked for stragglers.

Soon the colourful, wobbly brigade set out with George heading off to the right on the main road towards Hartstone Vale. This highway was an uninterrupted snake of a road, boarded with scrub, sometimes limestone walls, and boasted the early spring flowers. Winding, it seemed to Leela, over endless grey-black roads, occasionally a car would pass them, usually with a long "Peep" or two or three short "Beepeeps", sometimes a catcall for the girls from white-shirted young men, freshly oiled hair spinning in the wind as they craned from the vehicle's windows.

CHAPTER TWO

After 5 miles they met the steepest of their climbs for this trip. As if to give cruel hope, the road at first gently sloped downwards and the task was easy, and pleasant, and one could take in the cool breeze, and the fresh spring countryside. Then a short levelling off, followed by at first a gentle, then rapidly increasing upward climb. Edmund watched as he stood up to his pedalling, to see one, two, then three or four, of the group give up the mechanical option, and determined to walk the steepest slope of the hill. In particular, he noticed Kitty wobbling almost over the whole width of the road, and soon her bike fell away from her, and she, red and damp with sweat, giggling and gasping, picked up her bike and made way to the left side of the road to push her cycle up the hill. Ahead of her, Leela was now in difficulties, but attacked the burden with forceful zeal, and actually accelerated slightly up the hill. Edmund stopped by Kitty and the others who were now off their cycles.

"We'll have a steady walk to the top. It's about quarter of a mile", he lied, it being nearer half a mile to the summit. Even the prospect of half this distance had elicited a groaning chorus of "Ohhh!" from the unseated cyclists. They soon caught up with Leela, who had now forsaken her bike and waited for the group to join her.

"You liar Edmund", she laughed in low tones as she joined him, "it's at least half a mile or more!" "I know, Leela, but perception is important in the psychology of stress."

"From where are you quoting?", she asked.

"Oh! Some sort of manual I read an extract from some years ago. Something to do with the commandos in the war, I think. You seem to know this road, anyway."

"Yes, and I rarely make it to the top. But it is worth the effort. Hey!" she exclaimed "why are your peddles going round all the time. And...", she continued, looking more closely at this bike "why have you only one cog on the rear wheel and no gears - and, only one brake?"

"Oh!" he replied "this is called a fixed wheel. It gives you more control of the bike, and the gear is quite low, so it's not too bad. The fixed cog is the rear brake. Well, I'm now used to it I suppose."

"Weird!", exclaimed Leela, but smiled her approval of his 'difference'.

After some more minutes, peppered with groans, and gasping breath, and laughter, and vows never to cycle again, and being passed by one or two struggling motor cars grinding their way to the summit of the hill, they reached the top, to view to their left, the lush valley of the river which formed the Hartstone Vale. They could now hear the gurgle and splash of the stream falling nearby, and down the hillside, to open into a wider river, and down there were more cyclists, and a few motorcars. Further on, a proud blue and cream bus, sporting a beautifully painted swirling "Parkinson's Tours" on its side, was in attendance for the day trippers. And further still, by the open water, children called and splashed in pleasure as the sunshine danced on the rippling river in a merry chorus.

All Edmund's party could now sit astride their machines,

and freewheel down to the valley bottom without effort, although Edmund had to cycle, of course, to the glee of Leela, and Kitty, who she had told, and they both looked at his peddling quickly, both thinking what a waste of effort there was here! Young Tim, about Leela's age, held out his legs in a comical fork aspect, to let *his* fixed pedals chase each other around unattended:

"'Ey! Look 'ere!", in a broad Yorkshire accent as he took his hands also from the machine, holding them aloft in a great 'V' as he screamed: "I'm Superboy!"

George looked around, and his black gaze was enough to restore feet to pedals and hands to the bars:

"Do that again and you're banned!", exclaimed George. But amongst the other boys, Tim was the hero of the day.

The cycle party clustered in a small wooded area near to the grassy bank of the river, and George counted the group, and seeing all was as it should be, announced:

"Can we synchronise watches, people? By me it is now... ten minutes to twelve o'clock. Good time to eat! Leave your machines here. They'll be quite safe, as I'll attach this long cable and padlock them all up. But remove any water bottles or slide-on lights you have or you'll lose them. There is I see a snacks and drinks hut over there, and the borders of the woods and river Eden offer a lovely glimpse of spring flowers and other plants. Water is lovely, fresh and clear, but if you paddle close by the river, take care as there are many leeches. Don't worry if you get a passenger, he won't hurt you, he only wants to suck your blood!" he laughed, and the party laughed lightly, and groaned quietly, and buzzed to each other with stories of leeches and other horrible things there might be in the water.

"Hope I didn't seem to be so awful to that friend of yours. Kitty, I mean.", said Gerald, quietly into Edmund's ear as the latter gathered his sandwich bag and water bottles from his bike.

"She wasn't known to me before today", replied Edmund "but I think she'll be alright. It was better you did it now than stringing her along."

Gerald nodded, his brow furrowed as if in deep thought and contemplation. He went on, quietly, hoarsely, in a faltering embarrassing way:

"I mean, I didn't spoil it for you, did I? I don't know how you and Dot are at the moment?"

"Oh no... don't worry, Gerald at all about that" said Edmund, patting him lightly on the back. The other smiled and walked away.

Dorothy (Dot) Burns came into Edmund's thoughts for the first time that day. Dot at 21 years, was a little older than he was, and had brought a little sexual experience with her, and had enthusiastically persuaded him to have intercourse with her after they had know each other for only a few weeks. As well as this, he did have a happy relationship with her. She was interested in foreign films and liked smoking French cigarettes. Edmund didn't smoke, but approved of her doing so, and liked the smell and taste of the tobacco in her mouth when they kissed. His mother chastised him for smelling like "an ash tray", but did not totally disapprove of Dot, who she thought was the sort of girl to help bring her son to manhood. These and other related images and sounds were flitting inside Edmund's head as he walked towards the river, when he felt a gentle prod in the small of his back.

"Only me!", said Kitty, smiling, blue eyes glistening, her hair-bobs, newly tidied, bouncing slightly on either side of her round face. She continued:

"Could you do me a favour? Leela will be here shortly... she's just gone over there... ", she was pointing to the toilets," before she gets back, because she'll kill me if she hears me suggesting it. Anyway, Edmund, you seem like a really kind, good man. So... will you come with us next weekend on a cycle trip to Brough Cove? And if so, can you bring another man. I wouldn't expect someone as nice as you, but you can try?"

Edmund was taken aback, and why had he been put with Leela? ... but thinking quickly as Kitty looked nervously around:

"I'll do my best with another male. And I can certainly make Brough Cove next weekend. If fact, if the weather is good, it will be an ideal trip!"

"Oh ... great!" And she jumped a little on both feet, and squeezed Edmund's arm and pulling him closer, kissed him on the cheek. They were soon joined by Leela, and decided to get some tea and sit down near the river, in a spot Edmund knew well. Having all sat down, they were eating and drinking, and Edmund was aware of those blue eyes flashing towards him, and smiling at him, and so he said, after they had talked of small things for some minutes:

"This has been a good weekend, girls. What if we had another trip, we, and maybe I could arrange a foursome?"

"We were planning to go to Brough Cove, Edmund. You could join us, couldn't he, Leela?"

"Why not? Who's the fourth?" asked Leela, not betraying for an instant that she realised what had happened before she had joined them.

"Er, well, I'll find someone. A good chap! Don't worry!" And he laughed, feeling acutely uncomfortable.

"Where will we meet?", asked an increasingly enthusiastic Kitty.

"Where do we all live?", asked Edmund, looking at each of the girls in turn.

"I live at Parkleat, on the Brough road, but Dad can bring me and my bike to town. That makes it easier for Kitty, as she lives in Markham."

"Oh, then we'll meet in the car park, as we did today", said Edmund.

"Does that give you a long ride to town?", asked Kitty.

"Not really. I live out on the Spikedale road."

"Miles away!", exclaimed Leela.

"It's not too bad. And anyway I cycle to town most weekends to join the club, before a trip, like we did today. I won't suffer. Let's say... town centre car park, at 9 o'clock, next Saturday."

On their return, they stopped at an Inn, the elders taking beer, the others lemonade or dandelion and burdock.

The following Monday, Edmund asked a friend from his school, a colleague in the 'A' level technical drawing class called Barry Wooley, if he'd like to complete the planned foursome.

"I would, Edmund. Sounds like it could be good fun."

So it was settled. Edmund didn't know Barry too well, but he seemed 'pretty stable', he thought, and honest, as far as he knew. Anyway, one day-trip shouldn't be too bad.

At the car park on that Saturday morning, Edmund was

the first to arrive, 15 minutes early, and took the opportunity to observe the early morning bustle of town. His father, a general practitioner, had an early call, and he'd heard his car leave at seven o'clock, and couldn't get back to sleep, so he had set off early from home. The morning was fine, and not too cold. His bare legs were already pink and warm from the ride to town, and he felt good. Kitty and Leela arrived together, and joined Edmund in bright and cheerful mood. It was only five past 9 when Barry arrived, and the introductions done, they set off, girls ahead, as usual, so they couldn't fall behind.

Barry and Edmund cycled abreast of each other, and chatted easily at the leisurely pace set by the girls.

"Must say it's a nice view from here!", laughed Barry, observing the two females waddling and swaying in their saddles.

"I wonder what we look like?", said Edmund.

Once away from the town centre, this road to Brough Cove was narrow, but level, and the destination, everyone knew, was not too far. It was a favourite bike ride for all town cyclists. As they turned off the main road towards the cove and the sea sands, Edmund sprinted ahead and waved them down in the direction of a large wooden hut, which was a Café, perched where the grass is just beginning the give way to the sand. The group stopped, and Edmund suggested they took some tea.

They sat around a wooden table inside the hut, and swapped stories of their lives, of school, exams, future, films they had seen lately, and so on. Edmund told Leela of his father, who was a local GP, and mother, also a doctor, but who had retired from full-time medicine, and who loved flowers and gardens. Leela, he learned, was the daughter of a local fruit and vegetable merchant, William Drake, and she was studying for her GCE 'O' levels in the coming summer.

"Hey!" said Kitty, remembering something "do you realise that 'Rock around the Clock' is on at the Regent next week?"

"What's that? American music?" asked Edmund.

"Oh, it's Rock and Roll. It is an American craze.

Suppose ..." Barry said, looking to each of them in turn "we could go and take a look-see?"

"Sounds brilliant!" exclaimed Kitty "you'll go as well, Leela? And Edmund?"

"I don't mind, I suppose," said the other girl "do you want to go, Edmund?"

"Well, I think... yes, why not?"

Later, leaving their bikes in the safety of the café car park, they walked the half mile across the grass and sand to the beach, where a brisk breeze was blowing, and the sharp sand hurt their bare legs.

"Let's run to the sea, to get away from all this sand!", shouted Kitty as she ran down the beach. Barry looked around, and Edmund nodded, and Barry ran after her, as Leela laughed lightly, eyeing him curiously:

"You didn't look too sure about going to the pictures.", began Leela.

"Not really my music. If fact, I don't like music very much I suppose. If it's got a beat, it will keep me awake."

"If not I'll pinch you!" she laughed, and jerked his arm, "You really are the coldest fish in the sea, Edmund!"

“Sorry”, and he was really embarrassed, and sad, to have been adjudged so wanting by his new companion.

“However”, she went on “I’ll bet there’s a little flickering ember somewhere down there!”

Edmund wanted to tell her that Dot had told him he was the most passionate man she had had, that he was very enthusiastic about sex, and that he found her increasingly attractive.

“Hm!” she exclaimed, now looking into his eyes, “there certainly are a few cogs grinding around now, lad!”

Edmund laughed, but of course did not share his thoughts. He realised that this 16 years old girl seemed to have more of a grasp of him in some ways than Dot, several years her senior.

“Kitty and Barry seem to have hit it off!” shouted Edmund, above the wind, which now gusted sharply, throwing the sand up into their faces. Through this cloud they could see Kitty and Barry, closely linked, and sometimes kissing, and even at this long and cloudy distance, the bright beaming smile of Kitty seemed to defiantly pierce the murky air.

"Well, Edmund, Kitty is... well, not meaning this as an insult to her at all, but she's very easy going... and, well quite frankly, very easy in every way, if you know what I mean. She is the most wonderful, warm person you could have as a friend and a lover. But because she can't play hard-to-get, so boys take advantage of her. She is only sixteen, but she's had so many boyfriends, usually a lot older than her, and not very nice people.", she stopped, suddenly "I really shouldn't have said all this to you, Edmund. I just wanted to say, she's one of life's tragic people, I think. Her friends should try to look after her."

"Barry is OK, I believe, and he doesn't have a girlfriend."

"Yes, Edmund, but ... well, she can't be kept on a lead!"

"No, she can't", he agreed "even though it would probably be the best thing for her ... we could tie some string around her ankle!" he laughed.

"Around *both* ankles, Edmund! If you know what I mean!" and she laughed and giggled furiously, leaning against his body. He pressed her close to him, against the biting wind, whilst the screams and yelps of Kitty seem to float directionless around them.

CHAPTER THREE

The following week the four went to the Regent cinema to see 'Rock around the Clock'. To his own surprise, Edmund watched with increasing interest, as he hadn't seen such a film ever before. The youngsters in the picture appeared to be in charge, he thought. Kitty and Barry were squeezed together so tightly that Leela and Edmund had a surprising amount of room in the back stalls. And all around them, in the preceding supporting programme, there was the sound and shadows of teenage love. Murmurings, followed by a rustle of clothing, the liquid snapping of juvenile kisses; and the crinkly shiny outline of a young male head, rolling with passion, against the squashed hair, stiff with lacquer, of his girl, who struggled less and less to keep his hands from her breasts. Kitty and Barry, next to Leela, were locked in mouth to mouth contact for much of this time, and Edmund noted that his Barry's hand seemed to be beneath Kitty's skirts.

Edmund and Leela, by contrast, did not touch during the whole show, and neither of them thought this unusual or strange.

At the end of the film, which they all enjoyed in various ways, they parted; Barry to walk Kitty to her bus stop, and Edmund to wait with Leela for her father to come in the car to collect her from the square, her last bus having left some time before the end of the film.

"Are you sure you have a bus?", asked Leela as they walked to the town square "Dad will be happy to run you home first."

"No, I'm sure. The last bus tonight is quarter past eleven, here, from the square. I've caught it before. When I've missed it, I've walked, anyway."

"Long way though." she said.

"Not more than three miles, although it is uphill. But, possible, if necessary; which it isn't tonight." Edmund paused, thinking, and went on: "Leela - do you have a phone at home? I mean, do you mind if I phone you sometime?"

"Yes - do that... here's one of Dad's letter heads", as she passed him an old shopping list she had kept in her pocket, and added:

"Anyway you wouldn't escape that easily ... I know your phone number. It's on the town chemist's window. You know, the notice giving the duty doctor's phone numbers."

"Oh yes, of course. Interesting you should know that. I didn't!"

"Why should you?" asked Leela, smiling, and shuffling close to him.

Soon enough a large, dark Humber saloon car appeared in the road, and Leela waved towards the driver. The car pulled over and stopped, and the driver, Leela's father got out of the car and first of all smiled broadly towards his daughter, then less broadly to Edmund, to whom he nodded slightly. He was a tall man with a big frame and flat, open face with clear blue, searching eyes:

"Alright, love?" he asked.

"Yes, Dad. This is Edmund, Dr Rice's son."

"Pleased to meet you, young man. Thank you for looking after my daughter. Can I give you a lift home?"

"No, Mr Drake. My bus will soon be here. Thanks, all the same."

Edmund watched the vehicle pull out into the empty road, and accelerate gently to the road junction, to turn left towards Parkleat. When he turned round, his Red and Cream double-decker bus had arrived.

* * *

Later that week on one afternoon Edmund (now on school holidays) saw Dot, his girlfriend, who seemed curiously bursting with anticipation on meeting him. They sat in a café in town, sipping barely warm almost tasteless coffee, and talked of Edmund's pending exams, which were soon after the Easter holiday. However, Dot was not really interested:

"I hear you're two-timing me!" she said to him, pursing her lips.

"Oh, yes, I suppose I am in way. I took this girl to the pictures. But really, only because we wanted to accompany her friend."

"I didn't realise how altruistic you were", laughed Dot,

her slender hands opening out in mock surprise. She was a tall girl, as tall as he, and almost plump in body, but thin limbed in a curiously incongruous way. Her hair was dark brown, thick and quite long, artificially curled in tight bunches, and her deep coloured eyes flashed with passion and enjoyment. Tonight she wore large pendulous earrings studded with crystal glass which bobbed and swung as she talked to him in her animated way. Smiles almost burst from her face, and her eyes twinkled mischievously:

"So I have to share you now, Edmund, do I? Or are you finishing with me?"

"No, Dot, I'm not finishing with you. Leela's just a friend. She's only a young girl. Hardly sixteen."

"Ah... sixteen. Only sixteen ....

"Even so, I would think you are a man who can only have a relationship with a woman which is also sexual, Edmund. Your passion, which I feel even now, as we speak, and sip this dreadful coffee, is so great you cannot control it, I think, even when society casts a curse on such feelings as lust."

"What about relations? Mother? Sister?"

"You probably do not have a relationship of any sort with your sister Marsha. I've met her. And with your mother.?"

"I don't have sex with her!"

"No? Not yet? In your mind?"

"No! It's ridiculous. It would not even cross my mind. Not for one moment."

"Perhaps it exists in your mind, though. Somewhere in that steady, calm body of yours. You have this great passion, Eddy. Mothers who give that to their sons do not like to share it. What does she feel? You do not know. But I have seen her look at you, and I'm not so sure she has merely protective feelings towards you. It's not to be spoken of, of course, Edmund! But you read Freud, Edmund. Much of what he says is, of course, ridiculous, but he does feel life, in some way. Like we do. And he has experience and knowledge to interpret what he feels. Do you know what I mean? ..." She grasped his hand and rubbed his fingers, and she smiled at him, a smile which he had to return, though he was feeling uncomfortable with these conjectures, and would have dismissed them from his mind, had he not had an intense feeling of respect for Dorothy and her thoughts and opinions.

It was she who had introduced him to some little talks on philosophy and psychology, and best of all, the classical French Cinema. He loved these films, which they regularly shared at the town's Film Club, as much as she did. It was on a visit to the club (taken out of curiosity on his part) that he had first met her.

Dot smiled at him, and lit a cigarette, and exhaled into his face, as he liked. He breathed the pungent French tobacco smoke with relish, and feeling almost drunk now, looked over to her lasciviously, and taking her hand into both of his he grasped her firmly.

"Are you having sex with this girl yet?"

"No! As I said, she's only a friend. And she's too young."

"She isn't, or you wouldn't waste time on her. I'm sorry if that seems cruel, but it's true. And you are a bit of a liar, Edmund. Especially when it's a point of principle for you."

"I don't think I understand that. I'm sure I should be insulted, though." he said, smiling.

"I suppose you're not having sex with her. Not yet, at least ... In some ways that's disappointing, as at this moment, Eddy, you have only me to compare me to. That is frustrating for someone as big-headed as me!"

She laughed, and blew a cloud of smoke high into the air. Others in the café glanced over to her, smelling the strange tobacco, hearing the loud conversation of this "funny girl". But Edmund now had senses only for her. He could smell the smoke, see Dot, as she threw her head back and laughed at him, feel her strong, warm hand in his. His mouth was dry, and he felt within his loins this unspeakable longing and lust for her, which seemed to take him over sometimes, which in some ways he could not reconcile with anything else he knew about himself. It was easy, too, since Dorothy was sterile. He looked away from her, and down towards the floor.

"Can we go? To your flat?"

"Yes, let's go, Edmund, or you'll implode, I think!"

They walked the short distance to her flat, which she had taken as her first place away from home. She was in her first job in Wellawnbury, leaving her home town of

Sheffield, to be a trainee commercial artist after taking an Art Diploma in her local Art School. Her extravagant "Artiness" had camouflaged the shortcomings she certainly had in her technique.

Inside, the flat was dark, but quite warm, and when she had switched on the lights, ghostly half illuminated images appeared on the walls. Bamboo curtains stood in the doorway between the living-cum-bedroom and the kitchen, and a smell of peppery olive oil pervaded the atmosphere.

"Go there and sit down, Eddy. I'll pour some wine."

He sat down on the chaise longue. There were few pieces of substantial furniture in the large room. An easy chair, three Victorian dining chairs, a very old, gate legged dining table, with an unlit candle in a saucer, in the centre, and a large bookcase, brimming with books and magazines.

"Let's toast Leela!", announced Dot, appearing from the kitchen with two glasses of red wine, and handing one of them to Edmund: "may she be the love of your life. For a few weeks, anyway.", and she laughed, sitting down next to Edmund, and he smiled, and drank some wine, and put his arm around Dot's shoulder as she leaned heavily against him.

He awoke, blinked and swallowed; tasting wine and sex; and then looking up, saw the huge pre-Raphaelite print of a girl, glued to the ceiling, staring down benignly on the spent lovers. Edmund smiled and could imagine her saying "Well that was very nice, now can we pick some flowers?"

He tried to slide quietly out of the bed, but instead stumbled, and Dot turned to him:

"Stay with me just long enough for me to have some good coffee and a cigarette. Then you can go, as I have some work to do."

She patted to the kitchen naked, and Edmund sat on the edge of the bed waiting for the coffee. They sat together talking little, Dot frowning as she smoked heavily, blowing clouds of the acrid fumes: "Just have a look at this, Edmund.", she said, handing him a stiff board of scraper work: "does it look... interesting?"

He glanced at the work, comprising a view of a pair of binoculars.

"Suppose so. Well, if I was going to buy some binoculars, it would be interesting."

"You think it's OK? The client apparently said particularly that he wanted them to look 'interesting'. I don't fucking know how you judge a picture of a pair of field glasses interesting or boring.", she threw the board onto a chair, and smiling, approached Edmund and put her arms around his bare body: "You must leave, or I'll have to have more of you, and I can't afford the time tonight. Call me next week, if you want to."

The following week they met at the film club, at Dot's excited insistence.

"Tonight they're showing one of the great films of all time, Edmund", she said to him, as he sipped a lemonade, and she smoked cigarettes, as they sat in the grimy foyer of the club, bedecked as it was in dozens of old posters of great film shows.

"You will, really enjoy this, I'm sure."

"What is it?" asked Edmund.

"'Les Enfants du Paradis'. 'Children of the Gods'. It's a French film, of course. Produced during the war, would you believe. I've seen it before, but it's a film you will want to see many times, Edmund."

Soon, they and the other members shuffled into the claustrophobia of the tiny cinema, already thick with cigarette smoke.

After the film they went to a nearby pub, and both settled for a drink of beer.

"You didn't like it?", she asked him.

"Yes, I did. However, some of it was too sentimental, and I think it's a bit too long. At least, it was for me."

"You need to have a mood, and maybe you can never have this mood, Edmund" she said quietly, as tears fell slowly from her eyes into her lap. She took out a handkerchief to dry her face.

"Is something wrong?", he asked anxiously.

"Yes, in some ways. I have the offer of a new job in Leeds with the same firm, but better money and perhaps more opportunities for the future ..."

"That's good, isn't it?" he enquired.

"For me, I don't know. For you, maybe it's irrelevant.", and she cried again.

"No, I was thinking of your career. And Leeds isn't so far away. I'm taking my test soon, and I'll be able to drive there, if you want to see me ....."

"Oh! Leeds or London, it doesn't matter!", she said, looking almost angry now: "We - you and I - we can't go any further. I'm nearly 22, several previous owners, a bit dumpy and well, I can't compete successfully with a sixteen year old virgin .... If you really like her, and I've seen how beautiful she is in the town the other day, and she falls for you, I'll not be in the picture, Edmund. And if it's not her, it will be someone else."

"I'm not thinking of finishing with you. I told you that. I wanted to go back with you tonight."

"You may not finish with me yet, but you will, Edmund. You perhaps do not realise your own ruthlessness. Perfection is cruel, Edmund. And that is what you are seeking.", and she broke into tears again. Edmund moved his seat next to her, and putting his arm around her, comforted her, and spoke little phrases of shared experiences with her, and she eventually smiled through her tears, and her red eyes shone again: "Thanks, Eddy. I'm OK now."

"Can I come back with you?" he asked.

"Silly boy! Do you think I'd let you go after all I've been through tonight!", she laughed, and grabbed his arm, and they left quickly into the cold night air.

CHAPTER FOUR

A week later, Edmund phoned Leela, suggesting a picnic some miles away up the coast, on the cliffs, to go in his mother's car, he having just passed his test.

As he drove to the town centre on that spring Saturday morning, he could seen her from afar, as she sat on a low wall, looking down, dressed in black skirt, dark pullover, white blouse ...

"Here I am! No bumps yet!", and she smiled at him, and got in the car, which set off with remarkable certainty, she thought, and they were soon on the open road.

"I sometimes cycle to this spot. It's some miles on from Brough Cove, and it's set high up on the cliffs, with a spectacular view, and some little hollows to shield us from the wind!"

The road undulated across Dales' country, with craggy limestone set in the rolls of grass on either side. Smatterings of spring flowers dotted the greenery, and Leela looking out said:

"I've been up here sometimes. There are carpets of yellow flowers."

"Cowslips", he said, nodding towards her: "and you'll have seen those butterflies here?"

"Oh!" she remembered:" yes - the blue ones. Yes. I know."

In half an hour they turned off to the right, and down a rough narrow road, which eventually petered out altogether, but Edmund continued a little, and parked the car on the grass, near a large out crop of rock, to afford them some shelter. Leela gasped as she got out as beyond where the car was parked, the sea was 200 feet below them now, and she could hear the crashing of the waves against the rocks, and venturing further she could see a great rock, Black Rock, which rose from the sea almost it seemed to their level, and white water swirled furiously all around the promontory. Herring Gulls screamed at the sea, and at them, in their usual bad tempered way. Even when they got their share of the picnic, Leela knew that they would still be petulant, and annoyed, and seemingly ungrateful of the world in all its forms.

"Let's eat", shouted Edmund above the sea's roar, and she joined him in the shelter he'd so craftily found. On a cloth, there were sandwiches, fruit, and a bottle of wine:

"I've cut some salmon, beef and cheese sandwiches for us... there are here various sauces and chutney, and of course mustard."

"A real feast, Edmund!"

They ate well, as both were hungry. Later, a squall blew up, and they sheltered in the car, each with a glass of wine.

"That was so good, Edmund! Lovely food, and such a dramatic spot. Pity it rained."

"Well, at least we have a car rather than out bikes!"

"Are we going out with each other, Edmund? I don't really care for the expression, as it seems to be pretty meaningless, but all my girlfriends are asking me. What should I say to them, do you think?"

She looked up at him, over her glass, knowing from

other boys her coquettishness was usually attractive, smiling. He looked back down at her, feeling the lust arise within him, and looked away, feeling she was too young, or inexperienced, or didn't know enough ...

"I suppose at the moment we're just friends, sharing days out together."

"And that doesn't mean we're going out together?"

"Not necessarily.", he said, looking forward, then to the side towards the sea, and the birds, and the wind and the rain.

<u>A storm in a coffee-cup</u>

She phoned him some days later.

"Edmund! There's a production of Shakespeare's 'Tempest' at the Playhouse next week. Would you like to go? It's the set play for English Literature this year, and I'd like to talk about what you think about it afterwards. Will you go? I'll pay."

Edmund picked her up at her house the following Friday, having borrowed his mother's car for the trip. She scurried out to the car as soon as she saw it arrive, in a full black dress with lace trim, black high heels and black stockings. Just a hint of red lipstick was the only artificial colour he could see on her.

"Why do you always wear black?", he said to her.

"I hate making choices, Edmund. Anyway, don't I look good enough for you? You have sort of brown, greenish, and... well, earthy colours. I am absent of colour. We go together perfectly, don't we?"

The play was merry, Edmund considered. Very colourful, and very musical, with a 'Minstrel Band' above the stage area, to the rear, playing music throughout, 'but not in a tiresome fashion', he thought. He didn't really understand or like Shakespeare, he thought, but this experience was 'alright', and indeed, made his inquisitive for more. Also, Leela was good company; laughing, telling him things, joking with him and acquaintances in the interval. And at the end of the play, she dragged him over to some girls of her year, who seemed to Edmund like his little sister really, although he knew they must be older.

"This is Edmund, and he brought me here in a car!", at which they all registered a mixture of approval, awe, contempt, jealousy and disbelief.

"Look!", she said, taking charge of the group: "let's go to the 'Eight Bells' for some coffee, and we can discuss the play with Edmund. This is OK, Edmund? It will help stimulate thoughts for our exam.."

In this rather strange, late-night coffee bar, a couple, both in pinafores, and who appeared to be extremely miserable throughout, served them all with coffee and for some, biscuits. There was some music supplied from a record player, with dance music from several years before, playing on this night. One of the party (Mavis) was a freckly, pigtailed girl who pointedly ignored Edmund, except for an occasional sneer, and talked quite loudly, laughing at her own observations, at a game she and one of the others had been playing that night. Her ally in this intrigue was a shortish, fattish girl, whose size of face seemed to stretch her mouth in an involuntary and painful, joyless smile.

"We make up conversations about the actors on stage. I mean, those who aren't speaking", said Freckles.

"Yes!", rejoined the other: "we imagined what the crew were saying to one another in the first scene.."

"And?", asked a bored looking Andrea, an attractive

girl with long blond hair: "what did you imagine they were saying?"

"Well", said Freckles: "...we ...", she stopped to laugh.

"Oh get on with it!" retorted Andrea.

"Ok, ok ... well, well we thought that the thin one in the orange coat was saying to the botswain. 'For heavens sake stop yakking and let's get off this bloody boat!'"

"Quite good", said Andrea: "for you, that is. I suppose Edmund has some reflections on the play?", she continued, looking slowly towards him, almost smiling.

"Edmund, you don't know this play, do you?", Leela asked him, and knowing the answer, didn't pause, but continued: "so tell us what you thought was the theme of the play?"

Edmund looked at the group who silently stared at him, apparently for enlightenment. He began:

"I've never even heard of the 'Tempest' before, so it's all new to me. I suppose it seems to say something about ... well, retribution, maybe ... the men on the ship seem to feel they're OK, then a shipwreck, and their past comes back to haunt them, if you like ... I'm sorry, this is so silly. I can't help you much. I'm sure your teachers will help you far more than I can."

"It makes sense to me, what you say", said an eager young girl, in wirey NHS spectacles, who (to Edmund) suddenly seemed to emerge from the gathering. Leela smiled at the girl:

"I know, Veronica, that's why it's good to have a fresh view of things. Edmund, what you said is very relevant, I think. This idea of the theme is an important one. There's no right or wrong answer, you see. We have to get ideas to discuss things ..."

"Edmund!", exclaimed Freckles: "what do you imagine Miranda said to Ferdinand before they appeared with that chess board?"

All the girls laughed, this event being a topic exploited by their teachers. Edmund frowned, then smiled at them:

"I can't remember what anyone said on stage at that point. But I suppose Miranda asked Ferdinand if he liked her dress."

There was great hilarity. Miranda's dress had been a made of leaves - at least a cotton-made imitation.

Soon after this, with some little more talk, and increasingly some personal questions for Edmund, the girls had to leave to catch their bus.

"Well, Edmund, you certainly made a hit with all of those! Do you fancy a harem?"

"Yes, providing I can have one night off a week!", he laughed, then continued:

"The music was good."

"Purcell. It was written especially for 'The Tempest'."

"Are Purcell and Shakespeare contemporaries?", he asked.

"Oo! I don't know. But I think they were living at about the same time."

"And the band was very good.", he continued.

"Yes, it's the area's 'Ancient Musik Band' ", she said, reading from the programme. "funny way of spelling 'music' - oh! I suppose it's the Elizabethan way - I'll make a note of it to ask in class next week... do you realise most of the pronunciations of words have changed completely since Shakespeare?"

"You know, Leela", said Edmund, thoughts coming to

him now from the play: "it could really be a dream, this play. It reminds me of a dream.", and Edmund remembered some film he'd seen which reminded him of a dream.

"Really? Yes, I suppose it does have that side to it ... Edmund, tell me truly, can you take me seriously? I know I'm very young, and I know my school friends look even younger, but I'd like to remain your friend as I need someone of your maturity to talk to about things. Not only Shakespeare, but things that I think sometimes, and ideas I have? I won't embarrass you, ever. I know you have a mistress, Edmund. But it doesn't matter. I don't need that from you, and I won't try to snatch you away. Not that I could. Just friends. Why can't boys and girls see more than one friend?"

"We are friends, I'm sure, Leela. You're young for a relationship, I suppose, anyway ..."

He looked at her, laughing lightly, because he did want her. And wanted her more every time he was with her... he could feel the warmth of her bare forearm as she leaned over to talk to him, and he was taken with her appearing as a young adolescent schoolgirl, and a young woman, and he himself found he was helter-skeltering through emotions of lust, protectiveness and guilt ...

"Anyway, I wouldn't want to spoil your relationship with... er... Dorothy"

"You won't. Don't think about it at all.", he patted her hand, and she smiled at him.

"Edmund! Who in this play would you like to be?"

"What? The Tempest? Oh... strange question...", but she was looking at him with a wide-eyed intensity he couldn't resist:

"Prospero. He has all the magic and all the answers."

"I'd like to be Caliban", replied Leela mischievously: "I like the idea of grubbing around a desert island for exotic berries and fruits, and being able to frighten my enemies away with a look or a roar!"

"Didn't he want to rape Miranda?" asked Edmund.

"She'd be so lucky! The idea of a woman like that preserving her virginity for ever and living with a pretty weird daddy - sorry, Edmund - is creepy ..."

"Let's have some more coffee!"

They talked some more, and agreed to agree that live

music in a play was wonderful, and that Edmund would take her to see more plays, especially Shakespeare, so they could discuss what he thought, and she could measure this against her reactions; and she in return would visit the film club.

The drive back Parkleat was, for Leela, pleasant, and dreamy... she fell into some shallow slumber, awaked sometimes to see headlights pick out the hedgerow, or a clump of rocks in the verge, and she found herself slumped in the passenger seat, almost asleep when they arrived home. She stretched herself upwards, and smiled towards Edmund, his face lit lightly and only by the dashboard illumination:

"That was so good, Edmund. Call me when you can...", and she spontaneously, without thought but inevitably, put her arm around his head and kissed him... "goodnight... drive safely, won't you?"

He drove slowly back home, thinking about Leela, and Dot, and sex, and life... and... his exams... he did need to do some Geography revision!

"Play any good?", asked his mother, Vivian, opening the French windows into the path which led to his parked car.

She was a tall, blond woman with slim figure and blue eyes and moved from her hips, like a fashion model. She liked good clothes, a well-laid table, and had a passion for flowers of all kinds. She too was a doctor, but had given up regular practice to keep house.

"It was very good, Mother. There was a band, as well. And the music was alright."

"Did Leela like it? Was it useful for her?"

"Yes, she did. We discussed it, and what we'd like to be in the play."

"And you chose Prospero, I suppose.", she said, smiling, and laughing as she could see she had hit the mark:

"And this Leela? Well, of course, I haven't met her, only seen her... from afar... She might have chosen... Miranda? As the only woman, I think, in the play."

"Caliban!" laughed Edmund, as his mother's thinking frown turned into wide eyed wonder, and then, with a little darkening of her expression:

"The monster! What kind of girl wants to be a monster! Be careful of this one, Edmund ", she said quickly, reddening slightly as she went on: "or she might gobble you up!"

CHAPTER FIVE

Not a Teddy Boy

Edmung was waiting to meet her one evening during the week outside her school.

"A brilliant surprise!", she exclaimed as she saw his standing there: "and how is my Great Lord?", she laughed, clutching a small pile of books to herself as she did so.

"What? Oh no! Even mother knew what character I'd choose. Am I really that superficial?"

"Probably!", she laughed again: "but does it matter?"

They began to walk together, down the hill, to the town bus stop where Leela was headed. Both were decked in their uniforms. She, navy blue, pleated skirt, white blouse, jacket; he light grey, prefect's pocket badge, pushing his bike, free hand in pocket.

"Will you come out tonight?", asked Edmund, "not too long. Just a walk in the park. Talk."

"OK. I could do with a break from revision."

"I'll pick you up in mother's car. About eight?"

"Fine. Edmund, that will be fine", she smiled at him, swaying coquettishly, swinging her books in front of her, and walking backwards before him, as schoolgirls will do to boys ...

He smiled, but looked down, not wanting to betray what he knew was obvious to her. There was but a small amount of leg for him to see, as he glanced quickly at her, just below a longish skirt, above dark neatly folded socks. Her dark skin glowed against the blue material above and below; skipping legs; singing a song now ... "just be my teddy bear" ... "well I jus' wanna...".

"What's that you're gibbering about?", he laughed, looking up.

"Latest Elvis' hit!", she said, striding ahead of him.

"Elvis?"

"Sensational singer for USA!" she exclaimed: "all the girls all crazy about him."

"Is he good looking?"

"He looks great from his pictures. But then, all stars are photographed to look good. His music's really brilliant to bop to. You must try. Try now!", she said, plopping her books on a low wall, grabbing his hand; he held onto his bike with the other; she whirled around on one spot, this way, then that; and he was enthralled, and bewitched.

"It's easy!" he exclaimed, having not moved since the start of the dance. She laughed at him, her eyes sparkled unashamedly, like only the very young can do, and held onto his elbow, prancing along with him, humming and singing "do-de-do-bop-bop" as they went along.

He began suddenly to feel constrained, for the first time in his life. He would see Leela again, without wondering what he would feel like in a few days time, with some rumination, some reflection; maybe some regrets. He did have the suspicion that this was all very silly. Of course, he met with her that evening, not thinking of cancelling; but not really feeling a great urge to go walking with her. Well, well.

He left the car in the street by one of the park's

entrances, and they walked together, in the early evening light, by the 'pathetic fountain', as Edmund had dubbed it, towards the circular paddling pool; now locked up, with the benches dotted around it like a great necklace.

"Let's go for a drink. You can have pop, if you don't want alcohol", he said to her as they strolled together.

"Good idea", she retorted: "oh! and bugger pop, get me vodka and orange. Well Dad let's me drink that at parties!", she sulked as he frowned at her.

They sat outside, in the closing dusk, to hear the laughter and yatter of the early evening revellers, or those late from work. The steel workers, their afternoon shift finished, clumped homewards past them in silence; their heads down; tired; some would have beer before home, others would dutifully trudge their way directly to wives or mothers.

"Could almost be a picture!", said Edmund, really speaking to himself.

"Of what?"

"Oh!", he exclaimed, almost surprised she was there with him: "of evening life in our little town ... but you need to freeze those images..." he went on, again forgetting she was with him: "...in your mind, hold them; as if they were the reality, the icons of a time, a time greater than a particular miniscule instant...", he started, as he was aware she was indeed listening to him, and was looking intently towards him: "sorry! I'm jabbering on."

"Yes, you are. Although I know what you mean. Some things you remember when you think about some time or place, and that thing, if you like, becomes that time and so on for you, doesn't it?"

"More than that, Leela. It sometimes supplants the real thing or time... I'm glad you see it in that way."

She stared ahead of her, looking now at the wisp of steam engine smoke as the train from York pulled in at Central Railway station, just 50 yards from where they were sitting. The engine sighed relief, it seemed, as it came to a halt.

They strolled together, speaking half-sentences and trivia.

"After your exams, how do you see the future Edmund?"

He laughed, but said nothing. He had no plans, and didn't want to think of school.

They walked into the park, and in the gloom of a clump of trees, he kissed her. She was passionate in her response, and the heat of her eagerness s which almost frightened him, was followed with a soft and tender embrace. He could not resist this. He could deal with lust, she was young, it was not maybe so good ... but he could not deal with this sweet weakness, the physical sickness he felt as this little adolescent pushed primitively the tip of her tongue in his mouth ... he wanted her so much, so much so he was now not even hard; he could now carry her off to bed, but only to kiss her goodnight ...

"I'm your girl, now, in some way, I suppose ... you have a mistress... that doesn't matter to me... anyway, it's not my business... ", she plunged her head into his shoulder as they sat together on that old green park bench in the dark, the one nearest the pool ... now she ran her fingers over his jacket lapels, and tugged at the buttons.

"Would you like to meet my family? Come to my

home?" he whispered into the warm, dark air, staring at the stillness of the pool.

"No, but I'll do it.", she said.

"I won't force you. I'd like you to come ... they know about you and I meeting, anyway. I've talked about our seeing 'The Tempest'."

"I'll come. This weekend?", she left his shoulder and looked up at him, seeing the still, statue-like profile of his face nod slowly in the half-light of one of the park lamps.

* * *

For that next weekend, Leela went to Edmund's by bus, having been told by Edmund that Oscar, Edmunds father, would take her home afterwards. She wore a dark-blue dress of a simple, straight cut, with single pearl earrings (borrowed from her mother) and a necklace of jet stone, and arrived in time for tea, at 4.00 o'clock on a cold, showery summer day.

Oscar Rice was a General Practitioner in this area of the Yorkshire Moors bounded to the east by the North Sea. He was a man of quite substantial means, having inherited money from his family before setting up his practice; and he was now the senior partner, at 41. He had not been top of his class in the finals year at University, but his wife had in hers, two years after him. She had been in General Practice too, but had retired to look after their children. Oscar was prematurely grey, but had a full head of shortly cropped hair. He was dapper in appearance and moved briskly about his business.

Edmund was the eldest, at 18, and had a younger brother Timothy of 7 and a sister Marsha, of 9.

Vivian answered the door when Leela arrived, and although she smiled, it was obvious to the young girl that Edmund's mother took an immediate dislike to her.

"Well", thought Leela: "perhaps that's the way it should be."

"I would hardly guess you were a schoolgirl!" said Vivian, in an awkward allusion to her appearance, as they walked into through the back porch and into the kitchen.

"Sit down, sit down." Vivian continued. Leela felt

uncomfortable at this initial 'interrogation' by Edmund's mother: "and please call me Vivian, if you don't mind."

"Well, you are pretty, Leela. But then, all of Edmund's girlfriends are, you know!"

"I hope so, Vivian. I'd hate to feel he'd got bad taste."

Vivian laughed lightly, but as Leela noticed, it was too lightly, and too short, and the girl felt pleased with herself.

"Are you missing your cycling today?" asked Vivian, frostily.

"Not really. I may go out tomorrow. But I've got to study for my GCEs."

"What plans do you have for next year? A-levels?"

"No. Well, almost certainly not. I'll get a job, I think."

"Sick of school?"

"Sick of the uniform, Vivian!"

"Really? And I saw you the other day in your smart blue outfit, Leela. You look very good."

"Well, I don't feel very good wearing it. And more than that. I don't want to study any more. It's a sort of pointless intensity I'd like to finish with."

"Good job people like my husband didn't agree, or they'd be no GPs!"

"I'm not meaning to appear superior, Vivian. It's just not what I want to do."

The door opened and Oscar entered the kitchen, giving Leela, who rose to greet him, a kiss on the cheek, and beamed at her:

"You look lovely, my dear. My son should feel himself honoured, as I'm sure he does."

Vivian cast look of resigned hostility towards Oscar, as he stared approvingly at the young girl. He went on:

"Shall we go into the lounge? Edmund and the others are there - can you do some tea for us, Vivian?"

Leela and Oscar left the kitchen, and joined the rest of the family in the lounge. Marsha, the 9 year old, stared expressionless at Leela, and the younger Timothy ignored her as he played with a toy lorry; and of course, there was Edmund; to whom Leela looked, slightly reddened, waiting for his approval:

"Edmund!" exclaimed his father: "she's arrived! And doesn't she look a picture!"

"Leela, you do look wonderful. What a lovely dress!" said Edmund, getting up from his chair, where he had been reading some of his A-level notes.

"The dress can only look good on a beautiful girl, my boy!", rejoined Oscar, to the merriment of the younger children, as he briefly introduced her to them.

"Yes, of course. I agree with you, father. Please, Leela, sit down here, by me."

She sat on a low chair by his side, Oscar placed himself in an upright arm chair near the unused fireplace, and the Marsha returned to her book, whilst Timothy stayed with his toy.

Soon, after the return of some pleasantries, tea arrived, to be served by Vivian.

"There are some fancies here", she indicated: "but please don't eat too many, as we'll have high tea within the hour."

Leela took the cup poured and proffered by Edmund, and after sipping, noticed the vessel:

"What a lovely cup!"

"Minton", said Oscar: "Vivian's favourite china. She

insists tea needs to be drunk from China, rather than a mug, don't you?"

"I'm sure it makes a difference", she agreed, smiling: "but maybe it's just psychological. Anyway, handling beautiful things is one of life's pleasures it's good to afford, if you can."

"How is your revision coming on, Leela?" said Oscar.

"Oh not too bad. I need five passes, with three good grades, to get a decent job. I think I'll manage that OK."

"Not going on the A-levels?" She shook her head.

"And our Edmund is also sick of academic work, aren't you?" He turned to his son.

"I am, but I may have to do a bit more to be a draughtsman."

"I wish you'd reconsider Art School", said his mother: "you are a very good artist, you know."

"I don't think I'm good enough, mother."

"Have you shown Leela your drawings?", asked Oscar.

"No, they're not for showing off, father."

"I disagree. Leela, you can decide, would you like to see Edmund's drawings?"

"If he doesn't object, Mr Rice."

"Oscar, don't do this. He did those for himself, and to show to us of course. But they weren't for general display. You'll embarrass him."

"Don't fret, mother. I don't mind Leela seeing them, as long as she doesn't tell me the truth of what she thinks about them."

"You must leave that to her", said his mother, getting up and leaving to get the drawings.

"There are only about thirty, Leela", Edmund whispered: "so if you spend two seconds on each, you'll only waste a minute of your life."

"As much as that!" she whispered back: "then they'd better be good!"

Vivian swept into the room, looking flushed with pride, and something else, deep within her, thought Leela, as she watched her gently place the portfolio against the wall. She removed the tea tray from the dining table, and placed it by the French windows, then retrieved the drawings and put them on the table. She opened the portfolio very carefully, and took out the first drawing:

“This is the crag, over to the north-west from here ... we’ve often walked over there.”

She was looking at the drawing in her hands, and talked almost to herself.

“No-one else can see them, dear!” said Oscar: “pass them over to Edmund, then he can tell Leela about them.”

Vivian did so, and left the room.

Edmund and Leela looked at his drawings, done in pencil and charcoal, and sipped tea and nibbled fancies, as he told her of the crag, where maybe they could go after high tea, and other landmarks. There were drawings of his family, with (what Leela considered) a simple yet gentle portrait of Oscar and Vivian together in the garden, which she recognised from the view from the French windows from where she sat.

“These are good, Edmund.”, said Leela quietly, after they had seen several of his pictures.

“In some ways, they are, Leela. But they’re just copies, really. They don’t have that quality that makes them different in effect from a good photo.”, he said, as he stared at the drawings, and remembered what Dot had said about them, most cruelly, but truly:

"I would love to say they are good, but they aren't. Oh, don't be so glum, my dearest! You are an artist. The way you make love to me, what you say, how you look ... it really is the greatest art, and gives pleasure to many women, I'm sure, but especially those who will sleep with you .... but this is not your art ...", and she had tapped one of his drawings of her, and had smiled, and wrapped him in her arms, as he cried into her shoulder.

"What are you thinking about?", asked Leela.

"I'm glad I did these drawings, anyway. They're a chronicle of things that have interested me over the past three years or so ..."

Dorothy's portrait was striking, Leela thought. She had seen her at a distance, but had not studied her closely, and she felt somehow this picture did have something of the quality Edmund said he lacked. The subject was standing, looking quite imperious, with her long nose like an eagle's beak, and strong arms half-clothed in a shawl. She was looking down, and Leela saw Edmund in her flat, sitting in a low chair, knees curled up as a board for his drawing pad, darting back and forth between the subject and the paper.

"This is good. I like it." she said.

Edmund smiled at her, and they looked through some more sketches of the countryside, garden and people.

"I'd like to draw you", he said to her, quietly.

"No, not yet. Sometime in the future, Edmund, maybe. But not yet."

Oscar had been reading to Marsha, and Timothy had disappeared, when Vivian came in again:

"Tea is served in the kitchen."

The high tea was delicious, Leela thought. Although she did allow that her mum couldn't cook very well so she didn't have much of a standard. However, informed by a beaming, proud hostess that all the food was cooked or prepared by her, she envied Edmund this standard of eating. He, however, never seemed to care about food. He wasn't disappointed if the cake he asked for had all gone, nor did he argue or fight for the best biscuits. She felt she was almost minute by minute falling under his spell, and that she needed him to realise how much power he could have over her, if he cared to exercise it.

"More Cherry cake, Leela?", asked Vivian: "your plate appears to be empty."

"And that's a sin in this house!", exclaimed Oscar, to everyone's delight.

Cherry cake, tasting as lovely as Edmund's kisses, thought Leela. This house was filled with wonderful food to eat, she thought.

After tea, they walked through the garden, to a small wicket gate, and over the field to the moors. In half an hour, they were at the crag which Edmund had drawn.

"You see, it forms a ledge, under which we can now shelter", he said, from beneath the hood of his waterproof, as a heavy shower had dogged their journey. Leela nodded her agreement, and they scurried to the shelter.

The hugged together, and kissed, and squeezed each other tightly. Edmund looked down at her, her fresh face, moistened with rain, and looking at him with eyes glistening with desire:

"This is such a wonderful moment in my life, Leela. I feel so much at one with you now."

"Edmund, oh my Edmund", and she buried her head to his chest: "you must know I want you so much. Seeing Dorothy, not feeling jealousy, but envy ..."

"She is a woman, Leela. You are still a schoolgirl."

"That's just a name. And remember", she said, smiling mischievously, "Juliet was only 14."

They stayed for some time there, talking nonsense as lovers do, with Edmund pointing out some visible landmarks which could be seen from this high point.

On getting back, it was quite late, and the children were in bed.

"Drink before you go?" asked Oscar, and Leela declined. After bidding goodbye to Vivian, the pair sat in the back of Oscar's Jaguar saloon, and sped on their way back home. They reached Parkleat in under one hour, and drawing up to the house, were greeted by Sarah, who ran from the kitchen, with the large silhouette of William, Leela's father, in the doorway.

"Thank you for phoning - so we were expecting you, Mr Rice ... Leela and Edmund! Welcome!"

"Would you like some tea or anything?", Sarah asked mechanically, obviously assuming the invitation would be declined. In a few minutes, the party had exchanged pleasantries, and father and son were on their way home.

When they got back, the house was silent. Vivian and the children were in bed, and Oscar offered Edmund a drink:

"Yes, dad. I'll have whisky and water."

"And I'll have brandy, I think."

Oscar had prepared the drinks, and the two men sat down in the lounge.

"Fine girl, Leela.", said Oscar: "do you think it will get serious, between you and her?"

"She's very young, dad."

"In body only, my boy. She's a smart one, and sensible, I would say, as well."

"I can't see myself deciding what I want to do for some time yet. And Leela isn't one to follow me around waiting for something to happen. But it's very good for now."

"I'm glad you feel that. Getting committed at an early age is a bad idea for either of you, I'm sure. Times are changed. Marrying the local girl is not the only option. How is your Dorothy, by the way?"

"She's ok. Do you think I'm wrong to have both her and Leela as friends?"

"Why ask me? Ask yourself, Edmund. Don't deceive them."

"No, of course not, father."

"Unless you are sure of getting away with it!", he laughed, but Edmund knew that he meant it. Oscar, he knew, had been associated with several nurse colleagues in the past.

"You don't feel guilty about... playing the field?" he asked, almost to himself.

"No, not at all. I'm discrete. So are my acquaintances. The relationships are fun, not to be taken seriously. I've told you this before, Edmund."

"'Boy's secrets', you call them."

"Vivian knows, of course Edmund. She accepts it as ... well, one of my aberrations. And no one is perfect."

But Edmund suspected Vivian despised him for his weakness, from things she'd said when Oscar had an especially 'late surgery', but he also accepted that it didn't seem to personally offend her.

"Vivian is a wonderful woman, and completely adorable. I couldn't wish for a better wife. I know I'm incredibly lucky to have her, as well as her professional support at times."

Vivian was a doctor also, graduating with very high grades, but had put her career second to Oscar's to look after the home and the children.

"I'm off to bed, Edmund.", he said, getting up briskly: "goodnight, my boy. And don't think about life too much, or you'll lose time living it!"

Edmund checked the doors, windows and lights before climbing the stairs, his half finished whisky in his hand. He undressed rapidly, climbed into bed, and brooded whilst sipping his whisky, before his tiredness overcame him and he went to sleep.

CHAPTER SIX

The following Sunday, Edmund joined Leela and her family for dinner, which was a traditional roast, at the traditional time of 12:30. It was the habit at Parkleat to eat dinner outside on a fine day. And fine it was: a cloudless, hot, mid-May afternoon. The party sat at a massive oak table, in the shade of the house and the shrubby trees nearby.

Edmund had become used to fine, adventurous food at his home, as both Vivian and Oscar were keen cooks. Thus it was, oddly enough, quite unusual for him to be faced with roast beef, cabbage, carrots, Yorkshire pudding and roast potatoes; with white sauce as an option. It was mentioned before the dinner, that it had been cooked mainly by Leela and her brother John. Leela had told him some time ago that her mother, although she liked to try, was a poor cook, and her food was generally to be avoided.

"Mother will boil the cabbage till it evaporates!", she had once told him.

Well, Edmund liked the roast very well, especially the Yorkshire pudding, which he had never had at home, only flabby offerings in mediocre restaurants. The only time he had to endure Sarah's (Leela's mother) food was a Madeira cake she had made for after dinner. This, he admitted to himself, was dreadful. Forewarned, he had taken a small piece only, and managed to eat it without grimacing.

Throughout the dinner, which was conducted for the most part in silence; although Edmund did notice close scrutiny from William (Leela's father), and to a lesser extent, from Sarah. After the meal, as was the custom, iced drinks were brought out in large glass jugs: Draught ale, from a nearby off-licence, and Apple juice, prepared from William's own orchards.

"Can we go and have a quite word over there, lad?", William asked Edmund, placing his huge hand gently on his shoulder, and indicating a rough wooden bench some way off, beneath the trees.

They walked over there, and sat down, Edmund feeling the strain on the seat as William's great weight settled down.

"You and Leela have been going out for some time. You're young, but she's very young, and a girl, so you'll understand I'm sure that I'd like to be put in the picture about your plans."

"No special plans, Mr. Drake. I'll have to see how my A-Levels go. Leela and I are very good friends. We enjoy each other's company, and going out together."

"I'm glad to hear that, lad. I did hope that both of you would leave any plans of well - a more permanent nature - until you were a few years older."

"And I'm sure you're right. You don't object to my taking out Leela?"

"Me? That's up to her, Edmund. I'll support her in whatever she does. I'll give advice and so on. But these days, parents don't tell youngsters what to do. At least, not if they know what's good for them!", and he laughed, and patted Edmund's knee, and took a large drink of beer.

"Let's go back to the family, Edmund!"

As they got back to the group, Sarah looked up, almost apprehensively, smiling at William, to receive assuring smiles, and grunts, and an approving nod towards Edmund. She now looked at Edmund, and smiled broadly towards him. Leela joined Edmund at the table, and smiled, and squeezed his hand.

'With a hey and a ho and a hey!'

There were of course more meetings for the young lovers. They told each other more of their likes and dislikes, things they had done and wanted to do, and underlying all this, and always as a conclusion, there was the passion which had kindled between them so soon after their first meeting. He would squeeze her breasts through her blouse: she wanted more, she sighed deeply, exaggeratedly, so he would notice: always she wanted more.

But he dared not. He sometimes, with her, felt more out of control than with Dorothy.

The end of May. The playing had to end. Examinations for both Edmund and Leela were approaching, and there were thus fewer meetings. During the two and a half weeks of their exams, there were none, although at weekends they did phone each other for several minutes, swapping feelings of yearning for each other, and impressions of exam papers they'd already taken. During this time Leela wrote a poem to Edmund:

"Trees, trees, trees
Silent sentinels to the morning sun
Shivering grass, blades of green
Congregate at their feet
While we, side by side, sitting here
Touches exploring one another
Would I wonder so much if you
Weren't you?
Ah, Edmund!
Lovely, and loving
Silent sentinel to my maidenhood
Is it that which draws me to you, so much?
How quaint, that in the age of Rock and Roll

I feel like a Princess in a tower
When you look up to me
(Oh come to me, come inside my tower!)
And smile, a smile so tender, and distant, and receding into the cool, bright air
When you kiss me, and stroke my flesh,
I want all of you
Like a freshling foal, hooving the turf,
Willing the game on,
To go pelting forward:
Does that not quicken you, my love?
Perhaps to passion, or maybe to fear.
Hold me, anyway, and anyway
You want to ...
I am yours
You are my lord
My whole body and mind loves you, Edmund.

Today I feel that even if I live a thousand years, I will never feel like this with anyone else.

And I am happy, and complete, in this life of mine."

Edmund had replied with a drawing especially for

Leela. He took her opening reference to trees, and drew them grouped on the edge of a woodland. He had sketched it rapidly in charcoal, and depicted (quite pleasingly, he adjudged) a bright, fresh spring day, like the ones they had shared that year. The trees with their early foliage, were shot through with bright shafts of early morning sunlight, quite low in the sky for that time of year.

CHAPTER SEVEN

The Wimbledon Lawn Tennis Championship was over, and the examinations were completed. Schoolboys and girls anxiously giggled their exam stories to each other, some of the more worried or serious feverously scanned their note books to check their efforts. There were groans, laughter, hoops of joy; above all a great feeling of relief that the ordeal was at last over.

To celebrate, Edmund had arranged a picnic. They would go to the edge of a wood which Edmund had used as inspiration for his drawing to her. It was some miles, so he had borrowed his mother's car.

He was dressed in a floppy beige jacket and trousers, with a soft, white cotton, open necked shirt. When Leela saw him for the first time for weeks (years, it felt like!) as he appeared at her door to pick her up, her tongue stuck in her throat so she could not greet him coherently, as she was taken aback by her feelings on seeing him again.

"How beautiful he is", she thought as she collected a few things to take with her: "And how sweet he looks!"

When they arrived at the wood, it was already noon, and quite warm, so they set out rugs and blankets.

"What is that?" asked Leela as Edmund produced a wooden case, about the size of a small suitcase, but square in section.

"My surprise!", he replied, and unhinging the box at one side, produced a bottle of wine surrounded in its case by pieces of ice.

"Got the ice via the refrigerators your father uses at the depot." he laughed, as Leela's eyes opened wide. "Didn't say it was for wine, of course!"

"How brilliant, Edmund!" she studied the label: "Can't read French even though I've just failed my O level in it!" she laughed.

"It's 'Chablis'. Supposed to be very good. Dad sorted it out for me."

As was their wont, they nibbled and browsed their

salad food, more interested in each other than food or drink.

"Your father is right about this wine, Edmund. It's delicious!", Leela said as she drank her second glass, and found the effect totally pleasing.

Later, they walked into the woods, where humming flies and scurrying squirrels disturbed the silence of the afternoon sun. They found a large area dense with bluebells. Leela gasped:

"I've never seen so many! And the smell, so fine! I didn't know they had so much scent!"

"I often came here with Mother and Father when I was very young", he replied: "these bluebells are so beautiful."

They sat down amid the carpet of flowers, the sun warming them. Leela, dressed in dark-blue skirt and white blouse, leaned back on her hands and lifted her head to face the sun:

"Mmmm! Lovely", she exclaimed.

Edmund sat by her, on his side, facing her, and picked at the grass:

"Edmund!" she sat up suddenly, and turned to him: "Will you be called up?"

"I can defer it, according to Father. Anyway, I think it will end soon."

She laughed, and rolling over, pinned his arms to the ground:

"Now I have you!" she cried.

"I surrender!" he laughed, rolling over himself to take Leela with him, and she now looked up at him, eyes misty with love, and lust; the early teenage tingle of desire overwhelmed her

They were drawn together by an inexorable force of feeling which affected both of them. Clasping him tightly, Leela dug her fingers into his shirt, sighing with relief to be close to him at last.

.... These slow-motion images, part now only of their memories, play out the ritual of summer lovers

And he, pulling her to him, running his hands up and down her back, feeling her body

She pulls aside her blouse, 'Edmund, dear, here, here.'

He rubs her breasts over her bra, then deftly unclasping

it, squeezes her bare flesh, and then, sucks her there, tenderly, then more firmly, and gently bites

She in turn will squeeze his sides and back in ecstasy at each new wonderful experience of new love, new sex.

Now he will venture up her thigh, and she will sigh, of such pleasure, of such contentment, this is what she wants, she feels, she must have and she has everything ...

'These warm-long days, weeping with words of love for you

Feel I only the occasional surfacing from reality into the breathless sunlight

Feel this as I feel, Edmund.

Wherever you are now, my love, my lover ...'

They could meet now more frequently, and more feely, and did so.

Leela was keen to see much of Edmund, and eagerly wanted him to fulfil her newly aroused physical desires. He would not have intercourse with her, he had said; and he appeared to be in control in a way she had not experienced before. Previously, her boyfriends, usually a year or two older than she, seemed to be driven to a desire for sex often only frustrated by her urgent resistance to their groping hands and pressing body.

Of course, she loved Edmund, he was her first love, and the others she had known were just 'boyfriends'. But she was aware of a desire as strong for him, as, she mused those boyfriends had had for her. She was by no means frightened of this, and did not consider her youth clouded her judgement on what she most certainly wanted in her life at this time. But knowing Edmund, she would have to wait. And she did not wish to seduce him, and then be faced with his guilty introspection. She knew that their relationship already had raised uncertainties in him, feelings of responsibilities he did not know how to fulfil ....

However, she smiled to herself, that was his problem.

One day they met and took a long, slow and noisy bus ride on a sunny day to a place on the moors, where they knew they could be alone.

"Last bus back 9 o'clock", shouted a wiry female bus

conductor as they alighted. Neither heard nor cared what she had said.

When they arrived that day, the beauty of the limestone and flowers, and the tender bright clumps of grass, and the soaring joy of the skylark; all this was for the most part, lost on them. They could, mused Edmund later, have been in a damp, cold cellar and still enjoyed their day as much as they did.

Leela clung to him as they walked to a certain spot, known now to both of them, not too far from the road. She felt so much that day, she hoped he knew at least the power of the emotion she had for him, and for their love ...

This shadowy, lust-filled love... she wanted him.

For Leela there was no thought of shame nor was there any thought of hesitation, nor unsureness ... no thought of anything but him... not even him, now, but only the warm darkness of the sensation, of the touch... the rustle of clothing, pushed aside in the haste for fulfilment. The feel of the warm, moist grass on the backs of her bare legs ....

This lovely love, the first time Leela had felt not held by

gravity to the earth, nor to anything, floating as in a dream, which could never end, nor ever began.

It is what she had always wanted, yet never even knew.

He was now forcing his finger into her, she noticed, as she sighed and swayed against him limply, as she heard the rubbing lapping of her love ... she smiled... a small childish curious smile.

More and more and more insistent, and now she was involuntarily pushing herself down onto him, or rather onto his finger.

Then, down there, then over her whole body, she began to feel a mysterious tingling, sweetly painful. Wave after wave within her body, now into her mind, a kaleidoscope of whirling of coloured sensations. She found herself gasping aggressively, demanding of him.

And Edmund, as she remembered, years and years later:

"Ah Edmund! How perfect you were, and doubtless still are!"

If she had to lose her mind in her first real orgasm with anyone, surely this was the perfect choice.

"As good as fresh cream, home made scones, home made jam, and Darjeeling tea."

She smiled to herself although now worlds away as she looked through the window. And she recalled, she remembered taking his finger, that lovely finger, from herself that night, and rubbed the slippery essence... could now smell herself so strongly and for the first time realised how deliciously intoxicating sex was, and she almost involuntarily took his finger, and place it in her mouth, and sucked gently to taste herself .....

This was *her* night, *her* experience .... Edmund was beautiful; but this pleasure, this ecstasy, was hers alone.

She talked little to him afterwards as they walked, side by side, in an awkward hug, to her bus stop. She wanted to be alone now, and brushed a brief, kissing farewell to him as she boarded the bus, and climbed the iron staircase to the top deck without looking around.

She often, later, when she was much older, thought back to that bus journey home. The bus conductor, she remembered, was tall, dark and thin, and didn't smile at her, although he did seem to her to scrutinize her more closely. She smiled to herself... perhaps, she surmised, he could tell something of what she, a schoolgirl still, had been up to on the moor that night.

She always remembered vividly, for some reason, the noisy, relentless grind on the bus's engine.

As she was jogged forward and back, and side to side by the vehicle's motion, she looked down from her high viewpoint at the lessening blobs of lights as they left the town and climbed the moor towards Leela's home.

Edmund got home, having walked, and sat alone in the front room, staring into the darkness of the garden, through the French windows, and again mused on his relationship with Leela.

"Yes I want, but do I love? Yes I care but is this love, Yes I feel, but is it love? Her words are beautiful to me, but does this mean she is also? What is love? Is it anything? Does it matter? Is caring for her loving her? Am I too old for loving her? Am I too young? I miss sex with Dot - was this love? Sex with this young girl ... she is not a woman ... it would be too easy... and there would be no passion?

What did Dot say? She regretted I was not having sex with someone else for me to compare her to... is that experience, sophisticated pleasure, is the only true lust and love that which is open and dangerous... Everyone knew about Edmund and Dorothy... His relationship with Leela was, in contrast, totally private ... And he often lied about it.

'A close relationship, mother, that's it. We like and respect each other. We share pastimes and so on ... She is too young to be involved... and I am as well!'"

Edmund felt his brain was exploding, and he was unable to rationalise his thoughts. Perhaps he should finish with her. He did so, temporarily, but didn't tell her, instead he just kept quiet for two weeks, not contacting her at all.

Leela noticed the avoidance, but felt she understood, and did not disturb him. During the long summer that year, she got a job in a William Deacon's Bank in Wellawnbury, though she would have to do some day release study at the local Technical College.

Edmund admired her for this step to independence, and decided to 'stop finishing with her'.

He met her in town one evening, and saw that she did appear to be more confident.

"Working in a bank is probably the world's most boring job", she said to him, laughing, as she looked at the workers scurrying to queue at the bus stops on their way home.

"Yes, I should think so", agreed Edmund: "then why did you choose it?"

"Oh, brother John is very keen on banks. He works in Westminster Bank, you see, and seems to be doing very well for himself. He takes some sort of protective interest in me I suppose, which I'm grateful for."

"I'll see you on Tuesdays at the Tech, anyway" said Edmund: "I'm full time at the Tech for a year to get some qualifications I need to get into the drafting office at the Local Council."

"And that sounds almost as deadly as working for a bank!" she exclaimed.

"Well, maybe. I may use the experience to take an architecture degree or something like in time. I could start my own practice. But that's pie in the sky at the moment. I just need a job, Leela. And this one is about the best I can get."

"We have to make a solemn promise that we will ensure neither of us goes mad!" she said, squeezing his hand.

"But Leela, we're both completely and totally mad already!" he exclaimed in mock seriousness. They both laughed, and she fell onto his chest, as he put his arm around her. Not now at school, she felt a new freedom on what affection she could show for him publicly, although in the dash homeward no-one seem to notice them at all. And she, with a splash of lipstick and makeup, no longer looked like the schoolgirl he had so often walked to town with on the way from school.

In the weeks following, their meetings became more formal, in an unplanned way. There seemed to be less physical love. Edmund had become scared of touching her because of his uncertainty, exacerbated by his mother's subtle jostling his feelings for Leela. And Leela, noticing the cooling of their physical love, asked him one day as they strolled together after seeing a film:

"How do you feel for me, Edmund? Answer the first thing you think of, mind!"

"My dearest, dearest love, Leela... confused! ... beautifully confused."

"Poetic, I suppose, but where is your passion."

"I have passion, great desires for you... when you are a little older... my responsibility for you is part of my love."

"To protect me from myself! My Edmund is a great white knight, when sometimes I want a great white shark", and she snarled at him, squeezing his hand, and laughing at his discomfort.

That night, when the sun had disappeared, a cold breeze bustled around their legs, as they hung together on a park bench.

"Where do you make love to Dorothy?"

"At her place."

"Nice to have a place. Especially on such a cold night."

"I suppose I won't see her again, anyway. You and I are very close now, aren't we?". He seemed to seek reassurance.

"I'd prefer you to continue sleeping with her, if and when you want to."

"Really?"

"Edmund! Choosing is so boring!", and she laughed at him; her eyes, he felt, piercing into him with a defiance he felt almost intimidating.

"What do you use? To stop a baby?" she asked looking down.

"Dorothy can't have babies. She had a problem, and they operated when she was 12 ..."

He felt bad at divulging a confidence like this, but it was done ...

Leela nodded, smiled and lent her head against his shoulder.

When he saw Dorothy again, it was with a searching longing he reached out to her. So passionate was his loving that it disturbed her:

"Please do not cling to me, Edmund. That would spoil my whole life. I love you with all my heart and soul. Please don't destroy me ... you don't know how much I feel for you ... Take me like fine wine ... sip me, then just put me aside for a while."

At home, later that night, Edmund felt quite oddly desolate. His two women seemed to want him to be a part of their life, but neither, it seemed wanted them to be part of his.

One night, and in the car, Leela took the lead, asking him what is the matter, why doesn't he touch her? She gently takes his hand, and places it on her breast, and then lifting it, unbuttons her blouse.

"I feel I have taken advantage being older..." he stutters, but when she tells him that he is not the first to feel her bare breasts, he is now happier about it. Now he felt actually stimulated, having shed some of his accumulated guilt, and became more passionate. Their kisses are now longer, and softer, and there is no longer the need for the frenzied eagerness. He sucked her hardened nipples, to her exquisite delight, but goes no further that night, as he feels he could not stop himself making love to her. And he still felt the time was not right, maybe that it would never be right. And so there was a routine. To take each other to the edge of full sex, never further, because of him, because of guilt, because of his mother, because of the need to look forward to something, not break the spell .... anyway, Dot.

CHAPTER EIGHT

In the months that followed, and up to Christmas 1956, Leela dropped into the habit of her new job at the bank. She would see Edmund at the Tech on college days, and they would go out together regularly. Her passion for him did not dim, however, and while he seemed steadfastly resolved to abide by his pledge of not having full sex with her; their physical love, while limited, continued to their mutual satisfaction. She would now often make him come, and was fascinated, almost in awe, she felt, at the peculiar mechanism of the male ejaculation, and all the associated paraphernalia.

"It is an odd shape, Edmund!" she laughed: "and seems too big to go into me."

She rubbed the sperm between her finger and thumb:

"Slippery... and", she said, smelling her fingers: "smells very strong ... like bleach!"

They both laughed at this.

"Edmund", she said softly; gently massaging his penis in her fingers: "you will make love to me, one day, won't you?"

"As soon as I'm happy you're old enough not to regret it."

"Mmm" she murmured, taking him into her mouth, and gently sucking at the softening organ, tasting and drinking his sperm. The only way, she thought, she could take him into her body.

"You taste very pleasant, my love", she said, kissing his lips: "such nectare shouldn't always be wasted in this way."

"I'd have to wear a durex, anyway" he replied.

"Not always, Edmund", she smiled at him: "sometimes, I'll need all of you."

During that autumn, Edmund studied at the Tech. He was now, he felt, as he was told by his mother, becoming a young man, as opposed to a boy. His mother did not speak about Leela, although Edmund felt she thought about her. He also felt an increasing responsibility towards his Leela.

He could not, for example, afford to lose control either sexually, or emotionally.

Leela was now working in William Deacon's Bank in the centre of Wellawnbury. She worked as an office junior and trainee cashier. She studied on Thursdays at the Tech., and always took lunch with Edmund on that day. They were 'going steady', she thought. He thought they had become good friends, as well as 'teenage lovers'. They had done things that many others of their age only whispered and giggled about. Kitty had left a job ('she hated') serving on a market stall to join Leela at the WD's bank, which was good news for both of them as they continued to be very good friends.

A Dorothy Autumn

Leeds main Railway Station, October 1956.

As he walked towards Dorothy, who waited for him on the platform, he was bracing himself for what he was going to tell her. And it did not make it easier to notice something in her fleeting smile towards him, and her gait: too straight, composed, he thought; all this impressed upon him the realization that she knew what he was going to tell her.

Click, click, click ... the echo of his footfall before him.

He had prepared himself for a soft, seduced, lovingly painful scene of farewell over the next few days.

"Are you hungry? Would you like a drink?"

She had gently hooked her hand into his forearm. He knew she would wait for him to tell her. He never felt he understood her very deeply, but this he felt directly, instinctively.

"Let's go to the pub. It's not two o'clock yet."

They got into Dot's car, which was parked just outside the station. Edmund noticed a burly commissionaire standing by the station entrance, giving him a belligerent sneer as they set off. Edmund began to feel wretched, and almost felt panic, as his elaborate strategy suddenly lost its 'invulnerability'.

"I prefer this city to Welly-Belly." she said.

Edmund laughed. Dorothy had often regarded his home town of Wellawnbury with a mixture of disgust and contempt.

"Much busier." he said

"The people are more interesting", she replied: "they know they're ordinary. Well-Belly's think they're special."

She glanced towards him very briefly, and smiled a joyless smile.

They chose to stop at a city centre public house.

"Get me a double brandy!" she exclaimed as they sat down there.

He went off to the bar, to order, and Dorothy looked out of the window at the people, the big buildings, the busy traffic.

She felt lucky, in an objective way, but subjectively, depressed... ill-used ... deserted. How could he? Why should he?

She looked round, as he placed her brandy before her, and sat down in the adjacent seat.

"I've got a wonderful week planned for us, my boy!" she said, her eyes now twinkling, as she squeezed his hand. He felt more relaxed now, and happier. Sex gave him comfort, and security; and the rich, aching anticipation made him feel totally at one with himself. He laughed lightly.

"What was so funny?" she asked, smiling at him.

"Oh, I just suddenly feel smug!" he replied.

"You're a bastard", she laughed: "a real, fucking bastard. But I can't hate you all the time, Edmund. You really are too beautiful!"

They arrived at her rented terraced house, not far from the centre. He smiled as he got out of the car as the setting sun lent the modest street a pleasantly mellow aspect. Dot was opening the door as he turned back towards her. Passing through the tiny entrance hall, and bypassing the stairs, he followed her into a spacious kitchen. He saw onions hung from hessian strings attached to hooks in the ceiling. A smell of garlic and coriander tickled his nostrils, and made him smile again. The ceiling and the walls were white-washed, and he sat down on a large wooden kitchen chair, more typical of a farmhouse than this small terraced cottage.

And on these walls, he looked at the large, looming, self-serious pictures of the Pre-Raphaelites' hung by Dorothy.

"I'm sure you're hungry", she said, opening the door to a tall, pine cupboard.

"How did you guess?"

"You kept glancing over to the man next to us in the pub, eating his chips. You're not a homo, so I suppose it's his chips you're after."

Edmund watched her as she skipped deftly from pot to pot, vegetable to vegetable: chopping, grating. She was so swift, and sure. She would glance over her shoulder sometimes; aware that this was one of her last performances for him, and proud to hold him in thrall. As he watched, and waited for his food, he sipped a glass of Chablis she had poured for him. And when he finished the glass, she noticed, and poured out more for him:

"Good and dry, isn't it?", she asked, lifting his chin lightly with the tips of her fingers, and kissing his lips, looked lingeringly for a little time into his eyes, before resuming her bustling preparations.

Yellow hissing flames illuminated the bottom of the saucepans as the cooking began. Dot meanwhile hacked at a large brown loaf and cut off rough, jagged slices of bread.

"Ratatouille and bread. Very good for you. I only hope you'll like it."

"Smells wonderful", replied Edmund. And the food was delicious. They ate the Ratatouille slowly. Edmund munched at the bread, glancing, smiling; feeling suddenly self-conscious and exposed:

"Why not say it?" she asked, not smiling, nor frowning: just blank, flat. She was not going to spare him.

"Should I have come?", he stuttered, bread crumbs pattering down rather comically from his lower lip, and onto the wooden table.

"Did you really want to?", she asked, now irritated by him.

"Yes I did, and still do."

"Then that's your answer. Never don't do what you want to do, Edmund, as I'm sure someone or other has said."

He laughed slightly: "I don't suppose I can do this again. I want to be with you sometimes. Sometimes I ache for you. There's no substitute for you, Dot ... But the strain on both of us is too great. I want a great week of films and fucking!"

She threw her head back, and laughed loudly, feeling much relief:

"That's my boy. There are substitutes for you, though. But they're not nearly so shallow or beautifully corny as you are, Edmund!"

Edmund felt hurt by her jibe, but this was her party:

"I'm glad about that, anyway."

They went to bed soon after the meal, and more wine. Edmund felt in some ways he just wanted to get it over and done with, but he still found Dot attractive. For Dot though, this was important - a defining moment of her life, she felt. She needed to be in control. Above all, she needed to win.

They undressed quickly, without fuss. They lay on either side of the bed, symmetrically each had their legs draped out to the side. She took his face in her hand so very gently, and lovingly (she could not help it), and kissed him warmly, longingly ...

She carefully kissed his ears, his closed eyes, his neck, and down his body; but not so quickly, until she reached his penis: soldierly stiff, ready for duty. She smiled, and rubbed it with her fingers. She rubbed her lips over the tip, and kissed it, and took it right into her mouth, and sucked gently; hearing him sigh, and feeling his hand on her head, squeezing and letting go, squeezing and letting go ....

She felt his penis stiffen more, and she sucked harder, and held it in her mouth, gently squeezing with her lips, as he came with such force that she felt she would choke, but she held him there ....

She swallowed most of his spunk, but had some in her mouth as she kissed his lips, and forced her tongue into his mouth. She felt some little resistance as he tasted the sperm.

"Don't you like the taste of yourself?" she asked, impishly.

"Not used to it, Dot", he laughed at her, and pulled her closely to him, and kissed her passionately.

"Can you get hard again soon, my love?" she asked, gently squeezing his penis, and looking into his eyes as they lay together on the bed.

"I'm sure I can... but" he whispered: "I need some more wine."

"And I need to go and powder my bum!", she laughed

as she got up, and returned briefly, bringing in another opened bottle of Chablis, before disappearing again.

Edmund, now on his own, lay on the bed, sipping Chablis, feeling as good as men feel when they have come, and then emerge from that uncontrolled ecstasy in a warm, bed, the smell of sex around them. Edmund, unlike Dot, did not smoke, but liked to drink wine in the intervals between sex. As he mused there, he remembered his father had confided to him that Vivian, Oscar's wife, liked to smell whisky on his breath when he kissed her during sex.

There was, of course, a darker side to this visit. He would not see Dot again, he was sure, and he had to tell her. Well, she knew, but he had to... discuss? Talk about? Ask what she thought? Couldn't she see the difficulty with his seeing Leela so much now, and so seriously? And if with Leela he had sex, as she wanted so much, he felt morally he could not carry on with Dorothy, could he?

He looked around the room. On the ceiling, above the bed, was a picture of a couple making love. He could not decide the style, except to note that it was not the usual Pre-Raphaelite image that Dot seemed to prefer. Or maybe no longer preferred, as he noticed now that none of her old pictures were here. A more daring, less safe style of portraiture was there. (Almost all the prints were people in poses). Well, he was not surprised. Dot had often ridiculed his liking for Titian as "porcelain beauty without heart or true passion". Maybe, he thought, for the first time as he recalled her saying this, that she had really meant he had no heart?

But surely he did feel about others. After all, he could take what he wanted from each of these women and not care about what they wanted. He had been tempted more than many times, he thought ruefully, to fuck Leela, just as she wanted, but had stopped himself feeling it was not right. And he could now simply take a holiday with Dot, and look forward to their next meeting, avoiding all this negative jabs from her, and knowing that Leela accepted the current situation anyway. Perhaps he had been wrong, and this is what he should do.

Edmund lowered his head to the pillow, took a fleeting glimpse of the erotic coupling directly above, and closed his eyes. He did not sleep, but was not really awake for those next few minutes. He saw himself standing on a railway station. Not big, like the one he had arrived on that day; but a tiny country one, and although it was daylight, the air around had a dismal and thick consistency of a grey soup. Here was the train, puffing relentlessly towards him, as he waited on the platform, clutching a newspaper in his left hand. The train came closer and closer, and leaning from one of the carriage windows he recognised Leela. She was propelled towards him, her head (or rather face) seemed to fill the dream screen, smiling at him, and he at her. Her image grew larger and larger, before it enveloped and swallowed him. He looked around, then suddenly saw the face looking back at him, as it and the train sped onwards. She smiled at him again, and waved towards him, and said something, but he couldn't hear ....

Then from that same direction, the train appeared to reverse, and the images got closer. Leela seemed to have disappeared, but Dorothy was there now, playing cards, and invited Edmund to join her. Now he seemed to be on the train, so he did so, but did not understand the game. Dorothy told him "not to worry", and eventually they stopped playing, and Dorothy looked out of the window. Edmund followed her view, and saw nothing but the grey-white soup.

"Knackered already?", said Dot, prodding him in the arm.

"No, I'm not. But I did have a .... well ..... waking dream, I suppose."

"Wet dream?"

Edmund grunted a suppressed laugh, as she went on:

"Open spaces or confined?"

"Both, I suppose... there was a railway st..."

"Don't say anything else, Edmund. I shouldn't have tempted you. Talking about dreams destroys them. We need our dreams."

Edmund thought a little, took a sip of wine, and went on:

"Freud wouldn't have had much to write about if his patients hadn't told him their dreams."

"Seems so terrifically sad, though ... all those precious, private tails of hope and fantasy."

"Some dreams are bad, though"

"Only after you eat cheese or drink bad wine, Edmund!" she laughed: "And now I want you again ... Come here ..."

She caressed him closely. He could smell the faint perfume of her soap, and felt the moisture on her skin, and realised she had taken a bath.

"Oh my love, my darling", she whispered, pressing her body against his: "I will take you to the highest and the lowest ... ", she kissed him as she spoke to him in a low monotone:

"I need you ... a lifetime in seven days ... it couldn't be more wonderful."

They caressed tenderly, passionately. He rubbed her cunt with his finger. She was slippery-wet, and feeling an almost painful urge, he rolled her onto her back and plunged into her. He did not have to guide himself, he was so hard.

She looked at him, enjoying the sex, but obvious to him, she had something else in mind.

"That's enough of that!" she said, almost coldly, wrenching him out of her by pushing away his hips and pulling herself back ... He was shocked, but before he had time to speak, she had rolled onto her front ...

"There, there ...." and she guided him towards her.

"Oh! This way... yes, yes why not?" said Edmund, helping her to find her cunt.

"No! No, not that, my little boy ... this... ", and she rubbed the end of his hardened penis against her anus: "This is what I want, Edmund!"

He was taken aback, he was unsure, he never had ...

But now, wet and hard, he was in her anus.

"Now, fuck me! Fuck me you bastard! Fuck me for all the years I'll live without you! Go on, go on!"

He felt her around him, a new, strange sensation ... yet not unpleasant, not repulsive, as he always thought this sort of thing would be .... and so he went into her hard, and found her gasps of pain no longer stopped him, almost encouraged him ....

He thrust into her as much as he could, and when he came, he wanted this new receptor of his seed to feel it, to feel *him* there .... he stopped, sweating and breathing deeply. But he had not pulled out from her in disgust or shame. He stayed there, kissing her, as she sighed and moaned in pleasure. She was facing to one side, and he could see she was smiling with some contentment, her eyes closed, her need fulfilled.

They lay like this for some time, and eventually went to sleep in this pose, only to flop to their usual side-by-side when Dorothy awoke, found herself now free of his shrunken penis, and eased away from his weight to curl into a more comfortable position for sleep.

The next night, Edmund wanted to go to bed early, about eight o'clock.

"But Eddy, dear... you have not yet had your wine."

"Fuck the wine."

"No, fuck *me*, Eddy ... but I think I look better after you've had one or two glasses ..."

She was deliberately coquettish, speaking, moving like a dim-brained youngster. And he responded, even though he saw the game, and he pulled her clothes off her, quickly got out of his own, and clasping her closely, kissed her lips, then her breasts, now her cunt, lifting and opening her legs ...

And he lifted her higher, and licked along and into her cunt, then further, and his tongue entered her there also. He was no longer revolted by this intimacy. The new tastes and smells indeed seemed to stimulate him, and the realisation of that troubled him less ...

"This is lovely, Edmund," she said, clutching his scalp with her hands so strongly it was hurting him. He moved his mouth to her nipples and lightly bit them. She involuntarily flinched, but then pulled him closely into her breasts. They kissed now, mouth-to-mouth, and she reached down, and pulled his penis towards her. He entered her, and very slowly moved up and down on her she looked up at him, and smiled, her eyes glazed with love for him.

"You prefer this way, don't you... in my cunt."

He stopped his movement, and pulling out, roughly turned her over. She laughed lightly:

"Oh my boy... I see you have a taste for the real thing, now."

He guided his penis into her anus, and slowly at first, so as not to hurt her too much, he fucked her there, feeling her buttocks flap against his body with an audible 'slap'.

He came in her and then turned her over to face her, to look at her:

"Before this, I was some sort of virgin", he said, smiling. She remained impassive:

"I wasn't", she said, as she bent down to his penis, and sucked it.

She lit a cigarette while he retrieved some wine from downstairs. He brought up the bottle of Chardonnay and two glasses, setting them down by the bed, as he smelt the pleasant acrid odour of Galois. He passed her a glass, and took one himself as he flopped down on the bed. She smiled at him as he approvingly sipped the wine, and rested her head on his shoulder.

"Do you like fucking me... in the 'new' way?"

"Yes... yes, I do."

"Would you tell your mother you'd fucked my up the arse?", and she burst our laughing as for a moment, Edmund's face set in serious contemplation. He also laughed, adding:

"She knows we have an intimate relationship. Maybe

that's as far as it should go. I mean, for anyone apart from those in the relationship."

He glanced down towards her as she stared into the distance:

"Am I making any sense?"

"No. Not for me, anyway. I've always wondered what my friends got up to with their boyfriends and girlfriends. And girls often talk about the most intimate things between each other, Edmund. So, think about it, Edmund. Would you be ashamed to tell your mother you'd sodomised me? Or anyone, for that matter."

"I hope not, but I don't think I'd do it. What about you?"

"Yes, I told my mother the first time I did it."

"And?"

"Oh, like only mothers can do, I think, she refused to understand what I was talking about and changed the subject. The next generation will probably have a weekly magazine devoted to the topic!"

"Is it... well... that... popular. I mean, between men and women?"

"I think so. Well, in my experience. I had an affair with

a married man who only ever fucked me that way. He was religious and said that fucking a woman like that didn't amount to being unfaithful."

"That sounds ridiculous."

"Well, he believed it, and I liked it. Although it hurt me at first, and I was worried about being damaged. Since then many of the men I get seem to want it."

"And I want it." He had put down his glass, and rubbed his erect penis against her. She turned on her side, and continued to smoke her cigarette as he fucked her in his newly favoured fashion, coming with great passion, into her, as she still smoked her Galois.

"What a perfect evening", she said, turning onto her back: "Smoke in my lungs, spunk in my arse!" She laughed, and turned to him:

"I'm very crude, sometimes Edmund. But I need life to be fun, as well as challenging. You are always serious and analytical. I'm synthetical!", and she laughed again: "And I need more wine. Go and open a bottle of Merlot. There's one in the kitchen."

Next day they walked into the city centre mid-morning. They had decided to do some shopping:

"Tonight we'll have pasta, Edmund. And some vegetables and spices for a sauce. And something else .... maybe some minced meat." They were in the market, and dodging from stall to stall, looking at fruits and vegetables:

"Oh! I need some lemons! And I know a little corner... over here, Eddy!"

And she dragged him to a small stall at the back of the main thoroughfare. A small man with grizzly grey hair, long and unkempt, in a very old suit smiled at them and rubbed his hands together:

"Carlos... have you some Olive Oil?"

He bowed slightly, and disappeared behind a curtain, to return with a large cylindrical can, with a coned top. She removed the screwed top and smelled it, then poured a little into a tiny cup which Carlos proffered towards her. She tasted it:

"Mm very good. Peppery and sweet. Here, Edmund, see what you think."

He sipped a little, and it tasted good to him, so he nodded in appreciation.

"Carlos gets oil for Italian restaurants. Probably all smuggled. But it is very good.", she said, giving Carlos some money:

"Now, let's get some spaghetti, sweet peppers if we can, tomatoes... spices ..."

When it came to getting the meat, they went to the butcher's stall and picked out some lean beef, and waited while the shopkeeper minced it by hand through a large mincer attached to the counter. The meat squirted slowly through the numerous holes in the machine. The strands of meat almost seemed to regain some of the life they had lost that morning, as they squirmed, worm like into the catching bowl.

"That's enough", said Dorothy, and the butcher scraped off the surplus meat from the machine, into the bowl, and scooped in into some grease-proof paper on the weighing scales.

She paid, the meat was wrapped and bagged, and they went on their way.

“Let’s get the bus, Dot”, said Edmund, as he struggled to comfortably carry the large can of oil.

“It’s only round that corner ... can you manage?”

He nodded, and they were soon queuing for the next bus. It was a muggy evening, with a scent of warm rain in the air. It had not rained yet, which was fortuitous, since neither had a raincoat nor umbrella. The bus stopped not more than 50 yards from the house, and it had started to spit rain as they arrived.

“Seems we got back just in time”, she said, smiling at him as she unlocked the door.

While Dorothy prepared the meal of spaghetti Bolognese, she exiled Edmund to the front room to be out of her way. This room had a window onto the street, and as Edmund sat there, half reading a newspaper, he could hear the approaching footfall, and sometimes conversation, of passers-by. When they were near to the window, he could even discern some of the words:

“.... get more chips at the corner of Jackson Avenue but I ...”

"..... she had the nerve to say I looked like a tart because of my lipstick when she goes all the way with ....."

".... a nice hot bath, and get you to bed young man before you catch cold. And I don't want to hear ..."

'Man dies after fight at City baths', screamed the headline of the story he was reading. A man had a fight with a soldier, was knocked down and suffered a fractured skull. He had apparently suffered from a thin cranium. The story went in to the detail of his family, and had a picture of his holding a football, grinning into the camera with a squint, as the sun was obviously shining in his eyes. Involuntarily, Edmund's hand was now gingerly massaging his own head, as he wondered if he had a thin cranium.

Reading further, no-one seemed to remember what the fight was about, except that drink was involved, but there was disagreement as to whether the soldier or his victim had been drinking. The victim's mother said he was a 'good boy', and was an apprentice fitter in a local boiler works. There was a picture of the front of the works - "Appleyard's Boiler Factory".

Edmund put the paper down, and drank some

Darjeeling tea Dorothy had prepared for him. He had noticed as soon as he had entered the room that there was a film screen set up in one corner of the room, and had assumed it was something to do with the advertising work Dorothy did for a living.

"Food's ready, Edmund", she said, popping her head around the door.

They ate in relative silence, the food being so good, and the wine so smooth. After some strong, Turkish-style coffee, Dorothy said:

"We can see a film show tonight. French. Hot and sexy. Like you! Can you take the projector into the front room? I'll bring the film." She had indicated a large projector hidden from his view at the side of the kitchen cupboard. When they got into the room, she showed him how to place the projector on a small, high table strategically placed, and she deftly wound he film ready for the show:

"It's not exactly 35 mm quality, but it's entertaining!", she said, as she adjusted the projector so its beam landed squarely on the screen.

They sat together on the sofa, which faced the screen:

"Ready?" she asked.

"I am." he answered.

She switched off the room lights, sat down in the soft glow from the street light, and then clicked a switch on the camera from her seated position, and the film flickered into life. The show was dubbed into English from the original French, and the sound was thin and scratchy from a small speaker.

It was a black and white show, and was the story of a high-class, wealthy married woman who fantasised about being a prostitute so enthusiastically, she became one, in her spare time, telling her husband she had a job selling books. Touchingly, thought Edmund, he believed her.

"Very over used French film story", Dot whispered, almost as if there were other people watching with them: "but it's well done here, and ... well, you'll see."

Marianne, the would-be professional lady, was to meet her first client, arranged for her by her Madame. Edmund noted that Marianne looked as if she was dressed for dinner at the Ritz, and wondered if this ('in real life') would unsettle her customer.

It did not seem to in this story as they went to the pre-arranged room in a small hotel, although he was dressed like an insurance salesman (he turned out to be a tax inspector). After some amusing and embarrassed undressings - he in the bathroom, she in the bedroom, she lay on the bed waiting for him. She was frankly naked, and Edmund was impressed with the clarity of the image of the whole of her body. No modesty draping of sheets or camera angle. And when the tax-man came in, Edmund realised this was not the usual sort of film he had seen in the Film Club at home. The man was naked, and sported the most unbelievably large penis which was in full erection, and was bouncing around right in the middle of the screen.

Marianne expressed her concern with the size of him on the outside compared to the size of her on the inside, but Edmund notice her eyes never left her client's appendage, and soon she was caressing it, licking it and sucking it; showing a rather unconvincing rapid loss of embarrassment. The whole event was expertly and explicitly photographed, although the dubbing seemed to be increasing less related to the action.

When they had sex, this again was photographed with enthusiastic candour, and indeed, thought Edmund, the actors obviously had to position themselves in very odd ways to show the detail of exactly what was happening. However, the story itself was entertaining in other ways, and Edmund found the story line surprisingly strong, for what he considered was a pornographic film, which he had previously only heard about.

"Phew!" he exclaimed, after it was over, and said: "how did you get hold of that? I thought they were completely illegal."

"In a way they are. We can't show them at the film club. So we swap them around between ourselves."

"The only thing like that I ever saw was a magazine called "Health and Efficiency"", he added.

"You dirty little boy! Well, I hope you are now in the mood .... ", she got up and turned to him, smiling enigmatically:

"I have a few things to do in the bedroom. Well, help yourself to whatever you want to drink from the kitchen ...

make yourself at home down here. I'll call you when I'm ready."

She left the room, and he heard her climbing the stairs. Edmund, grinning to himself, suitably intrigued, went to the kitchen and finding some brandy, poured himself a generous portion and returned to the front room. He settled in an armchair and reflected on the film they'd just seen. How could anyone do that sort of thing, in front of the cameras and so on? Wasn't it embarrassing? Did they enjoy it?

It was about half an hour before a call from the upstairs bedroom came:

"Come to bed, Edmund!"

He put down his glass, left the room, and stepped slowly up the stairs, his heart beating heavily. He went to the bedroom, and had to open the door. There was music playing there, he guessed it was Indian or Persian. The room was so dark, it was almost difficult for him to find his way:

"Give me your hand", Dorothy said.

Her hand felt cool, and light, and he shuddered slightly

with excitement. She gripped him surely though, and guided him to the bedside. His eyes were now used to the dim light, furnished as it was by several candles placed on shelves around the walls of the room. He discerned the wisping trail of burning incense, and smelled the sweet odour of jasmine and sandlewood. Looking to the bed, he saw it was covered completely with a large, seemingly heavy white cloth. And at his side Dorothy stood straight and erect, and seemed taller than he. She stared ahead, not meeting his gaze:

"Get undressed, Edmund. Quickly."

He did so. Why not? He noticed as he took off his clothes that Dot was draped in a Victorian style nightgown, high necked with long sleeves, of crisp, white linen and which made a reassuring rustling sound when she moved. He was now naked, waiting like a baby by her side. She turned to him:

"Lie on the bed, my love. On your front."

He did so, head to one side, staring at a flickering candle, listening to the music; feeling part of its rhythmic journey ....

Not in his full vision, he discerned her, in her great, noisy, rustling white; lift her hand high above him, above his head, he guessed... he knew then, and reflected so later, that he was not sure there was no danger, but that even knowing this, he was frozen, unable to take action, unable to break the spell. He was as much a conspirator in this anyway. He heard a heavy, liquid sound; then felt a cold, sharp sensation on the back of his neck... he stiffened, knowing it was too late ... Then more liquid sound, and he realised, almost with some sense of disappointment (as absurd as this seemed to him) that she had poured some harmless - quite pleasant and warm - oily liquid on him. Now he felt her finger tips rubbing the oil into his skin; the back of his neck, his shoulders... then more oil, and he could smell it, inside the tunnels of jasmine, sandlewood, candle wax, and woman, he could smell the peppering olive oil they had bought that day.

She carefully rubbed the oil into the whole of his back, then poured more, from a jar with a long, narrow spout, down the small of his back, and between his buttocks; a breathtaking sensation as it trickled past, around and into his anus, and then to his genitals. She rubbed the oil into him, all over and into his body, in a dispassionate but gentle way that excited him intensely. She applied the oil to his legs, and turning him over, lovingly rubbed the liquid between his toes:

"Christ chose the most beautiful way to show love." She seemed to say this to herself, as she looked intently at his feet while she massaged the oil into them.

All over the front of his body she spread the oil, and finally, throwing off her white gown, she knelt before him naked:

"Kneel up"

He did so, and she pulled and pushed his legs into the position she wanted:

"This is a Karma Sutra position"

So saying, she turned her back to him, and lowered herself onto him. The sensation of her cunt softly swallowing his penis had this time (for him) a new sensation of love ... pleasure ... sensuous indulgence ....

"You stay still ..."

She rode up and down on him, his penis now so hard

it almost hurt. She stopped, and slightly turned her head, holding his testicles from between her legs.

"Don't come. I don't want you to come tonight. Do you understand?"

"Yes... I can come again if ..."

"No. Edmund, I don't want you to come tonight. It will spoil the experience."

She rode him again, and she could feel expertly inside her, when he was too close, and she would stop, and hold his testicles, almost hurting him sometimes.

Time and again, and in different poses, she would bring him to the brink of ejaculation, but stopped him, leaving him, after two hours, with aching loins, but otherwise in a drug-like daze of ecstasy.

"And now, just as I rubbed your feet, so you must do something for me, my love"

"Anything"

She rolled off the bed, and reaching underneath, retrieved a cane about a yard long, and offered it to him:

"Hit me"

"What?"

"Edmund, I want you to hit me. Wherever you prefer ... I would like you to cane my buttocks... quite hard."

"Dot... I can't... I could never hurt you."

"What? You can't hurt me? Then why are you leaving me, you bastard", and she thrust the cane at him again:

"Hit me!"

Edmund got up, taking the cane gingerly, and turned it so the thicker end was in his hand, and saw her laying on her front, smiling towards him:

"Imagine you're a teacher, and one of your pupils has been naughty... it's as simple as that, Eddy."

He started to tap her bare buttocks a little.

"When are you going to start?" she teased, sarcastically.

He hit her harder.

"Better... hit me harder"

He did so, and then harder, and soon there were red weals across her buttocks.

She turned over to look at him, tears running down her cheeks:

"See, you can do it, my darling, can't you?"

And she took the cane, and threw it aside, and pulled him down onto her:

"Now you can fuck me, and come."

"And this time we'll do it my way", he said, turning her over, and pushing his penis into her anus. She smiled and sighed:

"So my little boy has learned how to suck a lollipop!"

Afterwards, they lay together, her head on his shoulder, his arm around her. She was smiling, rubbing her face into his chest, smiling, joking, laughing:

"You've got three days left of me, Edmund .... Do you think you can face it?"

The following day, they had a lazy morning, and in the afternoon Dot had to go to see a client with some drawings she was doing for an advertising campaign:

"I'll be a couple of hours or so, Eddy. Make yourself at home."

CHAPTER NINE

The sun streamed through the front-room window. The street was busy. Housewives with scarves and shopping bags scurried back and forth, stopping to exchange information, nodding, laughing; sometimes shrieking. There were no young people. Long before they had gone to school. Edmund imagined them at morning break, with their little glass bottles of milk and wax-paper straws. He remembered the gurgling noise as he drained the bottom of the bottle. He turned back into the room, feeling the need to get down some record of these moments ...

In a corner of the room he saw a folder which he knew contained some thick sketching paper. He could do some drawings of the street, which in the morning, autumn sunshine struck a beautiful, mellow image.

He worked with growing enthusiasm, using sticks of charcoal Dot kept in a tin on the shelf. He had completed three views of the street, and was surprised to see the darkening skies when he saw Dot walking back home, down the street. He decided quickly to put her into the picture, and by the time she had taken off her coat and put away her folio covers, and come into the room, her image was almost finished.

"Let's see how you spent your time", she said, looking over his shoulder: "This is good, Edmund. Much better than your usual work."

"I'm glad you like them."

She had taken the last drawing and was looking closely at it:

"And is this me?"

"Yes ... done very rapidly ... from your returning home just now."

She kissed him: "That's really touching, Edmund. Can I have this one?"

"Yes. And here are two more. You can have them all,

if you want. They belong here anyway. Or maybe in the dustbin!", he laughed as he handed them to her.

A tear came to her eye, he noticed, but she quickly turned and left the room, saying: "I need some tea."

They had a light meal of salad and cheese. Chomping on a stick of celery, Dorothy looked over to him: "I'd like to get drunk tonight, Edmund."

After the meal, she opened a bottle of white Bordeaux she had selected from the kitchen cupboard, and poured two full glasses for them:

"Cheers! Here's to tonight, may I surprise you yet again!", and drinking half a glass of the wine in one draft, kissed him on the forehead, and said, wine bottle dangling from her free hand: "Come into the other room."

When they had entered the front room, Dorothy put down her glass and the wine bottle, and went over to a corner of the room where a record player stood on a small table. Next to it, on the floor, was a box of records, which Dorothy flicked through, and choosing one, placed it on the turntable, and pulled back the playing arm till there was an audible "click". The record started to rotate, and she carefully lowered the stylus on the beginning, with some little difficulty and a certain amount of rasping noise through the speaker.

"That's good music", said Edmund, tapping his foot to the pre-war dance music, as he sat in the chair, sipping wine. Dorothy smiled, looked round to him, and sat on the floor, by his feet. She took his free hand, and rubbed it on her cheek, kissed it and held it as they listened to the record.

"Let's dance!", she suddenly exclaimed, almost startling him.

"O.K.", he said.

They danced a clumsy 'lingering blues', knocking into chairs and tables: she hummed the tunes, and laughed when they stumbled. He was straight and tall, and smiled sometimes, looking ahead. Dorothy could barely look at him. She wanted to remember this feeling all her life, but to forget about Edmund, and all that they had shared. And as they danced, she drank wine, and so did he, and then another bottle was opened.

"Midnight ... perfect, Edmund... let's go to bed."

In the bedroom, she took off all her clothes with excessive care, folded them, and looked at them as she placed them on the chair by her bed. She lit a candle and placed it in a small reflector on a low shelf in the wall. Edmund watched her:

"Come on, my boy, I want you!"

He had undressed, and quickly joined her. There was some tender foreplay. She was quite silent, moving within his hands and caresses like a serpent, wriggling and straightening out, kissing, touching, stroking.

"Make love to me, Edmund ... here, on top of me... I want to feel your weight on me ..."

He entered her.

"Do I feel good, inside?" (She sounded almost coquettish.)

"Very good."

"Do I feel *wet* inside?"

"Yes."

"Look at me, Edmund, let me kiss your eyes... your mouth... Edmund, push hard into me."

He did so, and she pulled at his buttocks, and pushed her nails painfully into his flesh:

"Edmund! Do you feel that cunt you are fucking, eh?" she said, in a horse, urgent whisper: "You feel it around you? It's full of spunk, my love ..."

"Not yet, not yet."

"Not yours, not yours, Edmund."

He slowed his thrusting, but did not stop:

"How do you mean?"

"I mean that I made love with someone else this afternoon, my love ... now fuck me."

He was not put off by this revelation, which puzzled his mind, but not his body. He had become harder, and fucked her harder, and took her head in his hands, and kissed her open mouth... then he almost snapped out:

"And I suppose his prick was here too, in your mouth ..."

He could not believe what he had said.

"Right in, right down, Edmund... everything, of course my love ... Why would I spare you anything?"

He made love to her longer than he usually did, and

enjoyed her, and felt nothing but tenderness and love for her as he lay quietly afterwards.

"I've been a naughty girl, Eddy. Beat me."

"I feel only soft things for you, Dorothy. It doesn't matter about this afternoon."

"It's meant to matter, Edmund... ", and she carefully, gently, pushed him off, and reached for the cane:

"Beat me.", she demanded, holding out the stick towards him: "You're the only one who can do this to me. You're the only one who can hurt me."

After he had finished, she cried profusely, and clung to him ... he needed to hold her more than ever, and they fell asleep tightly in each other's arms.

The following day was sunny and cloudless, and quite warm. They had a lazy, late morning, and walked in the park in the afternoon, having coffee by the lake. They returned home for a light tea, and went to the city again in the early evening to go to Dot's favourite Italian restaurant for dinner. They took a table in a dark corner, with a few flowers and a candle:

"This is the best restaurant in town, I think", she said,

reaching over to Edmund, and squeezing his hand: "I'll order the wine if you like."

"Do you mind if I pay the bill?"

"Darling, I insist!", and they both laughed.

The meal was languorous, with many courses, and even some live music from a man with a fiddle.

"Can we go home soon?", asked Dorothy, as they drank coffee.

They caught the bus home, which got them to the end of the street by 10:30. They alighted the bus, and walked slowly to the house, as if to savour every step, every door of every house, every sound, every odour, and every lighted window: and all those sounds - the Radio, a variety show or pop music, sometimes a record player; often the sound of voices: chatting, arguing, sparring.

Occasionally, too, a motor car or motor cycle would drive down the street, and past them. There were several push bikes, with their wobbling front lights, carrying factory workers back home at the end of their afternoon shift, 2 - 10 pm, as Dot remembered from her father back home in Sheffield.

When they arrived at her door, they went in: "Make yourself cosy in the front room, Eddy. I'll get some brandy, if you like." He nodded approval, and went to sit down. She soon came in, with two brandy glasses. She sat opposite him, and smirking, said: "Feeling naughty?"

Edmund raised his eyebrows, grinned and nodded. Dot went over to her art cupboard, and in the top shelf, behind paints and bunches of brushes, she retrieved a tiny parcel, wrapped in silver paper, and from the bottom shelf, a large piece of white paper. She then got some rolling tobacco and cigarette papers from a pot on the mantel shelf, and on the paper she took out a cigarette paper, put in some tobacco strands, and then from the (obvious) precious parcel in the silver paper, broke away a little of the dark-brown substance, and sprinkled it in the cigarette. She deftly rolled up the cigarette, and tidying her knee, and putting aside all the ingredients, took a lighter from a table beside her chair and lit the cigarette:

"Try it!", she said, having taken a very heavy drag herself.

"I don't smoke."

"This isn't a normal cigarette. Come on. Don't be queasy!"

He took the cigarette gingerly, and took drew on it very lightly, shivering with the taste and sensation never known except years ago, in his school's old air-raid shelters, and never enjoyed.

"Try to take more smoke, Eddy ... it's not for the tobacco... it's this you go for ..."

"What is that", he asked, obediently drawing heavily on the cigarette.

"Cannabis resin. From Afghanistan. Illegal but well .... let's wait."

They shared the cigarette for the several minutes it took to smoke it.

"How do you feel, Edmund... ", she asked, as he had become quite still, and stared with apparent contentment at the floor.

"Very strange... but beautifully strange ... great and beautiful .... bright and beautiful ..."

She smiled at him, and they sat together there for two hours, talking nonsense sometimes, but usually nothing at all. When they went to bed, it was to sleep, and Dorothy held Edmund to her like a baby, as he fell asleep almost as soon as he had lain down there.

At breakfast, Edmund asked her: "Why didn't we do this before?"

"Because I was afraid you might finish with me."

Tears trickle down her face, and Edmund looked away:

"This week has been the time of my life, Dorothy, and whatever happens to me in the future, I'll never forget it nor regret any of it. You have given me a sense of freedom I never knew I never had..."

"And that's why I believe we will never meet again. Even after you have tired of your Leela. I'm sorry, but I think you will, some day. You have a ruthlessness that you can't handle, and I don't think anyone will ever tame that in you. Your beauty and unconscious sensuousness is perfectly matched by your shallowness of emotion and feelings... That sounds very bitchy, but I think it's true ... It all makes me love you so much, Eddy ... I think we've shared everything you could ever want to do with me, and so I don't think you'll ever find any reason to see me again."

At the station, she cradled his head in her hands, and looked into his face, and smiled, and laughed: "What a bloody wonderful time we had, eh, my boy?"

She left to walk away, not looking back, not waiting on the platform for his train.

He sat in a carriage crammed in with noisy, garrulous passengers who talked to him, shared jokes and so on ... he did feel unaccountably sad and empty, and even desperate, in some ways, for a short while, and thought of meeting Leela with some trepidation.

CHAPTER TEN

Familiar things

When he first saw her after those days with Dorothy, he looked into Leela's face, and discerned that instantaneous, fatal pause of recognition.

"Oh my love, it's so good to see you again."

She had clasped his waist with eager earnestness. He held her close to him and felt her warmth; her blue cardigan tickled his nose.

"Let's go out tonight", he said to her.

"Whatever you want", she said looking at him steadily: "as long as we're alone."

Edmund was still slightly afraid of being alone with her. Would he now be content with juvenile fumbling around after the eroticism he'd now experienced?

The winter of 1956 was cold, and they did not cycle much. Facing each other, perched often as not on a carpet, between them a few feet away, a coal or wood fire would burn or smoulder; and there on the carpet, too, a game board, or playing cards. They still loved being together, even though "certain assumptions" meant that the early electric spark of uncertainty had died.

"What should we do on Saturday afternoon, Edmund? We could go to 'The Stadium' as usual, but Pauline wants us to see her play in the school hockey match."

Leela had loved "Dirt Track" motor bike racing at 'The Stadium' since her Dad first took her as a toddler. Now Edmund was hooked: to the intoxicating smell of the motor oil they used, the snarl of the engines, and the sliding clumsy ballet of the race itself. However he was not, he had found, adverse to any Saturday sporting activity, because they never lasted too long, and he could always 'get involved' in some way or other.

"Hockey it is!"

Christmas Day was spent apart, as both Edmund and Leela were expected to be with their families. The occasion was one, however, which offered a chance for each of them to buy the other a present. Leela bought Edmund a print of a Renaissance picture she knew he liked, and Edmund gave her a framed portrait of herself, which he had secretly made of her. There were other little pleasantries exchanged, when they met on Boxing Day. Leela gave a large bag of fruit, and Edmund presented her with some popular records.

"This parcel is heavy!" she said as he gave it to her. She opened it to reveal four of the heavy 78 rpm records - two of these were Elvis P, of course "Blue Suede Shoes" and "Love me Tender".

* * *

When spring came, and they looked forward to the first anniversary of their meeting, they would spend more of their time together outdoors. Even when it was cold, when he could, Edmund would borrow his mother's car, and they would go to their favoured places on the moors, and find in each other the intense physical pleasure which was so central to their relationship.

"But it's not all sex, that I love you for..." he said one evening in the car, as they looked over the edge of the hill, down towards Wellawnbury.

"Not sex at all, really, love!" she laughed: "unless my education has been sadly lacking!"

"Well, we do most things I suppose ..."

"You don't do to me what you do to... your other girlfriends."

"Well, you're my only girlfriend now, you know... and, well, I'd like to give us just a bit more time to be sure ... Many girls still like to be virgins when they get married, even it they do play around a bit with their boyfriends."

"That's what most of my girlfriends say, I suppose... but, Edmund, being a virgin isn't any more interesting for a girl than a boy, you know... so why did you sacrifice your innocence, eh?"

"It's different for a man. Unlike a girl, he's the pursuer, and ...."

"Try telling Kitty that!" she laughed.

"Well, yes, but Kitty's... unusual .... and maybe she's just too desperate for affection."

"Or sex."

"I didn't want to say that, Leela. I don't know her and I don't like insulting her ..."

"Why is that insulting her? Why is sex shameful, Edmund? And if it's shameful for girls, why not for men?"

"Not just that, love... I am older than you. I know you work now, but you're still a young girl, you know." He took her in his arms and squeezed her, and she smiled, and cooed with delight as she buried her head in his breast.

'Wait for it!'

It was shortly after they celebrated their anniversary with a dinner out at a restaurant that Edmund found a peculiar looking envelope waiting for him at the breakfast table.

"Good heavens!" he exclaimed: "I've been called up!"

Oscar soon joined Vivian and Edmund and after sipping his black coffee, shook his head and handed the letter back to his son:

"Well, we deferred it, and I hoped I'd managed to

get you out of it... but it's no good. Now if you'd studied Medicine."

For some reason, Edmund was slowly, but surely, feeling a warm comfort from this news, which he knew would wrench him away from home, from job, friends, and, of course, Leela for two years. He even felt some trickle of excitement, burying all those depressing stories of those he knew who had done or were now doing, National Service.

"I'll make a few phone calls, Edmund. See what I can do." said Oscar, smiling and patting his son on the arm as he left the kitchen to get ready for his morning surgery.

Vivian looked closely at her son, and smiled slightly:

"You don't seem too worried about this, Edmund."

He looked up and smiled at her, and sipped his tea:

"It's easier not to have to make decisions if they can be made for you."

CHAPTER ELEVEN

Spring 1957

Edmund had his basic training in a large camp near to London. After the initial shock, and the grindingly dull routine of marching and 'kit-care', he settled down, and found he was indeed having a good time. He and friends he had made regularly went drinking in the evenings and played football at the weekends and some weekdays. There were some written tests to take, which Edmund liked, although the others found dull:

"Why is an egg-head like you in a place like this?", asked Rob Hockey, an excessively extrovert and vulgar member of his circle: "couldn't your old man swing it so you got a nice cushy number in Whitehall?"

"Because I've not *enough* egg, Rob. If I had, I'd have done medicine I suppose and escaped call-up."

"You can drink beer as well as any fucker I've met, anyway!", reposted Adrian Wadsworth, a fellow Yorkshireman and keen rugby league player: "and you're not a bad prop."

On his own, he did manage to cycle sometimes (on an army machine), through wooded lanes and the little villages which reminded him of home, and sit in the pubs being eyed by locals who wondered who he was and why he was there.

After six weeks, the first part of this training was deemed to be over, and he was sent for interview to the Ministry of War in Whitehall, London.

"Said you should be in Whitehall, Eddy!", observed Rob.

The journey by train was a short one and he walked from the station across some of the centre of the city to his destination. There he had to wait for 40 minutes in a musty, wood-panelled room for his interview with a Major Dillon. He was ushered into the office by a young Captain, who closed the door behind him to leave him alone with the Major, who read carefully a paper which he held flat to his desk: "Edmund Rice?", and he nodded in response. The major waved him into a chair, and took several more minutes to look at the paper, then removed his glasses and looked at Edmund, and smiled:

"Understand you have a flare for Languages"

"No, Sir, I'm a surveyor." replied Edmund in surprise.

"Of course.. You'll have to take a test anyway.", and the Major chuckled: "That'll be tomorrow morning. You can go now, Rice"

He left the room, and saw the Captain seated at his desk, scribbling something down.

"Ah! Rice. You'll stay in London tonight of course. Here's the address."

Edmund looked at the piece of paper and noted the instructions on what transport to take.

"It's a hostel. Not a bad place. Pretty clean. About half an hour away by the Underground. See you tomorrow at 9."

Edmund had a reasonable night in that Spartan place, which was guarded by two military policemen behind a reception desk, who glared at him suspiciously as he first entered, and spoiled their chatter, gave a cursory glance at his papers, and then glared at him with even greater suspicion:

"Up the stairs, two floors. Swing doors straight ahead, right, first left and number 12A is the second on the right."

They then returned to their interrupted conversation.

The bed was not too bad, there was a bath and plenty of hot water down the hall, and after writing some letters home, and reading a book, he undressed and lay down. Images and ideas flitted in and out of his brain, though, and he couldn't sleep much. By 6 he was washed and dressed, and at the reception desk, asking about breakfast. An older man, not in uniform, was now on duty, and smiled at him over his newspaper:

"Down the road, on the left. About 50 yards. You can leave that bag here, if you like."

The café had only one other customer at that hour, and Edmund ordered a full cooked breakfast and tea, and sat down near to the window, so that he could look at the early bustle of commuters up and down the street. He decided to walk to the Ministry as he had plenty of time after his meal, and his overnight bag was not so heavy. It took him well over an hour, but he felt refreshed and ready for the test. He was joined in the examination room by another 20 or so soldiers. The captain sat at the front of the room as they completed their exercise. As far as Edmund was concerned, the test seemed to consist of a series of pictures to arrange correctly, with odd questions such as "What is the Taj Mahal?" and "Where does a S - W wind blow towards?"

After the exam, the captain called him over:

"Major Dillon would like to see you"

He made his way to the office, knocked, and was told to come in.

"How did you get on with the test?" asked Major Dillon: "Which question did you find most difficult?"

"The one with stripes and circles!" exclaimed Edmund, without hesitation, as he found that question incomprehensible.

"Really! Hmm ... ". Dillon's brow furrowed and he looked away: "You're off tomorrow. We'll forward your kit."

"Where to?"

"You'll know soon enough.", and he smiled at Edmund, almost in a fatherly way, for the first time.

"What about my test?"

"Haven't a clue", said the Major, picking up his pipe and tapping it vigorously against the side of the desk:" Anyway, you'd better get going. Things to arrange. See Warberton."

On leaving the Major's office, he found Captain Warberton in his usual place in the outer office. Warberton smiled towards him:

"Here are your papers. Read this one now and ask if there's anything you don't understand."

Edmund read if quickly, noticing "boat train" and some German name which he couldn't pronounce:

"Boat train! But where am I going?"

"No idea. Immediately you'll go to this place (he fingered the itinery) just outside Cologne. Then... who knows?", he laughed: "Anyway, your kit will be forwarded in good time for your arrival to wherever it is! . And compared to most post-basic trainees I'd guess you'll have a good time!"

He arrived at 5 am for the 5.30 boat train, after one more night in the hostel. He'd also managed to get a few more clothes to change into, after speaking to the old man at the reception desk.

There were plenty of other service men around. There were mostly still on the platform, sitting on their kit or other object, usually with friends or sweethearts, or relatives. Edmund, alone, boarded the train to find he had his pick of several empty compartments, as he didn't seek immediate companionship. He sat down, shuffling for several seconds until the inherent discomfort of the carriage seats were reduced to a tolerable level, and looked out of the window. It was still dark. The silver streaks of the rails glinted in the low light of the station. Over on the far platform, the stooping figure of a uniformed railway worker trudged in a resigned fashion, from the rest room to his next duty. Screeching and clanking of iron wheels and couplings echoed in the cavernous void. And then, a shouting: incoherent to those outside the small group of station workers, followed a loud clash of two carriages as a train was being made up on the adjacent platform.

Edmund settled down to a novel he'd brought with him - "Vatican Cellars" by Andre Gide - a book given to him long ago be Dorothy, and which had lain neglected until now.

Just before the train was due to set off, he was joined by three fresh-faced, beaming young conscripts who nodded greetings as they heaved their bags onto the luggage racks. He read his book, interspersed with glances through the window, as early light changed to the full light of morning. His three companions chatted excitedly at first then gave an enthusiastic rendering of "Tipperary", then snoozed, although one of them did read a newspaper, before finally laying it across his lap, and falling gently to sleep.

Edmund could not sleep. His mind was filled with anticipation of his new life. The thought of two years, and abroad, excited him. And what would his job be? He smiled to himself and returned to finishing his book.

"Good read?", asked the only other to be awake: "My name's Alec Groves. Pleased to meet you."

"Book's OK", smiled Edmund in return: "although there's a rail journey described here as well, but not a bit like this one!"

The other frowned, then smiled: "We're off for tank training. They say the Russians might attack any day. Suez and all that!", and he laughed and looked out of the window.

Much later, after some little conversation, they were separated on changing trains, and hours later still, long after he'd finished his novel, and had had some sleep, the train stopped in Southern Germany, and he recognised the station name as his destination.

He was met, as were many other National Servicemen, by a British Army bus to take them to their new posting. A bumpy ride, along dark roads boarded by ghostly skeletons of destroyed buildings, they reached a gate, and heard shouting and scraping of the gate, and were then put down next to a long wooden shed, very brightly lit inside. A sergeant was in there to meet them, and Edmund together with five others, was ordered to wait while the rest were billeted there for the night. The larger group was taken away by a corporal, and the sergeant shuffled the others into a room, where a lieutenant sat at a desk:

"You people have been selected for special duties. To help you achieve this, you will from now on take the rank of corporal …."

* * *

"We can pull rank on the other buggers now", said Archie, a tall thin Londoner and part of Edmund's group, after the briefing.

"Wonder what we'll be doing?", queried Edmund to himself, but overheard by the others as they sat on their bunks doing various things: writing letters, cleaning shoes, sewing stripes onto their sleeves …

"Tell you what", said one: "it'll be better than square bashing!"

"Maybe there really is a war coming", said another in a concerned voice: "maybe the Russians are going to invade, and we've been put in the firing line!"

"They've got the Sputnik now", he went on: "years

ahead of us. Makes sense for them to attack before we can catch up!", said another fuelling mounting consternation.

"Well, they can blow me up while I'm asleep, then!", exclaimed Archie, stretching himself on his bunk and shutting his eyes.

For two days there was little to do. There was some general classroom training on weapons of war, of techniques, of loading and firing guns of various kinds, repeating some of the basic training they'd had in England. On the third day, they were each issued with new orders by the Captain, who had gathered the group in their barrack mid-morning for that purpose:

"You'll be going your separate ways today", he announced, as each received their own envelope: "open up and make sure you understand what you have to do."

Edmund's instructions were to catch a train, for which there'd be a car to take him to the station; and he was to disembark at a station with a German name he didn't recognise, to meet with a Sergeant Vickers. He noticed that estimated journey time was six hours. Another long journey, which did not altogether displease him:

"Where is this place?" he asked, approaching the Captain, and pointing to the name.

"Vienna", answered the Captain, and turning back to the group: "OK now, get your kit together and be prepared to set off. Best if luck, wherever you end up!"

'Goodnight, Vienna!'

The train to Vienna was almost full when he boarded, and more bodies squeezed aboard as it made its way, sometimes juddering, often speeding, through the afternoon and into the early evening. Vast areas of industry, much still merely the remnants of bombed factories, flashed by, followed by mountains and planes, and farmers with horses or tractors tilling fields in the fading light of day. Edmund had found a seat in an otherwise full carriage. The luggage rack was full too; showing suitcases and bags; together with the occasional pack of belongings held together by lengths of string, and sporting labels in German. All the others in his carriage were civilians, and he felt out of place, and under hostile scrutiny, in his uniform, which he'd been ordered to wear for the journey. So when an elderly looking man stumbled along, peering around for a seat, he offered his place, and went out into the corridor himself, noticing a murmur of approval from those in the carriage, together with a touch of his hat and smile by the recipient of his sacrifice, as he made his way into the corridor, where he would spend the rest of the journey. There were several other servicemen there, British and American, for him to chatter to and exchange information.

"How'dyer like Germany?", quizzed Pete, a grizzly, mid-thirties, American soldier.

"Didn't see much of it."

"Well, it's not bad. Girls are nice, beer is good ... and best of all, we won, and they know it!"

He laughed at first heartily, then seemed to regret it, and looked more sombre:

"But I'll be glad to go back home. Pennsylvania ... Here's my place, Eddy, with the wife, kids and a dopey dog called Skip!"

Edmund looked at a large crumpled snapshot, bearing signs of much handling, picturing a family group: wife, with short, curly blond hair and quite plump, smiling and hugging a large boxer dog; along with the two boys, 5 and 7 years, standing straight and looking serious. Pete's house was wooden, detached and colonial style and had a motor car parked before it. A banner "Come home soon, Dad" was stretched over a timber frame and rested against the motor.

Pete was very loquacious. Indeed the topics he talked about, and how much he had to talk about them, had Edmund in quiet awe.

"He has more thoughts in his head than I ever have had!", he thought, as Pete talked about farming barley after they had passed a tractor, chugging its smokey way across a large field. (And when he told Leela of this on his later return home she had quipped "More thoughts than you could think about!")

Pete left the train soon after on a station in Southern Germany. For the rest of the journey Edmund chose to spend alone, looking out into the dimly lit countryside musing over his experiences, and of Leela. It was some time since he had thought too much about her. He wrote to her each week, and received twice as many letters from her. She seemed cheerful: lots say, lots to do. She cycled regularly with the club, and went to dances at "The Carlton" with Kitty.

"Sometimes, Eddy, I <u>do</u> dance with boys, but I don't go home with them! Kitty has a steady boy at the moment, so we go as a threesome. I really only go for her sake, you know. I don't like dancing any more. I spend quite a lot of time in our garden (or rather, since you've seen it, our wilderness!) and Dad cut me a plot which I'm populating with all sorts of things - flowers to look at and things to eat. It's the first time I've tried this and I'm getting to like it. I saw your Mum the other day, and she promised to give me some seeds from your garden. By the way, she said she feels you can't manage on your own without home cooking and washing etc ... Ah! Poor boy!

Well, my garden. Edmund, don't expect to find a paradise like your Mum's when you come home. It's just a little hobby, and maybe I'll get sick of it.

You asked me how work was. I don't like writing about it. Or talking about it. Or even <u>thinking</u> about it!!!

But you asked - so here goes. I passed all my banking

exams so far. Brother John (my John - not a monk!) is doing great guns at Westminster bank. Well at least he says he is. He seems to be some sort of assistant to the assistant manager, if that makes sense. I'm sure he will do well, though, as he has that look in his eye, if you know what I mean. You have a look in your eye, but it ain't to do with banking!!! Eddy, I hope you still have that look for me, don't you? I love you so much, Edmund, and I want you. Is that so bad? Your letters are very proper, although there're nice and I couldn't do without them. Your should see the letters that some of my old school mates get! Phew!!..."

As the train jerked clumsily to slow down as it approached Vienna, Edmund mused that he was missing home, and especially Leela; and hoped his promised two weeks leave at Christmas would be honoured. He had a niggling worry now about the possibility of a Russian attack in Europe. Pete, the American, had also alluded to this possibility because of their new found superiority in space satellites.

"They can fire down on us from space, Eddy. We can't defend ourselves against that."

So at his destination, it was with gloomy thoughts he stepped down with his kit bag, and spied immediately a large white notice with "Cpl Rice" in large letters, and held be a stocky young sergeant, with a round, clean-shaven pleasant face, apparently perpetually smiling, who introduced himself to Edmund with a smile and an incongruously gently voice:

"Sergeant Vickers - had a pleasant journey? ... Good. We've got transport here ..."

As they drove along, the sergeant and he looked out on the still ruined city, but thought Edmund, seemingly retaining a dark dignity in defeat.

"You've got an apartment near the Embassy. That's where you'll work from, by the way. Quite luxurious for you and I, Rice - but it suits the job to have us close by."

He paused and nodded to himself. Edmund could only wait in silence for a few seconds:

"Sergeant - what am I to do here?"

"There'll be a briefing tomorrow morning. We'll get you settled in your digs, I'll show you where the Embassy is, and we'll meet there at 0800 hours. And get a good night's sleep. If you'd like a stroll and a drink or snack, I recommend that place."

He pointed to a large café in the street along which they sped:

"And it's fifteen minutes away by foot. They'll take English money ... do you speak any German? ... well, you'll learn, soon enough.", he added emphatically: "and here we are."

They had stopped at a high tenement block, half of which was now rubble.

"Don't worry, Rice. The bit you're in is quite safe."

Their car drove slowly away, as Sergeant Vickers led the way up a short flight of exterior stone stairs, then unlocked a large outside door, and ushered Edmund inside, locking the door behind them:

"Keep this locked, or you'll have refugees bedding down here."

The staircase was massive and impressive. Heavy wooden and (peculiarly, thought Edmund) shining through the dust, a highly polished very thick hand rail, held up beside the stairs by swirls of wrought iron, some of which were missing, or had been prised away and jutted out like a loose teeth. On each floor there was an impressive balustrade, and the two khaki-clad men seemed totally out of place in such a setting. Above them, the creak of an opening door drew their attention, and a tall bespectacled man with thin fair hair, serious and impressive, left his room, glanced at them without remark or change of expression, and locking his door, clattered down the stairs, then passed them, almost nodding towards them in recognition of a similar species, then out of the door. Vickers gave a wry, low laugh, and turned to Edmund:

"Place was built for the well-to-do. I'm afraid you'll be bloody cold in the winter, but we'll see what we can do to help ..... here you are, just one flight up, number 6 ..."

The light revealed a large room, sparsely furnished, with a high ceiling. He was shown the kitchen, bathroom and bedroom.

"It's not brilliant, but it's clean, and it's more than most Viennese get."

"It's fine, Sergeant... I like it."

"Settle down tonight, see you tomorrow. There's a

cleaner. She'll let herself in at 0900. She's honest, but don't leave any official papers here. If you don't want to carry them, store them at the embassy. Laundry etc, we'll discuss tomorrow. Come on, I'll show you a 'strasse' or two, and where the embassy is."

They left the building, and walked along the street, which was half rubble, and Edmund heard the bark of dogs, and saw a few of them, clambering to the top to a pile of bricks and stone, monarchs of the ruins, sniffed defiantly, stared down with some disdain at Edmund and others who walked the streets that night.

"Dogs are OK, Rice. They keep the rats under some control."

"Reminds me a bit of Sheffield. That's still bombed out in some places."

"This place is bombed out in more ways than one, Rice, believe me. The Russians have only just left. I think it was better straight after we'd flattened it!"

"Sergeant", he said, tentatively: "do you think they'll be back?"

"What? The Russians? Don't know. Don't know why

they left. Maybe it was to throw us off guard. What with this sputnik, well it makes you think it might all be starting over again."

"But this time with the Atomic bomb."

"Sure.", he shook his head as they walked briskly along: "but at least we won't feel anything, Ricey! Now, you see where we've come, down this road quite a way, after turning right from your apartment's street. I'll write down all the names - real and phonetic - when we get to the embassy. Are you OK so far? Now, this next one, two three ... the third street from where we are now is where the embassy is. Not far."

They continued their walk, passing some late commuters, parties going out to the town ...

They got to the embassy, and after some checking, were let in via armed servicemen, and through a reception area and into a side interviewing room. Sergeant Vickers took his cap off and sat down at the desk, and waved Edmund to sit down, who removed his own cap, and held it in his lap as he listened. After scribbling for some minutes on a notepad, he turned to Edmund and handed him the paper: "Make sense to you? Good. You'll probably not need it, but if you get lost, you can ask the locals. Most of them are OK, some will ignore you or swear at you. Well, we bombed the place after all, didn't we?"

He smiled at Edmund: "That's that, Rice. You get on, there's a good fellow. Have you got a passable civvy suit and whitish shirt? Come in that tomorrow, even if it is a bit crumpled. And bring laundry and ironing in the white bag in the bathroom, when you need to. It's collected daily, and returned the following day."

"I don't mind doing my own, Sergeant."

"Up to you. You can't use an iron, though. Fuse the whole building."

"As we came here, I noticed in the distance, a large open area."

"Belvedere Gardens. Very nice. Music there sometimes, too. Now tomorrow you'll meet the boss, as far as we're concerned anyway, the British Military Attache. Important man, Rice. Colonel Jack Clements. He's a good man. Good night, Rice. See you at 8."

Edmund left the embassy with almost uncontrollable

excitement. For some reason, this place had filled his eyes with vivid images, and his head with ideas. He could not articulate his thoughts at all, or even if it made sense, or even if it was just a temporary aberration, but he walked, of course, to the Belvedere Gardens, though it was now dark, and it was obviously about to be closed. A workman said something to him, and pointed to his watch, showing he had one hour before they locked the gates. He walked back a long circuitous route, but found his way back quite easily. There seemed to be much going on which had escaped him on his initial tour. Lights from restaurants, theatres and concert halls poured into the dark streets, and there were some trams running, and buses, taxis and cars... here was a bustle, where before he had seen only the silent monument of defeat.

His bed was hard, but he was tired, and after a hot bath, he turned in and was soon asleep. He awoke as usual at 5, and washed and shaved, then dressed and after patting carefully out of the silent tenement, was soon in the street with the first light of dawn and the early commuters. Under his arm he held all his papers, wrapped in small document case he had brought from home to carry his drawing paper. He could walk around, get some early breakfast - could he find an English newspaper? The café, "Sabina's" recommended by Vickers, was an early destination. A waiter, small, dapper and very dark, approached him, smiling.

"Do you speak English?"

"A leetle.", grinned the waiter: "Menu?"

"I'll have the English breakfast", he said, happy to see his usual food displayed on the list, amongst the buns and cheeses which seemed to form the continental breakfast.

The food was very good, and the tea was strong and sweet. He beckoned the waiter over:

"English newspaper?"

The other did not understand, but he pointed to another customer, reading a German newspaper, and mimicked reading:

"Ah! OK.", and he returned with "The Times".

He read the paper avidly, and left the café at 7:15, so that he could walk slowly to his appointment, and see a little more of the city. Thus he arrived early at the embassy, and waited in the reception area. Soon, Vickers also arrived, dressed in civilian clothes, and he was ushered into a large room, comfortably furnished, and invited to sit down. The other sat down near him, and flipping through his papers asked Edmund if there were any problems:

"The colonel will be here late. He's a good man, but he's very intellectual, so he's late for everything. However, don't you ever be!"

Just after this, as if prompted, the door opened and in walked a man in a dark suit, seemingly of very ordinary appearance, but with a zealous glint in his grey eyes, and a straight, determined nose, to be met by a salute from Vickers, and a belated similar greeting from Edmund.

"Corporal Rice? Good! Come through to my office, and we can get down to business."

They followed him through a door into a large office, large window, heavy curtains, with wood-panelled walls. Near the window there was a large wooden desk, and over the other side of the room, a small table with soft chairs clustered around an ornate fireplace. It was to this little haven that the two were directed by Colonel.

"Rice - I assume you know nothing about your duties here? That's good, oddly enough. At least some of our security is working, then. You and Vickers aren't involved in anything too sensitive, but I like to keep control, if you know what I mean... I am the British Military Attaché to Austria, and hold the rank of Colonel. You are on the embassy staff list while you're working for me. Well, Rice, you and Vickers, who's got some experience already, will be responsible for interviewing civilians who we find interesting, or who we're just curious about. None of them will be heavily involved in crime or espionage, as far as we know, but we get useful info from them - refugees, mainly. Are you following everything so far? Ask immediately if you need to know anything. Good - now - do you speak any language other than English? Doesn't matter. We can teach you all you need to know. Native speakers are used all the time. You need to know something of the lingo though. And the translators don't know how much of the language you'll understand - and you're not to let them know - OK?"

"How do we persuade them to be interviewed, Sir?"

"Bribery, normally. Or threats, or extortion. Yes, it's

not brilliant, I agree, but as far as possible we avoid placing them at risk because of our efforts. So most of the nasty stuff is bluff, actually. Now, Rice, are you on board with this sort of thing? Can't have you flaking out on us. If necessary, I can get you back to Cologne by tomorrow night."

"I'd rather stay here, sir."

Edmund felt suddenly he was in a totally different world to the one he had grown used to for the past 19 years. He felt frightened, for really the first time in his life, as if he were in the sea, far from any shore, and unable to swim. He gulped.

"Let's have some tea, shall we?" said the Colonel, opening another door and calling through:

"Alice - pot of tea here, will you?"

He came back in, and smiled at Vickers, then at Edmund, and patted his hand:

"You're very young. You've missed the wars we've been having. Thank god, you should! Wars are bloody awful. What we are doing here is being better informed to prevent the next one d'yer see, Rice?"

Edmund smiled, and retrieved his composure, but he never saw the world in quite the same light again.

They drank tea together, and joked and chatted about England, and Edmund's visits to Belvedere and Sabina's.

"Now, to work. Rice - unless you are ordered otherwise by me or Vickers, dress in civilian clothes. The folk we get are terrified of uniforms. Luckily you don't look very military anyway.", he laughed: "your base is here at the embassy. Vickers will tell you what rooms you can use. Don't go anywhere you not cleared for, though. You'll begin with some general German language instruction, then this afternoon interview techniques, and this evening Vickers will acquaint you with the City. Normally, you'll report here at 0800 and you're on duty till I say you're not - OK? Good. Administrative things like pay and so on, Vickers will arrange and tell you. You'd better let Rice have your address in case he needs you when you're at home .... Any questions? Good, now on your way as I've got an appointment for which I'm already late ...."

Vickers showed him to 'Lecture Room B': "See you in reception at 12:30".

In the classroom, he found four other students (embassy staff, he discovered), who swapped pleasantries, and soon in walked the course leader, a woman of middle years, foreign accent, blond hair, thick glasses, quite good figure for her age, thought Edmund, but it was a little squeezed into a very tight dress she was wearing. Her features were large, and her makeup overdone. Everything about her, he thought, was very nice, but just a little too much ....

"You - Herr Rice - you try now."

"Strasse"

"Not bad. Again." ....

And so on. That day they learnt about the adventures of Rumpelstilzchen, and how to buy ice cream and coffee. She gave them all books to write in, books of language and a small dictionary with phonetic pronunciation and a thick, soft pencil, which, he considered, would make a good drawing pencil ...

At 12:30, he met Vickers and the two set off for lunch at Sabina's.

"How did you like Frau Helge Sheppan?"

"I learnt a word or two."

"She's very good. Her husband, Wilhelm teaches as well. You might see him this week. For the Russian you'll get Svetlana Gruber. She married a German, that's why she has the surname."

"Russian?"

"We get a lot of Russian speakers. Don't worry. As the Colonel says, you only need know enough to avoid appearing stupid."

They had reached Sabina's and went inside, it being chilly outside that day, and sat by the window:

"Corporal - we ought to be on first names now. Alan's my name. Are you called Eddy or Edmund?"

"I prefer Edmund, Alan."

"That's that then. Edmund, what would you like to eat?"

After eating, they drank strong black coffee, and walked back to the embassy:

"Alan, tell me what's the name of this street?"

"This is Schwarzenberg Strasse ... try it!"

"Schwarzberg."

"Schwarzenberg Strasse ... again... very good! We'll be crossing Schwarzenberg Platz and onto Rennweg."

"Rennweg... bordering Belvedere."

"Very good. Tonight we'll be able to take the car. I'll show you main roads, city hall, stations, museums, and so on... and you'll get a book with a detailed map. In two weeks you need to know the city as if you've lived here for 10 years."

"Why?"

"Those we interview will often refer to things - if they're just inventing things, we need to know that. Vienna centre isn't so big, so it's not too bad. This afternoon you'll be learning the job itself. John Wadsworth. An army psychologist. Studied in America for years. Involved with interrogating Koreans, I believe. Seems to be effective."

"How do we know if the job we're doing is any good?"

"The Colonel will tell you pretty quick if he doesn't think so... !"

Sometime later they reached the embassy. Edmund had begun to learn his new trade.

So that evening, Edmund was chauffeured in an Embassy car (a Humber, no less) by Alan Vickers on the first of many night time sorties around the city of Vienna.

This night, a trip Edmund always remembered vividly, they made their way to the Hofburg district.

"Old Austrian Empire, all these buildings", Alan said as Edmund looked around. In one hour they'd driven around the quarter, often stopping for Alan to teach Edmund some new names or words. Finally, they stopped in one of the main streets, called "Graben", and Alan turned to Edmund:

"Down here there's a nice coffee house which usually has some music. Let's go!", as he led the way down a side road. They had to pass through flurries of excited night revellers. The girls were speaking a mix of German and broken English, the men pure American. Edmund smiled to himself as they approached a dingy, unprepossessing entrance sporting the name "Die Perle" (The Pearl) over the doorway, illuminated by a beam of light tightly directed from a single bulb by a long, narrow shade on a lamp fastened just above the top of the doorway.

CHAPTER TWELVE

They went in. The serving area was down half a dozen steps, and was darkened. Each table had a single candle to afford illumination, and at the far end a trio of musicians played jazz with almost exaggerated enthusiasm. They sat down near to the stage, and an immaculately dressed waiter; black tie and crisp, white shirt, nodded soldier-like on his approach.

"This place is run by Hungarians", whispered Alan: "and a bit of a haven for refugees from last year's revolution. Coffee is excellent, though."

Edmund decided to have coffee and whipped cream, whilst Alan ordered Turkish coffee. He gave the order to the waiter in German, who didn't speak nor smile, but nodded sharply (and, thought Edmund, clicked his heels), turned and quickly left them.

Relaxing in his seat, a substantial wooden chair with soft seat and high back; he jigged his head in sympathy with the music ("Smoke gets in your Eyes") and glanced around the café, at the gloomy tables, and noticed the half-lit faces, like pale half-moons, flitting from side to side, up and down, as they chatted, or ate, or took a sip of coffee. Most of the tables had two or more customers. This was a café for socialising, thought Edmund, rather than eating, drinking or music. His eyes flitted back towards the stage, then back again, as he had caught something in his vision, he didn't know what, and then he looked, and saw again: the reflected flash of metal. A cigarette holder as he could now see, held by a man who was seated on his own, right by the stage; smoking heavily and staring steadily at the musicians. He seemed at that time to be different in some ways from the rest of the clientele - not really belonging, although he couldn't think why. The man seemed to have a large head, topped by an untidy but impressive mass of black, swirling hair. Edmund looked away again, towards the stage as the trio were about to begin their next numbers. They were all young men, Edmund noticed; diffidently smiling down from the low stage. The oboe player shuffled forward slightly, and made an almost inaudible announcement, in German, of which the only words familiar to Edmund were "Jerome Kern". They then proceeded to render a very slow, but quite persuasive, account of "Can't help lovin' dat man".

Edmund glanced back towards the table where the solitary smoker was sitting. He had now Turkish Coffee, kept warm in a little copper pot above a candle flame; and a glass of water, which he was now sipping. The face in the dancing half-light was more clearly illuminated from the additional candle flame. He appeared in those heavy shadows like a bird of prey; his black eyes seemed to dance and sparkle, his nose, peeked into the candles' beams and seemed sharp as a beak, almost hooked; and his lips, appearing blackish-red, larger than you'd expect for a man; but above all the head, too large (thought Edmund), crowned with a mass of black, curly hair which cascaded over his skull before softening into a shower of gentle curls.

Edmund started visibly, as the object of his scrutiny suddenly (for no apparent reason) glanced away from the stage, and the unfinished song, to look directly at him.

"Look at those two girls over there", whispered Alan, as Edmund averted his look away from the man, and followed his companion's gaze, and saw two giggling young girls at a table some yards away, taking brief glimpses, blinking up from drinks, and meeting his look, and now his involuntary smile, and dipped their heads, and exchanged gleeful glances.

"Stay here . I'll bring them over, if you like!"

"And if they like!", Edmund said as he smiled assent. He watched as Alan stooped over to speak to them. They smiled at him, looked again towards Edmund, and nodding to one another rose to join them.

Alan did all the talking in those first few minutes, speaking German, judged Edmund, quickly and with apparent ease.

"Edmund", Alan said quickly, turning to face him: "This lady is Hildegard, and this is Sophie."

The two girls smiled across towards Edmund. Both, he guessed, were in their early twenties. Hildegard had long, thick and curly, dark hair, and Sophie was ash-blonde. Her hair was even longer, though hers was straight.

"They've kindly accepted my offer to join us, Edmund. Neither speaks much English, so you'll have some incentive to try your German!"

There was some self-conscious small talk, with Edmund stumbling along in German, and both girls' English on the other hand seemed to get better as the conversation progressed. Alan explained they were British Army, working from the Embassy.

It was just as Sophie was explaining the recent history of the club to Edmund, when he looked towards the table where the lone dark stranger had been, and noticed he had gone. There was now just a candle.

Sophie seemed to take more interest in Edmund than Alan, and anyway she spoke better English. She was, thought Edmund, plainly beautiful. All features were accurate, in proportion and straight, or gently curved. She smiled a lot, seemingly naturally, and she had large white, shining teeth, and her eyes sparkled as she nodded in emphasis, or shook her head in merriment. She was vital and vivid, and gradually completely tunnelled Edmund's attention. ("You're a sucker for a nice girl", Leela would say to him about this years later.) Sophie explained to Edmund that her family owned a small bakery, and she worked as a baker and sales girl there. She said she liked the work, but did not eat cakes as she did not want to get fat.

Alan had got up, and was ushering Hildegard out of her chair:

"We'll go, Edmund. See you tomorrow!"

A girl vocalist had joined the band, and began to sing "My funny Valentine". Edmund tried some German when he inquired:

"Sophie, would you like some more coffee?"

She grinned, and declined: "Let's go after this number, shall we", she said, and squeezed his hand gently.

The night was bright and crisp, and Edmund felt happy, and so confident he continued to speak in German:

"I can take you home by taxi… ", then, impulsively: "Or will you come home with me?"

She smiled, and nodded. (Had she understood what he had said? Or rather, meant to say?)

He had phoned for a taxi before they had left "The Pearl", and soon the car drew up and asked for him by name. The journey was short, and soon they were outside Edmund's street door. He led her up the steps to the door. It had rained, but had now stopped, and the clip-clop of drops of water from the roof of the tenement block echoed strangely loud across the street. He unlocked the front door and motioned Sophie inside. He switched on the light.

They climbed the stair. The uncarpeted wood clattered eerily beneath their feet.

"Come in, Sophie", said Edmund, holding open the door to his rooms.

She walked in, quite boldly, he thought: looking around, smiling at things, even laughing at his army cap, hanging on the corner of the wardrobe door.

He brought in some red wine which he kept in a scullery in the kitchen: a red wine, "Blaufrankisch" he had got from his local Café, at their waiter's recommendation. She knew it, and expressed her approval "Ooo", and eagerly took a glass from him: "Churs" she chortled briefly, before taking a drink.

"This is sehr good!" she exclaimed, sitting on the sofa, at his direction.

"Let's speak German, Sophie, even if you have to speak slowly and repeat things. It'll help my language."

She grinned, and poked him playfully in the ribs as he sat down next to her. He took a drink of the wine, and nodded his approval.

"What kind of buildings do you design in your job at home?"

"I don't really design anything. I just plan where houses and factories are going to be built. Town planning."

"You could have a job for life in Vienna, Edmund!"

"Hm! Specialist job, I feel, Sophie. I just do the simple things."

She drank again, and leaned against him.

"Do you want to stay here with me?" Edmund asked, mirroring his thoughts.

"Tonight, you mean", she said, looking up at him in gently mocking surprise: "All night?"

"Yes, I'd like you to."

"Well", she smiled, sipped her wine : "I suppose I would like also ...."

They drank the wine slowly, and talked a little, and kissed gently, and squeezed each others' hands.

"Shall we go to bed?"

"Where is the toilet?"

Edmund went alone into the bedroom, and tidied up a little, switched on the bedside light, switched off the main light, to give the vast room an air of cosiness. Soon she appeared, and began to undress: "Can I leave my clothes on this chair?", and he had nodded his assent.

They undressed slowly, unaffectedly; and without inhibition; almost as if they had been married for some time. They glanced towards each other, smiling, laughing slightly sometimes when removal of clothing revealed a breast or penis.

They made love eagerly, energetically; sometimes ferociously, as young people do when they first meet ....

Both experienced nothing really new, of course; but for both of them it was a significant night, and an important one.

Edmund felt he belonged in Vienna more than before, he felt less of a fraud, or interloper. And she, Sophie, had brightened her hectic, sometimes drab life in the family shop, with meeting this pleasant, handsome "conquering soldier".

And Edmund, of course, was in love with her .... How could he not be? She asked nothing, gave nothing; simply enjoyed herself in his company... flattered his lovemaking, fucked him like an Amazon.

She was out of their bed before 4 o'clock: "I have to begin baking, now, Edmund ... I need no taxi, I can walk from here - it will help clear my head..." and she laughed.

"Uh-oh" Edmund himself a relatively early riser, was still half asleep, and peered, tousle-headed, from beneath the bedclothes. She kissed him, smelling sweetly, quick and sparkling, as she bobbed around the bedroom to collect her things:

"Here is my address", she said, carefully placing a piece of card on his dressing table; with a loud "click" as Edmund noted, ruefully.

She opened the door, and turning, with a smile, added: "We are open from 7 o'clock for bread and confectionary, and nice visits!"

Edmund, as was his wont as soon as he awoke, whatever

the time, got up and turned the big brass taps of the bath tub, and heard the deep throaty gurgle of water as it made its way up to his room. The hot water gushed with its usual steamy, scalding spurt. He was soon settled in the bath, staring at the ceiling above his head. The cavernous white flat, devoid of all but a few trinkets and clothes of Edmund, and a small amount of essential furniture, at first seeming cold and empty for him, was now seen as a soft white cocoon of secret decadence, almost criminally shameful, he mused, in a city still suffering the ravages of war and occupation.

There was a restrained, but persistent, knock at the door. Before he could say anything, the door was unlocked and a highly pitched, female voice called out something in German.

"In the bath!" he shouted.

"OK!", came the crisp, calm reply: "I come back later".

He heard the door slam shut as the cleaner left. He rose from the hot water gingerly, anticipating the sharp chill of the cold air.

"Whoof!" he cried to himself with a shiver, as he

carefully trotted over to a wooden chair inside the bathroom which held his clothes and his watch. He took up the latter and had to wipe away a film of steam which had covered the dial as he picked it up. He noticed it was already eight o'clock. He got ready quickly and on leaving, saw the cleaner vigorously polishing the balustrade. She smiled at him, almost coquettishly, and brushed a wisp of hair from her cheek. She was a tiny, middle-aged woman with blue eyes which sparkled in the murky light of the house, the only illumination at that time coming from the tall, thin windows in the side walls which threw long shafts of dusty light across the stairs and the entrance hall.

"Hello", he said to her: "I'm Edmund. I usually leave before you arrive."

"My name is Martha", she said, taking his hand: "Your room is often untidy" (they both laughed): "but at least it's clean!"

CHAPTER THIRTEEN

As he stepped down the wide wooden staircase, he could see the marbled hall floor, with its restrained red, black and white circular pattern. He noticed Martha had put the mail neatly on the small oak sideboard. There were letters from Leela and his mother Vivian, forwarded from the army PO box in Germany. He descended the eight stone steps to the street below, and into the morning light, and the bustle of the city open for business, and pleasure. He glanced back at his tenement, as it was now in full light, to see if he was inspired to draw it for perhaps a present for his mother, or even for Leela.

He was by now seeing Sophie once or twice per week, and being busy and interested in exploring the city by bicycle, did not involve himself seriously in other relationships. He received regular letters from Leela, who had no idea where he was (at the insistence of Colonel Clements), but she seemed to assume he was marching endlessly on some parade ground in Bavaria:

'Dear lovely Edmund

I listen to "Family Favourites" every Sunday now (Jean Metcalfe in Cologne, and Bill Crozier in London) and imagine you at BFPO23 or whatever, taking a break from peeling a barrel of potatoes, and getting shouted at for thinking too hard!

How are you, really, Edmund? I miss you so much, and I'm sure I love you, as I think about you all the time and sometimes cry myself to sleep. Also, I'm certainly not interested in any other boys.

I go biking every Sunday and some Saturdays (if I'm not helping Dad in the warehouse) and (WAIT FOR IT !!!!) .... I've got a new bike ! It's top of the Raleigh range... like you told me to get .... lovely yellow and black... beautiful saddle (are you jealous of the saddle, Ed, eh ??)... it's got Reynolds 531 tubing, of course, or I'm sure you wouldn't speak to me again!... and EIGHT speed (2 x 4)... just a small, light bell..

and I CAN lift it with TWO fingers, rather than the one I'm ashamed to say, but I'm only a poor, weak girl after all, aren't I? Dad bought it for me because I help him (actually just keep him company, really!) on Saturdays.

Pauline will inherit my old bike, although she doesn't show much interest in biking. Music, music, music ...... (Put another nickel in!)...... well, she plays the piano all the time and she also plays the recorder sometimes. She is very good, she puts me to shame. BUT! she doesn't have you, does she? But do I, Ed? Have you run off with a girl from the NAFFI, or maybe lusty Fraulein?

All my love, my kisses, all of me, for you, dear Edmund XXXXXXXXXXXXXXX etc.'

He would write regular, short affectionate notes to his mother, almost always including s tiny thumb-nail sketch, and wrote of flowers and trees he recognised there, and assuring her of his domestic comforts. As for Leela, Edmund often answered her letters promptly:

'Leela!

Such a lot is happening to me. I am enjoying City life, I'm allowed to say, but not which city!

I do have an interesting job... not peeling potatoes, though!

Some very exciting news! I've made an officer - a Lieutenant, no less! I wasn't expecting it, but I'm very proud all the same.

I'm thrilled to hear about your bike. I've got a nice German bike second hand to use while I'm here, and I cycle just about everywhere in the day time. There is some countryside to see, but I find the City centre more interesting. I can't say much, you know, as my letters are checked; but buildings, streets people, parks .... and millions of beautiful starlings! Well, I miss you, Leela, as you do me. I've got a Leica camera (also second hand) and when I come home (if I'm allowed) I'll show you where I've been and so on ...

I'm learning German and I'm getting quite good at it. I speak it all the time in the City and everyone understands me. So I've achieved something from the Call-Up!

Love you, Edmund X'

Edmund was at this time, approaching Christmas 1957,

in two moods. On the one hand, he looked forward to the festive season as usual. On the other, he had heard of his promotion (and Alan Vickers') in a disturbing way as he talked with Colonel Clements:

"You can take your Christmas leave unless something urgent turns up", said the Colonel, after briefly congratulating Edmund on his promotion, and walking over the other end of the room, gazing downwards, deep in thought: "You and Vickers are being promoted for two reasons. Firstly, I need you two to have real authority in your work, with those you'll be interviewing, and with the native speakers you'll work with. By the way, that will happen straight after Christmas, so make sure you're ready for the job by then."

Edmund nodded, and felt very pleased with his promotion, and looked forward to interviewing. Clements breathed in deeply, and returned to his desk, and sat down heavily opposite Edmund:

"The other reason to promote you is more serious. Things are moving rapidly. There could be war soon. This is strictly confidential, Lt Rice."

Edmund nodded, and Clements continued:

"If the Russians are convinced they can launch a massive land attack without incurring a nuclear strike from the Americans, our intelligence suggests they may well move. Here I need a small caucus of officers to be ready to deal with any emergency. Do you understand?"

"I suppose so, Sir. But what would be our role?"

Clements brow furrowed and he looked at the young man:

"Organising the evacuation of most of the Embassy staff and", he paused:

"'Others'. Let's leave it at that. This is strictly confidential, Rice. You're to discuss this with no-one." He paused, looking for confirmation that Edmund had understood the gravity of what he was saying.

"You mean, we'd run away, Sir?"

"That's it. We'd have no choice. After the Hungarian revolution, we estimate the Red Army could easily emulate what the Wehrmacht did in Europe in 1940. And they have the A-bomb. And the best rockets in the world – more important, the best Germans! And we know some of their senior officers want to do it."

Edmund was shocked to his core, and felt that because in this short acquaintanceship with Vienna, a part of Europe had become a sort of home for him, he was visibly shaken.

"Getting to you is it, Edmund?" said Clements, walking over to him and standing by his chair, patted him on the shoulder, addressing him by this name for the first time: "Let's hope it doesn't come to that."

"Surely, Sir, the Americans will fight the Russians?"

"Don't bank on it, Rice. If you were sitting at home in Kentucky or whatever would you want to start a nuclear shoot-out with the Russians? After Sputnik? You know, a senior American officer said to me recently:' Hey, we spent 4 years bombing Germany flat. What the hell if the Russians want to do that? Let 'em!' He didn't add to that, but that sort of thing, if it was a policy, would mean the U.S. withdrawing totally from mainland Europe."

"But Colonel, they saved Berlin in 1948 didn't they?"

"First law of History, Lt Rice, is that there are no Laws in History. What happens at one time won't necessarily happen again. In 1948 the U.S. had just fought a spectacularly successful world war. Their blood was up. And the Red Army didn't have the A-Bomb. And they didn't have the means of attacking mainland U.S.A. That's the crunch. At that time, and for some years, some Americans even wanted to launch a nuclear attack on Russia, just as they had on Japan. Would they now? Not on your life, Lt Rice, not on your life!

"And as for fighting the Red Army in Europe, I don't think anyone would want to suffer a fate similar to the Germans when they had a go, eh, Lt.?"

There was long silence. Colonel Clements resumed his seat:

"So Lt., this might be the last really happy Christmas for some time."

Edmund looked down, and trying to collect his thoughts:

"Do you have any idea when .... ?"

"Could be any time. But there's almost certain to be some sort of diplomatic and military threat type standoff. That'll be in Berlin again, of course. The Russians will raise the stakes in the hope that the Allies will let the Russians have West Berlin."

"Will they?"

"Maybe. There're a lot of people - and some of them English - who'd like to be rid of the Berlin problem altogether."

"Sir, can you confide in me, what are the chances of this happening, in your opinion?"

"I'm sorry, but I think it's likely. The crucial factor isn't us or the Yanks. It's the Russians. If they feel they can do it, if their war-games scream 'attack now', then they may do it. They know Hitler lost the war because he hesitated at crucial times. They don't want to miss the opportunity. But their political leadership at present could be our salvation. They seem to be unsure of what to do. And at least one highly-placed politburo member believes there will be a Communist Revolution in Europe anyway."

Edmund went home that night with a numbness of mind he was anxious to shake off. So, he cycled over to the Bakery to ask Sophie out:

"Let's go dancing, Sophie."

Edmund left his cycle at the Bakery, and they walked together, her arm linked to his, to catch the tram to take them to the night spot - called "Jitterbug", in deference to the U.S. army's presence. Ironic, felt Edmund, after what he'd been told that day. However, his hidden desperation had little time for irony or other reflections. So to the rough rhythm of the "Blues Boys of Boston" he rocked and rolled with an intensity and enthusiasm he had never before known. After a while he approached the band and asked them to play (and sing) "Heartbreak Hotel".

"Why do they call themselves 'Boys of Boston'? They're German, I suppose?" asked Edmund as they had finished dancing to the request.

"Because Boston is America. No one here wants to be anything but American", Sophie said to Edmund, as she looked at him, her eyes sparkling with joy, and she squeezed his hand:

"We'll have a long night of loving, my dear. I'm not at work tomorrow."

In bed with her, he felt her innocence, her freshness, her ignorance... After a deeply passionate lovemaking, in the middle of the night, he burst into tears, and swung his legs round out of the bed, to sit weeping, head in hands, as she came up to him, stroking his back, and said in broken English:

"What's wrong, my baby? .... You can tell me. Maybe it will help. You could say me anything."

Edmund was not consoled. He could not tell her, and he knew to say to her that he was restrained would be unacceptable to her, or Colonel Clements. He decided to lie about the cause, but be otherwise truthful:

"I feel so guilty, Sophie. About my girlfriend at home. I think I'm being cruel to you, and to her..." He looked towards her, feeling ashamed at his dissembling, but hoping she would believe him. She reverted to speaking in German, just slowly enough for Edmund to understand:

"I guessed you had someone, Edmund. We are not pledged to each other, are we? And I don't expect it. I had boyfriends in the army before. They go away promising to write. They rarely do, and I rarely want them to. So let's just enjoy what we have together now, Edmund", and she kissed his shoulder and stroked and flicked his hair, and smiled at him, and called him: "Mein Liebling ".

It could not wash away his guilt, of course, and his frustrated feeling of wanting to protect her.

"Are you sure this is all that troubles you?", she asked as he continued sitting on the side of the bed, staring downwards, his head cupped in his hands which he held like blinkers to the sides of his face. He continued to weep quietly, involuntarily, for some time; and she murmured soothing tones, and stroked his back and neck so gently, that eventually he lay down again, facing away from her, clutching a pillow to his head, as she pressed her warm body into his.

CHAPTER FOURTEEN

The following weeks leading up to Christmas 1957 were filled with more interviewing training for Edmund. He found himself part of a small group of about a dozen, with only one female amongst them, sitting on hard chairs in a cubical room with bare walls, washed with pale paint covering a rough plaster:

"We'll teach you to develop a 'Poker' mentality", said John Wadsworth, the psychologist. Edmund now noticed he had a peculiar mixture of English Midlands' and American accents: "What you never let your opponent, or your interviewee in this case, know what you're thinking. It's hard, but with techniques I've developed and tested, it's possible, if you're prepared to make the effort .... Remember, you can't threaten, as you've no power to do anything. Your job is to find what they might want that we can give them. And, with subtlety, to withhold it until they tell us what we want to know. All happy so far?"

The small group showed very subdued approval.

"Good. I've got the film projector here today to show you a film about interviewing without showing your hand, and persuading the other fellow to show his. The film has actors in it. We aren't allowed to show the real thing, unfortunately."

He switched on the projector, and as the black and white leader film sent flickering sign and number images onto the board at the front of the classroom, he deftly switched off the lights from the back of the room and took his place on a high stool next the machine.

Two men, the interviewer and the translator, were pictured sitting together, both in dark suits, and discussing who they would be interviewing:

"The first one is a someone who claims to be German, a refugee from the Hungarian revolution, but who wants help to get accommodation and a job because the area of Germany he lived in is now in Poland. He says his family are all missing, and he has no papers. We need to find out first of all if we think he's telling us the truth"

The translator nods, and the man is led in by a soldier in uniform:

"Herr Kempff, Sir"

'Herr Kempff' had glasses and a sports jacket and twill trousers, and looked unconvincingly nervous. He spoke in German but most of it was translated in a subtitle on the film. He was asked to relate his travels since 1945 and how he had (he claimed) ended up fleeing to Hungary after being ejected from his house by the Poles.

"And why did the Poles take your house?"

"The Russians told them to, I think", he said.

"Did you abuse these people in the war?" the interviewer asked.

"No, no"

"What did you do in the war?"

"I worked for a local watchmaker. I clean watches."

"How do you clean a watch?"

The interrogation lasted some minutes, during which there were several close ups of the interviewer as well as the Herr Kempff. Eventually the latter was told to wait outside after some more questioning. The translator left, and in came an army Captain:

"Well, Lt, what do you make of our Herr Kempff?"

"Hard to say, Captain. I'd like to check out the towns he referred to and see if there's any obvious inconsistencies. Then we could have him in again."

"Right. Next one for you is a female. She says she's from Moldavia but she speaks some German. She wants asylum in England as she says she's not safe here because her father fought for the Wehrmacht. No chance of checking that, I fear. Just see what you can get from her."

'Mrs Grunig', as she now called herself, was a dark, plump woman dressed in a dark overcoat and headscarf. She claimed to have fled from Moldavia through Eastern Europe for several years as she felt the authorities (and hence the Russians) had had suspicions about her true identity.

"I want to get to England for safety, and get a job in my trade.", she said, leaning across the table towards the interviewer, and looking earnest.

"What is your trade?" asked the interviewer.

"I was a weaver in a cloth factory", she said.

She was quizzed about where she had lived, and how long and where she had been since she had been in Austria. As before, at the end of the interview, in came the Captain, out went the translator:

"Mrs Grunig- what do you think, Lt?"

"Well, sir, I reckon she's OK. You know we've already checked her home town. It does have a weaving factory. Some men from there did join the Germans, but we don't know if her father was one of them. Her travels across Europe seem to make sense. And we cross-checked her movements with events we know happened and would have been known to her if she was telling us the truth."

The Captain smiled, and nodded sagely:

"Well done, Lt. I think we'll recommend our Home Office to take her case in a sympathetic light."

At the end of the film, they took a break, and smiled and chatted together, and drank coffee, before going back in the room to reflect on the points the film. They were told that the key to success was:

"Keep cool. You'll rarely know if a lie is a lie from how the story's told. So keep facts in focus.", in the words of John Wadsworth.

CHAPTER FIFTEEN

There was a time before he left for his vacation at home that the weather was not so cold, but very clear, and he and Sophie cycled through some of the most delightful countryside Edmund had ever seen, and thrown into almost unbearable exquisite relief with the winter snows. They had taken a train, with their bikes, to the outskirts of the Vienna woods, and had cycled and walked their way through miles and hours of crisp pure air:

"I can see you are a great cyclist, Edmund", gasped his companion as he thoughtlessly powered his way up a long climb. He apologised, smiled and kissed her, as they dismounted their cycles and walked up the hill, surrounded by a shallow drift of snow beneath the trees:

"Let me take your bike. I can push for two!" he laughed,

as he took her bike: "And this is certainly more comfortable than my freezing flat!"

He learned German very rapidly now that he had Sophie to speak to almost every day, and read simple novels and newspapers.

"You will soon make love in German", said Sophie shortly before his real work began.

Ask me another

His first real interview was a young girl, who had with her a small child (about 2 years) she claimed was her daughter. She spoke German with some difficulty, saying she was Romanian and fled the Communists as her life was in danger.

"I need money and papers", she said: "I have none. I have no money. I've nowhere to stay. How can I buy food? The Austrians send me to you. Will you assist me?"

Edmund talked to her, with his young German speaker (an Austrian named Klaus) with him, and soon realised how tedious this job could be. He thought the girl was lying. But so what? He didn't think she was a spy. She was not attractive enough, he thought, to be planted to seduce diplomats. Her daughter didn't look like her and didn't seem to react positively towards her. However, he decided to give her some money, and another appointment with him, after she'd got work, if she could manage it. He gave her some addresses he'd found out to stay in and possibly with a landlady who'd look after the baby if she found work. He also gave her some names of possible employers. Why had she been sent here? She left, thanking him several times and smiling, and pushing her hair more tidily now as she spoke to him, and left the room.

"Let's have some coffee, Klaus!"

"Yes, sir"

Soon after, interrupting their break, Alan came in and announced another person for Edmund see.

"Come, come this way", he could hear Alan saying to someone just outside. Into the doorway stepped a shabby, shambling figure. His dark eyes peered quizzically under heavy eyelids as he looked at Edmund. He wore a dirty white shirt, as well as raincoat and trousers too long for his frame. His wispy beard pecked up and down as he chewed an empty mouth, showing his uneven teeth, browned with heavy smoking.

"Why don't you sit down here?" asked Edmund in German. The reply came swiftly and surely back as the man took his seat, and Alan disappeared, closing the door behind him:

"I am called Frederik Denktash. I am Hungarian. Pleased to meet you.". He offered his hand to Edmund, who briefly shook it, and sat down behind his desk, flanked by Klaus. Edmund looked at him for a few seconds, and Denktash at first sat back, as if to relax, then came forward and planted his elbows on the table.

"Would you like anything? Glass of water? ", asked Edmund.

"Water, please. Yes."

Klaus got up and left, to return quickly with a flask of water and a glass. He put these down on the table and poured some water for the man.

"Thank you. I have no passport. No documents of any kind. I managed to get here from Hungary after the revolution. The Austrians send me here for help. Do you have a cigarette?"

Edmund took some from a supply kept in the drawer of the desk and handed it to him, and leaned over to light it for him.

"Thank you. My wife is still in Hungary. I would like her here with me. My children are gone - maybe dead. Who knows?"

He sat hunched over the table, leaning heavily on his elbows, and conducted the conversation with dipping and waving hands like an orchestral director.

"The old have no permanent home. They can't stay in their house, they're sent away. Their friends are gone .... At least I can try to get a room or two here and bring my wife .... Can I have money? Enough to eat. Somewhere to stay?"

"There is a room here that's available.", said Edmund, taking from his pocket a piece of A4 paper with the property details: "It's clean and quite comfortable. The rent is at the just here", and he pointed to the place as Denktash scanned the document. Unusually, he did not query the rent, or say he could not afford it, or ask for money for rent. Instead his furrowed gaze looked at the address, then the small map:

"Where is this? Is it near a station? I can't walk easily and the trams upset me. Buses are too rough. When I was young I could go anywhere. On anything ..."

And so it went on for several minutes, until Edmund stopped him:

"We don't have so much time to talk about everything today, Mr Denktash. However, I can give you some money to cover the first month's rent and food. Come and see me in two weeks or earlier if you have a problem. We'll give you some temporary documentation for now."

Denktash looked steadily at him:

"Who are you?"

"My name is Lt Rice. I'm on the embassy staff here."

"And where is your father?"

"Oh! Well, he's in England." Edmund had answered a personal question which was normally not allowed, but he couldn't retract it. He did not, as he was first tempted to, curtail the interview abruptly, as that would be giving way to emotion, he thought:

"And I am here in Vienna, as are you, Mr Denktash. I have someone waiting for me, so I'll have to say farewell, for now."

Denktash grunted, and nodded towards Edmund as he got up and left the room, followed by Klaus. When the latter returned, he asked his reactions to Denktash:

"Be good to keep an eye on him. He speaks too much."

For Edmund this was too enigmatic, but he did not quiz further as officially the native speakers were not cleared to share information with. Klaus looked over to him:

"Lt, you have one more interview before lunch time. Lt Vickers said he will bring him along when you're ready."

"Ready now, Klaus."

Edmund was surprised, but hoped he had not shown it, to see the man who he had spotted at the nightclub, smoking cigarettes from a holder and drinking strong Turkish coffee. ....

The man was dressed in a dark suit and white shirt. He showed a day or two of dark stubble in his beard, and walked across to take the seat he was offered, meanwhile looking around not only at his two interrogators, but at it seemed every nook and corner of the room. He sat down, his medium height, slender frame fitting loosely into the chair. He glanced at each of the other two men in turn.

"I'm Lt Rice, and this is Klaus. You've been told who we are in this process, I hope?"

The other man nodded, again looking around him as if he were judging the décor in great detail:

"My name is Kep. That's the only name I use. I want your help in registering as a citizen of Vienna. I'm a refugee. Even if I can't stay for ever. It makes my work very difficult sometimes, not having passport and so on." He stopped talking suddenly, as if he felt he had already said too much. He was using a German accent Edmund didn't recognise, although he had understood most of what he had said. He tapped his hands, which he held together at the finger tips, on the desk, and looked at Edmund.

"How do you make a living, Kep?"

"Journalism. Features. Reflexions on Vienna life. Jazz, and so on ..."

"And have you always done that?"

"I don't want to talk about life before Vienna."

"And when did you arrive here?"

"About two years ago."

Edmund noted that this could have been about the time of the Hungarian Revolution.

"Why did you come here?"

"I don't want to say."

"It will be easier for me to help if I know more."

Kep shook his head and looked down. There was silence for a few seconds.

"You need papers? To establish yourself officially in Vienna?"

"Yes, yes. That's it." He looked unblinkingly at Edmund.

"I would like to know more about you. Something of your past, where you were born, and how and why you got here. And your full name. Without this, it will be difficult to do anything."

"I can pay. I have money.", he said, almost eagerly.

"We don't accept money, Kep. Is there nothing else you can tell me?"

He didn't answer.

"You could try the Austrians again. Even then they would probably need to know more."

Klaus got up, and showed him out. He did not protest at the ending of the interview, and was calm and courteous as he left, bidding good bye to Edmund as he left.

When Klaus returned, Edmund asked him:

"What sort of accent is he using?"

"South Austria. Hungarian border area. Some in that area speak their own dialect known only to them. He might have learned German there, though, so you can't be sure he comes from that area."

Edmund was puzzled as to why he had come. He would have known the embassy couldn't help someone who won't even supply their name. He saw the Colonel before going to town for lunch. Clements, it transpired, had already seen Kep briefly before the interview:

"What do you make of him, Rice? Strange fish!... Could be Hungarian... we have no translator to try him out. He speaks German well, with an unusual accent. Could mean anything, of course. He might be a Soviet spy. He's interesting, clever ... and maybe, innocent."

Edmund was about to tell him of his seeing Kep at the nightclub, but simply bade goodbye and went for lunch directly.

Sophie was to work early the next morning, so that evening he had gone to the city centre on his own and had chosen a café he had not used before, just off Friedrich Strasse near to the Opera House. There was an upmarket, bohemian atmosphere that he felt almost as soon as he had entered the large café, elegantly lit from wall and table lights. Some recorded jazz music quietly threaded its way through the noisy conversations, and he smiled, looking around in approval, and now saw a small thin man waiting to take his order:

"Espresso, bitte", and he sat down at a small centre table.

He settled down the read his Austrian Newspaper, a task he was finding now quite easy to do, at least for the most part, although he had got used to Sophie or Alan being around to help his way through some of the articles and stories. He studied German quite avidly now, but he found Russian more difficult and less interesting since outside the embassy lessons, no-one spoke the language to him. On the other hand, studying psychology was good,' but most of this is obvious 'he often thought' and if it's obvious to me, it'll be obvious to <u>them</u> 'he mused. His coffee having arrived, he drank, and had begun to read a story in his paper when a loud argument arose from one of the tables on the far side of the café. He looked up and towards the noise, and saw a fat man dressed in dark suit standing up and shouting at a man opposite him:

"How can you say that to me? I was there, and I saw it too. But more than that, my friend, I felt it. Felt the kick in my back and terror of the chase, knowing what would happen if they caught me. And you, how can you? Some say you were part of it .... I wonder myself. If I knew it, I would kill you!"

With this the fat man turned round and left the café, knocking against protesting people and passed close to Edmund, so he could see his face. He was, he saw about 40 years old or so, with prominent features and deep brown eyes. His hair was dark brown and dishevelled, and his eyebrows were deep and bushy beneath his furrowed brow. He was tense and very angry, and swore as he gained the street, glanced back at the café, and was gone. Edmund looked back to the table on the far side, which was now empty. The excitement over, everyone, including Edmund, returned to their own business. After a few seconds, however, he was again disturbed by a calm "Lt Rice" at his side. He glanced to see Kep. They greeted one another, as if they were old friends:

"Please call me Edmund, Kep", said Edmund, who then went on to tell him of the row he had just missed.

"Oh, that!" Kep exclaimed, his face breaking into a great smile: "there are often arguments here, about philosophy, literature, and above all, the opera."

"No, Kep", replied Edmund: "this was a personal argument. None of my business I suppose ... you mentioned opera. I've never been or heard an opera. Is there something easy I could start with, to see if I liked it? I mean, every other person here in Vienna seems to talk about it."

"Near to Stephansdom there is a little opera house.

I'll take you there after we've finished here. I think they're doing Mozart's Figaro this evening. It's a good place to start, or end, for anyone."

"Sounds good, or at least I hope so!" joked Edmund.

They chatted a little more, as Kep settled down in a chair at Edmund's table, when the angry man returned, flustered and remaining standing, not seeing Edmund to his side, said to Kep:

"This is a stupid row, Kep! The past is a place we can never revisit. So let's .... Oh! I'm sorry!"

He had now noticed Edmund, and his big face and wide mouth broke into a huge grin:

"I am Hugo. I saw you and rudely passed by you after my argument with my friend here."

He shook Edmund's hand, and stepping back, nodded and smiled towards Kep, who smiled thinly back at him. Looking round, he found a chair and placed himself between the others:

"You are English or American, of course, aren't you? Can you understand Kep's German?"

"I can get by. Hello, Hugo. I'm called Edmund, and I'm English.", replied Edmund.

"I speak correct German. I grew up in Berlin and went to a good school. Have you been to Berlin?"

Edmund shook his head.

"Well, you're too late anyway. It was a beautiful city, for a while. Now everyone wishes it didn't exist. Including many of the inhabitants. The great capital of Prussia! Well, that's what our little Russian doll Ulbricht wants, isn't it, Kep, eh?"

Kep shot a glance at him, then broke into a laugh.

"Hugo, this is Lt. Edmund Rice, from the embassy. He will not put up with your nonsense though, so behave!"

"Then he is our Third Man, is he not?"

Edmund laughed, as one of his favoured films was mentioned.

"You've been on the famous ferris wheel, I suppose?" asked Hugo.

"Of course, Hugo. Orson Welles is one of my favourite directors. And I like films.", answered Edmund.

"But now you are going to the opera." said Kep, getting

up. I'll see you later in the week, Hugo", he said to the other man.

"Which opera?" asked Hugo as they walked away.

"Marriage of Figaro."

"Best of them all, Edmund! Goodbye, my friends!"

Kep walked with Edmund to the small opera house, less than a mile, and Kep talked incessantly, although never referring to their first meeting in the embassy the previous day.

"Here is the magnificent Opera House. Rebuilt about a year ago. If you are lucky enough ever to get tickets, go there ..."

"We are now in Graben. And down there are some nice little art galleries and cafes, as you probably already know. I'll give you some names of galleries to visit ... And film clubs! Ah, yes, I can give you some names as well!...

"A short detour! There is the Neue Burg - you know the place? It's from there Hitler declared Austria part of the Third Reich ..."

They walked quickly to Stephansdom, and paused to admire it.

"You have been inside of course? Good, I assumed so. Well, down here and ..."

They passed by the great cathedral, some way further and then cut into a narrow side street:

"And here we are!"

Edmund looked up at the sign "The Little Opera House", and smiled.

"See you again sometime around town I suppose", said Kep as he left him: "and I'll leave details of galleries and film clubs at the embassy. Goodbye!"

He stepped into the small, shabby foyer of the theatre, and found a smiling bespectacled blond waiting to issue a ticket from an old fashioned ticket box.

"Figaro?", and she smiled even more broadly and nodded:

"Starts in 15 minutes", she said. He paid his admission, and was given a simple paper programme rather than a ticket. He was guided through some swing doors into a small, raked auditorium. He sat down about half way down the slope, near to the aisle in case he wanted to get out quickly, and looked around. The theatre was over half full.

Most of the people were above 50 years old, he thought, although there were dotted around little pockets of what looked like University or Art College students. It was a mix not unlike the film club in Wellawnbury, he thought, although the audience here was larger.

After a few minutes, the lights faded, and the lights went up on the faded red curtains as a small orchestra began to play the overture. As the performance progressed, although he liked the music for the most part, he was bored as he could not understand the German. (Kep had warned him that languages are difficult to understand when sung.) Also, he did not like two other things. He could not take seriously girls playing the part of men, especially when they seemed to desire one another (and obviously weren't lesbians), and was also irritated by even small-talk being sung.

"However. This is my first one, I suppose. Maybe I'll like it in time." And he stayed to the end, which in retrospect did surprise him. On reading the programme, he was somewhat relieved to discover that in its first performance which was in Vienna, it also failed to excite the Viennese.

CHAPTER SIXTEEN

Butterfly or Gadfly?

The following day Edmund related the conversation he had had with Kep.

"Would you like a drink of whisky, Edmund?", asked Colonel Clements. Taken aback, Edmund concurred. The other man gave him the drink, heavy with chunks of ice, and took his place in his chair behind the large desk:

"Time I put you in the picture. First of all, Kep and Hugo. I know something of them. Not important anyway as far as we know." Edmund interrupted him, even though he could see the Colonel was annoyed:

"But I must ask, Sir. Who on earth is Ulbricht?"

"Oh him. East German leader. Or rather, Russian representative in East Germany. We suspect he might actually be a Russian. Anyway, Hugo's joke is that he once said his dream was to redefine his new state as not a new Germany but a new Prussia. Silly bugger... Understand now? Oh! Their argument. Maybe interesting, maybe not. Just store those details away in the mind, Edmund. Perhaps it'll make sense later. Well now, to business. The interviewing we do here is of little point, I suppose you realise?"

"Yes, Sir. It doesn't seem to matter what we think of them unless they actually want to come to England."

"Wrong. It doesn't matter anyway. Immigration don't take any notice of us. This unit is my baby......".

Clements broke off and brought over the whisky bottle, filling Edmund's glass and his own. "More ice over there. Help yourself to either as you please.", and he plonked the bottle of whisky on the desk, between the two men.

Edmund nodded, and turned to see a silver bowl full of ice on the side board.

"We help some poor sods sometimes. Bit of money, word in the right Austrian ear. However, the real, important point, Rice, is that we may be on the brink of war. And anything we can find out about what's happening beyond the East European border is important. That's why one of these interviews every month or so may be useful." Clements drank his whisky, and poured another immediately: "Not yet? Well, help yourself when you need to. To get back to the point. We all need to take everything seriously, and remain alert, for those nuggets of info that might be really useful. Get the idea? Good man.".

Clements walked over to him, and patted him on the shoulder, then over to look out of the one window, a large expanse of glass facing onto the street below.

Edmund tingled, and smiled, and poured himself more whisky. The Colonel was fiddling with the curtain, and without turning round, said:

"Could be a career here for you, Rice. If you want it."

"Can't see myself in the army for long, Sir."

"Think about it.", and he turned round, and returned to his chair: "Good life for someone like you.", and he leaned forward across the desk: "chance to be rootless for the best twenty years of your life, Rice."

"Assuming the Russians don't attack"

"That won't matter, if you aren't caught in the initial assault. We'll still be needed back home."

He had poured some more whisky for himself, and filled Edmund's glass. The latter nodded and smiled, and now had that warm, pleasant feeling of his brain elevating gently above and beyond his physical body.

"Do you know what you have in spades, Lt? Poise. Bloody in-yer-face poise. It unsettles, yet also reassures. That's why you're good at this job."

"Why did you choose me, Sir?"

"You mean why didn't I choose an Oxford or Cambridge graduate with a commission? If they're trustworthy, they're mad, and if they're not, they're treacherous. Too much education is a dangerous thing, Rice. I wanted an ordinary, intelligent likeable man who I can trust absolutely. I think you're that man."

"But how ..." began Edmund, but the Colonel interrupted him:

"I know a good deal about you. One of the officers your Dad approached to try to get you out of call-up is one of our European team, by co-incidence. That's how it started. Oscar spoke about you, of course. We filtered out the usual 'noise factor' a Dad says about his son in these cases. But, we did get what we thought was some good info. One of the interviewees, by the way, was a set up. I suppose you realised that? No? Well, it's for you to guess which one! Anyway, we checked you out. And you seemed to fit the bill." He paused, and looked at Edmund:

"I'll tell you something, Rice. Have some more whisky. Cheers. Intelligence work is a job, like any other. Don't for God's sake mix it up with Queen and country and all that baloney. That's for the 'Intelligent' boys. You know, the ones who work for the Russians."

"Where were you serving in the war, Sir?"

"Special services, Rice. Small units. Often working behind enemy lines."

"Sounds dangerous."

"But exciting. But, yes, bloody frightening."

"Helping to save Europe from the Nazis?"

"We weren't doing that, Rice. We were simply staying alive. We decided we were saving Europe from the Nazis *after* the war was over. Made a better story. Anyway, a few politicians invent the philosophy. We soldiers just fetch the wood."

Edmund thought about this for a few seconds, while Clements remained silent for several seconds, then got up, and looked at Edmund with a steady piercing stare from his grey eyes:

"You can travel back to London by air for Christmas, Lt. and" he grinned, draining his whisky: "you can let your Austrian girl say goodbye at the airport."

He was in a mind now to go on leave for Christmas. He had bought a small watercolour of Vienna by a nineteenth century artist, which he was intending smuggling home with him, as a present for Leela. He would get her a card and one or two other things when he got home. And he had not forgotten Dot. He had sent her a card, although he had not heard from her.

Edmund and Sophie spent the day before his departure together. She carried around with her a transistor radio which played, as Edmund always was to remember "Oh please stay by me Diana" by Paul Anka, time and time again. That day he presented Sophie with a silver bracelet he bought for her the week before, and a card on which he had drawn a view of Vienna she particularly liked. She was bubbling with joy at his gifts:

"It's perfectly delightful, Edmund. Will you one day draw me?"

Edmund shook his head slowly, smiling at her: "Sophie, I'm not good at drawing people. Really I just copy things."

"I bet that's untrue. Even so, this is the best goodbye I ever had!", she said, kissing him. She had given him comprehensive city guide, designed for walkers and bikers: "After all", she said: "you can read maps better than me!"

In the square in front of Stephansdom, Sophie and he ate roast chestnuts and fish soup, before taking a taxi together to the airport.

CHAPTER SEVENTEEN

Christmas 1957

After the flight, he took a long, cold train journey bound for York. They had stopped at Nottingham. And from now on, the further north the train went, the colder and darker it got, and he saw more snow on the fields and roofs of houses, and noticed that there were fewer passengers waiting in the stations. And he began to breath the air of home. He was reminded of an article he'd read of the theory of cats being able to get back home, even over huge distances, by their ability to smell the air so sensitively that they knew in which direction to go.

"Each place or thing does have its own, smell, it's true", he thought: "favourite pub, weekend jacket Dot's cigarettes."

After jerky intervals of slumber, he arrived at his destination, most thankfully; and saw, on the platform as he alighted, a figure with long, dark hair, and wearing a dark blue coat, smiling and waving towards him.

"Oh Edmund, love, my dear, let me taste your cheek!"

And she kissed him almost maternally at first, then clasping his face, kissed his lips most passionately, and stepping away, hands still on his cheeks, pouted:

"Do you love me still, Edmund?"

"I do, I do, I'm still travel shocked and tired, Leela ..."

She smiled, cuddled up to his side, and taking his arm, led him away to the station exit:

"Good. I'm glad you've been sensible and kept your feelings for me, Edmund."

She squeezed his arm, as he realised how much more of a young woman she now was, grown from the schoolgirl he first met less than two years ago. Outside the station, his father Oscar was waiting for them in the Jaguar.

"Heave that suitcase into her, Lt Rice!", he joked as he opened the boot of the car.

The couple sat in the back, holding hands, whispering;

as they spent the half hour journey engrossed in each other. Edmund had been nervous of his reaction to Leela, as he thought he might have cooled towards her after his experiences. But he found she was all that she had always been to him, and even more, with her greater assurance and maturity.

The weather for their holiday was seasonally cold, with icicles and snow. The couple would go sledging on the moor side slope, where all the local youngsters congregated, and here there was screaming and the swish and slide of the toboggans, and the cries of the child who falls off, and the smell of wet wool, the glow of cold noses, dripping with dew. As the parents looked on to the antics of their children, they would be jumping from foot to foot, and squeezing and slapping their gloved hands:

"Time to go now, Michael! Tea time!"

"No you can't stay anymore. I have to fetch Granny at three!"

In the evening, at both their houses, there were log fires, lights on a Monkey Puzzle tree in the garden at Edmund's house, and a great spruce tree in the lounge at

Leela's. There was, of course, some cycling on the better days on a tandem borrowed from the cycle club. They spent Christmas morning at Leela's and the afternoon at Edmund's. They had time to exchange their recent experiences and thoughts. They had some time alone together, to renew their experiences of each other, and to mutually feel warm and happy in their growing closeness.

Edmund began his journey back to Vienna in January, from a cold, comfortless York station at 5 o'clock in the morning. He'd (easily) persuaded Leela not to see him off at such an inhospitable time, so Vivian was pleased to be the lone tearful female bidding goodbye to him that morning:

"The house will again miss you, my love.", she said to him, as she kissed the side of his face.

<u>'Won't you wear my ring around your neck?"</u>

Sophie met him at the airport, and was wearing the bracelet he had given her:

"Let's go straight to your flat, Edmund. I've missed you ………"

During his first week back, Edmund began to think

about getting her out of Vienna in case of war. The colonel had told him that much of central Germany will be obliterated if it happens:

"It's been an unwritten understanding between the US and Russia for some time now that Germany will be the battleground. So you're better off here. Austria might well escape the bombs, although the Russians will be back. Some might think that's even worse."

One night, Edmund was on a solo trip into a city bar to drink beer, and met a Captain Terry Tidy, with whom he has a drink:

"Grab the world, Ricey boy. How old are you? Nineteen? Do the things you dream of doing, and do them now. Don't wait. To quote someone or other: 'All that there is worth to do, you'll do before you're twenty-two'."

This only pushed Edmund into a greater crisis of conscience on if and how he can help Sophie, or at least somehow tell her that there could be danger in staying in Vienna.

"It would be difficult to do, and risky." he thought. He found he was easier with not to doing anything, and gradually found himself worrying about the issue less and less.

Jazz in January

It was a clear, cold January morning, and Edmund had some time to take coffee at "Sabina's". He had not been there too long, when Kep accosted him. He was wearing thick twill trousers, white shirt, and a long dark grey woollen coat seemingly two sizes too large for his narrow frame. He stood for a few seconds, looking and smiling at Edmund:

"How are you?"

Edmund smiled in reply, and invited the other man to join him. Kep turned round and ordered Espresso, then looked hard at Edmund, and smiled. For the first time Edmund noticed the deep blueness of his eyes. They twinkled and explored him as his said:

"And how are you liking Vienna?"

"I've grown to love it, I suppose", replied Edmund, feeling smug and comfortable.

"Oh don't *love* it, Edmund!", exclaimed the other, leaning forward towards him: "love your mother, love your dog... but don't love things that can let you down. It's a waste of energy!"

"How can a city let you down?"

Kep fell silent, and seemed to lose his exuberance as he said quietly: "It can reject you."

There was a hiatus for a some seconds, and Edmund drank some coffee, and thought of home. Suddenly changing his mood, Kep looked at him again in his intense way, and with some obvious impishness said:

"Are you not supposed to be careful with me? I mean, professionally."

"Yes, of course", replied Edmund quickly, almost involuntarily: "And I am. Careful... !"

Kep looked down, slowly taking a cigarette from his left hand pocket, and his cigarette holder from the other pocket. He lit his cigarette before placing it in the holder, and drew a deep draught of smoke before resuming the conversation:

"Vienna doesn't have much good jazz."

"I don't know", replied Edmund: "I've no real taste for it, although I don't mind listening to it, I suppose."

Kep almost snorted and inhaling more smoke, looked around the café which was now filling up:

"I love jazz, Edmund. I find it has a way of putting everything into perspective. And the tunes are bloody good!" He laughed, and knocking off some ash from his cigarette, turned to face Edmund:

"New Orleans Jazz is the best, as far as I'm concerned. There once was a musician called Johnny Dodds ... have you heard?" Edmund shook his head:

"He played the clarinet like Michelangelo draws..." And he laughed, as he recognised having touched something Edmund did care about:

"Your liking of lines and forms, Edmund. Stirring within you, maybe love, passion, guilt, tenderness, sentimentality ... all the paraphernalia of being alive ... well, I suppose, I think, that the purity of the notes of an exquisitely played clarinet, or oboe, can prick alive the same senses, don't you think?"

"Well, perhaps, but great classical art will live for all time. Some of this music, maybe, will fade away."

"Perhaps not, Edmund. But anyway, that doesn't prove

anything." He seemed to be about to add something else, but fell silent:

"If we indulge each other, Edmund, I can help you."

"How?" Edmund was uneasy about the suggestion:

"I can show you or tell you how to get to galleries, buildings and so on which will satisfy your classical tastes, I hope, and in return you will, please, indulge me by accompanying me to the few refuges of great jazz in this city."

Edmund felt relieved, and nodded his acquiescence, smiling, and ordering more coffee for both of them.

Edmund was happier to encourage Kep to talk about jazz, which he happily did, and just as happily smoked incessantly as they drank coffee. Kep also told him about places of interest in Vienna, how to get to them, and even drew maps and noted tramcar numbers for him to find his way around. Around mid-morning, after talking together for over two hours, they parted, as Kep said he had to get away, and so Edmund left, to spend the rest of his day's leave exploring some of the places he'd been told about. He had his bike with him, and donned a waterproof cape as it was now raining hard, and cycled slowly around the city, before eventually alighting on a small café he thought would be nice for lunch.

When he got to work the following day, he thought of his conversation with Kep:

"Better talk to the Colonel about it", he decided.

Later, in Clements' office, Edmund related his most recent encounter with Kep. The older man thought for some time, sitting at his desk and drumming the thumbs of his clasped hands against his lips. He suddenly looked up at Edmund:

"Cultivate this friendship, Lieutenant. But carefully. Don't let him see your knickers - know what I mean?"

Edmund smiled, and nodded, as the other continued:

"Find out what you can, but subtly. He's obviously intelligent, and clever; so he knows your interest in him might not be just to talk about King Oliver's jazz band."

The next meeting with Kep was sooner than expected. Edmund and Sophie were walking in the city centre, on a clear, cold afternoon in February, after visiting the Cathedral:

"I'd like to do some sketches of this Church sometime. We could picnic on the causeway while I work, when it gets warmer."

Sophie squeezed his hand, he kissed her lightly, and looking forward again, saw Kep coming towards them, his long dark coat bellowing out at this sides like a bird's wing:

"Edmund, my friend, and your lovely companion!", he said, as he kissed her hand: "come with me, as I am on my way to a little place, where they play real jazz!"

After a little while, they were guided into Domgasse by Kep, who jerked a finger leftwards as he strode quickly: "That's Mozart's house!" indicating a tenement in the street; then he advanced a few paces, and swung left and down as he descended some steps into a basement house. Through an open doorway they came, through a short corridor with half-open doors on each side, then a small lobby area, dimly lit, with a grim couple, seemingly man and wife, to grudgingly take hats and coats. They knew Kep, and he introduced his two companions. The saturnine pair smiled slightly and briefly, and took their coats. Edmund and Sophie then followed Kep, and the sound of music, into and then across a large room with subdued lighting, and impressive vaulted ceiling:

"Please, sit here!", he said in a hushed voice, bringing them to a small table with three chairs, near to the stage. They settled down just as the band finished their number, and left the stage to appreciative applause.

"Next group is a black band from the U.S. army. They play New Orleans' Jazz like only young black guys can! .... What would you like to drink?", he added, as a young woman appeared in a crisp waitress' uniform, blond hair, pony tail, sparkling grinning visage:

"Can I have beer, Edmund?", answered Sophie, to Edmund's questioning glance.

"Two beers please. Small and large."

"And a Gruner Veltliner for me, please.", added Kep: "Large and large!". He laughed, and the waitress smiled.

After some talk of their recent experiences, visits, people they'd met, Kep said excitedly:

"Here they come!"

They looked towards the stage as six young black men,

all smiling sheepishly as they nodded towards the audience to acknowledge the enthusiastic applause:

"Ladees and Genlemen!", said one of their number, clutching a shiny brass cornet in his right hand: "We are 'The Velvet Vienna's!"

There was now another burst of applause, and even some 'hooray', or so Edmund seemed to hear. The speaker was puffed up by the reception, and almost screamed the title to the first number:

"Here's 'Needin' my baby back home'"

They began to play. Piano and brass began, with a vocal by the cornet player, and which Edmund could not easily understand, although every word was English, or rather American-English, or really Mississippi-American. The trombone started, raunchily rasping, the player swinging the instrument up and down, then clarinet; with a clear, firm tone audible through all the other sound, and finally, after a phrase or two of vocals, in came the cornet.

"Do you like this music?", Kep asked his companions.

"Yes, very much, we do", said Edmund, noting the reaction and smiles of Sophie.

Kep listened intently to the music, but in breaks, he would be intensely conversational:

"How do you decide what's the right thing to do?" he asked, at one time, and Sophie answered:

"Depends on the circumstances. It it's a friend, I try to do what's best for them."

"Example?"

"If there was danger, I'd help them, I suppose."

"Go on!"

"Well, a girl friend of mine, say, may be seeing some man who I know is no good. So I warn her, even though she might at first resent it."

"What if she was about to be killed", asked Kep, sipping his coffee: "and you could save her, but putting yourself in danger also."

"If I could help her, I would do so.", said Sophie, thinking hard and speaking slowly.

"Even though it might be bad for you?"

"I... well, I hope so. That's what being good means, I suppose. Putting others before yourself."

"And what about you, Edmund?"

"I think good and bad are complex. There's always a balance."

"And who does the balancing?", Kep asked, laughing: "Well, no more philosophy. Here come the band again."

"Do you like films? Movies?", asked Kep during an interval.

"I do, of course." replied Edmund, and he looked at Sophie, who nodded:

"I love the movies."

"In England we call them the 'flicks', not movies.", laughed Edmund. Kep explained:

"There's a small private cinema I know nearby. Tonight I'm going to see a Czech film - called 'The Railway Station'. It's dubbed into German ... Will you both join me?"

"It's a good idea, Kep", said Edmund, after a very positive indication from Sophie: "We'll eat first, though."

They had a simple but adequate meal at a small Italian restaurant nearby, and saw the film. A touching, tender story of simple young love, concerning a factory worker and a girl from the country. He liked it, but thought 'This really is just a film', but did not share this reflection with the others.

Over the following weeks he found he had indeed settled to life in Vienna, and found it most amenable. His job was vaguely interesting, very easy to do, and he had enough money to entertain Sophie and explore the city and its surrounds. He was all the more happy to realise its essential impermanence - a fleeting moment or two in his life for which he would not have to pay. There was still, of course, that nagging doubt about his pushing away his idea of taking Sophie back to England, if he could arrange it, where she would possibly be safer in the event of a Russian attack. But he consoled himself, fairly easily, with the considerations that (a) it might not happen anyway, in spite of what Clements had said; and (b) maybe if it did England would be 'no hiding place'. Still, why not tell her, and see what she says? Well, maybe ...

A young man's fancy

Spring flowers, cycling in the lanes decked with colour and alive with birdsong. With and without Sophie, this was

Edmund's most pleasurable activity. 'Even including sex', he thought, and wondered if he was normal, in this sense. Oh he was in love with Sophie, of course. She and he were young and beautiful, in a beautiful place, however temporary that might be, and this time of year had always given Edmund a feeling of how enjoyable and fresh everything really was ...

He thought that maybe sex, 'young love', was essentially a personal, selfish thing, and that perhaps green, fresh nature was there anyway, whether he took part or not, and so drew him into 'the great, secret treasure house of the world outside oneself', as he remembered someone said in a film he had seen in England some time ago.

"You think a lot, my love", said Sophie once when he was lost in this sort of reverie.

There was a trip he was always to remember. It was his first visit to Salzburg, and he took it with Sophie, who knew the city well. They took a train, together with their cycles, and drank coffee in the squares, and climbed to the top of the castle; and when Edmund saw the view from there on that cloudless day, he took her hand and scurried them both down to their cycles, waiting in one of the streets below:

"Now, let's see what's in this countryside, Sophie!"

And they set off. Some of their journey was easy and flat, sometimes they climbed into forests up narrow tracks.

They found a farm, which sold them bread and cheese for their lunch, and some beer, and later Sophie showed him the little known paths, woodlands and meadows she had frequented when she was much younger:

"Here, later, this sheltered area will be covered in mushrooms", she said, beaming at her re-discovery of her childhood idyll: "I always dreamed of one day living here, in a small cottage in the woodland, with goats and geese!" she cried, and hugged Edmund as she dreamed of a future long since passed ...

They saw some little of Kep, and some of his friends and acquaintances, in the evening when they were in town. Kep had declined offers from them to join their picnics in the countryside. Edmund, on the other hand, had grown fond of jazz, and the jazz clubs of Vienna; and happily joined Kep on several occasions, as well as in their other shared interest of (mainly) non-American films.

"'Birth of a Nation' is a great film", opined Edmund over Coffee, talking to Kep and some of his friends: "but apart from Orson Welles' films, the Americans have produced mainly rubbish."

"Then thank God they won the war!", said Kep: "or we'd have the film market flooded with classics, and that would leave us no time to talk about things! ... however, what about some of the pre-war musicals? and Bogarde? 'Casablanca', and so on?"

"Formula films, in my book, Kep", replied Edmund: "Good guys with impeccable English (even when they're not English), bad guys looking sinister, with German accents, girl meets boy ..... and so on. Maybe the technique and acting are brilliant, I agree... but they don't take us anywhere new, do they? They're propaganda for the status-quo." he added, borrowing a phrase he'd learned from Dorothy when she was talking about American films.

Kep looked down, thoughtfully nodding, then the band returned:

"Play it, Sam!" he said to Edmund, and they both laughed.

Edmund wrote each week to Leela, and got at least two from her in return:

May, 1958

Dearest Edmund

Why do I have to wait for you? I know it's selfish and un-ladylike, but I want you NOW.

I'm worried about some stories in the press. They say there might be a war, and Germany will be attacked. I suppose that's where you are, my love. Please take care of yourself.

Oh, Ed, I wish you had made love to me - passionate, wanton love - and that I was now carrying your baby. Then you could never be taken away from me!

Anyway, I'm still a virgin. Just. I did kiss boy after a dance the other Saturday and he got very excited and it was difficult to ward him off. Funny, really! I spend all the time when I'm with you trying to get you to take me, and all the time I'm with other boys stopping them. Hope you appreciate this sacrifice, Edmund.

The weather is nicer now so I'm getting out and about at weekends or my days off. I'm a vintage cyclist now and there's not many hills defeat me. Dad and Mum and Pauline and I sometimes get out on Sunday to the Dales in the car. Dad has beer, Mum has lager and lime, and I have the same, and Pauline has Dandelion and Burdock. Pauline and I often go off into the woods and meadows, to see the flowers and insects. She loves anything that creeps and crawls. As I said to her last week, she'll like most of the boys in Wellawnbury when she's old enough!

A few weeks ago we found a dead sheep on the moor. Its eyes were wide open, and it looked as if it could be just resting. Pauline said that if there are such things as souls, then the sheep has one, too, and where would it go to now it had died? She was crying, and I tried to comfort her, but none of it makes sense to me, Edmund, and I prefer not to even <u>think</u> about it. To end on a happier note, Dad has promised us SCARBOROUGH next week, we Pauli and

Stephen Holden

I have vowed to go swimming in the sea for the first time this year.

The grass looks so green, and the blue sky is bluer than usual and the cowslips are coyer than ever as I think about your return. Of course, I might be assuming things!! Maybe you don't love me anymore. Well, if so, I'll wear black and live in a cottage on my own on the moors. I'll have a bicycle, a cat and hollyhocks around the door. So be warned!!!!!!!!!!

Need to wash my hair before going to bed. Wish you were with me. Love, Leela XXXX

May/58

Leela, dearest

I love you and miss you. I am enjoying my (short!) time in the army, but there's much here I could share with you, which I know you would like. It's frustrating I can't tell you where I am or what I'm doing, but I'll soon be home for good.

I've done lots of drawings, and taken some quite good

photos. I've learnt to develop pictures and it's interesting the sort of effects you can get when you do it yourself.

I'm very proud of my German which is now quite good. I can easily understand most of the conversational German I come across, and I can speak well enough to get 90% in my latest test. I have begun reading German novels. I hardly ever read a novel in English!

I entered a bike road rally last week and came in fifth. I think this was good because the first three are professionals. It was nice to know I'm keeping fit, anyway.

Kisses for you, my love, Edmund

Towards the end of May, whilst he was visiting one of the city centre art galleries, he met with Kep, Hugo and a woman he had not seen before, called Anna. She was a slim, dark-haired woman, in her late twenties, dressed in cream cheese cloth dress and was effusive in greeting him, offering her hand to be kissed, and giggling as he did so:

"Do you like these pictures? Any of them? Pah! Come to the Modern Art Gallery, around the corner from here, Edmund, if you want to see some good pictures!"

The foursome went to a coffee bar within the gallery, and chatted about art, films and philosophy.

"Kep was right. You *are* handsome!" said Anna, looking at Edmund as she sipped her coffee.

"Is that an advantage?" he smiled. Hugo leaned over to him and said:

"Not at all, my friend. I am totally ugly. Yet I have enough money, and plenty of women!", and he laughed. Kep smiled towards Edmund and tapped his hand:

"Use well any compliments you can get. Only appearances count in this world.", and he gestured towards Hugo: "he does have enough money to persuade the women to forget about his body!" And both he and Hugo now continued a conversation about a book Kep was reviewing.

Anna looked away from them, and pouted as she drew her finger in around the rim of her empty cup:

"On the subject of that film we were talking about, what is really important to *you*, in your world, Edmund? Can you tell me?"

Edmund thought for several seconds:

"Change and difference, I suppose. Light and shade. The transformation from night to dawn ... but is this all too pretentious?"

"Yes, but let that pass. You look forward to change, then."

She talked slowly, with a clear, low voice. Her lips moved carefully and seductively as she went on, looking at him directly:

"Are you afraid of things being the same?"

He smiled, and looked away. She continued:

"You are quite ordinary, and, I would say, ashamed to be so ... however, Edmund, you are, I think, in a way searching for some great cause ... Is that what you are trying to say?"

He did not answer.

"Of course, you can't talk about yourself. I understand this. I wonder what if would take to blow your complacency apart?", she added, sharply.

"Nothing ordinary will bring him out, Anna", enjoined Kep. Hugo muttered to himself and left the group. Kep followed him as he disappeared, then turned to Edmund:

"Tell, Edmund, have you added to your operatic repertoire since 'Figaro'?"

"I haven't Kep. The tunes are quite good, but the whole form of Opera ..... well .... I don't like it."

"You think it is unreal?", asked Anna.

"Unreal in that we talk together now, we don't sing!", he laughed.

"But art is of its nature, unreal, isn't it?"

"Yes", replied Edmund: "but mimics life so we can recognise it, and identify with it. I can sympathise and empathise with characters in films, although the situations are fictional."

"Oooo ... Edmund, you sometimes talk like an old man!" Anna laughed, and reaching over, with a cold, boney grasp, squeezed his hand.

"Comes of watching continental films, Anna ... and talking about them."

Kep hit the table with the tips of his fingers, almost like a histrionic piano chord:

"Don't lose your youthful ignorance, Edmund!"

Hugo was now scurrying over to rejoin them, scribbling

something into a small, green backed book, which he quickly pushed away into his pocket as he re-joined them.

"Hello again, Anna, Edmund ... and Kep... I just saw an acquaintance of mine ... you know her, Kep ... Christina ... well, it seems there is a flat available near Liechtenstein Park... near to where my old friend Freud used to live ... I would love to live there... amongst my friends ..."

"You knew Sigmund Freud?" asked Edmund, completely surprised, but Anna giggled and then laughed out loud:

"Don't tease him, Hugo ..."

"I must say the truth, whatever that is, however..." said Hugo, holding both his hands out towards Edmund: "I never met him... But I read every single thing he ever wrote... it was as if I was with him sometimes. So, I count him as a friend. I'm sure we would have got on!", he said, his smile breaking into a laugh.

"And, my friends, it will be easier for me to write, surrounded by the people I know, and trust."

"What do you write?", asked Edmund.

"Plays... I'm a playwright, and a poet .... so of course I need people."

"I had no idea..." said Edmund: "you write plays... which are performed here, in Vienna?"

"Yes, and Paris and Berlin."

"And, I, Edmund, sometimes act in them", said Anna.

"A bohemian quartet, then", said Edmund.

They talked more, and later, in the afternoon sun, lounged in the open air drinking beer and wine. Finally, Edmund bade goodbye to the trio as he left to go to a dinner date with Colonel Clements, Alan and others at the Embassy.

CHAPTER EIGHTEEN

Same again, please!

During his second, and last, year in Vienna, he became a minor personality of nightlife. Many coffee bar waiters and proprietors remembered his name, and he accumulated several good friends. One of those he found most useful was Sabina, owner of "Sabina's". She was a buxom Bavarian woman of about 40 years, with a fearsome glare, but otherwise pleasant to look on:

"Edmund! I have that special Chablis you wanted. A whole case! It will cost you, though!", and she winked at him in exaggerated way, and swayed her hip in his direction, to the glee of the group of customers near to Edmund's table.

Sabina's husband was a small mouse-like Austrian, and

Edmund and others speculated that he was completely controlled by her:

"They say that when she is on top of him, he has to wear a snorkel to survive!", Kep had surmised; and certainly one could imagine his face being completely engulfed by those two, huge jelly-fish breasts as they made love.

Sophie was almost keener than Edmund on "classical" European films, and sometimes bullied him into visiting the cinemas two or three times in one week, which was sometimes (he felt, silently) too much for him. She was happy to dominate their relationship in a way, though, and he accepted the position almost gratefully. Despite the constant threat of war, on which he continued to receive updates from Colonel Clements, he was more relaxed now that nothing very serious had happened in the previous year.

"There's a suggestion they'll wait till the USA get a new President. Then they may move, and probably decisively. So no, Edmund, the situation isn't any better. All we can say that it didn't happen yet ..."

Edmund nodded, and looked down, and wondered if

Clements enjoyed some sort of security in his constantly forbidding predications...

Kep and Anna seemed to be a regular couple, and they would go to the jazz clubs with Edmund and Sophie ...

"I'm not too keen on Jazz, myself, Edmund", said Anna whilst the four of them were dining together one evening: "but Kep loves it completely. And to be with someone who just loves something, and to experience his enthusiasm, well... it's better than expending the energy of enjoyment myself!"

For Edmund, his work was usually routine, and tedious. Scared, helpless, hopeless (often useless) flotsam drifted in and out of his world of interviews, and most of them never to be seen again, of no interest to anyone; not even to themselves in any convincing sense.

There were some 'jewels'. One of Edmund's interviewees had worked in a farm in East Germany, and seen work on the border with the West, and had 'useful' information, according to Clements. And then there was the secretary from Hungary, who'd worked at one time for the Deputy Head of State Security, and gave some information to Edmund, before being taken off by 'The Men from the Ministry' for 'a full debriefing' in London, only to die on her arrival there of 'Asian 'flu'.

"Fucking bastards!" exclaimed Clements to Edmund as he told him in the privacy of his office: "*they* killed her, of course."

"What? Our people?"

"Our people! In the Ministry of Information, Edmund, it's a toss up whether an officer is working for them or us. Most them work for both sides, I believe! ..... How did they know we had her? You didn't say anything? ... No, no of course not. ... Could have been KGB or our lot, trying to get the glory. That's the trouble with dealing with juvenile public school air heads who consider themselves superior to everyone else! ... Saving democracy, saving mankind ..."

"Surely there are principles, Sir", asked Edmund.

"Mistrust them, Lt. Rice. Question them, especially in yourself."

He found lots of time to indulge his loves of cycling and sketching. He filled ten large sketch pads with his work, and felt he was improving his technique. He had also albums of dozens of photographs of the city, carefully catalogued and arranged with his own attached anecdotes.

Sophie did not enjoy cycling as much as he, and so often he would venture out alone on his longer jaunts, with the guide she had given him, and would explore the streets, or visit a village, or immerse himself in the countryside. He had got to know Sophie's parents. Both were industrious, smiling and overweight from their constant eating of cakes and bread they had made.

"I don't want to get like Mum", said Sophie, as they drank Coffee after a night at the pictures: "so I never eat cakes nor bread, even though I'd love to. When I was a young girl I became like a little ball because I ate sweet things all the time."

They had several trips to Salzburg that year, and had gone sailing on Lake Worthersee in Carinthia in the South of Austria.

"These two years have been like an extended holiday, Sophie!", he remarked to her: "and you have made my life here so happy ... we've had so much fun together."

She kissed him and smiled: "That's what makes our

parting when you go so easily bearable, in some ways. We couldn't be happier together, Edmund ..... so quite frankly", and she laughed: "it's all downhill from now on!"

He laughed, and hugged her, and briefly felt almost tearful, as he knew the time of his leaving Austria was fast approaching.

In one of his last private conversations with Colonel Clements, he was told that:

"If ever you want 'in' again in the next few years, let me know directly. You know my phone number here, and if I'm moved, get in touch with Colonel Dillon... he was a Major when you met him in Whitehall a couple of years ago. Good man. Tell him anything you'd tell me."

However, for all his newly found love of Vienna, he did miss home, and he missed Leela. Their brief days with each other in his leave times seemed to have drawn them more tightly together. They seemed to have developed a sense of understanding, anticipating thoughts, needs, desires, fears; often without any words, or even a look...

"You're quite a Victorian Gentleman, Edmund!", she said to him: "apparently they always had a woman or two on the side, as well as a wife. Well... I'm not a wife yet, but I do seem to be permanent... at least", she laughed: "for the time being!"

Goodbye, Vienna

Colonel Clements, Alan Vickers and others in the Embassy that Edmund had got to know gave him a little party in the Colonel's room on the eve of his leaving. It was June, and was a hot, sultry day in Vienna.

"You're a good man, Rice", said the Colonel, taking him to over to the window area, where they were away from the others, and where the late afternoon sun streaked in, forming long bright patterns on the wooden floor:

"It's a pity you're leaving. If you change your mind about this sort of work, get in touch!", and he shook his hand warmly, and smiled at Edmund paternally: "Back to the party!"

All the next day in early June, the last day, Sophie and Edmund had spent together. They had stayed in bed till mid-morning, and had a pasta and salad lunch, with white wine, at what had become their favoured restaurant.

They walked the streets and the parks, and tears welled in Sophie's eyes, as she felt that Edmund had in some ways already left her.

And now it was time to go, and Sophie, tears on his shoulder, as they stood in the airport, waiting for his plane to take him home.

"There's no point in writing to me, Edmund, as we won't meet again. Let's now say goodbye, my love. I will never forget you, and I'll always wish you well."

She kissed him lightly, so softly, so warmly; pressing herself tightly into him as they waited near the embarkation queue.

"Goodbye, Sophie.", said Edmund, feeling detached, though sad, and with some remnant of guilt: "look after Vienna for me!"

CHAPTER NINETEEN

He had to report to Whitehall, much to Leela's grief, and briefly return to a training camp near London to effect his final discharge from National Service. He finally returned home permanently to complete his studies at the Tech in July 1958. Leela and he continued in their relationship, from Edmund's point of view not diminished by time, nor by his knowing Sophie, who was now simply a happy memory for him.

By the end of the month, Edmund was offered a permanent job with Wellawnbury Town Council prematurely, the council being short of draughtsmen to cope with the boom in house and road building. He was given a desk next to Jeremy Jones, an irascible Welshman, who found the rather taciturn though amiable Edmund a perfect foil for his boisterousness.

"It's not a bad job, boyoh!", he exclaimed, sipping coffee, and peering at Edmund over his drawing board:

"Often you'll go out on site with the surveyors, so you're not always stuck in here. And let's face it, Eddy, where'd you rather be, here or down a bloody coal mine!"

He laughed again.

Edmund smiled and looked down at his undrunk coffee. The tea trolley appeared again with biscuits. Jeremy enthusiastically took a handful of the arrowroot, which Edmund declined.

"No bickies, love?" quizzed Margaret, the tea lady, she shuffled past.

Jeremy nibbled on his biscuit, and looked over at Edmund:

"Aren't you thick with Greengrocer Drake's daughter?"

"Leela. Yes. We're going out together."

"Tell me, Eddy, did you ever consider a career in medicine, like your parents? Better paid than this.", he added, tapping the drawing board he was working on with his pencil. Edmund shook his head, and laughed ruefully:

"Not got the brains, I'm afraid."

"Is your girl following Daddy in the grocery trade?"

"No. She works in a bank."

"Banking ..... Wanking. Banking and wanking. Funny you know, Eddy - even the *words* are similar!", and he broke out into a loud laugh, which attracted attention from the rest of the draughtsmen. One of them, called Eric Wooldridge, in his mid-thirties, tall, big, dark, rugby-player, came over to them:

"What's he telling you, Edmund? Dirty stories? Don't worry about that. At his age he can only tell jokes about it!"

Jeremy smiled, and bit on his biscuit before going on:

"Away next Saturday, Eric?"

"Aah. Cobb's Coppice."

"Good side. Reckon you'll beat 'em?"

"Should do. We can run faster! Can't interest you in tickets, Edmund?"

"No. I'll be cycling, hopefully, to the seaside. Steeple Bay."

Jeremy drew a breath:

"Long way, Eddy. Save something for your girl, boyoh.

All that saddle work, you know. Bad for the old engine room."

"It's only 35 miles, Jerry!" he smiled: "and that's not so bad. Anyway, I'm hoping Leela can meet us there, if she goes on by bus."

"Young people nowadays, Eric! Bloody enjoyment, that's all they think about!"

He had been in his new job for less than a month, when he was asked to attend a week's seminar titled 'Managing Planning in Rural Areas' to be held in Edinburgh.

He was captivated by the beauty of the city, and was taken back to his time in Vienna, and he began to be wracked with pain and confusion. He did not feel guilty, of, for example, greediness, selfishness or callousness; nor had he been accused of such... although Dot had given him a hard time... and what of Sophie? Had he left her in possible danger because he 'couldn't be bothered'? Leela ... well, she was young, so to keep her at arm's length was good for her .... and he was sure her parents approved of a slowly-developing relationship.

"Ah!" he sighed to himself, still unable to expunge the

little gnawing worm inside his brain, and vowed: "I'll fuck both Dorothy and Leela from my system!"

He would, he decided, take a prostitute while he was in Edinburgh. He felt that sex would not only distract him from wasteful thinking, but may (he guessed) focus his psyche, although he could not explain why.

He did not seek the first meeting. After his first day, he had a drink and socialised with his fellow students in the bar of the hotel in which they had been accommodated. He drifted into a small dark corner, his melancholia driving him to drink alone. Whilst there, as the time approached midnight, a waiter approached him:

"Drink, Sir?"

"Oh! No, better not. Have a full day tomorrow."

The young man hesitated, and glanced round. He was, Edmund noticed, dapper and quite small, with black, greasy hair and darting brown eyes:

"If you're missing your girlfriend, Sir. I can get someone to be with you. I mean, just for company, or more if you like ..."

"How much?"

"Ten pounds. She'll stay for two hours. Nice girl."

"How do you know?" smiled Edmund, thankful for the diversion.

"She's my fiancé, Sir."

"Bit unusual, isn't it?"

"We're making all the money we can. Saving up. We want to go to America, when we've saved enough. I can run my own bar there. Make a living. There's no future here, Sir."

"Maybe you're right. OK. Send her along."

"The money, Sir"

"Bring her to my room. If you're worried, come with her to the door. I'll give you the money then."

The young man hesitated, then relented:

"What time, Sir?"

"In about half-an-hour."

Edmund had bathed, and was sitting on his bed in his nightgown when he heard a low, tentative knock at the door. He walked over and opened it. The waiter, looking fearful as his dark eyes darted this way and that, and he introduced his girlfriend. She was taller than he, and not so nervous. She had long, copper-coloured hair, and big features. Although overweight, thought Edmund, she was not unattractive:

"Here is the money", whispered Edmund, handing over two large, white English five pound notes, and smiling at the waiter, as the girl walked passed Edmund calmly and entered his room: "What is your name?"

"Henry, Sir", he said, smiling: "please look after her, Sir."

"Don't worry, Henry", smiled Edmund: "no whips nor scorpions!"

Henry laughed nervously, and turned away, walking swiftly towards the stairs.

Edmund turned round to see the girl sitting on the bed. She had already taken off her dress, which hung (rather symbolically, Edmund thought) over the back of a chair.

"You tell me what you want to do, Sir", she said, quite steadily: "but I won't do perversion."

"What do you categorise as 'perversion'", he asked, out of curiosity, as he only envisaged straight sex with her anyway.

"Nothing in my back, Sir. And no pain. No instruments. OK, Sir?"

"Fine. Do you do oral sex?"

"It's alright, Sir. I do that with Henry. I'm used to it", she said, smiling slightly, as if it were an ordeal which she had grown to accept.

"I'd prefer things you like to do with Henry. I don't want to upset you."

"I don't think you will, Sir. Do you mind my asking? Will you kiss me first, Sir."

"I will. Please call me Edmund, Mary?"

"OK Sir".

(She in fact never called him 'Edmund' while they were together. He considered it was her way of keeping a distance from him, and of remaining true, in this sense to Henry.)

"Just one thing, Sir. I'm clean. Are you free of disease?"

"Why yes, yes of course."

"Do you have johnnies, Sir?"

"Yes... in the top drawer over there", he indicated the small side board next to the bed.

She didn't check, but nodded, and smiled: "Well, come on then, Sir."

She took off her slip, and stood before him in her bra and knickers:

"You now, Sir"

He was obedient, and undressed till he was naked. She watched him, interestedly, but didn't move.

"Take off your bra, now, Mary"

She did so, and small pear shaped breasts bobbled down.

"Knickers"

She stepped out of them at his bidding, and stood there, calmly waiting his next command.

He stepped forward, and took her in his arms, and found he was caressing and kissing her, and that he didn't think of the sex. He wasn't even hard.

They made love twice. Once he was on top of her, the next she on him. It was good, surprisingly good. She came screamingly:

"I always come when I do it, Sir", she said, which he found reassuring.

"How many clients so far?" he asked her, as she dressed.

"Oh, about fifteen, Sir. I only do it with nice men." She grinned at him mischievously, and unexpectedly kissed his cheek: "I'll be off now, Sir. Henry will be waiting for me."

He fell asleep that night amidst the warm smell of their two bodies, and felt contented, and tired. He dreamt about sex, but with Dorothy, and saw her smiling face filling the whole of the dream image, and he heard her voice, with the characteristic throaty, smokers' tone, sensual and enveloping in everything she said. She was talking constantly .... (and in reality, Dot did speak all the time during love-making):

"Is this what you really want, boy? Is it this... do you feel me around you?" and he noticed her mouth close slightly as she snatched an intake of breath, with a slight hissing sound:

"I'm around you all the time... Go right inside me, boy ... that's it ..... more inside me, more... right."

He awoke with a start, feeling surrounded by darkness, suffocating:

"Maybe I was sleeping with my face on the pillow", he mused, walking over to the wash basin, and bending over, sucking some water from a running tap.

Three days later, and he decided to pick up a prostitute in the manner usually suggested on the films. He talked to the head of reception, a bald-headed man called Stone:

"I thought I'd take a walk around the city tonight. Is there any streets or places to avoid?"

"Well, Sir ..."

Stone told him about the historic buildings, the famous streets, the views that could be had at night ...and, of course, the red-light districts "you wouldn't like what you'd find down that street at night, Sir"

He was in that very street within the hour. He walked slowly, noting few walkers, but girls in groups of two or three standing on the intersections. The first girl who approached him had a great bunch of red hair in untidy curls, and mainly worn up, above her shoulders.

"Want a nice time?", she said in a deep voice, and broad Glasgow accent.

He shook his head as he noted she had some of her

front teeth missing. Further along the road, another girl approached. She was older, probably near to forty, but was smiling, he noted as she looked at him. She stepped to his side as he walked, and walked a little with him, then said, almost in a whisper:

"Would you like to go with me? Anything, five pounds".

He stopped and looked at her under the light of a street lamp. He had noticed her accent was less broad than the other girl, and that she was, short, but standing middle height in very high heels, slight in figure, long, straight dark hair, dark eyes, with a frozen smile, which gave her, he thought, an attractive vulnerability.

"Ok", he agreed, simply. They had walked side-by-side for 50 yards or so along the main street, when she gathered her breath, and uttered a stifled "Oh", then she whispered to him urgently:

"Can I link your arm? There's a police man coming." She had already done so, as he mumbled his assent. The constable passed them by, and she had now hid her face in a head scarf which had before hung over her shoulders.

"Goodnight, Lilly!", the tall, dark clad figure said as he passed close to them.

"Bastard!", she whispered, and turned to Edmund anxiously: "he won't tell anyone about you .... anyway, he doesn't even know you ..."

"Don't worry, Lilly", he assured her.

"Lillian, please, and now, what do I call you?", she said, quite relaxed, almost tripping along the pavement as they walked along, arm in arm.

"I'm fifty years old", she told Edmund as they approached the door of her small terraced house: "but don't let that put you off, young man!"

They had simple sex, pleasingly for Edmund without durex, because Lillian was barren after producing two children:

"Both gone south, of course," she said as they lay in bed after sex, she sipping fruit juice: "John is a chef in hotel in Petersfield, a trade learned in the RAF, and Robert is a coal-mining inspector in Doncaster. They're good lads, to me, Edmund."

When they made love, her smile brightened her whole

face, although she looked older than her fifty years, as her long hair fell over the pillow; and she always looked at him, looking (he thought) joyful. She was certainly enthusiastic:

"Oh, ride me like the cowboy you are, Edmund ... go on, go on ...", and she came twice in their night together, pulling his shoulders as she did so, so his full weight was on her, and she caressed his neck, and kissed his cheeks, and he felt the perspiration on her face as she rubbed against him.

"There, there, my boy ..."

He got back to the hotel at 5:00 o'clock, as some staff were arriving there.

"Good morning, Sir!", said the receptionist, as he nodded to her, and went up to his room. He showered and shaved, and prepared for the duty of the day: "Resolving interests in planning disputes."

Having completed his course and returned home, he met with Leela one evening, meeting her from work:

"Did you learn anything from your course? Did you fall asleep?"

"No, and no!", he answered laughing; "Look, let's go to

the film club tonight. It's lowering over, and I think it might rain."

"And I don't mind skipping our cycling date, Edmund, as long as I'm with you!"

The show that night was a Swedish film, only a few months' old, but was obtuse even for Edmund's taste. And it was dubbed, which he always found annoying:

"I wish they'd always use subtitles", he complained.

"Hm .... glad you can't see the sub-titles of what I'm thinking!", she whispered, eagerly into his ear, as she squeezed up to him in the tiny auditorium, which was almost empty that evening.

Afterwards, they walked to the park, it being still quite early, and Edmund had his mother's car to take Leela home. Sitting on a bench, they talked about everyday things, then kissed and caressed, and loved all they could, all he could dare.

Sometimes people would walk quickly by, not obviously looking, but they did not care, and Leela was defiant:

"Maybe we can teach them something, Edmund!"

"Leela", said Edmund: "I'm going to see Dot again, I think. How do you feel about that?"

She did not move, but continued kissing his neck:

"Up to you, Edmund. I'm not jealous of it."

"But... why not?"

"Because you're not with her now, are you?", and she kissed him again.

"I'm not trying to make you jealous or be unkind ... I suppose I need to see her, and I want to be straight with you."

"Enough said..." and she kissed his mouth, and forced her tongue between his teeth. Leela, noted Edmund, loved to kiss, and French kissing was (she said) her favourite kiss - 'As long as the boy's breath is good!' she had said.

During that week, he phoned Dorothy at her home in Leeds, and discovered she was visiting Sheffield soon for a week to look after her mother's cat, while she was on holiday:

"Do you like cats?"

"We never had pets. Cats seem OK to me, though."

"I'm like a cat, Edmund. I scratch your back, remember."

"But that's when I'm good. Cat's scratch when they're upset, don't they?"

"No, they do it when they're playing, as well."

"Anyway, Eddy, what do you want to see me again for?" she asked

"I want you. I want sex. Well, I want sex with you. That's all, to he honest."

"That's everything we ever had, my boy. Let me give you some directions on getting to me ..."

He stayed with her for a some days, during which he phoned his mother, as he had promised:

"I'm glad you've seen Dorothy again. She will always be good for you.... Autumn is coming, Edmund. Leaves are turning gold and coppery. I love that faint first chill breeze don't you, Edmund? You're twenty years old. I wish I could give you the experience and insights I gained in my twenties, to protect you, to give you all those advantages, Edmund."

Vivian was happy now her boy was home, and joked with him ...

"Back in a big city again, Edmund. And so soon. You'll be a real town boy!"

Edmund had taken the train to Sheffield, and Dot met him there, waiting for him in her car, outside the station:

"Well, Eddy, here we are again...", and she leaned over to him, as he sat in the passenger seat, and kissed him, resting lightly both her hands on his cheeks. "and we parted for ever only a few years ago."

She drove them to the house which had been for twenty years her home, an imposing old house in a suburb of the city bordering the moors.

"Almost like home!" he said, having got out of the car, and gazing to the distant hills. The sky was still August bright:

"I thought you might want to eat here, it being quite late now?", she asked.

They had a peppery rice dish, with small, whole fish:

"Whiting" she said, as he asked: "hope you like them?"

"Hmm. Very good. Mum does fish and rice sometimes, but whiting is new to me."

They had a very good, dry white wine with their meal,

as was the habit when they dined together. And as was the other habit, they were both thinking, as they ate, of being in bed together, so each of them, in different ways, delayed the finishing of the meal slightly, to heighten the anticipation. And they had not seen each other for some time, and both of them were hungry for each other after their meal. They did not dally much after finishing the wine, she said:

"Let's go to bed, eh Eddy?"

And soon they were in bed, naked:

"I wanted to smell you again, Dot, more than anything else, and taste you ...."

"Taste away, Eddy", she said, pulling his head into her as he licked her: "There's no one like you, Edmund. I thought I'd managed to finish with you for good. Although in way I have."

She sighed as he moved his attention upwards, kissing her body, and biting her nipples:

"I can take you or leave you now, Edmund... and taking you is just as great as it always was ... he kissed her passionately, and they stayed together, still for some time, before making love

They were different together, it was obvious to both of them. Not worse, nor better, but they had grown into new lives, and were left with little of that familiarity of culture, language and sense of humour which gave them so much rapport before. Of course, such things can be rebuilt. But why would they be?

"I'm over you, Eddy", she had said as they lay in bed one morning: "I can be with you. Or not be with you", and she looked coldly at him, and drew on her cigarette.

"Good.", he said, though felt some loss within his breast, but tried to ignore it: "Do you resent me being here? Was I too cheeky to ask?"

"Of course not, you fool!" she laughed, and kissed him: "I mean that I don't get torn open by you anymore. That's good, isn't it?", and she stubbed out her cigarette, and rolled on top of him.

He sat on the train to go home feeling refreshed and happy. It was a Sunday afternoon train he'd caught, so it stopped sometimes for track work; but he was quite contented to look out on to the fields, or buildings, or stations ... the whole vista was an amusing picture show for him that day. He was cured. He felt much better......

Leela spent the week thinking of his being with Dorothy. She did not usually do this, but it seemed that this time she couldn't help it. She spent time in her bedroom at home, and on her own, thinking about her feelings:

"I'll tell Edmund about what I feel ... oh, I don't know what I feel... not jealousy... I could stand that .... no ... it's something else... his place is here with me, now... oh, no, that's not the way."

So, and here she is, waiting on Monday evening, sitting on the bench by the main entrance to the Technical College, that day being one of Edmund's study days. He appeared at the entrance, and smiled as he approached, but looked concerned:

"What's the matter? You look sad"

"I'm confused and resentful, Eddy. Can you tell me why?"

"My seeing Dorothy. I may never see her again. I've no plans ... but ... well... do you think we should finish?"

"What good would that do, Edmund. I'm crazy about you.", and she burst into tears, and buried her head into his soft, thick corduroy jacket.

"I do love you, Leela. As much as I seem capable of doing, anyway."

"Why can't we make love? That would put me on a par with your other girl friends."

"You're still young."

"Eighteen, Eddy. And", she laughed: "If I did a Ruth Ellis, and shot you, I could be hanged... so why can't I have sex?"

He had no excuse, and suddenly wondered why he needed one. Perhaps his original feeling, that he shouldn't take advantage of a young girl, was no longer why he was holding back. Perhaps he was afraid.

"I can't go on much longer like this, Eddy. Not with your women, I mean. With not making love. We're at a point when I'm sure we need to take our relationship seriously, or finish forever.", and she burst into tears again: "although that would tear me apart, I'd have to do it, Eddy, I'd really have to do it."

Part 2

“OH BOY!”

CHAPTER ONE

Monday, August, 1959

A high, pulsating dome of water arose, thick with foam, and broke over the sharp, black rock. Splashing down; it crashed, its cry echoing in a grating, showering hiss of bellowing sand and shingle.

The rock was the first witness.

Edmund stared at the scene: not thinking, nor comprehending. Leela was sitting, gazing at the fresh, bright new grass; leaning on her hip; and now looking up she brushed her hand across his cheek. His gaze was drawn further out to sea; towards the horizon and the distant fishing boats. Gradually he became aware of himself once more, of the fresh breeze on his hand, of the touch of Leela's fingers on his face. It was those fingers wasn't it? It *was* those white slender ribbons which had tugged his hair a few moments before in a passionate expression of her virgin love. He ran his hand over the spots of her maiden's blood which stained their flattened grassy bed.

He felt, nothing. His complete lack of any reaction surprised him and yet he felt calm, and warm. He grasped Leela's hand lightly, and kissed her. She pulled herself closely to him, and kissed him several times about his face, her warm breath fanning his nose and lips. He held her warmly and against him, rubbing his lips across her hair.

They sat in silence for ten minutes as the cloudy summer day grew darker. Leela drew her legs in a tight curl against her body.

"Cold" she said, leaning on Edmund's upper arm.

"We'll go back now" said Edmund; and the couple returned, arm-in-arm, to the gate against which their bikes were leaning.

They cycled abreast of each other for most of the five miles back to Edmund's house and when they reached there, laid their bikes to the wooden wicket which stood at the entrance of the large front yard.

She alighted first. As she waited his joining her, she looked down at her feet, and her hair fell across her face:

"Better not be too late home" she said.

He took her hand, and led her towards the door: "I'll take some tea and then ride back with you"

Leela followed him inside, brushing a tear from the end of her nose. She was feeling less cold, at last. Edmund ushered her into the kitchen, where she sat down by the window, staring into the darkening sky. Edmund had gone, but then returned:

"Father's on call, Mother and the children are playing Monopoly in the lounge", he said, smiling at her. He took up his tea and sat facing her, turning slightly towards the window. He saw the fading light, and felt uneasy. This was a very significant point in their lives, wasn't it? All this. Not just the sex, but the feelings .... He glanced furtively and briefly towards her. She looked at the deepening yellow-blue sky. It was perfect, she mused.

Edmund saw her almost smiling. Would this not always be with them? And then why had he already begun to forget? He could truly feel for her, for Leela. But he could feel only, sorrow. Nothing, had ever been so breathtakingly painful, as the bitterness he felt at that moment.

Leela touched his arm tenderly, and smiling at him, eyes misty-glistening with lingering love, said:

"What do you see?"

"Oh! Clear sky ... colours you see only in reality ... too outrageously beautiful to be invented or copied."

"Precisely! ... Oh my Edmund ... are you as happy as I am? Is the intensity of my desire, my lust, my love too great for you? Or is it not enough? Brush those furrows from your forehead!", and she stroked the spot gently and firmly.

"When you reach the end, the goals, there's nowhere to go, is there? Is that sad, or joyful? ...."

"You mean, is the pleasure of taste as you eat, or afterwards when you remember?", she laughed. "when do we live, now, in the past, or in the future?"

"Some say we only have the here and now," said Edmund

CHAPTER TWO

The Following Monday, August, 1959

Edmund put down his pencil and looked out of the window. He could not keep his mind on his work today and he longed for the coffee break which would give him time to relax. He glanced back at the drawing of a small housing development he was trying to complete and sighed.

"Ugly, isn't it?" Ralph Jones, a fellow draughtsman, asked him in a rounded and lilting South Wales accent. Edmund smiled slightly as he looked up:

"Somebody loved it. Enough to design it, anyway."

"No they didn't. Somebody saw a way of making lots of money. Handouts, corruption, once-in-a-lifetime grab for a pot of gold, Edmund. You and I are part of the scheme, boy.

It's that, that irks me", and biting his lip he banged his pencil on his drawing board and leaned his head on his hands.

"What about some coffee!" Ralph shouted across the office. A few heads looked up, like mice peering from holes in the ground.

"I suppose you and the fruiterer's daughter will be married soon, boy?" He smiled at Edmund, taking his coffee from the rattling refreshments trolley as it stopped at their desks.

Ed|mund didn't answer. He stirred his coffee meticulously.

After work he met Leela in the town and they walked together to her bus stop.

"I'd like you to come for dinner tonight", he said to her, "Father will bring you and take you back."

"Lovely, Edmund!" Leela answered, and kissed him.

"Here's my bus ... What time?"

"Is seven o'clock too early?"

"Not at all", Leela said "Just enough time to get ready for you! Bye!" And she skipped onto the bus, smiling and waving her hand.

Edmund sauntered back to his bus-stop, having still fifteen minutes to wait. He posted himself in the bus queue, staring across the street at an old man dragging a reluctant dog away from a butcher's door. At his shoulder, a woman hectored her daughter. The woman's head was covered with a thin scarf, drawn tightly around her ears. Edmund did not listen to the words she spoke, but saw the jerking and pecking silhouette, and guessed she was very angry with the young girl. The latter, he could now see, was a teenager: dark hair, dark eyes, sullen and near to tears of frustration. She would occasionally murmur a low protest or rejoinder, only to be attacked afresh by her indignant mother.

The bus had now arrived, and Edmund ran upstairs the vehicle, jumping two steps at a time, and slumped heavily into the rear seat. Pulling his knees up to press against the backrest of the seat in front of him, he stared fixedly out of the window, above the roof-tops of the office blocks and into the far distance.

That Evening

"Do you like soup, Leela?" Edmund's father asked. "Truth is, it's my contribution to the cooking tonight."

Leela smiled towards him, sipping the hot soup as she listened.

"It's from a very old recipe. Mainly cabbage and turnip. Dutch cuisine, probably. Fancied trying it out on somebody, and you came along!" Oscar laughed, and his eyes twinkled as he looked at Leela and then towards Edmund.

"She doesn't say whether she likes it or not!" he said to his son.

"At least she isn't objecting to it, father." said Edmund, smiling towards her.

Vivian looked briefly and intently at her husband

"Since it took two hours to make, I hope she likes it!" she said, and then smiled, and turned to Leela, "If you don't like it my dear, don't be afraid to say so." She shook a lock of stray hair from her cheek and resumed eating. Her long, thin fingers moved almost hypnotically before her as she scooped a spoonful of soup, followed by a bite of bread.

After dinner, Oscar partnered Leela against his wife and Edmund in a game of bridge.

"We play lots of games in this family, Leela" said Vivian "And if the children were home tonight it would be Monopoly, since there would be too many for bridge." She paused and frowned questioningly at Edmund:

"The problem with bridge, Leela, is that it takes years to understand your partner's intentions. Especially if he's a man..." Vivian pouted in Edmund's direction:

"Even more especially if he's your own son!..... Edmund! What are you up to? Leading a low spade!"

Oscar laughed and looked towards Leela: "We are having no difficulties, are we, Leela?"

Leela smiled and played her reply. Vivian played a card, and then attempted to retrieve it.

"Not allowed. We've already played a practice hand," said her husband.

"Oh damn it, Oscar! It's surely better to amend a stupidity than to go on with it just to satisfy the rules?"

"If we disobey them, it gets absurd. Anyway, Vivian, I don't see it's such a bad card - the one you played?"

"It's obvious to me it's wrong. Never mind. Let it rest." She sighed and looked anew at her hand.

Eventually, Vivian and Edmund won the rubber, and Oscar suggested a drink in the garden, it being a very warm evening.

Edmund was standing by the gate, looking our across the moors, when Vivian joined him and gave him a glass of whisky.

"We won." She said, smiling at him, and squeezed his arm.

"You mean <u>you</u> did, mother. You're a much better player than father," Edmund replied, looking deeply into the night.

"Yes, I am." There was a pause as she stepped away from her son, towards the house; and then stood, her slender figure silhouetted against the light from the kitchen. It was in that room than Leela and Oscar were standing facing each other, talking and laughing. Vivian glanced downwards:

"But it's not always the best players who win the game, Edmund. It's not always like it was tonight!" Vivian lifted her glass and turned to face her son:

"Cheers!"

Edmund strolled into the kitchen, where he found Oscar and Leela completing a duet of laughter, obviously at the conclusion of an amusing story. Oscar turned to his son

"Edmund, why not take Leela for a walk in the gardens before I take her home? The romance will catch you, I'm sure." Edmund hesitated, and Oscar added:

"Look, if you don't want to, then I will!" and laughing, led Leela over to join her lover. She raised her mouth to his ear:

"Come along, Edmund. Take me into the hot summer night and woo me."

As Edmund walked Leela through the yard, he felt the veil of night air, heavy and hot, settling around them. They drifted towards the path, and into the low avenue of late flowering azaleas.

"I feel so wonderful, Edmund ..... so much in love"

"With me?" he asked, squeezing her closely to him.

"Hmmmm. With everything", she murmured, rubbing her head deeply into his breast. They had stopped moving, and Leela prodded a bush, and twirled a leaf around her finger:

"You'd better get something, Edmund, before too long. Or I'll be a mother."

"Wouldn't you like to be?" he asked her as they strolled further, in an ungainly fashion, his long stride being compensated for by two smaller and quicker ones from Leela.

"No, not yet. Maybe, not at all. She kissed him and they had paused now they had reached the lawns, and they embraced again beneath the cover of a large walnut tree.

"I think it's good, just as we are, Edmund. I don't want to change anything. It's too precious."

"How do you mean? Precious?" he sounded surprised.

"Precious, love, because I feel it must end, sometime."

"Everything must end," he reflected; but she turned to him more earnestly:

"Yes, but I feel I'd like to have melted into your body when you made love to me yesterday. I know you didn't feel that, Edmund. I know you were away from me, feeling it wasn't complete, or something of that kind. There's no sense of compromise, in you, is there? I'm glad about that. I'm in love with you and the whole world, and that's all that matters to me. It's complete, for me." She looked away from him and then began slowly:

"I don't mind. Your not feeling the same. It's selfish, of course. I'm using you to fulfil my dreams. Do you mind that?"

She grinned up at him, took his hand and pressed it against her lips. He looked down into her eyes, and laughed:

"Leela, Leela! .... If only ..." and with that he hugged and kissed her, and felt her warm breast, and swayed his body against hers, and cursed his feeble spirit.

It was now time for Leela to return home. Edmund steered her, his arm around her and resting on her shoulder, towards his father's car. They settled closely together in the big front seat; Edmund facing forward, sitting well back; Leela pressing her cheek and breast into his body. Her hand reached across his chest, pinching and caressing him:

"I could go to sleep. Just like this", she murmured.

The crunch of crushed gravel was heard and the driver's door opened. Leela lifted her head and sat upright, leaning against her lover:

"Soon have you home, young lady!" said Oscar, smiling at the couple.

The Jaguar turned into the deserted tree-lined road and sped towards town. There was no illumination save the headlamps of their vehicle, and the road ahead with the luxuriant greenery on either side forming a canopy above, seemed like a long tunnel, with no sign of escape. They accelerated rapidly, and to Leela's dream-filled mind the changing shapes which the moving lights afforded entranced her, as the silent films had done to others cradled, as she was, in her lover's arms.

Quite suddenly they were in open moorland, the roadway was high above the surrounding turf and heather, and the headlights picked out the sparkle of animals' eyes, and the flickering whiteness of the barn owl. To the right and below them the silent couple gazed at the distant street lights of the town, dotted in glinting strings which radiated from the commercial centre.

"Beautiful sky!" said Oscar, speeding to 90 miles an hour on the long, straight road. Leela felt herself pushed deeply into the backrest of the seat, and squeezed herself against Edmund as she did so. He hugged her and kissing her hair, quietly moaned his satisfaction. The rush of air from the heater warmed Leela's ankles, and she stretched herself in the intoxicating comfort of the big limousine.

She was awoken by the slowing down of the car as it prepared to park in the long driveway in front of her home. The young couple alighted and walked towards the house. It was a modern, detached construction set in large grounds, and of generally unkempt appearance. Leela turned to the two men:

"Would you like a drink before you go?"

"Not for me, but I'll say hello" said Oscar, and strode towards the open kitchen door, through which he had seen Leela's mother. Their greetings were soon muffled as he shut the door, to leave the lovers alone.

Leela took Edmund's face in her hands and pulled down, kissing his lips and rubbing her mouth over his cheeks. He squeezed her body passionately, digging his fingers into her breasts and quickly passed his hand up her naked thigh, penetrating her to bring a groan of pleasure from her. She laughed, despite her own intensity, the furtiveness of lovemaking greatly amused her. She could hear her mother's voice, not more than ten yards away, whilst she, her daughter, swayed and slid herself on his fingers, feeling the warmth and the excitement. And this excitement was made more as she again heard her mother's talking to Edmund's father, in the kitchen. She gasped for breath, and found pleasure in feeling she had to keep as quiet as possible. What did her mother talk about? About what she had done today. How the town was busy. How Pauline always seemed to need bigger sizes as she grew so quickly!

"Edmund ...." Leela came with delicious relief. "No." she grasped his wrist "Stay inside me ..." He kissed her softly:

"I must make love to you as soon as possible!" he whispered.

"I don't believe your father will wait for you!" said Leela.

"No, no" replied Edmund, unable to catch the joke cleanly, as they got out of the car. Eventually, he laughed, kissed her, and clasped her around the waist:

"Tomorrow" he said, smiling down into her eyes,

"Tomorrow I'll call for you at seven, and we'll go onto the moor."

"Oh-ho!" she exclaimed, eyeing Edmund with a sideways look, as if she should beware:

"Can I expect the worse to happen to me? Can I expect to be tormented and ravaged, my great Saxon?"

Edmund grinned, and hugged her strongly:

"You can, woman!"

"In that case I'll come to you" she said, kissing him, "And with you..." She added, licking her tongue into his mouth. They were soon disturbed by Oscar's appearance. He discreetly passed them and got into his car.

"Goodnight, Leela" said Edmund, turning and descending the doorstep to the drive where the car was parked.

"Goodnight!" Leela stood in the doorway, silhouetted sharply by the indoor light. As he turned, he saw her waving: "Goodnight, Mr Rice. Thanks for the lift!"

She continued to stand in the porch way, one foot raised onto the toe, holding on to the step rail, swaying slightly, until as she looked the rear lights of the car were all she could see of the vehicle. Even these now disappeared as far down the driveway, a bend took the car behind the bay hedge. She heard the scraping on the gravel as the car stopped at the main road; then, after a short pause, she could discern the scudding acceleration so typical of the machine, and of Oscar's driving. She closed the door gently behind her as she went into the house.

"There's a glass of Apfelsaft, Leela." Sarah, her mother, was calling in a piping voice from the kitchen.

"Thank you" said Leela, and greedily drank the cold juice on that sultry evening:

"Where's Dad?

"In the lounge" replied Sarah. Leela left the kitchen, and walked into the long entrance hall, into the lounge.

Her father was sitting in an armchair, reading a newspaper. He was a gigantic man; very tall and heavily built. He was 51 years, overweight, with a big, red face, huge blue eyes and thinning fair hair:

"Alright?" he said in a broad North Yorkshire accent.

"Yes, Dad" said Leela, sitting opposite him in the other

armchair: "Why didn't you come into the kitchen? Say hello to Mr Rice? Didn't you realise he'd brought me home?"

"That's three questions." He drew his enormous hands together - they almost covered the tabloid he was reading - and carefully picked and blew until the pages separated, and he re-opened the newspaper to read another story.

"Oh Dad!" said Leela, kicking his foot. William was silent for a moment; then, lowering his newspaper, said:

"Is it serious, Leela? You and Edmund?"

"Might be" she said, smiling at him.

"Bloody soft answer" he grunted, and added: "Mind you, you're a bloody soft woman!"

"Thanks, Dad" she replied.

"Well, it's probably true. Sulking won't alter the truth, Leela"

"All I asked was why you didn't greet Mr Rice after he'd driven me all the way home" said Leela, disapprovingly.

"Because I don't like him very much." And William resumed his reading.

Leela looked down at her feet, and sitting back in the armchair, stared at the ceiling. She had fallen from the height of elation to sudden and unexpected depression. She had known for a long time that her father hadn't like the Rice family, so why did she feel so sad? And she could see, although reluctantly, she could see her father's attitude in herself, and Edmund was Oscar's son...

Tears, bitter water; trickled down her temples as she stared fixedly upwards. She had given her virginity, her love, her passion and she couldn't even see why she had done it. She could find no reason, nor excuse. It would have been more bearable had she been forced, had she been raped or duped. But this incompleteness, this feeling of shallowness, or ordinary inevitability ...

She felt warmth and weight on her arm. William was there, by her side, looking at her with concern in his eyes. He said nothing, merely squeezed his hand around her shoulder, and then left the room. Moments later she could hear his heavy, measured steps as he climbed the stairs.

CHAPTER THREE

Next Morning - Tuesday

"Leela! Leela!"

Her name, shouted at a high pitch, penetrated Leela's slumber.

"Yes, mother, coming. Coming now."

She threw the covers back, off her body and down to the foot of the bed. The she lay still, her hand combing through her tousled hair. In another minute she was sitting on her bed, still trying to re-arrange her mind. Perhaps things hadn't happened in the way she had thought. Maybe it was usual for someone like her, young and lacking experience, sheltered ... maybe she just asked too much from life. She could love. She would love. And possibly, at this moment, she did love...

"Leela! Eight o'clock!", Sarah called up the stairs. Leela rose and crossed the landing to the bathroom. There she drenched herself in the hottest shower she could bear, before vigorously towelling down and dressing.

At the breakfast table sat William, his large white mug half filled with coffee. He greeted his daughter, then fell silent as Sarah served her tea and buttered toast.

"Late this morning, Leela?", Sarah looked at her: "Not ill, are you?"

"No, thanks, mum. Just overslept"

Her father finished his coffee and got to his feet:

"I'll wait for you"

"No, dad, be off! I'll catch the bus."

"Sure?", he asked, and smiled: "Goodbye, then." He kissed his wife, and Leela, and left.

"What time do you have to be in today, Leela?" asked Sarah.

"9.30, Mum. Why?"

"If our John's not taking you, then I will. Could do with a trip into town."

"Oh don't fret, Mum. I'll be fine." Leela glanced

through the window at the garden, bright and green in the morning sun.

Sarah made no remark; simply inclining her head slightly and returned to her dish washing. She was small and plump, and at 49 was two years younger than her husband. She often looked ill because of a pale complexion, contrasting against her short, dark hair, which was just greying at the temples. By the time she had finished dish washing, John, her eldest son, entered.

"Morning, Mother" he said, stooping over her and briefly kissing the top of her head: "Morning Leela"

"Hello, John," said his sister: "Can you give me a lift in today?"

"Alright. Why didn't you go in with Dad?" he asked, but Leela was drinking her tea.

"Did you want breakfast? Or just tea?" Sarah asked her son.

"No, Mother. Thank you", John had strode to the window, and was staring out.

"You've breakfasted, then?" There was a hint of accusation in Sarah's voice.

"Dad and I put a kitchen in my flat so I could do just that, Mother. And so I have done." He cut short his gaze through the window, and abruptly walked to the other side of the room, his lips drawn tightly:

"Ready?", he asked Leela.

"See you later, Mum!" she said, and left to wait for John in the yard outside. A minute later he had left the front door and went to open the garage to retrieve his car. Leela looked at the garage, above which she saw the pink curtains of his kitchen window. The flat was a mixture of conversion and extension to the large family house.

"How are you getting on at Barclays?" he asked as they drove into the road.

"Alright", she answered: "How are you getting on with Angela? Wedding plans well advanced?"

"Hopefully April. There are definite tax advantages in an April wedding."

"Oh" Leela said, softly.

"About you at the bank, Leela. If you want to advance, take the professional exams. They'll let you have time off to do it. Look at me. I'm an assistant manager already. I'm only 30. It's worth thinking about."

They drove the rest of the journey in silence until they reached the town outskirts.

"Look at that notice!" exclaimed John as they veered slightly to the right: "Five star petol's four shillings and eleven pence a gallon here! We'll try the next station!"

Leela sighed: "Can you drop me first?"

On her arrival at the bank she was sent to the counter from opening time to ten thirty. But it wasn't too bad. The bank was busy, and the customers were in good humour, and she found the task of account checking afterwards lightened by working with her long-time, and indeed only, friend at the bank, Kitty Hopeness. She had very pretty features, but her overall appearance was indefinably ordinary. She was unmarried, and in her mid-twenties:

"I've been checking all morning!" she complained, "And to be frank, Leela, I'd have preferred more time on the counter."

"Only half-an-hour to coffee!" laughed Leela: "And if we talk about something pleasant, it won't be too bad!"

"Then tell me about Edmund", answered Kitty: "That will be nice for you, and I have no man to think about at the moment, so it will be good for me too!"

"I'm seeing him tonight", Leela smiled as she scrutinised one of the forms on her desk:" But why be bored with my stories?"

"Because I've always liked hearing about romance." Kitty paused, and still looking down to her desk, added: "Do you think you'll marry Edmund?"

"I don't know", replied Leela: "Sometimes... well. Sometimes I think I really want to. But, not always..."

Kitty stared steadily at her friend, who at first returned her gaze, then glanced down at her hands:

"I can't put it better than that, I suppose ..." She was almost talking to herself, and now fell silent.

The peace was interrupted when the manager came to them, and asked Leela to help at the counter: "Can't Miss Hopeness do it, Mr Clark?" called Leela: "She's had to sort accounts for most of the morning"

"Very well. Miss Hopeness! Serve at the second place, will you?"

"Good girl!" whispered Kitty to her friend: "See you at coffee time!"

That time came, and Kitty approached Leela's desk walking very slowly as she was carrying two large mugs of hot coffee, both brimming full.

"Most welcome!" said Leela, drinking quickly.

"I don't know how you can do that when the coffee's so hot!" exclaimed Kitty, and then fell silent.

"Gloomy? Grumpy? What's the matter?" asked Leela.

"I suppose I'm envious of you. With Edmund. I don't think I'll ever be able to attract an exciting man like that. Even though I'd like to."

"That's a peculiar thing to say." Leela sounded surprised: "Edmunds isn't *exciting*. Not especially so. And you are an attractive woman. Truly, you are."

Kitty didn't believe her, on either count:

"Your Edmund is brooding, and taciturn." Kitty nodded this, to herself, with some satisfaction, sipping deeply and slowly at the brim of her coffee cup. She looked down at her distorted image lapping slowly on the surface of her drink: "You feel he'd take you, without a word, and you'd feel hot, and wet, and excited; and he'll say nothing. He'd not kiss you.... He might bite, though!" she laughed, and looked at Leela, who smiled, and looked down. Kitty gulped back a tear. "But it's never been like that for me, Leela." She looked across at her companion, who still inclined her head, and would not look at her. Kitty didn't mind. She had her own agenda: "Men like to marry virgins, Leela. At least, all the good ones I've ever met do. I'm not a virgin. And most men think you're no good unless you're a virgin."

Startled at suddenly realising what Kitty was saying, and surprised at her own unease, she coloured slightly and said awkwardly: "I don't think it's important in that way, Kitty... and anyway, you're not the only one, you know." Leela's voice was almost inaudible now. Kitty looked up quickly, and wide-eyed, as a child who is told a favourite story, said breathlessly:

"So ... you too. You've done it."

"Yes." Leela said it, and felt uncomfortable at Kitty's obvious relish at the drama: "Yes, I've done it. And I don't mind about it. Some people get a fixation for things like that."

Kitty smiled encouragement as Leela continued:" It's

stupid. It makes no sense. Women who re-marry are often happy. And the rule never seems to affect men."

Kitty smiled warmly, friendly, almost matronly: "Then you really are happy. You and Edmund."

Leela was thrown deep back into her own thoughts: "Not completely. To be honest, I'm confused. But it may pass. I hope it works out alright. I've wanted to love for two years. Ever since I first spoke to him. I may not be in love with him, after all. It may be a mistake. But I'm going to enjoy him, Kitty. I'm going to take him and his kisses and his childishness and his longing and his lust. I'll consume it all, Kitty."

Part 3

“BUTTERFLIES”

CHAPTER ONE

That evening

It was a warm, clear evening in summer. The sun was not so hot now, as the swift dipped and drank from the moorland pool. All seemed to be quietly enjoying the most perfect part of the day.

Along the road, which swayed around the biggest hills in an undulating white curve, the soft swishing of the two cyclists, restrained in their gasps for breath. They had stopped now to hide their bicycles in a cleft in the rock. Here they were propped together, and locked with a padlock and chain.

He led the way. Up the steep, dry footpath, hurting their softly clad feet where stones emerged proud and shining. Often, too, a low cord of bramble scratched or tore at their bare legs, or pulled persistently at an ankle sock. Soon the path levelled out and walking was easier; the path was wider and there were less brambles. Edmund walked quickly - almost striding ahead of Leela - who had to run odd steps to keep within a yard of him. But still, he hurried on. He knew where he was going and what was going to happen there. So there was no need to rush: but he did so. It was as if he had to get there before it was too late... To capture, To claim something that might be slipping away.

Leela knew where they were going. And the purpose. No agreement had been formally acknowledged. They would be going for a bicycle ride. On the moors. A beautiful evening!

She was curious about sex and had enjoyed having intercourse with Edmund. She was sure to like it again, so why not plan ahead? Why not this *arrangement*? She had felt that times like making love were precious. Too precious to be planned or exploited. But she was curious. And Edmund... well, he seemed to expect.

But Edmund felt desperate. That's why he strode so swiftly, why he did not look round too much. He held aside large whips of sharp brambles so they would not cut her, but he would not look into her eyes. He smiled and spoke odd words, but looked down.

They reached the place he had chosen. Dug deeply into the hillside, hidden behind large clumps of gorse, a platform of soft earth covered in fine, thick grass. This was the place. There was to be no pretence by either why they had come here. They both lay down slowly, in silent honour of the purpose. He kissed her with open mouth, rubbed his hand into the small of her back, and with the other hand felt her breast beneath her shirt. He then rapidly unbuttoned the front of her shorts and, freeing his other hand from beneath her back, he pulled her shorts and knickers off. She raised her knees to help him, kicking off her plimsolls as she did so.

He undid every button on her shirt and pulled it apart so he could lay open her breasts. He gazed avidly over her naked bosoms. Pink, proud nipples rose on them. He smiled, licked them, and then gently sucked them. Leela squirmed and squeezed her thighs tightly together. He tugged at her knees and pulled aside her legs. Kissing at the dusky-pink, licking at the rough acid saltiness ...

The sweet, sharp smell intermixed with the warm evening air and the grassy earth ....

She cried out, tantalised by, it seemed, a million sensations. She wanted more. Much more. So much did she want at this moment she could hardly bear the feeling.

Edmund smiled at her, and moved his face toward her. She kissed him and licked his lips. She tasted her sex on him, she breathed herself from his mouth, and she pulled herself up to him. He broke away from her, and threw off his shoes. He impatiently shouldered his way out of his shirt, and let it fall on the grass. He smiled briefly at her before taking off his shorts and pants. Leela stared in fascination at his penis. It was rubbery and half-erect, and as he jogged down to his knees, it bounced in a comical fashion. She giggled. Edmund pressed himself against her belly:

"What's funny about it, eh?", he said deeply and slowly.

"Nothing" she said "it's beautiful!" ; and she wriggled and squeezed her hand between their bodies, took his penis in her fingers, and rubbed her thumb across the loose skin which hooded the end. He kissed her face and licked his tongue into her ear. He heard her breathing quicker. She moaned and murmured her love-lines:

"Edmund. My Edmund... Oh, my love... my love..."

A surge of blood filled his desire so tightly he felt he might burst, and waiting no longer he threw his hips forward to sink into her till he could enter her body no further. She gasped and cried out: then with her hands on his buttocks, urged him onwards.

They made love until he felt the exquisite jerk of his seed. Up from the root of his being and along his member; squirting into her hot, dark place. She felt it coming, she felt it come. She raised her body to catch it, to claim it for her own.

The two bodies were now still: the quickness of their breathing had subsided. Edmund felt warmth and closeness. Leela felt a beautiful burning in her middle body. She hugged the heaviness of the body mounting her, and sighed. Edmund kissed her lightly...

Leela woke up several times from her sleep, before

craning her head upwards, to see beyond her dozing lover's shoulder her wristwatch:

"Edmund! Edmund, love! It's nine o'clock..."

There was a lark, high above, who had witnessed their lovemaking whilst he sang, and Leela saw him descend to his nest-place, silently.

The next day was hot and clear. After finishing work, Edmund met Leela in the town square, and they sat together on a low wall, looking at the people; talking, and drinking Coca-Cola. They stayed there until Leela's bus came, but they had decided to go to <u>the</u> place again on their cycles the following evening.

This time, the first time, he took her slowly; and having spent himself, they lay together on their sides, facing one another. Edmund listened to his breathing and felt perspiration trickling down his breast. He looked at Leela, who had closed her eyes and was quite still. He was inside her, even now, as they rested together. She murmured and shook her head as she was awakened by the stroke of his hand along and up the back of her thigh. He smiled at her and squeezed her.

"I was asleep" she said.

"You always go to sleep" he said.

The movement of her lips and the sound of her voice aroused him again, and he grew stiff, inside her still. He made love to her with the minimum of motion, and simply pushed his hips forward slightly as they lay there on their sides, facing each other. She had lifted her upmost leg, slightly; but she did no more than take her breath deeply and noisily, until at last she felt the urgency of this nearness to coming and then she held herself strongly as he slapped himself into her. He pushed harder as he felt the wet seed leave his body. She groaned and dug her nails into his bare shoulders, kissing the flesh there and murmuring her satisfaction.

It was cooler, now. The sun was much lower in the sky and Edmund was comfortable in the warmth of Leela's body. Nestling there, he too found himself asleep. When he awoke, the sun was setting.

"Should we go?" she asked when she saw his eyes flicker into life. He mumbled something and kissed her. As he moved, he was still within her body, and he thought again of his seed within her; swimming and womb-warm. He rolled on top of her and she could watch the setting sun deepen in its redness as he made love to her once more, for the last time.

They cycled back together to Leela's house. It was now dark, and Edmund did not enter the gateway. Leela leaned on the top plank of the gate, and kissed him coquettishly on his nose:

"Goodnight, Edmund. I must get to bed or I'll oversleep tomorrow morning."

"Tomorrow. On the wall." He said, mounting his bike. He waved to her as he weaved his way down the hill, and she stayed there to watch as the flitting beam of the headlamp chased and danced on the hedgerow. After a few seconds, it had disappeared; and she strolled slowly to her home, pushing her bike, and feeling warm, elated and content.

CHAPTER TWO

The next day Edmund had some news for her:

"Mother and Father are going away next week. Couldn't you spend some nights with me, at the house? They'll be no-one there."

"Yes. It would be good" she agreed: "Where will everyone be?"

"They're staying near to Timothy's summer camp, to have some time together."

"Won't they miss you?" Leela asked, squeezing his hand and laughing.

"No. Mum and Dad argue when I'm around."

"How do you know they don't when you're not there?" she said.

"Oh, maybe they do. At least I don't feel guilty about it, though" he replied, looking downwards. There was silence for some minutes, and Leela stared across the town square to the birds, washing themselves in the fountain. She turned to Edmund:

"I'll tell Mum I'm staying with Kitty"

"Why not this weekend?" said Edmund "They're away tomorrow morning"

"Fine! That's fine!" she answered "Here's my bus!"

When she got home she told her mother she was staying with Kitty-from-the-Bank, as her mother would be away for the weekend and she didn't want to be alone, her father having died some years previously. Leela would go there from work on the bus as it was quite a distance.

"Where does she live, now?" asked her mother, apparently not suspicious:

I've forgotten"

"Markham-on-the-Moors" replied her daughter.

"Well of course you must go. Poor girl. I remember her sister as school. Always a good scholar. When will you be back home, Leela?" Her mother gave her tea. Leela smiled at her mother but felt uneasy about lying to her.

She would like to have told her where she was going to be that weekend:

"I'll be home on Monday evening, Mum"

"And you'd better leave the address, just in case there's an emergency"

Leela wrote down Kitty's address on a piece of paper and put it into the letter rack:

"There it is Mum. I think I'll go out into the sun before it disappears"

On the following day, Friday, Leela asked Kitty to cover for her if anyone called.

"Of course I'll do it, Leela. I wish it was me. Alone for a weekend with Edmund! You'd better watch it my girl. If I got a chance – even for one night – I'd do it. Truly I would. Even if you are my best friend!" Kitty grinned as she sorted some papers on her desk, pleased to be involved.

Leela finished at four thirty that Friday evening and was surprised to find John waiting for her as she left the bank building:

"Jump in ! Kitty's not out yet, I suppose?" asked John, leaning across to open the passenger door. Leela was prickly and irritated at her brother's appearance, not only on account of her planed deception, but more because John tended to take charge.

"I don't know!" She had wanted to say 'Mind your own, John' but hadn't the nerve. She bit her lip and flashed burning glances as her brother, on whom they were lost, and on a waiting schoolboy, who retreated reluctantly into a doorway:

"What are you doing here, John?" Leela asked, stifling much of her anger and indignation.

"I finished early and so I thought I'd take you and Kitty over to her house. Mum told me you were staying there for the weekend," John smiled. Leela felt he was smirking at his triumphant intervention. He was now at the centre of the arrangements, she thought:

"I - well, Kitty may not be here for a while. So you can carry on home, and we'll catch the bus as usual." Leela blushed at her lying, at her being caught out, and especially being caught out by her brother. She was going to tell him that neither she, nor Kitty, needed John to solve their transport, nor any other problems:

"Look, John, you go .....", but she was interrupted by events:

"Here's Kitty!" John nodded towards the Barclays' Bank building.

"Hello, John!" said Kitty, beaming innocently at him.

"Kitty! I came to take you and Leela home. Save your catching the bus."

Leela was so furious she almost swore at him, but the arrangement was the important thing ...:

"Tell you what, John. You can take me back to Parkleat"

"Our house?" he returned, puzzled: "But why?"

"I want my bike for the weekend. We're going for a ride ... to Edmund's ... on Sunday." She turned to Kitty: "You don't mind, do you love?"

Kitty shook her head, surprised, admiring, gleeful ... so proud at being part of the story ...

"Of course, not, Leela. I'll get some tea ready for your coming. Cheerio John!"

But John knew it was not so straightforward, and did not say a word, but looked intently at his sister. She was uncomfortable at his stare, and wanted to hit back at him.

But there was the *arrangement*. Edmund. Her parents. Her lying and her shame at her deceit. So she said nothing in response to his attitude to her, but silently got into the car.

They had driven off before Leela remembered her meeting with Edmund:

"Can we go by the square? I'd forgotten. I'm to see Edmund"

They pulled into the square, and Leela ran from the car to where he was waiting for her on the low wall by the fountain. She told him not to wait for her, and that she would be going straight to his house on her cycle:

"Twelve miles!" he laughed and took hold of her hand: "Sure you can make it?"

"I had to think of something when he appeared" she laughed in return, feeling happiness and elation in his presence: "Anyway, the fresh air will do me good!"

She kissed him and waved as she ran back to her brother's car. There was a silent, strained atmosphere between them as they drove home.

"You should have left your bag with Kitty, Leela" said John, annoyed at not having thought of this point earlier."

You'll have to take it on the bike, now. I can't take you. I've got ...."

But as Leela looked out at the white rock she did not hear anything else he said. Flooding her vision now was the rich grass, and then the curious sheep which they passed on their journey to Parkleat. Her spirit had left that car; and was drifting upwards to the distant hills. At that very moment, she felt absolutely invulnerable.

When they got home, John went abruptly up to his flat, and her mother greeted Leela with an excess of fussy excitement:

"Hello, dear! But I thought you were going to Kitty's? Nothing wrong? Well, whatever the reason, this is a lovely surprise!"

"I want to take my bike, Mum."

"What?" laughed her mother: "Can't you manage without it for a weekend?"

"Oh – well" Leela went on, reluctantly drawn into the complex deceit: "I thought Kitty and I would go to Edmund's on Sunday". She looked away from her mother beaming face, and nibbled on a piece of carrot being prepared by the sink.

"Ah! I see!" said Sarah: "It's not the bike, it's Edmund!"

Leela did not reply, but broke off some more of the vegetable she was chewing, and stared out of the window, away from her mother's gaze. She decided to leave, and turned towards the door. Her mother continued:

"I think it's really good of you to stay with Kitty." Sarah did not look up, but engrossed herself in cleaning more vegetables for the stew.

"Yes." replied Leela.

"Especially considering you'll not be able to see much of Edmund, his being so far away ..."

"Goodbye, mother", Leela said quickly, and kissed her briefly on the side of her head.

"Yes you'd better make a start. I suppose it'll take you a good half hour to get there!."

Waving, paring knife in her hand, she was smiling her goodbye "Cheerio, love! Remember me to Kitty!"

Leela tied her bag of clothes to the saddle rest of the bike, and began her long journey to Edmund's ...

Kitty had got home at five o'clock, and after a bath, she helped her mother with the household chores. At about six, as she was ironing some clothes, she heard a knock at the door. She felt slightly on edge, and moved rapidly to intercept her mother who she knew would be quick to answer: "Alright mother! Leave it to me!"

Kitty opened the door. A thin, pretty, dark-haired girl stood there, clutching a vacuum flask, which Kitty recognised as belonging to Leela. The young girl, about nine years old, said:

"Are you Kitty?"

"Yes?" Kitty looked at her blue-black eyes, and felt even more nervous. The child stretched out her arm slowly, proffering the flask:

"This" said the girl, and then something fell onto the step: "And this" as she picked up the envelope which had fallen to the floor, and handed it to Kitty.

"Leela?" said Kitty, staring at the name on the envelope. She looked back at the girl, and suddenly saw the resemblance:

"Oh! You're Pauline! Leela's sister!" The little girl

nodded. "Well, I'll give these to her. Thank you for bringing them." Kitty stood in the doorway as Pauline turned away very slowly and walked off: "Cheerio, Pauline!"

What else could she do? Leela was not coming here, so there was no point in the child waiting ... But how was Pauline to get home? There was no bike, and now she looked further, she could see Pauline sitting on the wall, watching the road. Kitty ran up to her:

"I forgot to ask. How are you to get home?"

Pauline looked down the road:

"Dad will pick me up on his way from the orchard. That's how I got here."

Kitty was relieved, but did not want to leave the child alone:

"Come in, then, and I'll give you some orange juice." Kitty held out her hand, and the child took it with apparent reluctance.

"Where's Leela?" she asked as her drink was poured.

"Oh! Out on her bike" said Kitty, glancing away. Pauline said no more, and sat silently sipping her fruit juice.

"Hello!". Kitty's mother had re-entered the kitchen,

"Who's this, then?". She beamed at the little girl, who grinned briefly back at her.

"This is Pauline, Leela's sister"

"Really! Well, what took you so long to come and see us, eh, young lady?" asked Mrs Hopeness; and Pauline grinned again, and then blushed and slurped at her juice. But Kitty was far from happy, and taking up a cotton petticoat, asked her mother:

"Mam, please do me a big favour. Starch and iron this, will you? Right now? I've got cramp in my hands through counting all day, and I've just remembered that I'm going to the Carlton tonight."

"What?" said her bewildered parent.

"Please. It's a big night, and I forgot. I'll keep young Pauline happy – she was outside, waiting for her Dad to come back from the Orchard. Leela's out cycling and she thought she'd be here, you see?"

Eventually, to Kitty's enormous relief, her mother left them. Pauline had finished her drink by the time William knocked on the door ...:

"Hello, Kitty!" he exclaimed, his huge body filling the

doorway. The little girl ran to meet him, and he scooped her up with one arm, so that she rested in the crook of his elbow, like a perched sparrow.

"Is Leela around?" William's eyes grew wide in greeting, and hope that he would see his bigger daughter.

"Oh, she's out riding her bike, Mr. Drake"

"I see", he replied, frowning. He stood there looking over Kitty's shoulder, into the kitchen behind her. Pauline, expressionless, stared at Kitty.

"W-would you like some tea, Mr. Drake?" asked Kitty.

"No, I don't think so, Kitty. Will Leela be out for long?" He frowned as he looked down at the young woman.

"Er ... she might be. She'd only just gone out when Pauline came."

William looked back into the kitchen, Pauline blinked her eyes at Kitty, and a nervous silence fell over the company. Kitty turned and awkwardly busied herself with brushing the kitchen floor, a job she had already completed. William breathed out noisily before he next spoke:

"I'll be off, then".

They had left. Kitty went to the window to check they

had gone. When she saw they had, she felt relieved, and proud, too, that she'd been able to help her friend. She carefully secreted away the flask and note, and laughed to herself as she realised she was now forced to go to the Carlton that evening. Never mind, maybe someone nice would be there.

CHAPTER THREE

Leela arrived at Edmund's at half past six. She parked her bike in the corner of the garage, and tugged at the bell stop. Edmund let her inside.

"No more hitches?" he asked. She shook her head:

"I've brought a few bits of clothing. Where can I put them?"

"Oh! Er ... in the bedroom."

"Which one will we be using?"

"The one at the back. Mine."

Leela smiled and climbed the stairs. He called to her as she reached the top:

"Use the wardrobe!"

She nodded and disappeared from his view. He returned to his chores in the kitchen, where he was preparing the meal. He had completed the salad, tossed it in oil, and was now to cook two omelettes, filled with mushrooms and cheese. He greased the frying pan, but broke the eggs into the cooking pot too soon, and they did not set. He cursed to himself. Leela had now joined him:

"Problem?" she asked, looking into the pan.

"The pan was cold. I hope it will be edible." Edmund grimaced as he peered into the pan:

"Should I start again?" He turned to her. She laughed and shook her head:

"I'm so hungry, even a rubbery omelette wouldn't put me off!"

She found she had overestimated her hunger, however, and could not finish meal because of its harsh texture. Edmund looked across the table at her:

"Dreadful, isn't it?" She nodded emphatically:

"It is." She smiled, and reached over the table and squeezed his hand:

"It was good of you to try. Anyway, the salad is enough."

The evening was warm, and after finishing eating, they went into the garden. They sat on wicker chairs, and drank Leela's favourite *Apfelsaft*. They didn't say very much. The gardens were in prime show and being there, amongst all the activity, was sufficient to occupy their minds and senses. The ground here was thickly lawned and sloped away from them to the fish pool. There, huge water lilies were in flower and masses of duckweed glistened in its greenness around them. Occasionally, a bubble broke at the water's surface.

A crumbling garden temple gave adequate home to much flowering growth, and a climbing old rose tree, carrying rich red flowers which had no apparent centre. Their petals were folded many times across their breadth, and the colour was so dark that in parts it appeared to be almost black. Beds of irises and daisies of many varieties grew on the far side of the water, and behind these an old yew stood silent sentinel as bees sawed their low way between the flowers, ready to give the ungainly, fluttering butterflies plenty of space in their short love flight. The swallows, too, were now active, dipping down to feed on the dancing hordes of midges. A heavy fragrance of the honeysuckle, which tucked around the kitchen doorway, seemed to invite Leela's eyes to close in a less cluttered appreciation of its richness, and after half an hour, she had fallen asleep.

She awoke to find Edmund was no longer with her. She rose stiffly to her feet, and looked to the west. Venus was so brilliant she felt almost dazzled by its contrast with the dark-blue summer sky. She turned to the house, and heard the metal ring of kitchen pans. She stepped into the doorway:

"Need help?" she asked, as he looked at her, his hands thick with soap:

"No. You go up, if you like." He returned to his task. She swayed against the door, and stepped outside:

"I'm going for a short walk, before that."

She walked around the pool, and the house, as if to say goodbye to the flowers and the life out there. When she got back into the kitchen, she said nothing to him, but she climbed the stairs slowly, listening to each padded step she make as she went to the bedroom. She unfolded her night dress and bath bag, and once in the large bathroom, she locked the door, and taking off all her clothes, she stood still before the long mirror on the wall, and stared at her body. She hadn't really, closely looked at her naked form since she'd seen the first sprouting of adolescent breasts, and the spreading of pubescent hips. She looked at her front form, then turned to the side, then right round; screwing her head to the back so she could see the rear of her body. Although she felt no pride, she could see the conventional beauty of her figure. And her skin, full cream ebony white: and clear, so that her grey eyes and dark hair were so much more distinctive. She showered and powdered her body, smiling to herself as she thought that since she would soon be covered in sex, it was a lost effort. When she returned to the bedroom, Edmund was already in the bed, sitting up, looking ahead. He turned as Leela joined him:

"Did you find everything you wanted?"

"Yes, Edmund." She smiled at him, and began to place some clean clothes for the following day. He looked at her profile and saw the rapid movement of her eyelashes as she blinked down into her travel bag, and felt his throat tighten as his desire for her rose in him. It was *pure* enough, surely? He enjoyed her sex, but he wanted *her*, not just her body. She was rummaging around in her bag........

Perhaps he wouldn't live with her for all his time, who could say? But he felt he did love her.

She had found something, and was looking at it ...

He was not misusing her. All these things troubled him, and the greatest trouble of all was that he felt instinctively that he *shouldn't* worry, that everything was always as it should be, that thought of action was worse than no action at all ...

"This photograph of me is dreadful, Edmund!" She picked up a framed snapshot from the bedside table:

"If you must have one, I'll have a proper one taken!" She put the photo back. Edmund laughed, leaned over onto his side and kissed her just beneath her chin. She breathed very deeply, lifted the sheets, and pressed herself against his body ...

Leela lay alone, looking at the old master prints on Edmund's bedroom wall. She recognised the Goya and the Renoir, because they were so famous, but the third, which she considered most beautiful, she did not know. She stared at the picture, and daydreamed, so the images of the picture, whilst in her sight, were misty and blurred. She became aware of her feet, which were feeling cramped, and she stirred from her musing and stretched them. She looked towards the curtained window. Although it was almost ten o'clock, the sky seemed still reluctant to grow dark.

The door rustled open, nudged by Edmund's knee. He was carrying two mugs of hot chocolate in his hands:

"I left the light on, and the door open, so the kitchen was full of moths when I got down! It's taken me until now to set them free."

"I've been studying your prints. Tell me, what is the one on the right called?"

"Danae" answered Edmund: "It's painted by Titian."

Leela looked again at the print: "It's so beautiful, Edmund. I wonder you can compromise with me!"

Edmund settled down and caressing his chocolate, seemed lost in his own thoughts, and Leela looked around the room again. She had been here before tonight but she had never abided here. Now she, too, like the Titian, was part of this room. She sipped her chocolate. Opposite the bed, pinned to the wall, were some of Edmund's architectural drawings. The wall next to the bed was white, and unadorned. You could shut out this room, she thought, merely be turning onto your side, towards this wall ...

Next Morning, Saturday

Leela and Edmund decided to go to the beach that day, since they both had their bikes. They visited a tiny deserted cove, never seen by strangers or tourists because it was so hard to find. Here they could dare to swim naked, and bask uncovered in the hot sun. They rolled together in the ecstasy of summer worship, and their damp bodies tingled with particles of sand. They both felt mad, there, with the heat of the season and the pounding of the waves. Now they played a childish game, and she scampered around the sand dunes on all fours, chased by Edmund, baying like a dog. Then he caught her, by the ankle, and pulled her back, towards him. He felt his erection grow strongly, almost at once. In the dim, dark ancestry of his passion, there existed this desire. To dominate a woman and subdue her, to assault her and take possession of her ....

He was not now thinking. Not as he mounted her like a dog mounts a bitch. He found the place he wanted and rubbed his penis there till moist enough to enter ...

She held still. She didn't want to move, and she felt a great thrill not only with the feel of her lover inside her, but even more so because she could not see him. It could have been anyone, fucking into her, stretching her inside till it hurt. Perhaps some farm labourer or stray walker could be up there, on the cliff, secretly watching them.

When it was over, Edmund rolled to one side and lay back there, panting and looking up into the sky ... It was alright, no need to feel guilty ....

Leela, now flat on her stomach, breathed through her mouth, heavily; and relished the soreness she felt inside, and of her grazed knees. She had a round and warm feeling of consummated destiny as she lay there, exhausted in mind and desire. It was complete, and she was afraid, in some sense, of anything more happening. She almost hoped that when she finally turned round, he would not be there, but could have gone forever, even though she knew this would be almost unbearable.

She stayed there for some time, picking up her head as she heard voices: far off, but getting closer. She felt panic, and said:

"Edmund ...", but he was not there. She wasn't dreaming. The voices were getting closer. Her feeling for convention urged her to scramble to her feet and rush back down the hill to the beach and get her clothes ... but she could not. She did not really want to. She wanted the walkers to go by without seeing her, but she had to stay there, naked, damp, thrown-down. They had traversed the rise now, and were making their way to the beach. She could hear what they said, they were so close to her. She could see them. They were a couple in their mid-thirties, and they strode swiftly down the path some yards away from where Leela was lying. She pushed herself up onto her side, propping herself up with one arm, and stared at the pair. They were now quite near to her, and engrossed in conversation. Soon, they would be gone. Then, for no obvious reason, the man looked straight at her. He might be able to see down as far as her breasts, but no more. She did not move. Without blinking, she looked into his face. He was wearing thick lens glasses and a close-cropped beard. He seemed to stare through her and his eyes did not flicker, nor did he interrupt his conversation. She felt a warming inside her as she realised that he knew she was naked, that he might have seen her breasts. She did not want anything more from this man, and she lay down feeling a secret and guilty sense of gratification. Now she could hear another voice. Edmund was talking to them. A few seconds later Edmund, fully dressed, ran quickly up the hill and tossed Leela her clothes:

"Sorry, Leela!" He smiled and raised his eyebrows: "They came just as I'd finished dressing. I've never known anyone come down here before."

He stood by as she pulled on her clothes, and they walked back up the path to their bikes.

The following day showed a break in the weather and there was a torrential downpour of rain. In the morning, Edmund and Leela played Monopoly, and in the afternoon they made love. She realised, as she lay there in his bed, holding his body, how fortunate she had been in having him for her lover. Sometimes she feared of feeling too much for him. He turned to her:

"I've not taken any precautions, Leela, as you probably realise."

She laughed:

"I think I would have noticed that, Edmund", and she kissed his forehead:

"I feel you have to decide ..." . She looked at the ceiling:

"You've made me cowardly, Edmund. I feel frightened of passion, now I've experienced it." Edmund frowned:

"I never thought you'd feel that ... perhaps there's something I could do .... differently?"

"I don't want you to do anything about it, Edmund. I like to feel afraid. I like the feeling of your being in control. So whether you use contraceptives or not, I'd rather leave that up to you." And she closed her eyes and stroked his body.

"I have bought some", he said, quietly:

"But I felt it wasn't right to use them. Not for us. Here, in my bed, making love ... I fell there's nothing wrong about it,

Leela. So why be ashamed? ... Perhaps, you'll get pregnant. I'll not desert you. You know that, surely?"

Leela smiled: "You sound a bit morbid, really..." She had opened her eyes and glanced at him mischievously:

"Tell me, have you made a girl pregnant, or will I be the first?"

Edmund frowned:

"You're the first girl I loved, as I think of love .... Anyway, there's only one other girl, and she didn't get pregnant.

So I'd be the first?" asked Leela, her dark eyes now wide as she mocked his solemnity:

"Yes", he replied: "but not the last!"

And he turned her over onto her back and laughing, he squeezed her roughly and kissed her face. He made love to her so gently she could close her eyes and let her tired body go limp. She loved everything so much and she could want no more, and yet she was glad, that the following day she would have to go. Perhaps she would never feel happy, she thought, unless there was a way out ...

And they slept roughly folded together, until later he awoke, and again felt the consuming urge to take her. He kissed her forehead and face, then her lips, and rubbed her breasts roughly. He didn't want to see her face. He turned her over. And yet dreamily, she liked his taking charge of her. She was growing conscious of a sharp excitement and anticipation within herself. She could feel his close to her. He pushed against her buttocks. He was not hard enough. He pinched the end of his penis and pressed in between her thighs, and felt the sweat and love juice there. But he could not get hard. This was artifice, he thought. Leela's hand felt and patted around behind her till she found him, and after a few seconds, laughed lightly and turned over: "Let me help you."

Stroking her hair from her face, she moved down and rubbed her lips across the end of his penis, then licked slightly, and blushed with pleasure as she tasted herself on him, and now took him in her mouth, and sucked, and played, until she felt he was ready, and lifted her head, and said: "There you are" and now she turned back over, and waited...

He began uncertainly. It was good, it was full of pleasure, but he could not experience it. Not fully, anyway.

There was magic, there had been magic, but the spell was broken. Now there was concentration on the act, and the exquisite pain of his orgasm was so brief, and in its way so slight, he did not really notice it...

Leela could feel him on her, and in her, and she saw the white cotton of the pillow. White then dark, white, dark, as her head bounced down onto it. She felt him inside her as she had not before. It was good. She wanted him to stay still, but she wanted the excitement of his lunging into her. Better than the penis, she liked his weight against her, the thrusting of him, the petty violence ...

He had come, and rolled away from her. His sperm was everywhere, and the smell of sex hung over them. He looked at her, on her side now and facing away from him. He wanted to feel something deeply. He wanted to feel lots of different things. He was unsure whether to feel disappointed ...

Leela was calm, and warm. She had not come, but felt satisfied and complete. She wanted to sleep. She did not need to see his face:

"Cuddle me, my love, come close ..."

Of course he did so, and her body was hot and damp. He could feel her breathing, and moving nearer, he rubbed his face into her hair.

Leela was quickly asleep. Edmund counted her breaths, then glanced over her shoulder at her picture on the table there. Capturing moments – is that what happiness is? Can they be here and then go away ? Could they be here for some but not for others?

He felt there was a greatness about life, and he wanted this fulfilment.

Leela opened her eyes to see the white wall, and moving legs she felt Edmund next to her, limp and cool, and obviously asleep. She pulled herself up and looked across the room, through the window. The sky over to the east was white with the first rays of the sun. Some of the birds were making their early, tentative calls; and Leela did not want to stay in bed. After showering and dressing, she made up a breakfast of fruit juice and toast, on a tray, and took it to Edmund's bedroom. He was up now, sitting on the side of his bed, rubbing his face. He smiled sleepily towards her:

"Do you always get up this early on weekdays?" She put the tray on the table at the side of the bed:

"Let's cycle to work, Edmund, since somehow I've got to get my bike home, and it is a lovely morning!..." He staggered over to the window and looked into the garden, and then to the sky:

"Alright", he yawned:

"I'm sure I'll agree with you when I've woken up properly." He returned to his bed and sitting there, began to eat his breakfast. Leela sat by the table too, on a chair on which Edmund normally used to hang his clothes; but for her visit, he had hung them all in the wardrobe. She looked at his crunching his toast, her head cocked to one side and resting on her hand. If she ever had a son, she would love him to be like Edmund; gentle, kind, clever ... but if she had to have a lover? Surely, she did not deserve such beauty, had not earned, nor sought such, either. It was, she sometimes felt, too rich and full for her ...

CHAPTER FOUR

They rode together through empty morning roads to work. He kissed her before she went to the bank, and she hugged him closely:

"Leave me alone for a few days, Edmund. I'll see you later this week."

"Say .... Wednesday?" He asked, not surprised at what she had said. She nodded, and smiled at him, kissing his lips again:

"Yes ... Yes! Whatever you like, love!" She entered the bank, and was early enough for a cup of coffee. She looked forward to Kitty's coming, but she arrived later than was usual, and clutching Leela's flask. Kitty beamed her good morning towards her friend, and swiftly told her about the events of Friday evening.

"Good Grief!" exclaimed Leela, with open-mouthed admiration: "How did you manage to stay so cool?"

"Well, Leela, I had no choice. It happened so quickly. It wouldn't have been so bad if Mam hadn't come in!"

"That must have been really awful!" rejoined Leela, and pursing her lips tightly together, she looked down at her feet. Kitty gently squeezed her arm:

"Oh don't look so glum, Leela! It was fun, in the end!" Leela looked up and smiled slightly. Kitty resumed her tale:

"And I had to go to the Carlton, although I wasn't planning to!"

"Yes, of course." Leela felt more cheerful. Kitty was tingling with glee, and had more to relate:

"And I met up with Ted Barber..."

"Your old flame!" said Leela.

"Right. And he's unattached at the moment, so we're going out together! So you see, triumph came out of disaster in the end!"

"I'm so glad about that, Kitty. Ted's nice", Leela swivelled her chair around and looked away: "I didn't ought to have deceived Mum, though. She'd be so upset if she ever found out."

"She won't find out, though, Leela", Kitty moved to her and put her arm round her waist to comfort her as she was now crying: "Hey, love. I've never seen you cry before!... Just because you folks nearly caught you out ... He's just as much to blame, you know."

Kitty went on for some time longer, but Leela did not listen. Kitty did not understand, and Leela was glad she did not.

Edmund had arrived early at his offices, and he sat on a nearby wall, waiting for the key holder to come. Now at his drawing board, he basked in thoughts of the weekend. He felt it had been very beautiful, very positive ...

He could not decide, however, if this was why you married someone. Jeremy looked across:

"Thoughtful today? Accepted that £5,000 job in the USA yet?"

Edmund frowned quizzically, then smiled and put down his pencil:

"You're married, Jerry. What do you think makes people well married?"

"As opposed to bloody miserable, you mean?"

Edmund laughed, and nodded. Jeremy lit a cigarette, and leaning on his board, stared into the distance:

"Very much depends on what you want. You only get what the other is prepared to give. Some can't give what the other wants." His eye returned to view his colleague:

"But why, my boy, on such a perfect sunny morning, are you being so morbid?"

"Morbid", Edmund though aloud. That's what she had said... :

"But your marriage isn't morbid, Jerry. Is it?" The other glanced over to him, and snorted:

"It's perfect, boy. As a marriage goes, perfect. Question is, was it worth the trouble? Why not stay friends. Have your fun, Edmund! Don't tie each other down ... I think if I had my time again, I'd not marry."

Edmund was puzzled at this philosophy. It seemed illogical:

"Why not end it, then? If you don't mind my saying so."

"Because, boy. Because ... Because it's done. And it's not so bad. And... it's not important, really."

But Edmund felt it could not suit him, to compromise so completely. He would have to be sure that all was so good, there would be no choice. He looked over to Jeremy:

"Perhaps I should go away for a while. That would teach me something, I suppose... No friends, family ... No contact with roots ..."

"You're talking I riddles, Edmund. And I think you know that. There's no easy answer to life, you know ..." He looked at this young friend, whose head had now drooped over, and was staring downwards:

"And don't feel sorry for yourself! Think of most of the poor bastards out there. They haven't your sense or sensitivity. Nor the resources to indulge in this cheap philosophy. So just get on with things, best you can." He drew heavily on his cigarette, and deftly blew three smoke rings into the air:

"Follow your nose! Don't take yourself so seriously!" He dug Edmund in the ribs, and the young man grinned reluctantly. Edmund regarded his plan to go abroad very seriously. He would do it, one day, he thought. Not like his time in the army. Alone. Free. He'd not write to anyone while he was gone. He'd cut off all ties. He had to do that to get completely away, to break cleanly. He would come back, of course. That was the point of going away.

Leela ... What of her? Of it? Of the relationship? He couldn't feel happy about it now, unless there was some kind of continuation, development... some sort of growth. He didn't want it ever to end, nor to stay still ... And it had occurred to him that maybe marriage, or a child, was the only way this growing could take place ....

He didn't care for convention; but situations occurred which affected other people, and so it would affect Leela, and himself.

Part 4

“SON AND LOVER”

CHAPTER ONE

That Monday evening, Leela went straight home, without meeting Edmund. The weather seemed to be changing, and the early evening was dull and cool.

"Hello, love!" Her mother greeted her as she entered the kitchen:

"Did you and Kitty have a good weekend?"

Leela nodded: "Mmmm. And thanks for sending my flask. Sorry I happened to be out."

"It doesn't matter. I knew you'd need your flask for Monday, and Dad had to pick up some apples ... Pauline was most disappointed not to see you, Leela."

"I'll be with her tonight. I'm not going out." Her mother looked at her in astonishment:

"What? Not to see Edmund? After not seeing him over the weekend?"

Leela glanced back sharply:

"I did see him. We cycled over."

"Yes. But you're usually so keen. There's no problem, is there?"

"No, Mum. Of course there isn't. I just felt like some time here."

"Well that's lovely, dear. I wouldn't like anything to be amiss between you and Edmund. That's all."

Leela left the kitchen and entered the lounge. Pauline was already sitting there, her diminutive frame looking even tinier as she sat at the centre of one of the huge armchairs. The little girl looked up blankly at her sister, before resuming her studying of a musical theory book. Leela sat opposite her in the other armchair and smiled:

"Not speaking to me?"

Pauline turned over a page of her book, and read with even greater intensity. Leela sat back and contemplated her sister. Her long, dark hair hung untidily down her face, and her thin body hardly seemed to affect the shape of the cotton dress she was wearing.

Spindley legs rested loosely on the armchair front, and

Leela could not help feeling the vulnerability of the child to the Adult Conspiracy. She gently prodded one of those white, bony knees:

"It's rude not to speak to me. When I'm in the same room as you."

Silence. She went on:

"Even if you don't like me at the moment, you could say hello. Or ask me if I'm feeling well." Silence still, although Pauline's eyes had raised their lines of vision, to Leela's feet, and had then resumed reading her book. Leela got up and sat on the floor, next to Pauline's chair and near to her feet, and tapped her book:

"Please say something to me, Pauline. You're not the only one who needs attention, you know!"

Pauline looked at her with steady eyes, and glum mouth:

"Why didn't I see you on Friday?"

"Because I wasn't there. I didn't know you'd be along, did I?"

Pauline looked at her again, but scowled not so much as before:

"Mum said you'd be there. So did Dad. The woman didn't seem to know about you."

"It was a mistake, love. My fault, really. But not meant to hurt you or Dad."

Pauline was silent for a few seconds. She then lifted her book over to one side, so that Leela could see. It was bars of music, interspersed with explanatory notes. Pauline was about to take her Grade 5 exam in 'a few weeks' time' according to her teacher. She was the most advanced pupil they'd had at the school, and was under pressure from all, except her family, to do 'exceptionally well':

"What does that word mean, Leela?" She looked towards Pauline's spiny finger pointed:

"'Briskly' : that means .... with lots of energy, quickly." Leela went on with her explanation. She too had studied the piano, having achieved Grade 6. But she never showed 'exceptional promise'.

"You're well ahead with your study, Pauline. I never finished this book completely. Even for Grade 6."

"I want to try to cover all I can.", replied the younger girl, "You can't say what will come up, so it's better if you've done more than you need to ..." She turned over to the next page.

"Yes, love. But don't become too bogged down in study. There's other things in life besides music and schoolwork."

"Like Edmund." Said Pauline, grinning broadly at her sister.

"What makes you mention Edmund?"

"Well, you spend a lot of your time with him, don't you?" She stared at Leela, who looked away nervously, and replied quietly:

"Yes ... that's because I'm grown up. I don't say you should be thinking of boys, yet, love. There are other things in life, you know. Like reading your favourite books. Or pressing flowers. You don't have to study all the time, Pauline."

"I don't study all the time!" The little girl responded sharply:

"I do at the moment, but all you want to do is chatter!"

Leela turned away. There was a long silence. She felt so lonely, sitting there; and she thought she might go to Edmund. Maybe her idea of being away from him was wrong: or at least, something she couldn't see through. She'd phone him. She had begun to raise herself, when Pauline said:

"I'd like a break now. Can we do some flower pressing? There's some beauts in the garden." Leela turned and laughed:

"'Beauts'. Where did you get that word from?"

"Oh, there was an Australian teacher in school the other week. When we showed our tadpoles she said they were beauts. It means they were very good ones."

They left the lounge, then down the hall and into the garden. Theirs was not such a tidy, nor grand garden, as the Rices'. William had no time for it, and Sarah, Leela's mother, was not keen. Twice a week an old man came to tend it, and so there were some flowers growing, and a few shrubs.

"This is a likely candidate!" Shouted Pauline, indicating a bed of blue Pansies. They collected specimens of Iceland Poppy, Clarkia and tiny fern leaves, too, before deciding to begin the pressing. Leela stood up after stopping for some time, and grimaced as she cricked her back. Pauline looked up:

"What's the matter?"

"My back ... I just have to stand straight for a minute." And she drew herself erect, handing over her flowers to Pauline.

"These are beauts alright." Said the little girl, and shuffled around, so that her she and her sister were back-to-back:

"What are you up to?" Leela smiled at her over her shoulder.

"Seeing how much I've grown since Christmas," was the reply.

"Yes, I remember," said Leela: "your head was two inches above my waist."

"It still is," said a disconsolate voice: "I haven't grown at all."

Leela turned round. Her small sister was pouting. She was never mardy, and Leela realised she must be disappointed at still being so little:

"Look, I never really grew up until I started at the Grammar School. That's probably what will happen to you." Pauline looked at Leela:

"When will my breasts start to grow, like yours?" Leela laughed. It was Leela who had been given the task, which she had completed some time ago, of explaining the 'Facts of Life' to her young sister:

"Not for a long time." Pauline looked away. Leela put her arm round her shoulder:

"There's no point in having breasts if you can't have babies. And you can't have babies." Pauline glanced up at Leela:

"Let's go in now, Leela, and get the flowers pressed before dinner."

CHAPTER TWO

Wednesday, Wellawnbury Town Centre

Leela waited in a cool northerly breeze, sitting on the wall in front of the fountain, as Edmund ran up to her:

"Sorry to delay, but there was a meeting. Went on past the usual time."

"I'm cold," said Leela, not moving from her huddled position on the wall.

"The summer seems to have gone already," said Edmund, standing awkwardly by the girl. She reached out her arms:

"Hold me in your arms, Edmund. Please comfort me." She said, staring up at him. She felt suddenly alone again, like she had felt at home two days ago. He complied, and they sat there in silence for some minutes, cuddled together closely on the stone wall:

"We could go to my house", said Edmund at last: "Father and mother will be out till later. Dad told me to bring you round. He'll take you home when he comes in."

"So we can go to bed." Leela said, flatly, staring into the ground at her feet.

"If you want to", said Edmund, steadily, quietly: "or we could talk. Sit and talk. Or listen to music, or watch Television ...." He fell silent and waited as if inviting her to say something. She simply sat there squashed and crouched on the wall, held tightly in his arms. She still looked at the ground:

"And what do we do afterwards?" She murmured, almost in whisper.

"Afterwards?" He asked.

"What do we do after we've gone to bed?" She asked. He gently disentangled himself from their embrace, and walked towards the fountain. Leela lifted her gaze; not quite enough to see him. She wanted something from Edmund, although she knew he couldn't give what she required. Sometimes it was good to have thick, sweet icing sugar. Pink and sickly. Leela smiled to herself as she remembered yesterday, making curly sticks of home made toffee with her sister ...

"Would you rather go home?" Edmund was asking, standing in front of her. She looked softly at him. He'd got drunk once and tried to make love to her. He'd been over her, breathing whisky fumes and mouthing unintelligible words as he'd slid his hand up her leg. She'd lain there, on a carpet in an empty room, stinking of beer and cigarette smoke ...

He had eventually collapsed onto her and fallen asleep. She laughed as she recalled this ...

"What's the matter with you?" Asked Edmund, having returned to her after a short walk around the square. Her eyes, bright as demons', coal-black and sparkling, looked over him as she got up and pushed her arm deeply into his and squeezed his hand into hers ...

"Let's go to your bed, Edmund!" And she lifted his hand to her mouth and kissed with warm, damp lips ...

There was a high wind, and the milky-barked birch, which stood by the old yew tree near the pond, was bent over, low and wavering, in its wake. Leela drew her arms around her as she looked on, from the window of Edmund's bedroom, covered only by his dressing gown. She retreated from that scene, and turning round, her languid gaze fell on the Titian. She shivered. The room was cold for her. There was no sun that evening, and there was no music. She heard the muffled thump of Edmund's bare feet on the stairs, and looked towards the door. He came in, draped in a towel, carrying two mugs of coffee. He sat by her and looked out of the window. They talked a little, before Leela said she was going home. He walked with her to the bus stop and waited until the bus disappeared, Leela aboard, down the long slope towards the town.

CHAPTER THREE

He was not too sorry to see her go. She had been strange that evening and was obviously not completely happy to be with him there. And in any case, he had work of his own to do. He strolled back to the house and around the garden, easing his mind from the intangibility he had grown to love, to prepare to tackle a drawing left undone because of the afternoon's meeting. After a few more minutes, he went back in and began work in his room. He did not even stop for another coffee, and he'd almost finished by the time he heard the familiar crunch of his parents' car as it drove to door. Soon he heard the far-off, high voices of the children: Timothy, aged ten, and Marsha, twelve. Vivian and Oscar had been to play bridge, whilst the children had played elsewhere in their friends' house. Edmund went to the window and looked down. Almost immediately below him was the Jaguar, black and still, like a huge beetle.

Oscar was just closing the car door, talking to Vivian who was standing just behind him. Timothy ran noisily up to the front door, and slammed it shut behind him. Marsha stood by the car, looking at her mother, then glanced downwards and walked slowly to the door. Edmund went back to his drawing board. Soon after, there was a knock at the door. It was his father:

"Leela been?" He asked, his head leaning round the door, glancing around the room. Edmund glanced across:

"Oh ... yes ... earlier on ..."

"Shame she's gone!" retorted Oscar, "I can't flirt with her tonight!"

"Not tonight, father", responded Edmund, smiling towards him.

"Goodnight, boy!" And his head vanished from the doorway.

Edmund had finished his drawing, when his door opened again and Vivian walked in, bring a tray of drink and biscuits. She smiled handsomely at her son, who was still sitting at his board:

"I feel almost guilty, Edmund." She placed the tray on the table, and stepped slowly to his side: "whilst you've been working, I've been amusing myself playing bridge." She put her arm around his shoulder, and kissed and nuzzled his head as she admired his drawing. He grinned and looked up at her:

"You ought to feel ashamed!" He said. She stood, slender, tall and strong, next to him, towering over his hunched form as he leaned on his desk. Moving away, she took a biscuit:

"Leela came?" She asked, superfluously, sitting on the edge of his bed and biting hard on the biscuit.

"Yes. She went early, though." He replied, and began to collect his instruments together.

"How is this friendship with Leela, Edmund? Is it for now, or for ever?" There was a 'crack' as she took another bite of biscuit.

"I hope it's for ever, mother. Otherwise, it's not really worth pursuing any more."

"You mean you've made love to her." Said Vivian, biting hard at the biscuit again. Edmund didn't answer. He detected his mother's jealously quickly, but hadn't learned how to placate it. He felt he should understand, and so even from his earliest girlfriends' days, he had not condemned nor even scolded her because of it. She now waited, sitting on the bed, looking at him, swaying back and forth slightly.

"You brought her back here to make love to her, didn't you? I can smell her here, in your bed!" She arose slowly, defiantly, and crossed towards her son. She pinched his arm, and her face broke into a smile:

"You look positively petrified, Edmund! ... I'm not angry. I'm not going to attack you!" She laughed, and examined his drawing.

"It may help to talk about it", he said, quietly.

"If you need help to bed the girl, Edmund, I'm not sure I can assist. Perhaps you should see a Psychologist!"

Edmunds was not listening to her. He had walked over to his bedside chair, and sat down.

"I feel it's so good, but I think Leela's afraid. I want to explore. All I feel we're doing now is 'going on' ."

Vivian strode over to him, and sat on the edge of the bed:

"And what makes you believe she wants, or even capable of, such richness? Perhaps like most women, she'd like to be able to despise in her life, once in a while."

"Is that what you want?" Asked Edmund, looking at her steadily. Vivian turned away and picked at her hand in a nervous fashion:

"Why not address all this to her?"

"Lately I've felt unsure about saying anything like this to her. I don't want to upset her. Anyway, it's my problem."

"Lucky girl!" Vivian said sadly, as she looked out of the window:

"I mean, you obviously love her very much.", she turned: "Edmund, if nothing seems exactly right at the moment, why not forget your worries and see what happens naturally ..."

He had clasped his hands together, and stared down at his feet. Vivian came to the arm of the chair, and sitting on the floor beside him, looked up and went on:

"What happened to this dream of going abroad?"

"I'd still like to do something like that. That doesn't rule out Leela though."

"She's supposed to sit and wait, eh?" She smiled, and her voice was now deep and warm:

"I know I would, Edmund ..." She patted his hand and sighed. He glanced down at her:

"That would be her choice, of course. But it wouldn't mean I didn't care for her."

"Edmund", said Vivian, getting to her feet: "The next time you meet her, take her a huge bouquet of flowers. I'll make it up for you."

"It seems a bit irrelevant, Mother!"

"Edmund, sometimes you are stupid. Of course it's irrelevant, Lad!"

He looked towards her and smiled: "I'll trust your judgement. What flowers?"

"Leave it all to me, Edmund. I can still do a good bouquet. It'll give me great pleasure. I'll cut them on the morning of the day you're to take them to her, and keep them cool all day ..." She went to the window again:

"I'll give you some white lilies ... Yes! And roses. 'Peace' in the centre... and perhaps some red carnations ... Well, my boy, it seems as if I may be able to help you in your wooing!" She turned to him, laughing.

He remembered how she had tutored him in what to say to his girlfriends when he went out on dates some years previously, and he laughed with her. He felt a responsibility to protect her from being hurt .... He nodded and smiled towards her:

"Thanks, Mum. I don't know when I'll be seeing her again, though ..."

"As long as it's before the end of the month. By that time our lilies will be finished."

CHAPTER FOUR

Edmund did not meet Leela until Saturday. She invited him to have lunch at Parkleat, Leela's home, and they had decided to walk in the nearby woods. Edmund borrowed his mother's car for that afternoon, and thus he was able to deliver his huge bouquet without embarrassment.

"Gracious me!" Exclaimed Sarah, Leela's mother, when she saw the figure of Edmund nursing the exquisite present in his arms:

"Come in, come in Edmund! Let me have those after Leela's seen them, will you? And I can put them into water. They are so beautiful!"

Edmund smiled at her, and then went through to the lounge to where Leela was waiting:

"Oh! Edmund!" She cried, as he came into the room: "If they're not for me, you've finished it!"

He laughed as Leela kissed him.

"It's good to see you, Edmund. And these flowers are a wonderful surprise. I never expected anything like this from you!"

He sat down in one of the big armchairs. Leela took the flowers into the kitchen, and came back with a vase of water: "I hope they will last. They're really beautiful. Are they from your garden?"

Edmund nodded. She glanced up from her admiring the display: "I don't have a present for you, Edmund, but you can have a glass of Dad's whisky." He smiled and sat back into the armchair. He studied her profile as she poured the drink. She'd fringed her hair since he'd last seen her, and she seemed pleased to see him. But in some ways the bouquet had fudged things, he thought. And anyway it was his mother's idea. Leela had sat down by his feet, and he caressed her hair:

"New style?"

"Well, I had it cut. That's all, really. Do you like the fringe?"

"It suits you, I think." He sipped the drink, smiled, and began to feel very warm, and relaxed. They sat there: he, stroking her hair, she, resting on his legs; until half an hour later, Sarah shouted through that the meal was ready.

Pauline was already there. Father was busy in town with his shops, so there would be four only to eat:

"Never know when Dad'll be back. Of course this time of year's always busy, but each time it seems to get worse." Sarah talked to herself quite happily as she prepared the salad lunch. Pauline looked at Edmund sitting opposite to her:

"What do you do in that office all day, Edmund?"

"I draw plans of things", he replied.

"What sorts of things?"

"Buildings, fields .... I make maps showing people what to build and where to build it. You know, block of flats, a road. Something like that."

"Sounds like Geography", said Pauline, grimacing.

"Don't you like Geography?" Sarah asked her daughter.

"It's not that I don't like it. It's just that I can't draw!"

"No-one in this house can", said Leela.

"But not to worry, Pauline. Edmund can't play the piano!"

"What?" Pauline asked in wonder: "You can draw but you can't play the piano? I don't believe it!"

Edmund looked over to Leela and laughed. Pauline finished her lunch quickly and without much talking. She then sat back in her seat, placed the ends of her fingers on the edge of the table, and announced:

"Edmund, if you teach me to draw a little, I'll teach you to play a tune on the piano."

"I agree", he nodded and glanced round to Leela:

"If Leela doesn't mind waiting for our walk for a while, we can start after lunch." Leela nodded:

"I'll join you two in the music room after Mum and I have tidied up in here."

Pauline and Edmund left the kitchen table, and Leela began to clear the food away. Sarah bustled back and forth between the table and the sink area:

"He's a really nice man, your Edmund.", she said. Leela

felt pressure within that house when Edmund was there, particularly from her mother. It didn't worry her, but upset her mood and irritated her. So she stayed silent, but there was nothing she could now do to stop it:

"He's good with children, isn't he?" Sarah was by her daughter's elbow, and looked into her face. Leela had to reply. Her mother was quite capable, once she had started, in carrying on this sort of conversation with herself.

"Pauline isn't really a child. She's not typical of children, anyway", said Leela wearily.

"No, but he can talk to her. He's prepared to give her his attention. I noticed that tendency in William, your Dad, the first time I met him."

"Yes", said Leela, quickly: "but I may not marry Edmund. We've not decided anything yet."

"Well, don't leave it too late. It's better to be a young mother than an old one."

"I may not choose to be a mother, though", said Leela, rubbing a pan vigorously.

"You've said that before and it saddens me, Leela", said her mother quietly: "an attractive, healthy girl as you are should produce at least one or two. At least, Leela. I could understand if you were ugly or sickly. Twenty years ago many of us thought there may be no more children. Now there's prosperity and good education, some of you youngsters want to ditch the values we almost lost in the war."

Leela said nothing. Her mother often talked about her having children, especially if Edmund was mentioned or was around. Sarah was now silent also, and pressed her eyes tightly together to fight back some tears of sorrow. Leela quickly finished her tasks and joined Pauline and Edmund in the music room. Her sister was seated at the piano, and Edmund looked on over her shoulder. He was shaking his head:

"I don't think I can do it", he said: "but I'll teach you to draw something."

Leela sat down away from them and watched silently as Edmund drew on a piece of paper, while Pauline looked on in obvious admiration: "I don't think I could do that either." She grinned broadly at her sister, and looked down again: "I'll try to copy it while you're out for your walk."

The path to the trees led from the garden at the back of the house, and went across a large field before reaching a very old deciduous wood. Leela strode ahead of Edmund, and on reaching the first belt of trees, stopped by the base of a massive beach:

"I often came to this tree when I was a little girl", she said, smiling at Edmund as he came up to her: "it's so strong and tall I suppose I found it comforting." She took his hand and they walked on.

"You seem upset about something", he said to her after they had walked some distance into the wood. She glanced at him and laughed:

"It's mother. Wanting me to marry."

Edmund grunted in reply: "Maybe she's right. Perhaps we should be planning for the future."

"That doesn't bother me. It isn't what she said exactly ... I think she's afraid of my womanhood. She treats it like some sort of disease to be cared for by giving birth to half a dozen babies."

Edmund laughed, and shook his head: "You're being

unjust, Leela, I'm sure. It's good that she worries for you. It's natural for her to want you to have children."

But Leela looked away and thumped her feet down as she resumed walking:

"Mum's alright on most things. But she's bloody annoying about me and what I should be doing with my life. After all, it is my life, Edmund, not hers."

"Well, it if helps, my mother is curious about what we plan to do as well. I'm sure it's just natural. They're not able to forget the time their children were babies."

They walked for some time without speaking.

The spongy crackle of their footfall broke the backdrop hum of insect sound, and splinters of sunlight occasionally blinded them, or highlighted their pathway. Most of the birds were strangely silent, except sometimes a disturbed slumberer, or enthusiastic songster, broke the cosy, grassy peacefulness.

Leela stopped, and looking round, turned to Edmund:

"Isn't it strange how all the woodland flowers disappear so soon after springtime."

Edmund smiled. They continued, and attained the

summit of the hill in the centre of the wood. They sat down, and Leela pressed her head into Edmund's shoulder: "I want no change, Edmund. None that will spoil this."

He stroked her hair very gently: "would you like to live with me, Leela?"

"No, Edmund", there was no pause as she spoke, nor no surprise for her lover: "I'm happy as we are. I can't see any point in changing."

Edmund continued to stroke her, and stared into the distance. The leaves and branches swayed in the breeze, intermittently masking the sun's rays from his face. It was cool, and another puff of wind made him shiver. Leela pressed herself more closely to him. He pulled her hard against his body, but she felt cold. He suddenly felt that he did not know her. He continued to rub her hair between his fingers. She murmured something he could not hear, and his gaze fell upon the forest floor. There, dead wood and foliage lay in a rough carpet, and often a spiralling leaf would forsake a branch to find rest there. Over to his left he looked to the plain, gently sloping away into the distance. He could imagine them, at sometime- never-time, walking hand-in-hand, down that plain, feeling the gently squeak of grass beneath their feet, so clearly he could almost call out to that couple, and tell them not to wait for him ...

CHAPTER FIVE

Saturday. Sometime in September.

Edmund was up early that morning. He walked around the gardens and then over the fields, and by the time he returned, Vivian had already served lunch. He ate his meal quickly as his mother finished tidying the kitchen:

"What time are you going to the fair?" She asked, taking his empty plate.

"I'll be at Parkleat by two", he answered.

"And you'll be back here for dinner? You, Leela and Pauline?"

"That's it", he said, checking the contents of his pockets:

"I'll go now, mother", and he added: "is there anything I can get you from town?"

She was looking steadily at him, and he felt guilty to take her car, since Oscar and the children were out:

"You might bring me something. A surprise. Now get on!"

It took him twenty minutes to reach Leela's house, and he did not ring the bell when he heard voices around the back of the house. There, the whole family had gathered for after-lunch beer, and were sitting at a large wooden table. Edmund was embarrassed at his intrusion; but William waved him over to his side:

"Come and sit here, Edmund. Between Leela and me! Have a beer with us before going to the fair."

Edmund was glad to concur; and looking around, saw John and his girlfriend. Next to John, his mother smiled rosily at everyone, and greeted Edmund with an enthusiastic kiss. Facing Edmund as he clambered into his seat, an ebullient Pauline giggled across to him, showing a glistening array of white, but uneven, front teeth.

"You aren't afraid to take me on the fast rides, are you, Edmund?"

He nodded, smiled, and took a draught of beer. It was malty and cool. William kept it by his feet, in a large jug standing in a bowl of ice. He was jolly and laughing today. Edmund turned to him:

"Not very often you take Saturday off, Mr Drake." William laughed and inclined his head towards Edmund:

"It's not every day your son announces his official engagement!"

"What's the lady's name?" Edmund whispered in his ear.

"Angela", he replied, and after another drink, said to Edmund: "I'm also celebrating a good season for my business. If you and Leela get married... Well... Are you interested in trading?"

"I'm not at all", he answered: "not at the moment, anyway. Thanks for your concern. I'm ticking over in my job, Mr. Drake, and I may go abroad... and ... nothing is decided."

William looked down as he poured himself more ale, and seemed to be deeply considering something:

"Oh, aye", he took a glass proffered by John, filled it

carefully, and returned it. Edmund glanced over to Leela's mother, who was still in high spirits:

"You'll have no trouble with John, Angela!" She beamed at the girl: "since he's moved into the flat, he's had to look after himself. Food, ironing .... I take in some of his washing, of course, twice a week; but he does everything else for himself .... "She looked at John and laughed. He stared straight ahead, and said something to his father, who nodded as he poured another glass of ale.

"On Sundays", continued Sarah: "he eats with us. But rarely during the week. He does keep irregular hours – as you'll find out, I'm afraid ..."

John took up his drink, and glanced down at his mother: "You can't have an executive job in the bank and have 9 to 5 hours. Angela knows that." As he mentioned her name, she squeezed his upper arm into her, and kissed his cheek:

"I'm resigned to it, Mrs Drake!" She chirped: "the one thing I do worry over is how I can have dinner ready prompt and fresh; since I'll never know when he's due!" She smiled widely up to him, and he smirked, glancing to her, and then his mother:

"I'll try to phone you, dear, before I leave the office."

The two women laughed, and John once more smiled to each of them.

Pauline had just returned from the house to show off her pressed flowers. She stood by Edmund's side, flashing a great grin at him: "These are the ones I did last year, Edmund. This one is called Livingstone."

"I think I've seen this one alive, today. By the gate?" He asked her. She nodded:

"That's right. They are beautiful flowers, aren't they?"

Pauline turned the specimen in her hand and gave it to Edmund: "I wish I could draw, Edmund. I'd love to draw all these flowers. Will you teach me to draw?"

He looked at her and smiled: "I'll keep trying, Pauline!" He laughed, and pulled her onto his knee: "but when you're playing the piano at The Carnegie Hall, you won't have time for my drawing lessons, will you?"

Leaning over Edmund's knee, Leela clasped Pauline strongly in her arms: "and if you keep monopolising him, her won't have time for me, either! And I can't do anything, can I?"

"No!" Pauline agreed: "but you've got Edmund."

On hearing this, he threw back his head, crying 'Ohhhh', as he laughed off the child's flattery. Leela laughed as well, saying to her sister: "wrong, Pauline. No one's got him. You can't press him and put him into one of your big, heavy books, you know!"

It seemed as if Pauline might laugh with them, but taking up the daisy from Edmund's hand, ran back into the house. Leela's look followed; she smiled and turning to Edmund said: "lucky man! You've not only me to dote on you, but her too. And Mummy's got a soft spot for you, as well."

Edmund grinned at her: "we ought to go soon."

Leela nodded, hoisted herself to her feet and stepped over to her father:

"We're off now, Dad. I'll take the glasses in before I leave, if everyone's finished." She took most of the glasses, and went into the kitchen, where she was soon joined by Edmund:

"I'll help you with the washing, Leela."

She smiled, and dipped the vessels into a bowl of hot

water. He looked at her profile, her darkened skin, and high cheekbones. She was looking down, splashing suds and water over the drinks glasses, and he was struck by her beauty: the beauty which had first drawn him closely to her, in the beginning. It seemed almost despicable to admit such a thing, even to himself. Cheap; it had no substance .....

"Leela", he said as he dried the glasses: "what did you mean you told me some time ago that you wanted to 'melt into me'. It was after we'd made love. For the first time, on the cliffs ...."

"Yes, I remember", she said, not looking up: "I was glowing. I felt warm, and loving. Towards everything ..."

"I know", he said: "I felt that, too .... but ..... why did you use those words? They didn't occur to me, and I couldn't understand them. You remember?"

"Time stopped for me, Edmund", she said, looking steadily at him, and standing quite still:

"I was petrified ... not by the cold, of course, but by the unity felt, then. I wished not to gain, nor lose, at that moment ..."

"Then why did you say I couldn't compromise? As if it were a difficulty between us?"

She laughed and squeezed his hand:

"You always wanted more, Edmund! Even when you have all there is to have, you want more! That's why I can't live with you. Not yet. You look away, beyond the moment. I haven't the scope to take all that, Edmund. Not even for you, who I really do love." She kissed him softly, tenderly ....

He left her side, and walked towards the open door, and looked out onto the lawn, where the family were still sitting. William glanced at him from the corner of his eye, and tilted his glass towards him in salute.

Rattle and slap! The panting of an excited child skipping her way into the kitchen. Edmund turned. Pauline stood still and grinned at him, then at Leela:

"I've washed and got my purse", she said:" can we go now?"

"Yes, Pauline, but you won't need the purse, will she Edmund?"

"Certainly not. This afternoon is a treat on us."

Pauline smiled mischievously: "I was hoping it was! But I'll take it along to buy Mum and Dad a present."

They left by the lawn; and Sarah, Leela's mother, wanted to confirm the arrangements:

"You're to stay at Edmund's, tonight?"

"That's it, Mum."

Sarah nodded at Pauline in a matronly fashion: "You be no trouble, will you?" Pauline shook her head, and took Leela's hand, and dragged her a step or two nearer to Edmund, so that she could hold his hand, too. After more farewells, they went round to the front of the house and got into the car. Leela carried Pauline on her knee, so that she could see better .....

CHAPTER SIX

The fair was pitched in a recreation ground, just outside the local town of Wellawnbury. Edmund parked his car in a corner of the field set aside for the purpose, and the three set off for the fair in Pauline's favourite formation: she in the middle; grasping Leela on the one side, Edmund on the other. Before them, on that grey autumnal afternoon; two tall, white poles held aloft a canvas banner heralding 'Billy Stockdale's Fair'. They walked beneath this and between the two creaking poles; into the screams, catcalls and hubbub of the visiting crowd, and breathed in the sweet smell of diesel smoke, and looked around eagerly as they entered the brilliance of the arcades, warding off the solicitations of persistent stall-holders.

There were cheap trinkets for sale, or to win. Edmund stopped at one of the games' stalls:

"I wonder if I could do that?" He muttered. Pauline, her finger ends hooked over the edge of the counter, stared at the prizes at the back of the stall:

"What do you have to do?" She asked.

"Get the ring to fall over the block, so that it falls flat", he answered. Pauline looked at one of the active contestants: a young boy, self-consciously and desperately trying to impress his mates who looked on, occasionally jeering at his efforts. He was not successful. All the rings fell on blocks, but none fell flat. The boy was now red in the face, and seemed to be frustrated and angry:

"Can the bloody rings get over the blocks?" He demanded of the smirking stall-holder, a wiry young man with a bony nose and big lips, who showed him of course, that they would. The youth and his party slouched off: they laughing, he muttering threats of revenge.

"Have a go, then!" said Leela, nudging him.

He bought four tries for a threepenny bit, and with the last chance, won a prize.

"You choose", he said to Pauline, and she decided on a small, wooden doll: "He can live on my bed post."

Leela and she tried to win on shove hape'ny, but just failed. Behind this stall, there was, above the general level of noise from voices, machines and jerky music, the raising to a crescendo of female screams, followed by attendant and falsely loud giggling; and raucous, boyish laughter. They went to discover the cause of the excitement, and found the Waltzer Ride. Pauline stared at the sickening spinning of the passenger cars, and the closed eyes, falling heads, and contorted faces of their occupants:

"I would like to go on that", she said. They concurred, and Leela vowed not to take her sister's advice on anything at all, after the experience. Pauline was not only elated by the ride, but was now hungry:

"Over there", said Edmund, almost on tiptoe as he strained to see over the heads of the crowds: "Candy Floss!"

They went to the floss machine which was also a new experience for Pauline: "It's really good!" she cried:" he twirls the stick around the bowl, and it grows and grows!"

The Candy man took a shine to her, and gave her a sample free of charge, but she didn't like the taste:

"I'd rather have a bread roll, or something", she said.

Just a little further along from the Candy stall, a heavy sweet smell led then to the dough-nut counter. The uncooked rings travelled down to the hot fat on a conveyor belt; after one side was done, they entered a section which housed a lever, and this device flipped over the cake so its other side could be cooked. Pauline lifted her nose into the air, and closed her eyes: "Mmmm!" she said.

The man served them to her in a large, white paper bag, dipping them into powdery, white castor sugar before putting them away:

"That'll be four times two ... eight pence, please, sir!"

Pauline handed them round: "Who has the spare one?" she asked.

"You do!" Declared her sister: "We're content with three meals a day!"

Pauline grimaced towards her sister:

"Jealous because you aren't as slim as I am!"

"Slim! You're skinny!" Replied Leela: "still, you're right. You'll never be too fat, that's for sure."

At Pauline's insistence, they went on the Bumper Cars,

and at Leela's insistence, on the 'Love Ride' – a very short trip on scraping rail-cars through a very dark, damp, canvas tunnel. Leela also insisted on relegating her sister to being outside them for this ride, and in return Pauline made sure she was next to Edmund. She squirmed her tiny body close to him, while he leaned over the other side, and kissed Leela softly and passionately. She moved her mouth close to his ear:

"You have me on this side, and the little one on the other, if you get fed up. Doesn't that please you?"

All three now squinted their eyes as they emerged into the light of the later afternoon again. Over on the far side of the ground, some distance away from where they now were, they could see alternate flashes of the Union Jack, then that would disappear, followed by the Stars and Stripes. Leela noticed it, and turned to Edmund:

"What's that, over there?"

"A really awful ride called 'The Big Baskets'", he replied, sickened by the memory of his only ride on them some years ago. Pauline was keen to see, of course, and so they made their way to the ride, to get there just as it was slowing down. Soon the passengers were alighting from the sides of the two cars. These were shaped like two huge loaves, constructed from a wood-planked lower boat and canopied with steel frame, covered in canvas sheets across the tops with coarse hessian rope for the sides. They could carry more than fifty people, and the ride consisted of the cars simply rocking; but rocking until they were vertical. It was then, at the height of the hysteria and nausea, that the bottom of the baskets displayed the flag motifs.

Leela looked grimly at the people coming off: "they all look green!" She said, tugging at Edmund's arm. On his other side Pauline pulled at his hand:

"This we must experience!" She cried enthusiastically.

"Not I!" Said Leela emphatically; and stood firmly; arms folded, showing some apprehension as her sister, held by Edmund, sat down at the back of the Basket which had the Union flag painted on its underbelly. The same drive powered both boats, and they began by being rocked in complementary style to and fro, finally gathering so much momentum that they drove each other from their own volition. When the ride was finished, Pauline ran down the stairway to the ground, followed by Edmund, who progressed rather less steadily:

"I told you so!" Leela laughed as he wobbled towards them. She embraced him warmly, and the three walked slowly through the gateway, past the mechanical noise and human din, and the leering youths in greasy hair and mock-velvet collars, to the car. Their vehicle was now packed in as the evening trade had drawn in many more visitors. It was now seven, and the coloured lights of the fair were beginning to dazzle and streak enchantingly into the darkening sky.

On reaching his home, Edmund saw Vivian stooping at the pool, trowel in hand, thin woollen scarf on her head. At his side, two snoozing bodies, slumped together and unaware of the journey's end. On hearing the approach of the vehicle, she put down the trowel, and looked up. She stared silently at Leela, as she stumbled sleepily out of the car, while Pauline recovered instantly and was soon looking down, searching the pond intensely:

"Well the cat hasn't eaten any more of the fish", said Vivian, Edmund held Leela closely as they stood before her. His mother got up from her knees, and walked towards the house:

"Come along. Have some wine? Just a taste?" Leela nodded and they relaxed in the lounge as Vivian poured three glasses of white wine:

"Cheers!" Said the hostess. Leela smiled at her, and added:

"I'll toast youth, since I seem to have become an old lady at twenty-five!" She drank the wine and nodded her appreciation:

"Wonderful! It makes up for being made sick by a little sister who takes me on nauseous rides at the fair, who steals my man, and who's able to leap out of sleep as if she was in the middle of a forest fire!"

Vivian smiled at her, then beamed at Edmund: "you'll have to excuse me. I must prepare the dinner", and she left the couple alone. Leela finished her wine:

"This is lovely wine, Edmund!"

"Dad knows his wine", he replied.

"Where is your Dad?" Asked Leela. He shrugged:

"Study I suppose. Now we've got T.V. he's put it in

there. He may have decided to watch something. It's a bit of a fad at the moment, being so new."

"I don't like it", said Leela: "I find it hurts my eyes. And on most of the sets, the picture's blurred."

Pauline skipped into the room: "what's blurred?"

"We were talking about T.V., love", said Leela.

"I love T.V.!" exclaimed her sister: "Brenda's got one, and you can see all the matches from Wimbledon!"

The door opened, and Oscar came in:

"Leela and Pauline! Nice to see you! Edmund, now why didn't you tell me you'd come back!"

He laughed as he strode over to them, and kissed Leela with obvious enthusiasm, and Pauline with a genuine affection. He noticed the opened bottle of wine:

"Ah! I'm glad you chose this before dinner!" He offered re-fills, gave Pauline half a glassful, and poured a full one for himself. He took a mouthful, and looked round at the door:

"Excuse me. I'll prise that T.V. addict of a son of mine to join us. And my daughter, who's upstairs pinning a dress - she should be with us, too ..."

He left the room and shouted their names from the hall:

"Timothy! Marsha! Our guests have arrived! Come and be sociable, will you!", and then he returned, smiling at Leela: "Everyone will soon be here. I'm sorry they weren't ready to welcome you ...." He turned as the door opened and in came his younger son, Timothy. The lad was ten years old, and like Oscar he had a large head for his stature. His face wore a permanently sour expression; almost a smug, scowling general appearance. He strode jauntily across the room, helped himself to wine, and toasting the company, seated himself in one of the armchairs. Leela smiled at him:

"Been watching T.V.?" Timothy nodded. His father looked at him:

"It would be polite to say what you were watching. Make conversation, my lad!" He laughed quietly at Leela. Timothy glanced upwards. "Oh, yes. Well, it was just a comedy show." Leela smiled and nodded.

There was now a sound of voices in the hall, and after the door opened uncertainly, Marsha came in. She was long legged and thinly built. She was most unattractive, with freckles and short brown hair. She smiled self-consciously at the company:

“Mum asks if smoked Haddock is generally acceptable?”

Everyone was happy with the suggestion, and Marsha backed out of the room to tell her mother. Oscar serviced all the glasses, and ushered the company into the dining room:

“Bring the wine in with you”, he called out from the doorway as he waited for the group to file out. He beamed again at Leela, and looked down on her sister as she grinned up at him on leaving the lounge:

“Not too much wine, have you, young lady?” He addressed the little girl with mock sternness.

“No, I’ve got a long way to go, yet”, she replied, remembering the evening she drank a whole two-thirds of a pint of beer.

As usual at the house when guests came to dinner (and often when there were none), the dining table had each place comprehensively set, and was decked with a vase of fresh flowers, and a full bottle of wine. Vivian, tall and slender, hair taken up at the back and wearing a tightly fitted grey-green dress, swept into the dining room carrying two tureens of hot food. When they were all seated, Vivian served out the food, while Oscar chatted to Leela at the other end of the table, and the rest looked to the food they were anticipating eating shortly. Behind Marsha, the Carriage Clock which stood on the sideboard, struck eight o'clock:

"There!" Exclaimed Vivian triumphantly: "we are to begin dinner precisely on time!" She brushed strands of hair from her face, and added, smiling broadly:

"Let's start, shall we?" She dug her fork into the fish and soon there was a clatter of cutlery and china as the party began their meal. Oscar offered more wine around, and Leela and Edmund ate their food heartily:

"Beautiful fish!" said Leela, admiringly: "and perfectly cooked!"

Pauline, however, was picking at her food, and looked unhappy. She had been silent for over ten minutes, and Oscar, leaning across the table said to her, quietly:

"Do you not like the fish? No need to eat it. We can easily get you something else."

She shook her head, and looked dolefully at him:

"No. No. It's alright."

But she did not eat the fish. Leela, next to her, lowered her head and whispered:

"What's the matter? Are you ill?" Pauline turned to face her saying;

"No. I've been thinking about the fish. The ones in the pond, in the garden out there." She wagged her thumb towards the window, and spoke quite openly. Vivian frowned at her:

"The fish in the pond? What about them?" Pauline continued:

"Why are they cared for, whilst these fish are killed?" Vivian looked aggravated:

"Because they're pets." Pauline looked at her:

"Yes, I know, but I think I'd feel these were pets if I saw them swimming around, as I did the goldfish earlier tonight."

"Then don't eat it", said Oscar: "and we'll get something with cheese or whatever."

Pauline had pushed her plate away by now, and shook her head:

"Thanks. But I'm not hungry anyway", and she added, grinning towards Edmund:

"I had an extra dough-nut." Edmund smiled at her, and continued eating his meal. Vivian appeared more irritated than before. Leela looked at her sister, with some displeasure:

"I had no idea you felt this way. You're embarrassing people. It isn't like you."

"Yes, and I'm sorry, Leela; but I haven't felt this way before. Obviously now I can't eat fish." Leela gave a sigh of exasperation:

"Then you'd better become a vegetarian!"

Pauline looked downcast. She was upset not at what Leela had said, but her tone in saying it.

"Cattle are not kept as pets, but they too are alive, like the goldfish", Oscar went on: "and you eat their meat." He stared at her with wide eyes, waiting for her to respond. She looked back at him steadily:

"I shan't anymore."

"That's stupid!" Exclaimed Timothy: "you'd die without meat of some sort."

"That isn't strictly true", said Oscar, smiling in a patronising way towards his son; then turning to Pauline: "but it does mean you'll have difficulties with your diet."

"There'll be no difficulties", replied Pauline: "I'll just not eat anything that moves around."

Timothy scoffed, to be chided by his mother, but went on to say: "What about vegetables? They have life, too. You'll have to kill them."

"It isn't the same thing", she said. Timothy scoffed once more. Turning to face him fully, she continued: "it isn't the same thing to me, Timothy. The fish and cattle move. They have eyes, too. I've never liked the thought of eating anything that had eyes ...."

Marsha coughed nervously, and leaning forward, said: "I'd like to stop eating meat. But I enjoy it too much."

Oscar lifted his eyes to the ceiling: "Then you wouldn't

like to stop eating it at all, Marsha. You can't have it all ways."

"That's unfair, Oscar", interjected Vivian:

"Marsha is expressing a feeling that she has. You and Tim are being clever. You're not entering into the spirit of the discussion at all."

Oscar cast a brief smile towards his wife:

"Alright, Vivian. Now that we've finished eating, let's go into the lounge, drink some wine, and carry on with talking there ..."

The party moved to the lounge, and spread themselves freely on the chairs and carpet. Oscar, sitting in an armchair, smiled across at Pauline who was sitting on the floor near to Edmund's feet:

"Well, young lady. I'm going to tell you something. I hope you're not squeamish about blood and things like that. But I feel I ought to say it anyway."

He glanced around at the group. Leela seemed sleepy again, Vivian looked irritated still; but Edmund and the children were keen to continue.

During my first year in Medical School", said Oscar:"

I had to learn all about anatomy. That's all about the bits and pieces that make up the human body, Pauline. And do you know the first thing we had to do? To cut up a human body! Yes! Cut it up. Just like meat on a slab. You realise, when you do that, how similar our insides are to animals. I'd seen inside an abattoir, and the parts aren't much different, really. You could have roasted them in the oven, and served them up, and they would have looked the same. So I know that all we animals are the same, Pauline. But surely that's not the point?" Pauline seemed about to say something, but Oscar quickly went on:

"You can think of cooking the human bits until you take off the cloth which covers their face. When you see they're one of you, I don't think you'd do it. You see, it's not the eyes. It's seeing the similarity to ourselves that puts us off. The same with things we regard as pets. They're not to be eaten. They're part of our world. We wouldn't think of eating a dog or cat: although some other groups of people would!" Pauline winced, and Oscar laughed:

"Everything has its place, Pauline. Some things are pets, to be cared for, to give us pleasure. Other animals are used by us for food. We're naturally meat eaters, you know!"

Pauline, while obviously listening to what he said, did not look at all convinced. Timothy leered silently in a corner of the room, unable to see how anyone could not be converted by his father's argument. Vivian murmured her agreement with her husband's words, and leaned down to speak to Pauline who was sitting on the carpet, tightly packed as she pulled her legs close to her, so that her knees rested beneath her chin:

"It's true, Pauline. All flesh is doomed to die, anyway. Everything has a share .... Why look! When you die, you body will be eaten by the grubs, beetles and worms! It isn't wrong for us to have our share ..." Pauline looked at her, then her gaze fell downwards, and she blinked and stifled a yawn. Vivian smiled, and looked relieved, as she took hold of the little girl's hand:

"Come along, young lady! You are to go to bed, now, I think!"

Pauline offered no resistance, and soon the two of

them had left the room. Leela had smiled goodnights to Pauline, and now turned to Timothy:

"Are you going to study medicine, Tim? Like your Mum and Dad?"

"Oh no", he smirked: "you deal with poor people all the time. I hope to become a lawyer and deal with rich people." Oscar laughed uneasily, and added quickly:

"Leela's the job for meeting rich people. She works in a bank!"

There was an awkward silence, broken by Vivian entering the room saying:

"The little thing only just got to the top of the stairs!" And she smiled towards Leela:

"You're in the same room as Pauline ..... your usual room, you know!"

Leela smiled back with heavy eyes, and fought back a yawn, saying:

"I'll go up now, if no-one minds. Goodnight, darling...", as she kissed Edmund: "Good night, everyone! ...." She had turned towards the door, swaying against the handle as she did so; sleepy eyes half-closed, one of her shoeless feet with toes curled under, scraping on the floor; and Edmund wanted so much to take her in his arm, and guide her to his room ....

CHAPTER SEVEN

The following morning, Edmund arose at six; and with the sky showing its first streaks of dawn, he dressed quickly and went downstairs, out into the garden. He walked across the fields and over the river, then down, following the water course till it dipped down sharply in a shallow fall. Here, he drank at the water and looked eastwards towards the sea and sun. In the distance he could now hear the persistent call of a cockerel, and some throaty and grumpy 'rawk!' from the rookery further down the hill, towards the town. He turned back to head for home. He was hungry, and looked forward to a good breakfast. Crossing into the field which adjoined the garden of his home, he saw an old man loading wood onto a field trailer. The man did not look up towards him, and he headed for the far side, where there was a gap in the hedge. He had almost reached the hedge when, glancing down, he saw at this feet a black object, about the size of a woman's handbag. He stooped down to see more closely. It took a few seconds for him to realise that he was staring down at a dead rook. It lay on its side, and the upmost eye was half-open. He gently nipped the tip of the upper wing in his hand, and gently pulled, so that it was outstretched, as it would have been when the creature had last flown.

"Ee'll not aweken nu moore!"

Edmund started, and looking around, over his shoulder, saw the old man standing a few yards distant. His hands were on his hips, and he grinned broadly. He was dressed roughly, as for his work, in a dark cloth suit. He face was prickly with a day or two's growth, and his teeth were discoloured dingy yellow.

"Seems strange to think he once flew above the trees", Edmund remarked, casting his eyes downwards again, to look at the dead creature. The old man came forward and looked down at the carcase:

"Ah dunt know abaht that, young'un! It's certain 'ee an't nu use nu ornament nah!", and he took the bird from

Edmund's hand, and flung it into the hedge, voicing a weird, almost painful sigh with effort as he did so. He did not look at Edmund again, but turned and trudged heavily away across the field. Edmund frowned, and stared into the hedge for some time before resuming his journey home.

Arriving back, he found Leela in the kitchen, dressed and talking to Pauline. He greeted them, and was about to take off his boots when he stopped, saying:

"Oh! Help yourself to breakfast, if you like ... Mother will insist on all the trappings if she catches us, but she won't be up for a while yet .... we have most things: eggs, bacon, cereals .... in there"; he had pointed to the pantry door: "or in here", he went on, as he tapped the door of the refrigerator. The two sisters smiled at him, and Leela opened the pantry door and they looked inside. Pauline did not seem overtly interested, but at Leela's bidding, inspected the contents of the fridge.

"Well, love?" said Leela, inviting a choice of food from her sister.

"Oh, just cereal for me."

"Wouldn't you like bacon? I'm going to have some", and

she glanced quickly at Edmund, who was standing to one side of the fridge:

"And I'm sure Edmund will be having some."

"No, thank you. Just cereal, please..." said the little girl.

When the trio had settled to eat their food, Leela looked at Pauline, who was spooning her cereal with obvious enjoyment:

"I hope this refusal to eat bacon isn't anything to do with this idea of vegetarianism you talked about last night."

Pauline said nothing, and did not appear to hear the remark. Edmund looked towards her sympathetically; and Leela, noticing this, scolded him:

"It's no good your feeling sorry for her, Edmund. She's skinny enough as it is. If she stops eating meat I'm afraid she'd disappear!"

Pauline ate her cereal with even greater relish.

"Well", said Edmund, smiling: "although I've no intention of giving up meat, if Pauline has such an original idea ..... well, it's original to her", he added, answering a scowl from Leela, "and she didn't read or hear of it. It came to her ...

well, I believe it should be given some scope to develop, don't you think?"

"No!" Exclaimed Leela, vehemently: "what does she know of diet and what it is to have enough protein and so on? She's best to do as she's told till she's older, Edmund. Then she can decide."

The little girl did not look up, but she ate with more deliberation now, and Edmund noticed as he looked at her sitting at his side, in the corner of the eye nearest to him, the tiny sparkling of a tear.

CHAPTER EIGHT

December 1959

Edmund had arranged to take Leela and Sarah (her mother) to town that Saturday, to do some seasonal shopping. Coloured lights and broadcast music overwhelmed the town square, and a huge fir tree proclaimed anticipation of the festival. The store windows were filled with exhortations to buy their fancy goods; to buy big, and to buy now. Edmund pulled the collar of his overcoat to cover his cheeks as a harsh wind swirled around the shop front into which the two women were gazing: pointing, chattering and laughing excitedly at the displays. He had to step to, fro, and sideways as scurrying clusters of people passed the shop, or tarried to see what was offered for sale there.

By mid-morning they had completed some of the shopping, and Sarah suggested they take a drink:

"Let's go to Dad's warehouse", she said: "he'll be there by now, and give us a hot cup of tea or coffee."

The other two readily agreed, and so they walked, braced against a frosty wind, across the square and down the high street, turning at the bottom of the hill to cross the railway bridge; and reached the road where William's warehouse stood. The building was an old stone barn house, and huge wooden sliding doors had been fitted across the front opening to secure its contents, yet allow access to the goods vehicles at loading time. These doors were opened when they arrived; and standing there was a small, balding man with large ears; burnt red by the bitter wind. His lips nipped tightly on a damp, self-made cigarette; three-quarters smoked; as he stood at the entrance and looked at them as they approached. His hands were sunk deeply into the pockets of his brown storeman's coat, he was huddled tightly against the cold, and he squinted his eyes as he looked closely at the three people coming towards him. His face soon relaxed and he grinned, showing big, tobacco-stained teeth:

"Hello Mrs. Drake! Mr's upstairs! Good afternoon, Miss Leela! Afternoon!" He chuckled and stepped aside as they passed by, Sarah declaring a 'Hello, Mr. Hoyland!' as she did so. Just inside the entrance, a dusty, steep wooden staircase led to a cubical shaped office, glazed on two sides and illuminated by a small overhead sky-light in the warehouse roof itself. Sarah opened the door and looked in:

"Can we beg a hot drink, love?"

"Ah! Course, course!" Edmund heard the muffled remarks as he stood on the top landing of the staircase. The three went in, and William ushered them to various chairs around the office. He sat back behind his wooden desk, which was covered with several shallow stacks of papers. On the rear wall, there were two clip boards; one holding invoices, the other brown clock cards. To the side of these was a calendar, carrying the photograph of a girl in a swimsuit; legs immersed in water, and showing little naked flesh. The visitor had to wait while William ticked off some items on an invoice. Having finished, he looked up at Leela, staring at her over the top of his spectacles:

"Alright?"

"Yes, Dad. Cold though." She had shuffled towards a small electric fire, and was hunched over it as she spoke.

"I'll get some tea up ere", and he picked up the telephone receiver: "that you Barry? Bring us a pot of tea and four mugs, will you?"

He put the telephone down and rubbed his hands together:

"Getting colder! Here, Edmund! Come by the fire!" And they sat, huddled in their chairs chatting quietly. Young Barry Garner brought the tea, and the conversation halted briefly as they eagerly sipped their hot drinks:

"Spent all our money?" William asked Sarah, smiling and winking at Edmund.

"No, William. On the contrary", she answered, placing her hands emphatically together on her lap, as if to emphasise her frugality: "however, I haven't been to our shop yet. Can you recommend anything?"

William quickly referred to a list on his desk: "Greens

are very good ..... Roots aren't marvellous, though. Except spuds .... have a good look. They'll still be plenty left."

He dumped the list back on the desk, and pushed himself backwards, till the rear of the chair touched the wall:

"How's the town looking? They did it up this morning, I hear."

"Same as last year", replied Sarah, grimacing: "except now there's music blaring out across the square. It's so loud it's distorting. So you can't hear the words anyway."

"It makes no difference", said Leela: "you can tell what tune it is because they only seem to be half a dozen altogether. All popular Christmas things which everyone knows. I suppose it adds to the atmosphere."

"Get on with yer!" Responded her father, leaning his head back into his hands and laughing loudly: "second-hand stuff's never as good as the real thing. I'd rather hear the Sally Army in the square."

There was a pause. Sarah looked up and beamed across at her husband:

"Our Pauline was still practising when we left, William."

"She'd carry on all day if left alone", he muttered in reply, smiling and staring at his desk. There was a roaring noise beneath them, and William sighed and got to his feet:

"Anyway! I must go downstairs, now. The lorry's here to be loaded, and I like to see what's happening. You can stay here as long as you want."

"No, William, I think we'll go too ..... ", she exchanged glances with Edmund and Leela: "and finish the shopping... when will you be home?" She was addressing William just as he was at the door. He stopped and looked round:

"No later than six." He clumped slowly down the stairs, followed by the others. He waited at the foot of the staircase, proffering his hand to the women as they reached the bottom step:

"Cheerio!" He said, waving to them as they left, having to scrape sideways past the cab of the parked lorry which had backed into the warehouse to be loaded:

"Well!" said Sarah, standing outside as Edmund squeezed passed the vehicle to join the two women: "I feel refreshed! We'll go to the shop and get that over with. And if you don't mind, Edmund, we'll load the veg into the car... then we'll go to the market, and have a look around Swans'."

"That's fine", he said; and after visiting William's shop in the high street, they called in to the car-park, off-loaded the provisions, and prepared to set off for the market. Leela hugged herself against Edmund's body, and her mother gave a slightly embarrassed smile towards them, turned away and walked up the high street hill. They approached the market in this new formation; the lovers strolling closely together, and Sarah led the way, occasionally darting a glance into a window, or a brief look back to check they were still with her. She pushed her way into the market, through the crowd, and had soon disappeared from view. Edmund stretched himself upwards to see over the crowd:

"Can't see her", he said, looking back down at Leela. She looked up into his face, staring flatly, her eyes curiously devoid of expression, her lips tightly drawn:

"It doesn't matter", she said: "I know where she's gone."

"Are you feeling unwell?" Edmund asked her, frowning as he gazed at her.

"I'm pregnant!" she said, quite loudly, and two people turned round and looked at her:

"I'm going to join mother. Coming?" And Leela left his side as he stood there, very still, while the crowd pushed round him. He forced his way through to re-join her, and she was now standing next to her mother, looking at some cloth she had selected:

"Yes, mum. It's not that bad ...." Sarah took it back from her to re-examine it, and Edmund pulled Leela to him and talked closely and earnestly into her ear:

"We need to be alone to discuss it. Why did you wait until an inappropriate moment like this to tell me?" He felt frustrated and irritated as the women around him tried to push him out of the way so that they could see the fabrics on the stall. Leela said nothing, and did not even look at him now, but towards her mother, at whom she smiled and mouthed banal encouragements. Edmund pulled her round to face him:

"Will you please answer, Leela. Why choose a time like this for such important news?" She looked up to him with a defiant expression on her face:

"Because I wanted to get my own back!" She had shouted this and the cackle and hubbub of the adjacent crowd ceased. There were embarrassed murmurings now, though; and Edmund, feeling most uncomfortable, left the fabric stall and went back to the entrance to wait for them to come out. Oddly, Sarah had been so engrossed in scrutinising materials she missed the drama, and turned now to ask Leela if a blouse made from certain cloth would match her green skirt. They emerged from the market crowd. Sarah was bustling and fussy: excited by the atmosphere, and her purchases, and the thought of making some new clothes. Leela smiled unemotionally at Edmund, whilst he frowned, stood still, tapping his foot and biting at his lower lip. He nodded at Sarah as she came towards him, and then she went ahead, as Edmund took Leela by the arm. He walked her slowly by his side, looking fixedly ahead, and spoke quietly to her:

"I thought I understood you. I believed we had a relationship. You don't seem to trust me .... there's no danger, no battles to win! I'm here. I'll do whatever there is to do... I understand how you feel ..."

She looked back at him, grimly:

"You aren't the one who has it growing inside, are you? No, no Edmund! You can't understand. There's still a choice for you. And I suspect you're glad about that. Relieved that you can share the burden at a distance, whatever you mean to do with your life. But I have no such option. It's there, inside me!" She slapped her stomach and quickened her step so that she had now broken clear of him.

He felt helpless. He could have no sympathy with that she was saying, nor could he truly comprehend its meaning. He was unable to speak during the drive back to the Drakes', although Sarah and Leela talked throughout the journey. He stopped the car outside their front door, but kept the engine running:

"I'll help unload the shopping", he said, and having done so, got back into his car and left, without more than a cursory farewell. Sarah stared after him:

"I thought Edmund would have stayed for tea..." Leela was looking into the garden, smiling to herself.

Four days later, she met Edmund in a public house near to town. They sat in a corner in the lounge, and Edmund brought back two glasses of beer:

"It's almost a year to the day since we were last here!" said Leela, looking around the room, which was bedecked with tinsel, twisted crepe paper and branches of evergreen.

"Nigel Watson's party - New Year's Eve", he said, nodding and laughing. Leela sipped her beer, and putting the glass down very slowly, and carefully, began:

"Well, Edmund. You wanted to discuss it. My 'state', that is."

"I wanted to talk to you about your expecting our baby." he said, squeezing her hand.

"Talk then", she said quietly. He was silent for some time, then quickly finished off his drink:

"Like another?" he asked, noticing that her glass, too, was now almost empty.

"Gin please, Edmund. With orange."

He went to the bar again, and brought back their drinks:

"Mothers' Ruin!" she laughed as she drank.

"Leela", said Edmund, leaning over the table towards

her, "this baby could be for the best. For both of us. I love you. You must know that."

She looked back into his eyes, and felt the painful sweetness inside; that same feeling he had always aroused in her when she was most unready ...:

"Edmund, Edmund ... Love. Can't you see? Neither of us wants this baby. That is true, isn't it?"

"We didn't plan for it. Nor against it. Not seriously anyway. That's true also. But something doesn't have to be planned and thought out fully to be right."

Leela listened to his reasoning with mounting irritation:

"Edmund. You are not expecting this baby. I am. I am going to fatten like an overgrown tomato, not you. And I don't want it, Edmund."

"Leela. Don't get so distressed. It doesn't help..." She grabbed his wrist violently, jerking his hand so that some of his beer spilled, and bowing her head forward, fixed his eyes with hers, and said quietly, slowly and determinedly:

"I want to be allowed to curse this state I'm in, Edmund! That's why you are annoying me so much. For you, everything seems easy. For me, it's not, and I can't live with someone who doesn't experience that. It's this difficulty between us that makes the whole thing worse. It complicates itself so much in my mind. And it is my problem, Edmund. Not yours. Whatever you say, whatever you do, it's my body that will carry it, not yours. It may be my joy to touch him, and see his smiles. But it will be my guilt at his suffering, my crying over his weaknesses."

Edmund was about to interject, but she again grabbed his wrist, now tighter than before, and said, tight-lipped and baring her teeth:

"It will be my blood and bile that will spill out at his birth, not yours!"

He was silent. She inverted the glass so that the last drops of liquor trickled onto her tongue:

"Get me another drink, please, Edmund."

He nodded, and felt dazed as he went back to the bar.

She was not at their table when he returned with the drinks. He waited some time, but she did not come back, and he tramped across the fields; through the freezing damp grass and the marshes; across the stream, and finally through the field where he had found the dead rook some time before. He lingered in the garden; stood in the open space by the birch tree and the azaleas, heard the noisy perambulation of a hedgehog, and the screech of a fox in the field ..... he stared at the black sky, and was soaked by the cold drizzle.

He felt he could not sleep, nor did he want to go to his bed, so he remained in the kitchen, and made himself a hot milk drink; spending the night sitting there. He let his mind run free; over the hills to the fresh sea air, down to the crashing water and the smooth sand, clinging to the silver-grey rock, and chasing and calling with the sea-birds.

The following evening he telephoned her. She would meet him next day (Friday) after work, in the town square. He waited for her, but again she did not appear. The following morning, at home, he received a letter from her:

"Friday 6.30 P.M.

Edmund:

I regret not coming to meet you as we arranged. I felt I didn't want to go over the same ground again. We've never really argued before, and it seems pointless to start to do so now. However, I behaved cowardly tonight, as I did last time, in just running away. I'm hoping I can explain myself better by writing it down on paper. That way, it's there for good, isn't it?

I am disturbed, or upset, because I don't feel committed to you in the sense of a wife or fiancée should. I'm not even happy about bearing your child. That sounds awful to you, I know, but I feel it is the truth.

In time, things could change. I agree with what you said about planned events not always being for the best. But I'm not happy about it, and even on reflexion, I try to wish the whole thing away.

I've read through what I written so far, and almost destroyed it. However, I'll let it stand as it is. I hope it doesn't hurt you too much, because I don't wish to do that. I don't want to be without your closeness at the moment. I still need your love, and your passion. I'm not ashamed of this, but I don't expect you to be flattered. In any case, it's not that alone. But I do want us to <u>burn</u> into one another. To take and give as we please, and not to think of how we should behave or what we should be feeling. That way,

I think I can cope with the coming of the baby. I can try, anyway. As long as you don't put claims on me because of it, love.

Perhaps you'll finish with me now. That would be a terrible loss to me, but I can bear it, if you think it would be for the best. Don't stay for the sake of the baby. I would hate him then.

Leela

Edmund stuffed the letter into his trouser pocket and left the house directly, passing the kitchen to collect Vivian's car keys. She was there, drinking coffee:

"Out, are you?" she asked, looking surprised.

"Yes, mother. No lunch. Maybe back for dinner, but don't wait."

He'd gone, and almost slammed the door. She raised her eyebrows, then smiled to herself. On hearing the car start up, she went to the window in time to see it disappear down the drive.

He skidded to a halt outside Leela's front door, and

rang the bell. Pauline answered, and smiled greatly when she saw Edmund:

"You've neglected us!" she exclaimed.

"I suppose I have", he replied: "I've come to take Leela out for a drive. Is she at home?"

"She's in the lounge", said the girl. He passed her and went into the room to find Leela, sitting by a log fire, reading a novel:

"Edmund!" He smiled at her:

"We'll go for a drive. If you've nothing more important to do."

"That would be lovely. I can read, look out of the window, or talk to you", she said, getting up from the chair and following him into the hall:

"Mum! I'll be out for a while! Edmund's taking me for a drive!" she shouted up the stairs, while Edmund waited by the open front door. She looked at him, laughed and shouted up again: "if I'm lucky he'll buy me lunch out so don't wait for me! Goodbye!"

A muffled goodbye came back in response, and Pauline

ran out to the car to wave them on. Leela looked back at her as the car drew away:

"She behaves as though we'll never come back", said Leela, waving back at her. Edmund did not speak much during the drive. He didn't mention the letter, but drove high up, into the wild moorland.

"I haven't been here for years, Edmund!" she said as she looked around the jutting granite and grey sheep. He turned off the main road and climbed a steep, rough track. The car engine whined in first gear as it bumped its way upward. At the top of the track, he parked the car and turned off the engine. He got out of the car, and opened the passenger door. Leela looked up at him, and slowly got out. He closed the door after her and led her to a place he had known since he was a boy. He laid her down there, quickly pulling the clothes away from his middle; and she responded, eagerly drawing her skirt aside ... and then he was inside her. He sighed deeply as he felt her wet warmth encompass him. But this was not a time to be still, and he ravaged and plundered her body. She jerked herself violently up to him, hissing at him through tightly clenched teeth; and as he brought himself to the pinnacle of his frenzy in a series of long thrusts which stung her body, she whispered to him between snatching for breath:

"Tear me apart, Edmund! Take me with all the force you can muster! go on ... go on !"

Then he was still; throbbing inside her, saliva ran down the side of his mouth. The smell of sex drifted heavily around them, laying there; in that sheltered hollow of a schoolboy's fantasies. Had he ever been afraid, then, all those clouds ago?... He felt some dread now. Leela's lips were cold; and her eyes, he thought, danced unnaturally. She kissed him again. It felt like the cold, thin kiss of death, and he shuddered:

"Are you alright?" she asked him. He looked at her. It was the girl he had loved. It had been a misunderstanding. He smiled and held her closely. She too was now tender, and kissed his ears, and cheeks, and eyes, with soft, warm lips, murmuring: "beautiful, beautiful. Feeling so safe, now, Edmund ...."

They lay cocooned in a tingling haze of satisfaction for two hours, and then dressed and walked to the top of the crag. Here they stood in the cold noon day breeze, looking out to sea; and then came down the other side, to a stream. Edmund splashed his bare feet in the freezing water, and she joined him:

"It's so cold I daren't move. No! Not even to get out!"

He laughed, and then shouted:

"Let's walk to Wellawnbury!"

"What? How far?"

"About eighteen miles!" he exclaimed. She looked aghast, then laughed too, and snatched his hand, pulling him down and splashing cold water all over him:

"Alright, then, mi lad! And we'll have a meal in town. My treat today. We can catch a bus back to the main road to pick up your car!"

Edmund grinned ruefully as he dried his feet with his handkerchief:

"Don't talk about food! It'll take us at least three hours before we can get anything, and I'm already hungry!"

He quickly pulled on his shoes, and ran to Leela, who was now walking down the hill. She skipped and ran so that he couldn't catch up with her, but he finally made a rapid dash, and grabbed her with an outstretched arm, and whirled her down the slope. They both ran the steep bank, and their momentum hurried them across the meadow at the foot of the hill, after which they progressed more slowly through the valley woodlands:

"Here's where we picked bluebells, remember?" he said to her. She nodded:

"You never looked at girls then ..... I wanted you to notice me. I let another boy touch my tiny breasts in these woods, because of you." She smiled wistfully and looked at him as they trudged through the rich, heavy earth:

"For my sake?" he laughed in return.

"Yes, for you. He told me it would make them swell, if he rubbed and squeezed them. I thought you might look at me if I had bigger breasts."

They had left the woods, and crossed into some rough pasture. The animals looked quizzically at them, and keeping a safe distance, surveyed their journey southwards. After an hour, both were tired. They could see Wellawnbury Church in the distance, and felt justified in taking a rest. They sat on the downward edge of a massive hill, legs stretched downwards, lying back and breathing heavily with fatigue. Leela was the first to sit up:

"Where is your house from here, Edmund?" she asked him, looking round the horizon.

"Over the other side of this hill. Two or three miles eastwards. Your house is over there", and he pointed south-westwards, to the right of the church steeple.

"Yes, I remember", she nodded: "we picnicked here on a school trip. We parked the coach over there", and she pointed to a concreted flat, overgrown with brambles. Edmund looked, and could see the remains of the rough road, hewn for war, covered now with elders and nettles:

"You wouldn't get a coach up there now."

"Come?" Leela stood up, and held out her hand to Edmund. He took it, and she leaned back dramatically: "heave-ho!", and he was upright.

It took them less than two hours to get to town, and once there, they went to their favourite restaurant:

"We'll have a huge tea!" said Leela, passing the menu to Edmund. They persuaded the owner to specially grill for them two fillet steaks, with egg and chips. They waited eagerly for the meal, and when it arrived, both set into eating, with no pause for conversation. Edmund finished eating first, and sitting back, sighed deeply in his satisfaction:

"Would you like a glass of beer?"

Leela, mouth full of food, nodded. He ordered two pint glasses, and both were soon empty. Leela flopped in her chair and patted her stomach:

"Oooffff! I'm full, and bloated with ale!" she hiccuped, and giggled: "really, Edmund, I feel merry. That must be strong beer!"

"You'll need it! Have you seen this bill?" He laughed across at her, and tossed a slip of paper that the waiter had just given to him.

"Well!" she exclaimed: "seventeen shillings and sixpence! I've got enough left out of a pound for our bus fares."

"Let's split the bill, love. It's a lot for you to pay!"

"No, Edmund. I'll pay."

They smiled at each other, and walked slowly to the bus stop. They consulted the timetable, and found they had not long to wait. They stood together, chatting, smiling, joking.

The town bus, a red and cream single decker, pulled up and carried them away. They collected his car, and he drove her home. There they drank coffee with Sarah, Pauline and William; and to Edmund it seemed that the world was not so topsy-turvy as he had feared.

For the next three weeks, up to Christmas, he and Leela met several times. Each time, they organised being alone, hidden away; long enough to make love. They both needed this. It was like food and drink for them. Indeed, Edmund considered, it seemed that this was now the only priority, although he had not planned this to be so. As for the rest; the talk, the closeness. he did not feel the soft sac of intimate affection around them: only the cold heat of a feverish sex which left him increasingly unsatisfied, and uneasy. It was, to him, as if she was sucking his life blood as she drew his seed into her. She would talk little during their lovemaking, and rarely alluded to it in everyday speech with him; yet it was she who clawed at his back to urge him on as he thrust into her. She, it was, who assumed that every time they met, this was to be accomplished again, before anything else ...

CHAPTER NINE

Christmas Eve party at Edmund's. 1959

Vivian and her daily help had worked for some hours to produce a buffet supper with wine, spread out in caches around the huge ground floor, and near to the collections of food and drink there were soft chairs, and cushions on the carpets, and muted, coloured lighting. Throughout the festive area, recorded music was relayed at a level almost inaudible unless everyone ceased to speak. Vivian and Edmund had produced many interesting wreaths of holly, mistletoe, ivy and fir. There were over one hundred guests; mostly professional acquaintances of Oscar's: solicitors, vets, accountants and so on; and, of course, doctors, and their wives. Thus although they were mostly below 40 years old, the ripple and rhythm of the conversation was restrained; the laughter was never too raucous, the jokes were not excessively coarse. Edmund, being there without Leela, was subject to the attentions of the daughters. Sometimes even the mothers and wives would insist on his kissing them beneath a bunch of mistletoe, or dancing with them. Eventually, he managed to anchor himself by a University Lecturer, Dr. Karl Mejinsky:

"So. Here you are, Edmund. Twenty years old ....."

"Yes. Yes, that's right", he answered, smiling at him.

"And unscathed? No wounds? No scars?"

"A few", he smiled, ruefully: "but none mortal."

"Dear me!" said Mejinsky, his brow skinned face briefly wrinkling into a concerned expression: "you take it very seriously! That's bad, Edmund."

The young man pursed his lips, and averted his eyes:

"Parties aren't the occasion on which to joke. You have to *enjoy yourselves*", he said, putting great emphasis on the last two words of his sentence. Mejinsky laughed:

"That's better! You seem to be recovering!" The old doctor's eyes twinkled, and he smoothed back his long grey hair, which was thinning at the forehead. He laughed and nudged Edmund to look in the direction of a young girl dancing with another woman, quite near to them:

"There's a creature who would help you to recover from most things. And very quickly, too!" he grinned hugely; and his pointed, upturned chin almost met his large nose. He had reminded Edmund of a life-size Mr. Punch, with bulging brown eyes, always eager, it seemed, for something on which to rest their gaze. He was slightly taller than Edmund, but extremely thin and loose skinned. He looked back at Edmund:

"Yes, Edmund. Women were put here for the ultimate enjoyment and satisfaction of the human spirit .... I am convinced, you know, that all tyrants are haters of women! Don't you agree? Ahhh! Look at that!"

The young girl had whirled herself around, and her skirts had spun upwards. The doctor looked avidly at the legs as she danced:

"Wonderful! Wonderful!" he cried, applauding the girl for her performance, and she in turn curtsied to his appreciation:

"My dear girl! That was beautiful! Beautiful! You have

done wonders for my old constitution!" The mothers and girls giggled at his flattery, and the men smiled and nodded quietly to themselves. He had taken the girls hands in his, and held out her arms as she stood before him, smiling and listening:

"I am always afraid that I would suffer indigestion after eating pickles, like I have done tonight. But I am sure that after seeing you, my mind cannot be so low as to be frightened by rumblings of the belly, and so I will sleep well!"

The girl laughed, pulling one of her hands away and stifling her merriment. Edmund had been smiling inanely during most of this, his mind dwelling on other things. Karl turned to him:

"Wake up, my boy! Introduce me to this gorgeous young creature!"

"Oh! Yes .... Karl, this is Miss Manella Moon. Manella, this is Dr. Karl Mejinsky, who's supposed to be a University Lecturer, but spends his time looking at pretty girls."

The girl laughed, and Karl looked with mocked sternness at Edmund:

"My boy, you are only partly correct. I can fulfil my obligations to the University, and yet still admire an enchanting young lady like Manella!"

"What do you teach? asked the girl shyly.

"They call it 'Philosophy'", he said, whispering into her ear as if ashamed: "but I think we talk about ourselves in those classes, more than any other subject."

She smiled at him: "you have to be clever to discuss Philosophy. You don't just talk about each other. We all do that, all the time!"

The old man shook his head vigorously, and nodded towards Edmund:

"This fellow is near to you in age, and perhaps in outlook. He can tell you that talking about yourself candidly, truly; *brutally*; is the most difficult subject to discuss."

Manella looked at Edmund: "would you agree, Edmund, that people find it easy to talk about themselves?"

"In one sense, yes. I know what you mean. But it's the image of us we really speak about in this case. Our image of ourselves."

The girl nodded, and smiled, and then wandered back to her family.

"You see, Edmund, you are a liability. You frighten off all the young girls!" Karl nudged him in the ribs, and took his empty glass from his hand:

"Whisky?"

Edmund nodded, and Karl left him momentarily for the drinks table. He returned, proffered him the whisky, and in turn lifted a large glass of iced vodka:

"Here's to you, Edmund!" he took a long draught, and looked steadily towards the young man:

"It's a pity you decided to waste your time drawing plans for those who are gradually destroying our countryside", he began: "And you would have enjoyed my University course."

"I had to earn my keep, Karl."

"You ignore the salvation of the soul, Edmund, so that you can care for the body. It's the wrong way round." He paused and took another drink:

"For you, at least. Now the young girl, Manella. She ....

well - look at her. She is completely whole. At this time, I mean, right now. Do you see what I mean?"

Edmund nodded slowly, unconvinced. Mejinsky continued:

"Spirit and flesh are one. That is why she is so attractive, you see! In time, or at another time, if she is really conventional, she will no longer exude the essence of life, as she does now. She will grab, take advantage, sentimentalise .... for her, the problem is one of keeping her childlike simplicity. I am not insulting her when I say she obviously does not have the brain ever to be concerned with the deeper problems of self-doubt. You are worried about these problems, Edmund, aren't you? It's only natural that you should be. And just as you need the intellectual equipment for drawing your plans, so you need the facility to deal with yourself."

"I suppose you're right there", he replied: "I do find my life puzzling, sometimes."

Karl lowered his head, and looked deeply into Edmund's eyes:

"Life is never puzzling! You are thinking about

something specific. I believe you should have said: 'People are puzzling' - isn't that right?"

"Well. Their reactions to things. Yes."

"Which pre-supposes you are certain of the framework in which they operate. It isn't your world, it's theirs. That's why their reactions surprise you. We judge others from our own selfish point of view. It's a great mistake."

"Well. It is. But how are we to learn about their minds?"

"It's difficult, Edmund. They won't, they can't, tell you. Any observed fact has to have an observer, and that's difficult if the two are the same, is it not?" Edmund nodded, Karl continued:

"So maybe the best we can do is what I began by telling you: we must make every effort to understand our own selves more surely. That way, we shall at least be able to relate to others from a firmer footing."

Edmund was silent for a few seconds; then said slowly: "Let's say I followed your advice, though. How would I implement it? Talk to people like yourself? How?"

"Go into yourself, Edmund. Explore your mind. You can use various artefacts, of course - meditation is one ......"

"Is that the method you use?" Interrupted Edmund.

"Sometimes, I meditate. But nothing, in my experience, can substitute for dedicated introspection. Allow just an hour or so each week for this, Edmund."

Karl smiled at the boy, and left him alone. He was soon joined by his father.

"An earnest conversation, indeed, Edmund!"

"Yes, father. We were talking about understanding people."

"A rather over-long talk for such a subject", laughed Oscar: "and what conclusion did he come to?"

"Oh, the importance of sessions of introspection is to first of all understand oneself."

"My boy, I hope you won't do *that*! You will without any doubt drive yourself crazy. You above all others I know are too inwardly analytical already!"

"How do I cure myself of that?" Asked Edmund, smiling towards this father.

"I have no idea, and I don't even know if it would be good for you to try. However, I think another glass of that wonderful single malt will without any doubt be good for you!"

Oscar plucked the glass from his hand, and deftly shouldered his way through the crowd to get to the drinks table.

Edmund glanced to his side, to see Vivian had silently joined him. She was motionless and beautiful, and stared out into the room. She was wearing a very pale blue Grecian style dress, and held her head high to let the long tresses of hair hang down her shoulders. She turned and scrutinised Edmund's face:

"You look glum, my love. Please smile, if you can, and talk to Mark Kelderfelt's wife. He and Brian Lapping have been talking for half an hour, and she's left out on a limb. She prefers to talk to men, you know. Will you do it?"

Edmund left her and headed for the corner of the room where Angel Kelderfelt was sitting, staring at up at the two men who were locked in intense discourse. He bent over, smiled at her, and offered his hand to escort her over to a small free space. A waltz was playing on the hi-fi, and he drew her into a slow, swaying dance.

Angel K. (as most of her friends, and enemies, called her when they alluded to her) was a shapeless woman, with a white face, short dark hair and large dark eyes. She had produced her solicitor husband's children, and now struggled to fill her time with housework, gardening and morning coffee. Edmund could feel only intense sorrow for her, and hence found her gaze disconcerting. He looked away, and as he did so, something caught his eye. For the darkness on the far side of the room, he glimpsed a grey patch, and looking directly, saw a face; and two eyes shining, and looking at him. It was Leela. There was nothing surprising in her being there, of course; but the fall of light and shadow on her visage startled him. He stopped dancing, and Angel looked disappointed, but resigned, and nodded with an artificial smile. But Edmund didn't look at her:

"Excuse me, Angel. My girlfriend's just arrived ...." And he left her standing there, alone, as the slow tune continued to filter through the hum of party chatter.

"Who's the new girlfriend, then?" She asked as he

came to her. He grinned as she hooked her hand round his neck, and pulled his head down to kiss him:

"I didn't think I'd come here as I knew you wouldn't like it, even though I was invited."

"I was pretty sure you wouldn't. I wish in a way you hadn't", he said quickly, hardly realising what he was saying. She laughed:

"Well, Edmund. You are honest. I shall be very awkward and stay. So - you can get me a drink, please, and introduce me to a good conversationalist. I need stimulation."

He fetched her a glass of white wine:

"I'd better get back to Angel K.. It's part of my duty to dance with neglected wives." He attempted to smile at her, but found he could only stare back blankly at her own devilish grin:

"I'll introduce you to Dr. Karl Mejinsky. He talks a lot", he laughed, falsely, and added quickly: "He's a philosopher ....."

"He sounds boring. But it'll do for a start. Go on! Get back to Angel, my little gigolo!"

He wanted to repost, but couldn't. He wished even

more that she hadn't come, and he suddenly felt helpless against her.

He collected Angel K. from the drinks table, where she was halfway through the second of two vodka and oranges she poured since being deserted, and was also about halfway to becoming quite drunk.

"Edmund, you returned!" And she smiled enormously, and clasped his wrist with a moist, warm hand, and pulled him to her to resume their dancing. She now swayed and pressed against him with more confidence. Edmund felt bruised and badly used by women, but smiled and flirted with her, to her great delight.

Whilst talking and dancing, he could not resist looking over to the centre of the room, where he could see Karl and Leela in conversation, or laughing at some joke of Karl's, or flirting with one another. Edmund was relieved that she was amused, and that he did not have to be with her tonight.

"Take me into the fresh air, Edmund!" Angel said, quite suddenly, after they had been dancing for half an hour. She was, he noticed, now quite prepared to bully him.

"Er ... OK. It may be cold... and."

"I'll get my wrap on the way out ..."

They left the house into the garden. The air was windless and frosty, and not unpleasant.

"Cigarette?" She inquired, turning to him as he followed her.

"No, thank you."

She did not speak, but led the way to a garden bench, and sat down. Edmund remained standing.

"Poor boy! Fancy being foisted on an old trout like me!"

Edmund laughed. She hummed a tune, between heavy gulps of tobacco smoke:

"You could have done worse. Marie Gollembeck, I noticed, was on the point of having a frightful row with her husband, and she, my boy, she *smells*!"

Edmund laughed at this, and felt a new warmth for Angel, as he sat down next to her:

"Why does anyone get married?" He blurted out, not prepared for what he was saying.

"There are, I should say, many reasons," mused Angel, drawing heavily on her cigarette: "But your implication is correct, Edmund. Why the hell was such a stultifying, imprisoning, deforming mode of living invented? Or more interestingly, why has it survived so long? My beautiful man," she said, beaming through the darkness into his face, eyes sparkling now, cheeks blushing with excitement and pleasure:

"My beautiful man, let's raise our glasses to toast 'The End of Marriage'"

"I don't know. That's why I was asking, Angel ...."

"Oh bugger your don't know. I have twenty years, three children, a bloated waistline and no true vocation which says - end it! Now - don't argue, toast!"

Edmund laughed again, and again, he briefly observed, he could not resist a woman ...

After the toast, she stared out into the night, and said:

"Can you teach me to draw? I was good at art, and would have gone to art school ..."

"I'm a draughtsman, not an artist."

"You can draw figures, and trees and rocks I suppose?"

"Well, yes but it's not my speciality."

"Would you teach me whatever it is you know? I'd pay

you, of course. We could go for painting afternoons, if you want. I'll arrange everything, if you can get away."

"I'd be happy to, but I really don't have time. I have a girlfriend ..."

"You have a problem", she said, then bit her lip and frowning, turned to him:

"That was the drink talking."

"Drink talks what's thought", he said, looking down: "go on. Tell me what you think of Leela."

"She's a wonderful girl; brilliant, beautiful. Nothing amiss there. But you and her? Forgive me, but why not climb into the ring with Rocky Marciano?"

"I don't understand"

"Look. I know her well. And I know you also. She needs a different sort of man to keep her happy. You're too sweet, too beautiful, too naïve. I don't think it can work."

"That's pretty depressing, Angel."

"Well, it's what I think. But, I'm often wrong about these things. Look at the boring old fart I married!"

Edmund smiled, and nodded in agreement.

"So how about my art lessons?"

"I'll call you."

"I admit I'll try my damndest to seduce you, of course. But I never tell anyone about my affairs. Not that there's that much to tell. And, Edmund, I'm not brilliant to look at, even worse without clothes, I admit. But I promise, I'll fuck you till your eyes pop out!"

"I'm sure you will" he laughed, somewhat nervously, but he was happy to be with her in the cool night air.

She had lit another cigarette, and said:

"What kind of relationship do you have with Vivian?"

"Fine. Fine."

"She hates Leela, of course. But then I suppose I would if you were my son. Heck, I think I could hate her a bit at this moment anyway!" And she laughed, and looked down towards her shoes. She continued:

"I'm puzzled, or maybe I'm enlightened? At her performance tonight."

Edmund frowned : "What do you mean? She's the hostess, and she's always prided herself ..."

"Yes, Edmund. Don't be offended. It's not what I meant. She's dressed and groomed like a queen. She looks wonderful. And does she flirt with all those wonderful men in there, or even her husband? No. She only has eyes for you, my boy. And what eyes! It's more than a motherly glance she was giving you tonight, my boy."

Edmund felt uneasy. Angel had articulated something he had felt for some time. And now she went on to dig even more painfully:

"The real question is Edmund, do you feel the same about her", and she laughed uncontrollably, patting his knee, apologising, and noticing he was laughing, too.

"I'll say this for you, Edmund. You do have a keen sense of humour, and of the absurdity of life", she stubbed out a cigarette:" I'm pleased, because this sort of talk for someone of a different character could have driven them to suicide", and she could hardly control her giggling, and neither could Edmund, and they ended up in each others' arms, lost in laughter, and Edmund was marvelling how he'd missed so much of Angel K. in all those parties in all those years long passed ...

They chatted longer, and in the midst of talking of

art and proportion, and lines, distance, Angela nudged Edmund and lifted her hand towards the house.

There, haloed by the light from the door, striding tall towards them, was Vivian.

"I'm surprise how benign it is out here", she said.

"Oh, gosh, Viv, but you should have seen us earlier!" Angela laughed, and Vivian laughed too, as Edmund went on:

"Has our absence been noticed? Are we talked about?"

"I'm afraid not, my dear", smiled his mother: "most of them are concerned with matters financial or political."

"Can I get a drink for both of you?" he said as he got to his feet.

"Not for me", said Angel, winking at him, "Nor me", said his mother.

And he left them chatting and laughing in the garden as he re-joined the party.

At the stroke of midnight, there was a silence for a few seconds, then it seemed compulsory for each person to find someone of the opposite sex to kiss and wish 'Merry Christmas'. Edmund made his way to Leela, who broke off a conversation she was having with a young couple, and walked him away to a quiet corner of the room, and she sat on a soft chair, with Edmund perched on the furniture arm, next to her.

"I hope you'll stay, Leela. I've had too much to drink to drive you home."

She looked at him blankly:

"I suppose I'll have to, then. Or get a taxi ..."

"They'll be heavily booked tonight, love. Stay, will you? Look, would you like something to eat? The party will probably go on for a couple of hours yet. If you'd rather go to bed, use my room. I'll sleep down here."

"How romantic of you", she said, her voice heavy with sarcasm.

"Well, we can't sleep together", he said simply.

"No. But you could take me away from the crowd, couldn't you?" She smiled at him, and pulled him close to her. He flopped unenthusiastically against her, and said:

"It would be awkward. Mother or someone would want to know where we were."

"Mother and someone were very interested to know what you and Mrs A.K. found to do for over an hour."

"Well, mother asked me to look after her."

"Have you no energy left after Angel, Edmund? It that why I'm left dry and loveless?"

She got up and poured herself a huge glass of red wine before returning to him.

"You didn't even bother to fetch me. Or make arrangements how I was to get back."

He stared at her, unbelieving of her attitude:

"I invited you here, of course. But I didn't think you'd want to come. You never have before!"

"Which is why you didn't want me to come along, Edmund. I have no doubt what you were up to tonight. Distancing me from your thoughts. You can't deny it!"

"I don't", he answered: "but it's because I no longer understand you."

She looked into his face, her grey eyes shining brightly:

"I am an image of your mind, Edmund. Now we have to mature, the reality isn't so pleasant. I too am guilty. I know that. But I carry an extra responsibility, believing that to do nothing can't be wrong. Your high standards are built upon the assumption that everything has its own momentum. It doesn't. If you could only see me as I am, then you might cherish me."

He put his arm around her, and looked away from her gaze:

"I'll try", he said, helping her to her feet and leading her from the room. Vivian saw the young couple climbing the stairs together:

"Edmund", she called up from the bottom of the staircase: "if you come back down in a few minutes you can have a pot of chocolate or cocoa."

He nodded back down to her, and looked at the girl, and hidden in the folds of her dress, she clenched her hand so hard that her nails dug deeply into the palm of her hand ....

In his bedroom, Leela turned her back to him:

"Unzip me."

He did so, but felt uneasy, and completed the task falteringly and with reluctance. She glanced over her shoulder:

"What's wrong?"

"Someone might come."

Leela pulled away from him angrily, tearing the back of her dress. She turned to face him:

"I've taken the weight of your body many times, Edmund. I'm pregnant by you. No other man has touched my naked thigh. I'm not ashamed of that. Are you?"

"I prefer privacy", he said, looking away.

"Wrong!" she replied angrily:

"You prefer secrecy!..." she glanced down to the bed, her head swaying, and she looked up to him: "I need your passion. I need to be enveloped against the world, Edmund. You know that, yet you're still troubled at being caught out. You are afraid of what's thought about you, of how it's presented", she emphasised this last word, now almost hissing the words through clenched teeth: "your niceness is very precious to you, isn't it? And it is so easy for you. Handsome: you inherit your fathers' charm and your mothers' attractive features. But one thing you haven't inherited from her ..." She pulled him around to face her, and slapped him hard in his midriff: "there's no fire burning in your guts, is there? Your mother burns. She burns like I do. I can see it in her eyes when you're with me. She watched us climbing the stairs as if each step upwards was another lunge into her body. Thank God for that! Even if I don't arouse you, here, in your bedroom, at least I kindle something in somebody."

She collapsed onto the carpet and wept noisily. He knelt down and took her arm:

"I'm going to get a drink for us. Get into bed and I'll sit with you for a while."

He left her there, and she heard the door close quietly behind him. She got to her feet and climbed into the bed. It was cold to her bare skin, and she gave an involuntary 'Ooo' as she lay down. He was soon back with a pot of cocoa and two mugs, and sat down on the bed to drink:

"I was planning to come to your party tomorrow to give you a present. Would you prefer me to stay away? You can open it now, if you like."

"I'll open the present now, so when I've seen it I can decide if you deserve to be invited, still", she answered, grinning at him. He went over to the wardrobe, and fished out a parcel. She took it and examined the wrapping. Edmund always gave great care to preparing anything, and she smiled approvingly at the meticulous way the pale blue and brown paper had been folded and tucked around the present. She looked up at him, and kissed his face, gently:

"The wrapping is so beautifully perfect, it seems a crime to tear it off. So: will you do it for me, please?"

He laughed and taking the parcel, carefully pulled away the wrapping. He handed over the contents which were hidden from view by a layer of tissue paper. She peeled off the covering and exclaimed:

"Oh!", and then for a moment she was speechless. The present was a figure of Buddha, carved in wood, obviously eastern in origin and extremely old.

"It really is lovely, Edmund!" She weighed it in her hand: "and so heavy! But it's exquisitely worked..." and she continued to gaze on it in wonderment. Edmund stroked the statue and she turned it in her hands:

"It's Nepalese, I think", he said: "I got it in London a while ago for myself. Then I thought it would be a good present to give to you."

"You consider I need Redemption, then?" she laughed: "well, it will take pride of place in my bedroom shelf. Thank you, Edmund." And she kissed him again.

"That isn't all", he said, throwing another parcel into her lap. She quickly undid this for herself, and found a pom-pom hat, scarf and gloves: all hand knitted in wool, and colour matched in yellows, greens and blues.

"Just what I need!" and laughing, put them on. He laughed at her appearance in bed, saying:

"I should have got you a hot water bottle."

"I'd rather have you", she said: "even though I can't stand you sometimes!"

He took her empty cup: "You'd better get some sleep. I'll call you about ten."

She smiled at him as he backed out of the bedroom door:

"Goodnight, Edmund." She laid back her head on the pillow and tears welled up in her eyes, and stung her with their saltiness. She breathed deeply and looked at the dimly lit ceiling above her face. If only she could stop things happening, for a while, just to allow herself to take a rest.

She awoke to the sound of the tinkle and rattle of a breakfast cup by her head; and looking up, saw Edmund; dressed as he had been last night, and bright faced:

"Two boiled eggs, toast, tea. Sufficient?"

"Mmm", she murmured, lifting herself languidly onto an elbow, and squinting at him, before yawning and taking the tray. He sat by the window, looking out:

"Snowing quite fast, now", he said quietly. Leela could see the snow collecting on the panes as she crunched into her toast:

"Will you be able to get me home alright, Edmund?"

"I'll borrow Trevor Bartles' Landrover, just in case it's bad, down the slopes", he said, getting up.

"Stay in bed as long as you like, though. It'll take a while to get hold of him, and so on." He approached the bed and kissed her gently on her forehead before leaving her alone.

Leela finished her breakfast and wrapping herself in Edmund's bed robe, left the room to wash. She heard Vivian's voice as she stood on the landing outside Edmund's room, and paused; then quickly went down the stairs. She could now see Vivian talking over the telephone, and as she approached, she was saying goodbye, and then put the receiver down:

"Vivian, do you mind if I take a shower?"

"Of course not", replied the other woman, half-smiling in response: "and there is a clean bath sheet in the airing cupboard, by the bathroom door."

"Thank you", said Leela, turning away to climb up the stairs. Vivian stood at the bottom of the staircase, looking up at her; and shouted up, before leaving the hallway altogether:

"Please use my talc, and so on. Just as you please!" Leela smiled to herself, and opened the bathroom door.

Edmund drove her back home; and stayed there for half an hour to have a home-made scone and coffee, listen to a newly learned piano piece by Pauline, and leave with a promise to return for the family party in the evening:

"We'll save all your presents till then, to make sure you come along!" said Pauline, as he left by the front door, to step into an inch or two of snow. He climbed into the cab of the Landrover and waving through a snow-splattered window, left the Drakes' house for a slow journey home.

CHAPTER TEN

There was no more snow that afternoon, and so Edmund was able to fulfil his promise to attend the Drakes' Christmas Day party. He took with him a great parcel of assorted presents from Oscar, Vivian and his brother and sister. He arrived at seven o'clock. It was dark, of course, but not so cold; and the air was crisp on that windless night. Inside the lounge, arranged in a huge semi-circle around the log fire, was the party: family, elderly relations and a few close friends. They beamed at each other, and at Edmund when he came into the room, and three or four hands indicated the sideboard which carried food and drink. He first declined, but on seeing their apparent disappointment, went back and choosing a mince pie and glass of beer, squeezed himself next to Pauline and Leela.

"Merry Christmas to you, Edmund!" boomed William's

voice as he raised his glass, and most of the others present, joined in the salutation. Sarah tipped her glass in the direction of her elder daughter:

"And to Leela!"

Again, a disorganised chorus of cheers in agreement with this sentiment bubbled self-consciously around the room. The couple laughed, and both blushed, but soon the conversation had resumed its previous pattern of quiet and subdued chatter, and Edmund felt relaxed. He was sitting in one side of a great armchair, with Leela squeezed next to him on the other side: Pauline was perched like a sparrow on one of the arms. Now William approached Edmund, and handed over a parcel tied in a purple ribbon, with a sprig of holly stuck to the top:

"These are all our presents to all at Parkleat", he said, his great red face smiling down at Edmund, and his enormous frame obliterating sight, for that moment, of anything else in the room. He thanked William, then as the latter returned to his chair, he nodded a thank you to Sarah. Pauline, meanwhile, stifled a giggle:

"It's like the total eclipse of the sun, when Daddy comes so close!"

Edmund laughed, and so did Leela, whilst attempting in a half-hearted way, to chastise her sister's rudeness.

"You can't go yet!" shouted Pauline as Edmund stood up.

"Of course not!" He laughed: "I'm going to get your presents."

"Let me get them!" She exclaimed. He smiled, shuffled slightly, then sat down again:

"They're in the back seat of the car."

"Not the Landrover?"

"Not necessary any more. Weather's not so bad", he answered. Pauline skipped out for a few minutes, then came into the lounge again, almost staggering under the size of the parcel:

"These are all our presents!" she said, putting it down at William and Sarah's feet:

"Let's open it now, shall we Daddy?"

"I suppose so", he said, laughing and nodding towards Edmund. Inside the big box, they found all their gifts individually wrapped. There was a bottle of brandy for William, silk scarf and gloves for Sarah, peaked walking cap for John, French perfume for Leela and a record of Beethoven piano sonatas for Pauline.

"This is quite overwhelming!" said Sarah: "and it makes ours to you seem so unimaginative."

"Will you sign my record?" Pauline asked Edmund, pushing it into his lap.

"I hope you like these tunes", he said as he wrote his signature across the back of the cover: "because I chose them."

"They'll be good then, won't they?" She grinned toothily at Edmund, and carefully slid the record into the radiogram cabinet.

At ten o'clock, Sarah hushed the party, and announced that a small record player was set up in the other room and a 'little dance space' had been arranged. She looked pointedly at Leela, so she and Edmund make their way into the room, with Pauline following them. Edmund, then Leela, danced with her, then everyone joined in, and soon the small space was quite crowded. Leela and Edmund sat down in the recess of the bay window:

"Can we take a walk?" he said to her: "outside is quite fresh, but not too cold", she smiled at him and nodded her assent. They left the room, after Leela had had a brief word with her mother, put on their coats, and walked into the darkness. They went down the pathway, passed the kitchen door and to the trees at the back of the house. Edmund stood apart from her as they looked at the leafless branches etched in moonlight:

"I'll not contact you for a while, after tonight, Leela. You need to reflect. So do I."

She approached him, took his hand and squeezed hard with both her palms, then ran her fingers along the back of his hand and kissed and rubbed it against her cheek:

"Alright, Edmund, it's alright ... ", as tears fell onto his hand; hot splashes burning into his skin. He wanted to pull away, but she held herself to him:

"Why are we wasting this time, Edmund? .... Your car. Take me out in the car."

"It'll be more difficult, then...." he said. She took his face in her hands and kissed him:

"For you it will be, but for me it will be easier. And I deserve privilege, Edmund ..."

They drove the car to a nearby farm track, and he got out:

"We'll be more comfortable in the back."

She climbed into the rear of the estate car, and turned the back seat down. She arranged the rug that was always kept there and lay down. He was now next to her, and drew her close to him. He had unbuttoned the front of her blouse and pushed up her brazier to bare her breasts. She squirmed and wriggled, alive with desire:

"Edmund ... Edmund. I want to feel your nakedness warm against me!" and she pulled apart his shirt, and undid his trousers, and pushed them down to his knees:

"There, there!" she said, gasping for breath, pulling at his buttocks with strong hands, forcing him to roll over onto her:

"Stay... stay ... there... just wait..."

She tore at her garments. Off came her skirt and she pushed her underwear away from her:

"Come now, come into me, my Edmund... Just for this time, you're mine again ... Here ... here."

She had taken his hardened flesh, and guided it into her. He was gently pushing into her; but she, seething with greedy fire, catching the last drop of his love, made him hit her hard with every stroke; until, after his third orgasm, he could give no more, and they lay together, his flesh layered upon hers hot and wet, each having only sighs and murmurings left to vent.

They had lain, moving very little, for an hour more, when Edmund got to his knees:

"Ought to get you back. Sarah will wonder where you are."

"She knows, Edmund. She won't even bother asking. She'll be too embarrassed."

She laughed at him, and stroked the side of his face. He looked down at her, and she looked peaceful. The still, white shine of the moon gave her an unreal appearance, like a marble statue; and her deep, red smile: like a ghostly flicker falling upon his mind. He gazed: in wonderment at himself, and herself: at what they were doing; then, and later... To take, so much. To be able to get away with it .... Nothing to pay, nor to give ...

She was right, of course, and he could see that now. He had to do much better than this. He had to feel far more, than he did at that moment.

Part 5

“SALT”

CHAPTER ONE

January 1960

It was almost a year since Buddy Holly died, and although Pauline still played his records, her current favourite was "Cathy's Clown", by the Everly Brothers. This was playing, at discrete volume, early on that January morning. Of course, she liked the record that Edmund had bought her for Christmas, but that was 'music'. 'Music' was enjoyable, but it was not the same thing as 'Records'. This morning she had been first out of bed, and had completed half an hour of piano practice by the time William had come down. He usually had a large mug of tea at six thirty, and had sorted some invoices, or other paper work, before breakfasting with the rest of the family.

"Morning, love. Alright?" William had looked around the door, into the music room.

"Yes, Daddy. I'll do my other practice after breakfast since it's the holidays."

"What? Still on holiday? I'll complain to the government!" He laughed, and she could hear him clump heavily away into the kitchen. She looked back to her popular record newspaper, and re-positioned the stylus to the start of the record, which had just finished playing for the second time. She looked at her reading only briefly, then away, out through the window. The sky was grey, and the bushes cringed under the easterly wind, which blew fierce and cold: "Uff!" she exclaimed to herself, and considered she was lucky to stay home today. Leela would be down soon, maybe. Her sister had altered recently, Pauline thought; and she could not make up her mind whether she liked the old Leela better than the new one. It was funny what made you like some people and not others. She didn't like Aunty Grace because she made a hissing noise when she breathed. She decided to make a secret list, now, before anyone else came in, of the people she liked best of all, in order of preference. There was no doubt who was to be the top person. That was Edmund. He hadn't been around since Christmas day, and she was looking forward to seeing him again. Next on her list was Leela, she considered, but since Leela had definitely changed, she put the name down twice. She couldn't make up her mind which one she preferred, although one thing she had against both was that they kept Edmund to themselves! Daddy was next. She really liked him, and he never changed. She put her mother and John next. She couldn't decide how much she liked her mother. She was always there, around; but she didn't play the piano or collect flowers, and she didn't like modern records. Still, she had to be in the list. She was not as friendly as her Dad, though, so she'd come fourth and he was third. John was there because he was her brother, though he didn't come round to see her very much. He was nice to her sometimes, and often helped her with her maths homework. She looked at the list again, and realised they were all grown-ups. Her school friends weren't there at all:

"Stupid list!" she said aloud, and scribbled across it several times.

She had drunk her cup of coffee, and read her newspaper, when the rest of the house began to stir. John went down to the road to see if it was icy, and Sarah could be heard above tidying the bedroom. Suddenly a cascade of footsteps on the staircase was followed by the opening of the door, and Leela appeared:

"Like a cup of coffee?"

"Yes", replied Pauline: "even though I've had one already. But you come in here. I'll make it since I'm still on holiday."

She dashed out into the kitchen. Leela looked at her Pop Music paper, and tried to make out what had been written in the margin. She assumed it was some Pop Star's name; in any case, she couldn't decipher it. She put the paper down and strolled to the piano, and began pensively playing one of her own first piano pieces, when a sharp knock; as Pauline kicked open the door; was followed by the little girl: a stooping figure, padding carefully into the room so she would not spill the contents of the mugs she was carrying.

"This is the last Monday of my holidays", said Pauline, as she sat down on the carpet, beside her sister. Leela smiled wistfully towards her:

"Why are you wearing that dress today?" asked Pauline, frowning as her sister's purple and brown jersey dress: "it seems such a funny thing to wear, today."

Leela laughed: "Why do you say that?"

"It seems unusual in some way."

"Perhaps I'm unusual, this morning", murmured Leela.

"Are you? I mean, are you different this morning?" asked the little girl.

"I feel exhilarated. Perhaps that's why I chose this dress. You're right, although it's quite old, and I've rarely worn it. It seemed the right thing today."

"'Exhilarated', that's a mood, isn't it?" asked Pauline.

"No, not for me, today. I am excited because I have to do something, and other people will be surprised and shocked... pleased, perhaps?... I don't know. But I do have a secret that they don't have."

"You won't tell me, of course", said Pauline, sulkily.

"I can't. Not yet. Soon, I will. Later today, probably. You are part of my secret, you see. You are, in a way, the key to it."

"Really? That's good. That is really good." Pauline smiled broadly, and sipped her coffee.

In the lounge, William had lit the fire. It blazed up the wide chimney, and he sat quite closely to it as he worked there in the chair. He looked up as the door opened:

"Good morning, love. Come in and sit by the fire", he said to Leela as she came into the room. She smiled and sat on the carpet on the other side of the hearth to his armchair. He continued to make pencil marks on bits of paper:

"That's it!" he said, and took off his glasses: "how's you today, Leela?"

She looked at him as if she was making up her mind about something:

"Dad. I'd like to talk over something with you. Have you time, now?"

"I've always time, Leela", he said, a look of concern coming over his face:

"It's something important, I can tell. Is it bad?" he asked, folding his hands across his lap, and sitting back in his chair. Leela's head drooped forward, and she sat quietly and began to weep. William leaned to her, and placed his hand on her shoulder. She sniffed back the tears, and looked at him:

"Dad", she said, paused and took a deep breath: "Dad. I'm pregnant."

He looked at her. An expression of anger briefly came into his eyes, but quickly evaporated. He eyes rolled slowly downwards and he stared at the hearth rug:

"Will you pour me a brandy, Leela. And the same for yourself."

She did so, and resumed her sitting-place on the carpet.

"Very warming on a morning like this", he said; and smiled slightly, nursing the glass in his hands, his enormous palms enveloping the vessel. Leela smiled as she looked at him. She knew he could not be angry, and that it would not be painful.

They drank the liquor slowly, and both watched the fire crackly, splutter and blaze around the oak logs:

"*I'll* tell your Mum." said William, after some minutes of silence. He fell silent again, but thoughtfully so, before speaking quietly and with uncharacteristic hesitancy:

"Leela... Edmund, and you ... they'll be no marriage?"

"No, Dad."

William looked deeply into the fire, and sipped his brandy. Leela rose to her feet:

"I'd better go, Dad."

"No. Stay here, and finish your brandy. We'll have a good breakfast and I'll take you in. The bank can manage for half an hour or so if you're a bit late."

Leela sat down again, and they finished their drink in silence.

They went into the kitchen, and Sarah expressed surprise at seeing Leela:

"I thought you had breakfasted and gone!" she said.

"No, Sarah", said William: "I'm taking her in. We'll have a nice bit of bacon and egg, if we can."

Sarah seemed taken aback, but began to prepare the food: "Will you have mushrooms and tomatoes as well? I have to do those anyway for Pauline as she won't eat the bacon."

"I will. Yes please", said William, and Leela signalled her concurrence. Sarah set to, preparing the breakfast on a wooden board next to the sink. She glanced over her shoulder at odd times, towards William and Leela, who were sitting at right angles to one another at the corner of the table. Both were looking downwards; pre-occupied, it seemed, with their own thoughts.

"You two are quiet this morning", said Mother: but neither responded, and Sarah did not speak to them until the breakfast was cooked. By this time, she had called Pauline, and four plates of hot food were waiting on the table when she arrived. Both girls thanked Sarah for the meal, Sarah smiled briefly at them, and began to eat, glancing pointedly at William, who suddenly looked up:

"Oh! Thanks, Sarah. Nice breakfast."

She nodded back to him, then turned to Pauline: "is it alright for you ?"

"Just what I wanted, Mummy!" she cried, grinning. Leela looked across the table, and smiled at her sister. She was still so skinny, and seemed to struggle for easy use of the cutlery in her sprig-like fingers. She chopped a piece of mushroom and lifted it to her mouth, and then paused; looked at Leela, and grinned:

"You've decided to be late, then?"

"Yes, I have", said Leela.

"I knew you had", she continued, chewing at her mushroom: "because you had extra breakfast, and you aren't hurrying to finish."

When the meal was completed, William got up and took his coat down from the back of the kitchen door:

"I'll be back directly", he said to Sarah: "there's some paperwork to finish. I may as well do it here and go in after lunch. If you could phone Gordon Bibby and tell him, it'd be a help. I'll drop Leela at the bank, then I'll come straight back here."

Sarah stared at him, obviously puzzled: "yes...

yes. Alright", and she glanced at Leela also, feeling an atmosphere of unspoken thoughts, without comprehending their significance. They had all now left the room, Pauline hand in hand with her father; and Sarah looked out of the kitchen window, just in time to see the car reverse out of the garage. She stared after them, feeling afraid that something was wrong. She tried, but she could not brush aside the feeling. Perhaps William would come back and tell her about it. She shuddered. If it was anything too bad, she'd rather not know. She had finished washing up when William came back into the kitchen. He was looking stern faced, and breathed deeply as he heaved his hat off and place it on the back of the door:

"Sarah: please make us another cup of tea."

"What? But you've had two mugs, William!"

"Then I'll have a third, love. And do one for yourself, and then sit down at the table with me."

"Something's up, isn't it, William?" she said, her voice quavering.

"Nothing we can't handle, Sarah. But first of all, make the tea, then I'll tell you."

She put a full kettle of water onto the gas stove, and sat at the table:

"It's something to do with Leela, isn't it?"

William nodded: "she's going to have a baby."

"What?" said Sarah, aghast.

"Leela is expecting Edmund's baby. It should be born in August."

He walked to the stove to turn off the kettle. Sarah looked up from the table towards him, an expression of disbelief on her face. Whatever she had feared, this was not it. She had no experience of anything like this before, and was severely shocked at the realisation of what had happened:

"But they'll marry, of course. So it isn't like a .... "but William shook his head:

"She won't marry him, Sarah. She won't marry anyone for the time being."

Sarah felt helpless, and she stared ahead of her, unable to accept what her husband was saying:

"I can't believe it of our Leela", she murmured, denying even to herself what she had known for some time: "I thought they were just boyfriend and girlfriend ... like we were...it seemed they might get engaged this year, but..."

She cried, bitterly. William came behind her chair, and put his hands on her shoulders:

"What's done, is done, Sarah. Leela can't be blamed. Nor can he, I suppose. All we can do is to make things as easy as possible for her to have the baby."

"But I hoped her life with us was completely happy, Bill ... why did she have to do this? It makes me feel such a fool, having tried to bring her up properly."

There was a sharpness in her voice as she spoke through the tears.

"You aren't at fault, Sarah. But anyway, it's Leela who needs our support."

"What about Edmund? Surely he should help? Why won't he marry her?"

"She doesn't *want* to marry him. He's offered to. And if she can't be completely sure about him, she's better off without at the moment."

"William: have you really thought this through? The baby will be illegitimate. Leela will be thought of as easy game for any future boyfriends. And not many, even the decent ones, will want to take her and another man's baby."

"I'll make that clear to her, Sarah!"

He had, unusually, raised his voice; and she looked at him as he strode over to the far side of the kitchen. He turned and said very quietly:

"That will be *her* cross to bear, though. That's why we have to be understanding and loving towards her."

"I thought we had been", and Sarah wept again. William grew exasperated:

"Sarah: we've both got to be brave about it. For her sake. It's no good giving up, because the problem won't go away."

She rose slowly to her feet and lit the stove. She turned to her husband:

"I'm not good in a crisis. You know that. I feel sickened and ashamed by all this."

"The perhaps it's time for us to be especially courageous, as well as Leela. We have to face up to it, Sarah; and the better we prepare, the better we'll cope when the baby's here."

Sarah had turned away from him and was about to put tea in the pot:

"Did she say she wanted to keep the baby?"

"Of course she does. Well - I didn't ask her. But I suppose so. You think it would be better to have it adopted?"

"Lots of couples want babies, William. It might make it easier for Leela if she were to arrange for that, don't you think?"

"I don't know. We'll talk about it tonight, Sarah, and if she wants to do that, we can start making enquiries."

The knob on the kitchen door slowly turned, and the door opened slightly:

"Did I hear the kettle?" asked Pauline, her head poking around the door.

"You did, you scallywag!" and William chased her out of the kitchen, into the hallway and scooped her up into his arm:

"You weigh less than a blade of grass!" he exclaimed, laughing and kissing her, and carrying her back into the kitchen. He lowered her onto the table, where she sat, her legs swinging freely:

"The trouble with getting up early", she said: "is that you've finished everything before the day's really started!" and she smiled at her father, then glanced at Sarah, who ignored her.

"Mummy, why are you so glum?"

"Oh, nothing, love. Here's your tea."

Sarah looked at her daughter, her legs dangling as she sat on the table.

"Pauline - how much do you weigh?", she said, sternly: "because if you don't put on a pound or two on those scrawny legs, I'm not allowing you to skip meat at meal times. Even though you insist on doing so."

"I've put on one and a half pounds since last Monday", she said, swinging her legs in big arcs, so that the table creaked rhythmically. William smiled at her:

"You have to get fatter. Else you won't fill the pie!"

"What pie's that?" she asked, stopping her kicking, and picking up her tea cup.

"The steak and kidney Pauline!" he said, laughing at

Sarah, and nudging her. She had now managed a faint smile. Pauline laughed greatly at the remark:

"I'll get as plump as I can before you bake the pie!", she said, draining her cup; and jumping down from the table, went to the sink to wash up.

"Mummy", she said over her shoulder: "I'd like to walk across to Christmas Farm to see Maria. Can I go?"

"It might be slippery", said William:" but why not both of you go?", and he exchanged a glance with his wife.

"Oh, alright", she said: "I haven't seen Allison for a while. She does go on, though ... ", and she smiled at William as he put his arm around her, and drawing her closely to his side, kissed the crown of her head. Pauline had left the kitchen to get her woollen hat, coat and boots for the two mile walk.

"I'll go to work", said William, reaching for his coat: "I think it's best if we both busy ourselves in other business today. I'll see you tonight, love", he kissed his wife on the cheek: "I'm away now, Pauline!" he shouted: "cheerio!"

"Bye!" she cried from down the hallway.

Leela arrived at work that morning twenty minutes late. She was very quiet all morning, and Kitty expressed her concern:

"Man trouble is it?" she asked Leela, as they sat side by side, eating a cold lunch. Leela didn't answer immediately, considered something, then said:

"Kitty, how about the pub? For a change?"

"Yes. Yes, alright."

They picked up their handbags and coats, and went to a nearby inn.

"I'll buy", said Leela: "what do you want? ... Have something strong. I'm having gin."

"In that case, so will I!" said Kitty.

Leela fetched the drinks to a small table by the window, and looking into out the high street, said "Cheers" to Kitty, as she smiled and tilted her glass.

"To you, Leela", responded Kitty, and the other girl looked down, then took another drink:

"Truth is, my girl, I'm pregnant."

Kitty was silent for a while, then said quietly:

"And from the way you said that, Edmund won't marry you?"

"He wanted to. But it's no good pretending we'd be happy together. So I turned him down."

Kitty looked at her, astounded by what she had said:

"Well, Leela! If Edmund had asked me to marry him right now *I'd* say 'Yes'. He's as beautiful a man as you'll find, love. They don't sell those in Woolworths', you know."

"Yes, I know what you mean, Kitty. In fact, that's half the trouble. His very perfection, I find stifling. I can't really live up to it. It's like holding a piece of rare china in your hand all the time. You're so afraid to drop it, you eventually regret having it. You find you resent it, sometimes... Yes, I know I'll probably never find anyone like him again. Whatever it is, neither marriage nor Edmund is for me at the moment."

"Don't be so cocky, Leela! Sorry to rude, but you aren't thinking it out, are you? You'll end up like I've often dreaded. A baby on the way and no man in sight. It'll be hard for you after it's born. And if you want to marry later, you know how difficult it will be ...."

She stopped as Leela, head bowed low, burst into uncontrollable tears:

"There, there", said Kitty, soothingly: "it can't be mended. You must see Edmund at the earliest time. Even if you don't want to settle marriage plans at this time, he can still be around. And you need a man with you now, Leela. Honest you do."

She put her arm round the wounded girl, and one or two people in the pub looked round at them. Leela lifted her head, and stared with damp, raw eyes into the street:

"Why don't I do the sensible thing and get an abortion?"

"Leela! What are you saying? What a horrible thing to say!"

"Is it so horrible?" asked Leela, still staring into the street: "in some ways it's like cancer, growing there inside me, isn't it? Uncalled for, in the way .... fed by greedy enjoyment, not love."

"Stop it, Leela. Or I'll leave you here. You can't mean such terrible things!"

Leela ignored her:

"There's more, too, Kitty ... I don't think I could bear

being close to someone again, like I was to him. His baby would be a continuation of him, you see? It would wind itself around my heart, like babies do ... like he does. It would be another china bowl, Kitty. Killed now, it has no form nor brains: so what can it know? It can't matter to anyone, surely, Kitty."

The other girl, now herself close to tears, rose to her feet:

"Kitty! Stay here, by me, please?"

She sank back into the seat again, and Leela continued:

"Kitty, I need you. I'm very confused. I've not your faith in life, I know, but I appreciate your trying to help me. And talking about it is good for me. I can't talk about it with Mum or Dad. They're alright. I've told Dad, and he was understanding. But I need someone of my age, Kitty. Please forgive my upsetting you ..."

Kitty wiped her eyes with the back of her hand, and picking up the two glasses: "Same again?", and Leela nodded, and smiled.

While Kitty returned to the bar to buy the drinks, Leela took out her handkerchief and dried the tears from her face. The other girl now came back, carrying two glasses of neat iced gin, and Leela thankfully drank form hers before Kitty had sat down. They remained there for some minutes looking out into the bleak high street, and at the huddled figures, stepping briskly by; often hidden by the purchases they had made in the sales.

"We'd better go back to work", said Kitty at last: "and tonight, how about us going to the pictures? I was hoping you'd come with me anyway."

"Oh, I don't know... well, what's on?" Leela said as they walked into the street.

"An adventure film called 'The Pride and the Passion' is on at the Empire. I wanted to see that. The trailer was good, anyhow." Kitty gathered her collar up around her neck as an icy wind gusted down the pavement.

"Alright, Kitty. What time?"

"The programme starts at seven. So I'll meet you outside at five to seven", Kitty answered, as they stepped into the bank doorway, and each in turn shuffled through the revolving door.

CHAPTER TWO

Edmund left work that day at five-thirty, and on crossing the road, was surprised by the figure of John Drake walking towards him. Edmund groaned to himself. He was embarrassed by his own complete lack of ability to communicate anything to John, but he didn't feel he could simply ignore him on this occasion.

"Hello, John", he said quietly. The other man was looking serious and intense, and he had stopped walking as Edmund approached closely to him:

"Could I have a word with you, Edmund? About Leela and so on."

"Oh! Yes, of course. Somewhere out of the cold?" Edmund was now standing still, and he could feel the sharp bite into his legs, unprotected by his short woollen coat.

"My office is open", said John; and Edmund followed

him there. He opened the outer door of the bank. There were still several people inside, working; and they passed through to John's office.

"Please sit down", said John, sitting behind his desk, and facing Edmund:

"I went home early today and my mother told me about Leela. Mum's upset, especially since you don't intend to marry. Could I know why?"

Edmund disliked this situation, and felt an overpowering sense of distaste for the man opposite him. He reminded Edmund of some of the worst aspects of Oscar, his father. He looked across at John, and could find no image of sympathy there: thin, empty eyes; mouth turned down in self-satisfied sneer; and his hands, locked together in and impenetrable knot in front of his chest. Edmund, not looking at him, and in a voice so soft it was barely audible, said:

"There need to be good reasons for a marriage. Leela and I have none."

John's brow furrowed:

"Surely the prospect of a child is reason enough?"

Edmund took a deep breath, and John got up from his chair, walking to the corner of his room:

"It will be my sister - and my mother, too - who will bear the brunt of this, you know. You'll be out of it really. Apart from maintenance, which won't trouble your family I should think. All the emotional stress will fall on us."

He sat down again, and looked away from Edmund, who lifted his eyes and said:

"There's no way the course of events can be altered, John. We didn't plan this outcome, but it's with us now. I care for Leela, and I'm around to help her cope."

John raised his eyebrows:

"Let's you off the hook, I suppose?"

"How do you mean?" asked Edmund, puzzled.

"You seem to be eminently reasonable without doing anything at all", answered John.

"Tell me how I can do more", replied the other man, bemused.

"Of course it's too late to censure you for doing this sort of thing, without marriage. You are, however, completely irresponsible. It's *our* family that have to put up with the jibes of the crowd, not yours. And the work of looking after the baby will doubtless be laid at my mother's hands. She has enough to manage. Whereas you don't seem to want to become involved. Even given that you couldn't give a damn about Leela's - and the family's - good name, you could at least take an active interest in what is going to happen when the baby is born."

"I don't know what will happen. Nor do you", muttered Edmund. John strode over to the far side of the room again, then back again till he was near to Edmund once more:

"It would be better if the baby was adopted. Better for Leela, better for our family, and although I couldn't care less, better for you. Anyway, you could help by putting your weight behind the idea. Talk about it with her. Point out the advantages to both of you. A dark cloud in your past will be blown away ... with a baby around her neck, no man's going to rush to marry her, Edmund!"

His voice was raised as he saw and sensed the other's disapproval of what he was saying. He continued with a mounting but controlled anger:

"Perhaps it would satisfy some stupid desire of yours, for Leela to saddle herself with the problem? Is that why you're grimacing and frowning at what I 'm saying?"

Edmund lowered his face into his hands and was silent for some time. At last, he lifted his head and looked at the man standing not too far away from where he was sitting:

"Leela and the baby are the important individuals to consider. Everyone else - yes, myself included - will easily survive. I know something of your sister. Pushing her into any decision about the baby would be no good at this stage. The best thing to do is to give her support; not to get at her, and see how the situation develops. There's nothing to be gained by hasty action."

John turned away and rapped his hand against the desk:

"Which means you won't make the suggestion to her?"

"Yes. It means that. But just to console you, Leela wouldn't listen to any suggestion from me. Not at the moment."

"Damn you, man! I don't seek your consolation! You are the very centre of this problem."

"And you aren't, John. So it's best if you keep out of things for now. I'm not running away. Nor am I denying her. I'm doing nothing, because that's the only thing I can do, of any use, right now."

Edmund stood up: "Goodbye, John", and he turned away and left the room, and the bank; almost running away through front office. On reaching the street, he slowed his pace, but continued to walk quickly, and even though the early evening was cold and dark, he had completed a circuit of the town's shopping centre before he finally jumped aboard his bus. He sat at the front of the vehicle, squeezed into a corner, and stared through the window. The beam of the headlights caught the grassy verge as the bus climbed the steep hill towards his home. He was irritated, and felt inadequate to deal with the situation. John didn't matter, but there was some truth in what he said. Of course he never had liked Edmund. He'd not forgiven him for managing to skip the sort of National Service most others had, whereas John had been forced to go, marching around parade grounds and so on...

Leela and Kitty emerged from the doors of the auditorium of the Picture House ahead of most of the crowd who surged around them. They stood in the foyer for a moment to fasten their coats:

"Coffee?" asked Leela, and Kitty nodded and smiled. They made their way to a small café in one of the backstreets. It was the only place open in town at that time of night, where you could get freshly ground coffee. It was quite full, and the air was heavy and warm with the aroma of the powered beans:

"Mmmmm !", said Kitty, sitting down and pulling the chair close to the small table: "smells so beautiful!"

Soon they were served with their drink. They took the cups in both hands and felt the warmth of the liquid:

"This is lovely!" said Kitty; and sipped at the steaming surface of the coffee.

"Have you thought", she said after some obvious contemplation: "anymore about the baby?"

Leela trailed the tiny silver spoon in her cup and gazed unblinkingly downwards:

"I never think about it."

Kitty seemed not to hear what she had said, and continued in the same slow and quiet way:

"I hope you decide to keep it. I would love to fuss over it, or to take care of it while you were away."

"Perhaps it would be better if you had it, instead of me!" Leela responded, laughing.

"I wish I could, in a way..." said Kitty, smiling wistfully; then more earnestly:

"You are going to keep it, Leela?"

Leela continued to stare into her coffee, doodling the spoon in its surface:

"Mum wants me to have it adopted... she said it as a suggestion, but I could tell she really wanted to be rid of it."

"Shame!" said Kitty, very quietly.

"Oh, Mum's alright. She doesn't like babies... Dad's the one who loves them!" Leela smiled broadly towards Kitty: "you should have seen him with Pauline when she was small... clucking and fussing like a mother hen ... well, she was a gorgeous baby."

The other girl smiled, and holding her head on one side, said:

"There you are then. Why not have *your* baby. That'll be even more gorgeous. To you it will be."

"I don't know, Kitty. Not many youngsters are like Pauline."

"Did you like the film?"

The question came from behind Leela, and she twisted herself around so she could see who it was. A dark-haired man, in his early twenties, smiled across the shy profile of his younger companion:

"It was satisfactory", said Leela, smiling at them: "Where were you two sitting?"

"Just behind you. I noticed you in the interval, and said to Alan", as he indicated his friend: "... that I was sure you were the girl who works in Barclays'."

"That's right. So does Kitty." The latter had craned her head to one side to get into their sight-line, and smiled at the two men. Soon they were all squeezed onto the same, small table; and Victor, as the dark one was called, had ordered more coffee:

"We had difficulty deciding whether to go to the Empire or Odeon", he said as they waited to be served.

His friend Alan looked to the side and grinned, but apart from darting a glance at Kitty, did not look at the other three. The drinks arrived, and Victor passed them around, and organised the sugar and cream:

"We work at Arnolds'. You know it? The Chemical Plant? We're both trainee industrial chemists. We spend three days at work, two at the college. Studying for HND. It's hard work, but we have a good time, don't we Alan?" he said, nudging his friend, who grinned and nodded. Victor laughed and continued:

"We go out twice, or three times a week. Plus always on Saturday to the Rugby match."

"Isn't that expensive?" asked Kitty.

"Well, I'll tell you. Take me, for instance. I get thirteen pounds two shillings and sixpence, after deductions. I pay Mum three pounds a week, leaving me with ten pounds two and six. Saturday - Rugby is two shillings, and then sixpence for soft drink or tea. Travelling to an away game is about ten shillings on average. So I have nine or ten pounds left. You can have a good time on that. Even going out as much as I do."

"Yes, I suppose so... I only get about nine pounds after deductions. And we both pay board, don't we Leela?" She nodded in answer, and then stretched her head above the other people sitting down in the coffee room:

"Bus isn't here yet", she said to Kitty.

"Do you catch the same one?" asked Victor.

"No", said Leela: "Kitty lives at Markham. I live two miles out, on the Lorriby road. So I catch the number eleven, which goes before Kitty's."

"Yes, I know", said Victor: "you could catch the Scarborough bus, Kitty."

"I could, but I won't. It's too late for me. I have to work in the morning, you know!" She laughed, and Alan looked up, and smiled towards her:

"Here's my bus!" cried Leela, picking up her handbag, and standing up, as the pale blue and cream double-decker vehicle turned laboriously in a tight circle as it reached its terminus. Victor stood up also, and smiled at her:

"Maybe see you at the Rugby Match, sometime?"

"Maybe", said Leela: "but very much 'May' and not so much 'Be'." she smiled, and stepped towards the door:

"I'm coming with you!" said Kitty, edging her way out from behind the table: "I'll be sure of the eleven-fifteen if I do that", and turning to Victor: "Cheerio, Victor", and then to Alan, who had stumbled to his feet: "Cheerio, Alan!"

He had lifted his head, and looked at her: "It would be nice to see you again, sometime."

"Well", replied Kitty, smiling broadly at him: "We'll see. If it's to happen, then it will happen, Alan. Cheers for now."

The girls left the café, and the two young men resumed their seats, and continued to drink their coffee.

CHAPTER THREE

The following Saturday

Edmund had arranged to motor to London, sharing the driving with Oscar; to see the West End and watch Tottenham Hotspur playing at White Hart Lane. Spurs was Timothy's favourite football team, and Oscar and his sons set off early, with a grand picnic hamper aboard:

"I'm surprised Leela isn't with us", said Oscar, carrying a first-aid chest, which he placed on the boot of the Jaguar.

"We'll not be seeing much of each other for a while... ", Edmund replied, not looking at his father.

"Pity, Edmund. She's a nice girl. Still, at your age it's a good idea not to get involved. Love and leave 'em! Eh boy?" He laughed, and slapped the side of his son's leg. Edmund had just put the hamper in the car boot, and was standing next to his father, who now stared at the trees lining the driveway:

"Those could do with pruning off..." he muttered: "yes Edmund, at your age, in the medical school, I must admit I had many girlfriends! .... the was, of course, before I met your mother!" He laughed at Edmund, bearing his top front teeth, and his small moustache wrinkled under his nose. Edmund forced a smile, and made his way back to the house:

"Where are you going?" cried Oscar: "everything's loaded. Including your little brother, who seems to have claimed the back seat all for himself!" He laughed at the young boy, who was stretched out fully on the rear seat of the limousine:

"Saying goodbye to mother", replied Edmund, as he disappeared in the front doorway.

He stepped briskly down the long passageway, turning left to find his mother in her workroom. She was arranging various flowers from her hothouse, into several different vases which she had placed in a line on the large, old table before her. As soon as he had come in, she put down the huge spray of camellias and fern together with the scissors she had used for paring them, and beamed at him:

"Have a good time, Edmund. Don't drive too quickly", she came to him, kissing him lightly on the cheek.

"Cheerio, mother .... are you still sure you won't come?"

"I don't like the idea of such a long road journey, Edmund. And I've made no special arrangements for Marsha..." She looked at him, and was silent as she did so for several seconds:

"Some day you and I will go to London, Edmund. Just the two of us. So you can spoil me, my dear ... we'll go first class express train from Leeds. Alright?"

"Alright, mother", he laughed and waved to her as he left the room. Oscar had driven the car up to the doorway, and the engine was very quietly rumbling away as he waited for Edmund to get in:

"Tally-Ho!" shouted Oscar, and the car accelerated, with great rapidity, down the drive; skidding slightly as he had to stop at its junction with the main road.

It took them only five and three quarter hours to get to London, and a free parking space in Piccadilly, with

Oscar driving at 120 miles per hour when he dared, which was very often. Edmund had a grudging admiration for his father's devil-may-care attitude, although he was truly relieved to achieve their destination without any mishap.

Vivian was sitting by herself, in the workroom, drinking a mid-morning coffee. She stared out of the window into the garden. She was impatient for spring to come, and whilst she 'forced' many plants in the large, heated greenhouse, for her nothing compared to stepping across the lawns and selecting the choicest flowers to cut for her displays. The doorbell chimed, and she put her cup down and walked along the hallway to the front porch, where she found Leela waiting, flushed with the sharp air, and swathed in a heavy coat and scarf.

"Hello", she said to the girl, and smiling quizzically added: "come in. Come through to the workroom. I have some hot coffee."

Leela thanked her and followed her indoors, leaving her coat and scarf hanging in the lobby. When she reached the room where they were to have coffee, Vivian was already there, pouring out their drink. The room was typical of the rest of the ground floor, being richly appointed in wooden panelling and eighteenth century furniture, but with few ornaments or wall decorations. By the massive, mullioned window, a crystal vase, three feet high, and flared in great swirls of glass at the lip, showed off the most beautiful of Vivian's arrangements for that day, a spray of irises, full and golden in their flowering, like a deep yellow peacock's tail.

"Those are absolutely, stunning, breathtaking ... !" Leela stared, eyes wide open at the sight of such intense colour in the middle of winter. Vivian smiled at her, and looking back at the display, made a minor adjustment.

"These are for my bedroom ... if I can't have the sun, at least I've these to see in the morning!"

Vivian quickly explained that Edmund had gone to London.

"Of course, you're welcome to stay for lunch", said Vivian: "and I can take you home later."

"That sounds like a lot of trouble", replied Leela.

"I'm going to town for a couple of hours. So it makes no difference to me." Vivian said, pursing her lips. Why hadn't

Edmund told Leela of his arrangements? These flowers did not look right, and she had now a guest for lunch ....

"I'm expecting a baby." Leela had twisted her body around so she now faced the other woman, whose eyes and hands attended several camellia stems. She stopped her attention to the flowers, and looked ahead of her: not at the girl, but through the window ...

"I'm expecting Edmund's baby in August. That's why I came today. I had things to tell him about the baby."

The baby. Edmund's baby. She was expecting Edmund's baby. Inside her. Vivian looked around and stared into the girl sitting by the fire: "What? ... Oh. I see ..." she murmured, and her voice fell away.

"We don't intend to marry, Vivian. Nor be ... close again... I shall have the child, but I won't use it to embarrass you... ", Leela caught her breath, as in her emotion, tears had entered her eyes.

Vivian looked up at her again. What was she doing this for? She didn't need to show off so much about it.

The girl wiped her eyes and continued: "I hope this

hasn't spoilt your day", she sniffed and smiled at Vivian: "I really came to speak to Edmund."

"Don't be silly!" said Vivian, rather too sharply; then in a softer tone: "it's you who has most to worry about ... does all the family know?"

Leela nodded: "Yes. All except Pauline."

"Then you've crossed the worst bridge."

Vivian looked at her, then to her own hands. She brushed off pieces of foliage, then raised her head again. Leela was staring into the fire:

"Well ... there's no point in taking the dim view, Leela. You have a baby to look forward to ... I help bring these plants to life. But that's nothing compared to giving life to a baby of your own... it's really wonderful, carrying it there, inside you ... then, the experience of giving birth is marvellous, Leela. And you look at this little wizened ball of red skin! Amazingly, you love it! Immediately, you love it ... that feeling is always there, with you, even when he's grown up..."

Vivian stopped speaking, abruptly, and stood up:

"Leela. I've just realised. I must go to town right away, if you don't mind, so I'll take you home now. I'll tell Edmund you came to see him."

With this, she hurried from the room. Leela got to her feet and walked over to the table to look more closely at the flowers in their vases. The door opened sharply; and Vivian, muffled against the wind in her big overcoat, stood there, her hand on the door:

"Do you mind if we go now?" she asked, smiling thinly at the girl: "I've lots to do."

"Of course. It suits me better to go now", she answered, passing the woman standing in the doorway.

The two women did not speak for the first ten minutes of the journey, but as they approached a crossroads, Vivian had to skid to avoid a car which had pulled out in front of her:

"Stupid man!" She glanced over to Leela, who looked forward, and shrugged her shoulders.

"Are you alright?" she asked the girl, as they drew away again. Leela smiled and nodded. As they drove along, Vivian cast occasional glances in her direction:

"It's best for you to have the baby in hospital, Leela. If

you can. Please let us help in any way we can. We can get you a room in Moorvale .... Don't fret about the physical side of it. I'll give Edmund a book which is really good. I mean, it's helpful. You can always phone Oscar or myself if you're worried about anything."

Leela smiled again, over towards Vivian, in response; then looked out of her window again and said: "All the snow has gone from the bottom of the valley, hasn't it?"

Vivian dropped her at the front door. There was a brief wave of the hand as she turned the car round and disappeared quickly down the drive. Leela watched her go, then unlocked the door and went in. The house was very quiet, and both the kitchen and the lounge were empty. She was about to go to her bedroom, when she heard a sound from the music room. She looked around the door, and saw her sister at the piano, scrutinizing a score of sheet music.

"Leela! What a nice surprise!" she said, getting down from the stool: "I thought you'd be gone for ages. You usually are when you see Edmund."

Leela smiled and hugged the little girl firmly against

her side: "He wasn't there. He's gone to London to see the football match."

"Why didn't you go along with him?"

Leela had left her side and walked up to the piano. She looked down at the keys, and then played the first few notes of 'Fur Elise'. Pauline came by her:

"We can play a game, Leela ... you must play the right hand, I play the left."

"Oh no, Pauline. Not now. I have a lot to think about."

Pauline scowled at her: "Well, I suppose I have a lot of work to do anyway...", and she sat down on the stool. Leela looked back at her:

"Pauline!", and the girl lifted her head: "I want to tell you something... I'm going to have a baby. Edmund's baby. Do you understand?" Pauline nodded. It was Leela who had told her about people making love, and having babies. Pauline came close to her, and almost whispered:

"Do you mean we'll have a little baby in the house, soon?"

"During August", answered Leela.

"Will he live here?" she asked, obviously unsure of the full meaning of what her sister had said:

"Oh, yes. Yes, of course", said Leela.

"But that's really great!" cried Pauline: "A baby. All of our own. Well, it's yours, I know... but I'll be able to pet it and look after it..." she squeezed herself against her sister, who laughed down at her:

"It's good to know you'll be around to help, Pauline." The young girl looked at her sister:

"Won't this mean Edmund will live here, too?"

"No... "Pauline looked glum:" no, I'm afraid we aren't going out any more."

"Well, there'll be the baby, I suppose... yes, yes..." and she brightened up: "it is going to be really fantastic, having a baby at home, Leela!"

"I thought you might not like it so much, Pauline", said Leela: "you never had Dolls or Soft Toys as I did. I was afraid you wouldn't want a little baby around the place."

"Oh ... Soft Toys are stupid! But a real baby is something you can really love, Leela!"

"Good, good, good!" exclaimed Leela, picking her up in her arm, and hugging her again:

"You have made me far happier than I was a few minutes ago. I was worried that a baby would get in everyone's way... I'd considered living in town in a flat."

"Don't you dare do that, Leela!" said Pauline, laughing and squeezing her hand tightly.

The following morning, Leela went to see the Bank Manager in his office, and told him about her pregnancy and her intention to leave the bank in April, before her condition became too obvious.

"Even so, I'd prefer you to wear a ring from now on", said the manager. He was rotund in figure, with a pasty coloured face and eyes which flicked their sight line down to her ankles and up to her face as she sat opposite him:

"It will suggest to our customers that you're married, and protect our good name. That's not to be taken as an insult to you personally. You must live your own life. It's just that some of our customers take a strong view on personal relationships .... You don't mind about the ring?"

"I don't care about it, if that's what you mean, Mr. Clark."

"Good. That's alright then", he said, looking relieved, and smiling, pleased with himself, he continued:

"But you don't need to give up hope of a career at the bank, Miss Drake", and he leered slightly, glancing down at her legs, then quickly up again:

"You could well come back, you know."

"I'm not sure what I'll be doing. Other than give birth to a baby, that is."

"Well, we might be able to take you back, Miss Drake. Attitudes are changing ... yes, I could see, perhaps being able to re-employ. So don't lose heart, Miss Drake."

He approached her, and lightly pinched her arm:

"Had you confided in me sooner, Miss Drake, we could well have arranged a purely clerical job ... you could have continued here... I can't say I approve of what you've done, but things are changing... these freer relationships between people aren't regarded as being bad, are they?"

"Well, I've told you the worst!" she said, laughing lightly as she got to her feet: "I must get back to the counter now."

"Not at all, Miss Drake. Please stay for a while to talk it over. We're never too busy just now."

She sank silently down into the chair. He came close to her again, and standing behind her chair, leaned down and ran his hands over her arms. Leela shuddered, but felt riveted to her seat, as the man fondled her breasts in a peculiarly clumsy way from his position behind her. His face came close to her, and she could smell the pungent acridity of his breath. She pushed herself out of the chair, and without looking round, left the room, slamming the door. Later that day, she had to ask him to sign a document; which he did without looking closely at her. She felt she could now stay in the bank, if she agreed to wear the ring, until her planned resignation in April.

She went from work that day to the square, waiting for Edmund to come home to catch his bus home, and after half an hour he arrived there, smiling greatly at seeing her again:

"It's lovely to see you. Such a surprise. Mother told be you'd been over. I would have phoned in a day or so ..."

The couple embraced, and then Leela told Edmund about giving up her job, and keeping the baby at home:

"I'll stay in touch with you about the child... I'll not bother with maintenance .... you give me what you want to... you can, of course, come round whenever you want to, Edmund."

He stared at her, not hearing what she had said. He realised suddenly, that they really were going to part. Probably for good. And he felt a current of emotion surge through him. He took her and pressed her body close to his. He kissed the side of her face, and looked at the pale beauty of her profile. He tenderly kissed her ear, and held her head strongly in his warm hands. They stood in silence at the bus stop, he held her by the waist, she pushing her head against his chest. When the time came for him to go, they kissed briefly again, them simply said 'goodbye' ...

This had been even more final than if they had parted for good, for they had at last realised that what had been kindled by the mutual spirit was now finished.

Part 6

“MAYBE, BABY ....
WELL, ALRIGHT!”

CHAPTER ONE

August 1960

It had, so far, been a fine month. On this day, the band was playing in the park. The music was carried across the water of the small lake, and the people on this farther side dawdled and sometimes stopped, to see the band on the podium, and at the crowd which had now gathered around it. A red faced male of thirty years shouted towards his son, who splashed in the water, naked but for his trunks, and screamed with high pitched incoherence back at his father. Young men lolled and gesticulated near to the young girls, who had drawn their skirts up and tucked them into their knicker legs, paddling near the lake side, and screwed up their eyes or shielded them with a thin hand against the brilliant sun, to stare at the audience they had attracted.

Leela had a canopy to protect her baby in its pram, as she walked in the park. She had gone through a feeling of confusion on first becoming a mother; she had then felt relief; but now she enjoyed a warm, tingling happiness for most of the time. She could even feel some sort of excitement at her brother John's impending marriage.

John had changed into his second shirt of the day, and was seated behind his desk in a small office which connected directly with the manager's. He worked at the Westminster bank in Wellawnbury town centre. That evening, the manager and his wife were dining at John's flat, with John and his fiancé, Angela.

He left work at two thirty (with the manager's permission) to prepare the meal. Angela met John in the town square. She had been shopping, as being a schoolteacher she was at this time on her summer vacation:

"The shops are so busy, John! There seem to be more tourists here each year. But I've got everything we need."

She bustled at his side, banging the back of his knees with her shopping bags:

"Oops! Sorry, love! They're heavy..." John had grunted, and tutted as he glanced down at the small, smiling face.

"Oh! I could get no duck pate. So I got liver instead."

"What?" he exclaimed: "Angela: the whole point in getting pate as an entrée was that Mr. McGuire loves *duck* pate."

"Yes, John. I remember your saying; but since there was none, I thought liver pate would be as good."

"How can it be? I don't even know if he likes liver pate... Really, Angela! You should have used more common sense. Why didn't you get melon? Like we discussed? Do you remember talking about it last night, Angela?"

John had now stopped walking and faced her. She looked down at the pavement:

"Of course I do, John. But I thought liver pate would be better than melon. Since he likes pate."

"He likes *duck* pate, Anglela. *Duck*, not liver. That means we'd better get some melon."

"Then we must hurry, or they'll be gone", said Angela abruptly, and walked off quickly, back in the direction from which they had already come:

"And I hope", she said, in a prickly tone: "that you have got all the wines and cigars, and so on? And the coffee?"

"Of course", he retorted: "that was obtained yesterday, Angela"; his tone softer and defensive: "to you it seems a little thing, I know... but you'd be surprised at the things which will influence these executives when they come to consider people for promotion. I read an American article the other day..."

He broke off as they had to step into single file on entering the fruit shop:

"I wish Dad would do something about the layout of this place", he muttered to himself as they pushed their way to a stall at the back of the store.

They got back to John's flat at 4 o'clock, and had three hours and a half to prepare the meal. Angela put the melon to one side: "I'll do that just before the meal to keep it fresh", and she now put out lemons, cream, sugar and eggs:

"I'll make the mousse now. It will keep in the fridge and save doing it later on."

John watched her, and listened anxiously to what his fiancée was saying:

"As long as you're sure about that... let's have a look at the steak."

"It was three shillings and six pence a pound, John", Angela said, pointedly pouting and giving him an open-eyed look. He murmured almost approval at the high price, but still he examined it carefully:

"Are you sure it's pure fillet steak? Where did you get it from?"

"Carson's. Yes of course it's fillet. Stop fussing so much!" She slapped the meat into the greaseproof wrapping and put it into the fridge: "and it would be better if you left this to me, John."

He grunted, and lowering his chin, rubbed it slowly with his thumb:

"I'll get a shave. Also, I have some work to do, if I want to discuss the Sealy Brothers loan tonight", and he left the kitchen, giving one last thoughtful look towards the food purchases.

* * *

"Delicious, Angela!", proclaimed Mr. McGuire, Manager of Martin's Bank, Wellawnbury:

"I love steak! And this is a prime example of fillet. Of course, many would say that in spite of the fact it's cheaper, rump is best. Tastier." He chewed the flesh rapidly and grinned at his host:

"It *is* well cooked, John. You have the makings of a happy marriage. Food is the most important aspect of our domestic life, John. If we are well fed, we do our work better and enjoy life more. Truly, we do."

"More mushrooms, Mr. McGuire?" Angela smiled across the table at him, and his eyes bulged slightly behind his thick glasses:

"Yes, please, Angela", he said huskily, and grinned at his host: "this is quite a pleasant way to spend a Friday evening, isn't it, John? Eating well, drinking good wine."

"The wine is good, John", whispered Mrs. McGuire, a shapeless woman with a small, oval face, who had said very little during the meal, and when she had done so, had said the words in a hushed voice.

"Thank you, Mrs. McGuire. It is one of the finest French

wines produced from the Bordeaux region since the war...", John looked from the wife to Mr. McGuire, but the manager had returned to his food.

By ten o'clock, the four people were seated in a softly lit lounge, and a coal fire supplemented the radiators around the wall:

"I do love a coal fire, John", said Mrs. McGuire, smiling at him as he poured the last of the bottle into her glass. He went over to the sideboard, and took a box of cigars from one of the drawers: "Cigar, Mr. McGuire?"

"Thank you! Thank you, indeed!", he gloated as he read the label: "I hope, John, that you have not misappropriated bank funds to purchase these!", and he guffawed loudly, looking at each of the company in turn, who all laughed, after some little hesitation, as roundly as he had done.

The two men smoked their cigars, and John had opened the second bottle of wine, when he went to the sideboard drawer again, and produced the documents on which he had been working earlier that evening, before his guests had arrived:

"I've calculated the figures for the Sealy Brothers loan, Mr. McGuire."

"You should have shown me these before the second bottle of wine, John!" said the fat manager: "Still, let's see them ... mmm .... you've extracted these from last year's figures... well what would you say to him, Mr. Assistant Manager? Eh?", and he smiled, took off his glasses and rubbed then on his handkerchief with exaggerated vigour:

"I think we should grant only half. According to the valuations of the property they're offering for security", replied John, leaning towards Mr. McGuire, and pointing to some figures on the paper which the man was holding.

"Valuations should be taken with a pinch of salt, John. Be careful of them! What happens if the whole thing goes up the shoot? Forced sale of assets, etc? We wouldn't get the valuation price, John. And we don't need the business. If ever you're in doubt, don't do it! Cardinal rule of banking! You understand, eh, John?", he laughed, and smiled at him, and poured more wine into his glass:

"Yes. I can see that now, Mr. McGuire. Thankyou, I'll

put this away now... I was discussing, with my fiancée... we'll be married next year... hopefully in April."

"Ah-ha! You'll be getting a year's tax back!" said the other man:

"Oh! Yes! We will... well... we were discussing the possibility of moving to our own house, soon after that, if we could."

"And you want the bank to help you with raising the money? But there's no problem, John. You barely need to ask. You know we have arrangements for employees."

"Not from that point of view, sir. I was wondering if there were any plans, any possibility of a move in the next, say, eighteen months? Anything you might know?"

"Promotion! That's what you're talking about, isn't it, John? Eh?", said McGuire, smirking at the other man, who pursed his lips, and putting his hands together, looked down and nodded self-consciously: "I hoped that..." he started, but McGuire leaned forward and patted his knee:

"You hoped for a more senior post elsewhere. Bigger branch perhaps?"

John looked at him and nodded: "Yes, sir. I feel I'm ready for a move."

"Then I'm sorry, I have to disappoint you", said McGuire, grim faced. The conversation that had been progressing on the subject of children and public schools between the two women, suddenly stopped as they too became aware of the hiatus. The manager looked over to Angela, and shook his head:

"Did you plan to leave Wellawnbury? Your home town?"

"We didn't plan it. We didn't assume I'd be promoted, but I had hoped."

"Well, I'm the one who's going", he interrupted: "to London. Management course, senior appointment thereafter. But you, John, are staying here, as far as I know."

"I see", said John, very quietly: "what are the plans for me? Do you know, Mr. McGuire?"

"I can't say for certain; so you, and you too, Angela, must be pledged to secrecy."

He smirked, and looked over the top of his glasses firstly at the young woman, who sat with her knees press tightly together, with her hands clasped upon them; then at John, who leaned forward again as if he found McGuire's words difficult to hear.

"I think", began McGuire, taking a deep breath and sitting up in his chair: "I think that the Area Office have recommended your taking over as Acting Manager when I go..." he paused as Angela stifled a squeal of excitement, jerking her knee-hand arrangement to and fro rapidly. McGuire smirk widened, and he nodded towards her, and winked:

"And if all goes alright, then your appointment as my successor will be confirmed."

"Aah!" cried Angela, to be gently admonished by her fiancé:

"Do you mean", said John: "that I could be manager of our branch?"

"Within the year. If Area Office confirms... until then, my boy, better do all you can to impress me!", and he laughed loudly, and winked at Angela again, who blushed greatly, and brought her clenched hands to her mouth, and gently bit them.

CHAPTER TWO

Whilst her baby boy slept, Leela and her sister Pauline, were discussing John's marriage:

"What sort of dress will Angela be wearing, Leela?" asked the little girl, doodling some tiny sketches in her note book, as she sat on the floor while her sister attended some darning:

"I believe that she will wear a white dress, with a full skirt."

"Will I wear the same, then?" She had now finished the drawing and looked at it, swaying her head from side to side to get a different view:

"Of course not. She's the bride. You are a bridesmaid... they haven't decided, but I should think you'll have a pink dress."

"After St. James', where to then?" and she looked up

at Leela, whose eyes strained to see the work she was holding:

"What? Oh ... here, I think", and she looked more closely at her mending: "yes, Pauline. I think the reception will be here... it's usually the girl's house, but Angela's isn't big enough... There'll be a lot of people. Fifty. Maybe a hundred."

Pauline's eyes opened very wide:

"*That* many! Who'll do all the cooking?"

Leela looked up and smiled: "No-one here. Grangers, the caterers in town, will be used I should think."

Pauline looked disappointed: "And I was hoping we could have done something together."

"We can", said Leela: "Mum said that Angela's parents are overawed by the organisation. so it's up to us to do it all. And mum isn't all that keen, and Dad's busy, of course... So! I volunteered. And I assumed you'd help me of course."

She had now completed her darning and had put the clothing down by her side. Pauline quickly joined her sister:

"That's great, Leela!" she said, squirming with delight and hugging the other girl excitedly.

"We could start by putting down suggestions about food. Then we could think about how it's to be arranged..." Leela stopped, as she could see Pauline was frowning:

"What's wrong?"

"I suppose we can't have a vegetarian meal?" she asked.

"Oh, no Pauline... at least, only if the bride and groom agreed. And John wouldn't in a hundred years. I'm afraid you're going to be in a tiny minority for the rest of your life on that point. Most people like to eat meat."

"When I marry", said Pauline: "my reception will be vegetarian... big potatoes baked in their jackets and sprinkled with black pepper... grilled cheese and brown bread ... and beans. Oh! And lots of fresh fruit and biscuits."

Leela laughed: "Sounds very appetising. I'll look forward to your invitation."

"I don't think I'll be married in church, though. All the vicars I know seem to be so grumpy. I'd like to wear a huge dress with lots of white lace. Like those dresses the Victorian ladies wore... don't you agree, Leela, that it would be good to have a Victorian wedding?"

"Yes. The way you put it, it sounds splendid... however, it is our John's wedding next April, not yours."

"Well", said Pauline slowly, looking over her shoulder through the window, as a sparkling shower of rain spangled the foliage in the garden: "I might not be married. I would like the ceremony, though. Mind you, apart from special people like you and Dad, I think I'd rather have animals as my guests."

"What?" laughed her sister: "have lots of dogs and cats at your wedding?"

"Not only those. I'd invite crows, rats and foxes. The animals everyone dislikes."

"Ugh! I like foxes and crows, but I don't think I could stand rats as guests, Pauline!"

"I'm sure they'd be alright if we didn't hate them so much. Even Dad dislikes them, and he's the softest person I know."

"Maybe", said Leela, staring at the silver splashes on the window pane: "but people will always dislike rats, while they behave just as we do. Using our cunning to grab all we can."

She had fixed an unblinking eye on a droplet of water, which now rolled very slowly down the window pane.

"What are you staring at?" grinned the young girl, looking towards the window.

"Oh!" Leela jerked her head back with a start: "nothing specially. I was just day-dreaming about something I did."

"From the look on your face, you regret doing it", said Pauline.

"Yes. I do. But can't undo... but about your animals. Why don't we have a cat or a dog? I'm surprised you haven't insisted on having an animal yet. When I was little, we had an old dog called Benjamin."

"That's just it, Leela. I thought about it when dad asked me if I'd like one. What happens when they're ill? I'd suffer just as much as they would. If I didn't, I'd worry about not loving them enough. I couldn't bear them to die before I did. I don't seem to care too much about my own death, but I worry terribly about other creatures'."

"You should be careful about talking that way, Pauline. Some people will misunderstand, and simply make fun of you. You could find life difficult."

"Oh, don't worry. I know who it's worth talking too, Leela. Besides I don't much care about what people think about me."

"It's good to feel that, I believe, Pauline. However, don't shut *everything* out. Be prepared to give in ."

"Is having a baby like having a pet, Leela?" asked Pauline, quietly.

"I can't really say yet... anyway, it's a long time since I had Benjamin. There are some similarities, though. There's the joy, and the tediousness, and the dependence. But the big difference for me is the curiousness that I feel for most things that happen to you that you can't plan."

The little girl frowned: "I don't understand."

"Well. I didn't plan... say... to be a woman, rather than a man...to have black hair, rather than blond. To be good at English, but awful at Maths. You know what I mean. And then, there was the baby... I didn't plan anything about him, Pauline. Didn't plan to have, nor not to have him. So you see, he's very special. And Act of God, some would say: although I don't believe in God. The little one's here, and I didn't want him, but then I didn't want anything. He's there, that's all ... oh!... I'm sorry to twitter on. I find it difficult to explain."

"I understand you", said Pauline, looking seriously towards her sister: "I feel that about flowers. That's why I like to dry and press them. And. Uh-uh..." Pauline was silent for a few seconds: "Top B-flat!"

"What?" asked Leela, puzzled; and then she realised in the silence, that her baby was crying:

"Come along with me, Pauline. And we'll see what he wants."

Later that afternoon, Leela telephoned Edmund and arranged to go round after tea so that he could see the baby. Pauline was keen to go too, so they caught the four o'clock bus and were there before five.

"Come in Leela! And Pauline!" Vivian smiled and beckoned them inside. It had now stopped raining, and the family was having a drink of various kinds on the lawn, where they were sitting round a wooden table. Edmund and his father got up as the visitors and Vivian approached.

"Sit here", said Oscar, indicating a seat between himself and Edmund. She took the place and Pauline sat at her feet. Leela quickly spread a small blanket she'd brought, and laid the baby there. He was awake, and twisted his head to either side, blowing tiny bubbles of saliva as he did so.

"Oh, Leela! He is so beautiful!", exclaimed Vivian, bubbling with enthusiasm for the little child. Marsha, her daughter, now joined her, and observed the baby, who looked back and forth at the faces staring at him from the pale blue sky. Leela turned to Edmund:

"We went to the park today. It was so hot! He slept most of the afternoon."

Edmund looked down at the child, smiling, and gingerly, very gently brushed his cheek with his finger.

"You looked like that twenty years ago", said Oscar.

Edmund was struck by the beauty, the wonder, and the absurdity of this little creature; which had something of him within ... his pink perfect arms flapped around without co-ordination, and his face was expressionless, but, he thought, there was a hint of purpose about his existence. Edmund was secretly awed, and secretly embarrassed by his awe.

"He is our favourite thing", Pauline was telling Marsha: "and so we do all we can to make sure he's happy."

Marsha smiled at Pauline's words, and looked down at the child, then asked her mother:

"Why don't you and Daddy have a new baby?"

The question was impulsive, and took Vivian aback:

"Because I don't want another baby, Marsha! Don't you think I've had my share?"

"And in any case, we can't have more than three of you arguing over my will!" said Oscar, laughing. Vivian smiled slightly:

"The first baby is lovely. A wonderful experience..."

Edmund had got up: "Come on! Let's take the little thing for a walk!"

Leela also got up, and Pauline scrambled to her feet:

"You want to walk so you can hold the baby, Edmund", said Pauline.

"Yes! It's a good excuse, isn't it?" he retorted.

The three people, and one baby, walked off slowly in line abreast, into the garden. Vivian and Oscar watched them go:

"He resembles Edmund", Vivian said very quietly. Timothy, who had been silently eating cake and observing the group from the far end of the table, stared after them also, and then looked back to his father:

"I'm going to Derek Bartle's on my bike."

Oscar looked over to him and smiled: "Playing cricket?"

"Maybe", answered the boy, and left the table.

"Goodbye, Tim!" shouted his mother after him. Marsha got up:

"I'll go after Edmund. I'd like to see more of the baby", she said; grinning at her mother. Oscar poured himself some iced tea: "I'm surprised, you know, that they never got married."

"I'm not", said Vivian quickly: "he's always wanted the best ... if their marriage couldn't be the best, he wouldn't have it."

"I thought *she* turned him down?" he asked. Vivian breathed out noisily:

"He had to give her the privilege, Oscar. Can't you see that?"

"Even so, Vivian, she's a good looking girl. Intelligent and beautiful."

"Just your type", she interrupted. He was silent.

"You don't have the altruism of your son, Oscar. You would have made sure that the woman hadn't become pregnant, wouldn't you? There would have been no complications."

"As it is, she has no husband", said Oscar.

"She has my Edmund, Oscar! And the sort of man he is, that is more than most women get in a *lifetime* of marriage! Oh, he's told me of his fears and hopes... So I know of what he's what he's given to her. It's love I have never had from a man, Oscar."

"If you're referring to those silly little affairs."

"They're not, Oscar! They're the same sort of affairs you had before we were married. They are important to you, Oscar. More important than our marriage. You have a fond disregard for me. I fulfil the functions you required when you were looking for a wife. But that's it. You carried on with your life as you had before we were married. Never did I feel part of your world."

"You never wanted to be part of my world", he replied, turning and giving her a look of mild contempt.

She laughed: "That's true, Oscar... but there was a time when I had hopes."

It would have been truly wonderful to have been loved, she thought. But not by Oscar, hence she could not feel bitter. In any case she had no wish to ruin the truce under which they lived.

"I'd like to work again, Oscar. Only part time of course. I could help you in your practice."

He nodded and almost smiled. Vivian looked out into the garden. Edmund was holding the baby aloft, and Leela made a face at the child. Vivian smiled to herself and strode out towards them.

Later that same month, Pauline went to the town with her mother and Leela to get her new school uniform. She began at the 'Queen Anne Grammar School for Girls' on the 7th September next.

"It hangs very loosely on you, Pauline", said her mother: "but you'll fill it our fairly quickly I suppose."

The little girl stood in front of the mirror of the outfitters room. She was now taller that a few months ago, but she was still very thin, and her clothes appeared to be held up on her shoulders, then to fall down freely, covering no flesh nor bone. Leela looked at her face through the glass and smiled. That face now reflected the strength of her resolution. Her lips were large and almost sensuous, and the line of the mouth was strong. She had the high cheek bones of her sister, but her eyes were richly brown in colour, and just as striking as Leela's with their blue-grey hue. Around her small, dark face; her brown hair fell in its usual straggles. Leela smiled again as she looked. This woman would never fall victim to vanity!

"What are you smiling at? Do I look funny?" She was staring at Leela through the reflexion of the mirror.

Leela blinked: "Oh, no... but you might do something with your hair!"

Pauline pulled a face, and returned to pull at the collar of her uniform jacket.

"I think that's the best for you, love", said Sarah, her

mother: "if you do grow quickly, it'll save time getting a new one so soon."

Pauline glanced at her: "It's alright."

It turned out to be a busy autumn for Sarah and William Drake. Although Pauline settled quickly in her new school, there were the wedding arrangements to consider. Leela tackled these, so there was not much for Sarah to do. But she did have to check things, and insisted on worrying over the possibility of disasters.

William's biggest shop was being refurbished, and he had the usual business to cope with too. John and Angela were looking for a house to move to after the wedding. They decided on a semi-detached property that would be furnished by the time of their marriage, and which was situated on a small, brand new development just inside the town. Leela could have the flat for herself and her baby (as yet unnamed). She had considered the possibility of feeling lonely there, even though she could go down to the house when she liked, but she wanted some independence, and Sarah did not want a small baby around the house all the time. Sarah never broached the topic, of course; but

Leela could detect her hidden distaste for young children showing towards her baby. She remembered, even with Pauline, Sarah had not exhibited the 'Act of Motherhood' that seemed to be expected of all women. This aroused no ill feeling in Leela, however; merely sorrow that her mother's life did not seem to have been what, ideally, she would have wished it to be.

Edmund was working on some drawings for the council for the 'Piece of Plenty' housing estate, on which stood the plot for John Drake's first house. The local developer, 'Twigg Bros', was going to make an enormous amount of money from the houses, Edmund had been told; and he could easily believe it. The properties were not well designed. But then, he thought, neither is John.

He was still uneasy in his job, and still wanted to travel, but he felt the time wasn't ready for the journey. He could have gone on a month's holiday to India with his parents, but he'd stayed alone in the house rather than do it. He found his parents always argued greatly when they were on holiday, and so he'd resolved not to go with them again ...

Vivian was now acting as locum for Oscar's practice, and did some work for him on a regular basis, too. Edmund realised that both he and his mother were caught, albeit unwillingly, in the suffocating trap of assured, everlasting material comfort, whatever happened. He did not despise it, but he felt he must use it to achieve something worthwhile for himself, and that he was simply waiting, and that the wealth of his father was to be used to give him that time, and perhaps be of some direct assistance ....

He threw down his pencil. Through the window of his office he could see droves of schoolchildren leaving the bus that had just brought them from their camping holiday. They seemed to almost fall out of the bus door, then after moving away some distance, coalesced in little knots in the square before making their way to the various local bus stops. He noticed an old man in the doorway of the baker's shop, who looked at the children with some apparent distaste and disapproval. His head turned one way, then the other, as more of the youngsters arrived. Suddenly he looked up at the council window, and saw Edmund looking at him. He scowled and backed into the doorway so that he was now barely in view. However, Edmund had already returned to his drawing.

By Christmas time, he too felt the need for a holiday, and arranged to visit Aunt Beatrice, his father's sister, and her husband in their cottage near Tintagel, in Cornwall, for the first week in January. They were a childless couple, very quiet and simple in their habits, and most days Edmund went off early in the morning with a sandwich, to spend the day walking alone on the cliffs. He sometimes helped Jessup, as Beatrice's husband was called, on their smallholding, but it was obviously not expected of him, so he spent much of his holiday, as he had planned, alone. It was here on the massive grey cliffs of the North Cornwall coast that Edmund first felt the stirrings of the journey of a lifetime. There was a bleak warmth that this silent aloneness gave him, but he almost felt frightened by it, and so pushed it from his immediate thoughts.

The arrangements for John's wedding were almost finalised. Pauline had hoped to play the organ, rather than be a bridesmaid, but she found that her feet could not comfortably reach the peddles of the old church instrument. Thus at the service, she waited just inside the church door with Susan, Angela's younger sister, for the arrival of the bride. She was aware of the coldness of the stone bare walls next to which she was standing, and of the strange appearance of people she knew well, dressed in their dark suits or bright, pastel coloured dresses. The organ was being played quietly when suddenly a minor flurry took place outside the door, and the organ began to play very loudly. The echo was so great that Pauline did not take the cue, and had to be prompted to prepare herself for the arrival of the bride. She did not like the ceremony, which seemed to her to be very serious and quiet. But when she turned round to take the bride's train for the walk back down the aisle, she was surprised to witness tears in the eyes of many of the adults, including her own mother, who wept profusely as she was held in the arms of her husband. Pauline worried at what could possibly have upset her mother so much. However, at the reception back at the Drake's house, she noticed that she had now recovered and appeared to be enjoying the party.

She thought, too, of the little baby, left with Edmund and family for the day, and she hoped he wouldn't miss them too much:

"I'll be the only girl in the first year who's drunk real champagne", she said, raising her glass to Leela. The older girl smiled and lifted her own glass in return:

"Pauline, where's Susan?"

Pauline pulled a face: "With her mother, of course", she said: "but don't worry. I'd rather be on my own that with her anyway. All she does is talk about her stupid friends."

"Well", said Leela: "she's free to do that if she wants, love."

"Yes. And I'm free to dislike it, aren't I?". She grinned at Leela: "But if I drink more of this I'll not dislike much anyway!"

The table was littered with the debris of the meal as the two girls talked, while at the other end Gillian, Sarah's sister, Sarah herself, and William, were talking:

"It was a lovely service, Sarah", said Gillian, holding her head to one side as she said this, suggesting by her face that it was a very sad occasion. Sarah smiled:

"Yes. Yes, it was. And I'm so glad that he's found himself a good woman, Gillian. It's important to him, I think. It will help him in his career."

Gillian nodded her head slowly:

"Oh, yes ... Is there any news about Leela?"

Her voice had dropped into an almost conspiratorial tone, and her mouth was grimly set.

"Well... nothing. She manages alright, you know", Sarah said, casting a quick glance at William. He looked away from the two women however, and Gillian went on:

"She should put more pressure on that young man to marry her, Sarah. And you should have put pressure on her to ask him. She lives in your house after all ... and it's nothing to do with you."

"Yes, Gillian. I did ask her. But she has her own mind, and she and the baby are no trouble. In any case, she's got the flat after today, so she can be separate... Not that she has to be, of course."

"Yes, but it'll be better for you, Sarah. You're getting no younger, dear, and the strain of it all has shown itself you know."

William rose and left them, and poured himself another drink of whisky.

"Enjoying yourself?"

He looked round to see that he'd been joined by Harriman, Angela's brother, and Becky, his wife. William smiled and Harriman beamed up at him. He was of medium height, broadly built, and his eyes sparkled mischievously. His wife had short hair and a round face, with flat features but a perpetual grin.

"After all the worry, I'm glad it's all over", said William: "and I hope you're well catered for?", he added, indicating their glasses. Both nodded and smiled:

"The couple look very happy", said Becky in a broad Lancashire accent.

"Should hope so at this stage!" laughed her husband, with William joining in with a chuckle.

John and his bride were in conversation with Angela's parents:

"Aye, well", observed Harriman, in his Bradford accent: "he won't get much change out of them two. Mum and

Dad have always been shy to speak to anyone outside the family."

William looked towards the group. His son was standing very straight and appeared to be addressing his conversation to the whole room, although he was speaking quietly. Angela smiled shyly up to him, perpetually blushing and nodding; then saying the occasional word to her parents. Angela's father was very short and dark, and wore a moustache and a head of hair thickly plastered with 'Brilliantine'. He too stared out into the room, like his son-in-law, and sometimes moved his lips to show a measure of agreement with what was being said. His wife was altogether larger than he, and said nothing at all for long periods of time, but simply drank in many small sips from her sherry glass.

"See what I mean?" proclaimed Harriman: "Not a word!"

Becky laughed: "Oh, it's not as bad as that, Harri!"

"Yes it is!" he exclaimed: "I was two years old before he spoke to me!"

William smiled, and Becky nudged her husband: "Let them have their day", she said.

"When we were married", he went on: "they got horribly worried about who was to pay for the do. When they discovered it was Becky's dad, Father nearly died of relief!"

Everyone laughed, then in a lower tone, Harriman turned to William:

"Tell me if I'm being too nosey, but I'll bet you forked out for the lot? Yes, I thought you would. If you hadn't, it would've been The Miners' Welfare or nothing! There, you see! Look! Dad's looking round! I'll bet he's figuring out how he can sweep all the leftovers into his carrier bag without being seen!"

Becky was giggling, but attempting to hide her merriment: "Stop it Harri! Stop it!"

Even William was now laughing quite loudly as Harriman went on:

"It's true! Mr Drake, it's true! He always brings his carrier bag with him ..."

William lowered his head and shook it from side to side in his convulsion.

"You think I'm joking?" Harri pressed on: "You'll see if I'm not! He always pretends it's the principle of 'Waste not, Want not'!"

William was by now laughing so loudly that people turned their heads to see that the fun was. Leela and Pauline both smiled towards their father as they heard his familiar laugh:

"That sounds like a good joke!" said Pauline.

Soon they were joined by an earnest looking young man, who smiled nervously at Leela:

"You're John's sister, aren't you? Yes, I thought you must be. I'm Neil, Angela's cousin. There's music in the next room. Will you come and dance with me?"

Leela nodded and asked her sister:

"Want to come? We'll show you how to dance, won't we?"

The young man nodded rather uncertainly, but Pauline pulled a face to illustrate her distaste at the thought of dancing:

"I'll stay here!"

She was not alone for long, however. A very plump man, about middle age, was hovering behind the younger man; and once he had gone, introduced himself as Neil's elder brother. As he did so, he took a large handful of nuts from one of the dishes:

"Guess what my name is?", he asked, making grabbing gestures with his arms. Pauline stared at him, feeling he was getting angry:

"Don't be afraid!" he cried: "I was acting out a famous bible story!"

"I don't like the bible", she said.

"Why not? It's so beautifully written!", and he smiled at her: "Anyway, I suppose I've made a fool of myself. I was merely acting out the story of Samson, because that's my name, you see!"

"Mine's Pauline", and she took a drink of her champagne. Samson put down his glass:

"Please let me get you some champagne. Beautiful girls should always drink fine wine!", and so saying, he plucked the glass from her hand, and swept away to get a refill. Pauline leaned on the table, and looked towards her father. He was now looking at her, and mouthed an 'Alright': she grinned in response. She had a great affection for him, of course; but more than that: because of her own tiny size, having such an amiable giant nearby was, for her, reassuring.

"I see Samson's cottoned on to your daughter, William!", said Harriman. He faced Samson across the table, and raised his voice just as Samson had got back with Pauline's drink:

"Hey! Sammy! She's too young for you! And too good! And too pretty and too slim, too!"

"I've already started on a diet!" shouted the other man, laughing and then clumsily shovelling another handful of nuts into this mouth. Harriman toasted him extravagantly, and Samson responded with the most enormous bow. Harriman laughed, and turned to William:

"He's harmless enough. Although he'll probably propose marriage to her before he's had much more whisky."

"Don't be so cruel!", laughed his wife.

"It's the truth!", he replied: "And if it goes to form, he'll propose to all the women in this room before the end of the party... and if the replies go to form, he'll be instantly rejected by all of them!... No, no ... He's never managed to land a woman. Strange, isn't it William? I'll bet you didn't know what you were letting yourself in for when you allowed your only son to be married into our family!... Well, Sammy's a funny one. Sad figure, it must be said. He *did* try to lose weight. Went to Geneva for some sort of treatment... Fell in love with a nurse, forgot to follow the treatment. Came back half a stone heavier. Same old story... you would never guess to look at him, but he's a professional scale model builder! Yes, really. No kidding! Does all the government contracts. Not only here, but abroad too! Can't believe it, can you? Those fat, bulbous fingers... yet he's one of the foremost military scale model-makers in the country. His greatest desire is to fall in love... and he can't get a girl to go along with the idea, even though he is a good catch. Good job, honest... would doubtless be faithful and true."

Samson had been listening to Pauline's plans for the coming spring, and the flower pressing she and Leela would be hoping to do. He grinned sheepishly at her:

"I would have asked you to dance, but I gather you don't like it."

"I don't mind the dancing so much as the music!", she replied, smiling at him. She did not dislike his company now that they had talked for some time. He still looked at her in what she considered to be a 'strange way', but she felt no fear, and so it did not worry her. Anyway, he was, apparently, interested in musical instruments, and sometimes repaired very old keyboards in his spare time.

Everyone had, it seemed, lined the driveway to bid farewell to the married couple on their way to a honeymoon in Dorset. It was now getting dark, and was already very cold. Pauline shivered in her thin satin dress, and quickly went back in doors just behind Angela's father. She went into the kitchen as she was now hungry again, but finding nothing to eat, opened the door to the lounge, where the party had taken place. She was surprised to see Angela's father, oblivious to her having entered the room, carefully collecting pieces of food from the tables ...

END of BOOK 1

Milton Keynes UK
Ingram Content Group UK Ltd.
UKHW010907220224
438295UK00001B/10

9 798823 086097

Abo

Susan Stephens w
meeting her husban
of Malta. In true M
Monday, became e
three months later. Susan enjoys entertaining, travel, and going to the theatre. To relax she reads, cooks and plays the piano, and when she's had enough of relaxing she throws herself off mountains on skis or gallops through the countryside singing loudly.

Carol Marinelli recently filled in a form asking for her job title. Thrilled to be able to put down her answer, she put 'writer'. Then it asked what Carol did for relaxation and she put down the truth—'writing'. The third question asked for her hobbies. Well, not wanting to look obsessed, she crossed her fingers and answered 'swimming'—but, given that the chlorine in the pool does terrible things to her highlights—I'm sure you can guess the real answer!

Maya Blake's hopes of becoming a writer were born when she picked up her first romance at thirteen. Little did she know her dream would come true! Does she still pinch herself every now and then to make sure it's not a dream? Yes, she does! Feel free to pinch her, too, via Twitter, Facebook or Goodreads! Happy reading!

The Secret Heirs
COLLECTION

July 2019

August 2019

September 2019

October 2019

Secret Heirs: Royal Appointment

SUSAN STEPHENS

CAROL MARINELLI

MAYA BLAKE

MILLS & BOON

First Published in Great Britain 2019
By Mills & Boon, an imprint of HarperCollins *Publishers*
1 London Bridge Street, London, SE1 9GF

ISBN: 978-0-263-27680-0

MIX
Paper from responsible sources
FSC C007454

This book is produced from independently certified FSC™ paper to ensure responsible forest management.

For more information visit: www.harpercollins.co.uk/green

Printed and bound in Spain by CPI, Barcelona

A NIGHT OF ROYAL CONSQUENCES

SUSAN STEPHENS

For my most excellent editor Megan,
who is a joy to work with.

CHAPTER ONE

As funerals went, this was as grand as it got. As tradition demanded Luca, who was now the ruling Prince, arrived last, to take his place of honour in the packed cathedral. He was seated in front of the altar beneath a cupola with images painted by Michelangelo. Towering bronze doors to one side were so stunningly crafted they were known as the 'gateway to paradise'. Tense with grief, Luca was aware of nothing but concern that he'd pulled out all the stops for a man to whom he owed everything. Flags were flown at half-mast across the principality of Fabrizio. Loyal subjects lined the streets. Flowers had been imported from France. The musicians were from Rome. A procession of priceless horse-drawn carriages drew dignitaries from across the world to the cathedral. Luca's black stallion, Force, drew his father's flag-draped coffin on a gun carriage with the Prince's empty boots reversed in the stirrups. It was a poignant sight, but the proud horse held his head high, as if he knew his precious cargo was a great man on his final journey.

As the new ruler of the small, but fabulously wealthy principality of Fabrizio, Luca, the man the scandal sheets still liked to call 'the boy from the gutters of Rome', was shown the greatest respect. He'd moved a long way from those gutters. Innate business acumen had made him a billionaire, while the man he was burying today had made him a prince. This magnificent setting was a long way from the graffiti-daubed alleyways of Luca's childhood where the stench of rotting rubbish would easily eclipse the perfume of flowers and incense surrounding him today. The peeling plaster and flyposting of those narrow alleyways replaced by exquisite gothic architecture, the finest sculpture, and stained glass. In his wildest dreams, he had never imagined becoming a prince. As a boy, it had been enough to have scraps he stole from bins to fill his belly and rags to cover his back.

He inclined his head graciously as yet another European princess in need of a husband acknowledged him with an enticing smile. Fortunately, he'd retained the street smarts that warned him of advantage-takers. He wouldn't be chaining himself down to a simpering aristo any time soon. Though he could do nothing about the testosterone running through his veins, Luca conceded wryly. Even freshly shaved and wearing dress uniform, he looked like a swarthy brawler from the docks. His appearance had been one thing his adoptive father, the late Prince, had been unable to refine.

Well over six feet tall and deeply tanned, with a honed, warrior's frame, Luca couldn't be sure of his parentage. His mother had been a Roman working girl. His father, he guessed, was the man who used to pester her for money. The late Prince was the only parent he remembered clearly. He owed the Prince his education. He owed him everything.

They'd met in the unlikely setting of the Coliseum, where the Prince had been on an official visit, and Luca had been stealing from the bins. He had not expected to come to the notice of such a grand man, but the Prince had been shrewd and had missed nothing. The next day he had sent an *aide de camp* with an offer for Luca to try living at the palace with the Prince's son, Max. They would be company for each other, the Prince had insisted, and Luca would be free to go if he didn't like his life there.

Young and street smart, Luca had had the sense to be wary, but he'd been hungry, and filling his belly had been worth taking a chance. That chance had led to this, which was why honouring the Prince was so important to him. He held his adoptive father in the highest esteem, for teaching him everything about building a life, rather than falling victim to it. But the Prince had left one final warning on his deathbed. 'Max is weak. You will follow me onto the throne as my heir. You must marry and preserve my legacy to the country I believe we both love.'

Clasping his father's frail hand in his, Luca had given his word. If he could have willed his strength into a man he loved unreservedly, he would have done that too. He would have done anything to save the life of the man who'd saved him.

As if reading Luca's thoughts, his adoptive brother Maximus glared at him now from across the aisle. There was no love lost between the two men. Their father had failed to form any sort of relationship with Max, and Luca had failed too. Max preferred womanising and gambling to statecraft. He'd never shown any interest in family at all. He favoured the hangers-on who flocked around him, lavishing praise on Max in hope of his favour. Luca had soon learned that, while the Prince was his greatest supporter, Max would always be his greatest enemy.

Picking up the order of service to distract himself from Max's baleful glare, Luca scanned his father's long list of accomplishments and titles with great sadness. There would never be such a man again, a thought that made him doubly determined to fulfil his pledge to the letter. 'You are a born leader,' his father had told him, 'and so I name you my heir.' No wonder Max hated him.

Luca hadn't looked for the honour of being heir to the throne of Fabrizio. He didn't need the money. He could run the country out of pocket change. Success had come when he'd nagged his father to let him bring Fabrizio up to date, and had insisted on studying tech at university. He'd gone on to become one of the most successful men in the industry. His global holdings were so vast his company almost ran itself. This was just as well as he had to turn his thoughts to ruling a country, and to filling the empty space beside him.

'If you fail to do this within two years,' his father had said on his deathbed, 'our constitution states that the throne will pass by default to your brother.' They both knew what that meant. Max would ruin Fabrizio. 'This is your destiny, Luca,' his father had added. 'You cannot refuse the request of a dying man.'

Luca had no intention of doing so, but the thought of marrying a simpering princess held no appeal. The royal marriage mart, as he thought of it, didn't come close to his love of being with his people. He would leave here and travel to his lemon groves in southern Italy, where he worked alongside the other holiday workers. There was no better way for him to learn what concerns they had, and to do something to help. The thought of being shackled to a fragile china doll appalled him. He wanted a real woman with grit and fire inside her belly.

'There are good women out there, Luca,' his father, the Prince, had insisted. 'It's up to you to find one. Pick someone strong. Search for the unusual. Step off the well-trodden path.'

At the time Luca had thought this wouldn't be easy. Looking around today, he thought it impossible.

As funerals went, this one was small, but respectable. Callie had made sure of it. It was small in as much as the only people to mourn her father's passing, other than herself, were their next-door neighbours, the rumbustious Browns. It was a respectable and quiet affair, because Callie had always felt she should counterbalance her father's crude and reckless life. There couldn't be two of them wondering where their next meal was coming from. If it hadn't been for her friends, the Browns, laughing with her at whatever life threw up, and reminding her to have fun while she could without offending other people, as her father so often had, she'd have been tearing her hair out by now.

The Brown tribe was on its best behaviour today—if she didn't count their five dogs piling out of their camper van to career around the country cemetery barking wildly, but they'd given Callie a glimpse of what a happy family life could be, and, in her heart of hearts, love and a happy family was what she aspired to.

'Goodbye, Dad,' she whispered, regretting everything they'd never been to each other as she tossed a handful of moist, cool soil on top of the coffin.

'Don't worry, love,' Ma said, putting her capable arm around Callie's shoulders. 'The worst part is over. Your life is about to begin. It's a book of blank pages. You can write anything on it. Close your eyes and think where you'd like to be. That's what always makes me happy. Isn't it, our Rosie?'

Rosie Brown, Callie's best friend and the Browns' oldest child, came to link arms with Callie on her other side. 'That's right, Ma. The world's your oyster, Callie. You can do anything you want. And sometimes,' Rosie added, 'you have to listen to the advice of people you trust, and let them help you.'

'Anywhere ten pounds will take me?' Callie suggested, finding a grin.

Rosie sighed. 'Anywhere has to be better than staying round the docks—sorry, Ma, I know you love it here, but you know what I'm getting at. Callie needs a change.'

By the time they'd all crammed into the van, Callie was feeling better. Being with the Browns was like taking a big dose of optimism, and, after the lifetime of verbal and physical abuse she'd endured keeping house for her father, she was ready for it. She was free. For the first time in her life she was free. There was only one question now: how was she going to use that freedom?

'Don't even think about work,' Ma Brown advised as she swivelled around in the front seat to speak to Callie. 'Our Rosie can take over your shift at the pub for now.'

'Willingly,' Rosie agreed, giving Callie's arm a squeeze. 'What you need is a holiday.'

'It would have to be a working holiday,' Callie said thoughtfully. 'I don't have enough money to go away.' Her father had left nothing. The house they'd lived in was rented. He'd been both a violent drunk and a gambler. Callie's job as a cleaner at the pub just about paid enough to put food on the table, and then only if she didn't leave the money lying around for him to spend at the bookies.

'Think about what *you'd* like to do,' Ma Brown insisted. 'It's your turn now, our Callie.'

She liked studying. She wanted to better herself. She aspired to do more than clean up the pub. Her dream was to work in the open, with fresh air to breathe, and the sun on her face.

'You never know,' Ma added, shuffling around in her seat again. 'When we clear out the house tomorrow your father might have left a wad of winnings in his clothes by mistake.'

Callie smiled wryly. She knew they'd be lucky to find a few coppers. Her father never had any money. They wouldn't have survived at all without the Browns' bounty. Pa Brown had an allotment where he grew most of their vegetables himself, and he always gave some to Callie.

'Don't forget you can stay with us as long as you need to, until you get yourself sorted out,' Ma Brown called out from the passenger seat.

'Thank you, Ma.' Leaning forward, Callie gave Ma's cheek a fond kiss. 'I don't know what I'd do without you.'

'You'd do more than all right,' Ma Brown insisted firmly. 'You've always been capable, and now you're free to fly as high as your mother always intended. She used to dream about her baby and what that baby would do. It's a tragic shame that she didn't live to see you grow up.'

She'd soon find out what she could and couldn't do, Callie thought as the Browns and their dogs piled out of the steamed-up van. She couldn't stick around for long. She'd be a burden to the Browns. They had enough to do keeping their own heads above water. Once her father's debts were paid, she'd go exploring. Maybe Blackpool. The air was bracing there. Blackpool was a traditional northern English seaside town with bags of personality, and plenty of boarding houses looking for cleaning staff. She'd research jobs there the first spare minute she got.

It would have been a grim task sorting through her father's things the next morning, if it hadn't been for the cheerful Browns. Ma checked every room, while Callie and Rosie sorted everything into piles for the charity shops, things that could possibly be sold, and those that were definitely going to the dump. The sale pile was disappointingly small. 'I never realised how much rubbish we had before,' Callie admitted.

'Mean old bugger,' Ma Brown commented. 'He probably took it with him,' she added with a sniff.

'I doubt there was anything to find in the first place,' Callie placated. She knew her father's ways only too well when it came to money.

'Nothing left after he'd been gambling and boozing, I expect,' Ma Brown agreed, disapprovingly pursing her lips.

'Well, that's where you're both wrong,' Rosie exclaimed with triumph as she flourished a five-pound note. 'Look what I've found!'

'Well, our Callie!' Ma Brown began to laugh as Rosie handed it over to her friend. 'Riches indeed. What are you going to do with it?'

'Nothing sensible, I hope,' Rosie insisted as Callie stared at the grubby banknote in amazement. 'It's not even enough to buy a drink, let alone a decent meal.'

She would rather have her father back either way, Callie thought, which was strange after all the years of trying to win his love, and coming to accept that there was no love in him. 'I'll put it in the charity tin at the corner shop,' she mused out loud.

'You'll do no such thing,' Ma Brown insisted. 'I'm taking charge of this,' she said as she snatched the banknote out of Callie's hand.

'Think of it as an early Christmas present from your father,' Rosie soothed when she saw Callie's distress. 'Ma will do something sensible with it.'

'It would be the first gift he'd ever given her,' Ma Brown grumbled. 'And as for doing something sensible with it?' She winked. 'I've got other ideas.'

'Sounds good to me,' Callie said with a weak smile, hoping the subject would go away now.

Knowing her friend was upset beneath her humour, Rosie quickly changed the subject and it wasn't spoken of again. The next Callie heard of their surprise find was at supper with the Browns. When the girls had finished clearing up, Ma Brown folded her arms and beamed, a sure sign of an announcement.

'Now then, our Callie, before you say anything, we know you don't gamble and we know *why* you don't gamble, but just this once you're going to take something from me, and say thank you and nothing else.'

Callie tensed when she saw the five-pound scratch card Ma Brown was holding out.

'You'll need something to scratch the card,' Pa observed matter-of-factly as he dug in his pocket for some loose change.

'Close your eyes and imagine where all that money's going to take you,' Rosie urged, glancing at the other Browns to will them to persuade Callie that this could be a good thing if she got lucky.

'All *what* money?' Callie had to smile when the Browns fell silent. Silence was such a rare occurrence in this household, she couldn't let them down.

'It's time for a change of luck,' Rosie pressed. 'What have you got to lose?'

The Browns had been nothing but kind. The money she'd get from the scratch card would likely take her as far as the hearth to toss it in the fire when it proved a dud. 'Close my eyes and imagine myself somewhere I've always dreamed of…'

'Open your eyes and scratch the bloody card,' Ma Brown insisted.

As everyone burst out laughing Callie sat down at the table and started scratching the surface of the card.

'Well?' Ma Brown prompted. 'Don't tease us. Tell us what you've got.'

'Five. Thousand. Pounds.'

No one said a word. Seconds ticked by. 'What did you say?' Rosie prompted.

'I've won five thousand pounds.'

The Browns exploded with excitement, and the next few hours were spent in a fury of mad ideas. Opening a pie and peas shop next to the pub, a sandwich bar to serve the local business park. 'I want to give my money to you,' Callie insisted.

'Not a chance.' Ma Brown crossed her capable arms across her capacious chest, and that was the end of it.

Callie made up her mind to put some of it aside for them, anyway.

'You could buy all the rescue dogs in the world,' one young Brown called Tom said optimistically.

'Or a second-hand car,' another boy exclaimed.

'Why don't you spend it all on clothes?' one of the girls proposed. 'You'll never get another chance to fill your wardrobe.'

What wardrobe? Callie thought. Her worldly possessions were contained in a zip-up bag, but she smiled and went along with this idea and they all had some fun with it for a while.

'It isn't a fortune and our Callie should do something that makes her happy,' Pa Brown said. 'It should be something she's always dreamed of, that she will remember for ever. She's had little enough fun in her life up to now, and this is her chance.'

The room went quiet. No one had heard Pa Brown give such a long speech before. Ma Brown always spoke for him, if the dogs and his brood weren't drowning him out.

'Well, our Callie,' Ma Brown prompted. 'Have you got any thoughts on the subject?'

'Yes, I do,' Callie said, surprising herself as she thought of it.

'Not Blackpool,' Rosie said, rolling her eyes. 'We can go there any weekend we like.'

'Well?' the Browns chorused, craning forward.

Reaching for the television guide, Callie opened it out flat on the table. There was a double-page spread, a travel feature, showing vibrant green lemon groves hung heavily with yellow fruit. A young family of husband, wife and two children capered across the grass, staring out towards unimaginable adventures. The headline read: *Visit Italy.*

'Why not?' Callie said as all the Browns fell silent. 'I can dream, can't I?'

'You can more than dream now,' Ma Brown pointed out with her usual common sense.

But by this time, Callie was already putting her dream on the back burner in favour of a far more realistic plan. Perhaps a weekend in a small coastal resort nearby. She could look for a job while she was there.

'Think big. Think Italy,' Rosie insisted.

'That would be a proper memory, all right,' Pa Brown agreed.

Callie stared out of the window at a grey, dismal scene. Like the rented house where she'd grown up, the Browns' opened out onto the street, but the people passing by outside had their shoulders hunched against the cold. The photo in the magazine promised something very different. Rather than traffic fumes and bed socks, there'd be sunshine and fruit trees. She glanced at the page again. It was like a window opening onto another world. The colours were extraordinary. The people in the shot might be models, but they surely couldn't fake that happiness, or the sense of freedom on their faces.

'Italy,' Ma Brown commented, her lips pressing down as she thought about it. 'You'll need some new clothes for that. Don't look so worried, our Callie. You won't need to spend much. You can do very well on the high street.'

Rosie clearly had other ideas and frowned at her mother. 'This is Callie's chance to have something special,' she whispered.

'And she should,' Pa Brown agreed, picking up on this. 'Goodness knows, she's gone without long enough.'

'A mix, then,' Ma Brown conceded. 'High Street with designer flourishes.' And with that healing remark the family was content.

'Amalfi,' Callie breathed as copying the idea in the magazine took shape in her mind. The thought of a short trip to Italy made her head reel with excitement. A change of scene was what she needed before she started the next phase of her life, and the win had made it possible.

'All that wonderful sunshine and delicious food, not

to mention the music,' Rosie commented with her hand on her heart as she thought about it.

All that romance and the Italian men, Callie's inner devil whispered seductively. She blanked out the voice. She had always been cautious when it came to romance. She'd had too many duties at home to be frivolous, and too many opportunities to witness first-hand how violent men could be.

'Come on, our Callie. Where's your sense of adventure?' Ma Brown demanded as all the Browns murmured encouragement.

She was free to do as she liked, so why not don a glamorous dress and designer heels for once? A few days of being not Callie was more than tempting, it was a possibility now. Just this once, the good girl could unleash her fun side—if she could still find it.

CHAPTER TWO

HE NOTICED THE woman sitting at the bar right away. Even from behind she was attractive. It was something in the way she held herself, and her relaxed manner with his friend, Marco, the barman. He'd just ended a call with Max, and was in the worst of moods. Max had lost no time in Luca's absence causing unrest in Fabrizio. Max had been a thorn in his side since they were boys. Thanks to his mischief, Luca should not be visiting his beautiful lemon groves on the Amalfi coast, but should return immediately to Fabrizio, but this was an annual pilgrimage to a place he loved amidst people he cared for, and nothing, not even Max, could distract him from that. Though on this occasion, he could only spare a couple of nights here.

The woman was a distraction. She was watching everyone come in through the mirrors behind the bar. Was she waiting for a lover? He felt a stab of jealousy and wondered why he cared when she could just as easily be waiting for a family member, or for a friend.

He'd dropped by the hotel to invite Marco to the annual celebrations at the start of the lemon-picking season. He and Marco had grown up together, as Marco's father had worked for the late Prince. Standing at the end of the bar where he could talk discreetly to Marco when he was free, he saw the woman clearly for the first time. She was confident and perky, and obviously enjoying the chance to trial the Italian language. Laughter lit her face when she got something wrong and Marco corrected her.

Feeling mildly irritated by their obvious rapport, he returned to working her out. Her profile was exquisite, though she seemed unaware of this, just as she seemed unaware of the appeal of her slight, though voluptuous body. She was understated, unlike his usual, sophisticated type. He couldn't help but be intrigued. Dressed impeccably, though plainly for this setting in one of the coast's most famous hotels, as if she was playing a role, she was almost too perfect. Her red hair was lush and shiny, cut short for practicality, rather than fashion, he guessed. Her eyes were green and up-tilted, giving her a faintly exotic look. A light tan and freckles suggested she'd been here no more than a week and lived somewhere cooler.

This was a lot of thought to expend on a woman who seemed unaware of his interest. Or was she? His groin tightened when she turned to stare at him boldly and was in no hurry to look away.

Interesting.

'Good evening.' After politely acknowledging the woman, he gave Marco a look that left his friend in no doubt that Luca wished to remain incognito.

Sensing mischief afoot, Marco grinned. They exchanged the usual complicated handshake, while the woman looked on with interest. She was even more beautiful than he'd first thought. Her scent was intoxicating. Wildflowers. How appropriate, he thought as Marco left them to go and serve another customer. 'Can I buy you a drink?'

She levelled a stare on his face. 'Do I know you?'

The bluntness of her question took him by surprise, as did her forthright tone. Out of the corner of his eye, he saw Marco lift a brow. His friend would call security if Luca gave the word, and the woman would be politely moved on. An almost imperceptible shake of Luca's head knocked that idea out of court.

'My name is Luca,' he told her as he extended his hand in greeting.

She ignored his hand. Intelligent eyes, framed by long black eyelashes, viewed him with suspicion.

'I don't believe we've met,' he pressed, waiting for her to volunteer her name. 'I don't bite,' he added when she continued to withhold her hand.

'But you're very persistent,' she said, making it clear there would be no physical contact between them.

Persistent? Outwardly, he remained deadpan. Inwardly, he cracked up. Women referred to his charm and thought him attentive. Clearly, this woman had other ideas. 'What would you like to drink?'

'Fizzy water, please,' she replied.

Turning to Marco, he murmured, *'Aqua frizzante per la signorina, e lo stesso per me, per favore.'*

'Sì, signor,' Marco replied, serving up two sparkling waters.

Her gaze remained steady on his as she took her first sip. There wasn't a hint of simpering or recognition in her eyes, just that desirable mouth smiling faintly. Even now she'd had time to think about it, he was a man in a bar and that was it. She had no idea who he was, and would trust him as far as a glass of water was concerned, but no further. If she was unaware that his face had been plastered all over the news lately, since he'd ascended the throne of Fabrizio, something big must have happened in her life.

So, beautiful mystery woman, he mused as she returned his interest coolly, who are you, and what are you doing in Amalfi?

Straightening the short silk skirt on her designer dress, Callie wished she had worn the Capri pants Rosie had insisted were essential to Callie's Italian adventure instead. So chic, Rosie had said as Callie had turned full circle, wishing she could get away with a new pair of jeans and a top. The Capris were still in the wardrobe upstairs in the hotel, as she'd been unsure which shoes to wear with them.

At least Capris would have been decent. The dress was anything but. Far too short, it was enticing. She could only imagine what this incredible-looking man had thought when he'd first seen her perched at the bar. How could she convey the fact that she wasn't here for *that* type of business, and that this was, in fact, a holiday? The thought of an Italian adventure had excited her, but she hadn't envisaged such a dynamite opening scene. She fell well short compared to the other, more sophisticated women in the bar. There was barely enough fabric in her skirt to cover her fundamentals. She couldn't move for fear of it riding up, and with her naked thigh so close to the man's denim-clad muscles, that was a pressing concern.

'You didn't tell me your name.'

She turned to look at him as the dark velvet voice, with its seductive hint of an Italian accent, rolled over her. Strange how sound could send shivers spinning up and down her spine. Her chin felt as if it had half a universe to travel, as she moved from scrutinising his muscular thighs, to staring into a pair of mesmerising black eyes. Mesmerising and amused, she noticed now. He hadn't missed her fascination with the area below his belt. Her cheeks burned as she volunteered with a direct stare into his eyes, 'My name is Callista.'

His lips pressed down in the most attractive way, drawing her attention to the fact that his mouth was almost as expressive and beautiful as his eyes. 'Greek for most beautiful,' he remarked. 'That explains everything.'

'Really?' She did her best to simper and then hardened her tone. 'I've heard of people being born with silver spoons in their mouths, but yours must have been coated in sugar.'

He laughed, and then affected a wounded expression. 'I'm crushed,' he exclaimed, holding both hands to his powerful chest.

'No, you're not,' she insisted good-humouredly, starting to like him more now he'd proved to have a sense of humour. 'You're the most together person I've ever met.'

He smiled. 'So what is Callista the huntress doing on her own in a hotel bar?'

'Not what you think,' she flashed back.

'What I think?' he queried.

'What are you doing on your own in the bar?' she countered.

He laughed again, a blinding flash of strong white teeth against his impressive tan. 'I'm here to see the barman. What's your excuse?'

'A holiday.' She levelled a stare on his face. 'What do you do for a living?'

The bluntness of her question seemed to take him by surprise, but he soon recovered. 'This and that.'

'This and that, what?' she pressed.

'I guess you could call me a representative.'

'What do you sell?'

'I promote a country's interests, its culture, industry and people.'

'Ah, so you're in the tourism business,' she exclaimed. 'That's nice.' And when he nodded, she asked, 'Which country do you represent?'

'Are you staying here long?' he asked, changing the subject.

The fact he'd ignored her question didn't escape her notice and she gave him a suspicious look. Then, obviously deciding it couldn't do any harm to tell him a little more, she added, 'Not long enough.'

She was enjoying the man's company and decided to prolong the exchange. He excited her. It was no use pretending when every nerve ending she possessed was responding with enthusiasm to the wicked expression in his laughing black eyes. She'd never flirted before, and was surprised to find she rather liked it. This man could turn her insides warm and needy with a look.

'Have you been dancing yet?' he enquired, shooting her an interested look.

'Is that an invitation?'

'Do you want it to be?'

'No, sadly.' She gave him a crooked smile. 'These shoes are killing me.' Twirling a foot, she stared ruefully at the delicate designer shoes with their stratospheric spiky heels. *Could anyone walk in them?*

'You could always slip them off and dance,' he suggested.

As he spoke a band struck up for the evening's entertainment somewhere outside on the terrace. Imagine dancing beneath a canopy of stars, she thought. How romantic. She glanced at her companion, and immediately wished she hadn't. He really did have the wickedest black eyes, which, for some reason, made her think of slowly stripping off her clothes while he watched. She shivered inwardly at the thought. What she should be doing was making it clear that she didn't pick up men in bars. She should collect up her things, get down from the stool and walk away. It was that easy.

Sex with him would be fun. And seriously good.

What was wrong with her? This wasn't the type of simmering heat she'd read about in novels and magazines, but hot, feral lust, that promised very adult pleasures indeed.

'You are extremely entertaining, *signorina*.'

'Really?' Goodness, she hadn't meant to be. He certainly was. Sensuality emanated from him. If she embarked on her Italian adventure with Luca, it could only lead to one place. *Fantastic!* Callie's inner harlot rejoiced, so now the thought of lying close to him, skin to skin, with those strong, lean hands controlling her pleasure—

'Signorina?'

'Yes?' She blinked and refocused on his eyes…his disturbingly experienced eyes. However attractive and compelling she found him, she had to be careful not to take these newfound flirting skills too far. *So the adventure of a lifetime is over before it begins?* The adventure of a lifetime was great in theory, but in practice it threatened all sorts of unknown *pleasures*—dangers, Callie corrected her inner demon firmly. She had more sense than to let things go too far. Concentrating fiercely on her glass of water, she tried not to notice Luca's brutal masculinity as it warred with her inner prude. She gave up in the end. He'd won this point. He was far better at flirting than she was.

What else was he good at?

Stop that now! Didn't she have enough to contend with—a crotch-skimming skirt, and heels custom-made to prevent a stylish exit—without going head to head with a sex god in jeans?

'Another *aqua frizzante, signorina*?'

How did Luca make that simple question sound so risqué? 'Yes, please.'

Oh, so her sensible self was on holiday too?

She wanted to know more about him. What was wrong with that? Chances like this didn't come around every day. *So shoot me if I'm easy.* She wasn't ready to leave yet. And, anyway, why should she be the one to go?

Marco quickly refilled her glass and Luca handed it to her. She sucked in a sharp breath as their fingers touched. He was like an incendiary device to her senses. Using the mirror behind the bar, she surveyed the other men in the room to see if any compared. No, was the simple answer. They were all without exception safe-looking guys, dressed neatly in business suits. There was no one else slouched on one hip, wearing extremely well-packed jeans and a crisp white shirt open a few buttons at the neck to reveal a shading of dark hair. She jumped guiltily when she realised that Luca was staring back at her through the mirror.

'Taking everything in?' he suggested with that same wicked look.

He couldn't be interested in her. It didn't make any sense with so many attractive women in the bar. Had he heard she'd won some money? He might be a particularly good-looking con man on the make, though he didn't seem in need of cash and Marco the barman seemed to know him. Having survived her father, she had no intention of falling for a good-looking man simply because he was charming.

Falling for him?

'You're frowning, *signorina*,' Luca murmured in a way that made all the tiny hairs on the back of her neck stand to attention. 'I hope I'm not the cause of your concern?'

'Not at all,' she said briskly as his direct stare sped straight to her core where it caused havoc all over again. On any level Luca was concerning. Lacking airs and graces, with his rugged good looks he could easily be a roustabout from the docks. Equally he could be a practised seducer. And now was not the time for her body to shout hallelujah! Instead, she should be thanking him for the drink and walking away. 'Would you like a nut?' she asked instead. Luca grinned and raised a brow in a way that thrilled her. 'Before I eat them all,' she added in a tone that told him not to tease as she pushed the bowl towards him.

'It would be easier and far tastier to come out to supper with me,' he said, angling his chin to stare her in the eyes.

Not a chance. That would be courting danger.

'Supper?' Luca pressed. 'Or more nuts?'

She glanced with embarrassment at the almost empty dish—and gasped with shock when Luca took hold of her hand. She had never felt such a shock at a physical connection with another human being. The disappointment when she realised he'd only taken hold of her hand to steady it as he poured the last few nuts from the dish onto her palm was humiliating.

'Enjoy your supper, *signorina*,' he said, straightening up.

'You're going?'

'Will you miss me?'

'Only if I run out of nuts.'

He huffed a laugh that made her heart race like crazy. 'You could come with me.'

She could singe her wings and crash back down to earth too. 'No, thank you.' She smiled, a little wistfully, maybe, but she knew she was doing the right thing. Luca was like a magnet drawing her into danger with those dark laughing eyes. She was enjoying this newfound flirting skill far too much. 'Don't let me keep you from your supper.'

'I choose to be here.'

The way he spoke made breath hitch in her throat. The way he looked at her made everything inside her go crazy. It was everything about him, the Italian accent, his deep, husky voice, and his ridiculous good looks, and perhaps most of all the mesmerising stillness of his magnificent body. She was hypnotised—and determinedly shook herself round.

'Signorina?'

He was waiting for her decision.

'Enjoy your supper.' She wanted to go with him. She wanted to be a bad girl for once in her life. Bad girls had more fun. But then she would have to live with regret. How could she not? She would regret sleeping with him and not knowing him better. She would regret not sleeping with him, and never having the chance again.

'Enjoy your nuts—'

She couldn't believe it when he walked away. Oh, well, that was that, then. Everything went flat when he walked out of the door, and he didn't look back. He hadn't suggested they meet again, and he hadn't asked for her number. She'd probably done herself a favour, Callie reassured herself. He'd expect too much, more than she was prepared to give, anyway.

Saying goodnight to Marco, she got down from the barstool. She felt impatient with herself as she walked away. She couldn't miss a man she didn't know. She'd feel better once she was back in her room. She might have dressed up tonight, as per Rosie and Ma Brown's instructions, but she was still Callie from the docks inside. But not for long, Callie decided when she reached her room. She couldn't hang around the hotel aimlessly; she had to *do* something—get out, see more of the real Italy. This trip was supposed to be an adventure. She wasn't tied to the past, or frightened of the future. Roll on tomorrow, she thought as she climbed into bed, and whatever it might hold.

As soon as he got back to the *palazzo* he called Marco. 'Who is that woman?'

'Signorina Callista Smith? Staying at the hotel on her own, if that's what you're asking, my friend.'

'Am I so obvious?'

Marco barked a laugh down the phone. 'Yes.'

'Do you know anything else about her?'

'Only that she comes from the north of England and that her father died recently, so this is a rebooting exercise for Callie. That's how she described it while we were chatting. And that's all I know about her.'

'Okay. It explains a lot, though I'd guessed some of it.'

'And?' Marco prompted.

'And it's none of your business,' Luca told his old

friend. 'See you on the estate for the celebrations tomorrow night?'

'The start of the lemon-picking season,' Marco confirmed. 'I wouldn't miss it for the world, but can you spare the time? I thought Max was kicking off in Fabrizio.'

'I have controls in place to keep Max on a leash.'

'Financial controls?' Marco guessed.

'Correct,' Luca said calmly. Max's allowance was generous under their father's rule, and was even more so now that Luca had the means to increase it. Max had never liked to work and with no other source of income he looked to Luca to support him.

'And before you ask,' Marco added, 'Signorina Smith is booked into the hotel for another few days.'

'You've been checking up on her?'

Marco laughed. 'You sound suspicious. Do you care?'

He was surprised to discover that he did. 'Back off, Marco.'

'That sounds like a warning.'

'And maybe I've discovered a conscience,' Luca suggested. 'She's innocent and she's alone, and you are neither of those things.'

'You feel responsible for her already?' Marco commented knowingly. 'This sounds serious.'

'I'm a caring citizen,' Luca remarked dryly.

'I'll do as you say,' Marco offered with his customary good humour. 'And I'll watch with interest to see how long your concern for Signorina Smith's innocence lasts.'

He told Marco what he could do with his interest in Callista Smith in no uncertain terms, reminded him about the celebrations, and then cut the line.

What was he doing? He was a driven man with a country to care for, and a practically out-of-control brother to deal with. And he had to find a bride to provide an heir and continue the dynasty. He shouldn't be wasting time on contemplating an affair—wouldn't be, if he hadn't found Signorina Smith so appealing. He had to remind himself that she was an ingénue with her life ahead of her, and, yes, everything to learn. If they never saw each other again it would be better for both of them. She should learn about sex and the harsh realities of life from a man who could make time for her.

Just don't let me run into that man, Luca reflected dryly as he sank into the custom-moulded seat of his favoured bright red sports car. He'd have to kill him. *No!* He had no time to waste on romancing a woman who might have intrigued him tonight, but who would surely bore him by tomorrow when she proved to be as shallow as the rest.

Gunning the engine, he drove into town with his head full of Callista Smith. He planned to eat at his favourite restaurant. She should have been with him. Top international chefs worked at the *palazzo*, but Signorina Smith had put him in the mood for more robust fare. Tomorrow he would work alongside his seasonal staff in the lemon groves. In lieu of more challenging distractions, for which he had to thank Signorina Smith for providing some very entertaining images to keep him awake tonight, he'd fuel up on good food instead.

'Hey, Luca… Alone tonight?' The restaurant owner, who'd known Luca since he was a suspicious child tagging along behind his newly adoptive father, rushed out of the kitchen to give him a warm hug.

'Unfortunately yes. But don't worry. I can eat enough for two.'

'You always had a huge appetite,' the elderly owner approved.

True, Luca mused dryly as he ran his experienced eye over the women seated at the tables. They all stared at him with invitation in their eyes, but not one of them had the power to hold his interest. Not like Callista Smith.

She was surely the most ungrateful person in the world, Callie concluded as she woke to yet another day of sublime Italian sunshine. And frowned. She was staying in the most beautiful place imaginable in the most fabulous hotel, and yet still she felt as if something was missing. But how could that be, when she was nestled up in crisp white sheets, scented with lavender and sunshine, wearing the ice-blue, pure cotton nightdress trimmed with snowy white lace that Ma Brown had said Callie must have for her trip of a lifetime.

If money can't make me happy, what can I do next?

Well, she'd spent most of the money on staying at this hotel, so she wouldn't have to worry about her win on the scratch card and what it felt like to have some extra cash at her disposal for too much longer, Callie concluded with her usual optimism. Leaping out of bed, she threw the windows open and the view snatched the breath from her lungs. Steep white cliffs dropped down to pewter beaches where the shoreline was fringed by the brightest blue water she'd ever seen. Closing her eyes, she inhaled deeply. Flowers and freshly baked bread, overlaid by the faint tang of ozone, prompted her to take a second breath, just so she could appreciate the first.

What was so terrible about this?

She was lonely, Callie concluded. She missed the Browns. She missed her colleagues at work. Maybe it hadn't been much fun at home with her father being drunk most of the time, but the Browns more than made up for it, and even caring for her father had taken on a regular and predictable pattern. She still felt sad when she thought about him and his wasted life. He could have made so much more of himself with his natural charm and undeniable good looks, but instead had chosen to gamble and drink his life away, putting his trust in unreliable friends, rather than in his daughter Callie, or the Browns.

It was no use dwelling on it. She was determined to make a go of the rest of her life, which meant that decisions had to be made. She wasn't going to sit around in the hotel doing nothing for the rest of her stay. Nor was she going to monopolise Marco and risk bumping into the man with the devastating smile again. Luca was out of her league, the stuff of fairy tales. She had wracked her brains to try to find a film star or a celebrity who could eclipse him and had come up short. There was no one. It wasn't just that Luca was better looking, or had presence to spare, but the fact that he was so down to earth and made her laugh. And thrill. She liked him so much it frightened her, because that wasn't normal, surely? You couldn't just meet a man in a bar and never stop thinking about him…imagining his arms around her, his lips pressed to hers…body pressed to hers… That was ridiculous! She was being ridiculous, Callie concluded, pulling away from the window to retreat into the airy room. She could fantasise about Luca all she liked—well, had done for most of the night, but she had enough sense to stay well away.

'Room service…'

She turned and hurried across the room to answer the door. 'Sorry I took so long. I slept in today.'

'I can come back,' the young maid offered.

'No. Please,' Callie exclaimed. 'Your English is very good. Can I ask you something before you go?'

'Of course. My name is Maria,' the young woman supplied in answer to Callie's enquiring look. 'If I can help you, I will.'

Maria wasn't much older than Callie. Her long dark hair was neatly drawn back, but her black eyes were mischievous, and she had the warmth of Italy about her that Callie was fast becoming used to. 'If you wanted to work outside in the sunshine, Maria—we don't get very much where I come from,' Callie explained ruefully. 'Where would you look for a job?'

'Oh, that's easy.' Maria's face brightened. 'This is the start of the lemon-picking season when the demand for casual labour is at its highest. There's a big estate belonging to the Prince just outside town. They're always looking for temporary staff at this time of year.'

'The Prince's estate?' Callie exclaimed. 'That sounds grand.'

'It's very friendly,' Maria assured her. 'It must be for the same people to come back year after year.'

'Do you think I could get a job there?'

'Why not?' Maria frowned. 'But why would you want to work as a picker?'

Callie could see that it must seem odd for her to be staying at a five-star hotel, yet jumping at the chance to work in the fields. 'I need a change,' she admitted, 'and I'd love to work in the open air.'

'I can understand that,' Maria agreed. 'I'd go today if I were you, so you don't miss the party.'

'The party?' Callie queried.

'There's always a party at the beginning of the season,'

Maria explained, 'as well as at the end. Apart from exporting lemons around the world, they make the famous liquor Limoncello on the Prince's estate, and his parties are always the best.'

'Is the Prince very old?'

Maria snorted a laugh. 'Old? He's the hottest man around.'

Two of the best-looking men in one town seemed impossible, but as she wasn't likely to bump into the Prince, and was determined to avoid Luca, her heart could slow down and take a rest. 'I can't thank you enough for this information,' she told Maria.

'If there's anything else you need, anything at all, Signorina—'

'Call me Callie. You never know when we'll meet again,' Callie added, thrilled at the prospect of having a real goal to aim for.

'In the lemon groves, maybe,' Maria suggested.

'In the lemon groves,' Callie agreed, feeling excited already at the thought of working in lemon groves that she'd only seen in a photograph before.

She was excited and couldn't wait to embark on her new plan, Callie mused as she took her shower. She wouldn't be Callie from the docks for much longer, she'd be Callie from the lemon groves, and that had a much better ring to it.

This was his favourite place in the world, Luca concluded as he swung a stack of crates onto the back of a truck. Hard, physical labour beneath a blazing sun, surrounded by people he loved, who couldn't have cared less if he were a prince or a pauper. Max had been dealt with for now, and was cooling off after his drunken rampage in the local jail, Luca's royal council had informed him. He should take this last chance to celebrate at the party tonight, his most trusted aide Michel had insisted. 'I'll come back right away, if you need me,' he'd told Michel. Luca had never resented the shackles of royal duty. He felt humbled by them, and honoured that the late Prince had trusted him with the responsibility of caring for a country and its people. The only downside was picking a princess to sit at his side, when so far none of the candidates had appealed to him.

To lie at his side, to lie beneath him, to give him children.

He ground his jaw and thought about Callista. She could lie at his side and lie beneath him, though he doubted she'd remain calm or accepting for long. If he were any judge, she'd want to ride him as vigorously as he thought about riding her, with pleasurable thoroughness and for the longest possible time. Callista had more spirit in her little finger than all the available princesses put together possessed in their limp and unappealing bodies. But the fact remained: he had to choose a wife soon. His father's elderly retainer, Michel, had point-blank refused to retire until Luca took a wife. 'I promised your father I'd watch over you,' Michel had said. 'What this country needs is a young family to inject life and vitality into Fabrizio, to lead the country forward into the future.'

He'd sort it, Luca concluded. He always did. The buzz of interest surrounding him at his father's funeral suggested suitable breeding stock wouldn't be too hard to find. A very agreeable image of Callista chose that moment to flash into his mind. Callista naked. Giving as good as she got, verbally, as well as in every other way. She might be young and inexperienced, but her down-to-earth manner promised the type of robust pleasure that an insipid princess would be incapable of providing.

And how does this advance my hunt for a wife?

Loading the last crate of lemons, he groaned as he remembered Michel's words: 'Yours will be a bountiful reign with a harvest of children as abundant as the lemons on your estate,' Michel had assured him. Right now it was Luca's face that looked as if he'd sucked a lemon when he contemplated the current selection of brides.

Work over, he tucked his hands into the back pockets of his jeans and eased his shoulders, grimacing as he thought about the stack of neglected folders on his desk. Leafing through them had confirmed his worst fears. All the princesses were excellent contenders for the role of his wife, but not one of them excited him.

What would Callista be doing now? *She'd better not be sitting at that bar.* He'd drag her out, and—

Really? He grinned, imagining her reaction to that. There was nothing insipid about Callista. She wouldn't fall into line, or be content to bask mindlessly in luxury while working dutifully on creating an heir and a spare. Even Michel would find Callista difficult to lure into the royal fold.

Grazie a Dio! The last thing he needed was a headstrong woman fighting him every step of the way!

But a bolt of pure lust crashed through him as he imagined her in his arms. Finding a suitable princess could wait a few days.

Callie stared up in wonder at the royal gates marking the boundary of the Prince's estate. They were everything she'd expected and more. They were regal and imposing with gilt-tipped spears crowning their impressive height, while lions, teeth bared, grinned down at her. 'Hello,' she murmured, giving them a wink. The lions scowled back.

'Very welcoming,' she managed on a dry throat. Should she be using another entrance? Was there a back entrance? Well, it was too late now. She was here. And then she spotted a notice. It was only about twelve feet high. 'Numbskull,' she muttered. Turning in the direction indicated by the bright red arrow, she walked over to a disappointingly modern control box attached to the far side of the gate. Pressing the button, she jumped with surprise when a metallic voice barked, *'Sollevare la testa, si prega.'*

'I'm sorry, but I don't speak Italian very well…'

'Look up, please,' the same metallic voice instructed.

She stared at the sky.

'At the camera.'

Okay, numbskull squared, that small round lens just in front of me is a camera!

The metallic voice hadn't shown any emotion, but Callie could imagine the person behind it rolling their eyes. Finally, she did as instructed.

'The photograph is for security reasons,' the metallic voice grated out. 'If you don't wish to enter the estate, please step back now.'

'No—I do. I mean, yes. I'm here to apply for a job. I'm sorry if I should have used another entrance…' Her mouth slammed shut as the massive gates swung open.

'Report to the foreman in the first barn you come to.'

'Yes, *signor*…um…*signora*?' The sex of The Voice would remain a mystery for ever, Callie thought as she stepped into a very different world.

This was a world of control and order, Callie concluded, as well as extreme magnificence on every level.

Awestruck, she stared down the length of an incredible avenue composed of a carpet of glistening, white marble beads. At the end of this lay a pink stone edifice, bleached almost white by the midday sun. Both elegant and enormous, the *palazzo* boasted turrets and towers that could have come straight from a book of fairy tales. Cinderella's castle, she mused wryly. The driveway leading up to the palace was broad and long, with stately cypress trees lining the route like sentries. Butterflies darted amongst the colourful flowerbeds lining her way, and birds trilled a welcome as she walked along, but there was no sign of the barn The Voice had referred to.

'Hey! Per di qua! This way!'

She turned at the sound of friendly voices to see more pickers following her into the palace grounds. They'd halted at what she could now see was the shrubbery-concealed entrance to a pathway.

Callie scolded herself as she hurried to join them. There was another sign, and it was a huge one, but she'd missed it completely, being too busy ogling her surroundings. The sign read, *'Benvenuto ai nostro personale stagionale!'* Even she knew what that meant. 'Welcome to our temporary staff!'

It was certainly a warmer greeting than the stained sheet of lined paper pinned up on the noticeboard outside the pub, which warned staff to use the back door not the front, on pain of immediate dismissal.

The pickers had waited for her and were all in high spirits. She blended right in with denim shorts and a loose cotton top, teamed with a pair of market-find trainers. She was ready and excited for whatever lay ahead. This was an adventure. This was what she'd been waiting for. This was something to tell the Browns.

It was good news to hear she could start right away and be paid in cash if she wanted. That suited Callie. She planned to check out of the posh hotel and move to a small bed and breakfast in town to extend her stay. She'd already called to confirm the B & B had rooms. She wanted to get to know the real Italy, and, with her father's example behind her, she knew better than to fritter her money away. She'd tasted the high life, and was glad to have done so, but had come away feeling slightly let down. This was so much better, she concluded as she trooped out of the barn with the other pickers. There were no airs and graces here, and, more significantly, no need to wear those excruciatingly painful high-heeled shoes.

The Prince's estate was like a small town. She hadn't guessed how big it was from the road. There were dozens of gangs of pickers working throughout the spectacular lemon groves. This was heaven, Callie thought as she straightened up and paused for breath. Yes, the work was hard, but the sun was warm, the scent of lemons was intoxicating. She had thick gloves to protect her hands and a tool to pick the lemons that were out of reach. The camaraderie was incredible. Everyone wanted to help the newcomers. The party Maria had told her about at the hotel was definitely on tonight, and all the pickers were invited. What could possibly be better than this?

She soon returned to the rhythm of picking. With a lightweight bucket tied around her waist, dropping fruit into it as she went, she loaded the lemon gold into crates that were taken away on gleaming tractors. By the time the blazing sun had mellowed into the amber glow of early evening, she felt as if she'd been working there all her life.

She'd even made a new friend called Anita, a big, bonnie woman, as Ma Brown would have called her, with a ready smile as big as Texas. Anita came from the north of England each year to pick lemons, to feel the sun on her face, to prepare her for the long, cold winter, Anita said. 'I'm on my own,' she'd explained to Callie, 'but when I come here, I have a ready-made family.'

That was when Callie told Anita about the Browns. 'It's people that make things special, isn't it?' she'd asked.

This wasn't just a great way to extend her stay in Italy, Callie concluded as Anita offered to show her the way to the cookhouse, this was an entirely new slant on life, if she had the courage to seize it.

Seize it she would, Callie determined. Her limbs might be aching from all the unaccustomed exercise, but she felt exhilarated for the first time in years. This, *this* was freedom.

CHAPTER THREE

HER ADVENTURE HAD only just begun, Callie realised as excitement for the upcoming party built inside her. Anita had shown her to one of the many well-groomed courtyards surrounding the palace where the celebration was to be held. She couldn't help glancing through the brilliantly lit windows of the palace, to see if she could spot the Prince. Of course, there was no one who looked remotely like a prince, and there was no special buzz in the crowd, so he probably wasn't here. Anita and she accepted a small glass of iced Limoncello from a passing waiter and started to chat. They hadn't been talking long before Callie felt compelled to turn around. She gasped. 'Luca?'

'Someone you know?' Anita asked with surprise.

'Sort of,' Callie admitted. She'd just caught a glimpse of him, but now there was a crowd clustering round, so she could only see the top of his head. She wasn't surprised by all the interest. It was his magnetism that had first gripped her. 'He didn't tell me he worked here,' she told Anita.

'He's a regular—are you all right?' Anita had been about to say something else about Luca, but was responding to the look on Callie's face.

'I'm absolutely fine,' Callie insisted on a dry mouth. Which was an absolute lie. She had to put her glass down and cross her arms over her chest to hide her arousal as Luca looked at her. And he didn't just glance her way. Their stares locked and held.

'Uh-oh. He's coming over,' Anita warned. 'I predict things are about to change for you,' Anita commented sagely. She had to nudge Callie, who was as good as in a trance. 'Better make myself scarce…'

'No, Anita! Stay—' Too late. Anita had already disappeared into the crowd.

Luca saluted Callie with a bottle of beer, and his slanting smile of recognition was infectious and made her smile too. Her heart raced out of control. It was so exciting to see him again. *Too exciting.* She should follow Anita. What was she thinking of, standing here, waiting for a man who looked as if he ate brass tacks for breakfast with a virgin on the side?

Quite simple, Callie concluded, lifting her chin. She didn't run away from anything, and she wasn't about to start now.

And he was quite a magnet. Luca looked better than ever in his banged-up work clothes. Swarthy-faced, with an unruly mop of thick black hair and an indecent amount of sharp black stubble, he was everything better avoided for those in search of a quiet life. *But I'm here in search of adventure*, Callie reminded herself with a secret inner grin. Tousled and rugged, with scratches on his powerful forearms and hard-muscled calves, he even looked sexy when he wiped smudges of dirt from his face with the back of his arm. The bonfire behind him was throwing off flames that provided the perfect showcase for a man who looked like a dark angel from hell come to wreak havoc on novice flirters.

'Luca,' she said pleasantly as he came over, acting as if her senses weren't reeling.

'Signorina Callista Smith,' he countered with a slanting grin. 'What a pleasant surprise.'

'You know my name?' He must have been talking to Marco the barman, Callie realised. She wasn't sure how she felt about being discussed by the two men.

'You can't expect to be ignored, signorina.'

As Luca made a mock bow, she tried not to notice they'd become the centre of attention. She didn't flatter herself that he'd picked her out for any particular reason. If he was a regular as Anita had suggested, she was fresh meat.

His top was tight and skimmed the waistband of his low-slung shorts. It was impossible not to notice the arrow of dark hair that swooped beneath his zipper, or indeed the quite preposterous bulge that lay beneath. To say he looked amazing was an understatement. Even when she tried to focus on something harmless, like his tanned feet in simple thonged sandals, she realised they were sexy too. Her interest travelled up his legs to powerful calves, and on again to where she definitely shouldn't be looking. She had to stop this right now, and *concentrate*!

No! Not there!

She was about to meet a very challenging man for the second time, and she'd better be ready for it, Callie warned herself firmly. Fixing her gaze on Luca's darkly amused face, she determined not to let her gaze wander, but then thought, why not stare? Luca had never been shy about staring at her, and interest wasn't a one-way street. His bronzed and muscular torso, barely covered by the ripped and faded top, invited attention. He was an outstanding specimen. A statue should be raised in the town square for everyone to admire.

'Nice to see you at the party,' he said, smiling in that faint way he had that made her body burn. 'I hope they're serving nuts tonight.'

She gave him a look, half smile, half scolding. He'd stopped within touching distance. His heat enveloped her. And that voice. Dark chocolate tones strummed her senses until they were clamouring for the sort of pleasure she guessed Luca knew only too much about. He towered over her in a way that blocked out the light, which was enough to warn her to be careful. She didn't stand in anyone's shadow. 'Are you here on your own?' she asked, diplomatically stepping away.

'I am,' he confirmed.

His voice curled around her, making her skin tingle. 'No one waiting for you back home?' she enquired casually.

'My dogs, my cats and the horses,' he said.

'I think you know what I mean,' she insisted.

'Do I?' Luca stared at her in a way that made heat curl low in her belly. 'Do you always put people you've only just met through the third degree?'

When they look like you, and have who knows what secrets, yes, I do, she thought. 'That depends who I'm talking to,' she said.

'So why do I get the third degree?'

'Do we have enough time?' she demanded, and when he laughed, she said honestly, 'I just didn't expect to see you here, so it's a bit of a surprise.'

'A surprise I hope you're getting used to?'

His black eyes were dancing with laughter, so, responding in kind, she shook her head and heaved a theatrical sigh. 'I'm trying to be tactful, and I realise now that blunt is much easier for me.'

'I'm with you there,' he said. 'So be blunt.'

'Are you married?' she asked flat out. 'Or do you have a partner, a special friend?'

Luca grinned. 'You weren't joking about blunt.'

'Correct,' Callie confirmed. 'Before I say another word, I need to know where I stand.'

'Do I look married?'

'That's not an answer to my question,' she complained. 'In fact, I'd call it an evasion.'

'I'm not married,' Luca confirmed as she turned to go. She stilled when he caught hold of her arm. His touch was like an incendiary device to her senses. 'I'm unattached, other than being briefly joined to you,' he said as he lifted his hand away. She felt the loss of it immediately. 'Does that satisfy your moral code?'

'My moral compass is pointing in a more hopeful direction,' she agreed.

'You're an intriguing woman, Callista Smith.'

'Callie.' She enjoyed the verbal sparring with him. 'And you must have led a sheltered life.'

He laughed out loud at that suggestion, making her wish they could carry on provoking each other for the rest of the night. Electricity sparked between them. He made her feel good. Primal attraction, she thought. Sex, she warned herself flatly. Who couldn't think about sex with Luca?

He looked like a natural-born hunter who thought he'd found his prey. While under her blunt manner, Callie was sugar and spice and all things nice, and determined to remain that way. Her body could argue all it liked that sugar and spice could still enjoy verbal sparring, but she had no intention of taking things any further. Luca might be everything she'd fantasised about while she was on her knees scrubbing floors in the pub, but this was reality, not a dream world, and the safest thing she could do now was leave. 'I was about to go home,' she explained, glancing away down the drive.

'Aren't you enjoying yourself?'

Too much. 'I am.' She couldn't lie. She'd enjoyed everything about today, and now the food smelled amazing, the band was playing, and it was a beautifully warm evening beneath a canopy of stars. And then there was Luca. 'But I've got work tomorrow.'

'So do I,' he said smoothly.

'You're making this difficult for me.' And hard to breathe, she silently added.

'Why deny yourself the reward for a hard day's work?'

That depended on the reward. Good grief, he was beautiful! His stillness reminded her of a big, soft-pawed predator preparing to pounce. She didn't need a wake-up call, Callie concluded. She needed a bucket of ice-cold water tossing over her head.

'Hey, Luca!'

They both swung around to see Marco coming over. It broke the tension for a while as Luca greeted Marco, but once the two men were done with complicated handshakes and Marco moved on, the two of them were alone again. 'I thought you'd have gone in search of nuts by now,' Luca remarked dryly.

'I was waiting to say goodbye to you.'

'Ah.'

Was he convinced, Callie wondered, or had he guessed that she was trapped like a rabbit in headlights by his brazen masculinity?

'So why are you here, mystery woman? You're staying at a five-star hotel, but work in the fields picking lemons?'

'What's wrong with that?' she challenged.

'Nothing.'

'Well, now we've got that sorted out, I'll say goodnight.' To give him his due, there was no more questions. Luca shrugged and stood aside to let her go, but as she passed he reached out to smooth a lock of hair from her face. His touch thrilled her. Her skin tingled, and her nipples tightened, while tiny pulses of sensation beat low down in her belly.

'Stay,' he insisted. 'You'll have more fun.'

That was what she was afraid of. 'Should I be flattered by your suggestion?' she asked coolly, searching his eyes.

'No,' he said bluntly. 'You should be on your guard.'

She made a point of glancing around. 'Are there many predatory men at this party?'

'None that stand a chance of getting close to you.'

'Will you keep them away? I would have thought you had better things to do.'

'And I thought you were leaving,' he countered.

'I am.'

He could hardly believe it when she walked away. This wasn't a woman he could tease into his bed, but a woman to be reckoned with. Good. He needed a challenge. There was only one woman who could hold his interest tonight. He could hardly believe the transformation from butterfly at the bar, to working girl in the lemon groves. It was a good mix. That stubborn chin clinched it for him. He was done with insipid. She had a great walk too. He feasted his eyes as she walked away from him with her head held high and her shapely butt swaying provocatively beneath the simple clothes. She hadn't a clue who he was. He doubted it would have made any difference. Status meant nothing to Callie, as proved by her easy transition from luxury living in the five-star hotel, to some of the hardest physical work in the area.

The sun had been kind to her today. Flushed from physical activity, she looked good enough to eat, something he'd put on hold until later in the evening, he reflected dryly. He watched as she met up with her friends. She was more relaxed than she'd been at the hotel. Laughing easily, she mimed words when the different languages spoken became a problem. Nothing seemed to faze her. Apart from him.

She was comfortable around everyone, as he was, and far more beautiful than he remembered. Young and natural—even the smear of dirt on her neck only made him think about licking it off. It was time he stopped thinking about Callie naked in his arms, or he'd be walking around the party uncomfortably aroused.

And, before he committed himself to taking her to bed, there were questions to be answered. Why was she picking fruit for a few euros a day when she was staying at a five-star hotel? Was it just for the experience? Who was funding her? Why was she in Italy? Was this a holiday or an escape? If she was escaping, from what? He had no intention of allowing Max to lure him into a honey trap that could discredit Luca, and expose the principality of Fabrizio to corruption beneath his half-brother's rule. It was time to find out more.

As he approached Callie her friends melted away. 'Where are they going?' she asked with surprise.

They were diplomatically giving him space. Callie

couldn't help but be oblivious to the dynamics that existed between a prince and his people. However much he would have liked it to be different, obstacles between him and Utopia were not in his gift to remove.

'Anyone would think you'd got the plague,' she said, bringing a comic slant to bear on the situation.

'Let's hope it's not that serious,' he said, loving the way she could pop the pomposity bubble before it even had chance to form. She had raw, physical appeal, he mused as she stared up at him. It was all too easy to imagine her limbs wrapped around him as she sobbed with pleasure in his arms. 'Dance?' he suggested, curbing baser needs.

'Not if I can help it,' she exclaimed.

The response was pure Callie. 'Why not?' he demanded, play-acting wounded.

'Because I have two left feet and the sense of rhythm of a hamster on a wheel.'

He shrugged. 'Should be interesting. I'm a fast mover myself.'

She raised a disapproving brow, but her eyes betrayed her interest.

'Perhaps I can slow you down?' he suggested. 'Show you an alternative to racing to the finish?'

Her cheeks flushed red. She'd got the sexual message in his words loud and clear, but she hit him with a blunt response. 'You must be wearing steel-capped boots to feel so confident. And I'm going to sit this one out.'

He was nowhere near finished and caught hold of her arm. Momentum thrust her against him. She felt sensational, strong, lithe, and yet softly plump in all the right places. She was so tiny compared to him, but they fitted together perfectly.

'You're taking a lot for granted.' She frowned, but made no attempt to move away.

'I don't see you rushing off,' he countered softly.

'Caveman.'

'Nut freak.'

'Nut freak?' She stared into his eyes. Her lips were just a tempting distance away.

'You're quaint,' he said, meeting her jade-green eyes head-on.

'Quaint?' she queried.

'Old-fashioned.'

She appeared to consider this, and then said, 'There's nothing wrong with tradition. Someone has to take responsibility for keeping standards high.'

Yes. That was him. He stared at a mouth he could have feasted on until she fell asleep with exhaustion. 'Talk to me,' he murmured.

'About what?' she asked, her brow crinkling in enquiry.

He didn't care. He just loved to watch her lips move as she goaded him. The thought of teasing those lips apart with his tongue to claim all the dark recesses of her mouth, along with everything else, fired him up until the hunger to take her was all-consuming. 'That dance we talked about?'

'You talked about.' But she didn't resist when he steered her towards a space that miraculously, as far as Callie was concerned, had opened for them on the packed dance floor.

When Luca pressed her close she gasped at the intensity of feeling. She was conscious that people were staring at them and whispering, which she guessed was only to be expected when she was dancing with the hottest man at the party. Why he'd chosen her to dance with, she had no idea. She hadn't exactly made it easy for him. When he nuzzled her hair aside and kissed her neck, she didn't care what his reasons were. She didn't care about anything. The world and everyone in it simply dropped away.

CHAPTER FOUR

RISK VERSUS PLEASURE, Callie thought as she flicked a glance into Luca's eyes. Even the briefest look sent heat surging through her. She could trust herself for one dance, she decided, which might have had something to do with the fact that when Luca took hold of her hand a thrill raced through her. When his other hand slipped into the hollow in the small of her back, she could think of nothing but closer contact. Fighting the urge, she kept a sensible distance between them. Other couples had made space for them, so there was no need to cling to him like a limpet.

Luca was really popular, she realised as they started to move to the music. They were attracting lots of interested glances and smiles. In fact, she would call it more of a buzz, so maybe the Prince was close by. She glanced around and realised that she wouldn't know the Prince if she tripped over him. Everyone was probably wondering how she got so lucky, but she couldn't shake the feeling that she was missing something. There was no chance to dwell on it. It was far more important to keep her wits about her. Dancing with Luca was a high-risk sport, she concluded as the sinuous melody bound them closer together. There was only thing more intimate they could do and be this close, and that was to make love—

She could put that out of her head right now! She was going to have one dance, and then she was going home. To pull away from Luca before the music ended would be rude. To fall into the trap of relaxing in his arms was stupid. Control would be her watchword. *At least for now.* Another, far more reckless side of Callie wanted to know why she couldn't see this adventure out. She wasn't Callie who scrubbed floors for a living now, but Callie from the lemon groves, who had a whole world of adventure tucked up inside her.

She made herself relax. Luca was right about dancing with him being easy. For some reason her feet seemed to know what to do. Her body moved instinctively with his. They could have been alone on the dance floor. She looked up to see him smiling a lazy, confident smile. He was good. He was very good. Luca might look rugged and tough, but when it came to seduction, he was smooth. So long as she was aware of it, she'd be okay, Callie reassured herself as they danced on.

But he must feel her trembling with arousal. Her body was on fire for him. Her heart was banging in her chest. She'd never played such dangerous games before. Luca was so brazenly virile she couldn't think straight. She wanted to lace her fingers through his hair, and explore his body. She wanted to feel his sharp black stubble rasp her skin, and his firm, curving mouth tease hers into submission. *While his big strong hands position me for pleasure...*

No! She had to leave now.

But she didn't.

And then an annoying drone buzzed overhead. 'It's only just checking who's around,' Luca reassured her when she looked up.

'Like we're so important,' she said dryly. 'I guess the Prince must be around.'

'It's a natural precaution when there's a crowd,' Luca explained.

Hmm. She loved to watch his mouth tilt at the corners when he smiled. 'You've worked here before, so you're used to it,' she pointed out, 'but this is all new to me.' *And how!* And how fabulous, Callie thought as the music started up again, and one dance segued smoothly into two.

'Tell me about home for you,' Luca prompted.

'I'm from a small town in the north of England.'

'What's it like?'

His hands were looped lightly around her waist as he pulled his head back to stare at her. A sensible question was welcome. A return to reality was exactly what she needed when their bodies were an electric hair's breadth apart. But how to explain to a man who lived in one of the most beautiful countries in the world that her life back home was not like this? She settled for the truth. 'I'm very lucky. I have the best of neighbours, a good job, and wonderful friends.'

'So you live alone?' he pressed as they danced on.

It was hard to concentrate on anything while she was this close to Luca, but she shook her mind back to the facts. 'I lived with my father until recently. He died a short time before I came to Italy.'

'I'm very sorry.'

'He was killed in a drunken brawl,' she explained. Luca had sounded genuinely concerned, and she didn't want to mislead him, but her eyes brimmed as she said this. It had been such a tragic waste of life. 'The world keeps turning,' she said, to deflect Luca's interest from the confusion on her face. Guilt had always played such a large part in her thinking where her father was concerned. She had never had any influence over him, but had always wished she could have changed things for the better for him.

'And now you're spreading your wings,' Luca guessed, bringing her back on track.

'I'm trying different things,' she confirmed, brightening as she thought about the short time she'd been in Italy. 'I love it here. I love the warmth of the people, and the sunshine, the glamour of a party beneath the stars—who wouldn't love being here on the Prince's estate? I feel free for the first time in a long time,' she admitted carelessly. 'Sorry. My mouth runs away with me sometimes.'

'No. Go on,' Luca encouraged. 'I'm interested. I want to hear more.'

She was careful not to add the word adventure to her gush of information. He would definitely get the wrong idea. She told him a little more, and then his arms closed around her. His embrace was worryingly addictive and people were packed around them on the dance floor, making dancing close inevitable. Luca was easy to talk to and soon she was telling him things that perhaps she shouldn't, like the camaraderie down the pub where she worked that could so easily erupt into violence when people had had too much to drink.

'*Dio*, Callie, how could your father let you work there?'

She frowned. 'No one gave me permission, and it was a well-paid job. Good, honest work,' she emphasised, and then she laughed. 'They had to pay their staff well, in order to keep them in such a rough area.'

'It sounds horrendous,' Luca remarked, not seeing anything amusing in what she'd said.

'We needed the money,' she said honestly, 'and there aren't too many options where I come from.'

Luca was a passionate Italian male, Callie reminded herself, and they could be very protective. He might look hard as rock, but he was no brute. And she was no saint, Callie thought as his hard thigh eased between hers. She tried using force of will to pretend nothing was happening, but that was the biggest fail yet. He was so big and she was so small that relaxing against him soon became snuggling into him, which felt ridiculously good, almost as if it was supposed to be. Music quickly restored her moral compass when the beat speeded up. She thought he'd let her go, lead her off the dance floor, but instead he caught her closer still.

'You're a good dancer.'

'Only because you lift me off my feet.' She laughed, then reviewed what was happening to her body while they were brushing, rubbing, nudging. It was both sensational and addictive. She wanted more. She wanted to toss her moral compass away.

As if sensing the way her thoughts were turning, Luca whispered in her ear, 'I'm sure you've had enough dancing for now.'

She pulled back her head to stare into his eyes, which was dangerous, because now she discovered she was addicted to danger too. The camera drone chose that moment to intrude. 'If the person behind those controls wants to take a better look at us, why don't they just come down here and say so?'

'I doubt we're the sole object of the controller's attention.'

'You could have fooled me.' She glared at the drone.

'Do you think it's so interested because the Prince is here?'

'Possibly,' Luca agreed.

'I haven't seen him yet. Have you? I mean, you've worked on the estate before, so you must know him.'

'I'm offended,' Luca said, half grinning, which suggested he wasn't offended at all. 'All you want to talk about is the Prince.'

'It's something to tell them about back home.'

'What about me?' he growled.

'Don't look for compliments. You won't get them from me.'

He laughed and swept her off her feet.

'Put me down this instant,' she exclaimed.

'Not a chance,' he said. Amusement coloured his voice. 'Don't you want to know where your adventures could take you?'

'I've got a pretty good idea, which is why I hope your tongue is firmly planted in your cheek. Just for the record, I'll be sleeping on my own tonight,' she added as Luca strode on across the courtyard with her safely locked in his arms.

'Brava,' he said, showing no sign of slowing down.

The crowd parted like the Red Sea, she noticed. She should put up some sort of token struggle, but it was a magical night, a magical moment, and not too many of them came along.

Her senses rioted when Luca dipped his head to brush a kiss against her neck. She would see this adventure through, so long as it only took her from one side of the courtyard to the other. 'I have to go,' she insisted, when he lowered her to her feet to acknowledge some boisterous partygoers.

'No. You have to stay,' he argued when he was done, and so close to her ear that it tingled.

'Are you determined to lead me astray?'

'Would I?' Sweeping her up before she had chance to protest, he strode on towards the palace gardens.

She was dangerously aroused, but for one night, she was going to be Callie from the lemon groves, without fear or guilt, or any of the dutiful thoughts that had curbed her in the past.

'Where are you taking me?' she asked as Luca opened a gate leading to lemon groves.

'Wait and see.'

He didn't stop until they reached the riverbank where he set her down. She had free will. She could do what she liked. She didn't have to do anything she didn't want to. Conscious he was watching her, she smiled, but Luca wasn't fooled. 'What's worrying you?' he said.

'I'm not worried.' Apart from the longing to have more nights like this, which she knew in her heart of hearts would not be possible. Moonlight lit the scene. Sparkling water rushed by. The bed of grass beneath her feet was soft and deep, and the midnight-blue sky overhead was littered with stars. It was the perfect setting on the perfect night, and Luca was the perfect man. Reaching out, she linked their hands.

Luca soothed and seduced her with kisses, with touches, and with the expression in his eyes. She believed they were connecting on a deeper level. He made her want to know more about him, and for this to be the start of something, rather than the grand finale. His hands worked magic on her body. His strength seduced her, his scent seduced her… everything about Luca seduced her. He was a man of the earth, a man of the people, who worked with his body, his mind, and good humour, as well as unstinting loyalty towards his Prince, which he'd proved when he had refused to point him out to her.

This adventure might have its ups and downs, but Luca had featured large in every part of it. He made her spirit soar, and her body cry out for his touch.

They couldn't keep their hands off each other. There was no chance she was going anywhere any time soon. She was a woman with needs and desires, who saw no reason for self-denial. She hadn't prepared for this, but had taken the usual precautions, more in hope than expectation of a love life some time in the far distant future. She hadn't planned anything, because placing trust in a man was a huge deal for Callie, but Luca was different. He made her feel safe. He made her believe she could trust him.

His mouth was warm and as persuasive as sin, and, though she was tentative at first, she soon matched his fire. He was more controlled. She was not. She was new to this, and had had no idea how the fire could take hold and consume her. Luca kept his touch tantalisingly light, far too light for her frustrated body. The urge to know every part of him intimately was clawing at her senses. 'I want you,' she said as she stared up into his eyes.

He knew she was suffering. Of *course* he knew. He was responsible for it. She was hardly playing hard to get, and Luca was available for pleasure. Tracing his magnificent torso over his insubstantial top tipped the balance from caution to action. 'Take it off,' she instructed, 'and then the rest of your clothes.'

His eyes fired with interest and amusement. 'You first,' he countered. 'Or at least, match me.'

And so the game began. It was a game with only one

conclusion. Once started, it couldn't be stopped. Without breaking eye contact, she began unbuttoning her blouse. She did so slowly, and felt heat rise between them. It was her turn to make *him* wait. Pushing the soft fabric from her shoulders, she let it drop.

He frowned. 'You're wearing a bra.'

'I'd say you're overdressed too,' she murmured.

He smiled.

'You should have drawn up your rules before this started,' she teased, 'because now you have to take off your flip-flops too.'

Maintaining eye contact as he kicked them off, she whispered, 'And now your shorts.'

'Are you sure about that?'

'Absolutely sure.' She would keep her eyeline level with his.

'Take off your trainers,' he suggested.

'If that's a ruse to give me chance to have second thoughts, save it. I won't change my mind.'

'I'll take my chances.' Luca's stare was long and steady. 'By the time I've finished, you won't have a stitch of clothing on,' he promised.

She shrugged, pretending indifference, but her heart was banging in her chest. 'If you'd rather not?'

'Oh, I'd rather,' he said with a look that made her body flame with lust.

She toed off her trainers, wishing she'd dressed for the Arctic and had more clothes to remove. Luca was in serious danger of winning this game. How would such an experienced man judge her when he saw her naked? But it was exciting and fun, and every bit the adventure she'd dreamed about…the adventure she wouldn't be telling the Browns about.

She should have known he'd go commando. He'd lowered his zipper and allowed his shorts to slide down his lean frame. Currently, they were hanging on his thighs. Reaching down, he pushed them the rest of the way and, stepping out of them, he stood in front of her, unconcerned. 'You still have some way to go,' he commented.

She would not look down. 'My rules state—' She gasped as Luca yanked her close.

'Your rules count for nothing,' he assured her in a seductive growl as he nuzzled his stubble-roughened face against her neck.

'Oh—' Breath shot from her lungs. She couldn't help but rub her body against his in the hunt for more contact between them, but Luca held her firmly away.

'Not so fast,' he said, all control, while she was a gasping mass of arousal. 'I can see I have some training to do.'

'Please,' she said, making his eyes flare with amusement.

'Nice bra,' he commented as he deftly removed it.

Now that was definitely going to give him the wrong idea. She'd chosen something frivolous for Italy. It had seemed such fun at the time. And safe. When she had been shopping in a brightly lit department store with not a single good-looking man around, the flimsy bra and thong had seemed harmless. The brand was quite exclusive, meant for show rather than practicality. Designer lingerie in bright pink silk chiffon bordered with palest aquamarine lace was hardly Callie's usual choice. She was more of a sensible white cotton type. She could only imagine what Luca was thinking.

'You're beautiful,' he murmured, reassuring and disarming her all in one breath.

'No, I'm not.'

'I guess there's only one way to convince you,' he said, laughing softly.

He drew her closer, inch by inch, and then he kissed her. And this was not a teasing brush of his lips, but something more that drew emotion out of her, until she was happy and sad, excited and confused, all at once. She was happy to be here with him, and sad because she knew it couldn't last. He excited her. Her body was going crazy for more—which he knew. And she was apprehensive too, in case she got this terribly wrong. There were *so* many ways she could get this wrong.

'Stop,' Luca murmured against her mouth. 'Stop thinking and just allow yourself to feel for once. Go with your instincts, Callie.'

Her instincts were telling her to rub herself shamelessly against him, to part her legs and find relief as quickly as she could for the throbbing ache of frustration that he'd put there. And she had mightily encouraged, Callie conceded. She wanted this badly. Even more than that, she wanted the connection between them to last, but she had to face facts: Luca was an itinerant worker, as was she, and so they'd both move on.

He kissed away her doubts as he lowered her slowly to the ground. Stretching out his length against hers on the cool swathe of grass, he made sure that the world faded away, leaving just the two of them to kiss and explore each other. It was as if time stood still. Water still bubbled nearby, and a light breeze still ruffled the leaves overhead, but they were in another world where her senses were totally absorbed in Luca's warm, clean man scent, and the feel of his powerful body against hers. His chest was shaded with just the right amount of dark hair that rasped against her nipples as he moved. She was filled with desire for him, and only felt a moment of apprehension when he reached into the pocket of his discarded shorts and she heard a foil rip. She was glad he had the good sense to protect them both, because she had no intention of pulling back. She had no regrets. None.

When he dipped his head to suckle her mind exploded with sensation. Moving her head on the cushioned earth, she bucked her hips repeatedly, involuntarily, responding to the hungry demands of her body. In the grip of sexual hunger, she reached for his shoulders and held on tightly, as if she were drowning and Luca was her rock. She had stifle a gasp of excitement when he moved over her. The weight of him against her thighs was new to her, and a little frightening. She had to tell herself that this was what she wanted, and that nothing was going to stop her now, nothing.

'I'm right here,' he soothed as if he could sense her apprehension.

'Don't I know it?' she joked half-heartedly.

'Seriously. Stop worrying. I would never hurt you.'

She stared into his eyes and saw the truth behind his statement. It was as if that had opened the floodgates to hunger, to curiosity, which left her fierce with passion, as well as uncertain as to what Luca was used to. Goodness knew, her experience was limited, to say the least. She was on a journey of discovery, Callie consoled herself, and this was an adventure that would carve a memory so deep she would never forget this moment, or this man.

Luca whispered against her mouth, 'Trust me, Callie,' and then his hands worked their magic and she was lost.

'*Oh*…that's…'

'Good?' he suggested in a low, amused murmur.

Her answer was a series of soft, rhythmical sighs. ‘Better than good,’ she managed to gasp.

‘More?’ he suggested.

The hands cupping her buttocks were so much bigger than hers, and his skilful fingers could work all sorts of wickedness.

‘Would you like me to touch you here?’

His tone was low and compelling. ‘So much,’ she admitted, sucking in a shaking breath.

One of Luca’s slightly roughened finger pads was all it took to send her mindless with excitement. He knew exactly what to do. He started stroking steadily, rhythmically, applying the right amount of pressure at just the right speed.

‘Good?’

Was she supposed to answer? She daren’t speak. She was frightened of losing control.

‘Would you like me to tip you over the edge?’

‘I’m not sure.’

‘Yes, you are.’

Staring into Luca’s laughing eyes, she knew he was right.

He kissed her as he explored her, a shallow invasion at first with a single finger, and then deeper, with one, two, and finally three fingers. ‘You’re so ready,’ he commented with approval.

She rocked her body in time to the steady thrust of Luca’s hand. It wasn’t as good, or as immediate as when he attended to her achingly sensitive little nub. It was a different feeling, and one just as compelling in its way. It made her want him to lodge deep inside her. The urge to be one with him was overwhelming.

Nudging her thighs apart with his, he continued to

touch her in the way that took her mind off everything else. The delicious sensation of having him enclose her buttocks in his big, warm hands while he touched her lightly at the apex of her thighs was startlingly good. He found new ways to tease her, moving his body up and down until she was so aroused he could slide in easily, but then he pulled out again, provoking her more than ever. 'Don't stop!' she exclaimed with frustration.

He ignored this plea and continued to tease her. Wild for him, she begged for more in words she'd never used before.

'Like this?' Luca suggested in a low growl.

She gasped with shock when he sank deep. For a moment she didn't know if she liked it or not. He was very slow and very careful, but that only gave her chance to realise how much he stretched her. Every nerve ending she possessed leapt instantly to attention. The sensation was sudden and complete. She couldn't think, she could only feel. *'Yes,'* she sighed, moving with him.

Luca maintained a dependable rhythm, taking her to the edge and over, and he still moved intuitively, steadily, to make sure that her ride of pleasure continued for the longest possible time. She might have screamed. She might have called his name. She only knew that by the time she quietened her throat was sore, and with a gasp she collapsed back against the grass.

'And we're only just getting started,' Luca promised with amusement.

Still lodged deep, he began to move again, persuasively and gently to take account of her slowly recovering body. He kept up this sensitive buffeting until the fire gripped her again and she wound her legs tightly around his waist as he thrust deep. She didn't wait to be tipped over the edge this time, but worked her hips with his, falling fast and hard, while Luca held her firmly in place so she received the full benefit of each deep, firm stroke.

'Greedy,' he approved as she gasped for breath.

'You make me greedy.' Luca was still hard. She was still hungry. She reached for him and he took her again.

Callie was unique in his experience. It was as if they'd been lovers for years, but could enjoy the first, furious appetite that came with discovery of someone special. Not only could she match him, she fired him like no other. He was driven by the primitive urge to imprint himself on her body, her mind, and her memory. Pinning her down beneath him with her arms above her head, he thrust firmly to the hilt. She growled, and bucked towards him, as hungry as she had ever been. She was wild and abandoned, as he'd imagined Callie would be once he discovered what lay beneath her carefully cultivated shell. When they were still again, she turned towards him, as slowly as if her bones had turned to lead. Smiling, she managed groggily, 'You're amazing.'

'And so are you,' he replied softly.

CHAPTER FIVE

THEY BATHED IN the stream, seemingly unaware of the chill of the water, and dried off on the bank next to each other, kissing and staring into each other's eyes. Luca seemed surprised when she insisted she would go home on one of the staff buses, but she wasn't ready to spend the night with him. She needed to clear her head and come to terms with the fact that this might have been a life-changing experience, but it had no future.

Let this be, she thought as Luca smiled against her mouth before kissing her. Let it remain shiny and special. Allow nothing to taint it. She had those same thoughts when she boarded the bus, but by the time she walked into the hotel lobby her mood had changed, mainly because the concierge was waiting for her, and he looked worried to death.

'Thank goodness, Signorina Smith. This came for you.'

She looked at the envelope he was holding out. It was obviously urgent. She ripped it open and started reading. There was some confusion about her room at the bed and breakfast. She had intended to move hotels tomorrow, but now it seemed her room at the B & B was no longer available. Crumpling the note in her hand, she frowned as she wondered what to do next. She couldn't afford to stay on here.

'Signorina Smith?'

The concierge was hovering anxiously. 'Yes?'

'Forgive my intrusion, but I can see how concerned you are. Please don't be worried. The manager at the establishment you had hoped to move to left that note for you. He has informed us of a problem, and so it is arranged that you continue to stay here.'

Callie's cheeks flushed with embarrassment. 'I'm afraid I can't afford to stay here,' she admitted frankly. The concierge looked as embarrassed as she felt and this wasn't his fault. 'I'd love to stay on,' she added warmly. 'Everyone's been so kind to me, but I need to find somewhere cheaper. Maybe you can help?'

'Please, *signorina*,' the concierge implored, shifting uncomfortably from polished shoe to polished shoe. 'There will be no charge. You have been let down. This is a matter of local pride. The management of this hotel and the staff who care for you will be insulted if you offer payment.'

'And I'll be insulted if I don't,' Callie said bluntly. 'I really can't stay on if I don't pay my way.'

'The cost of your room has been covered.'

She swung around in surprise. 'Luca! Are you following me?'

'Yes,' he admitted.

'What do you know about this?' she demanded. Luca, tousled and magnificent, couldn't have looked more incongruous in the sleek, polished surroundings of the five-star hotel. She had to curb a smile as she glanced down at her clothes, and then at his. They both looked exactly what they were, labourers from the fields, which was another reason for decamping to another, much plainer establishment. Not that her body could have cared less what Luca was wearing. As far as her body was concerned, Luca looked better naked, anyway.

A million and one feelings flooded through her as they stared at each other. 'Are you responsible for this?' she asked, holding out the letter. Out of the corner of her eye, she could see the concierge, who'd returned to his booth, looking more anxious than ever. Something was definitely going on. Luca knew Marco. Had they pulled strings between them so that she would have to stay with Luca? She refused to be manipulated, especially by Luca.

'I couldn't help overhearing that you were having difficulties,' he began.

She bit her tongue and decided to wait to see what he said next. When he shrugged and smiled, threatening to weaken her resolve, she said, 'I don't suppose you know anything about my mysterious benefactor, or the fact that the hotel is refusing to charge me?'

He raised a brow. 'Don't you like it here?'

'That's not the point,' she insisted. It hadn't escaped her notice that Luca was speaking as calmly as if he were a tour operator dealing with a quibbling client, rather than a controlling alpha male who seemed to think that everything and everyone should run to his prescription. He might have quite literally swept her off her feet at the party, but post-party common sense had had time to set in.

'My only concern is that you have somewhere comfortable to stay,' he insisted.

She bristled. 'Well, thank you, but I'm quite capable of making my own arrangements.'

'They had a burst pipe at the small establishment

where you booked a room,' Luca explained while the concierge nodded vehemently. 'Marco alerted me to this, and the concierge was only trying to help.'

'How did Marco know I was planning to move to the B & B?' she asked suspiciously.

'I'm sorry, Callie, but you can't live in a small town like this and not know what's going on.'

'So Marco told you?' How could she have been so dim?

'Stay on at the hotel,' Luca offered, as if he were the owner of the sumptuous building. 'You'll be closer to the lemon groves here.' He shot her a questioning look. 'That's if you intend to continue working on the Prince's estate.'

'Of course I do,' Callie confirmed. She loved it on the Prince's estate, and was nowhere near ready to leave yet.

'So, come back with me.'

Luca was waiting at the lobby door, as if it were all a done deal. Did he mean go back to the party with him? Or did Luca have something different in mind? She had paid for the hotel until tomorrow, and packing could wait until the morning. Meanwhile...*adventure beckoned*!

More adventure? Why not? Luca was everything virile and masculine, drawing her deeper into the adventure she'd always dreamed about. 'Thank you for your concern,' she said, knowing she needed time to think more than ever now. 'And, thank you,' she added to the concierge as she walked away.

Callie avoided him the next day. His pride was piqued. However, everyone broke for lunch in the afternoon and congregated at the cookhouse. She was there, and they nodded to each other as they stood in line.

'Luca.'

Her greeting was cool. She hadn't appreciated his interference at the hotel, he gathered. He was hot from the fields, and hot for Callie, who had spent the morning in an air-conditioned facility the size of an aircraft hangar. Small, neat and clean, she slammed into his senses in her prim little buttoned-up blouse. Her denim shorts were short and they displayed her legs to perfection, as well as a suggestion of the curve of the bottom he'd caressed last night. That was all he needed before an afternoon's work.

'Excuse me, please,' she said politely, waiting with her loaded tray to move past him.

The urge to ruffle those smooth feathers and make her wild with passion again was more than a passing thought. Weighing up the bandana he wore tied around his head to keep his crazy hair under control, she moved on to scrutinise the ancient top skimming his waist, though was careful not to look any lower. He took charge of her tray. Her gaze settled on his hands, and then his wrists, which were banded with leather studded with semi-precious stones, collected for him by the children of Fabrizio so he wouldn't forget them while he was away. 'I can manage, thank you,' she said, trying to take the tray off him.

'I'm sure you can,' he agreed, 'but sometimes it's good to let people help you.'

Her brow pleated in thought as if she'd heard this somewhere before.

'Are you staying on at the hotel, or have you found somewhere else to stay?' he enquired lightly as he carried her tray to the table where Anita was waiting for Callie to join her.

'Is that why you're here? To question me?' Callie probed with a penetrating look.

For a moment he couldn't decide whether to shrug off her question or throw her over his shoulder like the caveman she thought him. He did know one thing. The tension between them couldn't be sustained.

'See you later,' he said, turning to go.

'Not if I see you first,' she called teasingly after him.

A little frustration would do them both good, he decided. Ignoring the buzz of interest that accompanied him to the door, he saluted the chefs and left the cookhouse.

Infuriating man! How was it possible to feel so aroused, and yet control the impulse to jump on Luca and ravish him in front of everyone? Which was probably exactly how he expected her to feel. The tension in the cookhouse had been high, and made worse because people were obviously trying hard not to stare at them. She had tried to start a conversation with Anita, but couldn't concentrate and kept losing her train of thought.

'If you take my advice, you'll get it over with,' Anita advised, glancing at Callie with concern.

'Get what over with?' Callie demanded, frowning.

'Sex. You need to sate yourself.'

'I beg your pardon?'

'Oh, come off it, Callie. You'll be no good to anyone, least of all yourself, until you do.'

'Anita, I'm shocked!'

'No, you're not, you're frustrated,' Anita argued. 'No one would think any the worse of you if you glut yourself on that one.' She glanced in the direction Luca had gone.

'This isn't an adult playground. It's a place of work.'

'Listen to yourself,' Anita protested with a forkful of crisp, golden fries poised in front of her mouth. 'Take precautions and don't involve your heart. You're here for adventure, aren't you?'

It might be too late to do as Anita said, Callie reflected as she left the cookhouse ahead of her friend. Her heart was already involved. She couldn't last a minute without wondering if she'd see Luca again soon.

Turning onto the dusty track leading through the lemon groves, she headed for the storage facility where she'd been working that morning, only to see Luca coming towards her.

'Shall I show you a short cut?' he offered.

A short cut to what? she wondered as he grinned and took hold of her hand.

It was no good. He couldn't get through the afternoon without it, without her, without Callie, without being up against a tree kissing her as if they were the last couple on earth and time was running out fast.

'Luca—we can't—'

'Yes, we can,' he insisted. Pressing his body weight against her, he slowly moved his body against hers until she was sucking in great gulping sobs of frustration.

'I need you,' she gasped out.

'I know,' he whispered.

He found her with his hand over the rough, thick denim shorts and stroked firmly. He could feel her heat and his imagination supplied the rest. He couldn't wait. Neither could she. They tore at her shorts together. Removing them quickly, he tossed them away. There was no time for kissing, or touching, or preparing, there was only this. He freed himself. She scrambled up him. He dipped at the knees and took her deep. She came violently after a few firm thrusts. Tearing at him with hands turned to claws, she threw back her head and howled out her pleasure as each powerful spasm gripped her. When he felt her muscles relax, and her hands lost their grip, he gave it to her again, fast and hard.

'Yes!' she cried out as he claimed her again. 'More,' she begged, blasting a fiercely demanding stare into his eyes.

'You can have all you want,' he promised as he worked her steadily towards the next release. 'But not right now,' he murmured, still thrusting, 'because we have to go back to work.'

'You're joking.' Her eyes widened. 'How can I go back to work after this?'

'That discipline we talked about?'

'*You* talked about.'

He ended the argument with a few fast thrusts, and she screamed out her pleasure as they both claimed their most powerful release yet.

'You're right,' she accepted groggily a long while after she'd quietened. 'They'll be short a team member if I don't go back, and I can't let everyone down.'

He could have sorted this out for her with a few words in the appropriate ear, but that would be taking advantage of his position, and so he huffed an accepting laugh and lowered her down to the ground. They were both bound by duty. Groping for his phone, he clicked it on to see the time. What he saw was a line of missed calls. Springing up, he dislodged her. 'Sorry, I have to take this,' he explained as he walked away. Sorting himself out as the call connected, he tucked the phone between ear and his shoulder and asked a few pertinent questions. Having cut the line, he beckoned to Callie. 'Sorry, but there's somewhere I have to be.'

'Your afternoon shift?' she queried, frowning.

'Something like that, but I'll have to leave the estate.'

'Is there anything I can do to help?' she asked, feeling his tension.

'Nothing.' He sounded abrupt, but there was no time for explanations.

Callie was hurt. She refused to meet his eyes. His sharp response had shocked her. And no wonder, when one minute they were totally absorbed in each other, even if that was up against a tree, and the next he couldn't wait to leave. It couldn't be helped. He'd see her again, if and when he came back.

She didn't have much experience of love affairs, but she knew enough to know Luca's behaviour wasn't acceptable. His intended departure was brutal and sudden, and only went to prove she didn't know the man she was with. She didn't know him at all. Shame and humiliation swept over her in hot, ugly waves as he paced impatiently while she struggled to put on her shorts as fast as she could. For Luca it was just sex, necessary like eating and breathing, and now it was done, he couldn't wait to leave.

What a mug I am, Callie thought as she pulled up her zipper. Even her well-used body mocked her as she dressed. It was so tender and still so responsive, while her mind continued to whirl in agitated spirals as she flashed glances at a man who seemed to have forgotten she existed. She'd been swept up in a fantasy, but as far as Luca was concerned they were two healthy adults who'd wanted sex. Now that was done there was nothing left. She couldn't even be angry with him. She'd been a more than willing partner. She was just puzzled as to how they could seem so close, and now this.

She glanced at him. He glanced back, but only to check on her progress. There'd be no more conversation or confiding, no more intimate jokes. Smoothing her hair as best she could, she looked at the time on her phone and grimaced. She was already late for the afternoon shift and would have to take a shower before returning to work. It must have been her heavy sigh that prompted Luca to say, 'There are facilities next to the building where you're working. You'll find everything there—towels, shampoo—'

Did he do this on a regular basis? Callie wondered. 'Thanks.' Why wouldn't he? Luca came here every year. She couldn't be the first woman to fall for his blistering charm. Her face flamed red as she pictured him with someone else. She'd thought they were special, which only went to prove how little she knew about men. She could understand he was in a hurry, but couldn't there be just the slightest pleasantry between them, to allow for an exit with dignity?

'So that's it?' she said as she checked her top was properly tucked in.

'Should there be more?' he demanded.

His response was the slap in the face she badly needed. Something had to bring her to her senses. Reality had landed. Hooray. He was right. What more should there be?

Callie was angry, but they were hardly at the stage where he could confide state secrets. She controlled herself well, but the tension in her jaw and the spark in her eyes told their own story. It couldn't be helped. News of Max's attempted coup was for his ears only. He strode on ahead as soon as Callie was ready. His mind was already elsewhere. Stabbing numbers into his cell, he told his staff to prepare the helicopter. He had to get to Fabrizio fast. He would just have time to shower and change before it arrived to pick him up. Max and his cronies had been causing trouble again, and, though they had been swiftly suppressed, the people of Fabrizio needed the reassurance of seeing their Prince.

'So, you're not even going to wait for me?' Callie called after him.

He turned around, shrugged impatiently then kept on walking. She was no longer his priority. However much he might want her to be, he couldn't put his own selfish pleasures first.

'What's got under your skin?' Anita asked when the two women bumped into each other outside the shower block. 'A man? One man in particular?'

Anita sounded so hopeful that Callie couldn't bear to disillusion her. 'Tell you later,' she promised as she hurried off for her afternoon shift.

'Wave goodbye to the Prince before you go,' Anita called after her.

Callie stopped and turned around. 'Where is he?'

Shielding her eyes, Anita stared up at a large blue helicopter with a royal crest of Fabrizio on the side.

'Apparently he's been called back to Fabrizio to deal with an emergency,' Anita explained as both women protected their eyes against the aircraft's downdraft, which had raised dust clouds all around them. 'Don't worry. It won't be an emergency when Luca gets there.'

'Sorry?' Callie froze.

'Prince Luca's will is stronger than any army his brother Max could raise, *and* his people adore him,' Anita explained. 'The people don't trust Max as far as they could throw him. I read in the press today that Prince Luca intends to buy Max off. Max will do anything for money,' Anita explained, 'and that includes relinquishing his claim to the throne. Max needs Luca's money to pay his gambling debts. He'd bleed the country dry, if he became ruler. The late Prince, their father, knew this. That's why he made Prince Luca his heir—Callie? Are you all right?'

'Why didn't you tell me that Luca was the Prince?' Callie stared at her friend in total disbelief, but how could she be angry with Anita when Callie was guilty of ignoring what had been, quite literally, under her nose?

'I'm sorry,' Anita said as she enveloped Callie in a big hug. 'I thought you knew. I thought, like the rest of us, you were being discreet by not naming him, or talking about him. We all know that's what Prince Luca prefers. If I'd guessed for a moment—'

'It's not your fault,' Callie insisted. 'I'm to blame. I only saw what I wanted to see.' She stared up at the helicopter as it disappeared behind some cloud. Luca hadn't told her anything, let alone that he was the Prince. What a fool she was. How could she have missed all the clues? They were as obvious to her now as the bright red arrow she hadn't noticed when she'd first arrived at the Prince's estate. Only worse, much worse, Callie concluded. She didn't blame Luca. Was he supposed to act like Prince Charming in a fairy tale? He was a man, with all the cravings, faults and appetite that went along with that, and she hadn't exactly fought him off.

'Why are you laughing?' Anita asked.

Callie was thinking that Luca didn't have to excuse his actions. He simply called for his helicopter and flew off. But into a difficult situation, she reminded herself.

Even if Luca and his brother had never been close, no one needed to remind Callie how much a barb from within the family could hurt.

'I thought he was one of us,' she admitted to Anita.

'He is one of us,' Anita confirmed hotly.

Callie smiled, knowing there was no point in arguing with Anita, one of Luca's staunchest supporters, but she still couldn't get her head around her own clumsy mistake. It was so much easier to think of Luca as a worker, rather than a prince, but how she could have been so wrapped up in her Italian adventure that she hadn't guessed the truth before now defeated her.

'Max's uprising was over before it began,' Anita explained as she linked arms with Callie. 'You can't fault Prince Luca for keeping his word to his father, the late Prince. Luca's been coming here for years to work alongside the pickers, but nothing's more important to him than the pledge he made to keep his country safe, and we all understand why he had to go back to Fabrizio.'

All except Callie, who was still floundering about in the dark wondering why Luca hadn't told her his true identity. Perhaps there were too many people who only wanted to be close to him for the benefits they could gain, apparently like his brother, Max. She could forgive him if that were the case. Well, sort of. Luca expected her to trust him, but he clearly didn't trust her.

And was she always truthful?

The only time she'd reached out since arriving in Italy was to text Rosie to reassure the Browns that everything was going well. She'd explained that she was going to extend her stay, but had kept her answers to Rosie's excited questions bland in the extreme. She was staying on because she wanted to learn more about Italy, Callie had said, which explained why she had taken a part-time job. She just hadn't expected to get her heart broken into pieces and trampled on in the process. 'I'll be leaving soon,' she mused out loud.

'Must you? Oh, no. Please don't. Was it something I said? I didn't mean to probe,' Anita assured Callie with concern, 'and I'll understand completely if you don't want to tell me why you're leaving.'

Callie responded with a warm hug for her new friend. 'You've done nothing wrong,' she assured Anita. 'If anyone's at fault, it's me. I could have asked Luca more questions, but chose not to. I didn't want reality to intrude, I suppose. It's better if I go home and get real. It's too easy to believe the dream here.'

How true was that? She couldn't believe she'd made such a fool of herself with Luca.

'Can't you stay a little longer?' Anita begged. 'We're only just getting to know each other, and I'll miss you.'

Tears sprang to Callie's eyes at this confession, and the two women exchanged a quick, fierce hug. 'I hope you'll come and visit me?' Callie insisted. 'I don't want to lose touch, either.'

'No chance,' Anita promised stoutly as they stood side by side on the dusty path that ran through the groves. 'When I go home, it's to a damp northern mill town not too far from your docks, so there's no reason why we can't meet up.'

'Come for Christmas,' Callie exclaimed impetuously. 'Please. I'll ask Ma Brown. The more, the merrier, she always says. Promise you will.'

'Are you serious?' Anita looked concerned, and then her face lit up when she realised that Callie meant every word. 'I usually spend Christmas alone.'

'Not this year,' Callie vowed passionately with another warm hug. 'I'll speak to Ma and Pa Brown as soon as I get back, and I'll send you the details.'

'You're a true friend, Callie,' Anita said softly.

'I won't forget you,' Callie promised.

Casting one last wistful look around the sun-drenched lemon groves, Callie firmed her jaw. She might be Callie from the docks when she returned home, but she would always be Callie from the lemon groves in her heart.

CHAPTER SIX

'WHERE THE HELL is she? Someone must know.'

The staff stared at him blankly. He was back in the warehouse where the lemons were stored. As soon as he'd sorted the problems in Fabrizio, he'd returned to his estate expecting to find Callie still working there. He hadn't realised how much he'd miss her until she wasn't around. 'Callie Smith?' he exclaimed, exasperated by the continued silence. 'Anyone?'

Apologetic shrugs greeted his questions. No one knew where she was. Or they weren't telling, he amended, glancing at Anita, who was staring fixedly six inches above his head. He'd made it back just before the end of the season when the casual workers left. Most of the pickers had already gone home, but some had stayed on to make sure everything was stored properly and they were set fair for next year. *Why would Callie stay when I've been so brusque?*

Wheeling around, he strode to the exit. Fresh from resolving a potential uprising in Fabrizio, he could surely solve the mystery of one missing woman. Max had accepted a pay-off equivalent to the GDP of a small country, and Luca had paid this gladly with the proviso that Max stayed out of Luca's life and never returned to Fabrizio.

He had the funds to buy anything he wanted, even freedom from Max, but could he buy Callie? In the short time he'd known her, he'd learned that, not only was Callie irreplaceable, she was unpredictable too. Her newfound freedom after years of duty to her father had lifted her, and in the space of a couple of days Luca had succeeded in knocking her down. Throwing money at a problem like Max worked. Callie was just as likely to throw it back.

He entered the office on the estate and everyone stood to attention. In a dark, tailored suit, Luca was dressed both as a prince and a billionaire, and not one member of staff had missed that change. 'Relax, please. I'm here to ask for your help.'

As always, his people couldn't have been more accommodating. They gave him Callie's home address from her file. Now there was just Callie to deal with, he reflected as he left the building. He doubted she'd be quite so helpful, and his smile faded. He'd never been unsure of an outcome before, but he couldn't be sure of Callie.

He took the helicopter for the short flight to the airport, where his flight plan to the north of England was already filed. He'd fly the jet himself. The thought of being a passenger appalled him. He needed something to do. Callie occupied every corner of his mind. The unfinished business between them banged at his brain. There was no time to lose. He didn't leave loose ends, never had.

Could it really be more than two months since she'd first met Luca? It was certainly time to take stock of her life. That didn't take very long. She was living in one freezing, cold room over a dress shop where she worked six days a week to fund her studies at night school. She was determined to get ahead by building on the Italian language she'd already picked up on her trip to Italy. Her love affair with the country was in no way over, and it had turned out that she had a flair for languages. She had moved to another town, because she didn't have a home to go back to as such. Her old home next door to the Browns had new tenants, and though the Browns had begged her to stay on with them, Callie had insisted that they'd done enough for her, and that it was time for her to go it alone. 'I wish I could have brought you more exciting news from my adventures,' she'd told them.

'Exciting enough,' Rosie had exclaimed, her eyes fever bright when Callie talked about the Prince.

Callie hadn't told anyone about the time she'd spent locked in the Prince's arms, and had deflected Rosie's questions by telling her that staying in a five-star hotel had kept her away from the real Italy. 'The posh hotel was lovely,' she'd explained, 'but it was bland.'

'Unlike the Italian men?' Rosie guessed, still digging for information.

'And so I looked for a job amongst the people,' Callie had driven on in an attempt to avoid Rosie's question. She had never lied to her friend, and she never would.

'You're too hard on yourself, love,' Pa Brown had insisted when Callie explained that without the young maid's suggestion she would still have been sitting in the hotel, rather than experiencing the lemon groves she had grown to love. 'You wanted to get out and do an honest day's work. You asked for help to find some. There's nothing wrong with that. We all need help sometimes.'

Pa Brown's words resonated with Callie more than ever now. He was right. In her current situation, she would have to ask for help at some point.

Yes. From Callie Smith, Callie concluded. Like millions of women who'd found themselves in this situation, she'd get through, and get through well. Though there were times when she wished she'd agreed to see Luca when he first flew to England to set things straight between them.

'Why won't you see him?' Rosie had asked with incredulity on the first occasion. 'He's an incredible man and he cares about you. He must do, to leave everything to fly here to find you. And he's a prince, Cal,' Rosie had added in an awestruck gasp, 'as well as one of the richest men in the world.'

Callie remembered firming her lips and refusing to add to this in any way. She had simply given her head a firm shake. The money meant nothing to her and neither did Luca's title. She couldn't risk her heart being broken again, and the feelings she had for Luca were so strong they frightened her. But Rosie knew her too well. Realising Callie wouldn't change her mind, Rosie had put an arm around Callie's shoulders and hugged her tight. 'I know you love him,' Rosie insisted. 'And one day you'll know that too. Just don't find out when it's too late.'

It hadn't ended there, of course. Luca wasn't the type to meekly turn around and go home. He didn't know how to take no for an answer. He'd called several times, sent flowers, gifts, notes, hampers of dainty cakes and delicacies from a famous London store. He'd even despatched an elderly statesman called Michel to plead his case. Callie had felt particularly bad about the old man, but Ma Brown had made up for her refusal, treating Michel to a real northern afternoon tea before politely telling him that his Prince had no chance of changing Callie's mind at the moment. 'You shouldn't even have given him that much hope,' Callie had insisted. 'I don't want to be any man's mistress and Luca's a prince. He's hardly going to take things in the direction I…'

As her voice had tailed away, Pa Brown had piped up, 'The direction you want is love, Callie. Love and respect is the direction you're entitled to want, when you give your heart to someone special.'

As Ma Brown had sighed with her romantic heart all aflutter, Callie had known it was time to move on. Her relationship with Luca, such as it had been, had started to affect the Browns, so she'd told them what she planned to do, and had packed her bags. And here she was three months later in Blackpool, the jewel of the Fylde coast. It was blustery and cold this close to Christmas, but there was an honest resilience about the place that suited Callie's mood. And there were the illuminations, she mused with a rueful grin as she glanced out of her top-floor window at the light-bedecked seafront. Known as the greatest free light show on earth, one million bulbs and six miles of lights brought tourists flocking, which meant there were plenty of part-time jobs.

The irony since she'd been here was that Luca was never out of the press. She couldn't believe she'd spent so much time in blissful ignorance as to his identity when his face stared out of every magazine and newspaper. Even when she went to the hairdresser's, she couldn't escape him. She had read every column inch written about him, and knew now that Luca had won his position in Fabrizio thanks to his sheer grit and determination. That, and the love of an adoptive father who had always believed his 'boy from the gutters of Rome', as Luca was referred to in the red-tops, was an exceptional man in the making.

Callie had become an expert in press releases and

could quote some of them by heart. Luca, who was already a titan in business, was now equally respected in diplomatic circles. A tireless supporter of good causes, he had just completed a world tour of the orphanages he sponsored.

The photos of him were riveting. Luca relaxing, looking hot as hell in snug-fitting jeans, or Luca riding a fierce black stallion, looking like the king of the world. He could be cool and strong on state occasions, when he was easily the most virile and commanding of all the men present. In a nutshell, the new ruler of Fabrizio currently dominated world news, which made him seem further away to Callie, and more unreachable than ever. Much was made in the press of his lonely bachelor status, but Luca clearly had no intention of changing that any time soon. Flowers arrived regularly at the Browns', a clear indication that he hadn't given up his search for a mistress yet.

The flowers were still arriving, Rosie had informed Callie only last night, together with the handwritten letters bearing the royal seal, which Rosie had insisted on squirrelling away for Callie. 'You'll look at them one day,' she'd said, not realising that Callie steamed them open and had read every one.

She'd never fit into Luca's glitzy life, Callie concluded, however much affection and humour he put into his letters. But there were deeper reasons. Her mother had died believing her father's lies, and Callie had listened to them for most of her life. 'Tomorrow will be better,' Callie's father would promise each day. But it was never better. He always gambled away the money, or drank it, and so Callie would do another shift at the pub. Did she want another man who lied to her, even if not telling her that he was a prince was a lie of omission by Luca to test how genuine she was? She would be the one lying if she couldn't admit to herself that each time she saw a photograph of Luca, she longed for him with all her heart.

'The trick is knowing when to say thank you, and get on with things,' Pa Brown had told her in their last telephone conversation, when Callie had asked what she should do about the flowers. 'You can send us your thank-you notes, and we'll pass them on. Don't you worry, our Callie, Ma Brown's loving it. She's like Lady Bountiful, spreading those flowers around the neighbourhood so they do some good. You can thank that Prince Luca properly when you see him in person. I certainly will.'

We won't be seeing him, Callie had wanted to say, but she didn't have the heart.

'Stop beating yourself up, girl,' Pa Brown had added before they ended their most recent call. 'You went to work in the lemon groves, which was what you'd dreamed about. You turned that dream into reality, which is more than most of us do.'

She should have kept a grip on reality when it came to Luca, Callie thought with a sigh. But she hadn't. She had allowed herself to be swept up in the fantasy of a holiday romance. And now there was something else she had to do, something far more important than fretting. Reaching into her tote, she pulled out the paper chemist's bag. She couldn't put the test off any longer. While her periods had always been irregular this was a big gap, even for her. Now, she had to know. It was a strange thing, becoming pregnant, Ma Brown had told Callie before the last baby Brown was born. There could be barely any signs for a doctor to detect, but a mother knew. For a couple of weeks now Callie had tried to believe that this was an old wives' tale, but she couldn't kid herself any longer. She might not be a mother, or have personal experience of becoming pregnant, but she did know when she wasn't alone in her body and there was a new, fragile life to protect. She had considered that this feeling might possibly be nothing more than the product of an overactive imagination. There was only one way to find out.

She stared at the blue line unblinking. Not because if she stared long enough it might disappear, but because she was filled with the sort of euphoria that only came very rarely in life. It was a moment to savour before reality kicked in, and she was going to close her eyes and enjoy every moment of it. When she opened them again, her biggest fear was that the kit was faulty. Surely, there had to be a percentage that were?

Leaning forward, she turned on another bar of the ancient electric fire and pulled the cheap throw that usually covered the holes in the sofa around her shoulders as she tried to stop shivering. Part of that was excitement, she supposed, though her hands were frozen. She couldn't believe it was December next week. Where had the time gone? It only seemed five minutes since she had been basking in sunshine in Italy. That was almost three months ago. Three months of life-shattering consequence, Callie reflected as she stared, and stared again at the blue line on her pregnancy test. One thing was certain. She'd have to see Luca now.

He knew Callie was pregnant since he'd tracked her down to England. He'd been tied up with his enthronement once the dispute with Max was settled. That stiff and formal ceremony was over now, with the celebratory garden party for thousands of citizens of Fabrizio still to come.

He loved being amongst his people and looked forward to it, but it was time to concentrate on Callie. They were similar in so many ways, which warned him to tread carefully, or Callie would only back off more determinedly than ever. And hormones would be racing, so the mother of his child, the one woman he could never forget, would have more fire in her than a volcano. Once more into the breach, he thought as the royal jet, piloted by His Serene Highness, Luca Fabrizio, the most frustrated and most determined man on earth, soared high into the air.

Blackpool Illuminations Requires Tour Guides. Callie studied the headline. She was going to need more money soon. Her bank account was bouncing along the bottom, and when the baby arrived… Touching her stomach, she was filled with wonder at the thought; when the baby arrived there would be all sorts of expenses. A wave of regret swept over her, at the knowledge Luca should be part of this. The sooner she told him, the better, but he must understand she didn't want anything from him.

But the baby might need things.

Might need the father she'd never really had, Callie mused, frowning. But what would that mean? Would Luca be a good father? Instinct said yes, but would he and his royal council control their every move? What about the lack of freedom that being royal would mean for a child? She wrapped her arms protectively around her stomach as, hot on the heels of excited disbelief and the marvel of a new life, came a very real fear of the unknown. What if she was a hopeless mother?

She couldn't afford to be frightened of anything, Callie concluded with a child on the way. Grabbing her coat and scarf, she quickly put them on. Leaving the bedsit, she locked the door behind her. The baby came before everything. She had to make some money, even save a little, so she could move to somewhere bigger, hopefully somewhere with a garden. Long before that, she had to buy clothes and equipment for the baby.

Remembering not to rattle down the stairs at a rate of knots as she usually did, she walked sensibly, thinking about the baby. She was already feeling protective. She was confident of one thing. She would not be separated from her child. Luca would have to know they were expecting a baby but, Prince or not, billionaire or not, she would not allow him, or his council, to take over. She would raise her child to have values and warmth, and teach it to be kind. The Browns would help. Maybe she'd have to move back to the docks, but not yet. Burying her face in her scarf to protect it from the bitter wind, she prepared to brave the weather to find a job.

And Luca?

He was an Italian male. Of course he'd want to be part of this. But he would also want to found a dynasty, and for that he needed a princess, not Callie from the docks.

She exchanged a cheery hello with the kindly shop owner who had rented Callie the flat and paused to help with a string of tinsel. 'Thank you, darling,' the elderly shop owner exclaimed, giving Callie a warm hug. 'I can't believe how you're glowing. You look wonderful. Don't you get cold outside, now.'

'I won't,' Callie called back over her shoulder as she stepped out into the street.

He saw the car coming from the end of the street. Driven at speed, it was being chased by a police vehicle, sirens blaring.

No!

He wasn't sure if he shouted, or thought the warning, but he did know he moved. Sprinting like a cheetah, he hurtled down the road. Shoving pedestrians from the path of the car, his sightline fixed on his goal. Time remained frozen, or so it seemed to him, with countless variables of horror possible.

Most people hadn't even realised there was a problem. Callie was one of them. She was still walking across the street, oblivious to the danger hurtling towards her. Launching himself at her, he slammed her to the ground. There was a thump, a screech of brakes, and for a moment the world went black, then the woman in his arms, the woman he had cushioned from the edge of the pavement with his body, battled to break free.

'Are you okay?' she exclaimed with fierce concern, lifting herself up to stare at him.

Winded, he was only capable of a grunt. She stared at him in disbelief. 'Luca?'

He gulped in a lungful of fumes and dust, mixed with Callie's warm fragrance, then, as his brain clicked back into gear, he had only one concern, and that was Callie. 'Are you hurt?'

'No.' She hesitated. 'At least, I don't think so.'

Colour drained from her face. He could imagine the thoughts bombarding her brain. She was pregnant. Was the baby okay? Could she reel back the clock and walk across the road a few seconds later or sooner? Did she have any pain? She squeezed her eyes tightly shut, making him think she was examining her body, searching for signs of trauma, particularly in her womb. She slowly relaxed, which he took to be a good sign. And then she remembered him. He saw the recognition and surprise in her eyes turn to suspicion and anger, and then back again, when she remembered where they were and how they had got there.

'You saved me,' she breathed.

'Grazie Dio!' he murmured.

Her gaze hardened again. *He* was back. The man she had thought she knew had turned out to be someone else entirely. She'd flirted with him, and had had sex with a man she had believed to be an itinerant field worker, who had turned out to be a billionaire prince, and an important figure on the world stage. He could imagine her affront when she'd found out. It wouldn't have taken her long. Settling back into her normal life, she could hardly avoid seeing his face in the press after his enthronement. In shock, she would be trying to process every piece of information, amongst which had to be what the hell was he doing here?

He followed her gaze as she glanced around to see if anyone else was hurt. He saw the tyre marks on the pavement left by the car as it had mounted the kerb, and realised how kind fate had been. Pockets of survivors were checking each other out. Numbers were being exchanged and arms thrown around complete strangers. This was human nature at its best. From what he could see, everyone was shaken up, but thankfully unharmed. Quite a crowd had gathered. People were calling on their phones. The emergency services would arrive soon. The police were already on the scene. The youth behind the wheel of the speeding car had been captured. Patrol cars had his vehicle boxed in.

'Luca,' Callie gritted out, managing to fill that single

word with all the bitterness and uncertainty prompted by his supposed deception. When she was calm, she might realise they'd both been escaping their normal lives during their time in the lemon groves. Both had seized the chance to escape and explore a different, looser version of themselves. But none of that mattered now. All that mattered was that Callie was safe. However, she, understandably, took a rather different view. 'I can't believe this,' she said, staring at him. 'What are you doing here?'

Ignoring her understandable surprise, he concentrated on essentials. 'Take it easy. Slowly,' he advised as she struggled to sit up. 'You might feel dizzy for a while. You've had a shock.'

'To put it mildly,' she agreed. 'Are you all right?' she asked tensely.

'Don't worry about me.'

'You came down with quite a bang.'

He wasn't interested in discussing anything but Callie, and was only relieved that he'd reached her in time.

'Sorry.' She started to giggle. Hysteria, he guessed. 'But we must stop meeting like this.'

He couldn't agree more. They were lying in the road on a bed of grime and oil patches. Hoping that laughter signified her body's resilience to the blow it had just received, he huffed wryly, and for a moment they weren't at loggerheads, but just two people caught up in an unexpected incident on a cold and wintry street.

'Oh, no!' Callie was staring at the stolen vehicle, which was planted in what appeared to be a dress shop window. 'My landlady,' she exclaimed, starting to get up.

'Let me help you.'

She pushed him away in panic. 'I have to make sure she's all right.'

'You have to get checked out first,' he argued.

'What *are* you doing here?' she demanded as he shrugged off his jacket and draped it around her shoulders.

'You're in shock, Callie. You need to go to hospital for a check-up now.'

'I'm fine,' she insisted, starting to pull his jacket off.

He closed it around her. 'You're shivering. You're in shock,' he repeated, 'and until the paramedics get here and check you out, I'm not taking any chances.'

'So you freeze to death instead?'

'I don't think it will come to that,' he soothed, 'do you? I'm just glad I got here when I did. I couldn't get here any sooner.'

'I heard you'd been busy,' she admitted.

A paramedic interrupted them. 'You all right, love?' he asked, proffering a foil blanket. 'Let the gentleman have his jacket back, or he'll catch his death of cold.'

'I've been trying to give it back to him,' Callie explained, 'but he won't take it.'

'Well, if he's happy for you to keep it.' The paramedic shrugged as he arranged the foil blanket over the jacket for extra warmth. 'Not too many gallant gentlemen left, love,' he commented. 'Better hang onto this one.'

Callie hummed and smiled, though Luca wondered if her smile was for the paramedic's benefit. 'Was anyone else hurt?' she asked. 'The lady in the dress shop?'

'Had just gone to make herself a cup of tea,' the paramedic reassured her. 'She was working in the shop window, she told me, only minutes before the car struck.'

'What a relief,' Callie gasped. 'I was with her. I live over the shop,' she explained.

'It's thanks to the quick thinking of your knight in shining armour that a young mother and her baby were also shoved to safety and saved from injury. He's a real hero. Aren't you, sir?'

'I wouldn't say that.' Luca had acted on instinct. There had been no planning involved. There'd been no time to think. He'd done what was necessary to avert disaster, in his view, and that was all.

'Accept praise when it's due, sir. You're a genuine hero, sir,' the paramedic assured him. 'Now, excuse me, miss, but we'd better get you to hospital for a check-up. If the gentleman wants to come too—'

'He doesn't want to come,' Callie said with a glance his way. 'You obviously know where I live,' she added, narrowing her eyes, 'so we'll speak later.'

Shepherding her to one of the two waiting ambulances, the paramedic steadied her as she climbed inside. 'What are you doing?' Callie demanded when he swung in behind her.

'Collecting my jacket?' Luca suggested dryly.

The paramedic gave him a broad wink, but had the good sense to appear busy with paperwork when the doors closed and the ambulance set off. Callie disapproved of him accompanying her to the hospital. Too bad. As she had been a member of his staff, he had a duty of care towards her, and with a baby on the horizon that duty had doubled.

'You saved her, mate,' the paramedic put in as he settled down.

This wasn't how he'd pictured his reunion with Callie. He just wanted her to be safe.

'Have you been spying on me?' Callie asked, careful not to let their companion hear her conversation.

He shrugged. He wasn't going to lie. It was a fine line between his security team's protection service and overstepping the mark. 'Your welfare and that of our child is my only concern.'

She blenched. He didn't think he'd ever seen anyone so pale. 'Are you all right? Pain? You're not—'

'No. At least, I don't think so.' Her eyes were wide with fear as she stared at him. She reached for his hand. For the first time, she looked vulnerable. This was a very different woman from the Callie he'd met in Italy. This was a woman afraid for her unborn child, and discovering she cared for that child far more than she cared for herself. 'Don't,' she said. 'Don't look at me like that.'

'Like what?'

'As if I'm special and you're glad you're here.'

'You are special. You're about to become a mother, the mother of my child. And if I am looking at you, it's only because you're covered in grit and filth and need a good wash.'

'Charming, mate,' the paramedic piped up, proving that he wasn't lost in his work after all. 'Which charm school did you attend?'

'I didn't go to school until I was ten,' Luca admitted wryly. 'And then it was the school of hard knocks.'

'Hey, wait a minute,' the paramedic exclaimed, turning to stare at Luca intently. 'Aren't you that billionaire bloke who started life in the gutters of Rome and became a prince?' And when Luca didn't reply, he added, 'What are you doing in Blackpool?'

He winked at Callie. 'I've been checking out a new set of gutters, mate.'

'Don't you worry,' the paramedic told Callie. 'I won't tell a soul. And you're going to be okay, love, we'll make sure of that.'

The atmosphere lightened a little, and Callie didn't resist when Luca put his arm around her and drew her close.

CHAPTER SEVEN

Luca was back. Callie's mind was in turmoil, and as for her heart… What a time for him to choose to come back! The best time, she conceded gratefully as the ambulance raced towards the hospital. She knew shock was playing a part in her mixed-up feelings, but on top of the accident and Luca returning to find her, and above all the fear that her recent fall had harmed the baby, her thoughts were spinning around and around.

'Okay?'

Had she really believed that putting distance between them would lessen her feelings for him? This wasn't the Amalfi coast where she could make the excuse of her senses being heightened by sunlight and laughter, but a grey northern coastal town in winter, and yet Luca was as compelling as ever.

'Hey,' he whispered. 'You're safe now.'

His arms seemed designed to protect. They had certainly protected Callie when she'd needed him. And now Luca's embrace was sending a very different kind of shiver spinning down her spine.

'Look at me,' he whispered. 'I said, you're safe.'

Even with his hair tousled and grazes down one side of his face, Luca looked what he was: a hero, her hero.

When they'd first met it had been lust at first sight for Callie, but now it was something much more.

'Callie?'

Instinctively nursing her still-flat stomach, as if to protect the child inside, she stared into Luca's eyes.

'We're here,' he explained gently. 'We've arrived at the hospital.'

'Oh...'

The paramedic stood aside as Luca helped her down from the ambulance. She clutched the foil blanket tighter as the wind whipped around her shoulders. The only part of her that felt warm was her hand in Luca's. His grip was warm and strong, and it was with reluctance that she broke free from him in the screened-off cubicle when a doctor came to check her over.

'I want an exhaustive examination. Whatever it costs,' Luca emphasised.

'She'll have the best of care,' the doctor assured him. 'We'll be careful that nothing escapes our notice.'

'She's pregnant.'

Luca knew everything. He probably had a drone positioned over the house. But when he thanked the doctor and turned around, she could only feel warm and thankful that he was back.

He was unharmed and impatient to leave, but first he had to make absolutely sure that Callie was okay. He'd wait as long as it took. Mud spattered his clothes. His jeans were ripped. Every bit of exposed skin had taken a battering. The nurses wanted to treat his wounds, but all he cared about was Callie. He sat outside the exam room while she was put through various tests. They were both ecstatic at the outcome. Babies in the womb were surprisingly well protected against trauma, the doctor told them both, and Callie had got off lightly with a sprained ankle and a colourful selection of scrapes and bruises. Apart from the shock, she was fine and could go home. The medical staff had been superb at every stage. He showed his gratitude with a generous donation, which was very well received.

'And now for your bath,' he told Callie as he escorted her off the hospital premises.

'My bath?' she queried, looking at him in bemusement.

'Yes.' They'd cleaned up her minor injuries in the emergency room, but like him she was still covered in dirt from the road, and he had plans. A short drive to the airport would be followed by a flight to his superyacht where Callie could enjoy a rest at sea. Heading south to the sun would be the perfect remedy, allowing her to chill out in privacy while they discussed the future.

'I can have a bath at home,' she said. 'Leave me here. I'll take a cab. Thanks for all you've done—'

'You will not take a cab,' he assured her. 'You can play tough all you like, Callie Smith, but the rules changed when you got pregnant.'

'It took two for me to get pregnant,' she reminded him.

'Which is why I'm prescribing rest for you.'

She gave him a look and then pulled out her phone.

'What are you doing?'

'Calling my landlady to check she's okay, and calling a cab. And guess what,' she added after a few moments of conversation with someone on the other end of the line. 'Turns out an unknown fairy godmother has waved a magic wand, so builders and window fitters are already on site at my landlady's shop, securing the building. I don't suppose you'd know anything about that?'

'Fairy godfather, please.'

She hummed and gave him a look.

'About that cab,' he said.

'Please respect my independence, Luca.'

'I do,' he assured her.

'Anywhere *I* want to go could easily turn into wherever you plan for me to go, and I need to get used to you being back first.'

He had no answer for that. She was right.

'Are you going to log my every move?' she asked with a welcome return of her customary good humour.

'Only some of them,' he said straight-faced.

'My lift is on its way,' she said. 'Give me a chance to think things through. It's all been such a shock. And I don't just mean the accident. Finding out your true identity, and then the months we've spent apart. The gifts you sent. The notes you wrote.'

'Would it have been easier if I hadn't contacted you?'

A brief flash of pain in her eyes said it would have been hell. The same went for him.

'I knew we had to talk when I discovered I was having your baby. I would never leave you in the dark. I just need time to process everything that's happened today. Just the fact that your security team has been watching me is unnerving. I realise you're a prince and I'm having your child, but that doesn't give you the right to put me under surveillance.'

'Your safety will always be my concern.'

'Just don't let it become your obsession.'

'My security team check out anyone I'm seen with.

They report to me, and I can hardly avoid reading what they put in their reports.'

'I accept that,' she said, 'and I thank you for being so honest with me. And most especially for saving my life,' she added in a softer tone.

'I don't want your thanks. I want your time.' He was impatient for a very good reason. The royal council was pressing him to find a bride. The country was waiting. He needed an heir, and Callie's pregnancy had set a clock ticking. He needed things settled between them before the ticking stopped.

'You left me without an explanation, Luca, and now you're back I'm supposed to snap to attention?'

'I never misled you.'

'You never told me you were a prince, either,' Callie pointed out. 'You allowed me to believe that you and I were on the same level.'

'As we are,' he insisted.

She laughed and shook her head. 'That's a fantasy. You're a prince and a billionaire, and who am I?'

'The most determined woman I've ever met.'

'Flattery doesn't wash with me, Luca. We had sex, the deepest intimacy of all, and then you simply turned your back and walked away. That means one thing to me. You're incapable of feeling.'

'You disappeared and pitched up here. Is that so different?'

'I was never going to stay in Italy for ever. It was a once-in-a-lifetime opportunity for me. I always knew I'd come home at some point. And now I intend to study and go on to make a purposeful life. You might be used to women throwing themselves at you, but—'

'Not in the way that just happened,' he said dryly.

She couldn't bear this. She couldn't bear the mash-up of feelings inside her. Her body was bruised. Her thoughts were in turmoil. She was in love with Luca. Their short, passionate time in Italy had left an indelible brand on her heart, but he was a man she could never have. He knew that as well as she did, surely?

'There's fault on both sides,' Luca insisted. 'You didn't reply to my letters. You refused to see me. You rejected my gifts. And, yes, I can see it must have seemed to you that I'd callously walked away, but I hope you can see now that there was a very good reason for my absence. Spend some time in Fabrizio. See the type of life our child will have.'

Fear speared through her at his words. *Hormones.* She knew she was overreacting, but he would sweep her away if she let him. He would expect the royal child to live with him. Yes, she should get to know his world. Luca was no ordinary man. She could never compete with his wealth, or royal status, but she believed just as strongly in her own values, and in her ability to bring up their child. They had to talk, but not right now. 'My cab's here—' She looked at his hand on her arm.

'What are you proposing, Callie?'

Luca's tone had changed, hardened. Their baby wouldn't benefit from parents at war. 'Truce,' she said. 'I'm proposing a truce. You're a hero. You saved me. You saved our child's life. I can never thank you enough for that. If nothing else, I'm sure we can be friends.'

'Friends?' Luca frowned.

'Please? For the sake of our child.'

Her cab rolled up at the kerb. Talking was done. He ground his jaw. Why wouldn't she take the lift he'd offered? He could call up a diplomatic limousine in minutes. Was this how it was going to be? He couldn't allow Callie a free hand. The heir to Fabrizio was too precious for that.

'I can't believe my new phone is still in one piece,' she said, glancing at it before putting it away.

'Give me your number.' He pulled out his phone.

'Give me *your* number,' she countered, 'and I'll call you when I'm ready.'

'Can I at least know where you're going,?'

'I'll call you,' she said as she climbed into the cab.

Seething inside, he gave her his number. After the accident and the shock of seeing him, he had to cut her some slack, but seeing Callie again was non-negotiable. He had every intention of keeping track of his unborn child. Grinding his jaw as the cab drove away, he had to remind himself this wasn't the end of anything, but just the start of their return match.

If her feelings had been mixed up before, they were ready to explode by the time she walked down the steps of the civic building to find Luca waiting outside. Lounging back against a sleek black car, he was staring at her with the lazy confidence that suggested he knew exactly what had happened at her job interview. *Of course he knew.*

Firming her jaw, she quickened her step towards him. The sooner they got this over with, the better. She'd had her suspicions at the start of her interview. It hadn't taken her long to realise she was never going to get the job, and the director of tourism was just curious to meet her. Even he'd admitted she was everything they were looking for; gregarious and well informed, she had read up on the history of the famous illuminations from the nineteenth century to the present day.

'And I know every nook and cranny of the town,' she'd assured him, explaining she'd visited Blackpool on numerous occasions.

'In short, you're perfect for the job,' he agreed, just before he shuffled awkwardly in his seat and explained that the vacancy was no longer available.

So why see her at all? Callie had wondered, until the director of tourism had added, 'Don't look so disappointed. I'm told you have a glittering future ahead of you.'

'What did it cost you?' she challenged Luca tensely. She'd come to a halt in front of him, and was determined to get the truth out of him, whatever it took.

'Cost me?' He frowned.

'How much did it cost you to spoil my chances for that job?' she demanded tight-lipped.

'Nothing,' he admitted.

'You're lying,' she said quietly.

'I think you should calm down,' Luca remarked as he opened the passenger door of his car. 'Climb in.'

'Not a chance.'

'Please.'

She started to walk past him, but he caught hold of her arm. 'Where do you think you're going?' he asked. 'You can't go back to the shop. It's all boarded up.' His voice was still low and even, but it had taken on an edge. 'Your landlady is spending the night in a very comfortable local hotel while my builders complete their repairs.'

'*Your* builders,' she snapped. 'That says it all. *Your* hand in my failure at interview just now. And you say you're not controlling? What else do you have in store for me, Luca?'

Releasing her arm, he stood back. 'I provided a faster

solution for your landlady than her insurance company could hope to offer, and that is all. As for your job interview, how are you going to work as a tour guide when you're heavily pregnant? I can't risk the mother of my child being exposed to people who might exploit her to get at me. Your situation has changed, Callie, whether you like it or not.'

'It certainly has,' she agreed. 'I was free and now I'm not.' She was furious. 'How did you get an appointment to meet with the Director of Tourism so fast?'

'His secretary recognised me.'

'Of course she did. Since your enthronement you're all over the news. "The world's most eligible bachelor",' she quoted tensely, 'who just happens to have a pregnant and discarded mistress on the side.'

'Very dramatic,' he said.

'Dramatic? Since you came into my life, everything's been dramatic—' She bit off her angry words, remembering that without Luca she'd probably be dead and so would their unborn child. Hormones again, she realised. Definitely hormones. The next thing she knew there were tears in her eyes. She drove them back. 'You said it cost you nothing to stand in the way of me getting that job. What *did* you do, Luca? You must have said something?'

'I did,' he confirmed, shielding her as the wind blasted them. 'I offered reciprocal marketing of our two very different holiday destinations.'

'There must be more.'

'There was,' he confirmed evenly. 'I told him I wanted you to work for me.'

'What?'

'Get in the car.'

She was shivering violently. It was freezing cold. They

stared at each other, unblinking. They both knew there could be no walking away this time. Callie had very little money left, and nowhere to stay tonight. Even a simple boarding house at this time of year, when the illuminations were drawing crowds to the resort, cost far more than she could afford to spend.

'Where will you take me?' she asked.

'I thought you had a sense of adventure.'

'I don't like surprises.' But her options were zero. They had to speak at some point. Why not now? Surely two intelligent human beings could come to an amicable agreement?

Seriously?

Yes, because this wasn't about either of them, but about their child, and with their histories Callie was prepared to bet that both of them would put that child first.

The passenger door closed with a soft clunk, enclosing Callie in a very different world. This was a world that only the super-rich could afford. It wasn't the spicy warmth of the lemon groves, or the anodyne interior of a five-star hotel, but was so comfortable that it could easily muddle her mind. It was far too tempting to relax and not think of anything but getting to her destination, wherever that might be, safely and warmly. Soft classical music played in the background, while the scent of soft leather assailed her senses. In spite of all the warnings to self, she relaxed and drank it in.

This was the scent of money, she thought as Luca swung into the driver's seat. He only added to her pleasure with his natural warmth, and the scent of warm clean man, laced with the light, exotic fragrance he always wore. He pressed a button and the engine purred. The sexy black car pulled effortlessly out into the flowing traffic. There were no brash noises, no sharp edges, nothing to alarm. The vehicle was precision engineering at its finest, rather like the workings of Luca's mind.

He drove as smoothly and as skilfully as he did everything else. They were heading out of town, she noticed, towards the airport. She had some decisions to make, and had better make them fast. She had agreed to get in the car, but had she agreed to travel out of the country? The thought of seeing Luca on his home turf was an exciting prospect, but she was wary of being seduced into giving up her freedom. Even now she knew his true identity, he was still the most brutally handsome and desirable man. Her body ached and longed for him. Her mind told her they needed to talk. Her soul said they were meant to be together. On a far baser level, pregnancy had made her mad for sex, and there was only one answer to that.

CHAPTER EIGHT

THE ROYAL JET was waiting. On this occasion he would not be the pilot. He escorted Callie on board as if she were already his Princess. He understood her need for freedom. Theirs would be a marriage for practical reasons, tying neither of them down. Its sole purpose would be to provide Fabrizio with the longed-for heir. Would she agree to that proposal? Better this woman he cared for than some unknown princess from Michel's list, and it would fulfil Callie's wish for independence.

Callie would certainly agree to sex. Pheromones were threatening to drown him. Electricity wasn't just snapping, it was threatening to bring down the national grid. Taking her by the wrist, he led her straight to the rear of the plane where his private quarters were located. He had given instructions that they were not to be disturbed under any circumstances, short of an aviation meltdown. They didn't speak. They didn't need to. Callie's needs were flashing like neon signs. They'd talk later. Opening the door to his lavish suite, he ushered her inside.

'Luca—'

'Too much talking.' She was still wearing high heels and her prim interview suit. 'Keep the shoes on.'

'What?'

'You heard me. Take everything else off.' She had the best legs on earth, elongated by the high-heeled shoes, and a figure to die for. The height of the heels thrust her hips forward in a way he found irresistible. Caging her with his arms either side of her face, and his fists planted against the door, he brushed his lips against hers for the sheer pleasure of hearing her moan.

'All my clothes?' she asked, snatching a breath.

'Yes.'

Erotic heat clouded her eyes. 'You haven't told me where you're taking me.'

'You're going to love the surprise.'

'Let me decide,' she insisted. 'Tell me, then I'll take my clothes off.'

She was teasing *him*?

'You don't play fair,' she gasped as he pressed his body against hers.

'Have you only just noticed?'

Rolling his hips, he rubbed his body against her while she groaned. When he pulled back she moved frantically towards him in an attempt to repeat the contact. The jet engines whined into life right on cue. The aircraft was ready for take-off. Any time soon there would be the most enormous thrust and they'd take to the sky. 'You're overdressed,' he commented.

'Why couldn't we talk in Blackpool?' she asked, playing for time, he guessed.

'In a hotel, somewhere anonymous and clinical? Wouldn't you rather be here?'

She gasped as he found her. 'I can't.'

'I think you'll find you can.' He dropped a kiss on her shoulder.

'Who lives like this?' she said, staring past him at

the designer-led living quarters on board his state-of-the-art jet.

'Stop trying to distract yourself and enjoy.'

'No. I can't. *I can't...*'

'You must. I insist.' Using his tongue to tease his way into her mouth, he deepened the kiss and pressed her back against the door. Every inch of her felt amazing. Had he really thought he knew how much he'd missed her, missed this? He didn't have a clue. Using his thigh to edge her legs apart, he finished what he'd started. She went quite still and then cried out repeatedly. It was some time before she quietened.

Her eyes remained closed, Her breathing remained hectic. He caressed her breasts while she recovered, teasing nipples that had tightened into prominent buds very lightly with his thumbnail. Gasping out his name, she rested her head against his chest as he stroked and teased her.

'I think we should take this to bed,' he said at last.

She gave him a teasing look.'Shouldn't we be strapped in?'

'If that's what you'd like?' he offered.

'You're bad,' she said as he took her to see the specially designed bed belt. 'For the billionaire who has everything, I presume?'

'For the turbulence,' he confirmed.

'Do you expect much turbulence?'

'I expect a great deal of turbulence.'

'You're worse than I thought,' she said, laughing and relaxed now.

'Worse than you know.' Bringing her into his arms, he kissed her. When he let her go she searched his eyes in a way that touched him somewhere deep. Callie didn't see herself as he saw her. She was a refreshing change. Most women of his acquaintance were overly self-aware, while Callie was oblivious to how attractive she was.

'Why are you looking at me like that?' she asked him softly.

'I'm anticipating having sex with you.'

'That's convenient.'

'Is it?'

'Yes.' She bit back a smile. 'Because I'm doing the same.'

He moved over her. She writhed beneath him. She opened herself to him, inviting him to explore. 'Now,' she said with a kitten smile that made him hungrier than ever. She quivered with arousal beneath his hands as he teased her lips apart with his tongue. As he deepened the kiss she melted against him. He pressed her into the bed to rediscover the contours of her body. She was driving him crazy with lust. He was driving them both crazy, with delay. Lifting her on top of him, he caressed her buttocks, stroking them as she sighed and groaned, until finally he clasped them to position her. Reversing positions, he brought her under him.

'What about your clothes?' she asked.

He started to undress, but Callie was ahead of him. Ripping off his clothes, she wasn't satisfied until they were both completely naked. Taking hold of her shoulders, he held her away from him so he could give her a long, hard look. 'I've missed you,' he ground out.

'I've missed you too.' She was trembling with excitement and anticipation, asking him with her body to be held, to be kissed, and to be pleasured until she was exhausted. He had no intention of falling short in any way. Throwing her onto her back, he hooked her legs over his shoulders. He took a long, appreciative look, and then dipped his head and feasted while Callie groaned and bucked.

'The bed straps,' she gasped out.

'Are you asking to be restrained?'

'Sounds as if we're about to take off,' she warned, turning her head on the pillows to listen.

He shrugged as the whine of the engines turned into an imperative roar. 'I think you could be right,' he agreed dryly. 'I definitely think you should be held firmly and safely in place.' Securing her in a few deft moves, he returned to finish what he'd started.

She didn't last long. *'Aaaah...'* The cry of pleasure seemed torn from her soul. It escalated into a series of rhythmical, primal sounds deep in her throat. They tormented him. She tormented him. His was a seriously painful state.

'Ah...ah...' she gasped out repeatedly, bucking so furiously that even the straps and his hands had a battle to contain her. Once she was capable of speech, she instructed, 'I need you inside me now,' with her customary bluntness.

This coincided with the pilot applying full thrust. Pinning Callie's hands above her head on the bank of soft cushions, he did the same. The sensation as the aircraft soared and they did too, was mind-numbing. Whatever he'd imagined about sex with Callie again was nothing compared to this. She was perfection. Her inner muscles gripped him with a vigour he could never have anticipated, and from there it was a wild, furious ride to satisfaction. By the time the jet had levelled out, Callie had enjoyed at least three noisy climaxes, and was ready for more. When she was done, he turned her on her side. 'Curl up and let me touch you. I want to watch.'

They were both blunt in bed when it came to what they liked. Callie didn't just agree to his proposition, she used colourful language to outline exactly what was expected of him. She lifted her thigh to tempt him even more, and angled her hips so he could see everything. He sank deep with a groan of contentment. 'More,' she insisted. 'More.'

He felt as if his climax started at his toes and then flooded his entire body. They were engaged in a very primitive act. He was claiming his mate. She was claiming hers. Where this could lead he had no idea, and he wasn't in any condition to reason things through sensibly. 'I only have one complaint,' he said, bringing her on top of him when they were quiet again.

'A complaint?' she queried.

'You should always wear more clothes so there are more to take off.'

She relaxed and smiled, and, sighing with contentment, she added, 'Well, that's your Christmas present sorted out.'

Then she fell silent. He realised it was only a matter of days before Christmas. There had been so much going on he hadn't even realised. 'Hey,' he whispered, seeing Callie frown. 'We're definitely going to be together at Christmas.'

'Are we?' Her voice was matter of fact. Her stare was deep and long.

'Yes,' he confirmed, stroking her back to soothe her. 'You're not going to be spending Christmas in one room over a shop. I want you to see where I live.'

'I know where you live.'

'I mean Fabrizio.'

'It's still a palace.' She sighed as if picturing a world filled with art treasures, flunkeys and hushed decorum, when the truth was a modern palace that was more of a workplace. He had homes across the world where he enjoyed complete privacy, but since his enthronement the palace had become his main residence. He had an apartment there. The palace in Fabrizio was the engine of the dynasty, but his wing was elegant and private. The boy from the gutters had come a long way. 'Where I live overlooks a lake and gardens, and has every comfort a child could need,' he reassured Callie.

Better than one room over a shop, he could see her thinking. 'I'm sure it's lovely,' she agreed, tense now. Turning her back on him, she pulled up the covers and pretended to sleep. She did drift off eventually, while he lay at her side with his arms folded behind his head, checking his plan to make sure there'd be no hitches.

When she woke, she sat up and spotted the selection of outfits on a rail immediately. 'Where did they come from?'

'The cabin attendant wheeled them in.'

'While I was asleep? In your arms?'

'You were well covered up. I asked my private secretary to make sure there were some dresses and accessories on board for you, for when you disembark.'

'I've got my suit.'

He glanced at the creased skirt and jacket, still lying on the floor where she'd dropped them. 'Well, I have to say, this is another first.'

'What is?'

'A woman refusing to look at a rail of clothes.'

'Chauvinist.' Grabbing a sheet around her, she swung

off the bed. 'I didn't say I wouldn't look at them, but I must insist on paying for whatever I choose.'

'I would expect nothing less of you,' he assured her, straight-faced.

'Are you mocking me?' she demanded.

'Maybe a little,' he admitted wryly.

For a few seconds as they stared at each other, he was stunned by how Callie made him feel. He had always guarded his emotions, but with Callie that wasn't possible. Even with the Prince, his late father, it had been very much a man-to-man relationship. He'd never had any softening influences in his life. Women had always been accessories in the past, a deal that worked well both ways, but Callie was different, special. Tousle-haired and flushed from sleep, she was drowsy-eyed with contentment, but still ready to take him on if she felt it necessary. His groin tightened at the thought. Unfortunately there wasn't time. They'd be landing soon. 'I'm looking forward to seeing which outfit you choose.'

She hummed and shot him a warning look.

That was all it took. He'd been inactive long enough. Crossing the cabin, he yanked her close to plant a hard, hot kiss on her tempting mouth. 'Surprise me,' he whispered.

'Don't I always?'

He kissed her again.

'What was that for?' she demanded.

'A down-payment on later.'

'I won't be bribed,' she warned.

He laughed as he left the cabin. They'd slept together, made love together, and been happy together. Now they had a deal to make that both they and Fabrizio could live with. He was sure of Callie in so many ways. She was full of light and love and passion, and was honest and direct to a fault. That didn't mean he could predict how she would react to the idea of raising their child in Fabrizio, but for him that outcome was non-negotiable.

She chose a simple outfit of jeans, crisp white shirt and a smart navy-blue blazer, teamed with a pair of mid-heeled boots. She felt comfortable, confident, and happy—until she saw the royal chauffeur, standing by the side of the big royal limousine. The imposing black vehicle flying the crimson and gold flag of Fabrizio on its bonnet, above a shield that displayed Luca's royal house in images of a lion, a rearing black stallion and a mandolin, was a real punch between the eyes, reminding her that Luca was a royal prince with all the money, power, and influence he could ever wish for, while she couldn't even get a job.

The chauffeur stood proudly to attention as Luca appeared at the door of the aircraft. He ushered her ahead of him. She felt exposed. The blazer and jeans didn't seem enough somehow now that Luca had changed into a smart, dark linen suit with a pale blue open-necked shirt. If he'd looked stunning before, he looked like a prince now. Then, she thought, *Stand tall, you've got as much right as anyone else to fall down the steps of an aircraft.*

'Take my arm,' Luca directed, making sure she didn't have another accident.

'Are you sure?' she asked, thinking he would not want to be seen with her in a way that could compromise him.

'Of course, so long as you give it back,' he said.

Lifting a brow as he stared at her, Luca made her laugh.

Turned out, it wasn't so hard, this royal business. Luca's humour helped. She smiled. The chauffeur smiled back. He saluted as he opened the door of the fabulous royal limousine, and she thanked him when he saw her safely inside.

'That wasn't so bad, was it?' Luca demanded as the chauffeur closed the door, enclosing them in the heavy silence Callie was fast becoming used to in these luxury vehicles.

'Not bad at all,' she admitted. 'Why are you doing that?' she asked when he lowered the privacy screen.

'Because I want you.'

Luca was as blunt as she was. Reaching across the wide expanse of soft cream kidskin, he dragged her onto his lap. 'You should have chosen a dress.'

'Luc—' She was about to protest, but he cut her off with a blistering kiss, and at the same time his hand found her. 'Oh, no,' she groaned, yielding to the inevitable as she opened her legs a little more. 'Oh, no?' he queried. 'Does that mean you want me to stop?'

'Don't you dare,' she whispered, rubbing her still-tender lips against his sharp black stubble. 'I wish I'd chosen a dress too.'

'I'm sure we can manage,' Luca said as his fingers worked deftly on the fastening at her waist. 'It's not as if we're stuck for space.'

'But do we have time?' she asked as he pulled off her jeans and she pulled off her jacket, this time remembering to fold it neatly.

'Enough time,' Luca ground out. 'Now your thong?' he suggested, settling back to watch.

'What about your clothes?'

'What about my clothes?' Lowering his zipper, he freed himself, proving he was more than adequately prepared. Reaching out, he brought her onto his lap. 'Straddle me,' he insisted, 'and make it slow.'

She felt deliciously exposed with her legs widely spread, and deliciously excited when Luca's hand found her. He was right about taking it slowly. She would never grow used to the size of him.

He felt so good. Linking her hands around his neck, she allowed him to guide her carefully down. He decided the pace, while she concentrated on sensation. She cried out with disappointment when his grip tightened on her buttocks, and he lifted her almost off him. Her cries of complaint brought a smile to his face, and he slowly lowered her again. Pressing down on her buttocks made sure that the contact between them was complete. And then he began to move. His hips thrust, sending him deep inside her, and he upped the tempo with each stroke until she could only bury her face in his jacket and wait for release. When it came it was incredible, and he knew just how to prolong it.

'Better now?' he asked quietly as she subsided into a series of soft, rhythmical sighs.

Callie lifted her head. 'Is there time for more?'

With a soft laugh against her mouth, Luca obliged.

CHAPTER NINE

FABRIZIO WAS BEAUTIFUL and quaint, with winding cobbled streets, and tree-filled parks at every turn. People waved and cheered when they saw the royal car, and Luca lowered the window when Callie was dressed again, so he could wave back. His timing, as always, was impeccable. She had caught her first sight of his fabulous palace when they were a few miles away. Surrounded by ancient city walls, the royal palace of Fabrizio sat atop a hill from where the defenders of old could see their enemies coming for miles around. It was the most beautiful building she had ever seen with a grandeur that even his *palazzo* in Amalfi couldn't match. Where that had been wedding-cake pretty, this was royal splendour cast in stone, wrought iron and stained glass. When the royal limousine drew up in front of a wide sweep of stone steps, Luca helped her out of the car and then left her in the care of his housekeeper and a maid, while he hurried off into the building.

Having crossed an exquisite hall, full of shields and swords and ancient portraits, Callie was taken up a sweeping staircase to the first level where she was shown into the most beautiful light and airy apartment. Knowing it would be hers for the duration of her stay was just incredible. The delicately decorated French furniture, the Aubusson rugs yielding softly underfoot, the twinkling glass and antique ornaments, the gilded mirrors—*what was she doing here?*

She thanked the stiffly formal housekeeper and the maid tasked with looking after her. Waiting until the door closed behind them, she headed for the unbelievably beautiful bathroom to take a shower in an enclosure big enough to house an entire rugby team. There was every conceivable type of potion, cream and bath foam, not in their original containers, but in the most exquisite cut glass jars and jugs. Lifting the fragile lid on one of these, she inhaled deeply. And sneezed. She was a little bit allergic to scent. But not to Luca's scent, Callie reflected wryly as she turned full circle to admire the pink-veined marble walls. What was he doing now? she wondered as she glanced at the internal telephone. She didn't want him to think her desperate. Let him call her, she decided. *Please.*

There was no such thing as the hot water running out at the palace. She basked in the luxury of heat and fragrant scent until she felt thoroughly clean, cosy, and fresh again. Then she donned a fluffy robe and wondered what to do about clothes. Pushing her feet into slippers she found ready in the bathroom, that matched the robe, she returned to the bedroom with its panelling and paintings, and floating silk voile, drifting romantically in front of the open window. She suddenly felt incredibly homesick and reached for her phone. What she needed was someone down to earth to confide in, someone she could trust to act as an honest sounding board. Ma Brown answered on the first ring.

'Ma...'

'Yes, dear?'

Ma Brown's concerned tone both bolstered Callie and provided a much-needed wake-up call. She had never been a moaner, and she wasn't about to start now that she was about to become a mother. 'I don't want you worrying about me,' she stressed, 'so I'm giving you an update.'

'Ooh, lovely,' Ma Brown enthused.

Callie could just picture her dear friend, pausing mid baking, or ironing, or dusting, or stirring a pot of something delicious on the stove, to hear what Callie knew she had to make into a Christmas fairy tale so that Ma Brown would smile and share it with the family, rather than fret about Callie over Christmas. 'I'm in Fabrizio,' she began.

'I knew it!' Ma Brown exclaimed. 'You're with the Prince.'

'Yes. But there's something else—'

'You're pregnant!' Ma Brown shrieked before Callie had chance to say a word.

'I had intended to break it to you gently—'

Ma Brown wasn't listening. 'Has he proposed yet?'

'No,' Callie admitted.

'Why ever not?' Ma Brown demanded good-humouredly. 'Do you need me to come out there and prompt him? I will, if you like. I can easily catch a flight.'

'No,' Callie said again, this time laughing. Ma Brown's voice had soared at least an octave. She probably didn't need a phone to be heard in Fabrizio. 'I promise I can deal with it.'

'Tell me about his country, then,' Ma Brown compromised, snatching a noisy breath as she attempted to calm down.

To a casual listener, their conversation might have

seemed a little blasé under the circumstances, but Ma Brown could always imply more by her tone than she said in words. The simple phrase, tell me about Fabrizio, for instance, promised that the subject of Callie's pregnancy had not been forgotten, but merely put on the back burner for now. One thing was certain. Ma Brown would always be on Callie's side. Missing out the fact that she should have been planning her future, rather than scrambling over Luca, having sex in his jet and then in his car, Callie cut straight to the particulars. 'Everything in Fabrizio looks as if it has been polished to a flawless sheen. Think Monte Carlo with a touch of Dubai—'

'Oo-er,' Ma Brown exclaimed, breathless with excitement. 'Go on,' she prompted.

'Luca's palace looks like something out of a fairy tale. It's like Cinderella's castle with turrets and crenellations. There's even a drawbridge over the moat.'

'Imagine the staff needed to look after that,' Ma Brown breathed in awe.

'And everyone wears uniform,' Callie confirmed to add to the picture. 'Sentries stand guard wearing black velvet tunics braided with gold—'

'Goodness,' Ma Brown cut in. 'Isn't that all a bit intimidating?'

You have no idea, Callie thought, but what she actually said was, 'Poof! Not for you and me, Ma.'

'That's the spirit,' Ma Brown exulted. 'I've read about the palace and how fabulous it is. The countryside around it is supposed to be equally beautiful. Tell me about that now.'

Hmm. Difficult topic, Callie thought as the silence extended. 'I was so excited on the drive from the airport to the palace I didn't take much notice,' she admit-

had completely switched around. The baby came first. It always would. Every decision Callie made from now on would be in the best interests of her child.

Luca's child also.

Closing her eyes, she reviewed what she'd seen of Luca's life to date. From the vast, echoing hallway, with it frescoes on the lofty ceiling, to the foot of a wide sweep of crimson-carpeted stairs, her head hadn't stop whirring as she gazed around. Did she need more proof that she didn't belong here? It hardly seemed possible that just a few hours ago she had been planning to make do and mend to raise a child she already loved. In the palace she was surrounded by so much…*everything.* The five-star hotel she'd thought so lavish was a mere potting shed compared to this. She had to stop short of pinching herself to make sure it wasn't all a dream. When a knock came at the door and it opened without Callie saying a word, she sprang up guiltily.

'Oh, sorry, madam, I—'

'No—please, come in. And please call me Callie…'

Callie paled as the maid stood back against the wall to allow a team of footmen to wheel several gown rails into the room. These were laden with a sparkling array of full-length ball gowns. Cinderella had nothing on this, Callie concluded, frowning. 'There must be some mistake,' she said.

'No mistake, madam,' the maid assured her. 'As it's rather short notice, His Serene Highness apologises for not sending you an invitation to the ball, but he wants you to know that you are free to choose any of these dresses to wear.'

'His Serene Highness expects me to attend the ball?'

'He does, madam.'

Then, His Serene High and Mightiness could have the courtesy to come and tell her that himself, Callie thought, but she thanked the maid, who was the innocent messenger. 'I hope this hasn't put you to too much trouble?'

'None at all, madam. As soon as you've made your choice, if you ring this bell…' the maid indicated a silken tassel hanging on the wall '… I'll return immediately to help you dress.'

'The ball's tonight?' Callie exclaimed in panic.

'Oh, no, madam. This is just to give you chance to choose your gown and try it on. The Prince has instructed me to tell you that he will be with you by seven o'clock this evening to discuss your choice of gown.'

Hmm, Callie thought. And take it off, if she knew Luca. She couldn't imagine he cared less what she wore. He was far more interested in removing her clothes.

As soon as the maid had gone, she walked over to the rail to check out the selection of dresses. She'd never seen so many fabulous outfits before. There were gowns in every colour in the rainbow. Some were beaded, some had frills, and some had gauzy ribbon. Nearly all of them had low necks, and/or big slits up the side and plunging backs. She guessed she was ungrateful for thinking all of them a bit over the top. She was frightened to touch them in case she soiled them, but she had to choose one. Picking out an aquamarine gown, her favourite colour, she held it up against her, but it was so heavily beaded it weighed a ton. She had to admit that the scent of fine silk, and the sight of such expert tailoring, did take her breath. There was boning inside the bodice, so no need to wear a bra, and the skirt was such a slender column, she'd have to hop, Callie reflected wryly as she returned it to the rail.

One after the other she discarded the dresses. She couldn't see herself wearing any of them. They were far too fancy, and didn't look at all comfortable to wear. Crossing the room, she rang the bell.

'Yes, madam?' the maid enquired politely.

'We're around the same size. Could you lend me a pair of jeans and a top so I can go shopping?' There must be a high street in Fabrizio, she reasoned.

'Go *shopping*, madam?' the maid repeated as if Callie had suggested dancing naked in the street. 'I'll have a selection of outfits delivered to you within the hour.'

'Really?'

'Of course.'

'Okay, but be sure to give me the—' Before she had chance to say, 'receipt, so I can pay the bill,' the maid had left the room and closed the door.

Callie heaved a sigh. What was she supposed to do now? She tried to ring Luca, but that was like trying to get hold of the Queen of England. She went through half a dozen people and none of them would put her through to him. It was already nine o'clock in the evening. He'd left her alone to stew. Talking of which, she was hungry. Picking up the internal phone, she rang the kitchen to order a tray of sandwiches and a pot of tea. Hmm. So much for the high life! And so much for the discussions they were supposed to be having. Could matters of State be so much more important than their child?

She drank the tea, ate the sandwiches, then walked around the apartment until she knew every inch of it by heart. It was a gilded cage for the Prince's pet bird, Callie concluded. It was impersonal. The drawers were empty. There wasn't even a book to be found. There certainly wasn't anything as crass as a TV. Opening the glass doors onto her private veranda, she sat down at the wrought-iron table. Listening to the night sounds soothed her. It was a beautiful evening, but where was Luca? She should have known by now that sex meant nothing to him, and he could just walk away, forget it, forget her.

She went back into the room when it began to get chilly. She'd forgotten that the maid had promised to have more clothes delivered, and the room was full of them. She couldn't deny that rooting through the boxes and carrier bags was fun. Choosing a pair of jeans and a loose sports top, she exchanged her fluffy robe for a casual look that would take her through to bedtime.

More tea?

More tea.

She was just concluding, with a return of good humour, that wading through such a vast selection of clothes was exhausting, when the door opened and Luca walked in.

'Tea, madam?'

She almost jumped out of her skin. Even with a tray of tea in his hands, he was everything she could desire in a man. Dark, tall, and powerfully built. She would never get used to the breath-stealing sight of him. He'd changed into jeans and a crisp white shirt with the sleeves rolled up. *Those arms!* His jeans were cinched with a heavy-duty belt that drew attention to his washboard waist. His shoulders were epic and his powerful forearms were tanned and shaded with just the right amount of dark hair.

Those arms belonged around her, she concluded, forgetting her good intentions as he strode across the room. She was supposed to be having a serious discussion with him, not falling victim to his dazzling charm. *Be objective*, she told herself firmly.

'Ah, the dresses have arrived,' he commented as his stare swept over the gown rail. 'Now for the fashion show.' Throwing himself down on a finely upholstered chaise longue, he made a gesture she could only presume was supposed to goad her into action.

'Are you going to model them for me, then?' she asked. 'You mentioned a fashion show?' she prompted when Luca raised a brow.

For a moment he looked bemused and then he laughed. 'You never change, do you?'

'I hope not. Hooking up in a car does not a future make, Prince Luca. You and I have some serious talking to do.'

'Soon,' he promised. 'But first a toast,' he insisted, standing up.

'In tea?' she queried.

'I can send for champagne—'

'I can't—'

'Of course you can't.' With a grimace, he reached for her, and, jerking her close, he linked their fingers in a way she found very hard to resist. 'Forgive me,' he whispered, slanting a grin. 'I had forgotten why we're here for the moment.'

'Don't,' she warned with a straight look into his eyes.

'I was about to propose a toast to the heir to the principality of Fabrizio,' he explained.

She hummed. 'In that case, I'll forgive you.'

When Luca smiled his wicked smile, if it hadn't been for the sexual tension between them they were close enough in that moment to be just two friends enjoying a moment of trust between themselves.

'Have you chosen your ball gown yet?' he asked, turning to glance at the packed gown rail.

'I want you to feel comfortable. I know you'll look beautiful. It's going to be a special night for both of us, because this is my chance to introduce you to my guests.'

'As what?' she asked.

Luca appeared to ponder this. 'My personal assistant? No.' His lips pressed down as he shook his head. 'What about Keeper of the Crown Jewels? More accurate?'

'This is serious,' Callie warned. 'Please stop teasing me. If I'm going to attend my first ball with you, I need to know where I stand. That's the only way I'm going to feel comfortable.'

'Comfortable was the wrong word. I can see that now,' Luca admitted. 'I want you to feel sensational. As the ball is tomorrow evening you'd better choose one of these gowns to make sure you do.'

But that wasn't what she was here for. She had come to Fabrizio to talk about their baby.

What about the promise she'd made to Ma Brown to send a full report on the ball? Callie glanced at the glamorous gowns twinkling on the rail. She wouldn't be able to get into any of them in a few months' time, not that she'd have any use for a ball gown when she went home. 'I'll look ridiculous,' she fretted as she rifled through the rail.

'You'll look beautiful,' Luca argued, making himself comfortable. 'Let's make a start.'

'I'll change in the dressing room,' she said, picking out the aquamarine gown that had first caught her eye. 'And I'm not coming out if I look a freak.'

Safe behind the door to her dressing room, Callie stared at herself in the mirror and grimaced. The gown that had looked so pretty on the rail did fit well, but, apart from being so heavy, it was too tight. It pushed her breasts up and her confidence down. But that wasn't what really worried her. When she emerged from the dressing room, Luca agreed. 'You look like a mermaid,' he said as she wiggled her way across the room.

'Thank goodness that's a no.'

'Unless you plan to hop into position at my side?' he suggested.

'I could drift towards you in this,' she suggested when she had changed into the next dress, a coral number with long chiffon floats flying from each shoulder.

'Nah. You'll only get caught in the door.'

'You know me too well.'

'I'm getting there,' Luca admitted dryly as Callie chose another dress.

'This one?' she asked uncertainly, blowing fronds of fern-like decoration away from her face.

'You look like a market garden,' Luca dismissed as she performed a twirl.

True enough, the big floral pattern wasn't her best look.

'What about this one?' he suggested, selecting a plain, intricately beaded flesh-coloured gown.

'Yes. That's nice,' she agreed. 'I'll try it on.'

With the dressing-room door closed between them again, Callie stared at her reflection in amazement. She actually looked quite good. Smoothing the delicate fabric over her frame, she had to admit that the gown Luca had chosen was both elegant and sexy. She might have known he'd have exquisite taste. The shade of the fabric matched her skin tone so exactly it was almost possible to imagine she was naked. Naked and shimmering with a slit up the side of the dress that almost reached her waist. Taking a deep breath, she opened the door.

Luca said nothing at all. His face was completely expressionless. This was Luca at his most dangerous, she thought. 'No,' she warned when he stood up and prowled towards her.

'Why not?' he husked. 'It's not as if I can make you pregnant.'

'Luca!'

He swallowed her protests in a kiss, and it wasn't just a kiss but a whole-body experience that made her hunger for him eclipse everything. His hands were warm on her body. He knew every slope and curve. The gown was so sheer, so delicate, that his touch transmitted effortlessly through it as if they were both naked. Memories bombarded her, memories of pleasure, memories of trust.

'I want you,' he growled. 'Right here. Right now. I can't wait.'

'Neither can I,' she assured him fiercely.

Luca had already found the slit at the side of the dress. She only had to move slightly for his fingers to brush dangerously close to where she needed him. Her breath caught as he handled her with the skill that promised so much more. She was wearing nothing beneath the gown but a flimsy thong. Held together with not much more than a hope and a prayer, the thong stood no chance against Luca's assault. Ripping it off, he cast it aside and rammed her up against the wall. Breath shot out of her as his hand found her. With teasing strokes, he tested her readiness. That didn't take long. Freeing himself, he nudged his thigh between her legs and, dipping at the knees, he took her in one long, firm thrust. From there it was a wild, noisy ride to their goal, but even when she shrieked as she lost control he kept on plunging until her throat was hoarse, and her body was alight with pleasure.

'I can't feel you,' she complained when she was able to talk again.

'What?' Luca demanded, frowning into her eyes.

'Not that—' She groaned with pleasure as he flexed inside her. 'I mean your naked body,' she explained. Tugging at his shirt, she made her meaning clear. 'I want to feel all of you hot and hard against me.' They ripped his clothes off between them and tossed them aside. 'Better!' she approved as his heat rasped against her body.

'Still not enough for you,' he guessed. Taking hold of her hands, he pinned them above her head, and with his other hand locked around the front of her dress, he ripped it from her body.

The beautiful gown was shredded, ruined. Disaster. But she didn't care. All that mattered was this. Rubbing her breasts against him tormented her nipples until they were taut little buds, composed entirely of sensation. They had a direct link to her core, and her hips worked involuntarily in her desperation for more contact. She couldn't remain still. She couldn't remain quiet. She was noisy and demanding. Scrambling up him, she locked her legs around his waist.

'More?' he suggested in the deep, gravelly voice with its flavour of Italy that could always make her tingle.

'Are you purposely withholding pleasure from me?' she demanded.

Luca laughed softly. 'As if I'd dare.'

'Don't make me wait,' she warned.

His answer was to nuzzle her neck with his sharp black stubble until she was a seething mass of lust. 'I just asked, did you want more?' he reminded her.

He surely didn't expect an answer to that question.

CHAPTER TEN

THE BALL GOWN was ruined. No point worrying about that now. She'd skip the ball. That was the last thought in Callie's head as Luca made rational thought impossible. He was making love to her. This wasn't just sex. They were natural together. This was so good, so right. This was fierce. When the moment came, she was wild with fear of the precipice she was facing, but Luca husked soothing words of reassurance and encouragement in his own language as he kissed her over the edge.

'Greedy,' he whispered when she quietened.

'You make me greedy,' she complained, smiling with contentment as she crashed against his chest.

Finding the nook just below his shoulder blade, she snuggled close as he carried her to the bed. A deep sense of this being right filled her completely. They belonged together. He laid her down gently on the bed and came to lie with her. When he brought her into his arms, her breathing slowed and her limbs grew weightless. Problems nagged at the back of her mind, but they could wait until tomorrow. Right now she could do nothing more than close her eyes and drift away.

He held Callie in his arms all night, watching her sleep. As he did so, he went over what lay ahead of her.

It wouldn't be an easy transition for her from the freedom of a normal life to all the restrictions of royalty, but if anyone could cope, she could. And he'd be with her every step of the way. He was confident that Callie would adapt to royal life as quickly as he had. He'd rebelled at first, but then he'd been very young. Callie was clever and kind, and her sense of humour would ease her through the sticky patches. Her common sense would get her through the rest. Not only would he have the longed-for heir, but a new, fresh style of Princess who would care for the land he had come to love as deeply as he did.

Careful not to wake her, he left Callie at dawn. Breakfast meetings were the norm for him. With her hair tousled, and her face still flushed with sleep, she had never looked more desirable, but he was a slave to duty. Both his royal council and his business concerns called him this morning. And then there was the ball tonight. He grimaced as he glanced at the gown he'd ruined. But there were plenty more on the rail. Callie would have to forget about being understated for one night, and just choose one of them.

Callie woke slowly, cautiously. At first she didn't know where she was. Her head was ploughed into a stack of pillows scented with lavender and sunshine. The bed was firmer than she was used to, the duvet softer…and her body felt very well used. With a groan of contentment, she turned her face, relishing the touch of the smooth white cotton, and inhaled deeply. Slowly, it all came back to her. Reaching out a hand, she searched for Luca, and stilled when she discovered the bed at her side was empty. Sitting up, she could see the indentation of his head on the pillow, so she hadn't imagined last night. She really was at the palace. *The palace!* In the most sumptuous suite of rooms imaginable. *Incredible.* But it was very quiet. She stilled and knew at once she was alone.

Hearing a knock on the door, she hastily pulled up the sheet to cover her naked body. 'Yes?' It had to be the maid. Spotting what remained of the glamorous gown still strewn on the floor, she called out, 'Just a minute,' and leapt out of bed. Gossip would spread like wildfire in the palace. Why fan the flames? Gathering up the dress, she brought it back to the bed, and stuffed it out of sight beneath the bedding. 'Come in,' she called out brightly.

The maid entered carrying a breakfast tray. There was a single red rose in a silver vase on the tray. 'From His Serene Highness,' the maid explained as she set down the tray. 'He has suggested that you rest this morning in preparation for the ball.'

Recover, he meant, Callie thought dryly, showing nothing of her thoughts on the passionate night before on her face. 'Thank you for bringing my breakfast,' she said warmly, 'but I will be getting up.'

'Oh, and this arrived by courier,' the maid said as she handed Callie a package she had lodged under her arm.

'For me?' Callie exclaimed with surprise.

She bolted breakfast as the maid opened the curtains and threw the windows wide. She couldn't wait to open the unexpected parcel, but wanted to do so when she was alone.

'Anything else I can get for you?' the maid asked politely before she left.

'Nothing. Thank you.'

Turning over the large padded envelope, Callie smiled broadly. The bold handwriting gave the game away, as did the UK stamp. 'Ma Brown,' she breathed. 'What have you done now?'

What Ma had done was to go shopping at a popular high street store, where she'd found the perfect dress for Callie to wear at the ball. Callie gasped with pleasure as she held it up and saw her reflection. The dress was simple and elegant. At last, a dress she could feel comfortable in. She'd take a shower and then she'd try it on.

The fine flesh-coloured fabric slithered over Callie's naked body like a second skin. It couldn't have fitted her better. The design was uncannily similar to the gown that lay ruined on the bed. The popular brand was a known fast follower that could have catwalk looks available for sale within hours. She would go to the ball, Callie concluded with amusement as she slipped on a pair of high-heeled shoes, and in a dress worth infinitely more to her than all those expensive gowns on the rail put together. Picking up her phone to thank her best of friends, she smiled with pleasure. 'Oh, Ma Brown, you've really come up trumps this time,' she murmured as she waited for the call to connect.

It was the evening of the grand ball and all his guests had arrived, but where was Callie? He wasn't accustomed to waiting. Tonight of all nights, a late arrival was unacceptable. Her maid had been given strict instructions regarding timing. Royals were expected to be punctual. Everything ran to clockwork precision. There was no leeway for a few minutes either way. With impatience, he turned his attention from the entrance where Callie was due to appear, to the guests who were waiting to meet him.

Laughter and excitement filled the room. There was a huge sense of expectation. No one had refused his invitation to the ball. There were rumours of an announcement tonight and interest was running high. He felt a great sense of love and gratitude for the restoration his father, the late Prince, had carried out so efficiently on the glorious old building, and this did soothe him to some small degree. The ballroom was a glittering spectacle with huge chandeliers glittering like diamond globes beneath a domed sky of priceless frescoes. An orchestra of the most talented Viennese musicians set the mood. Waiters in black dress trousers and short white jackets, braided with the royal colours, carried solid gold trays bearing a selection of canapés prepared by the world's top chefs. There were two champagne fountains, as well as tall crystal flutes of vintage champagne being offered to guests at priceless French ormolu tables that lined the room. Nearly every country was represented. Splendidly dressed royals dripping in family jewels mingled with diplomats and top-ranking soldiers. No one was too proud to sup at his table. Guessing that tonight would be talked about for years had winkled out even the most standoffish royal. Everyone was keen to see how the boy from the gutters had transformed into a prince.

So where was she?

There was no excuse for this. He had instructed his private secretary to commission the finest hairdressers and beauticians to assist Callie with her preparations for tonight. He couldn't believe her personal maid had failed to get her out on time. Did Callie hope to slip in unnoticed? Was she coming at all?

He gave a grim shrug. Callie Smith was the one woman he could never predict. Summoning a footman, he sent a message to Signorina Smith's maid to ask how much longer she would be. The man hurried off, leaving Luca to seethe in silence.

* * *

Well, this was it, Callie concluded as two liveried footmen swung the gilded double doors wide. She had politely asked the hairdressers and make-up artists to leave, preferring to get ready by herself, and now there was just this small hurdle of a ballroom packed with the great and good to overcome. She inhaled sharply at the scene of dazzling glamour, and was almost blinded by the flash of diamonds and the light flaring from countless chandeliers. *Trust me to forget my tiara tonight*, she mused wryly. Lifting her chin, she walked forward.

'Signorina Callista Smith.'

Callie glanced around as the disembodied voice of a famous television personality announced her arrival at the ball.

'That's you, miss,' one of the friendly footmen who'd opened the door for her prompted in an exaggerated stage whisper.

'Thank you,' she whispered back.

In the time it had taken Callie to say this, every head had turned her way. Even the orchestra paused, leaving her at the top of a dizzying flight of marble steps. The solid mass of people below her looked impenetrable, and not exactly welcoming. Her throat dried. She clenched her hands into fists at her side. She could only pray the stiletto heels fairy was on her side tonight.

'Wait…'

Every head swivelled to stare at Luca. His familiar voice stripped the tension from her shoulders. Her gaze fixed on him as the crowd parted to let him through. Whatever remained of her breath flew from her lungs as he strode forward. In full dress uniform, with his sash of office drawing attention to his powerful chest, this was the man she remembered, the man her body rejoiced in, the man she laughed with, slept with, and enjoyed challenging, as Luca relished tormenting her, and right now he looked good enough to eat.

'May I?' he asked, offering his arm as he prepared to lead her down the stairs.

'Thank you.' She smiled—graciously, she hoped.

If a pin *had* dropped, it would most certainly have deafened her. It appeared that no one breathed, let alone spoke, as Luca steered her safely down the steps.

'You look beautiful,' he whispered.

'I'm sorry I took so long,' she whispered back. 'The hairdresser made me look like a freak, so I had to redo everything. And don't even ask about the make-up.'

'But you aren't wearing any.'

'Exactly,' she murmured. 'If you'd seen me with false eyelashes and red-apple cheeks you'd have run a mile.'

'Would I?' he murmured, sounding unconvinced.

They'd reached the dance floor by this time. Everyone was staring, but just being with Luca reassured her, and she didn't hesitate when he asked her to dance.

Callie came into his arms like a rather lovely boat floating effortlessly into its mooring. The intimacy between them must have been obvious to everyone, and the shocked silence that had first greeted her changed at once to a buzz of interest.

'I can just imagine what they're saying,' she breathed.

'Do you care?' he replied.

'No,' she assured him. 'I just wish I was barefoot. You're in serious danger of being stabbed.'

'Not a chance,' he whispered.

He laughed. She relaxed, and the glamorous ball continued.

'Where did you get the beautiful dress?' he asked. 'You look stunning. It's so elegant. I didn't see it on the rail. It's so delightfully simple, compared to other women's more elaborate gowns.'

'That's the secret of its allure,' she assured him with a cheeky smile. 'Ma Brown,' she whispered discreetly.

'Well, wherever it came from, you couldn't look lovelier.'

'Well, thank you, kind sir…you don't look too bad yourself.'

She was in his arms, and, as far as he was concerned, that was all that mattered. 'Do you find it warm?' he asked.

'Is this another of your euphemisms, which could be interpreted as let's find a tree?'

'Callie Smith,' he scolded softly with his mouth very close to her ear.

'You left me alone, abandoned me, and now you can't get enough of me?'

'Correct.'

'Don't you have any scruples?'

'Hardly any,' he confessed. 'I'm planning to take you to see a magical gazebo.'

'Filled with your etchings?' she guessed.

He laughed, and was further amused by the fact that people dancing close to them were hanging on their every word. Leading Callie off the dance floor, he led her through towering glass doors onto a veranda stretching the entire length of the palace. Even this late in the year, plants illuminated by blazing torches still flowered profusely, and their fragrance filled the air. He wouldn't usually notice such things, but being with Callie always heightened his senses. A pathway led through the formal lawn gardens, and where they ended there was a lake with an island at its heart. Lights glinted on the island, and a rowing boat was moored alongside the small wooden pier that stretched out into the lake.

'Really?' Callie queried with a pointed glance at her dress and shoes.

'Where's your sense of adventure?' he demanded.

Slipping off her shoes, she accepted his steadying hand as she gingerly boarded the boat. 'I used to escape the palace by rowing out to the island,' he explained when he joined her. He'd left his uniform jacket and white bow tie on the shore with his highly polished shoes. Freeing a few buttons at the neck of his shirt, he sat across from her and reached for the oars.

'I can understand why you might want to be alone here,' Callie agreed as she trailed her fingertips in the water. 'It's so beautiful and peaceful on the lake.'

'I didn't notice that when I was a youth,' he admitted, plunging the oars into the mirror-smooth water. 'It took time for me to trust the Prince, my father, and sometimes I was just angry for no reason and just wanted to get away. Now I think I was afraid of disappointing him. I'd only known rare acts of kindness on the streets, and the fact that he never gave up on me seemed to be just one more reason for me to put him to the test.'

'That's only natural.'

'I was lucky.' He put his back into the stroke and as he saw Callie's appreciative gaze focus on his bunching muscles his impatience to reach the opposite shore grew.

'How did you live,' she asked, 'back before the Prince found you?'

He shrugged and dipped the oars again. 'I cleaned around the market stalls in return for spoiled fruit, stale bread, and mouldy cheese. I had some good feeds,' he remembered, 'but the stallholders had many calls on their time, and I was proud even then. I might have been filthy and wearing rags but I vowed that I would never sink any lower and would always strive to rise. My bathroom was the Tiber, and my bedroom better than most people could boast.'

'What do you mean by that?' she asked.

'I slept at the Coliseum,' he explained. 'I came to know a member of the security staff, and he turned a blind eye when I curled up in the shadows of that great arena.'

'You make it sound romantic,' Callie said with a frown, 'but you must have been freezing in winter.'

'It was certainly a challenge,' he recalled, 'but atmospheric too. I used to sleep in Caesar's box, rather than in the dungeons where the poor victims used to languish as they awaited their terrible fate. I had nothing in the material sense,' he added as their small craft sliced through the water, 'except when it came to determination. I had plenty of that, as well as the freedom to change my condition, which I did.'

'What age were you when this was happening?'

'I was grubbing around the streets from the age of four. That was when my mother died,' he explained. 'The whorehouse where she worked kicked me out. In fairness, no one could spare the time to take care of me. I think now that I was better off by myself. The clientele at the brothel weren't too choosy who they abused, if you take my meaning.'

'I do. But how did you manage on your own on the streets at the age of four?'

'There were other, older children on the streets. They showed me how to stay alive.'

'How did you end up at the Coliseum?'

'A lot of homeless children slept there. I saw the tourist posters advertising this colossal building, and I wanted to see it for myself. Getting inside was easy. I just joined the queue of tourists and walked straight in. I soon learned that if I pretended to be a lost child, concerned attendants would feed me. It worked for quite a while until they began to recognise me, but by then they had developed a soft spot for the boy from the gutters and so they turned a blind eye. The people who worked at the Coliseum didn't have much money, either, and so they saved food from the trash for me to root through. There were plenty of half-eaten burgers and hot dogs for supper. I don't remember being hungry. The Coliseum was like a hotel for me, growing up, so don't feel sorry for me. I did fine. The Coliseum was both my home and my school. I saw everything you can imagine during my time there. I learned about sex, violence, thieving, unkindness, and great acts of kindness too.'

'Can you remember your parents?' she asked as he took a deep pull on the oars.

'Nothing I care to bring to mind,' he admitted dryly. 'My mother was always harassed and often sick. I think now that she was what we would call depressed. No surprise there, but a child can't understand why a person behaves the way they do. A child only knows that it's hungry, or frightened, and I knew I had to fend for myself long before she died.'

'And your father? Did you ever meet him?'

'He turned up one night,' Luca recollected. He huffed a short, humourless laugh. 'My mother's colleagues pelted him with rotten fruit and worse. I remember him standing on the street, shouting up at her open window.

I remember his angry voice, and his soiled white shirt and the glint of his gold earrings.'

'He doesn't sound very nice.'

He shrugged. 'Who knows?'

'And now you're a prince with a country to rule and a palace to live in. It must all seem quite incredible, even now?'

'No. It seems right,' he said thoughtfully. 'If there was luck involved, it was that I met the Prince, the best of men, and a man who changed my life. Though even that wasn't as simple as it sounds,' he admitted. 'After everything I'd seen, I wasn't easily impressed—not even by the Prince of Fabrizio.'

'How did he persuade you to leave the streets and come to live with him?'

'He was a patient man,' Luca said, thinking back. 'From the moment he found me stealing food from the bins and the buffet table during his royal visit to the Coliseum, he was determined to save me. He told me this years later.'

'What did he do about your stealing?' Callie asked as he shipped the oars.

'He asked his attendant to find me a shopping bag, so I didn't have to hide my hoard down my shirt.'

'Cool,' she said, smiling.

'Oh, he was that,' he agreed as he sprang onto the shore to moor up.

She placed her hands in his as he helped her onto the dock. He wanted to take her right there. Throw her down on the cool wood and make love to her until she didn't have the strength to stand, but delay was its own reward.

It was just a small island. She could probably walk around it in ten minutes, Callie thought. The grass was cool and green, and felt lush and thick beneath her naked feet. Picking up the hem of her dress, she stared around. The clustering trees were lit with thousands of tiny lights in celebration of the ball. And then she saw the gazebo he'd talked about ahead of them. 'Is this where you used to come and sulk?' she asked.

'How did you guess?'

As he swung around to face her, the pulsing heat of desire surged through her. 'I've been a teenager too.'

He laughed and held out his hands. She felt so safe and warm when he took hold of her, and Luca's kisses were always a drugging seduction. They seemed even more so here on this magical island. Just occasionally, fairy tales did come true. She wanted to believe it so badly as he kissed her again. She'd spent so much of her life bottling up emotion, but Luca knew how to set it free, and as his kisses grew more heated she knew she would take any and every chance to hold onto happiness.

He swung her off her feet and strode quickly to the entrance to the gazebo. Lowering her down, he steadied her and then pressed her back against the wooden structure. Caging her with his arms either side of her face, he brushed his lips against her mouth and smiled. It was the most romantic moment, but if she'd written the fairy tale herself she could never have predicted what he'd say next. 'Marry me, Callie. Marry me and become my Princess.'

At first she thought she was imagining it, and it was all a dream, until Luca repeated softly, 'Marry me, Callie.'

She stared into his eyes, struggling to compute what he'd said. Embarrassed, uncertain, she resorted to teasing him. 'Shouldn't you be down on your knees? Or, one of them, at least?'

'I need an answer,' Luca said, refusing to respond to

her lighter tone. 'Just a straight yes or no will do. Or are you playing for time?'

'No,' she argued. 'I'm playing for the highest of stakes of all. I'm playing for my heart, and for the future of our child.'

'Then, marriage makes perfect sense,' he insisted.

'Does it?' She frowned.

'You know it does.'

Smiling into her eyes, he kissed her again, and because she wanted him she was foolish enough to believe in the fairy tale for now.

CHAPTER ELEVEN

'TRUST ME,' LUCA said as he took her slow and deep. They had been making love on the soft cushions in the gazebo for what felt like hours. 'Trust me,' he said again as he soothed her down.

'Shouldn't you get back to the ball?' she asked. She was snuggled up tightly against Luca, whose protective arms wrapped securely around her.

'If you're ready, we'll go back,' he murmured as he planted a kiss on the top of her head.

'Bathe in the lake first?' she suggested.

They swam, then dried off together, and Callie dressed quickly, thanking her lucky stars she had short hair that didn't take long to dry in the warm night air. Slipping her simple dress on, she took hold of Luca's hand and they walked back to the boat; back to reality, she thought, but if he could carry this off—their absence would have been noted—then so could she.

'My lords, ladies and gentlemen, I have an announcement to make…'

Silence fell the instant Luca's deep and distinctive voice was heard through the hidden speakers in the ballroom. 'I realise the clock is about to strike midnight, so I won't keep you long.'

A ripple of laughter greeted this remark.

'I'm taking this opportunity to introduce you to the woman I intend to marry.'

Not the woman he loved, Callie thought, cursing herself for being such a doubter. Luca had to wait a moment until the exclamations of surprise had died down.

'Signorina Callista Smith is an exceptional woman, whom I am lucky to have found.'

As he beckoned Callie forward and she joined him in the centre of the ballroom, the surprise of the sophisticated onlookers gradually turned to muted applause. They were shocked to the heels of their highly polished footwear, she thought as Luca lifted his hands for a silence that had already fallen deep and long.

'It goes without saying,' he added, 'that all of you will receive an invitation to our wedding.' He gave a fierce, encouraging smile into Callie's eyes, before turning back to address his riveted audience. 'I invite you all to enjoy the rest of your evening, while I continue to celebrate with my beautiful fiancée.'

As if by magic the orchestra struck up a romantic Viennese waltz, which allowed Luca to prove that not only could he sweep Callie off her feet, but he could provide the prompt necessary to shake everyone out of their stupefied trance, and soon the dance floor was ablaze with colour and the flash of precious jewels.

Callie told herself that everything would work out. Yes, there would be problems, but they'd get through them. Luca was right. This was the best solution. It was only when the clock struck midnight, and he was briefly distracted by one of the many ambassadors present, that everything changed.

She'd seen pictures of Max in various magazines back home. In the flesh, he was even more striking. As tall as Luca, he looked quite different, which was only to be expected when they weren't related by blood. Where Luca's features were rugged and sexy, Max's face was thin and hard, and, quite unlike Luca, Max's manner was unpleasantly autocratic.

Dressed entirely in black, his blood-red sash of office the only bright thing about him, Max was the haughtiest man in the room by far. And he was heading her way surrounded by cronies, all of whom were viewing Callie with what she could only describe as amused contempt. There was a beautiful woman on Max's arm, who was also dressed in black, with the addition of half a hundredweight of diamonds. Her tiara alone could have settled most countries' debts, Callie guessed. Knowing she was the target of the advancing party, she stood her ground and lifted her chin, then shrank inwardly when Max stopped directly in front of her.

'Well, my dear,' he said, keeping his stare fixed on Callie as he turned to address his obviously heavily pregnant companion, 'this is the little snip my brother intends to put on our throne.'

'Surely not?' his elegantly dressed companion protested as she stared disapprovingly at Callie. 'Who is she, anyway? And *where* did she get that dress?'

Callie ground her jaw, refusing to demean herself by responding. Max's friends could laugh all they liked. They wouldn't drive her away.

'Goodness knows, my dear,' Max replied, still staring at Callie through mocking eyes. 'Perhaps she got it from the same thrift store that sold her the dye for that ridiculous hair colour.'

As everyone laughed Callie reached up instinctively to touch her hair, and regretted the lapse immediately. She hated letting them see they'd upset her. 'Well, at least I don't have a cruel tongue,' she said mildly.

'Oh, she speaks,' Max exclaimed, turning to look at his friends. 'I imagine she learned that skill in *the pub back home*.' He made each vowel sound grotesque and ugly.

As Max and his friends roared with laughter, Callie made sure to remain impassive.

'He only keeps her around because she's pregnant,' Max drawled, quirking a brow in an attempt, Callie thought, to elicit some sort of response from her. 'He's desperate for an heir, and when you're as desperate as Luca I suppose it's a case of any port in a storm. Seeing you pregnant,' he added to the woman at his side, 'must really have disturbed him. That's the only reason he's chosen this girl. He's trying to compete with me—imagine that?'

'He's quite obviously failed,' one of Max's cronies derided.

'That's all this is,' Max assured Callie, bringing his cruel face close. 'Don't think for one moment that you've bagged yourself a prince, let alone that this is a fairy tale. This is a cold-blooded transaction, my dear. Luca doesn't want you. He doesn't want anyone. The only thing Luca wants is an heir. That's the only way he can hope to keep the throne of Fabrizio. It's written into our constitution. Two years, one baby at least, or I take over.' Coming even closer, he sneered. 'You're nothing more than a convenient womb. Shall we?' he added to his gloating companions with an airy gesture. 'I've had enough of this ball. The quality of guests at the palace has really gone down. The casino beckons. A few spins of the wheel holds far more appeal than these provincials can ever hope to provide me.'

'She's gone? What do you mean, she's gone?' Luca stared down at Michel in surprise. The elderly retainer seemed more than usually confused. 'Take your time, Michel. I'm sorry. I didn't mean to shout at you.'

'I saw her talking to Max,' Michel told him in a worried tone.

'What?'

'You said you wouldn't shout,' Michel reminded him.

'You're right,' he admitted, placing a reassuring hand on the older man's shoulder. 'But who invited Max?'

'Does Max need an invitation to visit his family home?'

Luca ground his jaw. He should have known that Max would never keep to their agreement that he stay out of Fabrizio. 'So, where the hell is she?' he repeated as he raked his hair with tense fingers.

'I saw her running out of that door not ten minutes ago,' Michel informed him, staring across the ballroom towards the French doors leading onto the garden and then the lake. 'And that was straight after talking to Max.'

'Ten minutes?' Luca exclaimed, frowning. 'Did I leave her alone for that long?'

'The ambassador can be garrulous and difficult to get away from,' Michel said in an obvious attempt to placate him. 'And His Excellency was more than usually talkative tonight.'

Luca could not be placated. His one concern was Callie. He should have told her long before now what she meant to him. The convenient plan that had fallen into place when he found out she was pregnant hadn't figured in his thinking when he'd made the announcement that they would be married.

All right, so maybe it had, he conceded grimly as he made a visual search of the ballroom to make sure she'd gone. Would he stick around under similar circumstances? So, where could she be? In her room, or had she tried to return to the island? His heart banged in his chest at the thought that she might have taken the rowing boat. Navigation was easy for him in the dark. He'd been rowing on the lake for most of his life. So he knew about the clinging weeds and treacherous rocks. If Callie took the wrong route, she could be in serious trouble. He didn't wait to consider his options. Cutting through the crowd, he hurried away.

He ran to the shore. The boat was gone. There was no sign of Callie. Everyone had been shocked by his announcement of their engagement, and now Max was causing trouble again. He had a stark choice to make. Callie, or the future of Fabrizio. There was no choice. Stripping off his clothes, he dived into the lake.

Relief surged through him when he spotted her pacing the shore. 'Callie,' he exclaimed, springing out of the water. Striding up to her, he seized hold of her and demanded she look at him. 'What's wrong? What happened back there?'

'You happened,' she said.

Her voice was faint, but the fire in her eyes was brighter than ever. She was hurt, bitterly hurt. He knew all the signs. Max had always been an expert when it came to wounding with words.

'Thank you for telling me how badly you needed an heir,' she said tensely, sarcastically.

'Meaning?' he demanded.

'I'm told your constitution demands it, if you're to keep the throne.' There were tears of anger and distress in her eyes. 'I would have been quicker off the mark getting pregnant, if you'd told me.'

'Don't be ridiculous,' he flared. 'What on earth has Max said to you?'

'Only the truth, I believe.'

A muscle jerked in his jaw. He couldn't even deny it, and had to listen to his brother's poison flooding from Callie's mouth.

'Max said that making an heir is the only reason you had sex with me.'

'I didn't have sex with you,' he insisted. 'I made love to you.'

'Maybe.' She hesitated a little. 'But how do I know that's true, now I know you had a motive?'

'Why can't you believe in yourself, Callie? Why won't you believe how much I need you?'

'Because it's convenient for you to have me,' she exclaimed. 'A convenient womb, Max called me. He says your primary concern is to build a dynasty.'

'My primary concern is you,' he argued fiercely.

'It doesn't feel that way to me, Luca. You made the announcement of our engagement without asking me first, without giving me chance to consider what I'm getting into. My late father used to tell me what I could and couldn't do, and I swore that I would never fall into that trap again.'

'This isn't a trap. You're not thinking straight, Callie.'

'I'm thinking perfectly,' she fired back. 'It's just a pity I haven't been thinking perfectly from the start.'

'That's your hormones talking.'

'Don't you dare,' she warned him. 'What was your plan, Luca? We marry, I have the baby, and then your people organise a convenient divorce? You don't have much time to play with, do you? Pregnancy sets a clock ticking, and so does the constitution of Fabrizio, Max tells me. Tonight was the perfect opportunity for you to announce our engagement. I imagine you'd have had us married by the end of the month, so that everything would be finalised before my pregnancy becomes obvious.'

He couldn't argue. So much of what she said was true, but his feelings when he'd discovered Callie was pregnant had been real and strong. A baby. A child. A family. Everything he'd always dreamed of had been suddenly within his reach. For a man used to subduing or ignoring his emotions, he'd been overwhelmed, and not just because Callie would provide him with the longed-for heir. She was the perfect woman, who would become the perfect mother. She would be his perfect bride, and would transition seamlessly into a much-loved princess. 'What's so terrible about becoming my wife?'

'If you don't know,' she said, sounding sad, 'I can't tell you. I suggest you forget about me, and ask one of those princesses to be your wife. You'll hardly be short of replacements for me.'

'Aggravating woman!' he roared. 'I don't want a replacement. I want you.'

'You can't have everything you want, Luca.'

'Are you saying no?' he demanded with incredulity.

'I'm saying no,' Callie confirmed.

'But you'll be a princess.'

'Of what?' she demanded. 'All you're offering is a temporary position, an empty life in a foreign country with a man who only wants me for my child-bearing capabilities.'

'That's Max talking. Don't listen to him.'

'I don't want that for our child,' she said, ignoring him, 'and I don't want to be a princess in a loveless marriage. I can't snuggle up to a tiara at night. I'd rather be back home in one room with my baby.'

'That isn't your choice to make,' he said, adopting a very different tone.

'Are you threatening me?' she said quietly.

'I'm reminding you that you're carrying the heir to the principality of Fabrizio, and that neither you nor I can change that fact.'

'And thank God for it,' she whispered as blood drained from her face. 'But there is something I can do.'

'Which is?' he demanded suspiciously.

'Unless you intend to keep me here by force, I can return home to spend Christmas with friends I can trust. You took my trust and abused it,' she accused. 'And tonight I learned that you took my body and used that too.'

'*What? Dio!* Never!' He raked his still-damp hair with frustration. 'Don't we know each other better than this? Yes, passion drove us initially. And yes, your pregnancy was convenient. I won't deny it. But it means so much more to me now. *You* mean so much more. I'm still coming to terms with the fact that I feel—' He stopped. He couldn't even put into words how many feelings he was dealing with. For a man who'd spent most of his life avoiding emotion, he was drowning in them. 'I respect you and I always will,' he stated firmly. 'Please give some thought to what becoming my wife will mean.'

'I have,' Callie assured him quietly, 'and it's not what I want.'

'What do you want?' he demanded fiercely. He'd do anything to put this right.

'I want love and respect on both sides,' she said without hesitation. 'I want friendship that makes both of us smile, and I want trust like a rock we can both depend on. I want to honour the man who is my lover, my friend, and the father of my child, as he honours me. And I want my independence. I've fought too hard to lose that now.'

'You'll have it as my wife,' he asserted confidently.

'And as your Princess?' When he didn't answer, because he knew only too well the restrictions that royal life imposed, she continued, 'I've spent too much of my life caged, and I won't exchange one cage for another, however big an upgrade that might seem to you. And it's not what I want for our child. I want us all to be free. I know I'm a fantasist,' she added in a calmer voice, 'and I know I want too much. I should have realised that from the start.'

'Callie!'

'No. Don't try to stop me,' she called back as she ran back to the lake. 'We were never meant to be together. Max is right. I can't marry a prince—this is over,' she flared, trying to shake him off when he caught up with her.

'It doesn't need to end here,' he said firmly, holding her still.

'Yes, it does.' With a violent tug she broke free. 'Goodbye, Luca—'

'But I love you.'

She stopped on the edge of the lake. Whether she intended to swim back or row back, he had no idea. He did know she was furious. 'You love me?' she said tensely. 'Yet you didn't think to tell me this before tonight? It sounds like you're desperate to keep me here.'

'I am desperate, but not for the reasons you think. You're more to me than you could ever know, more than Max could even comprehend.'

She shook her head. 'You had to be sure of me, didn't you, Luca? That's why you made the announcement of our engagement tonight in front of so many witnesses.'

'You're not listening, Callie. I love you. And you're right. I should have told you long before now, but I didn't realise it myself. I didn't recognise the symptoms,' he admitted ruefully, raking his hair with frustration. 'I'm not exactly familiar with love in all its guises.'

'Your father didn't love you?' she challenged with an angry gesture.

'The Prince loved me, but it wasn't easy for me to trust him enough to return his love, not as soon as he wanted, anyway.'

'He must have been a patient man.'

'He was.'

'Know this, Luca. Nothing will change my mind. I don't want a work in progress, while you discover your feelings. I want the boy who made his home in the Coliseum and dreamed of what he would one day become. I want the man who made that happen. Don't you dare make your past an excuse. I haven't.'

That was true. She shamed him. 'How can I prove that I love you?'

'By letting me go,' she said with her usual frankness.

* * *

Back home at the Browns', the ache in Callie's heart at the absence of Luca was like a big, gaping wound that refused to heal. Even the Browns' famously over-the-top Christmas preparations couldn't do anything to mend it. Seeing Anita again had helped, Callie conceded as she smiled across the room at her friend from the lemon groves. Anita had become a most welcome fixture at the Browns'. On her return, Callie had persuaded Anita, who lived alone in a rented room, to take a job close by, and the Browns had offered to rent her a room. They always welcomed help with the younger children and Anita would never be alone again, Ma Brown had promised. Anita had a proper family now—if she could stand the noise and chaos. Anita could certainly do that, and had fitted right in.

'Come on, our Callie,' Ma Brown insisted as she bustled into the room they called the front parlour. 'Anita, I need you to help me in the kitchen, and, Rosie, you and Callie still have the rest of those crêpe paper streamers to hang.'

'And make,' Rosie pointed out as she glanced at the uncut reams of crinkled paper and then at Callie's preoccupied face. 'Come on, I'll help you.' Kneeling down at Callie's side, Rosie waited until her mother had left the room before putting an arm around Callie's shoulders. 'I know you haven't said anything in front of the family, but you can't keep bottling this up. And you can't keep refusing to speak to him,' Rosie added. 'If Prince Luca comes to England to see you—'

'Do you know something?' Callie asked. Her heart soared at the thought of seeing Luca again, even as her rational mind told her she could never be a princess, so it was better not to see him at all.

'Not exactly,' Rosie admitted uncomfortably. 'I'm just saying that if Luca did turn up, you should see him.'

'I don't have to see anyone,' Callie argued stubbornly, but her heart was beating so fast just at the thought of seeing Luca again that she could hardly breathe. Was he in the country, maybe somewhere close by? There was no smoke without fire, she concluded, glancing at Rosie, who refused to meet her eyes.

'We'd better get these streamers made,' Rosie said, acting as if the lack of paper decorations was the only crisis looming, 'or there'll be hell to pay.'

CHAPTER TWELVE

CALLIE FROZE. THEY had just sat down to the most mouth-watering Christmas feast when an imperative knock sounded at the door.

'I'll answer it,' Pa Brown insisted when Callie moved to get out of her chair.

'Let him go,' Ma Brown said to everyone with a calming gesture. 'Whoever's there, we can't leave a stranger on the doorstep today.'

That was no stranger, Callie thought, shivering inwardly with excitement as the distinctive sound of Luca's dark, husky voice made everyone sit up and take notice. The air changed, stilled, and was suddenly charged with electricity as, quite improbably, His Serene Highness, Prince Luca of Fabrizio, stood framed in the narrow doorway. Radiating glamour, presence, and an irrational amount of heat, Luca was a starry visitor to the homey Christmas at the Browns'. His stare locked briefly with Callie's. That short look carried more heat, more passion and determination than she could stand. It was almost a relief when he turned to greet everyone else in the room.

'This is wonderful,' Luca exclaimed, sucking in a deep, appreciative breath as Pa Brown relieved him of his rugged jacket. 'I didn't realise how hungry I was, until

I smelled this delicious food.' His gaze swept over Callie before he smiled at Ma Brown. 'Do you have room for one more?'

'Most certainly,' Ma Brown exclaimed, leaping up from the table.

In a midnight-blue fine-knit sweater that clung lovingly to his magnificent frame, and beat-up jeans moulding his muscular thighs, Luca was an improbable giant in their midst. Callie couldn't help but remember having those thighs locked around her as they made love, and her longing for Luca surged as his stare found hers and this time lingered. Her heart was gunned into action. She hadn't realised how much she'd missed him. Snow dusted his ink-black hair, making it twinkle and gleam. If she'd never met him before and didn't know his history, if someone had told her that Luca was a cage fighter she'd have believed them. He certainly wasn't her childhood idea of Prince Charming. But fairy tales were a long way behind them now. Sex radiated from him like sparks from a Catherine wheel, though his eyes were full of warmth for the Browns, and for Anita. 'Don't I know you from Italy?' he asked Anita.

'You do, Your Serene Highness,' Anita admitted, blushing.

'Call me Luca,' he said. 'You know the rules.'

As Anita and Luca laughed together, Callie thought him so infectiously warm, so vital and compelling. 'I hope I'm not intruding,' he said, noticing that the Browns were all staring at him open-mouthed.

'Not at all,' Pa Brown was quick to reassure him.

'Good,' Luca declared, 'because I'm here to claim my bride.'

The younger Browns stared at Luca, while the rest

carried on as if nothing unusual had occurred. Callie moved first. Pushing her chair back, she put down her napkin. If it hadn't been for Pa Brown's restraining hand on her shoulder, she would have left the room and taken Luca with her. What right did he have to come storming in like some medieval feudal lord, interrupting the flow of everything around the Christmas table and demanding that she be his bride. 'Steady girl,' Pa Brown murmured discreetly.

Everyone closed their mouths and pretended to concentrate on their food as Callie sat down again. All except one. 'You can have my chair, if I can have a ride in your sports car,' young Tom Brown told Luca.

'Sounds like a deal to me,' Luca agreed with a smile.

'My name's Tom,' the youngster supplied as he and Luca bumped fists.

'Come on, everyone…shuffle up,' Ma Brown instructed. 'Let's make room for the Prince.'

'Now, there's a phrase you don't hear said every day,' Pa Brown ventured, only to receive a stern look from his wife.

For a while everything was good-natured chaos as chairs were swopped around, and new cutlery was brought out of the drawer. Once crockery and glassware had been located, everything was settled for their guest.

'I envy you,' Luca told his hosts midway through the most succulent meal of turkey with all the trimmings.

'You envy us?' Pa Brown exclaimed, only to receive a second hard stare from his wife, who sensibly steered the situation.

'More gravy with that extra helping of meat, Luca?'

'Yes, please.'

With Ma Brown setting the tone, all the Browns began

to behave as if His Serene Highness were any other neighbour who'd called around to share their Christmas cheer. Now that was class, Callie thought. Stuff Max and his cronies. They couldn't hold a candle to these genuine folk. The meal could have been tense, and Christmas could have been ruined, but with Luca at his relaxed best, and Anita and the Browns just being themselves, the irreverent, good-natured banter soon resumed.

'So, what's it like being a prince?' young Tom enquired.

'Busy,' Luca told him economically.

'Don't you have to smile at people you don't like?' another boy asked.

'That's called diplomacy,' Pa Brown put in. 'Something you could all do with a lesson in.'

'No, he's right,' Luca intervened. 'That's why it's so good to be here.' He flashed a wry glance at Callie, who raised a brow.

'Didn't you have anywhere else to go at Christmas but here?' young Tom demanded.

Luca's lips quirked as he thought about this. 'I had a few places, but nowhere as special as here.'

'Pudding?' Ma Brown enquired.

'Yes, please,' Luca confirmed. 'But first…' He glanced at Callie, and then jerked his head towards the door.

'Of course,' Ma Brown agreed. 'I'll keep the pudding warm for both of you.'

Callie wasn't sure how she felt. She didn't feel any more forgiving towards Luca, but they did need to talk, and the sooner, the better.

'So now you know,' she said. Having wrapped herself up warmly in her winter coat and scarf, she was sitting in the front seat of Luca's bright red car.

'Know what?' he asked with a frown as he started the engine.

'Where I come from.'

'You're lucky. It's wonderful. That's the best Christmas I've ever been part of.'

'And it hasn't even started yet,' Callie said wryly. 'Wait until they start playing parlour games.'

'Parlour games?' Luca queried.

'What people used to do before TV.'

He shot her a sideways look. 'Sounds interesting.'

'You said you'd give me time, Luca,' she reminded him as he pulled into the light Christmas Day traffic.

'How much time do you need?'

'More,' she insisted.

'I'm afraid that's not possible. I have other places to be.'

'You said you'd let me go.'

'I didn't say I wouldn't come after you.'

Callie shook her head while her heart went crazy. 'I belong here, Luca.'

'You belonged in the lemon groves too. You belonged in the five-star hotel, whether you chose to believe it or not. The staff there love you. You belong anywhere you choose to be. You have a positive slant on life that infects the people around you. That's why they love you. That's why I love you, and want you for my wife.'

'And a royal princess, mother of your heir,' she said quietly.

'So you're going to believe Max, not me.'

'I make my own decisions. This has nothing to do with Max.'

'Who has been reminded that he'd agreed to stay away

from Fabrizio for life,' Luca explained, 'in case you were wondering.'

'Stop here.'

'What?'

'Here,' she insisted. 'There's a park. We can walk.'

Luca dipped his head to stare around. 'I had intended taking you somewhere more romantic.'

'It's all a matter of scale,' Callie insisted, 'and this is fine. This patch of green might not look much to you, but I can tell you that it's appreciated around here as much as you appreciate your royal parks.'

'I didn't play in royal parks as a boy,' Luca reminded her as he slowed the car. Parking up, he killed the engine. Getting out, he came around to open the passenger door. She accepted his help and climbed out.

The same thrill raced up her arm. Luca's quiet strength was so compelling. He broke the silence first as they went through the entrance into the small inner-city park, and her breath caught in her throat when he said, 'I refuse to believe you don't know how right this is between us.'

'But you're a prince,' she protested.

'I'm a man.' Wrapping his big hands around her lapels, he drew her close. 'And that man knows we belong together. But though I've confided in you, you've told me nothing.'

Shoulders hunched against the freezing wind, Callie lifted her head and stared into Luca's strong, rugged face. 'Why do you want to marry me, when you can have your pick of every princess in the world, and all the heiresses, if that grand ball was anything to go by?'

'I keep asking myself that same question,' Luca admitted dryly.

'This isn't funny,' she said.

'This I know,' he agreed. 'All I can come up with is that there is no reason to love. You either do or you don't.'

They had stopped in front of the bandstand where, only that morning, she'd sung carols with the Browns while the local band played their hearts out.

'I know why you don't trust easily, Callie. You had a hard life with your father. Ma Brown told me a lot of it over the phone.'

'She shouldn't have.'

'Yes, she should,' he argued. 'She cares about you, and the Browns thought I should know. When you didn't answer my letters, I got in touch with them. They told me to stay away and give you time to take everything in. Has it worked?' He gave her a fleeting smile.

'And love,' she said. 'What conclusion did you come to?'

He considered her question. 'I came to the conclusion that love isn't rational, and there are no answers. There's only this…' Dragging her close, he kissed her, gently to begin with, and then with increasing fire, until they were kissing each other as if they were the last two people on earth.

It felt as if they were finding each other all over again. 'I've missed you,' she breathed when they finally broke apart.

'You have no idea,' Luca murmured as he smoothed her hair back from her face. 'When I say that I want to know all about you, I'm not talking about the heavily edited facts you've fed me in the past, but the truth, all of it, good and bad. I want to face the trials and triumphs together, so we can share the feelings we've both steered clear of in the past. I'm still learning when it comes to emotion, but I owe it to my country to change, and I owe it to you most of all. If we don't know sadness, how can we recognise happiness, and if we don't feel regret, how can we look forward and plan for the future? Tell me everything,' he insisted. 'I'll know if you're holding back.'

She thought back, and started with her mother. 'I can't remember her…' She paused, saddened. 'My father blamed me for her loss. She died in childbirth,' Callie explained. 'And he could have been so much more,' she said as she thought about her father.

'But none of this is your fault,' Luca insisted. Taking hold of her hands, he brought them to his lips and kissed them. 'You don't need to tell me how hard you've worked. Your hands speak for you.'

Callie laughed ruefully. She didn't exactly have a princess's hands. They were red and work-worn, having never quite recovered from scrubbing floors at the pub, but they were part of her, and she would rather have her work-roughened hands than all the pale, floaty things she'd seen at the ball.

'What was life like before your father died?' Luca prompted when she fell silent.

'Life's always been great, thanks to the Browns. Well, most of it,' she conceded. 'But if I didn't have the Browns…' That didn't bear thinking about.

'Good friends are beyond price,' Luca agreed. 'But now you have to ask yourself what *you* want out of life now.'

You, she thought, but you without complications, and she knew that wasn't possible. 'I wish life were simpler,' she said. 'I wish we could go back to working in the lemon groves, when I thought we were both holiday staff.'

'We're the same people we were then.'

'But now you're a prince,' Callie argued.

'I'm a man in love with you.'

Or in love with the thought of great sex going forward with the woman carrying his child? she wondered. 'I just don't know if it could work out,' she said, speaking her doubts out loud. 'The Princess bit, I mean.' Lifting her chin, she stared directly at Luca. 'Being royal seems so confining to me.'

'Not once you learn how to pin on a tiara,' he said. 'I'm sure you'll soon get the hang of it.'

She shot him a warning look, but Luca was in no way deterred. 'I've got homes across the world where we can be alone as much as you want, and I've got a superyacht to escape to.'

'That's just the point, isn't it? This is all normal to you, but it's crazy mad to me.'

'So?' he prompted.

'So, no, thank you.'

'Think about it carefully.'

'I have,' she assured him.

'I realise it's a huge commitment to make. Most people would jump at the chance of marrying into royalty and wouldn't give a second thought to the practicalities. But that's not you, Callie. You're cranky, challenging, and real, and that's why I want you at my side.'

'Compliments?' she said dryly. It was hard to remain neutral when Luca was working his charm. She was already warming and thrilling inside, and she didn't need anyone to tell her how dangerous that was. 'Or are you saying I keep your feet on the ground?'

'That's not the reason I want you,' Luca assured her with one of his dark, gripping looks. 'And, in the interest of clarity, I should make it clear that your feet won't be on the ground for long.'

* * *

'So,' Callie murmured, shooting him a troubled look when they got back in the car. 'You love me.'

'I do.'

'And you want to marry me.'

'Correct.'

'And not just because I'm pregnant with your convenient heir?'

Pressing back in the driver's seat, Luca sighed heavily. He owed her nothing less than the truth. 'When I first found out, I'll admit that it suited my plan.'

'You needed an heir,' she supplied.

'Yes, I did. And great sex.'

'Luca—'

'Regularly.'

'You're impossible.'

'Seriously?' he asked. 'If you want to know what I want? I want a family like the Browns.'

'Fourteen children?'

'One at a time?' he queried, sliding her a look. 'That's not so bad.'

'For you, maybe,' Callie said, biting back a smile. But then she turned serious. 'Callie from the docks, the Princess of Fabrizio?'

'Callie from the lemon groves, and my beloved wife,' Luca argued as he pulled away from the kerb. 'So, what's your answer, Callie?'

'The same as it was before,' she said tensely. 'I still need time to think.'

'All you need is time to assess your character and abilities to realise that you have everything it takes and more to be my Princess. So I'll give you until we get to the Browns', and then I want your answer.'

'And if it's no?' she pressed.

'We'll deal through lawyers in the future.'

Her face paled. 'That sounds like a threat.'

'It's the only practical option I can come up with. Or you can give me your answer now, if you prefer?'

She refused to be drawn, and by the time he had stopped the car outside the Browns', he could feel Callie's tension. Helping her out of the low-slung vehicle, he kept hold of her hand as they walked to the front door. Each time they talked, he learned a little bit more about her, and what he'd learned today had confirmed his opinion that they weren't so different. They both had principles, loyalty, and trust printed through them like sticks of rock. Callie was honest to a fault, and still overcoming the scars of a difficult childhood. He'd had the most enormous stroke of luck when he'd met the Prince at the Coliseum, and Callie had experienced a small taste of luck with her surprise win on the scratch card that had allowed her to travel to the lemon groves. It was strange how fate set things in motion. Experience had taught him that sometimes it paid to go with the flow.

'Come in, come in,' Pa Brown invited as he threw the front door wide.

Luca might live in a palace with servants on every side, but he hadn't been joking when he said that he envied the Browns. This was the type of family he had imagined being part of when he was a boy on his own each night with only the ghosts from the past for company. He and Callie were welcomed back into the warm heart of the Brown family just as the Christmas gifts were being opened and happy noise was at its height. Dogs and children were racing around colliding with each other, while Anita tried in vain to keep up with the amount of wrapping paper flying through the air. Rosie was attempting, without much success, to dissuade the younger Browns from opening each of the crackers before they were pulled, to discover what gifts lay inside.

'We saved some crackers for you,' she explained to Callie and him, as Pa Brown insisted on taking Luca's jacket.

'And I've saved two big dishes of plum pudding,' Ma Brown added from the doorway.

'I'd like a few moments of Ma and Pa's time. If I may,' he said.

Silence dropped like a stone. Every head turned his way, and then the focus switched to Callie, who shrugged, giving him no clue as to what her answer would be to his proposal.

'Of course,' Pa Brown agreed, breaking the tension as he exchanged a look with his wife. 'Come into the kitchen where we can be private, Luca. Would you like Callie to join us?'

'No. It's something I want to ask both of you. It involves Callie, but she knows all about it.'

'Do I?' Callie demanded, making him wonder yet again if he had misjudged the moment.

She was unreadable, and where women of his acquaintance were concerned that was a novelty, and, for a man who had everything money could buy, novelty was the most valuable currency of all.

'You should know how I feel about you by now,' he insisted, and, grabbing her close, he kissed her, which in front of the younger Browns was tantamount to making a public announcement.

Before he had chance to leave for the kitchen, young Tom piped up, 'You'll need this…' Holding out a blue plastic ring from his cracker, Tom stared up at Luca expectantly.

'*Grazie!* Thank you, Tom. Your timing couldn't be better.' He stowed the ring away in the back pocket of his jeans, and left Callie to have his conference with the Browns. When he came back, he knelt at Callie's feet—which wasn't as easy as it sounded with all the toys scattered around. 'Will you do me the very great honour of accepting this priceless ring, which has been especially chosen for you by Signor Tom?'

'I'm overwhelmed,' Callie admitted, starting to laugh.

The situation was bizarre admittedly, and could only happen, he figured, at Christmas. 'Take it,' he muttered discreetly, 'or I won't be responsible for my actions.' As the younger Browns cheered he sprang up and put the ring on Callie's finger. There were a few tense moments when she didn't say a word, but then she laughed and threw her arms around his neck, and everyone cheered.

'A Christmas wedding, then,' Ma Brown exclaimed, clapping her hands with excitement.

'A bit late for Christmas, Ma. It will have to be New Year,' Pa Brown, who should have known he could never win, argued, frowning.

'Ah, that's where you're wrong,' Ma Brown assured him, 'because Christmas is celebrated in January in Fabrizio. Isn't that right, Luca?'

'Quite correct, Mrs Brown.'

'Still, not much time,' Ma Brown said, frowning as she thought about it. 'But enough time, if I know our Callie.'

'You do know Callie,' Luca asserted, giving Ma Brown the warmest of hugs. 'You know her better than anyone except me.'

'I'll accept that,' Ma Brown stated as Callie narrowed her eyes in mock disapproval.

'How long have you three been conniving?' Callie enquired, raising a brow as she looked at Luca and then Ma and Pa Brown in turn.

'Four,' Rosie put in. 'Don't forget me.'

'Why, you—' Callie was still laughing when Luca swept her off her feet. Swinging her around, which was quite a risky manoeuvre in a room full of Browns and Anita, he planted a breath-stealing kiss on her mouth. 'Have you kept my letters?' he asked as he set her down. 'I was just thinking that you might want to read them now.'

'Read them *now*?' Rosie exclaimed. 'The paper they're written on is almost worn through. Don't let Callie kid you, Luca. You are the love of Callie's life.'

EPILOGUE

It was unseasonably cold in the north of England. Brilliant white snow was falling in soft, silent drifts, slowing the traffic and muffling the noise of hooves as Callie's horse-drawn wedding coach arrived outside the Browns'. To counterbalance the frigid temperatures, every house on the street was brilliantly lit to celebrate the holiday season, which would go on well into the New Year. In the town, stores and corner shops were still crammed with reindeer and stars, and sleighs and plump-cheeked Santa Clauses, as if no one could bear to let go of the Christmas cheer.

There would never be another wedding like this one, Callie was sure of that. She was going to marry Luca in the area where she'd grown up, surrounded by her closest friends the Browns, Callie's landlady from the shop in Blackpool, and Anita, and Maria and Marco, who had travelled from Italy. She was wearing a dress chosen by Ma Brown and approved by Rosie. In ivory lace, it fitted her like a second skin—something she wouldn't be able to indulge in for very much longer, Callie thought, smoothing her hands over her slightly rounded stomach as Rosie arranged her veil.

The ceremony would be a simple affair in the local

church, followed by a small reception at the Browns'. Callie had wanted the people closest to her to know how much they meant to her, and that even when she became a princess and lived in the palace in Fabrizio, they would still be a big part of her life. As far as the world of royalty was concerned, Callista Smith would marry Prince Luca of Fabrizio at a grand ceremony in that country's cathedral in a couple of weeks' time.

'You look beautiful,' Pa Brown said as he took charge of the young woman he thought of as a daughter. 'I'll be a proud man giving you away—though I'm only lending you out,' he added, frowning. 'I want you to keep in touch, our Callie, and never lose sight of your roots.'

'I never will,' she promised, giving Pa Brown a warm kiss on the cheek as Rosie draped a warm, faux-fur cape around Callie's shoulders. 'And you must all come and visit me regularly in Fabrizio.'

'Only if I can watch the match while I'm there,' Pa fretted with a frown.

'I'm sure it can be arranged,' Callie soothed, knowing how much the Saturday football match meant to Pa Brown.

They stepped out of the house straight into a snowdrift. Callie howled with laughter as she pulled her foot free from the glistening snow. 'Not a great start,' she admitted, 'but nothing can spoil today.'

The day was so Christmassy, with crisp snow underfoot and robins chirruping in the trees. It was so evocative of all the optimism inside her. Luca had insisted she must travel to the local church by horse and carriage and she was glad of the hot-water bottle waiting for her beneath the blankets on the leather seat. Two beautiful dapple-grey ponies with white plumes attached to their headbands were waiting patiently to draw her to the church. There were silver bells on their bridles that jingled as they trotted along. People stopped to stare, and waved frantically with friendly approval when they recognised the local girl who was soon to become a princess.

She'd never change, Callie thought. She'd always be Callie from the docks and Callie from the lemon groves too. All that mattered was love and friendship, and the man waiting for her inside the church.

Luca's face was full of pride when he turned around as the grand old organ struck up the wedding march. She had never seen anyone more handsome in her life. In a plain dark suit, without any of his orders of office, or the royal sash with its ornate jewelled insignia, Luca couldn't have looked hotter if he'd tried. What more could she want than this? Callie thought as Pa Brown transferred her hand from his to Luca's.

'You may kiss the bride.'

'I may kiss the love of my life,' Luca whispered so that only Callie could hear, 'the only Princess I'll ever need.'

'The only Princess you're ever going to get,' she teased him softly before they kissed. She stared down at the band of diamonds that Luca had whispered could never replace the blue plastic ring from the cracker, but he hope she liked it. Liked it? She loved it. And there will be another ring, he'd told her. 'When we marry in Fabrizio, you will have a ring made in Fabrizian gold.'

'The blue plastic ring was enough for me,' she had assured him. 'What I feel for you is in my heart.'

As they stepped outside the ancient church hand in hand, a crystalline scene of snow and icicles greeted them. Luca turned to Callie beneath the stone archway decorated with white winter roses and floating silk ribbons, to draw her winter bridal cape more snugly around her shoulders. 'Warm enough?' he asked.

She gave him one of her looks. 'Is that a serious question?'

Pulling her close against his muscular body, Luca gave Callie the only answer *she* would ever need, in a kiss that was more than hot enough to keep out any chill.

Michel, Luca's elderly aide, had advised on all things formal to make sure that protocol was followed for Luca and Callie's second ceremony in Fabrizio, but the magic, as always, was provided by the Browns, who had a far more relaxed take on what went into making the perfect wedding day. Callie only knew that it took one man to make her day perfect and he had just snuck into her suite at the palace, when she was fresh from the shower and naked beneath her fluffy towelling robe.

'You shouldn't be here,' she whispered, glancing over her shoulder to check that the door was securely locked.

'Why?' Luca demanded, looping his arms around her waist. 'You're not in your wedding dress, are you?'

'Exactly,' Callie exclaimed, shivering with desire as he teased the sensitive skin just below her ear with the lightest of rasps with his stubble. He looked beyond amazing, wearing nothing more than a white T-shirt and banged-up jeans. 'You parked the shave?' she reprimanded in between hectic gasps of breath.

'I know how much you like a good rasping,' he murmured, transferring his attention to her lips, which he now brushed with the lightest of kisses.

And she did like a good rasping. Far too much. 'You have to stop,' she gasped out.

'Or you won't be accountable for your actions?'

'Something like that,' she agreed on a dry throat as Luca's experienced hands traced the outline of her breasts.

'Do you know how long it is since we made love?' he demanded.

'Too long?'

'That's right,' he confirmed. 'It must be an hour since. What's this?' he asked, frowning as he extracted the fine gold chain that disappeared between her breasts.

'My something blue?'

'The plastic ring,' he exclaimed, smiling. 'I hope you won't mind if I replace it with something more substantial today?'

Callie's heart beat nineteen to the dozen. What type of rings did princesses have to wear? Her knowledge of such things was confined to magazines and newspapers, and those rings always looked so clunky and as if they would ruin all her clothes. 'So long as it's nothing too flashy.'

Luca hummed and frowned. 'I'm afraid I can't promise that.'

And Callie couldn't fail to be impressed. In fact, she was speechless when she saw the obviously priceless diamond ring that Luca had so casually pulled out from the back pocket of his jeans. The large, blue-white oval stone glittered wildly in the light as if it contained countless hopes and dreams just waiting to be set free. It was the most stunning piece of jewellery she'd ever seen, apart from the diamond ring Luca had surprised her with in the church in England. 'I don't need this,' she felt it only fair to tell him.

'But I want you to have it,' Luca insisted. 'Our children will expect you to have beautiful gifts from their father, a man who loves you more than anything else in the world.' As he spoke Luca placed his hand on her not quite so flat belly, as if he were making a pledge to both Callie and their baby to love and protect them with his life. 'You'll have to wear the engagement ring on your right hand with the eternity ring from England,' he said as he brought her fingers to his lips. 'According to tradition in Fabrizio, your wedding band goes on this left hand, because it is said to contain the vein the ancient Romans believed connected directly to your heart. We still call it the *vena amoris*, the vein of love, and for that finger you will wear something very different.'

'Fabrizian gold,' she said, remembering as their stares connected.

'As strong and as direct as you are,' Luca confirmed in a way that made her heart go crazy. Thrusting his hand for a second time into the back pocket of his jeans, he brought out the simple band. 'No frills,' he said. 'Just plain, honest perfection like you. I hope you enjoy wearing it.'

'I love it,' Callie exclaimed. 'You couldn't have chosen anything better. This is the most precious ring I'll ever wear.'

'And the plastic ring?'

'I'll never forget it, but this,' she said as Luca drew her close, 'will be the ring of my heart.'

He dipped his head to kiss her just as Ma Brown called out from the other room, 'Are you ready to get dressed, Callie? We can't keep that carriage waiting.'

'Punctuality is the politeness of kings,' Luca teased.

'And my time-keeping's dreadful,' Callie fretted.

'Lucky for you I'd wait for ever if I had to.'

Luca had turned serious in a way that made her body ache for him, but with the briefest of kisses he was gone.

* * *

The second royal winter wedding was perfection, if a little grander than the first. The streets were packed with people eager to see their new Princess, and they weren't disappointed. There were food stalls and bands, and Christmas decorations still glittered everywhere. The theme was white and silver, which made everything seem filled with light. There might not be snow in Fabrizio at Christmastime, but beneath the flawless blue the gentle sunshine warmed the throngs of wedding guests as they cheered their new Princess dressed in yards of white silk chiffon that floated behind Callie as she walked along, and yet moulded her body so beautifully. The finest lace covered her arms and shoulders, while her train was almost twenty feet long. Anything shorter than that, and there wouldn't have been enough fabric for all the young Browns to take a handful of, Ma Brown had proclaimed ominously, but all the small bridesmaids and pageboys behaved perfectly on the day. There wasn't a spill or a smudge from any of them, and under the Browns' and Anita's prudent shepherding, Callie felt as if she were floating down the aisle of the glorious cathedral in Fabrizio before she finally halted at Luca's side.

'Who giveth this woman—'

'We do,' Pa Brown piped up, to be heartily shushed by his wife.

No one in the congregation noticed anything amiss, as they were all too busy watching the way Luca gazed at his bride. There was no doubt in anyone's mind that this was a royal love match, and one that would benefit all.

'Happy Christmas,' Luca murmured, and as Callie's gaze dropped instinctively to his mouth he added in a sexy whisper, 'Remind me. How long is it since we made love?'

'Too long,' Callie whispered back, her gaze locked on Luca's. 'Must be almost three hours now.'

'We may have to miss the reception,' he said with a mock frown.

'Almost certainly,' she agreed. And then the announcement rang out that His Serene Highness, Prince Luca of Fabrizio, could now kiss his bride. 'We may have to ask the congregation to leave,' Callie said dryly when Luca kissed her and she felt his very obvious impatience for herself.

Turning Callie, so that now they faced the packed body of the church together, Luca announced in a firm, strong voice, 'My Princess.' And as everyone applauded, he added, 'The love of my life.'

'There are no affairs of state for me to deal with for the next two weeks,' Luca told Callie as their horse-drawn carriage made its stately progress along the gracious main boulevard lined with cheering crowds. 'There's just my long-running affair with my wife to concentrate on now.'

'After our wedding feast,' she reminded him as she waved happily to the crowds.

'Did I mention we'll be delaying our arrival?'

'Really?' she asked, pretending to be shocked.

'I have commanded the carriage pause at our private entrance to the palace, so we have chance to…freshen up.'

'You think of everything,' Callie remarked dryly.

'I try to,' Luca confirmed.

If the staff at the palace was surprised by the sight of their Prince and Princess racing full tilt, hand in hand, across the grand hall, the bride with her tiara askew and her lengthy train bundled up beneath her arm, they of course made no comment. Minutes later, the happy couple had slammed their bedroom door behind them. Frantic seconds later Luca had opened every button down the back of Callie's beautiful gown. She barely had chance to remove her tiara before he swept her into his arms and carried her to the bed. The room was full of flowers and the scent was divine. 'And all for you,' he said.

'They're so beautiful,' Callie gasped when Luca gave her the briefest of chances to take everything in. 'Everyone's gone to so much trouble.'

'For you,' he declared as he took her deep, groaning with pleasure as she claimed him. 'For ever,' he whispered.

'Or even longer than that,' Callie agreed.

* * * * *

THE SHEIKH'S BABY SCANDAL

CAROL MARINELLI

PROLOGUE

'KEDAH, WHERE ARE YOU? That's enough, now!'

The royal nanny was getting exasperated as she again called out to her small charge, but Kedah had no intention of being found—he was having far too much fun!

Kedah could see the nanny's feet go past as he hid behind the large statue that she had checked just a few seconds ago. He could run like greased lightning, and he smothered his laughter as she now moved towards the grand staircase.

'Kedah!' The nanny was sounding very cross. As well she might—Kedah was a handful.

The people of Zazinia adored him, though, and they would all be lined up outside the palace hoping to get a glimpse of him. Usually there was just a small crowd when the royal plane landed but, thanks to the cheeky young Prince, the numbers had grown of late.

Never had there been more interest in a young royal. Kedah's chocolate-brown eyes were flecked with gold and his winning smile had drawn rapt attention from the moment the first photographer had captured it. In their eyes he could do no wrong—in fact, Kedah's boisterous boyish ways only served to endear him further to the public. He was as beautiful as he was wild, they often said, and it would seem that he could not stand still.

He tried to!

For the people of Zazinia, a dreary parade was made so much more entertaining when they watched little Kedah's attempts to obey the stern commands that were delivered out of the side of his father's mouth.

Just a few weeks ago there had been a procession, and Kedah had had to remain still for the best part of an hour. But he had quickly grown bored.

'Control him!' Omar, the Crown Prince had said to Rina, his wife, for the King had started to get cross.

It was so hard to control him, though.

When his mother had warned him to stand still, Kedah had merely smiled up at her and then held out his arms to be lifted. Rina had tried to ignore him—but, really, who could resist? In the end she had complied. Kedah had chatted away to her, despite being gently hushed. She had smiled affectionately and put her hand up to his little fat cheek, looked him in the eye. She'd told him to behave for just a few more moments, and that then it would be time to return to the palace.

The King's silent disapproval had been felt all around. He did not approve of his son's young wife, and certainly he felt that children should be seen and not heard. Omar had been tense, Rina had done her best to appease all, and yet Kedah had chosen to be impervious to the strained atmosphere and turned his attention to the crowd.

They had all been staring at him, so he'd smiled and waved to them. It had been such a break from the usually austere and remote royal shows that the gathered crowd had melted *en masse* and, quite simply, adored him. Kedah was funny—and terribly cheeky. He had so much energy to burn that he was the work of five children, and the royal nanny struggled with this particular charge!

'Kedah!' she called out now, to thin air. 'I need to get you bathed and dressed so that you can go and greet your father and the King.'

He crouched lower behind the statue and did not respond. He was not particularly looking forward to the senior royals' return. They had been gone for a few days and the palace felt so much more relaxed without them. His mother seemed to laugh more, and even the staff were happier without the King around.

Neither did Kedah want to change out of his play clothes just so he could watch a plane land and his grumpy father and grandfather get out. And so, as the nanny sped down stairs in search of him, Kedah ran from behind the statue and tried to plan his next move.

Usually he would hide in the library, but on this day he ran somewhere he should not. Jaddi, his grandfather, had his own wing, and there were no guards there today—which meant that he was free to explore. But his eager footsteps came to a halt midway there. Even though his grandfather was away, Jaddi was intimidating enough that Kedah chose not to continue. And so, at the last moment, he changed his mind and turned and ran to the Crown Prince's wing, where his parents resided.

There were no guards there either.

To the left there were offices that ran the length of the corridor, and to the right was the entrance to his parents' private residence.

Kedah rarely entered it. His parents generally came and visited him in the nursery or the playroom.

Knowing that he would be told off if he disturbed

his mother from her nap, for a second he considered the balcony—but then chose to run to the offices instead. He had long ago kicked off his sandals, so his bare feet made barely a sound.

Even though he was in a rush to find a hiding place, Kedah stopped for a moment and looked up at the portraits, as he always did when he was here.

They fascinated him.

He looked along the row of Crown Princes gone by. All were imposing-looking men, dressed in warrior robes with their hands on the hilt of their swords. All stared down at him with cool grey eyes and grim expressions.

He looked at a younger version of his grandfather, the King, and then he looked at his father.

They looked so stern.

One day, his mother had told him, *his* portrait would hang there, for he was born to be King. 'And you will be such a *good* king, Kedah. I know that you shall listen to your people.'

He had heard the brittle edge to his mother's voice as she'd gazed up at the portraits. 'Why don't they smile?' Kedah had asked.

'Because being Crown Prince is a serious thing.'

'I don't want it, then!' Kedah had laughed.

Now he looked away from the portraits and ran to a meeting room that had several desks. He went to hide under one, sure that he would not be found there.

Or perhaps he would, for there were noises coming from behind a large wooden door and he recognised his mother's voice as she called out. He knew that that was his father's private office, and wondered why she would be in there.

And then he heard a low cry.

It sounded as if his mother was hurt, and Kedah's expression changed from happy to a look of concern as he heard muffled sobs and moans.

His father had told him to take care of his mother while he was away. Even at this tender age, Kedah knew that people worried about her, for Rina could be unpredictable at times.

He came out from under the desk and stood wondering what he should do. He knew that the door handles were too high for him. For a moment he considered running to alert the royal nanny that his mother sounded distressed, but then he changed his mind. Often his mother wept, and it did not seem to endear her to the staff nor to the rest of the royal family.

And so, instead of getting help, Kedah selected a chair and started to drag it across the room. The chair was made of the same wood as the heavy door, and it felt like ages until he had got it close enough to climb upon it and attempt to turn the handle on the office door.

'Ummu…?' Kedah called out to his mother as he climbed onto the chair and turned the heavy handle. 'Ummu?' he said again as the door swung open.

But then he frowned, because his mother seemed to be sitting on the desk and yet she was being held in Abdal's arms.

'Intadihr!'

His mother shouted that Kedah was to stay where he was, and she and Abdal moved out of his line of sight. Kedah did as he was told. He was not sure what was happening, but a moment or so later Abdal walked past on his way out.

Kedah had never really liked him. Abdal was always cross whenever Kedah came to the offices and pleaded with his mother to take him for a walk. It was as if he didn't want the young Prince around.

Kedah stared at Abdal's departing back as the man walked quickly along the corridor and then, still standing on the chair, he turned and looked to his mother. Rina was flustered, and she smoothed down her robe as she walked towards him.

Kedah did not hold his arms out to be lifted. 'Why was Abdal here?' he asked. 'Where are the guards?'

There were no flies on Kedah—not even at that young age.

'It's okay,' Rina said as she lifted him, unyielding, from the chair. 'Mummy was upset and didn't want anyone to see. I was crying.'

'Why?' Kedah asked as he took in his mother's features. Her face was all red and, yes, he *had* heard her sob. 'Why are you always sad?'

'Because I miss my homeland sometimes, Kedah. Abdal is also from there. He is here to ease the transition and to help our two countries unite. Abdal understands how difficult it can be to get the King to agree to any changes. We were trying to come up with a way that will please all the people.'

Kedah just stared back at his mother as she hurriedly spoke on.

'Your father would be very upset if he knew that I had been crying while he was away. He is tired of arguing with the King and he has enough on his plate, so it is better not to tell him. It is better that you don't tell anyone what you just saw.'

Kedah stared into her eyes more deeply and tried to read her. His mother did not look sad. If anything, she looked scared, and that had his heart tightening in a fear for her that he didn't understand.

'I don't want you to be unhappy.'

'Then I shan't be,' Rina said, and brought a hand up to Kedah's face and cupped his taut cheek. 'After all, I have so much to give thanks for—I have a beautiful son and a wonderful home…'

'So don't you cry again,' Kedah said, and those gorgeous chocolate-brown eyes of his narrowed. He removed his mother's hand from his cheek and looked right into his mother's eyes. For one so very young, he spoke with command. *'Ever!'*

'Kedah, there you are…'

They both turned to the sound of the royal nanny's voice, and he did not understand why the nanny stammered and blushed as she apologised to Her Royal Highness for losing sight of her young charge.

'I've been looking for him all over the palace.'

'It's fine,' Rina said, handing Kedah over. 'We'll say no more about it.'

A little while later his father and the King returned, and life went as before.

Kedah continued to be boisterous, and yet from that day there was a defiant edge to his antics. From then on those brown eyes narrowed if anyone got too close. He kept his own counsel and he trusted no one.

A few years later his brother was born and that signalled happier times, for Mohammed was a model child.

Weary of the wilder young Prince, the King insisted he be schooled overseas, and little Kedah attended a boarding school in London. He somehow knew that he held a secret that, if ever revealed, might well destroy not only the people he loved but the kingdom his family ruled.

And as he matured Kedah knew how dire the consequences would be for his mother. If her infidelity was exposed she would be shamed, and the King would have no choice but to divorce her and separate her from her sons.

But secrets had ways of seeping out through even the most heavily guarded walls. Servants gossiped amongst themselves as children played at their feet, and royal nannies eventually married and indulged in pillow talk of their own. Rumours spread wide when they were carried on desert winds—and returned multiplied, of course.

And as Kedah grew, and returned to Zazinia during term breaks, the portraits fascinated him for a different reason.

Perhaps what was being said was true and he was *not* his father's son. After all, he looked nothing like any of them.

But his doubts were not because of the rumours that refused to fade with the passage of time—Kedah knew what he had seen.

CHAPTER ONE

You need Felicia Hamilton.

Crown Prince Sheikh Kedah of Zazinia had always made sure that he needed no one.

He was reliant only on himself.

That late afternoon he sat in his London office and rolled a rare spherical diamond between the pads of his index finger and thumb as he read a newspaper article on his computer. When there was a knock on the door and he called for Anu to come in he saw that she looked rather tense. He wondered if she had read the article too.

What was being discussed in it would distress her, he knew. She had been a loyal member of his team for a number of years and was also from his homeland. She would understand how damning this article was.

'Ms Hamilton is here for her interview,' Anu said, and her lips pursed a little.

'Send her in, then.'

'She asked for a few moments to freshen up.'

Oh, Anu tried, but she could not hold her protests in. All the staff who came into contact with Kedah had a preliminary interview with Anu first. Yesterday she had met with Felicia, and found the young woman did not tick any of the usual boxes that might get her through to a second round interview. She lacked hospitality experience—though she made up for it in attitude—and that would *never* do when working for Kedah. He was not exactly known for consulting with his staff. He had a packed schedule and he expected his team to work quietly and seamlessly in the background—which was something Anu could not see happening with Miss Hamilton.

Anu had reported this to him yesterday, and yet Kedah had told her to call Felicia back and invite her to come in this afternoon.

'Kedah, I really don't think that she is suitable to work as your PA.'

'Anu, I understand that you have concerns, and they have been noted. Can you please alert me when Miss Hamilton decides that she is ready?'

As the door closed behind Anu, Kedah replaced the diamond in the inside pocket of his jacket and returned to the news article that he had been reading.

It was in English. No one from his homeland would dare to publish such a piece. Not yet.

Heir (not so) Apparent!

Beneath the daring title there was a picture of Kedah, wearing a suit and tie and a rich, arrogant smile. It spoke of the recent death of Kedah's grandfather and how, now that Omar was King, certain difficult topics needed to be raised. It briefly discussed Kedah's British education and subsequent jet-set lifestyle and playboy reputation. It mentioned how, at thirty, he still showed no sign of settling down.

The article also spoke about his younger brother Mohammed and his wife Kumu and their two sons. Unlike Kedah, Mohammed had been schooled in Zazinia, and there was a considerable faction in the country who considered that, for stability, Mohammed would make a more suitable Crown Prince and subsequent King. The article stated that some of the elders were now calling for the Accession Council to meet and for a final decision to be made.

At the end of the piece there was a photo of Mohammed and Omar, but most damning of all was the caption below: *Like Father, Like Son.*

Apart from the years that separated them, Mohammed and Omar were identical—not just in looks but in their staid, old-fashioned ways.

The only change that Omar had made while Crown Prince had been an update to the education system. Over the years Kedah had made no progress with his father either. Kedah was a highly skilled architect, yet every design he'd submitted had been rejected and every suggestion he'd made either immediately turned down or later overruled.

He had hoped, now that his grandfather was dead, that things might change, but his latest proposal for a stunning waterfront hotel and shopping complex had been rejected too.

His father had pointed out that the new building would look onto the private royal beach.

'There are ways around that,' Kedah had insisted. 'If you would just let me—'

'The decision is final, Kedah,' the King had interrupted. 'I have discussed it at length with the elders…'

'And you have discussed it at length with Mohammed,' Kedah had said. 'I hear that he was *very* vocal in his criticism of my plans.'

'I listen to all sides.'

'Well, you should listen to me first,' Kedah had said. 'Mohammed is *not* the Crown Prince.'

'Mohammed is the one who is here.'

'I have told you—I will not live in Zazinia if I am to be ineffectual.'

Kedah turned off his computer so he did not have to see the offensive article.

Earlier today, when it had first appeared, he had called Vadia, his assistant in Zazinia, and had been assured that it would be pulled down from the internet. There was no denying, though, that things were coming to a head. Even before their grandfather's death Mohammed had decided that *he* would make a better Crown Prince and future King. Many of the elders thought the same, and—as the article had stated—there was a strong push for a meeting of the Accession Council to discuss the future of the royal family formally.

His father would have the final say, but rather than declaring outright that he would prefer his younger son to be King one day, Omar seemed to be pushing Kedah into stepping aside.

Kedah refused to.

Instead he was busy making plans.

He had many rich and influential friends, and he knew a lot of bad boys too. Matteo Di Sione was both. He had a reputation that rivalled even Kedah's.

They had met up in New York a couple of weeks ago—and not by chance. Kedah hadn't told Matteo the issue, just that he was expecting turbulent times ahead and needed someone tough who could handle things. Matteo had made some discreet enquiries on his friend's behalf and had come back to Kedah with his findings.

You need Felicia Hamilton.

Kedah glanced at the time. Usually a potential employee who arrived late for an interview and then asked for time to freshen up wouldn't even make it through the door of his office.

What the *hell* was she doing? he wondered.

She was reading.

Felicia hadn't actually *intended* to keep Sheikh Kedah waiting for quite so long. The West End was gridlocked—thanks to a red carpet awards show taking place tonight, the taxi driver had told her. So Felicia, sitting in the back and doing some final research on Kedah on her way to the interview, had decided to walk the last couple of blocks. But then a very interesting article had turned up on her tablet and, after arriving at his impressive office, she'd wanted a few more moments to go through it.

Now perhaps she understood why she had been called back after that disastrous interview yesterday. Anu had spoken to her as if Felicia wanted to *work* for Kedah—a real job, so to speak—and after an awkward twenty minutes, during which it had become increasingly clear that Felicia was not the type Sheikh Kedah employed, the two women had parted ways.

Still, her phone had rung this morning and Felicia had smiled to herself when she had been invited to return and meet with the man himself. Of course Kedah didn't want a PA—it was her troubleshooting skills he required.

Now she knew why!

It would seem that Crown Prince Sheikh Kedah of Zazinia was fighting for the throne—and Felicia was now sure he wanted to commence the clean-up of his reputation.

From what she knew of him, it would take more than industrial strength bleach!

If there was a scale for playboys, then Kedah was at the extreme top. In fact his partying ways were legendary.

How the mighty fell!

Today this oh, so arrogant man would reveal his troubles to Felicia. Of course she would look suitably unshocked as he did so, and assure him that whatever trouble he was in she could sort it.

Felicia was *very* good at her job because she had been doing it all her life.

She had been taught to smile for the cameras alongside Susannah, her long-suffering mother, long before she could even walk. She had on many occasions sat in the family lounge with spin doctors and PR people as they had debated how her father's multiple affairs and the trashy headlines and exposés should best be dealt with.

There had even been times when they had come to her school. Felicia could remember sitting in the headmaster's office with her parents, being reminded that cameras would be on them when they left. She had been told what to do as they walked, as a family, to the waiting car.

'Remember to smile, Felicia.'

'Susannah, hold his hand as you walk to the car and don't forget to laugh when he whispers to you.'

And her mother had done as she was told. Susannah had done everything that had been asked of her. But in the end it had all been to no avail. When Felicia was fourteen her father had decided to update to a younger model and had walked out on them.

A legal wrangle had ensued.

The lovely private boarding school that had been such a haven for her had disappeared when the school fees hadn't been paid, and with it had gone Felicia's friends and her beloved pony.

Susannah had fallen apart, and it had been up to her daughter to be strong. They had rented a small house while waiting for the money to be sorted out and Felicia had enrolled in the local school—but she hadn't fit in. Her dreams of being a vet had long gone by then, and she'd left school at sixteen. She had taken an office job to help with the rent.

Those days were gone now.

Felicia was highly sought-after, and her troubleshooting talents were coveted by the rich and famous. Her mother lived in a house that Felicia had bought and paid for, and Felicia owned her own flat.

Some questioned how she could defend these men—but, really, Felicia was just doing what she'd been taught.

The only difference was that now she was paid.

And paid handsomely.

She ran a comb through her dark blonde hair, touched up her lip gloss and added a slick of mascara to bring out the green of her eyes. As she headed out Anu told her to take a seat. Guessing the newspaper article would soon be taken down, she took a few quick screenshots on her phone as Sheikh Kedah now kept *her* waiting.

Oh, well! She had done the same to him.

Working with this type of man, Felicia had found that it was terribly important to establish early on that *his* ego had to be put aside and that from this point on *she* ran the show. It was even more vital to establish that they weren't suddenly best friends and, given the reputations of the men she dealt with, to make it clear they would never be lovers.

Felicia would be very nice at first, of course, while he told her what was going on, but then her smile would fade and she'd tell him what had to be done if he wanted to come out of this intact.

The truth was that Felicia despised these men.

She just knew, from wretched experience, how to deal with them.

'You might want to put your phone away,' Anu suggested.

Felicia was about to decline politely when a rich, deep and heavily accented voice spoke for her.

'I'm sure Ms Hamilton is just keeping up to date with the news.'

She looked up.

She had prepared thoroughly for this moment—determined not to let such a superfluous thing as his stunning looks sideswipe her. She had examined many photos to render herself immune to him. Only no photograph could fully capture the beauty of Sheikh Kedah in the flesh.

He was wearing an exquisitely cut dark suit and tie, but they were mere details for she had little interest in his attire. And it was not the caramel of his skin against his white shirt or his thick glossy black hair that forced her to try to remember to breathe. Nor was it cheekbones that looked as if Michelangelo himself had spent a couple of days sculpting them to perfection. Even sulky full lips that did not smile hardly mattered, for Felicia was caught in the trap of his eyes.

They were thickly lashed and a rich shade of chocolate-brown with golden flecks and—unlike most of her clients—he met her gaze steadily.

Oh, she was *extremely* good at her job. For, despite the jolt to her senses, Felicia did not let her reaction reveal itself to him and instead stood up, utterly composed.

'Come through,' he said.

And she smiled.

Widely.

She had a smile that took men's breath away. It was a smile so seemingly open that hardened reporters would thrust their microphones a little closer and their lenses would zoom in, so certain were they that it would waver.

It never did.

And long ago she had trained herself not to blush.

'I'm sorry I'm late,' Felicia said as she walked towards him. 'The traffic was terrible.'

He almost forgave her, for in turn Felicia was not what Kedah had been expecting. He had thought, given she had been invited for a formal second interview, that she would be in a suit, but Felicia looked rather more like a lady who lunched and was wearing a pretty off-white dress.

It was fitted enough that it showed her slender frame and pert bust, while short enough to reveal her toned legs. She was wearing high-heeled strappy sandals and looked nothing like the hard-nosed woman he had been prepared for. In fact she was as delicate-looking as she was pretty. She was so soft and smiling that Kedah was quite sure Matteo had got it all wrong.

Felicia Hamilton was the very *last* person he needed. Moreover, she was exactly the soft and submissive type he desired!

Naturally he had looked her up and had seen a picture of her in a boxy suit with her hair worn up. She had been coming out of court, with a terribly famous and thoroughly disgraced sportsman by her side. She had spoken for him and her voice had been crisp and to the point.

Today Kedah had expected brittle, and yet there was a softness to her that confused him. Her hair was long and layered and framed a heart-shaped face, and her fragrance was light and floral, meeting his nostrils as he held the door open for her and she passed him.

'Please…' Kedah gestured. 'Take a seat.'

Felicia did so, placing her bag by her side and crossing her legs at the ankles. Though he seemed utterly composed, Felicia was prepared for anything. Often the door had barely closed before her future client broke down. *'For God's sake, Felicia, you have to help me!'* they all too often begged. *'You have to stop this from getting out!'*

Yes—*client*.

Oh, she might call them her boss when she was in front of the camera lens but, as Kedah would soon find out, it was Felicia who was in charge.

Yet instead of begging for her help Kedah calmly offered refreshments.

'No, thank you.'

'You're sure?' he checked.

'Quite sure. I had a late lunch.'

And his troubles would be a very sweet dessert!

He walked around the desk and took his place and Felicia ran a tongue over her glossed lips as she waited for him to reveal the salacious truth.

'You come highly recommended.'

'Thank you.'

'Ms Hamilton?' he checked. 'Or can I call you Felicia?'

'Felicia's fine,' she offered. 'How would you like me to address *you*?'

'Kedah.'

She nodded.

They went through the formalities. He told her he was an esteemed architect, which of course she already knew.

'I used to sell them off, but now once I design a hotel I tend to hold on to it,' Kedah explained needlessly.

She just wished he'd get to the point.

'So I have a fleet of hotels across the world, which in turn means I have a lot of staff…'

Felicia nodded and wished they could lose the charade and get to the good bit.

'Do you have much experience in the hospitality industry?' he asked.

Felicia frowned. She'd expected a confessional—to sit, seemingly non-judgmental, as he poured out his past—yet he seemed to be actually interviewing her.

'Not really. Though of course I've stayed in an awful lot of hotels!'

Oh, she had. And if Kedah was going on word of mouth then he'd know that she worked for just a few weeks a year.

He didn't even deign to smile at her small joke.

'As I hope Anu explained, the role would involve extensive travel. If you work for me the hours will be very long. Sometimes there are eighteen-hour days. If we are away you would also work weekends. Do you have other commitments?'

'My current employer is my only commitment,' Felicia answered. It was the truth—whatever his crisis, it would have her full attention.

'Good.' Kedah nodded. 'How soon would you be able to start?'

'As soon as the contract is signed.' Felicia smiled. 'I trust Anu gave you my terms?'

'Indeed she did.'

Felicia Hamilton commanded quite a fee.

'What about your personal life?' he asked.

'That's not your concern,' Felicia answered.

'Be sure to keep it that way,' Kedah said. 'I don't want to hear that your boyfriend is upset because you missed his birthday, or that your mother-in-law has surgery next week and you need some time off. Care factor? Zero.'

Felicia's response was to laugh, and for once it was genuine. Honesty had been somewhat lacking in her life, and she would far prefer the truth than a dressed-up lie.

And now she waited—*how* she waited—for that cool facade to crack and for Kedah to admit that he had royally stuffed up and needed his past to disappear. But instead he spoke of hotels and designs, and she stifled a yawn as he told her about Hussain, a graphic designer he regularly used.

'He's excellent. He actually studied with my father many years ago. We have worked on many designs together—mainly in the UAE.'

Felicia stifled another yawn.

'Why don't I show you some examples of my work—as well as a few of the hotels we shall be visiting in the coming weeks?' Kedah said, and then dimmed the lights.

Felicia wondered for a brief second if refreshments might be in order after all. Was she about to get a private screening of the trouble Sheikh Kedah was in? A steamy sex tape? The Crown Prince bound and gagged in a seedy encounter, perhaps?

Kedah watched that tongue pop out and moisten those lovely lips as she sat straight in the chair, giving him her full attention.

Then he smiled unseen as her shoulders slumped and she sat through the forty-minute presentation that took her through some of his luxury hotels. She fought to keep her eyes from crossing as she watched it.

What the hell...?

'Do you have any questions?' Kedah invited as he flicked on the lights.

No! She just wanted him to cut to the chase and reveal the truth. 'Not at this stage,' she said.

'There must be things that you want to ask me?' he invited. 'Surely you have come prepared? You will have looked me up?'

'Of course I have.'

'What do you think your role might entail?' he asked as he went through her file.

Maybe he was shy, Felicia thought. Though that made no sense. He looked far from shy. But perhaps he needed a little help revealing his dark truths, so she decided to broach things gently. 'I would guess, from my research, that I'll be running a dating agency with only one man on the books,' Felicia said, and watched him closely for a reaction.

Kedah merely looked up from the papers and stared back at her as she continued.

'Though of course rather more discreetly than my predecessors.'

'Discreetly?' Kedah frowned.

'You tend to hit the glossies rather a lot.'

'That's hardly my staff's fault.'

'Well, they should monitor what's said. If a woman's upset...'

'As far as my sex life goes, you would just have to deal with the bookings and the brochure, Felicia…'

'Brochure?

He didn't enlighten her. 'What I am saying is that you do *not* police comments or apologise on my behalf. I am quite grateful for "the glossies", as you call them, for if women expect anything more from me than a night in bed, possibly two, then that is their own foolish mistake. They cannot say they haven't been duly warned.'

No, not shy, Felicia decided as he continued to speak.

'But I do expect discretion from all who work for me. Naturally you will have to sign a confidentiality agreement.'

'I told Anu yesterday that I shan't.'

Kedah, who had gone back to going through the papers, glanced up.

'Nobody would employ a PA without one.'

'If you look through my references you'll see that they do.' She gave him a smile, as if she was asking if he took sugar with his coffee—one lump or two? 'You either trust me or you don't.'

'I don't,' he responded. 'Though please don't take it personally. I don't trust anyone.'

'Good, because neither do I.'

Kedah was fast realising there was nothing apart from her appearance that was delicate. She was actually rather fascinating, and any doubts he might have had about her being up to the job were starting to fade.

He had no intention of telling her his situation just yet, of course, but he had decided that he wanted her onside. 'We can't go any further without you signing one.'

'Well, we can't go any further, then,' she said, and reached for her bag.

He didn't halt her.

'Thank you for wasting my time,' she added, and gave him another flash of that stunning smile.

Kedah noted that it didn't quite reach her eyes. They were a dazzling emerald-green—a shade that was one of a forest reflected on a lake…emerald, yet glacial.

He watched, quietly amused, as she began to flounce off.

'Sit down, Felicia.'

There was such command to his tone that it stopped her.

His voice wasn't remotely raised. If anything his words were delivered with an almost bored calm. But he might as well have reached for a lasso, for it was as if something had just wrapped around her. Oh, Felicia *heard* his words—yet she *felt* them at the base of her spine, and it tingled as he continued speaking.

'I haven't finished with you yet.'

CHAPTER TWO

If ever a voice belonged in the bedroom, it was Kedah's.

Not just a bedroom.

A boardroom would do nicely too.

For the second time in an hour Felicia was transported to that headmaster's office—but it was a far nicer version this time!

He was utterly potent. She almost wanted to keep walking towards the door, just for the giddy pleasure of finding out that she had a scruff to her neck as he hauled her back.

What she could not know was that the very controlled Sheikh Kedah was actually thinking along the same lines.

Felicia was absolutely his type.

He stared at the back of her head and then took in her rigid shoulders, let his dark eyes run the length of her spine. Her face was heart-shaped, and so too were her buttocks, and his eyes rested there for a moment too long.

Then he forced them away.

Kedah did not need the complication of a fake PA who turned him on.

He liked softness on his pillow and sweet, batting eyes, and he didn't care if his women lied as they simpered.

It was, after all, just a game.

And then he thought of the games he might play with Felicia.

He wanted to haul her to his knee and give her the job description as he ravished that mouth.

Know my hotels inside out, meet my staff, handle the press, and keep my world floating as I fight for my title. Now, let's go to bed.

Of course he did not say that.

This was business, and Kedah was determined it would remain so.

'Take a seat,' he said.

Felicia breathed out through her nostrils as he mentally undressed her. She felt as if he had even seen what colour knickers she had on. Flesh-coloured, actually. Not because she was boring, she wanted to hasten to add, but because of the white dress.

Oh, help!

And though common sense told her to leave now, to get out while she still could and most definitely should, neither had Felicia finished with *him*.

She wanted to know why he'd brought her here. She was positive that he didn't really want her working as his PA. So she turned around.

'Why are you so against signing a confidentiality agreement?' he asked, in such a measured tone that Felicia wondered if she'd misread the crackling tension.

'They're pointless.' She fought for professionalism and cleared her throat as the interview resumed. 'If, as you've stated, you trust no one, then a confidentiality agreement, no matter how watertight, cannot protect you.'

'It offers some level of security.'

'Well, it doesn't for me,' Felicia responded. 'What

if something is leaked and you assume that *I* was the source?'

He didn't answer.

'I'm pretty unshockable, but what if you do something abhorrent?' she challenged. 'Am I supposed to turn a blind eye just because I've signed up for silence?'

'I'm bad,' Kedah said. 'Not evil.'

That made her smile, and this time it reached those stunning cold eyes.

'Sit down,' he said again. 'We can discuss it at the end of your trial.'

'There's nothing further to discuss on that subject—and also I don't do trials.' Felicia did sit down again, though. 'A one-year contract is the minimum I'll sign.'

'I might not need you for a year.'

That was the first real hint that there *was* more going on here. Maybe he felt awkward about telling her about his past—but that made no sense. There was nothing chaste about that blistering gaze. Perhaps there was something big about to come out? A huge scandal about to hit?

Felicia was tired of playing games. She wanted to know what she was getting into before she signed.

'Kedah, I'm not a defence lawyer.'

He simply stared back at her as she spoke, and she thought that never before had she had a client so able to meet her gaze.

'You *can* tell me whatever it is that's going on.'

Still he said nothing.

'I'm quite sure I already know.'

'Do tell,' he offered.

'I think you need me to restore your reputation,' she told him. 'And I can. Let me get to work, and in a matter of weeks I'll have you looking like an altar boy,'

'I hope not.'

'So do I…'

She faltered. Her voice had dropped to a smoky level that had no place at work—actually no place in her *life* till this point. Felicia dated, but she preferred the safe comfort of feeling lukewarm to this feeling of being speared on the end of a fondue stick and dipped at his whim.

She cleared her throat. 'Well, an altar boy might be pushing things, but if there's anything you're worried about…'

'Worrying is a pointless pursuit—and, as I thought I'd made clear, I'm fine with my reputation,' Kedah answered smoothly, and although his expression did not display even a trace of amusement Felicia felt as if he was laughing at her. 'In fact I've loved every minute that I've spent earning it.'

Kedah was entranced, for Felicia hadn't so much as blinked, nor had she blushed, and he decided then that she was hired.

'Okay, no confidentiality agreement. But mess with me, Felicia, and I will deal with you *outside* of the law.'

Now she blushed—but at a point far lower on her body than her face. She was about to make some glib comment about being tipped over his knee but rather rapidly changed her mind.

'Six months,' Kedah said.

'A year,' she refuted. 'And when I'm no longer needed you pay out the rest of my contract and I'll be on my way.'

'Is that what generally happens?' For a moment he let his guard drop—just a little. He was curious about her job. Fascinated, in fact. 'You do a few weeks' work for a year's pay?'

She nodded and Kedah—albeit briefly—forgot his own dark troubles. He wanted to know more, but Felicia shook her head when he asked.

'I don't discuss my previous clients, and of course I'll provide you with that same courtesy.' Her voice sounded a little frantic now. 'Now you need to tell me what's going on if I'm to do my job.'

'Felicia,' he offered, in a rather bored drawl, 'I didn't hire you to tidy up my reputation. This leopard shan't be changing his spots. I want a PA and I hear that you're amongst the best. Do you want the role or not?'

Her smile slipped and those once glacial eyes clouded in confusion.

He pushed forward the contract.

'We need to discuss terms and conditions,' Kedah explained, and then went through them.

Basically, for the next year she was his.

Well, not *his*!

Just at his beck and call. Even if he was in Zazinia without her she would be working here.

There would be no reprieve.

Felicia wondered if now was the time to state, as she usually did, that she never slept with clients.

She looked at his long slender fingers as they turned the page and moved on to remuneration.

'Regarding your salary…' he said.

'Kedah.'

She watched as with a stroke of his pen he doubled it.

'I expect devotion.'

Now! she thought. He had given the perfect opening, Felicia knew. Right now she should smile and nod as she warned him that there were certain things out of bounds.

And there were.

Of course there were.

But actually to state that nothing could possibly happen might make her a liar. Even if *he* didn't, Felicia trusted her own word, so she refrained from her usual terse speech.

He crossed out the confidentiality clause, and initialled it, and then it was time for them both to countersign.

Felicia read through the contract again, and noted that her starting date was today.

Now.

'Kedah…' Felicia felt it only fair to warn him. 'I don't think I'll make a very good PA.'

'On the contrary,' he said. 'I think you'll be excellent.'

There was more to this.

Quite simply, there had to be.

And Felicia wanted to know what it was.

With a hand that somehow remained steady she used her own pen to sign her name and initial in all the right places and that was it—she was tied to him for a year.

Unfortunately not literally.

'Why are you laughing?' he asked, when she suddenly did.

'Just something I said in my head.' Felicia replied, and tried to right herself.

She looked out of the window to a bosky summer evening and knew the rush Kedah gave her was a giddy one. She wanted to go home now, to collect her thoughts.

'I'm looking forward to working with you, Kedah,' Felicia said, and held out her hand to shake his.

'Good,' he said, but did not shake her hand.

It became suddenly clear she was not dismissed.

'Anu will show you to your office. I believe my assistant in Zazinia will be free to speak with you in an hour.'

'I thought…' she started. But, as she was about to find out, the interview was over, the negotiations were done, and Kedah had nothing more to discuss.

'That will be all for now.'

It would seem that at five p.m. on a Friday her work day had just begun.

The gorgeous office would tomorrow have Felicia's name on its door, Anu told her, and there was an award-winning chef a phone call away who would prepare whatever she chose for supper.

And so she got busy.

It was late in Zazinia but Vadia, Kedah's assistant there, looked fresh and crisp on the video link.

'The offending article has been taken down,' she informed Felicia. 'If you could let Kedah know that?'

So she didn't use his title when she spoke of him either, Felicia thought as Vadia continued.

'I am trying to schedule the finishing touches on his official portrait. The artist is due to go overseas for surgery in a couple of months' time, so if you could tell Kedah that it is becoming rather pressing?'

'I shall.'

Then she went through his upcoming agenda, and it was so full that Felicia wondered how on earth he'd had the time to earn his reputation.

'I shall speak with you again tomorrow.' Vadia smiled.

Tomorrow was Saturday. Not that a little thing like the weekend seemed to matter in Kedah's world.

'If you can just push Kedah for an answer regarding the artist? Also remind him that the next time he's home we will be arranging the date for his bridal selection.'

As easily as that Vadia slipped it in. In fact she spoke as if she was trying to pin him down for a dental appointment.

'Bridal selection?' Felicia checked.

'Kedah knows.' Vadia smiled again. 'Just inform him that his father, the King, wants a date.'

As Vadia disappeared from the screen Felicia sat for a moment, trying to assimilate all she had found out today. While Kedah might insist that his reputation wasn't an issue, it might prove to be one for any future bride.

Especially if said reputation continued unchecked.

Was that why she was here? Felicia pondered. Was he soon to marry and she was to take charge of his social life here in England?

No way.

Felicia was used to putting out fires—not sitting back and watching them be lit.

Anu was the gatekeeper to Kedah's office, and as Felicia walked over to ask her something she saw that she was happily taking her supper break and eating a fragrant meal as she watched the awards show live on the computer.

'Oh, she won!' Anu smiled and put down her cutlery, and clapped as Felicia came to her side and watched a pretty young actress take her place on the stage. 'She's such a lovely person,' Anu said. 'Just genuinely nice!'

Please! Felicia thought, about to point out to Anu that actresses *acted*, and that was what Miss Pretty was doing right now as she thanked everyone—absolutely everyone…not just God, but her neighbour's blind cat too—in her little breathless voice.

'She's just acting…' Felicia started, and was about

to say what a load of whitewash it all was when Kedah stalked out of his office. 'I was about to come in and speak with you,' Felicia said. 'Vadia needs some dates—'

'Not now,' he interrupted. 'Felicia, can you find out what after-party Beth will be attending and get me on the list? And could you also call The Ritz and have them prepare my suite?'

'Beth?' Felicia frowned.

'The actress who just won that award,' Kedah said.

'Do you know her?' she asked, but he had already disappeared.

'Not yet.' Anu smirked as she answered for him.

And the oddest thing of it all was that Anu didn't seem bothered one bit. Anu—who had looked as if she was chewing lemons all through Felicia's interview—didn't seem to mind in the least about Kedah's wild ways.

The staff at The Ritz were also clearly more than used to him. His suite was already prepared, Felicia found out when she called. And the organisers of the after-party would be delighted to add him to the list. In fact they asked if they could send a car.

'I'm not sure,' Felicia said. 'Can I call you back?'

'Just check with him,' Anu suggested, and gestured to his door for Felicia to go in. 'Though I doubt he'll want one.'

Felicia knocked and entered and there Kedah was—all showered and cologned, as sexy as sin, as he pulled on a fresh shirt and she got her first glimpse of a heavenly brown and broad chest. Michelangelo had clearly been at that, she thought, as she tried and failed not to notice the fan of silky straight black hair. Straight? Yes, straight, Felicia realised as she glanced down to where his trousers sat low on his hips.

'The party is all ready for you,' Felicia said, managing not to clear her throat. 'They offered to send a car.'

'Tell them no. I prefer to use my own transport.'

'Sure.'

His shirt was now done up, and he frowned as he pulled out a tie and saw that Felicia remained. 'Can you call down for my driver?'

'Of course,' Felicia said. 'But can we quickly discuss a couple of things? Vadia needs a date for your portrait to be finished and also to arrange your bridal selection.' She watched for his reaction, for Kedah to falter and possibly tell her the real reason she was here, but instead he finished knotting his tie and pulled on his jacket.

'We can go through all that another time. I'll see you tomorrow.'

He had that hunter's look in his eye, and Felicia guessed there was no point talking business now.

Nor brides.

'Hey, Kedah!' she called as he went to walk off.

'What?' His reply was impatient—there was an after-party for him to get to after all.

'I don't think Beth *is* actually that nice,' she said, and on his way out he halted. In a matter of fact voice, she explained better. 'Usually I warn my clients if I think they're courting trouble…'

Now she had his attention, and she watched as he turned around and walked over to where she stood. She'd expected a question, for him to ask for a little more of what she knew about the woman, but he came right over and faced her, stepped into her personal space.

Too close?

He was a decent distance away, and there was nothing intimidating about his stance, yet her body was on high alert and his fragrance was heavy on her senses. Without saying so, he demanded that her eyes meet his.

'I'm not your *client*, Felicia,' he said, in a voice that held warning. 'I'm your boss. Got it?'

And she stood there, prickling and indignant, as he put her very firmly in her place.

'I was just trying to—'

'I don't need warnings,' he said. 'And, between you and me, I've already guessed that Beth is not *nice*. My intention tonight is to prove it.'

Then he smiled.

Oh, it was a real smile.

Her first!

It stretched his lips and it warmed her inside. It was like ten coffees on waking and it was the moment Felicia discovered the skin behind her knees—because it felt as if he were stroking her there with his long slender fingers, even though his hands were held at his side.

'Goodnight, Felicia. It was a pleasure to meet you and I'm looking forward to *working* with you.'

She heard the emphasis on the word working and let out a slightly shrill laugh. 'Fair enough.' She put her hands up as if in defence. 'You don't need another mother…'

'I certainly don't.'

'But know this,' Felicia said, and delivered a warning of her own. 'I shan't be arranging hotels and after-parties once you've chosen your wife.'

He stared at her for the longest time, even opened his mouth to speak, but then he changed his mind.

Kedah did not have to explain himself—and certainly not to a member of staff.

Which Felicia *was*, he reminded himself.

And a member of staff she would remain, for there were plenty of actresses and supermodels to be had.

'Be here at seven-thirty tomorrow and don't be late.'

He stalked out of the office. There was no slamming of the door—he didn't even bother to close it—but she was as rattled as if he'd banged it shut.

Oh, she would *not* fall for him.

Yes, if there was a scale for playboys then Kedah would be at the extreme end. The problem was Felicia could easily see why.

It was impossible not to want him.

It was the first time she'd realised she must heed her mother's advice.

'Never fall for a bastard. Especially not one who can make you smile.'

And Kedah did.

Oh, he most certainly did.

CHAPTER THREE

FELICIA BRISKLY MADE her way along Dubai's The Walk, towards the restaurant she had booked for their lunchtime meeting. There was no time to linger, or to take in the delicious view. Kedah's multiple assistants were kept far too busy for that.

At the age of twenty-six, Felicia Hamilton had a job.

A *real* one.

Instead of her regular four weeks or so of work for a full year's pay, and a long pause between jobs, Felicia now found herself working the most ridiculous hours as she travelled the globe with Kedah. Oh, their mode of transport was luxurious—Kedah had his own private jet—but even a mile up in the air there was little downtime. Kedah considered his jet another office, and it was the same at his luxurious hotels.

She'd never have agreed to a year of this had she known.

Except not only had she agreed to it—Felicia herself had been the one to insist on it. He had told her exactly what to expect at the interview. He'd even offered her a trial period, which she'd declined!

Oh, what a fool. Had she taken the trial then she would have been finishing up by now!

Or would she...?

Even after close to eight weeks spent working hard for him Felicia still didn't believe that Kedah just wanted her as a PA.

She wasn't even very good at it.

Felicia was the one who generally gave orders. Now each day she stared down the barrel of her to-do list, as did his other assistants. One PA would never be enough for him.

There had to be another reason she was here.

Felicia was trying hard to work it out, but really there was little time for daydreaming. Her schedule was relentless.

She was up at six each day, and it was often close to midnight before she crashed—just as Kedah hit the town with his sweet and oh, so pleasing date of choice for the night.

Felicia honestly didn't know how he did it.

Since meeting him she was on her second lot of concealer, to hide the shadows under her eyes.

There had been a tiny reprieve last night. Kedah had asked her to book theatre tickets for himself and his latest bimbo—which she had done. But while his absence had given Felicia an early night, she had spent it sulking.

This morning Kedah had been off looking at potential hotel sites, and she had sat in bed on the phone, liaising with his flight crew for their trip to Zazinia tomorrow.

Now she was meeting him for lunch, to go through the agenda for his trip home. There the artist would be able to work on his portrait, and there his father would discuss a wedding with his son.

That *had* to be the issue, Felicia decided. She was quite sure that Kedah had no desire to marry.

The restaurant she had chosen was dark and cool,

and uninviting enough to keep the less than extremely well-heeled away.

'I have a booking,' she said. 'Felicia Hamilton.'

'Of course.'

When she had booked the restaurant Felicia had told them she was meeting an important guest and would like their very best table. She hadn't told them just how important her guest was, though.

It was a little game she played, and she smiled as she was led through the stunning restaurant to a gorgeous low table.

Indeed, it *was* beautiful.

There were plump cushions on the floor and the table was dressed with pale orchids. As she lowered herself onto a cushion she could hear the couple behind her laughing and chatting as she set up her work station.

She took a drink of iced water as she waited for Kedah to arrive, and again tried to fathom what trouble his wedding could pose.

There might be a baby Kedah? Felicia pondered. A pregnant ex, perhaps?

But, no, she was quite sure that Kedah would handle that in his own matter-of-fact way.

What about a pregnant prostitute?

That would surely rock the palace and destroy any chance for Kedah to remain as Crown Prince. Though she couldn't really imagine Kedah having to *pay* for sex—or even caring what others thought if he chose to do so.

Felicia took another long sip of iced water. She tended to do that when she thought of Kedah in that way—and she thought of Kedah in that way an awful lot…

Despite her very strict 'Never mix business with

pleasure' motto, Felicia occasionally indulged in a little flirt with him—or rather, a very intense flirt. And there were odd moments when she felt as if her clothes had just fallen off. He made her feel naked with his eyes, although he was always terribly polite.

Felicia knew she'd have trouble saying no if he so much as crooked a finger in her direction. He hadn't, though—which was just as well, because he'd be in for a rude shock. There was no way Felicia would turn into one of those simpering *Your pleasure is all mine, Kedah* women he had a very frequent yen for.

Sweet.

That was the type of women he chose—or rather that was how they appeared until they were dumped. Then it was Felicia who dealt with their angry, tearful outbursts.

She had almost been able to picture Beth, the actress, kicking her neighbour's blind cat when she'd told her that Kedah would not be taking her calls anymore.

'Have you thought about a gift?' Felicia had asked her, while trying to keep a straight face.

Yes, she had found out on her third day of working for Kedah that his aggrieved exes were sent a brochure from which to choose a gift.

No diamonds or pearls from Kedah—jewellery was too personal, of course. But a luxury holiday brochure was theirs to peruse. After all, what better than a week in the South of France or a trip to Mustique to help soothe that wounded heart? The only downside was that Sheikh Kedah would not be there.

He had already moved on to the next.

Beth had chosen to take her broken heart for a little cruise around the Caribbean. Felicia might have told her she'd have stood far more chance of a repeat night with Kedah if she'd told Felicia to pass on to him precisely what he could do with his brochure.

No one ever did.

But, while Kedah seemed at ease with his wretched reputation, there *had* to be more to why he wanted her nearby than to introduce her to the managers of all his hotels around the globe.

Why did Felicia need to know that the Dubai hotel manager was an anxious sort but a wonderful leader? Why had he taken great pains to have her meet his accounts managers and his team of lawyers?

It just didn't make sense.

She looked up because, from the rustling and whispers amongst the patrons, it would seem that someone stunning had just arrived—and of course there he was.

She had recovered from the faint-inducing sight of Kedah in a suit, but here in Dubai he wore traditional attire and each day was a delicious surprise to the senses. On this fine day the angels had chosen for him a robe in cool, completely non-virginal white, and such was his beauty and presence that he turned every head as he made his way over.

His *keffiyeh* was of white-on-white jacquard, with knotted edges, and was seemingly casually tied. He was unshaven, but very neatly so. His lips were thick and sexy, the cupid's bow at the top so perfect one might be forgiven for thinking it tattooed. But this was all natural. Felicia had inspected that mouth closely enough to be very sure of that.

He looked royal and haughty and utterly beautiful, from his expensive cool head right down to his sexy leather-clad feet. Then his eyes lit on her, and the beautiful mouth relaxed into a warm smile—one that didn't just light up his features, but his whole being.

Auras were supposed to be indistinguishable, even non-existent, yet Kedah wore his golden glow like a heavy fur coat.

He was a wolf in prince's clothing. Felicia knew that.

Such delectable clothing, though!

And *such* a stunning man…

Of course it wasn't only the women who noted his suave arrival—inevitably the head waiter came dashing over, clearly troubled at the inadequate seating arrangements for such an esteemed guest.

'You didn't say that you were dining with Sheikh Kedah,' he admonished her.

'I *did* say I was meeting an important guest,' Felicia said sweetly.

'Then please accept our sincere apologies. We have given you the wrong table—it is our mistake. Allow me…' He was gathering up her phone, her tablet, the whole mini-office that she set up whenever she met with Kedah.

'Of course.'

Felicia smiled to herself as she was bundled over to a stunning table—one where there was no chance of hearing their neighbours' conversation. The only sound was the gentle cascade of a fountain, the view of the marina was idyllic, and here the floor was entirely theirs.

'You played your game again,' he commented as they sat down opposite the other.

'I did.' Felicia nodded, and then met and held his gaze.

His eyes were thickly lashed, and he had a way of looking at her that honestly felt as if she were the only person present on the planet. He gave his absolute full attention in a way that was unlike anybody Felicia had ever known.

'Why don't you just say in the first place that you are meeting me?' he asked, because this happened rather a lot when Felicia booked their meetings.

'Because I like watching them fluster when you arrive.'

Kedah would like to see Felicia fluster—and yet she was always measured and poised and gave away so little of herself.

He would like to know more.

The thought continually surprised him. Kedah did not get involved with staff, yet over the past few weeks he had found himself wondering more and more about Felicia and what went on in her head.

It was a pretty head—one that was usually framed with shoulder-length hair. But today her hair was worn up. It was too severe on her, Kedah thought. Or was it that she'd lost a little weight? And he could see that she'd put on some make-up in an attempt to hide the smudges under her eyes.

Gorgeous eyes, Kedah thought. They regularly changed shade. Today they were an inviting sea-green, but he would not be diving in.

He did not want to muddy things—he needed her on board and, given that his relationships ran to days rather than weeks, he did not want to risk losing her over something as basic and readily available as sex.

Yet all too often they tipped into flirting. Kedah usually didn't bother—there was little need for it when you were as good-looking and as powerful as he. Yet he enjoyed their conversations that turned a seductive corner on occasion. Though Felicia had promised him discretion, there were times when he wanted her naked in bed beside him. He wanted to laugh as she told him tales about her former bosses.

Or 'clients', as Felicia referred to them.

That irked him.

He had seen her list of references, and some of the names there had had his jaw gritting. And, yes—he'd wondered all too often how close Felicia might have been to them. That was another thing that irritated him, but it would hardly be fair to question her about it.

He remembered now that he was cross with her for last night.

'Felicia, when I ask you to make a theatre booking for my date and myself, please do better in future.'

She knew he was referring to the previous night. At five, he had suddenly decided he wanted two of the hottest tickets in town.

'I got you the best available seats,' Felicia said. 'And I had to call in a favour to secure them.'

'Again…' he sighed '…you declined to say for whom you were booking.'

'You told me at my interview that you expect discretion.'

'I *expect* the best seats,' Kedah said. 'Had they not recognised me, I'd have been stuck behind a pillar. When you ring to make any booking in future, you are to tell them that it is for me.'

'That will ruin my game.'

'Tough,' he said. 'Right, let's go through my schedule. I want you to arrange some time for me to go to the States in a couple of weeks.'

And as she stared at him a thought suddenly occurred to her. Maybe he was already married—maybe that was the scandal that was about to hit.

'Do you go to America a lot?' she asked.

He nodded.

'Where?'

'All over. Though mainly New York. My friend Matteo lives there.'

'The one with the motor racing team?'

Kedah nodded.

Wild Matteo, who was known for his penchant for gambling and high-octane living.

'Have you ever been to Vegas?' she asked him.

'Felicia…' Kedah sighed again. 'Where is this leading?'

'I just wondered if you'd been to Vegas with Matteo…' She gave him a smile. 'And perhaps done something there that you might regret?'

'I don't waste time with regrets,' he said. 'And I don't like wasting time—which we are. Let's go through tomorrow's agenda.'

They were saved from that, though, as the waiter somewhat nervously approached with mint tea. As Kedah looked up she felt the shifting of his attention. He was polite and engaged with the waiter, and as they spoke in Arabic she watched as he put the young man at ease.

He was arrogant, and yet he was kind.

Arrogant in that he expected the best and most often got it.

But then he could also be very kind.

'What would you like to eat?' Kedah asked Felicia.

'Fruit,' Felicia said. 'Something light.'

'Sounds good.'

He ordered, and when they were alone again he asked her how she was finding the hotel. Given he had not just designed the hotel but owned it, Felicia knew this was no idle enquiry.

'It's amazing,' she told him. 'Though I'd love to have some time to actually enjoy the facilities.'

Instead rather a lot of her time had been spent driving around to meet with the staff at his other acquisitions, or standing in the blistering sun scouring potential sites for Kedah to build on.

'I think I've found the site for its brother,' Kedah told her.

'Do buildings have a gender?'

'Mine do.'

'From conception?' Felicia asked. 'Do you decide before you start the design that this one is going to be a boy?'

He smiled, and for Felicia the rays were as golden as the sun outside as he pondered her question.

'I guess I do,' he said. 'I want to go and have another look at the site after lunch, and then meet with a surveyor. You'll need sensible shoes.'

Joy!

Their lunch was served—citrus fruit and dragon fruits and sweet plump figs, as well as a light lemongrass mousse that just melted on her tongue. As they ate he asked her more questions about the hotel and she answered honestly.

Most of the time he liked it that she did—he was terribly used to his staff pandering to him. Her opinion was always refreshing, as well as at times rather blunt.

Kedah was, of course, up in the royal suite at the hotel, where every detail was taken care of and his every whim predicted. He wanted to know what it was like for a Western businesswoman traveller, so she was slumming it on the luxurious twenty-fourth floor with her own lap pool and butler.

'It's gorgeous.'

'Tell me what I don't know.'

Felicia thought hard. It really was difficult to be critical about somewhere so divine, but she pondered his question for a moment and was finally able to find a tiny fault. 'I think the service is a bit inconsistent.'

He watched as she bit on a piece of dragon fruit and waited for her to elaborate.

She soon obliged.

'Like, last night there weren't any chocolates on my pillow.'

'Poor Felicia.'

'I'm just saying,' she told him. 'You come to expect these things. Now, if I'd *never* had chocolate on my pillow I wouldn't have missed it, but I really sulked last night when they forgot…'

Or had she sulked because Kedah had gone off, out to the theatre? She wasn't sure, but certainly chocolate would have helped if that had been the case.

'First world problem.' She smiled.

'Noted,' Kedah said. 'If you came back to Dubai would you choose to stay there again?'

He was rather taken aback when she immediately shook her head.

'I don't think so.'

'Why?'

'I like trying new things.'

'If you're satisfied there should be no need or inclination to try anything else. I want to know why you wouldn't return.'

'Well, it's stunning, but…' She let out a breath and then decided she should perhaps check before being completely frank. 'Kedah, do you *really* want me to criticise one of your babies?'

I dare you to, his eyes told her. 'Go on,' he said politely.

'Well, as nice as it all is, I find it to be a bit impersonal,' Felicia responded, and she watched his tongue roll into his cheek. 'You *did* ask.'

'I did.'

'It just needs those extra touches,' Felicia offered.

'Such as…?'

'I don't know.' She shrugged. 'Maybe coloured towels, or something. I'm sick of white.'

She was—for she looked at his robe and she wanted it gone. She looked down to her hands and wanted them to be suddenly wrapped in his.

And *that* was the trouble with Kedah.

Not the terribly long hours, nor the jet lag, and it wasn't even the endless little black book she ran for him.

It was *this*.

These moments sitting with him.

These moments when flirting was a thought away… when she felt every conversation would be better executed in bed.

'You can do better than that,' he said.

Felicia had to drag her mind back to their conversation, actually force herself to remember they were discussing his hotel and not lean across the table and tell him that, yes, she *could* do far, far better.

'I don't have much experience in hospitality, remember?' she snapped wondering for possibly the millionth time what the hell he had hired her for.

Kedah could be boring!

Truly.

It was a terrible thing to admit but, just as when he had dimmed the lights and, instead of thrilling her, had proceeded to numb her brain with his hotel presentation, now—when they were in sumptuous surroundings and there was all this energy present—they sat discussing, of all things, towels.

He was driving her to distraction.

'The décor is black and brown in my American chain of hotels,' Kedah mused. 'The towels there are too.'

'Yum…' Felicia snarked.

'It actually works very well.'

'Why am I here, Kedah?' She was exhausted with not knowing. 'Why are we sitting here discussing bloody *towels…?*'

'Décor is important.'

'Then hire someone who cares!' she snapped. 'And tell me why I'm here.'

'You'll know when you need to.'

'Are you married?' The question tumbled out. 'Was there a drunken mistake that turned into a Mrs Kedah that I'm going to have to explain away?'

'Is that why you were asking about Vegas?'

He put his head back and laughed and she wanted her mouth on his throat.

'Felicia, I'm not married.'

'Is there a baby…?'

'You have too much imagination.'

'Er… Kedah, I don't think you and your lady-friends are merely holding hands. Accidents happen.'

'Not to me,' he said. 'I make sure of that.'

He honestly admired Felicia, because even as they discussed his strict use of birth control she didn't blush.

'However,' he mused, 'it wouldn't be a problem.'

'Your father would *welcome* the news?' Felicia asked, in a somewhat sarcastic tone, but it didn't faze him.

'It would be dealt with. I wouldn't be the first Crown Prince in our history to have a child out of wedlock. But Vadia would deal with that sort of thing—not you. Enough now,' he said, and went back to his schedule. 'We'll meet in the foyer at five tomorrow morning and get to Zazinia around midday,' he said. 'My time will be taken up with family stuff. There won't be much for you to do.'

'So why can't I just fly home?'

She was itching to get home—for a night in her flat without the alarm set for the crack of dawn the next morning. For a full twenty-four hours away from the burn of his eyes.

'Because…'

He couldn't answer straight away. Usually he *didn't* bring his London PA home with him. Occasionally he brought Anu, because she was from Zazinia, but there was absolutely no reason for bringing Felicia other than that he wanted her there.

'It's cheaper to have you there with me than to fly you home separately.'

'Oh, please!' She smiled sweetly.

'The Crown Prince's wing is being refurbished. I might need you…'

'To haul stone from the quarries?' she teased.

'To take some photos and jot down my suggestions.' He was stern. 'If it's not too much trouble?' She really was a terrible PA. 'As I said, I'll be busy with formal stuff. My portrait needs to be completed. Then there will be a dinner with my family.'

'That will be nice.'

Kedah gave her nothing—not a roll of the eyes, not even a small smile at her slightly sarcastic comment—but she knew there was trouble between the brothers.

'And then there's the matter of your wedding.'

'Yes.'

'And will you?' Felicia asked. 'Be taking a bride?'

'I might.' Kedah nodded.

He was tired of his father using his marital status

as an excuse for things not to move along. Perhaps he would call his father's bluff and tell him to get things underway.

When he had said that he might be considering marriage, for the first time Felicia's expression faltered. She fought quickly to right it, but Felicia knew she'd been seen and so moved to cover it.

'I loathe weddings. I hope I shan't have to arrange that?'

'Don't worry.' He shook his head. 'The palace will take care of all that. You'll just be arranging a few final wild nights for me, leading up to it.'

'Look out, London.' Felicia rolled her eyes.

'Look out, world,' he corrected, for if he were to marry then he intended to use his last weeks of freedom unwisely. Except he hadn't been. Lately he hadn't. Last night it hadn't just been the seating arrangements that had got on his nerves.

It had been the company.

He had wanted Felicia beside him, and that might have been the reason he had dropped his date back to her hotel early.

'Then again,' Kedah said, 'if I am to choose a bride in a matter of weeks, perhaps it *is* time for me to be more discreet.'

She did not meet his gaze. Perhaps she had missed the opening, he thought, for she was signalling the waiter and asking for more water.

That was bold for here in Dubai. Usually only a male would signal the waiter, but then that was Felicia: bold.

Tough.

She was possibly the one woman who would *not* go losing her head if they were to sleep together.

'Felicia...' he said, and then, for once unsure how

to broach things, he asked another question. 'Are you enjoying your work?'

'Not really,' she admitted. 'It's nothing like I expected. I thought I'd be putting out fires after big Kedah-created scandals.'

'How did you get into all that?'

She hesitated. Usually there was no way that Felicia would discuss her personal life, and yet if she wanted to know more about him maybe it was time to reveal something of herself. And he *was* good company.

Terribly so.

She might not be thrilled by her job description, but there was no doubt that she enjoyed being with him.

It was when she wasn't that her issues arose.

And so she found herself telling him a little. 'My father had a prominent job, but as far back as I can remember he got embroiled in scandal. Affairs, prostitutes…' Felicia coldly stated the facts. 'My mother and I were regularly schooled in what to say and what not to say. How to react…how to smile. Now I get paid to tell others the same.'

'Did your mother leave him in the end?' Kedah asked.

'No, after all he'd put her through it was my father who ended the marriage,' Felicia said. 'All the times she'd stood by him counted for nothing in the end. He planned how to leave her and did all he could to protect himself and his new girlfriend. The family home went—as did my boarding school. And I found out that my friends weren't really my friends. By the time he had dragged out the court proceedings I was well out of school. I left at sixteen and got a job in an office to support my mother.'

'Yet *you* are the PA everyone wants. Why?'

'My first boss. I never even saw him much, apart from setting up a meeting room. Anyway, scandal hit—as it often does—and the PR people he had working for him were seriously clueless. I knocked on his door and told him I could sort it for him.'

'How old were you?'

'I'd have been about nineteen,' Felicia said.

'He believed you?'

'He had no choice. He was up to his neck in scandal. I spoke to the press. I laughed at their inferences. I dealt with it just as I'd been taught to while I was growing up.'

'How is your mother now?'

Felicia didn't answer. She just gave a small shrug.

He sensed that she was finished talking about it. The subject moved back to work and there it remained, even after their meal had concluded.

Yet Kedah was curious.

'You'll need sensible shoes,' he reminded her as they walked to his car.

'Then you need to buy me some.'

She attempted humour, but she was still all churned up from thinking about her mother.

A little while later they stood on a man-made island and Kedah told her his vision for the hotel he was thinking of building there.

'What do you think?' he asked.

Usually he cared for no one else's opinion, yet he was starting to covet hers.

'It sounds a lot like the other one.'

It was possibly the most offensive thing she could have said, and yet her honesty made him smile.

'That's why I call them brothers.'

'Can't they just be siblings?' Felicia asked. 'Could this one not be a girl?'

He thought for a moment and, as terrible an assistant as she was, Felicia gave him pause.

Perhaps he *could* consider a gentler version of the other hotel. The Dubai skyline was ultra-modern, and there were some stunning architectural feats. From tall rigid towers to soft golden buildings in feminine curves. Perhaps it was time to try something different.

'See over there…?' He pointed. 'That was my first design. Well, along with Hussain.'

'Now, that's *definitely* a he!' Felicia said, because it was a huge phallic tower, rising into the sky.

'You're getting the idea.' Kedah smiled. 'It was my first serious project. Well, my second. I had designed a building for my home, but it was vetoed.'

'Is that a modified version of it?' Felicia asked.

'No. That design could never have worked here. There was a mural and…' He shook his head. 'I worked on this with Hussain. He is from my homeland, and studied architecture with my father, but *his* hands are tied there too…' Kedah halted.

'In what way?'

He thought for a moment and realised there was no harm in telling her, and as they chatted they walked away from the car and towards the water's edge.

'There are so many regulations back home. No window can overlook the royal beach…no building can be as high as the palace…'

'I'm sure you could work your way around them.'

They had toyed with each other and, yes, occasionally they had flirted, and of course Kedah had wondered what it would be like to know Felicia in the bedroom.

Now with one sentence she had changed things.

It was as if she had a little jewelled sword in her hand

and had sliced straight through the chains that kept anybody from entering his heart.

She was the very first person who had not immediately derided his vision for his homeland.

Here was someone who did not instantly reject nor dismiss his ideas.

Even Hussain, to whom he had entrusted his visions, constantly told Kedah that he dreamed too big for his home.

'It's complicated, Felicia.'

'Life *is*.'

'We should get back,' he said, and he took her elbow to guide her back towards the car.

'What time are we meeting the surveyor?'

'Two,' Kedah said, and his voice was suddenly brusque. 'Though I won't need you there. Go back to the hotel and use some of the facilities.'

'You're giving me the afternoon off?' Felicia frowned. 'Why?'

'I *can* be nice.'

'I never said you couldn't.' She gave him a little nudge.

It was just that—a playful nudge. But Felicia did not play like that and neither did Kedah.

It was a tease—a touch that would have gone unnoticed had they been more familiar.

Yet they were *not* familiar.

They just happened to ache to be.

And so instead of walking they stood there, on an empty man-made island. His driver was some distance away, endlessly on his phone, and as the hot wind whipped at one of her loose curls Kedah resisted tucking it behind her ear.

'Will you tell me something, Felicia?'

'Maybe.'

'Do you flirt with *all* your clients?'

'I don't flirt.'

'I disagree.'

He was rather too direct.

'While I accept,' Kedah continued, 'that you don't tip up your face or bat your lashes—in fact you don't invoke any of the more usual tactics—you *do* flirt. And I just wondered if it was the same with all your…*clients*?'

She heard the implication. 'You make me sound like a whore.'

'Please forgive me for any offence caused—absolutely none was meant. I am just curious as to what you are here for. I employed you as my PA and yet you don't seem to want that job.'

'I'm tired of the games, Kedah, and I'm tired that even after eight weeks you still don't trust me with the truth.'

'Okay—here it is. I believe the Accession Council will meet soon, and that there will be turbulent times ahead as my suitability for the role of Crown Prince is called into question.'

'I know all that,' Felicia said. 'So where do I fit in?'

'I need someone who knows the business—someone who, when it all kicks off—'

'Kicks off?' she checked.

'I believe my brother will have the backing of the elders. More troubling for me is that I believe my father may support him also. If that is the case I shall be forced to take it to the people to decide. That would cause a lot of unrest and bad publicity…'

'You'd want me to convince your people that just because you've run a bit wild…?' She paused as Kedah smiled—a lightly mocking smile.

'Felicia,' he said. 'My people *love* me.'

She didn't get it. She could not see where she might fit in to all this. 'They love you regardless?'

'No.' He shook his head. 'I would never expect them to support me regardless. They love me because of what I stand for, what I can do for them.'

'Oh.'

Kedah did not want to tell anyone—unless he was forced to—that the scandal that was looming was not one of his making.

Correction.

Sometimes he *did* want to tell her.

Back in the restaurant, when Felicia had spoken of her father, he had wanted to share his own truth. But that was an unfamiliar route for Kedah and so still he'd held back.

He held back from revealing the full truth now.

'I am spending time in Zazinia. You can deal with the empire I have built and answer with ease the many questions that will be hurled.'

'That's it?' Felicia frowned. 'That's all you want me there for? To deal with the press? I don't believe you.'

That *had* been it.

Kedah had wanted someone tough and strong to take care of the press as he devoted his time to his country. He knew how bad things were likely to get if the elders and Mohammed called his parentage into question.

Never had he considered revealing that to another—especially not a lowly PA.

And he wasn't now.

Instead he was considering discussing it with Felicia—the woman who had held him entranced since she had stood outside his office eight weeks ago.

He was supposed to marry soon. He did not need

her tearful and scorned. And yet with every minute that passed between them he felt as if they were falling slowly into bed, into sex, into want. She could deny it, yet he *felt* it. And if they were about to cave then he needed to know she could remain strong, that sex could be separated from the vital tasks ahead.

And possibly, Kedah pondered as she stared back at him, Felicia was the one person who would be able to do that.

It irked him that she considered him a *client*.

And it troubled him that she might have been involved with some of her clients in the past.

Then again, if he wanted the toughest of the tough perhaps it should not.

There was no polite way to ask.

'Your eyes were the shade of the sea at the restaurant. Now they are hooker green.'

Her breath tightened and she flashed him a look of fire.

'It's an actual shade,' he said. 'And you *are* flirting, Felicia. Your eyes invite me closer at times.'

'Perhaps I'm just responding in kind.'

'I want you,' he told her.

He just stated his case.

Her clothes felt as if they had disintegrated again. She felt as if she were standing there stark naked even though his eyes never left hers.

'I am thinking now that unless you go I shall cancel the surveyor and take you up to my suite…'

'And you presume that I'll join you? You just assume I want you too?'

Felicia tried—she really did. But had his driver got out and started clapping she'd have joined him. Because it was a joke that she didn't want Kedah. She was *so* turned on.

Click your fingers and I'll come turned on.

And he smiled that arrogant smile that told her he absolutely *knew* she would join him should he so choose.

'The thing is I need you working for me more than I need you between the sheets.' Right now that was debatable, but although Kedah regretted little, he knew that *this* he might. 'I don't want tears in the morning, and I want you to continue to work for me rather than moping about in Mustique, so I suggest that you go back to the hotel and have a think. I don't want you agreeing to something you might later regret.'

'You've got a nerve.'

'I know I have.'

'Kedah, I've booked for your date to be collected for you at ten tonight…'

'That gives you several hours to make up your mind. She can easily be cancelled.'

Oh, yes, if there was a scale of playboys then Kedah would definitely be at the extreme end.

In all her imaginings—and, yes, there had been plenty—they were talking one moment and then somehow had moved seamlessly to bed. Never had she thought she'd be so frankly propositioned. That Kedah would have her cancelling his date so he could slot *her* in.

Thankfully he'd just made it a whole lot easier to say no!

'I don't need several hours to make up my mind,' she answered. 'Enjoy your night.'

She turned her head as a car approached. It would seem that the surveyor was here.

'I'm going to enjoy my afternoon off.'

'Do.'

* * *

She didn't.

The lap pool was paid a visit, but it did not clear her head, and a lengthy massage, although divine, did little to relax her.

Dinner for one felt lonely that night.

But she made herself sit through it.

Ten p.m. came, and when it had safely passed she went up to his suite.

He was out.

Clearly Kedah waited for no one.

The maid was there, preparing the bed, and the butler helped her to pack up his things for their early-morning start.

She stared at the bed with a mixture of pride and regret.

Pride that she had not succumbed.

Regret that she would never know how it felt to be Kedah's lover.

She set his alarm for four and headed down to her own suite. As she opened the door, still cross—*so* cross with him for his suggestion—still he made her smile.

There were chocolates on her pillow.

Many, many chocolates on her pillow. All perfectly wrapped.

But more than that, as she walked into the bathroom to strip, she was met with a rainbow of colour.

Kedah wasn't boring, and even towels could be sexy, Felicia thought as she showered and then chose from the selection.

There were deep crimsons and burnt oranges—but she bypassed them and reached for another towel…one possibly the shade of hooker green.

She should be offended, and yet Kedah had removed

that. From the day she had met him she had rightly guessed that he saved his issues for outside the bedroom. If sex was reduced to a business arrangement then so be it for him.

Could *she* do it, though?

Could she simply submit for the bliss of knowing what it was like to be made love to by him?

Kedah seemed to think it was doable. But then he assumed that she was tough and that he was simply another client.

Oh, no, he wasn't.

He was slowly stealing her heart.

What if she never revealed that?

Felicia had been trained to hide her true feelings from a very young age. This could possibly serve as the ultimate test.

Wrapped in her towel, she walked to the bed and peeled open a chocolate. As she tasted it, dark, sweet and silky on her tongue, she saw a note.

Handwritten by him.

Think about it.

She couldn't *stop* thinking about it—no matter how she tried.

CHAPTER FOUR

WHERE WAS HE?

A pre-dawn Dubai sky offered no answers as Felicia peered out through the window of her hotel suite. There were yachts lit up on the marina. No doubt there were parties aplenty still happening, and if Kedah was running true to form he might well be down there amongst them.

His butler had just called her to say that there had been no response to his wake-up call.

'Can you go in and check?' Felicia had asked, but the butler had explained that because the 'Do Not Disturb' light was on he couldn't, even though it was doubtful Kedah was there.

Apparently the Sheikh had returned to the hotel after midnight, but had been seen heading out again around two a.m.

When Felicia tried his cell phone it was off.

He was *always* on time, Felicia told herself as she headed into the bathroom and checked her appearance. She would have to change on the plane, as Kedah had told her the dress code was strict in Zazinia, but for now she was wearing a navy shift dress. Before heading out she would add to it a small short-sleeved bolero to cover her arms.

Felicia really needed her concealer this morning, after a night spent pondering their conversation, but she decided to do her make-up on the plane too.

Right now she was too busy ruing the hours she had spent considering getting further involved with Kedah if his reaction was simply to stay out all night.

Hell, yes, she was angry.

She had worked with him for eight weeks and the last four had been spent travelling.

Soon they would be back in London and a safer distance would be easier to maintain.

To think she might have succumbed at the last hurdle!

She wasn't just cross with Kedah, she was angry with herself as she marched out of her bathroom. She went to put up her hair, but simply didn't have the upper arm strength or the concentration this morning.

Another thing that could wait for the plane.

There was a knock on the door to her suite, and she opened it to the bellboy who had come to collect her luggage.

'Has Sheikh Kedah's luggage been taken down?' Felicia checked.

'Not yet,' the bellboy informed her. 'We cannot go in if the "Do Not Disturb" light is on.'

'Even if he's probably not there?'

'Even then.'

Felicia let out a tense breath as the door closed and she was again left alone with some choices to make.

She had access to his suite—of course she did. Last night she and the butler had packed his belongings there, leaving the necessaries out for the morning.

All Kedah had had to do was tumble into bed with the requisite blonde and then get up on time.

She headed out to the elevators, but instead of going down to the foyer, where they had arranged to meet, she used her security pass and pressed the button for the royal floor.

A rather worried butler greeted her.

'The "Do Not Disturb" light is still on. I really cannot go in.'

'Well, *I* can.'

The butler was slightly startled at her assertive tone, but she took out the swipe card for the room, gave the door several sharp knocks and then entered.

Please, she begged silently, *if he's in here then let him be alone.*

The suite was in darkness. There was the sound of running water and she wondered if he had fallen asleep in the sunken bath. The sound came from the pool, she realised as she saw the drapes gently billowing in the breeze and realised that the huge glass doors were open.

She walked silently over the thick carpet and out to the stunning alfresco area. It truly was an oasis. High in the sky, there was a colourful garden and a large pool that jutted out over the ocean.

It made her dizzy even to think of it, though Kedah told her he swam in it each day.

Felicia walked over. No, he was *not* practising the breaststroke.

She stepped back from the edge as the warm morning air dusted her cheeks and blew at her hair.

There weren't any signs of a wild party, though he must have been out here at some point for the doors to be open.

It really was beautiful, Felicia thought. So much so that for a moment she forget her mission to find the missing Sheikh and simply took in the stunning view.

The navy sky was fading and was now dressed in ribbons of silver and various shades of blue as the sun prepared to break into the horizon. Ahead, Felicia could see the island where they had stood yesterday and spoken.

She could stand and bristle with indignation, or she could wrap her arms around herself and try to hold on to the shiver within her that Kedah evoked.

He moved her.

Just that.

He took feelings and memories that were usually guarded and shook them. He jolted awake desires and emotions so that she was standing there feeling as if she was on the top of the world and convincing herself that she could handle it.

That a night or two would surely be worth it, just to have known that bliss.

And there was always the brochure. Yes, she would mope, but only for a week, and then she would circle Mustique and spend time there rehabilitating her heart.

No.

She could *not* sleep with him and then continue to work for him; she could *not* pretend it didn't matter when he discarded her and moved on to the next woman.

And there was no way she would be a filler between drinks.

She actually laughed at the nerve of him.

'Is everything all right, madam?'

Felicia turned and saw the butler, hovering in the doorway.

'Everything's fine.' She nodded. 'I'll just check to see if he's asleep.'

She headed back inside and with mounting trepidation walked towards the main bedroom in the suite. The double doors were closed and she glanced at the butler, who gave a worried shake of his head as she went to knock. He was certain that their most esteemed guest should not be disturbed.

'He might be unwell,' Felicia offered. She didn't think it for a moment, but it was the excuse she would give to Kedah if he called her out for disturbing him.

'Kedah!' Felicia knocked loudly. 'Kedah, the plane's scheduled to leave…'

When there was no response she opened the door.

Relief.

She wasn't disturbing an intimate moment.

He was not there, and yet she could see that he had been—the bed was rumpled and unmade and there were several thick white towels dropped on the floor. And his visit had been a recent one, for the musky, woody scent of his cologne lingered.

Perhaps he had come back from the party and showered and changed before heading out again?

Bedded his date, showered and changed, Felicia thought with a gnawing unease as she closed the door.

She was tired of playing detective, tired of putting the pieces together on his depraved life.

Tired of it all, really.

Especially saying no.

'I'll just pack up the last of his things,' Felicia said to the butler as she turned off the alarm.

She headed to the wardrobe and took out the case she had left. There wasn't much to pack. Most of it had been done last night, and once the bellboy had come to collect his luggage she headed back down to the foyer.

His vehicle was waiting, the engine purring, and his driver was—as always—on the phone. Felicia was grateful that the doorman didn't attempt small talk. Instead he handed Felicia her preferred brew in a takeaway cup and she said her thanks and took a grateful sip.

Dawn was breaking and Dubai was now pretty in pink. And then, as transfixing as the sunrise, Kedah appeared, walking slowly as if there was no King or country awaiting his imminent arrival, no jet on the runway ready and primed to carry him there.

She would have loved to say, *Look what the cat dragged in*—but, as always, he was immaculate. In fact he looked as if he were just leaving for the night rather than arriving back at dawn. He was a sight for Felicia's sleep-deprived eyes.

'Good morning,' he greeted her.

'You're late,' Felicia responded.

'So?' His response was surly and brief, and he glanced down at the coffee she held in her hand and then back up to her eyes. 'May I?'

Felicia handed him her coffee and he drained it, but then pulled a face. 'Too sweet.'

'It didn't stop you, though.'

Actually, last night it had.

Last night his mind had been on Felicia—so much so that he'd dropped his pouting date back at her hotel and returned to his room. Sleep had proved elusive, and a shower had done nothing to temper the urge to call Felicia and summon her to his suite.

The trouble was, he had known she was the one woman who might not take too kindly to his summons, and so instead he had headed onto the balcony and told himself to forget about her—at least for now. There was his trip home to get through first.

Zazinia had to be his priority—though he wasn't looking forward to this visit in the least. He knew there would be a confrontation with his father, and that there would be a push towards him choosing a bride.

Last night he had hoped to take his mind off his problems in the usual way, but he hadn't been able to.

Now the reason that he hadn't smiled back at him.

This morning her hair was worn down, though it was more wavy and unkempt than usual. She didn't wear a lot of make-up, but she had on none today.

She belonged on his pillow.

'Are you ready?' she asked him.

'Am I?' he asked. 'Did you finish my packing?'

'Yes,' she said. 'I went into your suite with the butler this morning. He didn't want to—he was worried we might disturb something.'

'There was nothing to disturb last night,' Kedah said. 'In fact there hasn't been anything to disturb for quite some time.'

'I don't believe you for a moment.'

'That's up to you. My theatre date bored me, as did my date last night. Did you get the chocolates?'

'You know I did.'

'Did you like the towels?' he asked. 'Oh, I apologise—I forgot there are things that bore you to discuss.'

She said nothing.

'Did you get my note?'

She nodded.

'And *did* you?' he asked.

And then he looked at the shadows under her eyes that were so much darker than before and the slight gritting of her jaw. The answer as to whether she had thought about it was clear.

'Of course you did.'

She wished she could go back to their first meeting, when she had been sure about never sleeping with him.

But she hadn't really been sure even then.

On sight she had wanted him, and that feeling remained.

'I'm going to freshen up,' Kedah said.

When he had left she stood there, as the driver made small talk and worried about angering Kedah's father, the King.

She remembered the tingle at the base of her spine at the way he said her name.

She did not mix business with pleasure, but he blurred all the lines.

He wanted the tough woman who had stepped into his office—which she still was—and yet Felicia was also aware that she liked him more than she should for such a relationship to work.

He didn't need to know that.

More than anyone, Felicia knew how to hold onto her heart.

'How long did he say?' the driver asked now. 'Apparently they're furious at the palace that he's so late. The captain's trying to sort out a flight path to make up the time…'

'He shouldn't be too long,' Felicia replied. 'I'll just go and see.'

She should text him, really.

It would be far safer.

Instead, just a few moments later, she stood at the door of his hotel suite.

She had the access card—of course she did—but usually if he was in there she'd knock first.

This morning she didn't.

She stepped into the entrance hall and saw Kedah was emptying his safe.

'You forgot my diamond.'

'Sorry.'

'Attention to detail, Felicia,' he said, and wagged his finger in a small scold.

'I told you on the first day that I would not make a good PA.'

'You did.'

He closed the safe and pocketed the stone, but made no move to walk towards her.

'You need to hurry up.'

His eyes met hers. 'Says who?'

'Word from the palace is that the King is concerned you haven't left yet. The pilot is going to try to make up the time…' All this was said as he walked towards her, and her voice was breathless.

'Oh, well.' He shrugged.

And now he stood right in front of her, and Felicia looked at his mouth and wondered what the rest of her life would feel like should she never taste it.

'Did you think about it?'

'Yes.'

It was pointless to lie, and the fact that she stood there rather than stepped back, that she met his beautiful gaze, spoke of the decision she had come to.

'We have to continue to work together,' he warned her.

'I know that. So there are things we need to discuss…' Felicia attempted, because she *would* be laying a few ground rules.

'There's no time for that now,' that beautiful mouth said. 'We can speak on the plane.'

But that was a full twenty-six minutes away, at best. And she looked at the dark pink of his lips and then the black roughness of his jaw. It would be cruel to look back on this moment and regret walking away.

And so she did not turn to go.

Instead she stood as his hand moved to her shoulder and he peeled away the strap of her bag. He placed the bag on an occasional table, and that gesture alone told her of the thoroughness of the kiss to come.

She was shaking—not outwardly, but there was a low tremble that seemed to start at midthigh and inch with every heartbeat nearer to her throat.

'Kedah,' Felicia warned again, 'we have to speak.'

'First we taste.'

There was no time for this. Kedah knew that. His father's mood would not be improved by his late arrival, and things were already tense.

And yet he too could not resist.

White-hot, Felicia turned him on. There had been a slow burn as he'd walked towards her. Now he was hard and ready, and he hadn't even tasted her mouth.

Now he did.

Their flesh, their tongues, finally met, and both were wet and wanting, and both moaned in mutual bliss as eight weeks of want found an outlet.

Their mouths moved slowly and appreciatively at first, relishing the heady taste that they made.

'That,' said Kedah, peeling his lips back just a little, 'was how I wanted to greet you on the first day.'

And there was something terribly freeing about it being a work deal, for she could be as provocative as all hell without being accused of being a tease.

'This,' she said, 'is how I wanted to greet *you*.'

She kissed him harder still, and Kedah loved it that she did not hold back from revealing her pleasure.

Her body was lithe, and it pressed into his as their tongues met. Provocatively, he ran a hand down her spine until it came to rest on one heart-shaped buttock while the other hand went to the back of her head so that he could kiss her more thoroughly.

It was more of a kiss than she had ever known.

She had a brief wish that their clothes would evaporate, because she knew herself that in that space of time when he removed her clothes common sense would kick in.

And she knew Kedah and where a kiss would lead.

She pulled her face away, and her mouth was wet and swollen, her skin pink and inflamed from the roughness of his jaw.

He was hard against her, and her breasts were aching for his touch, for his mouth, for any contact he cared to bestow.

He kissed her again, but this time his fingers tightened in her hair, and it was the roughest, most thorough kissing of her life.

He held her hips and rubbed her against himself.

She peeled her mouth away and still he held her. He could feel her body trembling as she fought the writhing want within. Her eyes were green and her mouth was open, dragging in air, and he held her hair taut in his hand and fought not to tug it—hard. He fought not to pull back her head and lower his mouth again.

He stroked her where his hand cupped her bottom, and then he pulled her further in so she could feel every generous inch of his hard length against her stomach.

And it was too late to worry about the time, for her fingers had moved to the row of small buttons on his shirt and she'd exposed his muscular chest.

Kedah loved the way her hands were not shy—how, as her mouth still merged with his, she toyed with his flat nipples and then, bored with them, let her hand creep down to the soft snake of silken hair that had entranced her from that first glimpse.

From her bag on the table her phone bleeped with a text message, just as the head of his erection nudged her palm.

'That will be the driver, telling me to hurry you up.'

'Hurry me up, then.'

And he felt her smile, for her lips stretched beneath his as he took her hand and ran it the length of his long, hard shaft.

His other hand pressed at her head, and she knew—because this was the kind of man she was choosing to get involved with—that from the direction of the pressure Kedah exerted she should be dropping to her knees—oh, right about *now.*

But he was in for that shock. For she had needs of her own and it would never be all about *him.*

'Kedah,' she said, and removed her hand as she lifted her head. 'We really don't have time for foreplay.'

She watched his eyes flare as she stepped back from his embrace and reached for her bag.

'Foreplay?' he checked.

'It's when—'

'I *do* know what it is, thank you,' he snapped.

'Good.' She smirked. 'I've got news for you, Kedah. I didn't come up here just to satisfy your needs. I have terms and conditions of my own!'

And she was doing it.

Somehow, against this very powerful man, she was holding her own.

'We need to get a move on, Kedah. I'll see you down there.'

CHAPTER FIVE

SIX FOOT THREE of sulking Sheikh boarded the plane.

Kedah did *not* need the complication of Felicia.

But he had tasted her now.

And *she* did not need the arrogance of him.

She wanted him, though.

They sat on his private jet and her skin was prickling—so much so that she almost went through her bag for antihistamines, till she realised this was no allergic reaction. She was on fire for *him*.

The take-off was smooth and he glanced up as a flight attendant came over.

'Can I get you anything, Your Highness?'

'Shaii.' Kedah asked for tea, and it was served in a long crystal glass and cold, as he liked it. It was refreshing and sweet but not soothing.

He took out the diamond that he carried and tapped it on the gleaming table. He saw Felicia glance over.

'That's a pretty elaborate worry bead.'

'I told you,' a surly Kedah replied. 'I never worry.'

The tapping resumed as he pulled up a file.

Not any old file.

He had been working on this for years, for it was Zazinia as he envisaged it.

Every plan he had submitted had been rejected, every

vision he'd had for his home discounted, and they were all compiled in this one stunning display. He sat there watching as buildings rose before his eyes and bridges connected them. He had designed all the infrastructure—the roads and railways were splendidly linked—and yet none of it had been implemented. At every turn he had been thwarted. This was the reason Kedah was rarely home.

He closed the file and worked instead on a skyline that he *could* change. He started on some preliminary designs for his latest Dubai project.

He was considering linking the hotels—either with a monorail or possibly a tunnel. It would be a huge venture. Yet Felicia was right. Why link two hotels that were basically the same? Now, thanks to her, the gender was no longer clear, for he was thinking of a more recreational facility. One families or couples might choose to visit.

His plane was usually a second office, but she was invading his headspace. She was even influencing his hotel's design. So he closed the file. Hussain could work on it further, or tell him outright if he was dreaming too big, Kedah decided.

He opened his email and flicked over to Felicia the files he wanted her to tidy up. He added a message telling her that he wanted her to write a cover note for Hussain, but then, distracted, realised he'd sent the wrong file.

For the first time since leaving the hotel he spoke to her.

'Delete the last email I sent,' Kedah said. 'The information I want you to forward to Hussain is in the one I am sending now.'

Always he could separate work and pleasure.

Not today.

He looked over to her and saw that the dress she was wearing was modest, but it would not be suitable for his home.

'Felicia?'

'Yes?'

'Did I tell you about the dress code in Zazinia?'

'You did.' She nodded. 'I'll change closer to when we land.' She turned and rather pointedly looked out of the window rather than prolonging their conversation.

'I'm going for a rest,' he told her. Normally Kedah just stalked off and it was left to Felicia to guess where he'd gone.

She turned and their eyes met as he stood and headed to the bedroom. He halted when he got to the door.

'There are three more hours' flying time,' he said. 'Is that sufficient for you?'

He walked into the bedroom and Felicia went into her bag and took out a book. But the words all ran into each other and after a few minutes of pretending she put the book down.

There were moments in life from which you knew there would be no coming back.

If she entered his suite it would be one of those moments, she knew, for his kiss had offered her more than a glimpse of what it would be like to be with him.

He assumed she had slept with previous clients because she had let him assume that.

And she was lying to herself now, Felicia knew, by telling herself she could handle this.

Yet she had to.

He came with a warning, and he had stated the same.

This would end—and no doubt at a time of *his* choosing.

She sat for a moment and accepted that fact.

Desire won.

And yet she did have rules.

She wanted to be behind that door, wanted her time with him, and so she stood and headed to the bedroom.

She didn't knock. Instead she walked in. And there on the bed lay Kedah as she had never seen him before.

He had a sheet covering his lower half, but she knew that he was naked beneath the sheet. For now she just stood and stared at him and took in his beauty.

His chest was toned and there was a smattering of dark hair across it. His nipples were a deep shade of red and he was utterly exquisite. She followed the dark trail down, and through the sheet she could see the thick length of him against his thigh. The thought of him inside her was intensely thrilling.

'Undress,' he told her, and his voice had a rasp of impatience for she had kept him waiting again.

'Not yet,' she said, and then she stated her case. 'Kedah, as long as we last, there's only me…'

He just stared.

'If you see someone else, don't expect me back in your bed.'

'I shan't.'

His response was surprising. She had expected debate, or for him to state that he would do as he pleased.

'I have no interest in others…' He didn't. He hadn't in a while. 'I do have to marry, though.'

'I know you do.'

'So how about a long fling before that…?'

It was what she wanted—more than she had expected—and yet a warning sounded in her head, because it was already more than sex for her, and a prolonged affair with Kedah could only hurt more in the end.

'A fidelity trial?' he said.

She wanted his kiss. She wanted him to stand and kiss her to oblivion as he undressed her with skilled ease. Yet he did not.

'Take off your shoes,' he told her, and she stood there for a few seconds before doing so. 'Now undo your buttons…'

'I do know how to undress myself,' she snapped. Her voice was tense, and her head felt as if she had stepped off a merry-go-round.

He was nothing like any lover she had known, and that secretly thrilled her.

'Undo the buttons,' he said, but with less patience this time.

Her hands were shaking as she undid the row of buttons at the side of her dress, and the tension in the air made her almost dizzy.

She recalled that tone now. It was the same one he had used on the day they had first met, when he had told her to sit back down and that he hadn't finished with her yet. The effect was the same, and yet multiplied a thousandfold.

'Take it off over your head.'

'It doesn't come off that way.'

And instead she peeled it down the arms and her dress slid to the floor. She stood there, cross with herself for doing as she was told, yet angrily awaiting further instruction.

'Nice bra,' Kedah said. 'Now, take it off.'

'You.'

He flashed her a look as he moved to stand and she took in a long breath. It was the kind of breath she might take in private, before making a difficult phone call. The kind of breath she might take before opening the door to a stranger.

Yet it was the right kind of breath to take before a lean, toned body rose from the bed and the sheet fell away, to reveal him aroused and hard and walking towards hers.

'Turn around,' he said.

She resisted, but only in the hope that he would touch her, for her skin was screaming for contact, yet contact he refused to give.

'Turn around,' he said again, and this time she did as she was told. 'Now, undo your bra…'

'You can do it.'

'Don't annoy me any more than you already have.'

'Why?'

His mouth came close to the back of her head and his low voice in her ear made her want to arch her neck, to turn to kiss him, but she stood staring ahead.

'For insinuating, back at the hotel, that I would have left you unsatisfied.'

She turned her head then, and found him smiling. And he smiled as only Kedah could. He smiled as he had when he'd walked into that restaurant and seen her sitting there waiting for him. He smiled as he did when he greeted her each morning.

Yet it was different today, for there was no mistaking the deep intimacy levelled at her. There was absolute seduction in his eyes, and Felicia knew that if all that was left was this—if the plane fell from the sky right now—she was glad for this moment.

Game over. For it was Felicia who turned and smiled and wrapped her arms around his neck. They were back to deep kissing as he removed her bra—easily. His fingers stroked her breasts with feather-light strokes alternated with pinches that made her gasp in shocked pleasure.

Now, the solid nudge of his body was guiding her to the bed, and though she wanted to be there so badly still she wanted to stand for just a moment and fully savour the feel of him naked against her. He felt like silk beneath her fingers, and there was a wall of muscle that warned of pleasures to come. His mouth was firm and his tongue expert as his hands roamed her, strumming her rib cage or toying with her hip as he enjoyed the body he had been resisting for what felt like far too long.

She could feel the mattress pressing into the back of her thigh and fought to stay standing against him. Yet like a domino he toppled her onto the bed.

It was Kedah who remained standing, and she felt the scorch of his eyes as they roamed her flushed skin.

'Let's get rid of these,' he said.

He placed her feet on his thigh and she lifted her bottom to allow him to peel off her knickers as if he was opening the most delicate gift. Down her thighs he slid them, with such a lack of haste that she let out a moan—an absolute whimper.

His shaft jerked in response to it as Kedah discovered that the sound of Felicia moaning was a sound he craved.

She was always so brittle, so contained, it was a pleasure to hear her unravel.

Past her knees came the knickers, and then he ripped them down the final stage. Now she was naked, and soon she'd be his.

He knelt between her legs and Felicia had never known such absolute scrutiny. It felt as if he were kissing her all over, yet only his eyes caressed her for now.

'Turn over,' he told her, and she rolled to her front.

She rested her head on her forearm and waited—for whatever he so chose. Anticipation thrummed as she heard his ragged breathing, and then he placed a wet kiss right at the base of her spine.

'Kedah…'

His tongue was hot and slow and it moved in long circles. Her free hand moved to touch herself at such bliss but he caught her wrist.

It was an attack of the senses. Because now he parted her thighs and slipped his long fingers into her as his mouth worked the length of her spine.

She lifted her hair, just so that he might have access to her skin, and did not know if it was the bruising kiss to her neck or the stretch of his fingers inside her that caused her to make a low choking noise.

'Please…' she said, not knowing how to say that she wanted—no, *needed* more and more of this.

But he removed the pleasure and rolled her onto her back. He opened her legs and moved so that he knelt between her knees. He wanted to take her there and then, and reached over the bedside for a condom, but the sight of her pink and glistening beckoned him for just a brief taste.

Felicia swore as he parted her lips and, instead of devouring her, licked her with just with the tip of his tongue. 'Don't…' she said, and her hands knotted into his hair as he teased her, scratched at her thighs with his jaw.

Kedah knew he was good, but he'd never enjoyed himself to this level. Hearing the panting in her voice and feeling the pressure of her thighs trapping him made him search deeper. Her sweet, musky taste was like nectar. Hot, she writhed, and his tongue devoured.

He was too slow, she decided, for she was suddenly frantic.

The sounds he made were low, and his possessive growl reverberated through her.

Her hands left his head and went to her own, tense fingers tightening in her hair as he raised her bottom.

He was relentless.

He should stop now, she thought as she started to come.

Please stop, she thought. Because she had never come so fully to a man's mouth—in fact she couldn't remember feeling like this *ever*.

She wanted to push him away, and yet she wanted for this never to end.

He felt the pulsing and the tension rise within her. And for Kedah there was a giddy triumph at hearing Felicia in the throes of the pleasure that he had procured for her. She made no logical sense as she pleaded for less while her body urged for more. And then it faded, and he felt her relax and grow calm, but this wasn't even close to being over.

He wanted his own release, and so he took her slowly, just kneeling up and pulling her in.

He toyed at her entrance and Felicia pushed herself up onto her elbows. She watched as he glanced over to the condoms scattered on the bed beside them, but they might as well have been in his office drawer back in London, for nothing must break the contact they made.

She told him that she was covered in ragged, breathless words. 'I'm on the pill…'

Both of them would usually have needed far more than that to continue. Felicia even let out a half-sob and a laugh at her own abandon. But both felt now that it was imperative not to lose the beauty of this moment.

They were on the edge of discovery, entering into uncharted water—and not just because of the lack of protection. It was the eye contact, the unbridled pleasure, and the care taken as he positioned her calves.

Kedah let out a moan as he slid into her oiled, tight warmth. His eyes came up to meet hers, but she was looking down at the blending of them.

'Felicia!'

He snapped her into eye contact with him, and she found there was nothing sexier than full-on looking into Kedah's eyes as he took her.

For a couple of moments that was exactly what he did. He moved to his whim along his thick length.

With anyone else she would have resisted, and yet he guided her so expertly and filled her so completely that all Felicia had to do was give in to the arm that held her up and lie back to receive the pleasure.

She felt the bliss of his weight and the reward of his kiss. His skin was immaculate as her hands slid down his loins and she knew that if she'd made a decision to do something rash then this was the right one.

He took her with force and passion and she returned the same—and almost a tussle ensued as they rolled so Felicia was on top.

'I want…' she said, but did not continue. She just wanted to come again, and there was such energy between them…such a mutual goal to give the other pleasure.

He had thought about what they might be like together and he had expected restraint, a tinge of regret too, and yet there was only fire and buried passion from Felicia.

'Slow down,' he said, and took her hips and jerked her down on his thick length over and over.

His hands moved up to her breasts and toyed with them, stretching her nipples as Felicia bit down on her lip. Then she leant forward to taste his salty skin as his hands roamed her buttocks.

He started thrusting upwards, and with that she had the pleasure of watching him release, and the sensation of the power of him within her.

She toppled forward, and as he came he slid her over and over down onto him, over the edge with him.

Their faces were next to each other and she could feel her hair was damp. Every part of her was more than warm, her skin was on fire, and she had never known anything like this feeling of silence and peace—this space they had walked into together.

He slipped her off him and she fell beside him, breathless, and looked him in the eye.

Then they smiled, because it had been better than they had hoped or dared to expect.

She wanted to touch and explore him, but they lay for just a moment, both thrumming in private bliss as they kissed each other down.

CHAPTER SIX

THEY LAY ENTWINED TOGETHER, and Kedah listened to the hum of the engines as the plane carried them to his home. Deeply sated, he found his mind was clearer.

Felicia's wasn't.

She lay with her head on his chest, listening to the steady thump of his heart as her hand toyed with the silky straight hair on his stomach that she had, right from the start, wanted to feel.

Now that she had, *still* she wanted.

'Can I ask you something?' Felicia spoke but, far too comfortable in his arms, did not raise her head.

'It depends what it is.'

Kedah was no open book.

'Do you want to be King?'

'Of course,' he answered as his hand stroked her bare arm. 'I was born to be King.'

'So why aren't you there all the time?'

'Because my plans to improve Zazinia are repeatedly turned down. I refuse to be an impotent Crown Prince…'

'I doubt there's any chance of that…' she said, and her hand crept down.

'I had a stand-off with my father and the old King some years ago,' Kedah told her. 'They had turned down every plan I had submitted and it was evident that they were never going to accept them. I asked for confirmation and they gave it to me—they did not welcome change. I love to design and so I chose to go it alone. That diamond I carry—it was from the sale of my first hotel. They loathe that I am self-made because it means that I am not beholden to them. I want, though, to make my land better for the people.'

'And now you can?'

'Perhaps.'

'The old King is dead,' Felicia pointed out.

'My father still chooses to listen to the elders and Mohammed.'

'I know you, Kedah—you could convince anyone of anything.' After all, she was in his bed. 'Your people love you.'

'I know they do.'

'What will happen when the Accession Council meet?'

'Mohammed shall state his case, and I shall state mine, and my father shall be asked to make a formal choice.'

'And if it isn't you, you'll take it to the people to vote?'

And it was then that she knew him. Or rather she knew for certain that there was far more to this than Kedah was admitting to.

She did not blush. She had been trained not to react from an early age. And Kedah was the same—he never revealed fear. And so the hand on her arm did not tighten, nor did his breathing change, but as she carried on speaking she heard his heart rate quicken.

'And who would the people chose?' she asked.

'I believe…me.'

'No problem, then.'

'None.'

His response was measured and calm. Had they been having this conversation standing and facing each other, she would not have known of the nerve she had just hit, but his heart beat like a jackhammer in his chest.

'So why are you busy making billions just in case?'

He did not answer, and she lay there listening to the rapid thud of his heart.

'Does Mohammed have something on you?'

'I told you,' Kedah answered evenly. 'I don't regret my past.'

'I know there's a scandal looming.' Felicia smiled. 'I can smell them a mile off.'

There was.

For the first time in his life he needed advice. The question as to how to approach his mother had been rolling around in his head like a ball bearing in a pinball machine. Ideas were bounced around and were rapidly dismissed, but over and over he returned to one small corner that said he should speak with *someone*.

Who?

And, though he kept flicking the thought away, always the ball rolled back and settled in a pocket marked 'Felicia.'

He trusted no one, and yet…

'Felicia?'

She was sleepy and warm in his arms, though her low murmur in answer to her name told him she was awake.

'If I were to tell you something, would it remain between us?'

'Of course.' She smiled again. 'Hit me with it—a pregnant prostitute?'

'Excuse me?' he said, and then smiled in the darkness as he realised she was still trying to guess what his secret was. 'Was that before or after I got married in Vegas?'

She pulled herself from his arms and onto her elbow and she looked at him as his smile faded. The truth was scary sometimes, and she felt its brief threat.

'What is it?'

He shook his head, and Felicia knew when to remain silent. Any guessing now would only irritate, so she lay back down and played with his chest instead as she thought how best to respond.

'If you decide to tell me it shan't go any further.'

'Thank you.'

The gift of time was the best he had known, and he was grateful for it. He was aware it would be all to easy to say what was on his mind in this post-coital haze only to regret it later.

Even that didn't make full sense to him, though, for he did not usually indulge in pillow talk.

There was a small buzzing sound. It would seem that their flying time was nearly over. He reached out and flicked on a light and for the first time Felicia took in their splendid surroundings. Apart from the hum of the engines there was no sign that they were on an aeroplane.

The bed was vast, and rumpled from their lovemaking, and there was no place in the world she would rather be.

'Can we be late?' she asked, and lifted her face for a kiss.

Kedah was tempted to lift the phone beside the bed and inform the captain there was a change of plan, and yet some things needed to be faced.

'Get dressed,' he told her, though it was said with regret. 'I'll have your clothes brought through.'

'Can you at least wait until I'm in the shower?'

He smiled at her modesty, but did as she asked and waited until she had gone through to the bathroom before calling for her overnight bag to be brought to his bedroom.

Felicia washed her hair and dried it, and then she came out.

Kedah lay on the bed with his hands behind his head, clearly deep in thought.

Another buzzer sounded, and now it was Kedah who rose from the bed and headed to the shower as Felicia put on the robe she had chosen to wear. It was a dusky pink with long sleeves and a high neckline. From neck to floor the gown was done up with a row of embroidered buttons, each one individually made. Felicia had bought it while they'd been on their travels and was glad to be able to wear it. Again she chose to wear no make-up.

Kedah soon reappeared, wearing just a towel around his hips. He wished she did not move him so. For the first time in his life he perhaps regretted sex.

She had never looked more beautiful.

Her robe was a light crushed velvet, and it was subtle, yet he had touched each curve that it gracefully concealed, and his fingers itched to undo each button and return her to his bed. Her hair was loose and the air was fragrant with the perfume she had worn on the day they'd met.

Today was not one for distraction, and Felicia was proving a huge one.

He was reeling from coming so close to telling her the secret he had kept for all these years, and—more troublesome for Kedah—he was still dangerously close to revealing it now.

'Why don't you go and have some breakfast?' he suggested. 'I'll join you soon.'

Felicia nodded, unsure as to the dynamics between them, but just as she turned to go he caught her and pulled her back into his arms.

'You know that nothing can happen at the palace?'

'Of course.'

'We will leave straight after dinner. You will be taken to the offices to work there.'

'Kedah,' Felicia said, 'I don't expect us to leave the plane holding hands.'

'I know…'

She stepped from his embrace and went out to the lounge, where she was served breakfast. She was too consumed by Kedah to be embarrassed by the staff, but she was a little worried that they might gossip.

When Kedah came out of the bedroom she was about to voice her concerns to him.

Then she saw him.

The man who would be King.

Always he was beautiful—he was exquisite now.

The robe he wore was silver, and over that was an embroidered coat. His *keffiyeh* was black, and a heavy silver rope fell to one side. She had never seen him carry a sword and it unnerved her—for this was not a Kedah she had ever seen before.

Not just exquisite…he was truly out of her reach.

He was regal, imposing, and it was hard to imagine that less than an hour ago she had lain smiling in his arms.

An attendant served him strong coffee and he declined the sweet pastry she offered.

'They won't say anything?' Felicia checked, and he frowned. 'I mean, what happened won't get back to the palace?'

'Felicia, why do you think I use my own plane? You don't report to my father—none of my staff do. The only exception is Vadia.'

Kedah's success was not reliant on his title. But it was his hope for the future, and his heart belonged to the people he loved.

His words had come out perhaps more harshly than he'd intended—he had not meant to relegate her straight back to being staff—but he was having trouble with his worlds merging.

He had only ever brought Anu to his home, and there had never been anything between them. Anu was close to his mother's age and happily married.

Felicia would cause eyebrows to rise, and he wanted to spare her that shame.

Not that she knew that.

As they sat in silence Felicia looked out on Zazinia as the plane banked to the right and she got her first glimpse of his land from the sky. She understood a little more how thwarted Kedah must feel. It was stunningly beautiful, and yet so ancient that it looked almost biblical.

And then she saw the palace.

It was easily the highest point in the land, set on a cliff along a stretch of white beach.

And it was huge.

As the plane lined up for its approach Felicia realised the palace had its own runway, with several private jets that bore the royal coat of arms on their tails.

The landing was a smooth one, and soon they prepared to disembark.

'Am I to call you Your Highness here?'

'We have already addressed that—you can still call me Kedah.'

'And when we get to the palace am I to—?'

'Enough questions, Felicia,' Kedah snapped.

It was a stern reminder that they had left the bedroom, and Felicia felt the sting of her cheeks at his reprimand.

They stepped from the plane, with Felicia walking a suitable distance behind him. Kedah was met by his personal aide, Vadia, whom Felicia had spoken to on several occasions.

There were no introductions for her, though.

The heat of the Zazinia air and the hot desert wind that whipped at her cheeks were not so hard for her to acclimatise to as her sudden relegation. An hour or so ago they had been in each other's arms, with Kedah almost revealing his darkest of secrets; now he didn't even glance over his shoulder as they stepped into the main entrance of the palace.

He indicated with a flick of his hand that she was to wait there.

A maid came over and she was informed in broken English that soon she would be taken to the offices in the royal wing.

And then Felicia stood, alone and ignored, as she heard a woman call out his name.

'Kedah!'

The woman who was walking towards him had to be his mother. She had the same winning smile as her son, and the robe she wore was a deep crimson. As Felicia glanced towards her she caught his mother's eyes and could see the question in her gaze.

Hurriedly she looked away.

Whatever was said was in Arabic as they embraced.

'Who is that?' Rina asked.

'That is my PA—Felicia.'

'Has Anu left?'

'No,' Kedah responded. 'But she wanted to pull back on the travel. Anu manages things in London now.'

'Well, your father and brother are looking forward to seeing you, Kedah. It has been far too long.'

Kedah doubted they *were* looking forward to seeing him, but they all tried to keep their troubles from his mother, and so he walked with her towards the main office.

Not once did he turn around.

Felicia felt less valuable than even his luggage, which was already being taken up to his suite. And it should not hurt quite so much, yet it did. To go from being his lover to less than nothing was not something she had prepared for. In all their time together he had never made her feel worthless.

He did now.

The guards opened the doors as Kedah and Rina approached, and inside Kedah kissed his father's cheek and shook his brother's hand.

Kumu—Mohammed's wife—was there, and she gave Kedah a small tap to the heart in greeting.

'Now we are all together,' Rina said, beaming, 'there is some good news that Mohammed and Kumu have been waiting to share.'

She clapped her hands and Kedah stood silent as his younger brother stepped forward.

'We have been gifted again,' Mohammed announced. 'In November we are expecting a child.'

'That is wonderful news.' Omar beamed, though at the same time managed to freeze his eldest son with a glare.

Congratulations were offered, and Kedah gave his own. It would be another boy—of course it would. Mohammed did everything to perfection, and had already produced a potential heir and a spare.

All the right things were said, though, and Kedah enquired after his young nephews.

'I hear you are looking to build another hotel in Dubai?' his brother said.

'Another one?' Omar frowned.

'It is early days,' Kedah announced. 'I haven't yet shown the plans to Hussain.'

That silenced his father for a moment.

Hussain and Omar had studied together, and on occasion Hussain had told Kedah about the fine plans his father had once had for his country.

Those days were long gone now.

A maid came in and announced that the portrait artist was ready, but Omar was not letting Kedah off that lightly.

'He can wait,' the King said. 'Now that he is finally here, I would like to speak with Kedah alone.'

'I don't mind staying,' Mohammed offered.

'That shan't be necessary,' Kedah said, and waited until he and his father were alone.

Omar cut straight to the chase.

'The elders are pushing for the royal lineage to move forward,' Omar said. 'Ours is a country that is divided, and there is unrest. Some want things to stay as they did under the rule of my father, and Mohammed is one of them—which is why the elders support him.'

'Your opinion is the one that matters,' Kedah pointed out.

'How can I support you when you are barely here?'

'You know why I stay away,' Kedah said. 'The people here need more infrastructure, healthcare, jobs—the list is endless. We have a country that could thrive, a tourism industry that could help people support their families. Instead they are poor while we continue to live in splendour. No, I cannot feast night after night in a palace when children go to bed hungry.'

'It is not so bad…' the King started, but then he saw Kedah's furious glare and hesitated.

It had been a long time since Kedah had lost his temper on this subject and Omar did not want a repeat.

'Kedah…' He trod more carefully. 'There have long been calls for the Accession Council to meet,' Omar told him. 'But it is becoming more pressing now.'

'Then give me the power I seek. Give me permission to make changes to our land and I shall return. You *know* that I would make a better Crown Prince and ultimately King than Mohammed.'

'How do I know that when you are never here? Prove your devotion…'

'I don't need to prove it—my country has my heart.'

'Choose your bride, come home and settle down. That would satisfy the elders for now, and perhaps delay the calls for the Accession Council to meet…'

'I don't need to appease anyone. I know my people—they want *me* as Crown Prince. If you vote otherwise at the meeting then I shall take it to the people to cast their vote, as is my right.'

'Have you *any* idea of the unrest that would cause?' His father was breathing rapidly. 'Kedah, why can't you just choose a bride and toe the line…?'

'What *happened* to you?' Kedah asked. 'Hussain told me that when you studied together you had plans and dreams for our land… What happened to them?'

'The old King did not want change.'

'But *you* are King now. So why do you bow down to the elders?'

'They are wise.'

'Of course they are—but they are also staid. You are King. Your word is law and yet you choose not to use it.'

'It would be easier—'

'Easier?' Kedah interrupted. 'Since when did a king choose the easy option? Whatever hold the elders have on you, share it with me, and then together we can fight. But I shall not return to Zazinia just to sit idle and wait for you to pass.'

Kedah would not be pushed around by anyone. He knew his father was doing his best to protect his mother's reputation—he was quite sure that was why the King held back—but if only his father would voice the problem, together they could face the trouble.

Just so long as Kedah was indeed Omar's son.

There was a knock at the door and he knew there was only one person who would disturb an official meeting between the King and one of the Princes.

The door opened and the Queen stepped in, smiling widely.

'Rina,' the King scolded lightly, 'I am busy speaking with Kedah.'

'Well, the poor artist is waiting. He's so old that I am scared he will die if we keep him much longer.'

Omar laughed, and even Kedah smiled.

'Come, Kedah,' Rina said. 'I will walk with you.'

They walked through the palace and his mother stopped at a large floral arrangement and chose a bloom, which she placed in her hair, and then she selected a few more.

'It is so good to have both my sons home. Stay a while longer, Kedah.'

She was oblivious to the tension between him and Mohammed, and the terrible rumours had been kept from her. Kedah did not know how much longer they could remain so.

'I cannot stay. I have been away for a few weeks, and Felicia…'

He halted. Since when did he take into consideration the fact that his staff had not been home for a while?

And while Rina was oblivious to many things she was alert to others.

'Careful, Kedah.'

'Careful?' He frowned and stopped walking.

He almost wanted to confront her—to say that he was old enough now to understand an affair—but it was imperative, if he was to fight his brother, to know first that he was the King's son. But then he looked into her smiling chocolate-brown eyes that were flecked with gold like his and he couldn't do it.

There was a fragility to Rina—an air of impulsiveness and a little river of vulnerability that ran through her that sometimes darkened that winning smile.

If he confronted her now, Kedah would watch her fold and crumple. If he questioned her about what had happened all those years ago their relationship would never recover. That much he knew.

Yet if Mohammed called his lineage into question her shame would be held up for the elders and ultimately the people to discuss.

He was scared for his mother.

'Be careful with Felicia,' Rina said. 'Be careful with a young woman's heart.'

Kedah shook his head. His mother did not have to concern herself with his sex life, and especially not with Felicia's heart. This was a business arrangement, and if anyone could handle it, it was Felicia—she was the toughest person he knew.

'You don't have to worry about her.'

'But I do. You have never brought one of your lovers to the palace.'

They walked on and Kedah said nothing. But his mother was right. It was in part the reason he would not be staying longer. He wanted Felicia in his bed, and that could never happen here.

'You are choosing a bride soon,' his mother warned. 'It is not fair to her to be here.'

'Felicia is fine.'

Rina wasn't so sure. She had seen Felicia's angry glare as Kedah had made her walk behind him and ignored her.

And now there Felicia was, standing on a balcony, looking out at the view.

'Think about staying for a little while, Kedah,' Rina said, and kissed his cheek. 'I miss you.'

'I know.'

'Come home.'

He wanted to.

'I cannot sit idle for years like…' He halted.

'Like your father has?'

He nodded, and after a moment of sad thought Rina cupped his cheek.

'I do understand.'

Could he ask his mother for the truth? If he *was* his father's son then he could confront the rumours and douse them before the sun went down on this day.

If he wasn't…?

Kedah was ready to know.

'Mother…' He stood there and felt as if he had removed his sword and now held it over her head.

'Yes?'

Rina smiled. And he did not know how to ask her.

'Why don't you give Felicia these?' she suggested.

'You tell me to be careful and then you suggest that I give her flowers?'

'I often pick some flowers to sit on Vadia's desk while she works.'

Indeed Rina did.

'I need to get on,' he said to his mother.

No, he would not go to Felicia with flowers.

Felicia didn't turn when he came to join her—she was still smarting. She was a very modern woman, and while careerwise she would have been fine walking two steps behind him and being ignored, having just left his bed she could not accept it—though she was doing her best not to let it show.

'I want you to take some photos of this wing while I go and have my portrait finished…'

'Sure.'

They walked around the Crown Prince's wing as the staff prepared his office and brought in the artist to add the final touches to the painting.

'I think this area could be better used,' he mused. 'Perhaps as a pool or spa area?'

Felicia tried to keep her features expressionless, though she was aghast at the very thought. It was an ancient palace and absolutely beautiful. To think he would consider tearing up these walls and floors to transform them into some modern gym was appalling.

'You don't approve?'

'I think that it's far too beautiful to risk spoiling.'

'You've seen my work?' Kedah checked, and she

nodded. 'So why do you think I would ruin it? I want to enhance what is already here. I want somewhere I can live rather than a museum.'

They stopped by the portraits, and possibly she could see what he meant. Cool grey eyes seemed to follow them, and they were a forbidding sight indeed.

'I'm meeting with Vadia in an hour,' Felicia said. 'We just spoke on the phone. She wants to take some time to go through your schedule. September is the King's birthday, yet that week you're booked to be in New York.'

'I have a friend's wedding.'

'Oh, and speaking of weddings… Vadia wants to go through potential dates for yours.'

She said it so calmly that Kedah honestly thought his mother was wrong and Felicia was fine with their arrangement.

'Tell Vadia that, given I haven't chosen my bride yet, it's a bit early to be discussing dates.'

'Sure.'

'I have a family dinner to attend after the portrait,' Kedah said. 'Your meal shall be served to you at your desk. Just call through with your order. We should fly out around midnight,' he told her. 'You'll be home by morning.'

But tomorrow was a day too late, Felicia thought.

If only this visit had been arranged for yesterday…if only she could have held out for a couple more days… Then she wouldn't be feeling as she did now.

She looked at the portraits of the men who had come before him. They were dressed in robes of black or white and the familiar chequered headwear. Kedah wore a gorgeous silken robe and an embroidered coat.

Somehow, even traditionally dressed, he made a statement.

'You're going to stand out amongst the others,' she said.

'I always do,' he answered, and looked at the portraits of his father and grandfather. The fact that he dressed differently had little to do with it. 'I don't look like any of them.'

He walked off and Felicia stood there, frowning—not at what he had said, more at *the way* he had said it.

She knew she was already in too deep, yet as she looked up at the portraits he dragged her in ever deeper.

She was beginning to understand.

Kedah stood for his portrait.

The artist was indeed ancient, and it was hard to believe that those shaky hands could produce something so beautiful.

'I have painted your grandfather, your father, and now you,' the old man said as he added the final touches. 'I hope to paint the next Crown Prince.'

'It might be Crown Princess,' Kedah answered. He was bored from standing so long, and ready for a little disagreement, but the old man just smiled at the provocation.

'That is something to stay alive just to see.'

Yes, Kedah thought, the people really were ready for change.

The painting had been done over many sessions and Kedah, who hated to be still for more than a moment, had found the entire process excruciating.

'Just turn your face a little to the left,' the old man said. 'And look out to the desert.' The sky was orange and he wanted it to light the gold flecks in Kedah's eyes.

And so Kedah sighed and stared out to the desert. No wonder the portraits were of men looking stern, Kedah thought as he dwelt on his problems and pondered again discussing things with Felicia.

A woman's view on things might help, and she might know better how to broach the subject with his mother.

And, given her own family and her job, if there was anyone who would not be shocked by an illicit affair it was Felicia.

But could he trust her?

Yes.

It was a revelation, for since the day he had discovered his mother and Abdal his childhood innocence had faded and trust had rapidly left his heart.

He had thought it gone for good, but now he looked back on his time with her and their conversations. He remembered sitting in the restaurant as she'd revealed the dark part of her heart, and then smiled as he recalled her forthright observations about his hotels.

And then he remembered her lying in his arms, and how close he had come to confiding in her.

Then he thought of her beauty today.

The sun was setting and the desert fired red in the distance as the old man put down his brush and his work was finally done.

'Would you care to see it, Your Highness?' he offered, but Kedah shook his head.

'I shall wait until it is framed,' Kedah told him.

He did not want to stare upon the truth.

CHAPTER SEVEN

THEIR DEPARTING FLIGHT from Zazinia was very different from their outward flight. Despite the pilot's best efforts to climb above it, turbulence carried them home.

Kedah tapped his diamond, cursing the missed opportunity with his mother, and Felicia looked out of the window to the seemingly black lake of desert below. She was still angry about being ignored and dining at her desk alone, while cross with herself for expecting it could be any other way.

As they bumped through the sky she decided to try to do some work and put on her headphones. She would look at the presentation that she had been asked to send to Hussain. But, without thinking, she opened the file in the first email that Kedah had sent her.

Realising it was the one he had sent in error—the one he had told her to delete—she was about to exit from it when she paused.

She had sat through a lot of presentations these past weeks. She had expected to see a proposal for the Dubai hotel and the walkway, and to label a few files, but instead she saw magic.

It was Zazinia, she quickly realised.

It was Kedah's vision of Zazinia.

With each passing frame the bare skyline was filled with graceful buildings, and each was a work of art in itself. Instead of gleaming silver or gold with mirrored windows, the buildings blended with the ancient surrounds. There were delicate artistic murals on the walls that faced the palace, and the city spread gently outwards rather than up. There were carefully thought out roads, railways and bridges to link communities, while the desert retained its remote beauty.

He had poured everything into this, Felicia knew.

It was a life's work in the making.

And she knew he had never meant her to see it.

She snapped off the presentation and then looked over. His eyes were waiting for hers to meet his. She pulled her earphones off, wondering if he somehow knew what she had just seen.

The truth proved to be just as disconcerting, and it troubled her how deeply he could bore into her heart.

'I apologise for the way I treated you back at the palace.'

Despite being strapped in, she almost fell off her chair in surprise. The apology jolted her, even if her expression barely faltered.

'I have never brought a woman there. Colleagues, of course, but…' He gave a tense shake of his head. 'If there had been even a hint that we were involved then it could have made things awkward for you. I didn't handle it well.'

Please don't be nice, Felicia thought, because her feelings were so much easier to deal with when she was cross.

'Well, it's done now.' She shrugged. 'And I shan't be back there again.'

'I doubt there would be any reason…'

'No,' Felicia said. 'You misunderstand. I *shan't* be going back there again, Kedah. We all have our limits, and your treatment of me in Zazinia far exceeded mine. Anyway, there's no need for me to be there.'

'No.'

It had been too far out of her comfort zone. Had she only been working for him, she might not have liked it, but of course she would have accepted his treatment of her.

But they were lovers.

Oh, it was a business arrangement, perhaps, but still she could not flick a switch. She refused to go from being his lover to a servant who walked behind him, being ignored. His little hand-flick had incensed her.

An hour out of London the turbulence finally eased, and by then Felicia was dozing. Kedah went to his bedroom, but there wasn't time to shower so he just changed out of his traditional clothing into a suit.

He could have slept for an hour, maybe, but instead he sat on the bed with his head in his hands.

Despite his brave words, he did not know what his response would be should his father back Mohammed.

Should he risk his mother's past being exposed by taking it to a public vote? What if the title of Crown Prince wasn't rightly his?

Usually Kedah looked immaculate.

Not this morning.

London was beautiful, Felicia thought from the back of a luxurious car, and yet it wasn't the same as when she'd left. The last few weeks had been spent exclusively with Kedah, and nothing felt the same.

This wasn't a date. He didn't drop her home first. Kedah was both royal *and* her boss, so they pulled up outside his apartment and she got out and ensured all his luggage had been removed.

Here, they always said goodbye.

'I'm assuming that I've got the rest of the day off?'

'Of course.'

It had been a very long business trip, and new boundaries needed to be established now.

'I'll see you tomorrow at eight,' she said, and as she did so Big Ben chimed and they stood there. It was seven in the morning, which meant a separation of twenty-five hours.

'Come up,' Kedah said.

'I'm really tired.'

'I know you are.'

He could see the shadows under her eyes, and he was exhausted too. But the turbulence on the plane was nothing compared to now.

They were on the edge of being stupid.

Sleep-deprived, wanting, holding back…neither really knew.

She should run, Felicia thought. Jump in the car and go home.

Go to her mother's tonight for a timely reminder on what falling in love with a certain type of man could do.

But, truly, she didn't know how to play tough today—especially when Kedah spoke on.

'You said that if I decide to tell you it won't go any further. Does that still apply?'

And just when she knew she should walk away, he beckoned her in.

'You know it does.'

He took her hand as he signalled the driver to remove her cases from the car too.

She stood in the antique elevator beside him, and even then she knew she should get out.

But it wasn't curiosity that had led her back to him. It was desire.

Every minute available to them she wanted to claim.

She would heal later.

Felicia had been in his apartment a couple of times, though never with Kedah there. Usually she went there to speak with a maid, or went with his driver to collect his luggage.

Now, she was a little unsure of her role as she stepped into the magnificent abode.

The drapes were open, revealing beautiful private gardens, and she gazed out at them as the driver deposited their bags in the hallway.

Felicia knew she wasn't here as his PA, and yet she wasn't quite sure if it was her troubleshooting skills that Kedah was seeking now.

'I'm going to shower,' he told her, and she nodded. 'Join me?'

She gave a tired laugh and carried on staring out of the window as Kedah headed off. His presumption should irk her, yet it didn't.

She wanted him, after all.

It was later that concerned her, not now.

Kedah walked into his large bathroom and removed his clothing. It should feel good to be home after all this time away, yet it never quite did.

Home was Zazinia.

He turned on the shower and the jets of water should have blasted him awake, but he was too tired for that. He stood soaping his body, still questioning the wisdom of telling the truth to another person.

But then he watched as Felicia, a little late, took up his offer to join him.

And for the first time it was good to be home.

'Wait,' he told her as she started to undress.

Kedah came out of the shower and she stood as he took care of the intricate buttons he had itched to undo so many hours ago.

This time he gave no orders. Instead he simply did what he must to get her naked. He peeled off her robe and then helped her out of her underwear.

'You're shaking?' he said, because he could feel the tremble in her as she stepped out of her knickers.

'I think I officially have jet lag,' she said.

She didn't.

Well, she probably did. But in that walk from the lounge through his bedroom to the bathroom she had known she was entrenching herself deeper into his life.

He lifted her hair and kissed her neck softly, deeply, intimately, in a way that made her dizzy. And she wished he did not take quite such care, so that later she could fault him, but instead he took her, tired and aching, into the shower.

First he washed her hair, and those strong fingers worked her into a quiet frenzy. He soaped her body and he missed nothing—not a finger, nor that patch of skin behind her knees that she had become aware of on the very first day they met.

And she did nothing. She didn't even touch him. She just felt the arousal that swirled around them thicken and knew of his increasing pleasure as his breathing tripped on occasion.

She faced away from him and he splayed her hands against the glass. He kissed down her back and it was the first time since childhood that Felicia had cried. Not that he could see that she did, for the water took care of that, and not that he could hear that she did, for she sobbed also with desire.

'Turn around.'

They were the only words spoken, and when she did she was met with a wall of muscle. He held her and lifted her hair and kissed her, so the sound of water was but a distant thrum. It was so distant that it took her a moment to realise that he had turned the taps off. Taking her hand, he led her dripping wet to his bed.

They would pay for this later, Felicia was sure. They would wake up in soaked sheets, with her hair in chaos, but she cared nothing about that now.

She shivered—not just from the cool of the air on her wet skin, nor her building need, but from the darkness of the bedroom that shut out the morning sun, from the upending of her senses.

In his room, she was deeper into his life.

He pulled back the covers and she climbed in, and then he wrapped her not in linen but in the cocoon of his body. He was barely on his elbows, their skin was in full contact, and his weight was pleasurably heavy upon her.

Then he took her, and Kedah had never meant to take her like this. He drove in on a kiss and told her her name. He told her just who he needed to chase away the demons.

And she said stupid words—like *yes* and his name.

All her anger and fury at being ignored and having to walk behind him was not eliminated by his kiss—in fact it was intensified. As he took her, hard and fast, there was almost a fight to the death taking place. Delicious anger burned and cleansed.

He pounded her senses until she could take it no

more, and she came but did not surrender, even while moaning his name and unfurling at her core.

He met her, matched her, he filled her deeply and she lay there beneath him, breathless.

And she was still angry.

Did he think this was a part of the service? Did he think she could just give herself to *anyone* like that?

Clearly he did, Felicia thought, for she assumed all his lovers were treated to such intimate bliss.

She could never have known she was the first in this bed.

He rolled from her.

He had spent a lifetime wishing he had never opened that door, wishing he had never seen what he had. Now he checked that Felicia wanted to come further into his world.

'Do you want to know?'

She glanced at the clock by the bed and it told her it was nine.

Her cases were there in the hall. She could easily dress now, make some casual comment and tell him it would keep and head for home.

Get out now, while she still had a chance.

It was already far too late for that.

Her tears in the shower had left her surprisingly clear-headed, and she knew now she could not leave him by simple choice.

'Yes.' She turned and nodded. 'I want to know.'

CHAPTER EIGHT

'THAT ARTICLE YOU read on the day of our first meeting,' Kedah said. 'Do you have it?'

'It was taken down from the internet.'

'Come off it, Felicia.'

He knew that she was savvy and would have taken a screenshot, and of course she confirmed it. 'I've got it on my phone.'

'Take a look.'

He got out of bed and it troubled Felicia how little it bothered her that he went into her bag and took out her phone, which he handed to her.

'Have another read of it while I go and make coffee.'

She moved over to the side of the bed that wasn't damp from the shower and read again about the very decadent Sheikh Kedah.

'What do you see?' He brought in some drinks and then climbed in beside her on the dry side of the bed.

'There's nothing I don't know. They're hinting that the Accession Council should meet…'

'Read on,' Kedah told her, and she frowned and read down.

'There's just a picture of Mohammed and your father.'

'And what does the caption say?'

'"Like father, like son."'

'There's a subtext there,' Kedah said. 'A warning that if I push for change then the truth might be revealed…'

Felicia frowned.

'The truth?'

'There is a rumour in Zazinia that I am not my father's son. It's not just that I look nothing like him—our visions are so different. Though the rumour persists, to date no one has dared voice it to my father or me. I believe soon they might. I need to be ready, and to quash it with the most withering riposte…'

She thought back to what he had said as they'd stood by those portraits—about looking nothing like any of them.

'I don't look like *my* father…' But Felicia knew there had to be more to it than just rumour, and so she asked the question no one dared. 'Is there a chance it might be true?'

'Yes,' Kedah told her, and he watched the swallowing in her throat. 'I caught my mother cheating when I was a young child.'

'Does anyone else know?'

Kedah thought back and shook his head. 'I was on my own when I caught them.'

'Does your mother know what you saw?'

Kedah didn't answer.

'Tell me what happened.'

'You don't need the details. I made a decision a long time ago never to speak of it.'

She saw his eyes shutter and Felicia let out a tense, 'What happened?' Then she continued. 'Tell me what you saw. You hate it when I discredit your work—well, don't dismiss mine. I deal with this type of thing a lot. Well, maybe not with royalty, but I know I can help. Though you have to tell me it all.'

She knew he didn't believe there was any difference she could make but, to his credit—or perhaps to hers—he told her some more.

'I was young.'

'How young?'

'Just turning three.'

He was hesitant to say more, but then he looked at Felicia. Yes, Matteo had been right about her. She was tough and experienced—he himself had seen that. And now they were lovers. But, more than that, he trusted her.

'The office where you worked yesterday…just outside the one where my portrait was done…?' He offered the location and Felicia nodded as her mind's eye went there. 'I was hiding from the royal nanny. My grandfather and father had been away and I didn't want to go and welcome them back, so I ran off and hid under the desk. I could hear noises coming from inside the office, and at first I thought my mother was hurt. When I opened the door she was being held by Abdal.'

'Abdal?' Felicia checked, but then, aware of her own impatience, she shook her head—she would find out in time. 'Go on.'

'Abdal walked off and she told me she had been crying and that he had been comforting her. She told me not to tell the King or anyone else. I don't think she knows that I remember.'

'What about the nanny?' Felicia asked. 'The one you were hiding from?'

'She came in then, and apologised for losing sight of me.' Kedah thought back. 'She was awkward, though I don't think she would have seen…'

'She might have seen Abdal leaving.' It was good that Felicia had been to the palace and could picture it properly. That corridor was a long one, and if the nanny had seen Abdal leaving then it might have been clear he had been alone with the Queen.

While the King was away.

It was immaterial now, but possibly this helped Felicia understand how important it was to Kedah that no one guessed what was between them.

They were still in bed together, and Felicia had never worked like this before.

They were trying to unravel the past, to work out how best to deal with the future.

Now she sat up cross-legged, with the sheet around her, trying to imagine that the Queen she had met would risk it all for a brief fling.

'Why, if you were only almost three when you caught them, do you think it was a prolonged affair?'

'You don't take the Queen over a study desk unless you're very sure…'

He looked up, and he saw that Felicia smiled.

It felt odd to smile about something so dark, and yet it helped that she did and so he told her some more.

'My mother comes from a much more modern country. Abdal was an aide also from there. He came to Zazinia to help with the transition and to ensure my grandfather upheld his agreements.'

'Did he?'

'Minimally. There was a lot of hope for change when the marriage took place, but little transpired. If he wasn't dead I would cheerfully kill him…'

Felicia didn't doubt him. Kedah's voice was ominous.

'Abdal had been in Zazinia ever since the royal wedding,' he went on.

'How soon after you caught them did he leave?'

Kedah thought back. 'A few days afterwards.' Even

at such a young age he had served his mother a warning that day, and it had been heeded. 'I look nothing like my brother or my grandfather. He must have been a risk-taker to do what he did. So am I—'

'Kedah,' Felicia interrupted, in a voice that was terribly practical. 'Let's assume you inherited your risk-taking behaviour from your mother.'

He gave a reluctant smile, because he had never thought of it like that.

'What about a DNA test?' she asked. 'You'd know once and for all.'

He liked it that she was practical, that she didn't judge his mother or wring her hands, just got straight to the pertinent facts and seemed to sense how vital it was that Kedah knew where he stood.

'I've already had my profile done,' Kedah admitted. 'Anonymously, of course. But you've seen how it is there. Can you imagine me creeping around trying to find a comb?'

'You can get it from other things,' Felicia said. 'One of my other clients…'

His jaw gritted. He loathed thinking of her other clients and their scandalous pasts—and he loathed, more than that, that she had ever been close to them. 'I don't need to hear about them.'

'Maybe you do. With one of them I got a sample from chewing gum.'

'He's a *king*,' Kedah said.

'I get that. I'm just saying…'

'Why don't I pull on some gloves and offer him a stick of chewing gum or snip off some hair? Do you think no one will notice?' He lay back and tucked his hand behind his head as he tried to think.

If there was a solution to be had, he would have come up with it by now.

'I'm thinking of asking her.'

'Oh, no!' Felicia shook her head. 'Kedah, even if she admits to the affair, she's never going to admit to *that*. Do you think your father knows about the rumours?'

'Possibly,' he said. 'But he still thinks my mother is perfection personified. He would defend her to the death. But I know that if he does then he could be made to look a fool. I need to know the truth.'

'Even if the result isn't the one you want?'

'I can handle the truth, Felicia.'

She believed him. 'But…?'

'I don't know that my mother could,' Kedah said. 'If even so much as the affair were exposed then my father would have no choice but to divorce her.'

'By the old rules?' Felicia said, and Kedah looked over to her. 'Does he love her?'

'Very much.' Kedah thought of how his father's face lit up whenever she came in the room. How he did all he could to shield her from the feud between her sons. 'I don't know how he'd be if the truth came out, though.'

He was done with talking about it.

'Come on,' he said. 'Sleep.'

And this time there was no thought of heading for her case, or making a feeble excuse that she needed to go home to water her plants.

Felicia slept.

CHAPTER NINE

FELICIA HAD NEVER known someone so able to separate the bedroom from work.

Kedah did it with ease.

And it helped.

At restaurants, her computer and her phone on the table served as a little wall between them. To remind her, as often as was necessary, that they were not lovers having lunch.

She was *working.*

Oh, but the nights!

In the evenings they ate at the best restaurants, without a computer between them, holding hands between courses and doing rude things under the table with their feet before returning home to his bed.

The bedroom was an entirely different thing. Her cases had long since been unpacked by his maids.

Her family and friends were very used to Felicia disappearing for weeks on end as she focused on her clients, so her absence was easily explained—even when she caught up with her mother for lunch.

'At least tell me who you're working for,' Susannah said.

'I can't just yet.' Felicia smiled and then looked at the time. 'I have to get back.'

Felicia *did* have to get back. Kedah had a two p.m. meeting with Hussain. But, knowing she needed supplies, after lunch Felicia decided to use lover's licence and dash back to her own flat.

Poor neglected flat, she thought as she grabbed some make-up wipes and tweezers from her bathroom cupboard. Two things that were sadly lacking at Kedah's.

Perhaps they should spend some time here…

And then she checked herself. It was easier that their time was spent at his apartment. She did not need constant reminders of him here when they were through.

And soon they would be.

Vadia's requests for a bridal selection date were almost daily now. The article that had been taken down from the internet was back up again, and there had been several more too.

Things were coming to a head, whether she wanted it or not.

Felicia opened up the cabinet and grabbed a fresh packet of contraceptive pills—the real reason she was there, for she was down to her last.

She went to grab some tampons too, but then remembered she'd already taken some to Kedah's last week.

She stilled as she realised she was down to her last pill and had nothing to show for it. Her tampons sat languishing in the glitzy mirrored cupboard in his bathroom.

Felicia stood for a very long moment and told herself it was the travel, it was exhaustion, it was being in love with a sexy sheikh who could never consider loving her back that had made her late.

And she *was* late.

Late with her period, late back from lunch.

And, because they kept things very separate, Kedah did not hold back from pointing this out.

'You're late.' He scowled.

'Indeed I am,' she responded.

'You haven't sent the file to Hussain…'

'No.' She sighed. She'd been too engrossed in that other file he'd mistakenly sent her to remember a small detail like that. 'I forgot.'

'Well, don't forget again,' he said, but then he halted.

He knew he was working her hard—both at work and in the bedroom.

Workwise… Well, he knew that time was running out, so he was trying to fit everything in.

And as for the other…

The same.

Still Felicia fascinated him. Still he wanted her over and over.

Usually his interest waned by the time the sun rose on a new day, but this fidelity trial was going exceptionally well.

Felicia did not wait for him to terminate the conversation. Every night she spent with him she felt as if she were handing over more and more of her heart, and she could not take it much longer.

She walked out and sat at her desk. She smiled at Anu, who brought some tea into her office and then left Felicia to work, but a few moments later Anu was back.

'Felicia…' She sounded concerned. 'That was Reception. Kedah's brother is here to see him, but he's in a meeting with Hussain and he told me that I am not to disturb him.'

'Well, he said nothing of the sort to *me*.' Felicia

smiled sweetly as she reached for the phone, which made Anu laugh.

Kedah was not impressed. 'I said that I wasn't to be disturbed.'

'Well, you might change your mind for this. Apparently Mohammed is down in Reception.'

Kedah looked over to Hussain. His first instinct was to tell Felicia to let Mohammed know he was in a meeting and that he would see him when he was ready.

But there was no point.

This was no idle visit, and Kedah had to show he had no reason to delay or hide.

'He can come up.'

He spoke to Hussain. 'I am going to have to cut our meeting short. It would seem Mohammed has flown in to speak with me. I hope you understand.'

'Of course.'

The men shook hands and suddenly, for Kedah, the design for a hotel in Dubai held little importance.

Hussain saw himself out of the office. He looked more serious than Felicia had ever seen him. Usually Hussain stopped and spoke, but today he just nodded to Anu, who also looked troubled.

Mohammed walked in, and when Anu did not move Felicia greeted the Prince and showed him through. 'Can I get you any refreshments?' she offered.

'No, thank you,' Kedah said. 'That shall be all.'

It was all supremely polite, but the air was so thick it was like closing the door on a tornado.

'Trouble is here,' Anu said once the door had closed.

'Not necessarily,' Felicia offered.

'I grew up knowing that this day would come.'

So had Kedah.

'This is a surprise.' Kedah's voice told his brother that it wasn't a particularly pleasant one.

'I only decided to come this morning,' Mohammed said as he took a seat. 'I sat in on a meeting about brides considered to be suitable as future Queen. It struck me as odd, given that I already have a wonderful bride, who would make an excellent queen, as well as two sons.'

'*I* am first in line,' Kedah answered smoothly. 'Why would you consider it odd?'

'Because I am the one sitting there discussing the future of our country and you are miles away, focusing on your own wealth.'

'As I have long said to our father, and to our grandfather before him, I am more than happy to devote my attention to Zazinia, and I shall do so when I am not thwarted at every turn. If I have to wait to be King to see my country flourish and thrive, then I shall do so—'

'I have been approached by Fatiq,' Mohammed broke in. Fatiq was a senior elder. 'I felt it only fair to warn you that there is a majority agreement amongst the elders that *I* would make a more suitable Crown Prince and King.'

'I could have told you that a decade ago.' Kedah shrugged. 'That is old news.'

'They feel that your interests are clearly removed from Zazinia…'

'Never.'

'And they suggest that it is time for you to step aside and make way for the most suitable heir.'

'Never,' Kedah said again.

'Some also say that I am the *rightful* heir.'

'Name them,' Kedah responded with a challenge.

Mohammed shook his head. 'I cannot do that. However, should an Accession Council meeting be called…'

'Why would that happen? Our father has stated that once I choose my bride I will have his full support.'

'Kedah, we don't *want* it go to the Accession Council. You know as well as I do that there are things that should be left unsaid. You have the power to halt the elders.'

And Kedah saw his brother's game plan then. Mohammed wanted the threat of his mother's exposure to force Kedah aside.

He had chosen the wrong man, though, for Kedah would never be bullied.

'You really think I would step aside to appease the elders?'

'No, but I feel you would for the sake of our mother's integrity…'

Mohammed had intended to prompt his brother finally to back down. Instead Kedah picked up his phone and called the palace. He was through to the King in a matter of moments.

'I am calling a meeting of the Accession Council,' he said to his father, and he stared his brother in the eyes as he did so. 'This shall be dealt with once and for all. Do I have your support or do I not?'

'Kedah…' The King had known his youngest son had flown out and had been waiting for this call. 'There is no need to call for a meeting. I have told you—return to Zazinia and choose your bride, appease the elders…'

Kedah had heard enough.

'The meeting will be held at sunset on Friday. You shall stand in support of your eldest son or not. If Mohammed is chosen it will not be left there. I shall take the decision to the people.'

He threw down the phone and looked to his brother. 'I mean it,' Kedah warned him.

'The elders say that if pushed they will demand a DNA test…'

He waited for Kedah to crumble, for the Crown Prince to pale, but his brother gave a black laugh.

'They embrace technology when it suits them.' He dismissed the threat with a flick of his wrist, though privately he fought to keep that hand steady. 'I am returning to Zazinia…'

'Even though you know what it might do to our mother?'

'Don't turn this onto me,' Kedah warned, and now he stood. 'Don't pretend for a minute that you are not behind this too. If and when I choose a bride—'

'You cannot!' Mohammed frowned, but backed off slightly as his brother approached. 'Why would you do that to her?'

'To whom?' Kedah frowned too.

'To your *wife*.' Mohammed had stopped even pretending he wasn't the one leading this coup. 'I was just saying yesterday to Kumu—*she* married a prince who might one day be King. Whereas *your* bride will marry the Crown Prince who might one day be a commoner. You are in no position to choose a wife.'

Kedah just gave another black laugh as he took his brother by the throat. He, too, had stopped pretending.

'If my mother's name is ever discredited I shall have you thrown in prison.'

'You don't seem to understand, Kedah. The power won't be yours.'

And Kedah's response…?

It had been banter when he had said it to Felicia, but there was no hint of that now, and he watched Mohammed pale as he delivered his threat. 'Then I shall deal with you outside of the law.'

CHAPTER TEN

FELICIA SAT IN her office as Kedah's other world intervened.

Or rather his real world.

This was all temporary. They had always had a use-by date and she had to remind herself of that.

Not any more, though, for now there was no hiding from the truth.

From her office she could see Mohammed striding out, one hand massaging his neck, and she guessed there had been a tussle.

Felicia honestly could not deal with it now. She had been going through her calendar and trying to work out when her last period had been. Her world was a blur since she'd been working for Kedah.

She *couldn't* be pregnant?

Surely!

'Hey.'

Felicia looked up and there he was. 'How did it go?' she asked.

'He stated his case.'

And, after weeks of wanting to know more, and a career based on revelation, suddenly Felicia didn't want to know what had been said. She did not want to hear that their time was running out.

'Shall we go and get dinner?' Kedah suggested.

'It's not even five.'

'Let's go back to my apartment, then. We need to talk.'

'I have a meeting with Vadia soon.'

'Well, cancel it,' he said. 'We need to talk. Things are coming to a head back home. My brother has spoken with the elders. They want *him* as Crown Prince.'

She said nothing.

'My father seems to think if I choose a bride then we can put things off…'

Very deliberately, Felicia did not flinch.

'I have called for a meeting of the Accession Council this Friday at sunset.' For once the arrogant Kedah was pale. 'I shall leave on Thursday.'

'For how long?'

'I doubt it will be dealt with quickly. If the vote is in my favour I expect that things will get dirty, and the elders will do their best to question my lineage. I shall be busy there for the foreseeable future.'

'Where does that leave *me*?'

It was the neediest she had ever been, but thankfully Kedah took her at her selfish, career-focused best.

'Your contract is for a year. Whatever happens to me.'

It was like a slap on the cheek, but a necessary one, and it put her back in business mode.

'And if it goes in your favour?'

'Then it is time for me to step up.'

And, whatever way it went, Felicia knew things would never be the same.

'We need to sort out—' Kedah started, but she interrupted him.

'Not now.'

Felicia wanted to curl up on her sofa and hide from the building panic. She wanted a night spent with chocolate, convincing herself that she couldn't possibly be pregnant.

She had been right never to mix business with pleasure, because she was finding it impossible to think objectively now—and that was what he had hired her to do after all.

'I need to go home and think this through.'

'You can think it through with *me*.'

'No.'

She couldn't.

Because when she was with him feelings clouded the issue. A part of her didn't even *want* Kedah to be the rightful King, because if he was not that meant there might a chance for them.

Oh, surely not?

She had become Beth, Felicia realised, or one of the many others who had hoped against hope that things with Kedah might prove different for them. She had fallen head over heels, even with due warning, and had hoped he might somehow change.

One day she would laugh, she decided.

One night in the future she would sit with friends, sipping a cocktail, and make them laugh as she told them how, even as he'd spoken of his future bride, even as he'd told her not to worry about her contract, she had hoped—stupidly hoped—there was a chance for them.

'I'm going home.' Felicia stood. 'I'll think about it tonight…' And then she did it. She offered the lovely wide smile that she gave to all her clients. The one that told them she'd handle this, that they could leave it with her. 'I'll come up with something.'

And Kedah said nothing. He just stepped aside as she brushed past.

He hadn't been asking her to come up with a solution! Conversation and something rather more basic would have sufficed. He'd never needed anyone in his life, yet tonight he needed Felicia Hamilton.

And she had walked off.

She'd had no choice but to.

It had been walk away or break down and cry—something she had sworn never to do in front of someone else, especially Kedah.

And so she headed for home, turned the key in the door, and stepped into the flat that had once felt familiar but no longer did.

She felt upended now.

At the age of twenty-six Felicia had fallen in love.

Real love.

CHAPTER ELEVEN

KEDAH ARRIVED FOR work a little later than usual the next day, and stepped out of the elevator to the aroma of coffee.

It had been a long night.

As much as it galled him to admit it, Mohammed had made a very good point—how could he marry when one day his title might be held up for question?

Kedah was proud, and the selection of royal brides from whom he would choose all expected him to one day be King.

His problems had kept him awake for most of the night, and this morning, just as he had been leaving, Omar had rung to try to persuade Kedah to call off the meeting. But he had refused.

It would just delay the inevitable.

He headed towards his office and there was Anu at her desk, drinking coffee. 'Good morning,' he said, and it took him a moment to register that Felicia wasn't there. Her office door was closed and the light was off.

'Good morning.' Anu went to stand up. 'Would you like coffee?'

'Later,' he said, and waved her to sit back down. 'You look tired.'

'I couldn't sleep,' Anu admitted. 'My mother called

late last night and said there are reports that the Accession Council are meeting.'

'On Friday.' Kedah nodded and thought of Felicia's response—*Where does that leave me?* 'Anu, whatever happens your job is safe. I shall be keeping all my hotels and—'

'I'm not worried about my job, Kedah,' Anu said. 'Well, a bit… But my mother was upset and my father is too. I worry for my country. Growing up, we all looked forward to the day you would be King…'

'And I shall be,' Kedah said, though he could see that Anu wasn't convinced.

She would have grown up on the rumours too.

'I would like to fly back to Zazinia tomorrow, some time midmorning,' he told Anu. 'Can you arrange that, please?'

Tomorrow was Thursday. He could possibly have left it another day, but he wanted some time in his country to prepare for the meeting. Perhaps he would go to the desert and draw on its wisdom. He was very aware that tonight would be his last in London for the foreseeable future.

'Can you ask Felicia to come and speak with me as soon as she gets in?'

'Felicia's not coming in today,' Anu said. 'She just called in sick.'

Oh, no, she didn't!

Kedah walked into his office and, closing the door behind him, immediately picked up his phone.

The first time she didn't answer, but he refused to speak to a machine and so immediately called again.

Felicia stared at her phone and something told her that if she didn't pick up then Kedah would soon be at her door.

'Hi.' Felicia did her best to keep her voice crisp, but she had woken in tears and they simply would not stop.

'Are you crying?' Kedah asked.

'Of course not. I've got a cold. I've already explained that to Anu.'

'It's summer,' he pointed out.

'I've got a summer cold.'

'You were fine yesterday…'

'Well. I'm not today. Look, I'm sorry it's not convenient, but I really can't work. I need to take the day off.'

'Felicia…' Kedah's impatience was rising. She had swanned off before five last night and now, when he properly needed her, she had called in sick—with a cold, of all things. 'I want you here within the hour,' he told her. 'I have a lot to sort out. You know that. I fly to Zazinia tomorrow.'

'I can't come into work,' she responded. She didn't need to be looking in a mirror to know that her face was red and that her eyes were swollen from crying. 'I have to take today off. I believe my contract allows for sick days with a medical certificate?'

Felicia ended the call and turned off her phone. Refusing to lie there worrying, she hauled herself out of bed and dressed. Grabbing her purse, she headed out.

Oh, she was doing her best to reassure herself that it was travel and exhaustion that accounted for her being late, as well as the uncertainty of being head over heels in love with the most insensitive man in the world.

A man who could hold you in his arms while discussing brides.

A man who had told her to her face that an unplanned pregnancy wouldn't faze him and that the palace would 'handle' it.

Though for all he had stated it wouldn't be an issue,

it might be a touch more scandal than he would want this close to a meeting of the Accession Council and the bridal selection.

Well, she didn't need Vadia to sort her out. Felicia would manage this herself!

She bought the necessary kit and, once home, did what the instructions said and waited, with mounting anxiety, trying to tell herself that she could *not* be pregnant.

Except just a moment later she found out that she was.

All the panic seemed to still inside her, and she waited for it to regroup and slam back. She waited for the tears she had sobbed this morning to return with renewed vigour, but nothing happened. She sat there, staring at the indicator, trying to comprehend the fact that she was going to be a mum.

It wasn't something she'd ever really considered before. A baby had never factored in her plans.

Her career had always come first and relationships had come last.

Till Kedah.

Only she wasn't thinking about Kedah and scandals and the damage this might cause right now.

Instead she thought of herself and her own wants.

And she wanted her baby.

She wanted this little creation that had been made by them.

It was, for Felicia, a very instant love, for someone she knew she must protect.

And she had been told, though had never quite understood, that love was patient.

Could it be?

When she should be calling the doctor, or demanding Kedah's reaction, something told her that her baby would still be waiting on the other side.

There were other things that needed to be sorted now. It was time to focus on the job she had been hired to do.

Even though she had only known she was pregnant for an hour, right now Felicia needed to be a working mum.

Kedah's future might depend on it.

Yes, Felicia was *very* good at her job.

She went over and over their conversations and thought back to her time at the palace—it all came back to one thing.

Kedah needed to know, before he went into battle, whether or not he was the rightful Crown Prince.

Without that there could be no clear rebuttal, and if he *wasn't* his father's son…

Felicia sat in her little home study late into the afternoon. The shadows fell over her table and she was just about to put her desk lamp on when there was a knock at the door. She went down the hall, opened the door and signed for a box, which she took back to her study.

It was as if she had let in the sun, for now it streamed through the window, golden and warm. She smiled as she opened the box and took out a gorgeous basket. She looked at the contents.

There was a bottle of cognac and a glass, as well as a warmer. There was a dressing gown, silk handkerchiefs and organic honey. Felicia felt as though she was going to cry as she held lemons so perfect that they might have been chosen and hand-picked by angels.

There was everything you could possibly need if you did indeed have a cold and weren't in fact crying over Kedah.

What was it with him that he moved her so?

And not just her.

She thought of how he walked into a room and the aura Felicia felt she could see, how heads turned when he passed.

It wasn't just his beauty.

There was more.

When he gave his attention it was completely, whether it was to her or to a waiter. Kedah had a way of giving full focus, and she had never witnessed it in another.

Kedah was his father's son. Felicia was sure.

She was as certain as she could be that he had been born to be King.

But how could she prove it?

There was a note too, handwritten by him.

And this was much better than choosing from a brochure or a huge bunch of flowers.

She could imagine the courier waiting as he penned it, and knew that whatever happened she would keep it for ever—because while he made her cry in private, always he made her smile.

Felicia,

Of course you don't need a medical certificate. I was just surprised that you were sick and disappointed not to see you. Things are about to get busy, but take the time you need to get well and return when you are ready.

It would mean a lot if I could see you tomorrow before I leave for Zazinia. If not, I understand, and shall be in touch soon.

Kedah.

Clearly he needed her on form to deal with the press and believed that she really had a cold.

Yes, he could be arrogant at times, she thought, but then he was so terribly kind.

And he must never know she had fallen in love with him.

It had never been part of the deal.

CHAPTER TWELVE

FELICIA WOKE LONG before her alarm, and after showering she dressed for battle.

And it *would* be a battle to keep her true feelings from him.

But there was work to be done and finally, after a long night spent tossing and turning, she had a plan.

She went to her wardrobe and chose the white dress she had worn on the first day they had met.

It was her favourite lie.

It made her look sweet when she wasn't.

It made her appear a touch fragile when in fact she was very strong.

And she was strong enough to get through this.

She rubbed a little red lipstick into her nose and saw the redness of her eyes had gone down, so hopefully it looked as if she were at the end of a cold rather than in the throes of a broken heart.

Instead of arriving at work early she lingered over her breakfast, and then headed to a very exclusive department store and waited until its doors opened.

There she made a purchase, before going to his office where the doorman greeted her as she walked in.

'Can I help with your bags?' he offered.

'I'm fine, thank you,' she responded.

She would not let the bag and its contents out of her sight for even a moment.

It was far harder than facing the press—far harder than anything she had ever done—to walk out of the elevators with a smile and greet Anu, who looked as tearful and as anxious as Felicia felt on the inside.

'Is he in?' Felicia asked.

'He flies in a couple of hours.' Anu nodded. 'I just took a call from a reporter. He was asking for confirmation that he is flying today to Zazinia. I don't want to trouble Kedah with it, but I don't know what to say…'

'Just tell him that for security reasons you are not at liberty to discuss his movements,' Felicia answered, and then she looked at Anu's crestfallen face. 'Have some faith—Kedah will be fine.'

'You don't know that.'

'Of course I do.'

'You didn't grow up in Zazinia,' Anu said. 'The people there have always feared this. You don't know what is about to come…'

So Anu knew of the rumours, Felicia realised. Possibly the whole country did, and had been waiting for the black day when their Golden Prince was removed.

'When does he leave?'

'At midday.'

As Felicia headed towards Kedah's office Anu, the gatekeeper, stopped her. 'He said that he doesn't want to be disturbed.'

Felicia nodded, but would not be halted. 'I need to speak with him.'

She knocked on the door and when there was no response opened it. Kedah was on the phone, and he gestured for her to take a seat and then carried on speaking in Arabic for the best part of ten minutes before ending the call.

'Are you feeling better?' he checked.

'Much.' She nodded.

'Good—because the press have got hold of it already and my staff are starting to become concerned. Let them know that nothing has changed and—regarding the press—clarify, please, that it was I who called for a meeting of the Accession Council…' He stopped talking then and came around the desk. 'I didn't think you were coming in.' He went to take her in his arms. 'It's good to see you.'

Felicia pulled back. She could not take affection and also do what was required.

'Kedah, I've been thinking. Take me with you to Zazinia.'

'Felicia, I am going to be busy, and you know as well as I do that when I am there we can't do anything. Anyway, you said you'd never go back.'

'I know I did, but I'm not asking you to take me there for a romantic holiday. Kedah, if you knew for certain that you were your father's son, would it change things?'

'Of course.' He nodded. 'I am fighting blind at the moment, but…' he shook his head '…there is no way to find out unless I speak with my mother.'

'And we both know that no good can come from that.'

He didn't look convinced.

'Kedah, I've worked with people who've been caught red-handed and they'll all admit to once, but…' She shook her head. 'You need irrefutable proof—DNA testing.'

'I've told you—I couldn't get a sample without his

knowing.' Kedah pressed his fingers to the bridge of his nose. 'Soon the elders will call for one.'

'Then find out *now*.'

'Ask him?'.

'No.' Felicia shook her head. 'I doubt your father would want to know, unless forced. What if you asked him to come to your office?'

Felicia took a large box from the bag she had carried in and opened it. Along with a stunning crystal decanter and glasses there was a pair of white cotton gloves.

'I've got the buffering solution. I can prep the glass, and if he takes a drink from it I can fly straight back and have the test done. You said they already have your profile?'

Kedah nodded to that question, but then he shook his head. It could never work 'Felicia, you've seen how it is there. There is no way he would come into my office for a discussion, let alone stay long enough to have a drink. No, he would ask me to meet with him in his.'

'What if you had your office set up for a presentation?'

Kedah looked at her. 'What sort of presentation?'

'The one you've spent years working on—your hopes for Zazinia. Your vision for your country. All the plans you have made.'

All the plans that had been knocked back. 'I told you to delete that file.'

'Since when did I do as I was told?' Felicia shrugged. 'And I'm glad I watched it…'

'You watched it?'

'Of course I did.'

Of course she had, Kedah thought. This was the woman who had taken a screenshot of that article that had only briefly appeared online. He was a work project, a problem to solve, and for a while he had forgotten that.

'Aside from obtaining a DNA sample, I think it's something that your father ought to see. He needs to know what he's taking on—or turning his back on.'

Kedah had grown too used to the other side of Felicia—the softer side he sometimes glimpsed—not the very tough businesswoman she was.

And this, although private, *was* business.

The business of being royal.

'Show it to him,' Felicia said. 'We can set up for a presentation in your office and ask him to come and view it. It goes on for an hour…'

It could work, Kedah realised. By the time the Accession Council met he could know the truth.

'Whatever the result, I shall fight for my people.'

'Ah, but it will make it so much easier, Kedah, if you're able to laugh in Mohammed's face…'

'Assuming the result is the one I want.'

'And if it's not?'

'I can handle the truth, Felicia.'

Could he?

She thought of the baby within her and wondered for a brief moment if it might be better to tell him—but then, in the same instant, she changed her mind.

Kedah needed to find out who his father was before she told him that he would soon become one.

There was no question of them whiling away the flight in the bedroom.

Kedah had not only his presentation to his father to edit, but also his speech for the Accession Council to prepare.

Aside from that, Felicia didn't know if she could

risk being close to him right now without confessing her own truths.

Not just the baby, but the fact that she loved him.

So she put herself firmly into Felicia mode.

Or rather the Felicia he had first met.

She only had one robe that complied with the dress code in Zazinia, so an hour from landing she went and changed into the dusky pink one.

Her hands were shaking as she did up the row of buttons and her breath was tight in her lungs. She feared that he might come in, for she was not sure she possessed the strength not to fold to his touch.

He did not come in.

Oh, he thought about it, but he didn't dare seek oblivion now. He knew he had to keep his mind on the game.

God, but he wanted her.

'Still working that worry bead?' she teased when she came out from getting changed and saw him tapping away.

'I told you—I never worry.'

'Liar.'

'I don't worry, Felicia. I come up with solutions. I've known for a long time that one day this would happen. While the outcome might not be favourable, I've prepared for every eventuality. I'm a self-made billionaire. I'll always get by.'

He flicked the diamond across the table to her and Felicia picked it up.

'It's exquisite.'

'When my designs for Zazinia were first knocked back I spoke with Hussain. He had studied architecture with my father, and when I told him the trouble I was having he said his struggles for change had been thwarted too, and he would not let history be repeated.

He invited me to come in on a design with him in Dubai. It was my first hotel, and a stunning success. Back then I sold it. I had never had my own money. I cannot explain that…I was royal and rich, but to receive my first commission brought a freedom I had never imagined, and with the money I bought this. I know each time I look at it that, if need be, I can more than make my own way.'

'People will be hurt, Kedah, even if the result is what you want. If Mohammed discredits your mother…' Felicia had thought about that too. 'She will be okay. It would be awful for a while, but—'

'No,' Kedah interrupted. 'She would *not* be okay. She isn't strong in the way your mother is.'

Felicia looked up from the diamond she was examining. She had never heard her mother described as strong; in fact she had heard people suggest she was weak and a fool for standing by her father all those years.

'It must have taken strength of character to go through all she did,' Kedah said, and after a moment's thought Felicia nodded. 'My mother doesn't have that strength.'

It wasn't something that had ever been said outright, yet he had grown up knowing it to be true.

'I remember when my father went on that trip. His last words were, "Look after your mother."' Kedah hadn't even been three. 'My father always said it, and I always took it seriously. She is a wonderful woman, but she is emotionally fragile. All the arguments, all the politics—we do our best to keep them from her. She does so many good things for our country. She worries for the homeless and cries for them, pleads with my father to make better provision for them. She takes their hurts so personally…'

There was no easy answer.

'She'll be okay,' Felicia said again, and watched as Kedah gave a tense shrug.

Had she even listened to what he had just said? he wondered.

She had.

'Your mother *shall* be okay, Kedah, whatever happens. It sounds to me as if she has the King's love.'

Kedah nodded. 'She does.'

Rina, Felicia thought, was a lucky woman indeed.

Kedah went back and forth to his country often. Usually they were short visits, so that he didn't get embroiled in a row, but he was a regular visitor and so as he stepped out of the plane he knew what to expect.

Or he thought he did.

But this time, as Kedah stepped from the plane it was to the sound of cheering. From beyond the palace walls the people of Zazinia had gathered to cheer their Prince home.

They wanted Kedah to rule one day, and it was their way of letting the Accession Council know that he was the people's choice.

Kedah would make the better King.

'Kedah!' Rina embraced him, but she had a question to ask. 'Why now?'

'Because the elders have long wanted Mohammed and it is time to put this to rest once and for all.' He stepped back. 'I have some work to do. I shall be in my wing.'

'Kedah…' Omar came out to greet his son.

'I would like to speak with you,' Kedah told him.

'Of course,' the King agreed. 'I have much to discuss with you also. Come through to my office.'

'I would prefer that we speak in mine,' Kedah responded but Omar shook his head.

'We shall meet in mine.'

'I have something I want you to see.' Kedah refused to be dissuaded. 'I will go and prepare for you now.'

He didn't even turn his head to address Felicia.

He just summoned her in a brusque tone and gave that annoying flick of his wrist.

He offered a small bow to his parents and walked off, with Felicia a suitable distance behind him.

Up the palace steps they went, past the statue where as a child Kedah had hidden, and then past the guards and down a long corridor. Felicia understood now why he wanted these offices destroyed, for events there had caused so much pain, and possibly were about to cause more—not just for Kedah, but for his family and the people.

He closed the heavy door behind them and dealt with the projector and computer as Felicia pulled on gloves and pulled out a decanter and glasses and filled them.

'If he asks for another drink don't top it up—let him do it. You don't want anything from *you* on this glass.'

'He'll call for a maid to do it,' Kedah said. 'He is King.'

Felicia was confident that Omar would not be calling for a maid. After all, she had seen the presentation and had no doubt Omar would sit transfixed as he watched it, just as she had.

'Are you nervous?' she asked, and then went to correct herself. Of course he wasn't nervous—Kedah never was. Yet he surprised her.

'Yes.'

It was possibly the most honest he had ever been. In some ways more open than he had ever been, even in bed. She went straight over to him and as easily as that he accepted her in his arms.

Kedah took a long, steadying breath as she leant on his chest. Here, once the scene of such devastation, he found a moment of peace.

'I'm sure the result will be as you wish it to be.'

'No one has seen my work before…'

'Kedah?' She looked up to him. 'It might not count for much, but *I've* seen it and, for what it's worth, I thought it was amazing.'

He was about to say that he hadn't meant it like that—more that no one important had seen it—but then, as he stood there, holding her, it dawned on him that the presentation had been watched by someone *very* important to him.

'Did you watch it all the way through?'

'Yes.'

'And…?'

'The truth?' Felicia checked, and he nodded.

'I saw it first by mistake and I have watched it many times since. The designs are stunning, Kedah.'

'I thought you said my work was impersonal?' he teased, and Felicia looked up.

'Your vision for Zazinia isn't work.'

It was everything.

There was the sound of the guards standing to attention and, when he would have preferred to hold her for a moment longer, Kedah had no choice but to let her go.

Felicia's eyes were glassy and, rather than let him see, she busied herself, walking over to check the projector was set up correctly and that everything was in place.

And then the door opened and in came Omar the King.

'Thank you for coming,' Kedah said, and he stood proudly. He had possibly been preparing for this moment for most of his adult life. Not just the confrontation, but sharing his vision for Zazinia with his father. 'I have something I would like you to see.'

'Not without first hearing your choice.' Omar thrust a bundle of files onto Kedah's desk. 'This is a shortlist of suitable brides.'

Even though Omar spoke in Arabic, this was not something Kedah wanted to discuss with a certain person present. 'Felicia, could you excuse us, please?'

'Of course.'

Omar hadn't even noticed that a lowly assistant was present, but he simply stood until she had left and the door closed quietly behind her.

Kedah broke the silence.

'If I choose a bride, then I shall have your full support at the Accession Council tomorrow?' he checked, and then let out a mirthless laugh at his father's lack of response.

He knew for certain that his father was bluffing, for he saw a rare nervous swallow from him as he reached for the files as if to peruse them.

'I need to know that, once I'm married, I shall have your approval to make the necessary changes…'

'First things first,' Omar said.

'Isn't that what *your* father said to *you*?' Kedah asked. 'Choose a bride, produce an heir, and *then* we can talk?'

Omar did not respond.

'Yet nothing got done, and all these years later still there is little progress in Zazinia…'

'I ensured an improved education system,' Omar interjected. 'I pushed for that.' Yet both men knew that he had pushed for little more. 'The King did not want change,' Omar said.

'What about *this* King?' Kedah asked, but again there was no response. 'Please,' Kedah said, 'have a seat.'

He dimmed the lights in the office and took a seat himself as the presentation commenced.

Kedah looked over to his father, but the King gave no comment—though he did, Kedah noted, take a sip of his drink. And, while that was supposed to be the reason they were there, suddenly his father's reaction to the presentation was more important to Kedah.

Felicia had been right. His father needed to see this.

And there it all played out.

Like golden snakes, roads wove across the screen and bridges did what they were designed to—bridged. Access was given to the remote west, where the poorest people fought to survive, and somehow it all connected.

Schools and hospitals appeared, and within the animation teachers, doctors and nurses walked. There were animated children too, playing in parks. Now, hotels rose, and there were pools. Restaurants and cafés appeared on bustling evening streets.

And the King sat in silence.

Kedah watched as his father took a drink, and another, yet made no comment. An hour later, when an animated sun had set on a very different Zazinia from the one they knew and the presentation had ended, it was Omar who stood and opened up the drapes.

Still he offered no comment. Omar just stared out to the golden desert beyond and it was Kedah who spoke.

'That is what you deny your people. All this is achievable and yet you do nothing…'

'No—'

'Yes,' Kedah refuted. 'Turn around and tell me that Mohammed would make the better Crown Prince.'

Omar did not.

'Turn around and tell me that you don't want a glittering future for our people.'

'That is enough, Kedah,' Omar said, but Kedah had not finished yet.

He picked up the files and held them out for his father. 'As I said to you when I was eighteen, you shall not force me to take a bride. I will never be pushed into something that is not of my choice. If you want me gone then say so, but let us stop pretending that it has anything to do with my choosing a wife.'

Kedah tossed the files down on the desk in frustration as again his father said nothing. He simply walked out.

He had shown his father his best—the very best of his vision, all that he hoped to achieve—and his father had offered no comment.

Felicia was startled when the office door opened unexpectedly. She did not receive any greeting from the very angry King who stalked past.

She had been seated at the very desk where years ago Kedah had once hidden, and now she took the same steps that he had at three years old—though she opened the door with greater ease.

'How was it?'

Kedah shrugged. 'Hopeless.'

'He didn't have a drink?' Felicia checked, and then Kedah remembered the real reason for the meeting.

He looked over to his father's glass, which was empty.

'I meant that the presentation was hopeless. He's never going to change his mind.'

Felicia pulled on her gloves and popped the glass into a clear bag, and then another, then placed it in her purse. On the desk she saw that there were some photos of dark-haired and dark-eyed beauties. One of them, no doubt, would be his bride.

Kedah was too incensed by his father's lack of response to notice where her gaze fell. His mind was on other things. 'What am I fighting for?' Kedah asked, and for the briefest moment he wavered where he had always been resolute. 'Am I the only one who wants change?'

'Your people want it also,' Felicia said. 'I heard them cheering you, Kedah.'

She was right—it wasn't just his ego that insisted he could do things better than his brother. And after his father's pale reaction to the presentation it was as if she blew the wind back into his sails.

'I am going to speak again with Mohammed,' Kedah said.

'Do so,' Felicia agreed. 'I'm going to head back to London.'

She was meeting a courier at Heathrow, who would take the glass to a laboratory where the samples would be analysed.

'I'll call you as soon as I get the results.'

And this was it, she realised. It was the very last time she would be in Zazinia—for certainly she would not travel here as his PA once Kedah had chosen his bride.

'Don't leave now.'

Kedah stood and came around the desk. He felt her resistance when he took her in his arms.

His fingers went to her chin and he lifted her face to meet his gaze. He was going to kiss her, she realised. Right now, when she was doing all she could not to break down.

'I have to go.'

'Not yet.'

His mouth was fierce and claiming, and she tasted salt at the back of her throat as she squeezed her eyes closed and held on to the tears he must never see her shed.

'Not here,' she said.

'Yes, here.'

He did not want her gone.

He could not picture the future. He just wanted a moment of the oblivion that they created together. So he did what Abdal should have done all those years ago.

Felicia stood as he walked over and turned the lock on the door.

Kedah turned her on in a way no one else ever had or ever would. He tossed his sword to the floor and was opening his robe as he walked back towards her.

His passion was so fierce and overpowering. His hands were at the buttons of her robe and he was holding back from tearing it open.

And she loathed herself for wanting him so badly.

Even with his future wife's photo on the desk she would do this. She *would*, Felicia decided as he lifted her onto the desk. Now, while she didn't know his wife's name, she would be taken for the last time.

His hands ruched up the skirt of her robe and lifted it over her thighs, and perhaps Kedah was aware that this was the last time because impatient fingers were tearing at the buttons.

She had to walk out of this office soon, so she tried to assist him. But the buttons gave way so that her legs and chest were exposed and he pulled down the cups of her bra. There was no time to take off her knickers. His erection moved the slip of fabric aside and he stabbed into her.

Felicia sobbed as he filled her.

Their mouths were frantic and bruising in their fast, urgent coupling.

He thrust hard, then pressed her so the desk was hard against her back and her hair splayed out. Now he tore at her knickers, and the sight of them, of himself deep inside her, almost made him come. It was intense, it was fast, and as he scooped her up her legs wrapped around him and she bit his shoulder to fight the scream as her body beat with his.

And it could never be over—and yet it was.

He was lowering her down, and she rested her burning face against his chest and listened for the last time to his heart. She told herself that she would never succumb to this bliss again.

'Felicia…'

She peeled herself from him and started to do up her robe. She wanted to be away from Zazinia, in the safety of the plane and then back in London. There she could sort out her head.

'I'd better get going.'

'In a moment. But first…'

'Kedah, the plane is waiting—there's a courier at the other end. If there's to be any hope of getting the results back in time…'

'Can't you stop thinking about work?'

'You *are* work, Kedah.'

Felicia took a mirror from her bag and ran a comb through her hair, and she saw her own lips start to tremble as he spoke on.

'In that case, if all goes well, then I am going to be spending a lot more time here in Zazinia. I will need someone to help with my overseas investments, and there will be an opening for an executive assistant…'

And briefly she allowed herself to glimpse it—an amazing career, a stunning flat and a night with Kedah whenever time allowed. A part-time father…yet she would be his full-time mistress…

She snapped the compact mirror closed and managed to sneer as she faced him 'You mean an executive *whore*?'

'Felicia…'

'I have to go.'

She really did—because otherwise she would say yes to him. If she stayed for just a few moments longer she would accept his crumbs.

'I'm going to go.'

'Of course.' He nodded.

'I hope you get the result that you're hoping for.'

And they were through.

She had but one more smile left in her, and she gave it to him now as she held up her bag.

'My work here is done,' she said.

'No,' Kedah said. 'You will be back in the office tomorrow. I employed you to look out for my people. This was…' He hesitated. 'A personal favour. Thank you.'

He could not quite believe that she knew. That he had asked for and received her help.

'I trust you, Felicia.'

And she waited for him to warn her, to remind her

that if she let him down then she would be dealt with 'outside the law', but there was no postscript.

'I hope it all goes well,' she said.

And maybe he shouldn't trust her, because right then she had lied—for there was a part of her that *didn't* want him to be Crown Prince.

No.

She wanted what was best for him.

'Hey, Kedah?' Felicia said. 'For what it's worth…' This was the hardest thing she had ever said, the least selfish words she had ever spoken, because she was very good at her job, and she could see another route even if the news for Kedah was not good. 'It's very hard to dissuade a loyal public.'

Kedah frowned.

'Your people know the rumours and yet they still cheered you home. Whatever the result, you can still fight.'

She walked out and she saw that Mohammed was deep in conversation with Kumu at the end of the long corridor. When he saw Felicia approaching Mohammed stalked off, leaving Kumu by the large statue at the top of the stairs.

'Are you leaving?' Kumu asked, for she had heard that Kedah's jet had been prepared to fly out and Mohammed had asked her to glean more information.

'Yes…' Felicia smiled politely, about to carry on down the stairs. But even if Kedah wouldn't let her help, it didn't mean she couldn't try. And so she paused and turned around. 'It's a relief, actually,' she said in a low voice, as if confiding a secret.

'A relief?' Kumu frowned, a little taken aback but curious.

'I always worry that I'll say the wrong thing,' Felicia admitted.

'The wrong thing?'

'You're very used to royalty…' Felicia sighed. 'It's just all so new to me. I keep worrying that I'm going to mess things up. I mean, King Omar has been perfectly kind, and he seems lovely—you just have to see how devoted he is to his wife to know that. Even so, I would *hate* to be the one to offend him.' She gave Kumu an eye roll. 'I mean, after all, he *is* the King.'

Kedah walked out of his office just in time to see the very end of a conversation between Kumu and Felicia, and almost instantly he doubted his thought process. Now Felicia was smiling and walking down the stairs, as confident as ever. Kumu, on the other hand, stood looking worried and clearly more than a little perplexed.

She hurried off, but Kedah's attention was no longer on Kumu. Instead he was looking again at Felicia.

Her slender frame packed a punch even from this distance. Confident, collected, she walked towards the grand entrance and nodded for the guards to open the doors. In her bag was the glass, the answer, but that wasn't all that was on Kedah's mind.

Yes, he would have to select a bride—and, given her response, that meant this was the end.

They were over—just as he had told her from the start that they would be.

'Felicia…'

The Queen called out to her as Felicia walked to the car.

'Your Majesty?'

'You're leaving already?'

'Yes, Kedah needs me to go back to London.'

The Queen frowned, for she had rather thought Kedah might need someone on his side here, for when the Accession Council met.

Felicia was driven the short distance to the private jet, which she boarded. It felt so odd to be there without him. Over the last few months they had flown together on many occasions.

The plane felt lonely without him.

Her *life* would from this point on.

'There's a slight delay getting clearance,' the steward informed her. 'It shouldn't be too long.'

But Felicia could no longer hold it in.

'I'll be in the bedroom. Call me when we're ready to take off.'

Felicia headed to the bedroom suite and lay on the bed and allowed the tears to come.

Oh, and they did come.

Except the slight delay wasn't in order to get clearance from Air Traffic Control—it was caused by a certain Crown Prince who did not like it that she had gone.

He was thinking of her on the long flight to London when, in truth, he would far rather she was here. For a moment he even considered the possibility of someone else taking the glass to have it tested.

But, no, that couldn't work. It would mean involving another person, and Kedah wanted it kept just between them.

She was crying too hard to hear her phone, but then there was a knock at the door.

'Kedah wishes to speak with you,' the steward informed her, and gestured to a phone by the bed.

Felicia furiously wiped away her tears and blew her nose before picking up.

'Hello?'

'Hey,' Kedah said.

'What do you want?'

Kedah had been about to talk dirty, to tell her to get back this minute, or maybe to be honest and tell her he wasn't ready to let her go. Then he heard her slightly thick voice and knew that unless Felicia had the most rapid-onset cold in medical history she was crying.

Which meant she'd been crying that other time. He knew that now.

It would seem that she did have a heart after all.

'How long will the results take?' he asked, and Felicia frowned.

Why would he ask when they'd already been through this numerous times?

'Overnight,' she answered. 'The results will be couriered to your office, hopefully by lunchtime in the UK.' Which would be late afternoon in Zazinia—just a few hours before the Accession Council met.

A few hours before he was expected to choose his bride.

'Felicia?'

'I think we're about to take off,' she lied. 'Speak soon, Kedah.'

CHAPTER THIRTEEN

KEDAH WAS VERY used to women falling for him.

He *wasn't* used to them proudly walking away.

He looked at the slight chaos their lovemaking had created and righted the crystal decanter that had toppled over. Then his eyes took in the files and the photos of the women his father wanted him to choose from.

Felicia had seen them, he was certain.

Their lovemaking had been fierce and angry, and now possibly he understood a little more why.

Yet she had known all along that he was to marry and had seemed fine with it.

Possibly she wasn't so assured after all.

Even though he generally didn't use it, Kedah was tempted to summon the royal jet, so he could be in London, or nearly there, when she landed. He needed to speak with her—he wanted to know what her tears meant exactly.

He needed space, and so he walked along the pristine white beach. Suddenly everything had changed.

Always he had wanted to be King; he had spent his life knowing it could be taken away and protecting himself from that possibility. Now, when the coming days should have his full attention, when he should be devoting every thought to the potential battle ahead, he was staring up at the sky that carried her.

He *had* chosen wisely.

Kedah had protected all the people he loved and cared for in this. Tomorrow, when the press were crawling and the staff were afraid, he would ensure that the best of the best knew his business inside out.

He knew Felicia could face this crisis.

In these past months she had crept into his heart, and now she belonged there so absolutely that it had taken her leaving to expose the fact.

And her tears made him believe that she loved him too.

What to do?

Omar stood in his own office, looking out on Zazinia and thinking of the presentation his eldest son had just shown him. He saw Kedah walking along the beach alone. As always, he cut an impressive figure, but for once his son's stride was not purposeful, and instead of looking out to the land he so loved Omar saw Kedah pause and gaze out to the ocean and the sky.

The King did not turn his head when the door opened and Rina stepped into his office. Instead he focused on his eldest son. There was a pensive air to him, and the set of his shoulders showed he carried a weight that was a heavy one.

Kedah was the rightful Crown Prince. Omar knew that.

Yes, the road ahead might be easier if he followed the elders' wishes and stood behind his younger son, but it would be the wrong decision.

He turned his head a little as Rina came in and walked over to stand by his side. She stood quietly beside him, watching their son, who cut a proud and lonely figure as he walked.

'Felicia just left,' Rina said.

'Felicia?' Omar frowned, for he had no idea who his wife was referring to.

'Kedah says she is his PA, but I am certain there is more to it.'

'Nothing can come of it. There are many brides that would be far more suitable.'

Omar's response was instant, but then he felt his wife's hand on his shoulder.

'I am sure plenty say the same about me,' Rina said. 'There are many who don't consider *me* suitable.'

So rarely did they touch on that long-ago painful time.

'You are a wonderful queen.'

'*Now* I am,' Rina agreed.

Omar turned and looked again to his son, and he recalled himself striding into the office brandishing files on potential brides. He hoped Felicia had been unable to understand what he had said.

'Kedah showed me a presentation that he has been working on,' Omar said. 'It was very beautiful. In fact, it reminded me of my dreams for Zazinia.' He looked out to the city. 'He has a gift.'

'So do you.'

'Perhaps, but I could not express it properly to my father. Of course back then we did not have the technology to make such a presentation…'

'Nothing would have swayed your father,' Rina said. 'Remember how you tried?'

Omar nodded.

'And then you stopped trying.'

'I chose to focus on the things I *could* change,' Omar said. 'I wanted my bride to be happy. And you weren't.'

'But I am now,' she said. 'And I am much stronger for your love. I shall always have that.'

And then Rina was the bravest she had ever been.

'Come what may.'

Still, even now, they could not properly discuss her infidelity—and not just because of pride or shame, but also because walls might have ears and whispers might multiply.

'Speak to your eldest son, Omar. Now. Before it is too late. Offer him your full support.'

Rina stood after Omar had left and tears were streaming down her face. Oh, she knew how her husband and eldest son protected her, but she was a *good* queen and it was time for the people to come first.

And Rina had not lied.

She *was* stronger for her King's love.

Nothing could take that from her. Even if the law dictated that Omar must shame and divorce her, still she would have his love.

'Kedah?' Omar caught up with son. 'Can I walk with you?'

'Of course,' Kedah answered.

'Your presentation left me speechless. I had never considered using murals on the east-facing walls. It would be an incredible sight.'

'They could tell the tale of our history,' Kedah said. 'Of course scaffolding would be required to shield the beach during construction…'

'We are not at war now,' Omar said. 'Those rules were put in place at a time when the palace risked invasion. I pointed that out to my father many years ago…'

He gave a low laugh. 'You are like a mirror image of me. When I see your visions it is like looking at my own designs…'

Kedah turned in brief surprise. 'We are nothing alike.'

'Not in looks,' Omar said. 'But we think the same.'

Kedah did not believe it. His father was staid and old-fashioned in his ways.

But Omar pressed on.

'You were right to challenge me in the office. When I studied architecture with Hussain we had such grand plans. My father said that once I had married he would listen to my thoughts. I returned from my honeymoon with so many plans and dreams. Your mother was already pregnant with you, and I can remember us walking along this very beach, talking of the schools and the hospitals that would soon be built. Your mother, being your mother, looked forward to the hotels and the shops. They were such exciting times. There was such an air of hope amongst the people. But even by the time you were born those dreams had died.'

'How?'

'My father preferred his own rules.'

For a moment they stopped walking.

Even though the old King was dead it was almost a forbidden conversation.

'He had always said that when I was married—when I was officially Crown Prince—then I could have input. And so I married. I chose a bride from a progressive country.'

'For that reason only?' Kedah checked.

'He was just delaying things, though. By the time you were born I knew he would never listen to what I had to say. It was a very difficult time…' Omar admitted. 'I was young and proud and I had promised your mother so many things—she had come from a modern country and I wanted the same. I wanted our people to prosper from our wealth too, but my hands were tied. I became very angry and bitter. I spent all my time trying to convince my father to listen to my ideas—travelling with him, pointing out how progressive other countries were. Your mother was in a foreign country with a new baby, but I had no time for either of you…'

They walked in silence as Omar remembered that difficult trip away, and coming home to a grim palace and a wife who had been utterly distraught.

And then had come her confession.

And as Omar remembered the past Kedah better understood his parents, for he could envisage how undermined his father would have felt. For a little while he pondered how he might feel, bringing Felicia here, to a land full of promises that did not come true.

'You have a good marriage now,' Kedah commented.

'We have worked hard to achieve that.' Omar nodded. 'I had been so caught up in my own ego that I forgot what it must be like for your mother…alone in a new country, with no one to speak of her problems with…'

Except Abdal.

'When did you realise you loved her?' Kedah asked—not just because he was curious about his parents' marriage, but because it was a question from his own heart. Suddenly he could not bear to envisage a future without Felicia. Their conversations, their laughter, their occasional rows…he just could not see himself doing those things with anyone else. And yet she was flying further away from him with each moment that passed.

'When?' he asked again, for his father was lost in thought.

Omar was thinking back to the day Rina had confessed what had taken place and his reaction.

'The moment I realised I could lose her,' Omar answered. 'It was then I knew I was in love.'

Perhaps they were not so different after all.

'Your grandfather was not a fan of your mother. He seemed to think I would do better to take another bride.'

Nothing was said outright, but both knew the rumours were finally being addressed.

Kedah could see how things might have happened. Perhaps he understood his mother more. And yet he realised it was not *his* forgiveness that his mother needed.

It was the forgiveness of the man he looked to now.

'Not only did I not want to lose her, Kedah, I was scared for her also.'

Kedah looked at him, and it was then he knew that he was his father's son.

They had the same fears for a vibrant, impetuous woman.

Kedah had never admired his father more, for it took a strong king to be a loving one too—especially when wronged.

'How did you resolve things?' he asked, for he needed his father's wisdom.

'I accepted that my time would one day come and I went back to concentrating on my family. All that time I'd spent fruitlessly clashing with my father I had neglected your mother—and you…'

Here was a man who was far stronger than Kedah had given him credit for.

'You have the same visions I once did,' Omar said. 'But I am older now. I need support. And I do not want you to have to wait, as I did, to make changes. That is not good for the people. Your presentation has reminded me of my own fire. Together we could change things. But there is Mohammed and the elders to consider…'

'You are King.'

'Yes, but there is your mother…'

And Kedah thought of Felicia's words. His mother would be okay. After all, she had the King's love.

'Together,' Kedah said, 'we can protect her.'

So much was said without words.

'But there is a condition,' Kedah said to his father. 'I shall choose my own bride.'

'Perhaps we could wait until after the Accession Council meets?' Omar suggested, for he was quite sure who Kedah's choice would be—which would make for an even more difficult meeting.

But Kedah, now that his decision was made, could no longer wait.

He excused himself from his father and walked into the palace. As he did so he saw Mohammed walking into his office with Fatiq.

'Mohammed.' Kedah followed him in. 'We need to speak.' He didn't even look over to Fatiq as he addressed him. 'Please leave.'

'You can say what you have to in front of Fatiq,' Mohammed told him.

'Very well.'

The timbre of Kedah's voice was so ominous that Mohammed's hand moved to the hilt of his sword as his elder brother strode towards him.

'Know this. It is very hard to dissuade loyal people… If I am forced to I will take the decision to them and I know I will win.'

'Not if we call for—'

'I don't give a damn about some test that was invented ten minutes ago compared with the rich history of our land. I was born to be King, I was raised to be King. And if I have to I shall take it to the people. Tomorrow my father shall offer his full support for his eldest son, and I hope he shall also announce that I have chosen my bride—Felicia.'

There was a hiss of breath from Fatiq at his side, but instead of an angry response Mohammed gave a black smile.

'The elders would never accept her…'

'They will have no choice.' Omar came in then. 'I will offer my full support.' He glared at the feuding duo. 'Your mother is on her way.'

Rina arrived then, with Kumu.

'Kedah, your father tells me you have exciting news…'

'I *hope* to have exciting news.'

'But Felicia does not understand our ways…the people…' Kumu, who rarely spoke, did so now.

'Felicia understands *people*,' Kedah said. 'Full stop.'

'And our people would adore to see their Crown Prince happy.' Rina smiled. 'Just so long as you are married here.'

'I haven't asked her yet,' Kedah said. 'I think it's a bit early to be speaking of wedding plans.'

'It's never too early,' Rina said.

'And I happen to like a good English wedding,' Omar mused.

And then, just as Kedah was about to roll his eyes and excuse himself, his father took his wife's hand and spoke on.

'What is it they say in the English service? Speak now or for ever hold your peace?'

Omar was looking directly at Mohammed as he said it, and there was challenge in his tone.

Never had Kedah admired his father more.

His father.

Kedah no longer needed proof, for Omar stood proud and strong and he maintained his sovereignty.

'Do you have anything you would like to say, Mohammed?' Omar enquired.

His son blinked.

'Come on, Mohammed.' Kumu pulled at his arm. 'We should go and check on the children.'

Mohammed stood there. They all watched and waited, but it was Kedah who walked off.

He had rather more important things on his mind than waiting for his brother to speak…

Or for ever hold his peace.

CHAPTER FOURTEEN

THERE WAS NO thanking God that it was Friday.

Felicia had deposited the sample at midnight and now all she could do was wait.

Kedah had told her to go in to work as usual. The one thing she didn't have to worry about was money. Felicia had worked hard for many years and commanded an impressive wage. But work was still important to her and, like it or not, Kedah was her boss.

Yes, her boss.

Somehow she had turned into a real PA.

She had rescheduled her meeting with Vadia and knew they would be talking at ten. Before that she had to liaise with the manager at the Dubai hotel and arrange for some signatures from the surveyor.

Felicia chose a boxy little grey suit. She usually saved it for court appearances, but she could use a little power dressing today.

Felicia came out of the underground and walked towards the office, but instead of seeing the doorman smiling at her, she saw he was obscured by the gathered press.

Felicia watched as poor Anu got out of her husband's car and shielded her face.

Finally, after three months, Felicia was being put to

work. *This* was the reason she was here and the reason she had been hired, she realised as she stepped in and faced the cameras.

'The proposed hotel in Dubai—will it still go ahead?'

'How will this affect the European branch?'

'Is the Crown Prince stepping aside willingly or is he being forced to stand down?'

Questions were coming from every angle, and Felicia stood there as the microphones and cameras clamoured for a response and did what she did best.

She smiled.

Widely.

'Of course I'll take your questions,' she said, and proceeded to answer them in turn. 'I'm actually just about to speak with the surveyor. Absolutely the sister hotel will be going ahead.'

'Sister?'

'Yes, I believe the new complex is going to focus more on holidaymakers than the business traveller. Next?'

Kedah watched the live stream and knew he had been so right to hire her.

His employees could not be in better hands. She was taking the edge off the fear that would be sweeping through his empire today.

One by one she answered the questions and then, for Felicia, came the hardest of them all.

'Is it correct that his marriage will be announced later today?'

Kedah watched her closely for her response.

It was flawless.

'I'm more than happy to answer, where I can, your questions about the business side of things, but I would never comment on the Sheikh's personal life without his authority.'

'You *must* know...'

'I'm his PA.' Felicia smiled. 'Certainly he doesn't report to *me*.'

With question time over, she smiled at the relieved doorman, who held the door open for her, and took the elevator to the offices on the top floor.

Anu was crying as she walked in, and Felicia knew exactly why she had been hired.

Not for the press but for his staff.

Kedah had made provisions for them even on his darkest day.

'He'll be fine,' she assured Anu.

'You say that for the cameras,' Anu wept. 'But what if they choose Mohammed? Zazinia needs Kedah. We all want him to one day be King. Even when he was a little boy everyone adored him so much, but never more than now.'

And Felicia adored him too.

Which was why, when her heart was breaking, she kept on working. She fired back responses to emails from worried managers and investors the world over, she took phone calls and video calls, and she even managed to hold her composure when Vadia stuck a virtual knife through her heart.

'Whatever the outcome of the Accession Council meeting, there will be an announcement from the palace later tonight as to his chosen bride.'

It was a hellish Friday, made harder when a courier arrived and she had to sign for a plain package. She opened it, and inside there was a thick cream envelope. And, for all that today had been hard, now it tipped into agony.

She blew her nose and put on lip gloss before calling him. She forced her mouth into a smile as she waited for him to answer, because one of the assertiveness courses she had been to had told her it forced a happier and more confident tone.

No matter how fake.

'Hey,' Felicia said at the delicious sound of his voice. 'Your results just arrived.'

'What are you doing?' Kedah asked. 'How has it been?'

'Not too bad. A lot of press and a little bit of panic from some quarters, but it's dying down now.'

'Good.'

'When do the Accession Council meet?' Felicia asked, wondering why he didn't have her tearing the envelope open now.

'An hour or so,' he said, as if it hardly mattered. 'I want to ask you something. What did you say to Kumu on the stairs? She hasn't been quite the same since!'

Felicia let out a low chuckle. 'I just pointed out that, as nice as your father is, he's still King and he clearly loves his wife. I said that I'd *hate* to offend him.'

He laughed, and then he was serious. 'Are you going to open it?'

'Sure,' she said. 'I'm just going to put you down.'

She placed the phone on the desk and put him on speaker, and then she took out a letter opener and sliced open the envelope.

Kedah listened carefully. There were no sniffles or heavy breathing. Felicia was indeed tough.

'Congratulations, Your Royal Highness.'

She smiled, and it was a genuine one.

No, she didn't want him to be King—but that was a selfish wish. She was also terribly pleased for him.

'Go get 'em,' she said.

'Hey, Felicia…?'

'I have to go, Kedah,' she said.

'You can talk for a moment.'

'No.' She smiled again. 'I really do have to go. Good luck!'

Absolutely she had to go. Because she was starting to break down.

He didn't need to know as he went into a fight for the throne that she loved him and would do so for ever. And neither did he need to be sideswiped by the news that she was pregnant.

In time she would tell him—somehow.

Yet she knew she was tough and could raise their child alone.

She thought of all the people who loved their Prince and needed change.

She just needed a moment to cry. And she put her head in her hands and sat at her desk to weep in a way she never had.

Oh, Felicia had cried before—of course she had—but she sobbed now.

There was no need to worry about Anu hearing, for Felicia's sobs were deep and quiet and racked her body. She wrapped her arms around herself, scared that if she let go she might fall apart.

She was so deep in grief that she didn't hear the door open.

'Felicia…'

His voice stilled her.

Kedah had been sure of her love, but as he'd watched her on the live stream and heard her speak on the phone moments before she had sounded so composed that for a moment his certainty had wavered.

She looked up, stood up, and there were so many questions.

'You should be there…' she said, and there was no way to hide her tears so she ran to him.

He held her tight in his arms and Kedah knew he had been right to return when he had. Sometimes you had to look after those you loved first.

'I'm not needed there. My father will go in and tell them who is the rightful Crown Prince…' He held her closer. 'But I *am* needed here…'

He kissed her, and there were so many things that he wanted to say, but right now not one of them mattered.

It was a kiss so deep and so passionate that it should never have ended, and yet there were too many things she needed to know.

And Kedah too.

'Were you crying the morning I called you and you said that you had a cold?'

Felicia nodded.

'I have spoken with my father. I have told him that I have chosen my bride…'

And as she winced, as she braced herself to hear the chosen name, he pulled out a diamond that was familiar. He told her that soon it would be mounted on gold and worn on her finger.

'Every time I looked at this I knew I would be okay, and I want the same for you…'

The diamond had reassured him that come what may he would be taken care of, and in handing it over to Felicia he afforded her the same reassurance.

'Marry me?'

Never in her wildest dreams had she thought she might hear those words from Kedah.

Liar.

Had his driver been there he might have stood and applauded—and, yes, she might have joined in. For, yes, in her wildest dreams she *had* hoped that one day he would say those words, that there might somehow be hope for them.

'I didn't want you to be your father's son.' It was a terrible confession to make. 'I feel so guilty, because I've been hoping and wishing that you weren't because then there might be a chance for *us*...'

'I make my own chances, Felicia, and there is no need to feel guilty. I am glad that you wanted a chance for us.' He thought back to Mohammed's cruel words. 'It is wonderful that you love me whether or not I might one day be King.'

It would make her a princess, who would one day be Queen, and an extremely worrying thought occurred.

'Kedah, there's going to be the most terrible scandal...' Even if they married this week there would always be a question over the dates. 'I'm pregnant...'

She was starting to panic, for no spin doctor could fix this—no dates could be changed—and it would be she, Felicia, who brought discredit to his name.

Yet Kedah smiled. 'Really?'

'I took a test. They're going to know that we...'

'Felicia.' Kedah still smiled. 'If my people are going to be shocked that we have slept together, that I am not a virgin, then they don't know me at all.'

He made her laugh through her tears.

'But they *do* know me, and they care for me—just as they will care for you.'

'You're not cross?'

'Cross? I am stunned, I am thrilled and I am scared that you might not have told me.'

'I was trying to work out how.'

'Together we will sort out our problems,' he said. 'And right now I can't see that we have any. Can you?'

Felicia thought for a moment, but not long and hard.

Oh, there would surely be problems, but they would deal with them together.

She could cope with anything.

After all, she had Kedah's love.

EPILOGUE

SHE WOULD ALWAYS express her opinion.

Though occasionally, Felicia conceded, only to herself, she did get it wrong.

His work was stunning, and nowhere more so than here in the palace.

There were now no offices in the Crown Prince's wing. Kedah had indeed had them torn down. They had been replaced by walls of soft stone from the quarries, and a trickling noise lined them, coming from the soft fountains from a deep spring the diviner had found.

The sound soothed both Felicia and the baby she sat with this dawn. It felt as if she was sitting in a blissful sanctuary.

'You've got a big day today,' Felicia said to her daughter.

Yes, they had been gifted with a little girl.

She had been born eight months ago, and her public appearances since then had been brief. She had been tiny enough to sleep through them, but she was bigger now—a bit more dramatic and clingy. Felicia was worried about how she would react to the crowds.

Kaina.

It meant both *female* and *leader*, and her name spoke of another of the changes that had been made.

She would one day be Queen of this magnificent land. But for now she was just a baby who really needed to sleep—except she had other ideas.

Kaina's long eyelashes were just closing when the gap in the half-open door widened, and Felicia watched as her daughter's little head turned.

'She was nearly asleep,' Felicia said as the baby smiled and wriggled and held out her arms.

'Go back to bed,' Kedah said as he took their daughter from her, for Felicia had been up for ages and he knew that she was worried about today.

'She's been fed,' Felicia said. 'She just won't settle.'

'Go back to bed,' he said again. 'I'll get her to sleep.'

He didn't suggest calling the royal nanny. Felicia was having none of that. And neither did their daughter sleep in a separate wing from her parents.

Times had finally changed, she thought as she climbed into their magnificent bed and closed her eyes.

And the landscape had changed also.

Kedah held his daughter and watched as the sun started to rise over Zazinia. A hotel had already been built and it was the most stunning building—his proudest work. No windows looked to the palace. Instead there was a beautiful mural that told some of the history of Zazinia. And close to the hotel in the modern city he was creating were the beginnings of a hospital, built with stone from the quarries of Zazinia but gleaming and modern inside. It was already functioning, but it would be a couple more years until it was complete.

'Today,' Kedah said, and he spoke in a low voice to his daughter, 'there are going to be a lot of people cheering and making noise…'

He didn't tell her that she was to behave and not cry. Of course Kaina was too young to understand, but there were other rules he had changed. Kaina would be herself, and go to school with her peers.

He looked down at his precious daughter, who was finally asleep, and walked out of the dark sanctuary and placed her in her crib.

There were no portraits on the wall as he walked back to his suite.

They were for the formal corridors now.

Here was home.

And home was a palace, and today the people would gather to see their beloved royals.

'You're going to be fine,' Kedah said to Felicia, who was very nervous.

Oh, she had faced angry press many times in her past, but facing these people was different. The men she had represented in the past had meant absolutely nothing to her.

This man did.

Her robe was that certain shade of green which brought out the best in her eyes, and Kedah had chosen white for today. He looked sultry and sexy, and the only thing marriage had done to tone him down was to direct all that passion to one woman.

'Felicia!'

Rina was chatting to Mohammed and Kumu as Felicia approached, but she was overtaken by a tiny little boy who had just found his feet.

'Abi…'

He called for his father and Felicia watched as Mohammed's austere face broke into a smile as his youngest son toddled over and Mohammed scooped him up.

For Mohammed was his father's son also.

When he had accepted that there was nothing he

could do to change the lineage, instead of plotting bitterly he had chosen to focus on what he could do best. He had always loved his wife and children, and now he let it show.

And he had worked with Kedah to build a new Zazinia, and Kedah respected his brother's sage advice.

'I like it that the portraits are here by the main balcony…' Rina said. 'My husband hated standing for his. And look at Kedah!' Rina suddenly laughed. 'He looks nothing like the rest of them…'

Oblivious.

Rina had been coddled, shielded from the fact that everyone knew her secret—the terrible mistake she had made many years ago. To this day she thought only her husband knew about that week many years ago, when Omar had been away, and lost and lonely she had turned to the wrong man for comfort. But he had brought none.

'Really,' Rina said, with all the assuredness of someone who had *not* been having an affair around conception time, 'Kedah doesn't even look related. He takes after my side of the family, of course…'

And Felicia caught Kumu's eyes and both women shared a smile.

They loved Queen Rina. Yes, she was dramatic and flaky, but she was also the kindest woman—even if at times she ran a little wild.

Like her eldest son.

'We should go out now,' Omar said.

The King loathed these formal moments. His whole life had been spent being told to behave or to keep his family in check.

Today they all walked out to loud cheers.

Kaina was startled, and Felicia hushed her, but of course she started to cry.

'Give her to me,' Rina said. 'So you can wave. It is you they all want to see.'

No, it wasn't.

The crowd cheered as their lovely Queen took the little baby, and they cheered more loudly on seeing Omar looking so happy and relaxed.

And then they called out for Kedah.

He waved and he smiled. He was so proud of his lovely wife, and the people just adored him.

They loved the way he came down to the quarries and spoke with the workers, how when the hospital had opened he had stayed for hours to meet with the staff.

Kaina was really crying now, and refused to be held in Rina's arms. Kedah took his daughter and held her so she was sitting on his hip. And Kaina, safe in her daddy's arms, buried her face in his chest.

But then she peeked out.

To see all the people.

There were so many that she put her little hand over her eyes, so she didn't have to see them, and then she put her hand down and saw they were still there.

And they were laughing.

So she put her hand over her eyes again.

Oh, indeed she was her father's daughter.

She was playing peekaboo with the crowd, and from this day on she would hold them in the palm of her hand.

'You,' Kedah said to little Kaina as they headed inside, 'were amazing.'

The nanny came and took her. Kaina would go and play rather than sit through a long formal lunch.

There was an hour, though, before they had to be seated, and Felicia wandered off to stand by the portraits.

The old artist was working on a portrait of little Kaina now.

All the portraits fascinated her, but one especially so.

She didn't turn as Kedah joined her. 'You *are* smiling.'

'No.'

They had argued about it often, but there amongst the stern faces of Crown Princes of old, she knew one stood out—and not just because of his attire. There was a certain Mona Lisa smile on Kedah's face, though he repeatedly denied it.

'Yes, you are,' Felicia insisted.

'I like your robe.' He did his best to change the subject. 'I love that shade of green.'

'I know you do.'

'We have forty minutes before we have to go through. Perhaps we should check on Kaina.'

'Kaina's fine.'

'We could make sure,' he said, and then he looked up at the portrait and conceded defeat. 'I was thinking of *you*,' he said in her ear, and Felicia resisted turning. 'And what had happened on the plane.'

She turned then, and looked into the eyes of the only man she had ever loved.

'Come on,' Kedah said.

There was love to be made.

* * * * *

THE SULTAN DEMANDS HIS HEIR

MAYA BLAKE

CHAPTER ONE

THE SULTAN DEMANDS HIS HEIR

MAYA BLAKE

[illegible] natural [illegible] had [illegible]

[illegible] her job [illegible]

[illegible] bor [illegible]

[illegible] before [illegible]

Am I [illegible] Emerald [illegible]

[illegible] near [illegible]

Who used her [illegible]

[illegible] anything [illegible]

[illegible] Al-Ameri [illegible]

CHAPTER ONE

ESME SCOTT JERKED awake in the split second between her phone vibrating and the bell ringtone blaring through her darkened bedroom. Heart racing, she lifted her head off the pillow and stared at the illuminated screen.

As a social worker, it wasn't unusual for her phone to ring in the middle of the night. The problems of her wards and an overstrained system required twenty-four-hour dedication.

Except she knew instinctively that *this* phone call had nothing to do with her job. The same gut instinct she'd been forced to hone for less altruistic purposes in her past.

But she'd left that life far behind.

After the fourth ring, she reached for the phone, willing her hand to stop shaking.

'Hello?'

'Am I speaking to Esmeralda Scott?'

Esmeralda. Her heart sank further. The only person who used her full name was her father. The man she hadn't spoken to or seen in eight long years.

She forced her jaw to relax. 'Y-yes.'

'Daughter of Jeffrey Scott?' came the deep, cultured, slightly accented query. The voice was stamped with enough authority and arrogance to make her grip tighten on the handset.

No, this was no ordinary phone call.

Sitting up, she turned on her bedside lamp, although she couldn't focus on anything but the ominous voice on the line.

'Yes. Who is this?'

'My name is Zaid Al-Ameen. I'm the chief prosecutor

in the Royal Kingdom of Ja'ahr.' The voice was filled with deep pride. Implacable purpose.

Esme's breath snagged in her lungs, but she refused to let the premonition lurking in her mind take hold. 'What can I do for you?' she asked, using the tone she reserved for calming her most agitated wards.

Momentary silence met her cool query. 'I called to inform you that your father is in jail. He's due to be arraigned in two days when formal charges will be brought against him.'

A thousand icicles pierced her skin, the boulder in her stomach confirming that even though she'd written him off when she'd walked away eight years ago, her father still possessed the power to rock her foundations.

'I…see.'

'He insisted on using his one phone call to reach you, but it seems the number he had for you is out of order.'

There was speculation in the crisp, no-nonsense tone but Esme wasn't prepared to inform him that she'd made sure her number was unlisted for this sole purpose.

'So how did *you* find me?' she asked, her mind swirling with a thousand questions. None of which she wanted to air to the deep-voiced stranger on the phone.

'I have one of the best police forces in the world, Miss Scott,' he replied haughtily.

I?

The possessive reply made her frown a little, but she couldn't put off the one question sitting on the tip of her tongue no matter how much she hated to ask. 'What are the charges against him?'

'They're too long to list. Our investigation unearths a new charge almost on the hour,' he replied, his voice growing colder with every answer. 'But the main charge is fraud.'

Her heart banged harder against her ribs. 'Right.'

'You don't seem surprised by the news.' This time the query held stronger speculation that snapped her spine straight.

'It's the middle of the night here in England, Mr. Al-Ameen. You'll pardon me if I'm struggling to take it all in,' she replied, transferring the phone to her other hand when her palm grew clammy.

'I'm aware of the time difference, Miss Scott. And while we're not under obligation to track you down on behalf of your father, I thought you might like to know about the incident—'

'What incident?' she blurted.

'There was an altercation in the jail where your father is being held—'

'Is he hurt?' she demanded, her stomach hollowing at the thought.

'The medical exam shows a mild concussion and a few bruises. He should be well enough to be returned to custody tomorrow.'

'So he can be attacked again or will you be doing something to protect him?' she screeched, tossing aside the duvet to get out of bed. She paced from one end of her small bedsit to the other before the man at the end of the phone deigned to answer.

'You father is a criminal, Miss Scott. He doesn't deserve special treatment and he will be given none. Consider yourself fortunate to be receiving this courtesy call at all. As I mentioned before, his arraignment is in two days. It's up to you to attend if you wish. Goodnight—'

'Wait! Please,' she added when the man didn't hang up. Esme forced herself to think rationally. Were this one of her young wards, what would she do?

'Does he have a counsel? I'm assuming he's entitled to one?'

The terse silence that greeted her told her she'd caused

offence. 'We're not a backward country, Miss Scott, despite what the world's media likes to portray. Your father's assets are frozen, as is the law in fraud cases, but he's been given a public defender.'

Esme's heart sank. In her experience, most public defenders were overstretched and overworked. Add the fact that her father was indubitably guilty of the charges levelled against him and the outlook was bleak.

The part of her that experienced the urge to end the conversation right now and pretend this wasn't happening was immediately drowned out by the heavy guilt that followed. But she'd cut ties with her father for a very good reason. She'd turned her life around. She wouldn't feel guilty for that.

'Can I talk to him?'

For several seconds, silence greeted her request. 'Very well. Provided he's given the all clear by the doctors, I'll allow him to make one more phone call. Make yourself available at six a.m. Goodnight, Miss Scott.'

The line disconnected, taking the authoritative voice with it.

A tiny knot in her stomach, caused solely by that charged, electric quality to her caller's voice, unfurled. She dropped the phone and returned to sit on her bed, her vision blurring as her hands shook. As Zaid Al-Ameen had loftily stated, Esme wasn't surprised by the news. If anything, she was only surprised it had taken eight years to finally arrive.

She exhaled roughly, willing the guilt and anger and pain to subside. When after a full ten minutes she still hadn't managed to wrestle her emotions under control, she rose and padded to the small desk in the corner of her bedroom.

Further sleep tonight was out of the question. The only way to prevent the vault of bad memories straining to crack open was to fill her time with work. Her work, which thankfully involved concentrating on other people's problems rather than her own, always managed to distract her. From the very first day she'd stepped into her junior social worker role four years ago, she'd welcomed that distraction simply because her actions produced positive results. Sometimes in indistinguishable ways, other times more meaningfully. Either way was good enough, although not good enough to ever wipe away the black stain on her soul.

Touch Global Foundation, the worldwide foundation she worked for, dealt directly with local organisations to help the disadvantaged, with numerous arms offering everything from drug rehabilitation to residential relocation.

Except working now, with her father's news fresh in her mind, was near impossible. Esme forced herself to finish up the notes recommending rehousing for a single mother of four to a better neighbourhood, and a dyslexia test for the second child. She set a reminder to follow up her recommendation with a phone call, and closed the file.

Calling up her search engine, she typed in the relevant information. Although during the frenzied pockets of time she'd spent with her father he'd often talked of the Kingdom of Ja'ahr, they'd never visited that country. It hadn't been on *the list*. Back then, decadent, well-established kingdoms like Monaco and Dubai and the brighter lights of New York and Vegas had been more desirable.

Within minutes, Esme understood why her father had taken an interest in Ja'ahr. The small kingdom, poised on the edge of the Persian Gulf, had gained as much international renown as its well-known neighbours in the last decade for all the right reasons.

Clever brokering of its rich resources of oil, gems and shipping lanes had seen it attain world's richest status, catapulting its ruler and royalty to extreme wealth, while the lower classes had been left far behind. Such a divide wasn't uncommon in such countries, but in Ja'ahr's case it was staggering.

Inevitably, the result of such a divide had caused political and economical unrest, some of which had escalated into violence. *All* of which had been ruthlessly suppressed.

Esme cautioned herself not to believe everything she read on the Internet. But disturbing stories about the Kingdom of Ja'ahr's judicial system were hard to dismiss. Stiff sentences were handed down for the lightest of offences, with even more ruthless punishment meted out to re-offenders.

'We're not a backward country, Miss Scott, despite what the world's media likes to portray.'

Except their judicial system seemed backward. Right back to the Dark Ages. Which didn't bode well for her father.

He deserves it. Remember why you walked away?

Jaw clenching, she straightened her spine.

She'd walked away. *She'd* changed her life for the better.

The reminder bolstered her up until her phone rang. Resolutely, she answered.

'Hello?'

'Esmeralda? Is that you?'

Her free hand tightened into a fist, her eyes closing at the deep, familiar voice.

'Yes, Dad, it's me.'

His exhalation was tinged with relief. Followed by a rough laugh. 'When they told me they'd actually managed to reach you I thought they were having me on.'

Esme didn't answer. She was too busy containing the cocktail of emotions that always swirled inside her when it came to her father.

'Baby girl, are you there?' Jeffrey Scott asked.

The endearment was so bitter-sweet, she didn't know

whether to laugh or cry. 'I'm here,' she managed after a minute.

'Okay, I guess you know what's happened?'

'Yes.' She cleared her throat, hoping her mind would follow suit. 'Are you all right? I was told you had concussion.'

Her father laughed, but the sound lacked its usual bravado. 'A concussion is the least of my worries. Not if the big man gets his way.'

'The big man?'

'Yes. The Royal Punisher himself.'

She frowned. 'I'm sorry, Dad. What are you talking about?'

'The chief prosecutor is gunning for me, Esmeralda. I've already been denied bail. And he's putting in a petition to fast-track my trial.'

The memory of the deep, powerful voice on the phone momentarily distracted her, made her breath catch a little. Then her hand tightened on the phone. 'But you have a lawyer, don't you?'

The laughter was starker. 'If you call a lawyer who told me my case was hopeless and advised me to plead guilty and save everyone the trouble a proper defender.'

Despite what she'd read about Ja'ahr's judicial system, she was still shocked. 'What?'

'I need you here, Esmeralda.'

This time her breath stayed locked in her throat. Along with the inner voice that screamed a horrified *No*.

When she'd tossed around scenarios of how she would conduct this reconnection with her father, she hadn't deluded herself into thinking he wouldn't want something from her. Money had been the most likely bet since his assets were frozen. She'd even mentally totted up her savings, and girded her loins to part with some of it.

But what he was asking of her…

'I've done a little research. They're very big on character witnesses over here during trials,' he continued hurriedly. 'I've put you down as mine.'

Déjà vu whispered down her spine. Wasn't this how it had always started? Her father innocently asking her to do something? And her guilt eating away at her until she obliged?

Esme stiffened, reminding herself of that last, indefensible thing he'd done. 'Dad, I don't think—'

'It could make the difference between me dying in prison or returning home one day. Will you deny me that?'

Esme firmed her lips. Remained silent.

'According to my lawyer, The Butcher is going for life without parole.'

Her heart lurched. 'Dad…'

'I know we didn't part on the best of terms, but do you hate me that much?' her father asked, after another long stretch of silence.

'No, I don't hate you.'

'So you'll come?' He latched on hopefully, his voice slipping into the oh-so-familiar smooth cajoling that even the hardest heart couldn't resist.

She closed her eyes. Reminded herself that in the end she *had* resisted. She'd been strong enough to walk away from him. But, of course, that didn't matter now.

Because no matter what had gone on before, Jeffrey Scott was the only family she had. She couldn't leave him to the mercy of a man known as The Butcher.

'Yes. I'll come.'

The relief in her father's voice was almost palpable, but the torrent of gratifying words that followed washed over Esme's head as she contemplated the commitment she'd just made. Eventually she murmured her goodbyes as her father's allotted time ended their call.

Almost detached, she typed another name into the

search engine. And forgot the ability to breathe as she stared into the brandy-coloured eyes of The Butcher.

The formidable authority in those eyes was just the start of the shockingly arresting features of the chief prosecutor of the Kingdom of Ja'ahr. She already knew what his voice sounded like. Now she saw how accurately it matched the square, masculine jaw that could have been cut from granite. It was shadowed despite the clean shave and, coupled with sharp cheekbones resting on either side of a strong, haughty nose, slightly flared in suppressed aggression, it was near impossible to look away.

Blue-black hair sprang back from his forehead in short, gleaming waves, the same colour gracing winged eyebrows and sooty eyelashes. But what captured her attention for a breathless moment was the sensual lines of his mouth. Although set in grim purpose in the picture, she couldn't help but be absorbed by them, even wonder if they ever softened in a smile or in pleasure. Whether they would feel as velvety as they looked in pixels.

The alarming direction of her thoughts prompted a hurried repositioning of the mouse. But that only revealed more of the man whose magnetism, even on screen, was hypnotising. Broad shoulders and a thick neck were barely restrained in the dark pinstriped suit, pristine shirt and immaculate tie he wore. Long arms braced an open-legged stance, displaying a towering figure with a streamlined body that had been honed to perfection.

He stood before a polished silver sign displaying the name of a firm of US attorneys. Esme felt a tiny fizz of relief at the thought that she'd got the wrong hit on her search. But clicking the next link revealed the same man.

Only he wasn't the same. His compelling features and hawk-like stare were made even more compelling by the traditional garb draping him from head to toe. The *thawb* was a blinding white with black and gold trim, repeated in the *keffiyeh* that framed his head and face.

With deep trepidation, Esme clicked one last link. Her gasp echoed in her bedroom as she read the biography of the thirty-three-year-old man nicknamed The Butcher.

Only the man who'd disturbed her sleep last night with bad news wasn't just the feared chief prosecutor of an oil-rich kingdom. He was so much more. Gut clenching, her gaze drifted back up to the mercilessly implacable face of Zaid Al-Ameen. Sultan and Ruler of the Kingdom of Ja'ahr.

The man who held her father's shaky fate in his hands.

CHAPTER TWO

Zaid Al-Ameen rested his head against the back seat of the tinted-windowed SUV transporting him from the courthouse. Only for a moment. Because a moment was all he had. His caseload was staggering. A dozen cases waited in the briefcase on the seat next to him, with dozens more waiting in the wings.

But even that was secondary to the colossal weight of his responsibilities as ruler of Ja'ahr. A weight that made each day feel like a year as he battled to right the wrongs of his uncle, the previous King.

A fair number of his ruling council had been shocked by his intention to carry on with his chosen profession when he'd returned from exile to take the throne eighteen months ago.

Some had cited a possible conflict of interest, questioning his ability to be both an able ruler *and* a dedicated prosecutor. Zaid had quashed every objection by doing what he did best—following the letter of the law and winning where it counted. Meting out swift justice had been the quickest way to begin uprooting the rank corruption that had permeated Ja'ahr's society. From the oil fields in the north to the shipping port in the south, no corporate entity had been left untouched by his public investigative team. Inevitably, that had made him enemies. Khalid Al-Ameen's twenty-year corrupt rule had birthed and fed fat cats who'd fought to hold onto their power.

But in the last six months things had finally started to change. The majority of factions that had strenuously opposed and doubted him—after all, he was an Al-Ameen like his late uncle—had begun to ally with him. But those unused to his zero tolerance approach still incited protestors against him.

His bitterness that his uncle had escaped Zaid's personal justice by falling dead from a heart attack had dissipated with time. It was an outcome he couldn't change. What he could change was the abject misery that his people had been forced to endure by Khalid.

Zaid had first-hand, albeit deadly experience of the misery crime and the greedy grasp for power could wreak. That he'd lived through the experience was a miracle in itself. Or so the whispers went. Only Zaid knew what had happened that fateful night his parents had perished. And it was no miracle but a simple act of self-preservation.

One that had triggered equal amounts of guilt, anger and bitterness over the years. It was what had driven him to practise law and pursue justice with unyielding fervour.

It was what would bring his people out of the darkness they'd been thrust into.

Lost in the jagged memories of his past, it took the slowing of the lead vehicle in his motorcade to alert him to his surroundings.

A large group of protestors was gathered in a nearby park normally used to host summer plays and concerts. Some had spilled into the street in front of his motorcade. Protests weren't uncommon, and, although regretful, it was part of the democratic process.

Zaid glanced around him as a handful of his personal security began to push back the crowd.

Ja'ahr City was particularly magnificent in early April, new blooms and moderate weather bathing the city in sparkling beauty. Giant sculptures and stunning monuments, surrounded by verdant gardens containing exotic flowers, lined the ten-mile-long central highway that led from the courthouse to the palace.

Except, as with everything else, this particular display

of Ja'ahr's wealth had been carefully cultivated to fool the world. One only had to stray along a few streets on either side of the highway to be met with the true state of affairs.

The grim reminder of the wide chasm dividing the social classes in his kingdom forced his attention back to the crowd and the giant screen showing a reporter surrounded by a handful of protestors.

'Can you tell us why you're here today?' the female journalist asked, thrusting her microphone forward.

The camera swung toward the interviewee.

Zaid wasn't exactly sure why his hand clenched on his thigh at the sight of the woman. In the previous life he'd led in the United States, he'd had numerous liaisons with women more beautiful than the one currently projected on the super-sized screen in the park.

There was nothing extraordinary about her individual features or the honey blonde hair tied in a bun at her nape. And yet the combination of full lips, pert nose and wide green-grey eyes was so striking his fingers moved, almost of their own accord, to the button that lowered his window. But still he couldn't decipher what had triggered the faint zap of electricity that had charged through him at the sight of her. Perhaps it was the determined thrust of her jaw. Or the righteous indignation that sparked from her almond-shaped eyes.

Most likely it was the words falling from her mouth. Condemning. Inciting words wrapped in a husky bedroom voice and amplified on speakers that threatened to distract him even as he strained to focus on them.

A voice he'd heard before, slightly sleep husky, over the phone in the middle of the night. A voice that had, disturbingly and inappropriately, tugged at the most masculine part of him.

'My father has been attacked twice in prison during the last week, while under the supervision of the police.

Once was bad enough, considering he suffered a concussion then. But he was attacked again today, and I'm sorry, but twice is not acceptable.'

'Are you saying that you hold the authorities responsible?' the reporter prompted.

The woman shrugged, causing Zaid's gaze to drop momentarily from her face to the sleek lines of her neck and shoulders, her light short-sleeved top clearly delineating her delicate bones and the swell of her breasts. He forced his attention up in time to hear her answer.

'I was given the impression that the authorities here are practically the best in the world, and yet they can't seem to keep the people under their care safe. On top of that, it seems I won't be allowed to see my father until his trial or until I offer a financial incentive to do so.'

The reporter's eyes gleamed as she latched onto the delicious morsel. 'You were asked for a bribe before you could see your father?'

The woman hesitated for a millisecond before she shrugged again. 'Not in so many words, but it wasn't hard to read between the lines.'

'So I take it your impression of Ja'ahr government so far isn't a good one?'

A sardonic smile lifted her mouth. 'That's an understatement.'

'If you could say anything to those in charge, what would you say?'

She looked directly into the camera, her wide eyes gleaming with purpose. 'That I'm not impressed. And not just with the police. These people here clearly believe that too. I believe a fish rots from the head down.'

The reporter's gaze grew a touch wary. 'Are you alleging that Sultan Al-Ameen is directly culpable for what happened to your father?'

The woman hesitated, her plump lower lip momentarily disappearing between her teeth before emerging, gleaming, to be pressed into a displeased line. 'It's apparent that something's wrong with the system. And since he's the one in charge, I guess my question to him is what's he doing about the situation?' she challenged.

Zaid hit the button, blocking out the rest of the interview just as his intercom buzzed.

'Your Highness, a thousand apologies for you having to witness that.' The voice of his chief advisor, travelling in the SUV behind him, was almost obsequious. 'I have just contacted the head of the TV studio. We are taking steps to have the broadcast shut down immediately—'

'You will do no such thing,' Zaid interjected grimly.

'But, Your Highness, we can't let such blatant views be aired—'

'We can and we will. Ja'ahr is supposed to be a country that champions freedom of speech. Anyone who attempts to stand in the way of that will answer directly to me. Is that clear?'

'Of course, Your Highness,' his advisor agreed promptly.

As his motorcade passed the last of the protestors, he caught one last, brief glimpse of the woman on a much closer screen. Her head was tilted, the sunlight slanting over her cheekbone throwing her face into clear, more captivating lines. His jaw tightened at the further sizzle of electricity, until he was sure it would crack.

'Do you wish me to find out who she is, Your Highness?'

He didn't need to. He knew exactly who she was.

Esmeralda Scott.

Daughter of the criminal he intended to prosecute and put behind bars in the very near future. 'That won't be necessary. But have her brought to me immediately,' he instructed.

As he hung up, he allowed the inner voice to question why he was going out of his way to trigger such a knee-jerk reaction. A second later, he smashed it away.

The why wasn't so important. What mattered was her maligning the fragile pillars of the very things he was fighting to restore in his country. Integrity. Honour. Accountability.

Esmeralda Scott needed to answer a few questions of her own. After which he would take pleasure in pointing out the errors of her ways to her.

Esme gave in to the frantic urge to slide her clammy palms down her skirt as the black town car with tinted windows sped her towards an unknown destination. She'd cautioned herself a dozen times against letting fear take over. So far it hadn't.

Perhaps it had something to do with the bespectacled, harmless-looking man sitting across from her and his reassurance that her interview had gained her the right audience on behalf of her father.

'Where are we going?' she asked for the second time, her mind still spinning at the swiftness at which her appearance on TV had earned her attention.

The question earned her a slightly less warm smile. 'You will see for yourself when we arrive in a few minutes.'

The fear she'd staunched looming a little larger, Esme glanced out the window.

She began to notice that the landscape was growing more opulent, the parks even greener and studded with staggeringly beautiful works of art. Why that triggered a stronger sense of trepidation, Esme wasn't sure. Sweat that had been steadily beading the back of her neck, despite the air-conditioning of the car, rolled between her shoulders.

'My father's prison hospital is on the other side of the city,' she attempted again.

'I am aware of that, Miss Scott.'

Alarm trickled through her. 'You never said how come you knew my name.' She'd only given the journalist her first name during the interview.

'No, I did not.'

She opened her mouth to press for a clearer answer but closed it again as the car swerved in a wide circle before approaching huge double gates painted in stunning gold leaf. They slowed long enough for armed guards to wave them through.

'This…is the Royal Palace,' she mumbled, unable to stop her voice from shaking as she stared at the immense azure-coloured dome that could rival St. Peter's Basilica in Rome.

'Indeed,' the man responded, not without a small ounce of relish.

The town car drew to a firm stop. The sweat between her shoulders grew icy. She cast another, frantic glance outside.

The penny finally dropped. She was here, at the Royal Palace. After publicly calling out the ruler of the kingdom.

Dear God, what have I done?

'I'm here because of what I said on TV about the Sultan, aren't I?'

A sharply dressed valet opened the door and the chief advisor stepped out. He signalled to someone out of sight before he glanced down at her. 'That is not for me to answer. His Highness has requested your presence. I do not advise keeping him waiting.'

Before she could answer, he walked away, his shoes and those of his minders clicking precisely on the white and gold polished stone tiles that led to the entrance steps of the palace.

Esme debated remaining in the car as alarm flared into full-blown panic. The driver was still seated behind the wheel. She could ask him to take her back to her hotel. Even beg if necessary. Or she could get out and start walking. But even as the thoughts tumbled she knew it was futile.

Another set of footsteps approached the car. Esme held her breath as a man dressed in dark gold traditional clothes paused beside the open door and gave a shallow bow. He, too, was flanked by two guards.

They seem to travel in threes.

She was tossing away the mildly hysterical observation when he spoke. 'Miss Scott, I am Fawzi Suleiman, His Royal Highness's private secretary. If you would come with me, please?'

The question was couched in cultured diplomacy, but she had very little doubt that it was a command.

'Do I have a choice?' she asked anyway, half hoping for a response in the affirmative.

The response never came. What she witnessed instead was the firmer, watchful stance of the bodyguards, even while Fawzi Suleiman bowed again and swept out his arm in a polite but firm *this-way* gesture.

Esme alighted into dazzling sunshine and a dry breeze. She took a moment to tug down her knee-length black pencil skirt and resisted the urge to adjust her neckline. Fidgeting was a sign of weakness, and she had a feeling she would need every piece of her armour in place.

Slowly, she raised her chin and smiled. 'Lead the way.'

He took her words literally, walking several steps ahead of her as they entered the world-famous Ja'ahr Palace.

At first sight of the interior her steps slowed and her jaw dropped.

Tiered Moorish arches framed in black lacquer and gold leaf veered off half a dozen hallways, all of which converged in a stunning atrium centred by a large azure-tiled fountain.

She dragged her gaze away long enough to see that they'd arrived at the bottom of wide, magnificent, sweeping stairs. Carpeted in the same azure tone that seemed to be the royal colour, the painstakingly carved designs that graced the bannisters were exquisite and grand.

Truly fit for a king.

A faintly cleared throat reprimanded her for dawdling. But as they traversed hallway after hallway, past elegantly dressed palace staff who surreptitiously eyed her, awe gave way to a much more elemental emotion.

She'd been expertly manipulated. With clever words and non-answers, but tricked nevertheless. Esme could only think of one reason why.

Intimidation.

They arrived before a set of carved double doors. She curbed the panic that flared anew, clutching her purse tighter as Fawzi Suleiman turned to her.

'You will wait here until you're summoned. And when you enter, you will address the Sultan as *Your Highness*.'

He didn't wait for her response, merely grasped the thick handles and pushed the doors wide open.

'Miss Scott is here, Your Highness,' she heard him murmur.

Whatever response he received had him executing another bow before turning to her. 'You may go in.'

She'd taken two steps into the room when she heard the doors shut ominously behind her. Despite the slow burn of anger in her belly, Esme swallowed, fresh nerves jangling as the faint scent of incense and expensive aftershave hit her nostrils.

She was in the presence of the ruler of Ja'ahr.

She forced her feet to move over the thick, expensive Persian rugs she was certain cost more than she would earn in two lifetimes as she emerged into the largest personal office she'd ever seen. Esme's entire focus immediately zeroed in on the man behind the massive antique desk.

From the photos on the Internet she'd known he was a big man. But the flesh and blood version, the larger-than-life presence watching her in golden-eyed silence, was so shockingly visceral, she stumbled. She caught herself quickly, silently admonishing herself for the blunder.

A dozen feet from his desk, his magnetic aura hit her, hard and jolting. She wanted to stop walking but she forced herself to take another step. And then she froze as he rose to his feet.

It was like being hit with a tidal wave of raw masculinity. At five feet five, she considered herself of average height but her heels added a confidence-bolstering three inches. None of that mattered now as she took in the towering man looking down his domineering royal nose at her.

He was dressed in a three-piece suit, but he may as well have been adorned in an ancient warrior's suit of armour, such was the primitive air of aggression Zaid Al-Ameen gave off as he watched her. Above his head, a giant emblem depicting his royal kingdom's coat of arms hung, emphasising the glory and authority of its ruler.

But even without the trappings of all-encompassing wealth and power, Esme would have been foolish to underestimate the might of the man before her.

She summoned every last ounce of composure. 'I… don't know why I've been brought here. I haven't done anything wrong. Your Highness,' she tagged on after a taut second.

He didn't respond. Esme forced herself to return his intense stare as she fought the urge to wet her dry lips.

'And I hope you don't expect me to bow. I'm not sure I can do it correctly.'

One imperious brow lifted. 'How would you know unless you try?' he drawled.

A spike of something hot and unnerving shot through her midriff at the sound of his accented voice. Deep, gravel rough, filled with power, it rumbled like ominous thunder. Esme's shiver coursed down to her toes.

'It may be the done thing, but I don't think I want to.'

An enigmatic expression crossed his face, disappearing before she could accurately decipher it. '"But I don't think I want to, *Your Highness*".'

She blinked, dragging her attention from his exotically captivating face. 'What?'

'You were told of the correct form of address, were you not? Or does your lack of respect for my country and my judicial system extend to my station as well?'

The throb of anger in his voice sent a chill over her nape. She was in the lion's den, faced with its incredibly displeased occupant. Regardless of her personal feelings, she needed to tread carefully if she wanted to escape with her hide intact.

'My apologies, Your Highness. I didn't mean to cause offence.'

'How is it possible that I've known of your existence only a short time and yet I'm ready to add *insincere* to the list of your unsavoury attributes?'

Her mouth gaped. *'Excuse me?'*

'Excuse me, *Your Highness.*' This time the command was coated in ice, his eyes reflecting the same frigid displeasure as he regarded her.

Esme attempted to curb the angry words tripping over her tongue. She failed. 'Perhaps it has something to do with being brought here against my will. *Your Highness.*'

With measured strides, he rounded his desk. Esme

couldn't help but stare. Despite his immense size, he moved like poetry in motion. Like a stealthy predator, focused on only one goal.

Vanquishing his prey.

CHAPTER THREE

ESME EXPECTED A cataclysmic event to occur in the seconds it took for him to prowl closer. Such was the power of the force field he wielded. Instead, Zaid Al-Ameen stopped a few feet from her, his gaze capturing hers as a frown pleated his brow.

'You were brought here against your will?'

'Well…yes. Somewhat. Your Highness.'

'The answer is either yes or no. Did my men lay their hands on you?' he enquired, his voice a touch rougher.

She had to lock her knees to keep from doing something stupid. Like crumbling into an inelegant heap at his feet. Because the closer he got, the higher she craned her neck, the more her brain scrambled. 'I…er…'

'Were you harmed in any way, Miss Scott?' he demanded in a near growl.

'No…but your emissary misrepresented himself.'

He stopped moving, his eyes narrowing. 'How?'

'He didn't tell me he was bringing me here for a start. He gave me the impression that he was taking me to my father—'

'But no one touched you?'

Esme couldn't understand why he was so hung up on that. But she shook her head. 'No one touched me, but that doesn't alter the fact that this is a form of kidnapping.'

He clasped his hands behind his back, but that didn't diffuse the power of his presence. If anything, his focus sharpened on her face, his eyes raking her from temple to chin and back again. 'You weren't told that I wished to speak to you?'

'Not until we got here. And I got the feeling that I wouldn't be allowed to leave even if I wanted to.'

He remained silent for a moment, hawk-like eyes probing her every breath. 'First you allege that the authorities wanted a bribe in order for you to see your father, and now you're alleging a potential kidnapping, even though you came here of your own free will. Are you in the habit of making assumptions about everything, Miss Scott? Or getting into the vehicles of men you think wish you harm?' The accusation was delivered in a low, pithy tone as he took yet another step closer.

The icy fingers crawling up her back shrieked at her to retreat from the wall of bristling manhood coming at her. But Esme had learned to stand her ground a long time ago.

So, even though her instinct warned that Sultan Zaid Al-Ameen posed a different sort of danger from that she was used to, perhaps an even more potent kind, she angled her chin and stubbornly met his gaze. 'No, Your Highness. I'm in the habit of judging a situation for myself. But if I'm wrong, here's your chance to prove it. I wish to leave,' she threw out.

That left brow arched again. 'You just got here.'

'And as I said, Your Highness, I thought I was being taken to see my father and not…'

'Not?'

'Bundled here for…whatever reason you've had me brought here. I'm assuming you're going to tell me?'

'In due course.'

Her response stuck in her throat as he strode past her. The mingled trail of incense, aftershave and man that sneaked into her senses momentarily distracted her. Esme found herself turning after him, her feet magnetically taking a step in his direction.

'Come and sit down,' Zaid Al-Ameen said.

The invitation was low and even, but another layer of apprehension dragged over her skin. She glanced at the closed doors through which she'd walked a few minutes ago.

'Just for the hell of it, if I said no, that I want to leave, will you let me?'

'You may leave if you wish to. But not until we've had a conversation. Sit down, Miss Scott.' There was no mistaking the command this time, or the inference that she wouldn't be allowed to leave until he was ready to let her go.

Esme gripped her purse tighter, her fingers screaming with the pressure on the leather. Pulse tripping over itself, she followed him to the sitting area and perched on the nearest seat.

Almost on cue, the doors opened and his private secretary appeared, bearing a large, beautifully carved tray of refreshments.

He set it down, executed another bow, then waited with his hands clasped respectfully in front of him.

Zaid Al-Ameen sat down in the adjacent seat and looked at her. 'Do you prefer tea or coffee?' he asked.

About to refuse because she didn't think she could get anything down her throat, she paused, keenly aware of the two sets of eyes watching her.

'Tea, please, thank you. Your Highness,' she hastily added after a sharp look from Fawzi.

His master cast her a sardonic look before nodding to Fawzi, who moved forward and prepared the tea with smooth efficiency.

Bemused, Esme accepted the beverage, almost afraid to handle the exquisite bone china. She refused the delicious-looking exotic treats Fawzi offered her, then waited as Sultan Al-Ameen's coffee was prepared and handed to him.

Fawzi bowed again and left the room.

Silence reigned as Esme took another sip, and attempted to drag her gaze from the slim, elegant fingers gripping his coffee cup. After taking a large sip, he set the cup back on the saucer and swung his penetrative gaze to her.

'Contrary to what you wish me to think, you know exactly why you're here.'

The muscles in her belly quivered, but she fought to keep her voice even. 'My television interview in the park?'

'Precisely,' he intoned.

Sensing the beginning of a tremble in her hand, she gripped her cup harder. 'I thought Ja'ahr advocated free speech among its citizens?'

'Free speech is one thing, Miss Scott. Skirting the inner edges of slander is another matter entirely.'

The quivering in her belly escalated. *'Slander?'*

'Yes. Disrespecting the royal throne is a criminal offence here in Ja'ahr. One that is currently punishable by a prison sentence.'

'Currently?'

'Until that law, like a few others, is amended, yes. Perhaps that is what you wish? To be tossed in prison so you can keep your father company?' Zaid Al-Ameen enquired in a clipped tone.

'Of course it isn't. I only wanted… I was frustrated. And worried for my father.'

'So you always leave your common sense behind when your emotions get the better of you? Are you aware that some of the allegations you made this afternoon are serious enough to put you in danger?'

The rattle of the cup had her hastily setting it down. 'Danger from who?'

'For starters, the police commissioner doesn't like his organisation or his reputation questioned so publicly. He could bring charges against you. Or worse.'

Fear climbed into her throat. 'What does *worse* mean?'

'It means you should've given your words a little more thought before you went on live television.'

'But…everything I said was true,' she argued, unwilling to let fear take over.

His lips pursed for a moment. 'It would've been prudent to take into account that you're no longer in England. That things are done somewhat differently here.'

'What does that mean?' she asked again.

He discarded his own cup and saucer then leaned forward, his arms braced on his knees. The action caused his wide shoulders to strain beneath his suit, drawing her unwilling attention to the untamed power beneath the clothes.

A hint of it emerged in a low rumble as he spoke. 'It means my magnanimity and position are the only things keeping you out of jail right now, Miss Scott, given the fact that some of the allegations you claim to be true are unfounded.'

'Which ones?'

'You said your father was attacked twice in the last week. But my preliminary investigation tells a different story.'

Her breath caught. 'You've looked into it already?'

'You maligned my government and me on live television,' he replied in icy condemnation. '"The fish rots from the head" I believe were your exact words? I don't take kindly to such an accusation, neither do I leave it unanswered.'

She felt a little light-headed. 'Your Highness, it...wasn't personal—'

'Spare me the false contrition. It was a direct challenge and you know it. One I took up. Quite apart from my intimate knowledge of your father's many crimes, do you want to know what else I discovered?'

The taunting relish in his voice told her she didn't. But she swallowed down the *No* that rose in her throat. 'You're going to tell me anyway, so go ahead.'

'I have it on good authority, and on prison security footage, that your father instigated both confrontations. He seems to be under some misguided delusion that his fate will be less dire if he's seen as a victim.'

She tensed as the words struck a little too close to the bone. Jeffrey Scott was a master at reading situations and adapting to them. It was the reason he'd survived this long in his chosen profession.

Eagle eyes caught her reaction. 'I see you're not surprised. Neither are you hurrying to his defence,' he observed. 'Perhaps some of what I've said rings truer for you than the picture you painted of him on live TV?'

She took a deep, steadying breath. No matter what she knew in her heart, she wouldn't incriminate her father by answering the question. 'That doesn't alter the fact that the guards didn't take action after the first incident,' she replied. 'Perhaps if he'd been released on bail—'

'So he could attempt to take the first flight out of the country? Your father is a veteran con man, which, judging by your continued lack of surprise, is not news to you. And yet he's named you as his principal character witness,' he mused, his eyes cutting into her.

'As the man prosecuting my father, isn't it unethical to discuss the case with me, Your Highness?' she parried.

His grim twist of his lips told her he'd seen through her evasion tactics. 'Nothing I've said so far contravenes the correct judicial process, Miss Scott. You can trust me on that.'

His biographer had called him a master tactician, able to mould the word of law like putty in his hands, but never breaking it. Esme needed to proceed with caution if she didn't want to be tripped up. 'Did you bring me here to point out the error of my ways before you throw me in jail, too?'

'I brought you here to warn you against indulging in any further public outbursts. If you wish to exhibit any more rash decision-making, wait until you're back home in England.'

Affronted heat crawled up her neck. 'That sounds distinctly like a threat, Your Highness.'

'If that's what it takes to get through to you, then so be it. But know that you're treading on extremely thin ice. I won't tolerate any further unfounded aspersions cast against me or my people without solid proof to back them up. Is that understood?'

The sense of affront lingered, attempting to override the same tiny voice she'd ignored during her interview. This time it urged her to be thankful that she wasn't being hauled over royal coals. She was struggling with the dissenting emotions when, taking her silence as assent, he rose.

His towering frame made her feel even more insignificant, so she scrambled to her feet. Only to lose her balance as one heel twisted beneath her. She pitched forward, a gasp ripping from her throat as her hands splayed in alarm.

Strong hands caught her upper arms at the same moment she dropped her purse and her open hands landed on his hard-muscled chest. She heard his sharp intake of breath and felt her own breath snag in her lungs as heat from his body almost singed her palms.

Esme's head snapped up, that compulsion to look into those eyes once again a command she couldn't ignore. His eyes had darkened, the light brandy shade now a burnished bronze that fused incisively with hers. This close, she saw the tiny gold flecks that flared within the darker depths, the combination so mesmeric she couldn't look away, despite the frisson shooting up her arm. Despite the lack of oxygen to her brain from the breath she couldn't take.

Despite the fact that she shouldn't be touching him, this man who was hell-bent on exerting his supreme authority over her. Who was hell-bent on keeping her father in prison.

Move!

Her palm started to curl, in anticipation, she told herself, of pushing back from him. But the infinitesimal tightening of his fingers stopped her. Absorbed by the gleam in his eyes, by his scent swirling around her, Esme remained immobile. His nostrils flared slightly as his gaze dropped to her mouth. Almost as if he'd touched them, her lips pulsed with an alien sensation that absurdly felt like excitement. Hunger.

She didn't…*couldn't* want to kiss him, surely?

He released her so suddenly she wondered if she'd spoken the thought aloud. Spoken it only to have it promptly, ruthlessly rejected.

She stepped back, silently urging her legs not to let her down, even as another wave of heat swept over her face.

She needed to leave. Now.

As if the same thought had struck him, Zaid Al-Ameen turned abruptly and walked away, his imposing figure carrying him to his desk. Released from the trap of his puzzling, spellbinding presence, she sucked in a much-needed breath then snatched up her purse. She straightened to the sound of him issuing a rasped instruction into his intercom. Seconds later, the door reopened.

His private secretary barely glanced her way, his attention focused solely on the Sultan and the rapid words of lyrical Arabic falling from his lips. Esme was so distracted by the exotic, melodic sound that she didn't realise they'd stopped speaking and were staring at her until the silence echoed loudly in the room.

For the third time in a disgracefully short period her face heated up again. 'I'm sorry, did you say something?' she addressed Fawzi, unwilling to catch another mocking glance from Sultan Al-Ameen.

The private secretary looked a little perturbed at being addressed directly in the presence of his master. He stood straighter. 'His Highness said you are free to go. I am to escort you to your chauffeur.'

Knowing it would be impolite to leave without acknowledging him, Esme reluctantly redirected her gaze to the Sultan. 'I… I'm…'

One sardonic brow elevated, the look he sent her haughty enough to freeze water. 'You pick a curious time to become tongue-tied, considering your desire to leave has been granted. The next time we meet will be in the courtroom when you testify on behalf of your father. Let us hope you're not as inarticulate under cross-examination. I would hate to see all the effort you made to come to the aid of your father wasted. Goodbye, Miss Scott.'

The dismissal was as final as the drive back to the hotel was quick. Even after she was safely back in her hotel room, Esme still couldn't force her heartbeat to slow. She'd been summoned, judged and found severely wanting.

And yet the righteous anger she'd felt in Zaid Al-Ameen's presence was no longer present. Instead, awareness from his touch clung to her skin, her mind supplying an alarmingly detailed play-by-play of the moment he'd stopped her from falling. With each meticulous recounting her body grew hot and tight, her breathing altering into shameful little pants that drew a grimace of disgust at herself. To distract her out-of-control hormones, Esme turned on the TV and channel-surfed, only to come face to face with herself in a replay of her interview. Forcing herself to watch, she experienced a twinge of remorse as her words echoed harsh and condemning in the room.

The stone of unease in her belly hadn't abated hours later when she was in bed, attempting to toss and turn herself into sleep. Sleep came reluctantly, along with jagged, disturbing dreams featuring a breathtakingly hypnotic figure with brandy-coloured eyes.

The intensity of the dream was so sharp, so vivid she jerked awake.

Only to find it was no dream. There was someone in her room.

Esme's breath strangled in her lungs as she battled paralysing fear and scrambled upright. The dark, robed figure outlined ominously against her lighter curtains tensed for a watchful second then launched after her the moment she scurried off the bed. Her feet tangled in the sheets, ripping a cry from her throat. She sensed rather than saw the figure rounding the bed towards her as she pushed at the sheets and crawled away on her hands and knees. A few steps from the bathroom she attempted to stand.

A strong, unyielding arm banded her waist, plastering her from shoulder to thigh against a hard, masculine body. He lifted her off the floor with shocking ease, her feet kicking uselessly as he evaded her efforts to free herself. Acute terror finally freeing her vocal cords, Esme screamed.

The large hand that clamped over her mouth immediately muffled the sound.

Terrified by the ease with which the intruder had caught and restrained her, Esme fought harder. She wrapped her fingers around the thick wrist and was attempting to pry him off when she felt his warm breath against her cheek.

'Calm yourself, Miss Scott. It is I, Zaid Al-Ameen. If you wish to remain safe, you need to come with me. Right now.'

CHAPTER FOUR

ESME SLACKENED IN shock for a handful of seconds before outrage kicked in. At her renewed struggle, he held her tighter. 'Be calm,' he commanded again.

She shook her head, her heart tripping over all the possible reasons for his presence here in her room, holding her prisoner. She came up with nothing remotely reassuring.

'You have my word that I mean you no harm, Esmeralda. But I need your reassurance that you won't scream before I release you,' he said, his lips brushing against her ear.

Despite her racing heart, she felt herself go still. She told herself it wasn't the effect of the deep but lyrical lilt to her first name as it fell from his lips, or the low, even way he spoke that finally soothed her, but the need to be set free from the deeply disturbing sensation of the body welded to hers.

No longer fighting, she was keenly aware of the firm strength of his body against hers. The splay of the fingers of his restraining arm branding her hips. Her bare legs dangling against his longer ones. Her back absorbing his unhurried breathing as her bottom snuggled between the widened stance of his hips. And the highly masculine, very proud organ cradled between them.

Heat surging up her body, Esme jerked her head in quick assent. He waited a beat then released her. She launched herself away from him, slapped her hand on the light switch in the bathroom before whirling to face him.

The sight of the Sultan of Ja'ahr, dressed from head to toe in black traditional clothes, every inch the dark desert warrior lord he was, threatened to rob her of the breath she'd just regained. The hand she lifted to push back her heavy hair shook as she glared at him. 'You may be the ruler of this kingdom, but you have no right to invade my privacy,' she condemned, a touch too shakily. 'Not to mention the fact that you scared the living—'

One imperious hand slashed through the air. 'I understand that you wish to express your outrage. But I highly recommend you do so once we're away from the hotel.'

'Why?' she demanded.

Not bothering to dignify her with a response, he strode to the small wardrobe on the other side of the room. Esme watched, stunned, as he began to rummage through her clothes.

'What on earth do you think you're doing? If you think I'm going anywhere with you after barging into my room in the middle of the night, think again.'

He turned from the wardrobe, his eyes narrowed in displeased slits. 'I caution you against using that tone of voice with me or my men will arrest you, with or without my permission.'

Her eyes widened. 'Your men?'

He jerked a head towards the door. Esme followed his action and for the first time she noticed the men who stood guard, their broad backs to the door but rigidly alert. Protecting their King.

Barring her way.

'Why are they here? Why are *you* here?'

He stepped forward and she saw that he held her black cotton dress in his hand. 'I don't have time to debate the matter with you. Put this on. We need to leave now, unless you plan on walking out of the hotel dressed in that wispy scrap of nothing?' he rasped. Although his expression remained stoically impersonal, his voice was a touch more raw than before.

Esme stared down at the peach night slip she wore. The silky, lace-edged material was short, barely coming to mid-thigh. The bodice consisted of two cupped triangles also edged in lace, with thin straps joining at her nape in a halter design. As nightwear went, it was intended to be feminine and sexy, hugging, flattering and titivating where necessary.

Except, with Zaid Al-Ameen's piercing gaze on her, Esme bypassed those middling sensations and went straight to fiery hot awareness between one heartbeat and the next. Mild shock rippled through her belly at the intensity of the feeling singeing her body as his gaze conducted a slow journey over her. When it rose from her feet to linger at her thighs, a heavy throbbing commenced between her legs. The sensation rippled outward, sparking tiny fireworks that exploded beneath her skin as it spread.

Dark golden eyes rose higher, over her stomach to rest on her breasts. Suddenly sensitive peaks prickled, then slowly tightened into hard nubs. Realising that the silk exhibited every reaction of her body, Esme hastily threw her arm up over her chest, even as she defied the hot flush staining her neck and cheeks to stare challengingly at him.

But she might as well have been a gnat challenging an elephant. The eyes that met hers may have been a touch more turbulent than they were moments ago, perhaps even gleaming with a hint of suppressed hunger, but the man who strode determinedly over to her and thrust her dress at her was once again the supreme marauder intent on having his way.

'You have two minutes to put this dress on or I will do it for you myself,' he pronounced succinctly.

Even though she caught the dress, Esme stood her ground. 'I'll put the dress on, but I'm not leaving this room until you tell me what is going on.'

At his curt nod, she stepped back into the bathroom and shut the door firmly behind her. About to put the dress on, she froze when she caught sight of her reflection in the mirror. Her long loose hair was in complete disarray, her colour high as her chest rose and fell in agitation. But it was the brightness of her eyes that shocked her most of all. Where she'd expected fear, she read something else. Something that made her skin tingle even more wildly. Her nipples were still tight twin points of blatant arousal and belatedly she realised that, standing in the light of the doorway, Sultan Zaid would have been able to see right through her slip.

With renewed chagrin and heightened disquiet, she turned away and tugged the dress over the night slip. There was no way she was going back in there to retrieve her bra so the nightgown would have to offer the extra protection she needed. Besides, she could feel Sultan Zaid's restless prowling through the bathroom door.

After sliding her fingers through her hair in a vain effort to control the unruly mess, she tugged it into a ponytail and left the bathroom to confront the figure pacing the room. 'Okay, I deserve to know what's going on, and I'm not moving until I do.'

'The chief of police is on his way to arrest you. And unless you come with me, you will be in jail within the hour. It won't be a pleasant experience.'

Her mouth dropped opened, but the stark words had shrivelled her vocal cords and killed any further protest in her throat. Her gaze swung to the guards standing at the door. They hadn't moved, but she sensed an escalated urgency in the air.

He'd turned on a lamp while she'd been in the bathroom and Esme hurried across the room to shove her feet into the heels she'd discarded at the bottom of the bed. Then she went to the wardrobe and tugged out her suitcase. It was ripped from her hand a second later.

'What do you think you're doing?' he demanded.

'I'm getting my things.'

'There's no time for that. Your belongings will be taken care of.'

Again she wanted to protest, but at the implacable look in his eyes she nodded. Her purse held her passport, credit cards and phone. He waited long enough for her to grab it before he marched her to the door.

Eight bodyguards immediately positioned themselves in a protective cordon around them. A lift she suspected had been held especially for him transported them swiftly to the ground floor.

They exited to a large, empty foyer with only a sleepy male receptionist stationed behind the desk. He straightened to attention, then bowed respectfully as they moved past him.

Sultan Zaid barely glanced at him, his focus on the revolving doors. And the small group of armed men walking through it.

Her heart leapt into her throat. Beside her, Zaid tensed, even though he didn't break his stride.

'Remain by my side and do not speak.' The words were delivered in a low, even voice, but the stern command that pulsed through them was unmistakeable.

She nodded as the small group drew closer. Their posture and uniforms announced who they were before she read the insignia on their attire.

The leader, a small, rotund man, came forward and in unison they executed a bow, but she noted that although the chief of police paid his respects to his ruler, the act was delivered with reluctance and more than a hint of antagonism.

'Your Highness, I am surprised to see you here at this time of night,' he said, slowly tucking the cap he'd removed from his head under his arm. His black, beady eyes swung to the Sultan's bodyguards protecting them before returning to Zaid.

'Matters of state do not always wait for civilised hours to demand attention.'

The man's gaze settled on her and Esme spied the distinct gleam of malevolence in the black depths. 'And that is what is happening here? A matter of state?'

Zaid's response was spoken in sharp, rapid-fire Arabic, his posture seething with unbridled authority. Esme watch the man shrink back slowly. The hostile expression in his eyes didn't abate, and his gaze darted to her many times during the conversation but he didn't attempt to arrest her.

Although only mere minutes passed, it felt like a lifetime before Zaid glanced her way.

'We're leaving now,' he said.

Relief punched through her and she gave a swift nod as she hurried to match her steps to his.

The moment she slid into the car he climbed in after her. A second later, after she'd slotted in her seat belt, they were moving with the smoothness borne of military precision.

She took a deep, shaky breath, but the thousand questions that crowded Esme's brain were momentarily suppressed when her senses were suffused with the very male scent of the man sitting next to her.

The man staring at her with silent, watchful intensity.

'What...?' She stopped and flicked her tongue over her dry lips. 'Why was he coming to arrest me?'

'Because he found out, like I did, that the allegations you made against his police force weren't entirely accurate. Your interview has been televised every hour for the past twelve hours. There are those who called for your arrest the moment it was aired. It came to my attention that the police chief was beginning to gather his forces.'

Ice cascaded down her spine. 'Oh, my God.' The hand she lifted to push back a swathe of hair shook badly. Tightening it into a fist, she placed it in her lap. 'What...what was he going to charge me with?' Not that it mattered. Jail was jail. And prison in Ja'ahr wasn't something she wanted to experience, even for a minute.

To her surprise, Zaid Al-Ameen's lips pursed before his powerful shoulders moved in a shrug. 'He would've found something.'

'What? You mean he could've just made something up?'

'It could've been something as simple as questioning you about what you said, or it could've been more. You supplied him with all the base he could have wanted. All he needed to do was capitalise on it.'

Her heart dropped to her stomach. 'But isn't that…illegal?' she questioned carefully, unwilling to add further fuel to the fire it seemed she'd started.

In the semi-darkness of the vehicle she watched his jaw clench harshly, his expression turn grave. 'The wheels of change are turning in Ja'ahr, but not fast enough,' he said semi-cryptically. 'True democracy comes at a cost. Not everyone is ready to pay that price yet.'

The bald statement left very little room for more questions after that. The convoy rolled swiftly along near deserted streets, silence reigning in the vehicle. Until Esme realise the familiar road they travelled on.

Her gaze swung from the elevated road and the familiar dome ahead to the man sitting next to her. He was staring at her, shrewd sharp eyes waiting. 'You're taking me—'

'Back to the Royal Palace, yes,' he confirmed.

Wild hysteria powered through her. 'So I was right. You *are* kidnapping me after all.'

She'd meant the words half-jokingly, a way for her tumbling thoughts to grapple with the events of the last hour and the enormity of what might have happened to her.

When he didn't immediately answer, she glanced at him.

The look he levelled at her was in no way mirthful. It

was filled with solemn, unwavering resolve. 'For want of a better word…and for the foreseeable future, yes.'

Zaid watched her process his reply. She may have been joking, but he was deadly serious.

Slowly, every trace of amusement drained from her face. He told himself the apprehension that replaced it was much more useful to him. It would keep her focused properly on what lay ahead of her. It would also serve to draw his attention from the luscious curve of her mouth and the tiny twitch of her nose when she was amused.

He was already battling with the heated tug of his libido at the way her skin had shone under the bathroom lights, like the pearls mined in the sea bordering his kingdom. The way the scrap of silk she had worn to bed had caressed her flesh had made him infinitely glad he'd been wearing a shrouding tunic. The urge to touch her, to relive the memory of holding her warm body captive in his arms was so strong it was a visceral ache deep within him. He smashed down hard on the unwelcome sensation and concentrated on the matter at hand.

'You're serious, aren't you?' Her eyes were widening, her hushed voice stained with burgeoning realisation.

'I have a kingdom to rule. I don't undertake missions like this just for the fun of it.' His words emerged clipped.

She flinched. He experienced the tiniest dart of remorse before he firmed his lips.

Before he could say anything further, his vehicle drew to a stop. His head of security jumped out and opened his door.

Zaid didn't exit immediately. For some reason, he found himself staring at her, taking in her pale features, the lower lip she was worrying as she stared back at him. The shadows under her eyes. 'It's almost two o'clock in the morning.

We will continue this conversation at a more appropriate hour, once you've had some rest.'

He stepped out of the car and held out his hand. Her gaze dropped warily. For a tense moment he watched her silently debate whether or not to take it, then she reached out, almost in slow motion, to finally accept his help.

The sensation of her sliding her hand into his ramped up the volatile tension inside him. Zaid ruthlessly dismissed his body's response, just as he'd dismissed almost all extraneous emotions since his return to Ja'ahr. He'd needed to, to be able to focus on rebuilding what his uncle had so brutally destroyed. It was the reason he hadn't taken a woman to his bed in well over eighteen months. It was the reason his work days were so long and sleep was a luxury he afforded himself only when necessary.

Nevertheless, he found his grip tightening, his touch lingering even after she stood before him, her face upturned to his. In the floodlights gracing the entrance to his palace, her unique beauty struck him all over again.

Enough.

He turned and started to walk away, leaving Fawzi and the rest of his staff to make the arrangements for her care and comfort. Right now there were a hundred other tasks that needed his attention. 'Goodnight, Miss Scott.'

He'd only taken a few steps when heard her rush after him. 'Wait. Please. Your Highness.'

Against his will, Zaid felt the whisper of a smile tug at his lips at the way she'd tagged on his title. Reluctantly. Grudgingly.

Recalling his insistence that she use it the previous afternoon, he grimaced. Although his veins pulsed with royal blood, Zaid had never forced the outer trappings of his nobility on anyone, until her. Something about Esmeralda Scott had made him want to assert his dominion over her. Perhaps, even absurdly, he wanted to see that defiant chin and insubordinate body lowered in the archaic, submissive bow he hated from everyone else.

'Your Highness, please.'

Zaid gritted his teeth and paused at the entrance to the hallway that led to his private lift. The small group of staff who found it necessary to follow him everywhere within the palace, night or day, paused at a respectful distance.

Esmeralda, however, kept coming, her lissom, curvy body swaying sensually beneath the cotton dress. Zaid dragged his gaze from her shapely legs and hips to her face, stamping down once more on the insistent tug to his groin.

'I know it's the middle of the night, but it may as well be the middle of the day for me. I won't be able to sleep. Not until I know more about what's going to…happen.'

To me.

Zaid silently applauded her for leaving those words out. She was determined to show no weakness, despite the precarious position in which she'd placed herself and her father. A situation he'd been monitoring since she'd left his office the previous afternoon. The repercussions of her interview had been more damaging than he'd initially thought. He'd been in the process of considering ways to mitigate it when he'd been alerted to the chief of police's intentions.

Recollection of their conversation in the hotel foyer made him grit his teeth. If Esmeralda Scott wanted to know what fruit her actions had borne, he would gladly apprise her. And since he hadn't been heading for his own bed, now was as good a time as any.

He dismissed his staff, although he knew Fawzi and his bodyguards would remain awake and in close proximity until Zaid himself retired to bed. 'Very well. We will talk now,' he said to her.

He caught her quick, nervous swallow before she gave a firm, responding nod. 'Lead the way, Your Highness.'

Zaid didn't know whether to commend her fearlessness or condemn her for it, because the spirit she'd displayed, which had led her into hot water in the first place, would be what she would need to keep her going in the days to come. He was still tossing the thought around in his head when he entered his private lift. She followed him into the small space, but immediately plastered herself to the wall farthest from him. Zaid would have been amused by the action if his senses hadn't been immediately assailed with the delicate scent of her cherry blossom shampoo and the elusive wisps of perfume that clung to her skin.

The moment the doors shut, her breathing altered. Her eyes darted to him and he noted that they reflected more green than grey with her suppressed agitation. When he leaned forward to press the button, she jumped and he smiled.

'I'm glad you find this amusing, Your Highness.'

'I will take my amusements where I please since I interrupted my night to come to your aid. A task for which you have yet to thank me.'

She hesitated for a moment before she answered. 'You told me less than five minutes ago that you've effectively kidnapped me. Pardon me for not reserving the right to find out first if I've been whisked from one undesirable situation into another before frothing at the mouth with gratitude.'

With a magnetic pull he couldn't resist, his gaze dropped to her mouth again. Rouged from the distressed biting of moments ago, the plump Cupid's bow was more enticing than he wanted to acknowledge. Again it took an irritatingly large amount of control to drag his gaze away.

'I look forward to witnessing this…frothing when the time comes.'

He exited the lift straight into the office he preferred to use when he wasn't attending to scheduled matters of state.

Zaid crossed to the extensive drinks cabinet and looked over his shoulder. 'Would you like something to drink?'

'No, thank you,' she murmured, a touch distractedly.

Her gaze was taking in the less formal layout of the room—the grouping of large cushions centred around a Bedouin carpet said to have been woven by his great-grandmother, with the rarely used hookah set on a bronze tray in the middle of it; the half-divan tucked beneath an arched window, upon which lay a set of papers and his reading glasses. The suit jacket hanging at the back of a chair, and the *keffiyeh* he'd discarded hours ago when he'd come upstairs.

Zaid wasn't sure why seeing her gaze on his personal effects strummed the pulsing hunger within him. But as he turned to pour a glass of mineral water, he considered that perhaps the time had come to attend to his baser needs. Before it impinged on clear and concise thinking. Just as quickly as the thought had come, he was already discarding it. He had neither the time nor inclination to pursue any of the women from his past life, nor did he feel compelled to entertain the advances of noble families both in Ja'ahr and its prosperous neighbours, wishing to marry off their daughters to the new Sultan.

The time was coming when he'd have to do his duty, marry and produce heirs. He knew that. But not before he'd attempted to bring change to Ja'ahr and set it on a much more stable course. He didn't just owe it to his people, he owed it to the memory of his parents, who'd been assassinated in the name of power and greed.

The raw reminder helped him suppress the primal hunger caused by the presence of the woman now turning to face him again.

'You have questions,' he stated, after finishing his drink

and setting down his glass. 'If you're going to demand to leave come morning, let me pre-empt that by saying I don't foresee this being a situation that will be resolved in twenty-four hours so, no, you won't be leaving any time soon.'

Her lips parted, but she didn't immediately reply. She took a moment to absorb his words before she spoke again. 'I understand now that things are done a little…differently here. But I need to know what *any time soon* entails. I can't stay here indefinitely. I have a life to get back to.'

'Eventually, but not immediately,' he said.

She frowned. 'What?'

'You flew to Ja'ahr to support your father, did you not? I believe you've taken a month's leave of absence from work for that purpose.'

Her eyes widened. 'How do you know that?'

'I make it my business to know pertinent details surrounding my cases. Of course, your conduct yesterday afternoon also warranted a little more research into you personally.'

Zaid couldn't recall moving closer to her but suddenly they were mere feet apart. He knew it because he could see the green-grey shades of her eyes much more clearly, read the bewilderment in her expression and the rapid pulse beating at her throat.

He shoved his hands into his trouser pockets to kill the urge to splay his fingers over that silken pulse.

'Surely you can't expect me to remain here for all that time? Besides, you spoke to the chief of police, didn't you? That's why he didn't arrest me tonight?' she pressed.

Zaid shrugged. 'I bought you a temporary reprieve, but let me lay it out for you so there's no mistake. Attempt to leave this palace before I deem it safe for you to do so, and you will be arrested and imprisoned. The chief has some influence in the right circles.'

Esmeralda shook her head, her puzzlement evident as her gaze probed his. The action caused the long sheaf of her ponytail to swing, drawing his gaze to the thick rope of hair. Zaid didn't welcome the reminder of the way it had looked unbound. After a moment, she turned away, hugging her arms to her middle as she paced to the edge of the floor cushions. In the silence that pulsed between them his gaze dropped, tracing over her slim shoulders to her delicate spine and the womanly flaring of hips and curve of buttocks to the shapely length of her legs.

The sudden image of her lying on top of his cushions, wearing nothing but that saucy little see-through night slip, with her hair spread out over his pillows, punched so hard through him that his stomach muscles clenched viciously.

The fists in his pockets bunched tighter, and he veiled his eyes as she whirled back around.

'I still don't understand. Why did you save…um, come to my aid at all?'

It took precious seconds for his mind to track long enough to refocus on the decision he'd made the previous afternoon.

Raising his gaze, he reaffirmed the fact that Esmeralda Scott would not be gracing his cushions or anywhere else in his personal space. Not unless he wanted to court trouble. The woman in front of him had been in his kingdom for only a short time, and yet she'd already caused ripples that could destabilise everything he'd worked so hard for. It was time to draw some boundaries and put her firmly in her place.

'No matter your failings, I've decided you're more useful to me out of prison than in it.'

CHAPTER FIVE

'USEFUL?' ESME ECHOED.

Dark eyes gleamed at her, the haughty expression having deepened between the time she'd paced to and from the stunning arrangement of cushions on the floor. But alongside that expression she sensed something else, something that accelerated her heartbeat. Something she desperately wanted to deny. But no matter how hard she tried, a part of her brain remained locked on the magnificence of the man before her.

In her hotel room, fear and adrenaline had ruled, dictating her actions, although the keen awareness of him had been present too. Now, in the soft, exotic luxury of the lamplit room filled with his towering presence, her awareness of him had heightened to far more disturbing proportions.

'Do you need the word defined for you? I have a need for you other than as an inmate wasting away in my prison cell.'

She shook her head in confusion, an action she seemed to have repeated a few times in his presence. 'Let me get this straight. You didn't come to my aid out of the goodness of your heart but rather on the basis of what I could give you?'

The moment she said the words she realised how needy and damning they sounded. But the all-powerful man in front of her didn't give an indication that he cared one way or the other.

Zaid Al-Ameen merely shrugged, his hands easing out of his pockets to remove the robe that layered his tunic and drape it lazily over an armchair. 'Primarily. But there's room to negotiate what you could stand to gain from this arrangement.'

Through the prickling of an even sharper awareness at the sight of the impressive chest and muscles straining beneath the black tunic, Esme absorbed his words.

He wanted something from her.

Just like her father did and had done for the endless years before she'd been forced to walk away from him. Just like everyone did at one point or another in her interaction with them.

The emotion that lodged in her chest felt absurdly like hurt. Absurd because in no way should this man have the power to wound her. She'd barely known him for a day.

Pushing the feeling away, she tightened the arms clasped around her middle and returned his stare. 'And what arrangement would that be, exactly? Your Highness?' She tagged on the title to remind herself of the vast differences between them.

'Reparations for the damage you've caused,' he stated imperiously.

'Reparations?' Damn it, she really needed to stop parroting his words. 'But I have nothing to give you.'

'On the contrary, I have a need for you that would restore some goodwill in your favour.'

Her spine tingled with premonition. 'I'm sorry, you've lost me.'

His long arms clasped behind his back, the movement tugging her attention once again to the ripple of muscle beneath cotton. 'You're a social worker, are you not?'

She frowned. 'Yes.'

'There are organisations here in Ja'ahr that could use your expertise. While you're here, you will work for me.'

'Work for you? Doing what?'

'Exactly what you do back in England, helping displaced families and offering practical guidance to young adults who need it.'

She reeled at his accurate description of her role at Touch Global. 'Just how much research did you do on me?' she asked, a thudding starting in her chest at the prospect of Zaid Al-Ameen finding out everything about her, including the one incident she could never wash from her soul.

'I know relevant details.'

The imprecise response didn't bring a single ounce of relief. But she clung to the hope that if he'd gone searching for facts about her work, then Sultan Zaid wouldn't have uncovered her most damning secret.

But the man you're dealing with is a ruthless prosecutor also known as The Butcher.

Her relief collapsed under the stark reminder.

'Do I have your agreement?' Zaid pressed.

She yanked herself from the black abyss of her past and shook her head. 'No. I'm not…' She stumbled to a halt, her mind reeling at what he'd demanded of her.

'It was your wish to speak now, instead of in the morning when you would have had some sleep. It's not too late to take that option if it'll help you be less confused.'

His faint mocking tone sparked heat in her cheeks. 'I'm not confused, just…' She stopped again and took a breath. 'Well, for starters, I have no clue how your social care system works.'

He paced closer. She had to tilt her head to meet his gaze. The sensation of being small in his presence registered once again. 'The basics of social care are the same no matter where you are in the world,' he said.

She couldn't disagree. 'Okay, but there are other things to consider.'

'Such as?'

'The language barrier, for one thing.'

'Children are taught English alongside their Arabic lessons. Every citizen in Ja'ahr speaks English. Communication won't be a problem.'

Esme couldn't deny that everywhere she'd been since her arrival, she'd been met with impeccably spoken English. 'I'm only here for a month. To support my father. Everything else would be secondary to that. What good would that do anyone? And even if that weren't an issue, where would I live?'

'Here in the palace,' he responded in a low, deep voice.

'With you?'

An inscrutable look fleeted across his face, gone too quickly for her to catch, but it didn't stop another tingle of awareness from stinging her skin.

'Under my roof,' he clarified. 'Under my protection.'

The tiny catch of her breath somewhere in her midriff told her she was affording far too much importance to his words. Dozens of people lived in the Royal Palace. She would be one of many. Nothing special.

'As to how long you intend to be here,' he continued, 'if you'd taken time to do a little more research, you would've found out that a month wouldn't be anywhere near an accurate timescale to give yourself.'

'That was all I was entitled to.'

'Then an extension will need to be obtained from your employer if you truly intend to be here for your father for the entirety of the legal proceedings. I can request it from Touch Global on your behalf, if you wish. Or you can see to it yourself. Either way, the only thing that'll happen in the next four weeks is the setting of your father's trial date hearing.'

She should have waited till morning to discuss this but, then, how much deeper would he have probed and strategised?

Esme frowned. 'It takes a whole month to obtain a trial date? I thought you were pushing for an expedited trial?'

'Yes, and that won't be for six months at the earliest.'

Shock punched the breath from her lungs. *'Six months?'*

'Yes. Were I to request a normal trial, he would be looking at two years in jail before his case was even heard.'

Her eyes widened. 'You have that many untried people languishing in your prisons?' She cringed the moment the guileless words left her lips.

His head jerked back anyway, his eyes growing a touch colder. 'I believe I've already mentioned the ways in which change comes. The pursuit of zero tolerance accountability also has its unique challenges.'

Esme bit her lip, and judged it wise to choose her battles. 'I'm…sorry, I didn't mean to criticise the way you run your country. Your Highness.'

She caught another gleam in his eyes at her use of his title a second before his lashes swept low and concealed his expression, but his answer to her response was to stroll past her to the conference table. As she watched, he pressed a button on a futuristic-looking gadget sitting on the polished surface and issued fast, lyrical Arabic before he turned back to her.

'My staff will escort you to your suite. We will speak again in the morning when you are better rested.' The dismissal was final.

'But I need—'

He gave a single, implacable shake of his head, his jet-black hair gleaming beneath the soft lit chandelier. 'I have other matters to attend to, Miss Scott.'

A glance at the grand antique clock proudly displayed on his wall showed it was almost three a.m. 'At this time of night?'

'The office of the King never sleeps.'

'What about the King himself? Does he sleep? Or is he

superhuman?' she asked, before she thought better of it. To be fair, she told herself, he *looked* superhuman enough to attest to the fact that sleep was a very minor impediment that could be overlooked at will.

A knock came on the door a moment later but, unlike before, no one entered. It became clear that whoever he'd summoned was waiting for his permission to enter. Permission he withheld as he stared at her for a long, charged moment.

'You wish to discuss my sleep patterns, Miss Scott?' The question was softly voiced, but the low rumble of his tone pulsed with a new, sensual danger that heated the blood in her veins.

Despite the shifting sands beneath her feet, Esme didn't heed the warning. Esmeralda, she wanted to say. *Call me Esmeralda.* She bit off the urge at the last moment, blindly stabbing at another, more grounding question. 'I wanted to discuss what you would do if I refused you come morning. If I say no, what then?'

Everything hardened. His eyes. His face. His body. In that moment, she became fully intimate with the reason he'd earned his moniker.

'I would advise you against it because if you refuse, we will be having a very different conversation,' he rasped.

She was gritting her teeth against the chill his words brought when the door opened and Fawzi entered. Despite the late hour, he was sharp-eyed and alert, his posture ramrod straight after bowing to his master. Without taking his eyes off her, Zaid spoke in low, firm tones to his private secretary, who nodded.

'If you would come with me, Madam, your staff is waiting to escort you to your suite.'

Surprise helped her break the power of Zaid's stare. 'My *staff*?'

Fawzi tensed, once again perturbed at her direct address to him in his Sultan's presence.

'Each guest in the Royal Palace is assigned their own staff for the duration of their stay,' Zaid supplied silkily. The timbre of his tone dared her to take umbrage with that.

Esme chose retreat instead, even though something inside her pinched in disappointment that their conversation was over. 'Goodnight, Your Highness.'

As she turned to leave, she caught the mocking tilt of Zaid's brow. She silently cursed the wave of heat that rose again, studiously keeping her face averted as she followed his private secretary to the door. The ripple of awareness down her spine told her Zaid's sharp gaze stayed with her until she was out of view.

At which point, she once again experienced a plummeting of her mood. All that disappeared the moment she was faced with two women wearing varying expressions of curiosity. The older woman, dressed in a deep purple *abaya* and headscarf, was more successful at keeping her expression neutral than the younger woman, who stared at Esme with open interest.

'This is Nashwa and her assistant, Aisha.' Fawzi introduced them. 'Nashwa is in charge of the guest suites in the south wing. I will leave you in their care.'

He hurried away, leaving an awkward little silence in his wake before Esme recalled that these two women most likely spoke English.

She attempted a small smile. 'I apologise if you were woken up because of me.'

'We are here to serve at His Highness's pleasure,' Nashwa replied, gesturing gracefully to one of the many well-lit corridors that led away from Zaid's office. 'No command will ever be too great.'

Aisha nodded enthusiastically, smiling as she cast a furtive glance at Esme.

'Well, thank you, all the same,' Esme said.

Nashwa nodded, the soft fall of her gown brushing the floor as she led the way at a brisk pace.

Esme couldn't help her gasp at first sight of the elegant salmon-pink and rose-gold room she'd been allocated.

The highly polished marble floor flowed from the doorway and into the large living room. Just before the gorgeously upholstered set of sofas arranged on a Persian rug, the largest bouquet of flowers she'd ever seen had been arranged in a giant vase atop a round console table made of black lacquered wood inlaid with mother-of-pearl.

'The bedroom is this way, Madam,' Nashwa urged in a soft voice.

Esme dragged her gaze from the white baby grand piano that adorned the room and followed through a smaller set of doors.

She barely managed to suppress another gasp as she was confronted with a king-sized bed whose carved posts were painted in swirling designs of pure rose gold. Muslin curtains fluttered in cascading drapes around the pristinely covered bed, while on either side, large Moroccan lamps glowed on twin bedside tables. Smaller bouquets holding long-stemmed exotic orchids sat on the tables and when she took a breath, Esme inhaled their delicate scent.

'We took the liberty of unpacking for you, Madam. Aisha will help you with your night things or, if you prefer, we have provided you with alternative clothing.'

Following Nashwa's direction, Esme spotted a set of lingerie folded neatly on the bed. She wasn't aware she'd moved over the plush carpet until her fingers caressed the silk and lace concoction. The slip was short and similarly styled to the one she owned but with a matching robe and made of far more expensive material than her own.

Beautiful, expensive things. All around her. Things meant to be admired. Decadently enjoyed. Except everything came at a price. She'd known it from the moment her father had given her an unimaginable choice on her fourteenth birthday—foster care or boarding school with her holidays spent on the road with him. With her mother's abandonment a fresh trauma in her reality, choosing her father for a few months of the year, despite the knowledge that he was prepared to abandon her too, had felt like her only option. Until that life too had come crashing down on her head.

'Would Madam prefer this set?' Nashwa enquired.

Esme snatched her hand away, the memories and the notion that things were spinning out of her control churning faster until she felt nauseous.

'No, thank you.' She stopped, cleared her husky throat and summoned a smile. 'If you don't mind showing me where my things are?'

The older woman nodded immediately, her diplomacy firmly back in place. 'Of course, Madam.' She led the way to a dressing room and adjoining bathroom that was bigger than Esme's flat back in London.

Amongst the vast square footage of empty shelves and drawers, her meagre belongings looked forlorn occupying a single shelf. The absence of her peach night slip reminded her she was still wearing it under her dress. Unbidden, her mind skipped back to the hotel room and the sizzling effect of Zaid's gaze on her just a few short hours ago. Heat threatened to fire up again as her body tightened in recollection.

'Do you need assistance in undressing?'

Esme jumped guiltily at the softly voiced question and turned to see Aisha gliding forward with a smile.

She shook her head, then raised her hand to rub the tension headache that was making its presence felt at her temples.

'Some chamomile tea perhaps, to aid a restful sleep?' Nashwa urged.

Esme dropped her hand as weariness seeped into her bones. 'Normally I would say yes, but I don't think I'll need it. I'm ready to drop off.'

Aisha took that as a sign to make herself busy elsewhere, and Esme emerged from a quick trip to the bathroom to find that she had indeed been busy. The covers of the bed were turned down, a crystal jug of water and a glass stood on her bedside table, and the lamps were dimmed to a pleasant glow.

Both women were standing just inside the bedroom doors. With twin curtsies, they bade her goodnight and left.

Alone at last, she slipped off her dress and slid between the sheets, replaying the day's mind-boggling cascade of events. Esme wasn't unfamiliar with how one decision could change the course of one's life. She'd lived through one such unforgettable event at seventeen, and wore the scars to prove it. But even she couldn't have foreseen how a three-minute interview could have set off such a roller-coaster.

A roller-coaster that had only slowed momentarily. Come daylight, she would once again be fighting to hold on, because Zaid Al-Ameen wasn't done with her. She intended to push for a visit to her father but whether or not that plea would be granted was another matter.

It was still uppermost in her mind the moment she opened her eyes. Contrary to thinking she would toss and turn for the rest of the night, she'd slept soundly, waking to the sound of a bath being run and the scent of eucalyptus and crushed roses in the air.

Nashwa's courteous greeting and apology for waking her was followed by the announcement that the Sultan wished to see her within the hour.

After bathing, she secured her hair in a neat bun, slipped into her short-sleeved chocolate shirtdress and cinched the wide gold belt in place. The three-inch leather wedges and a touch of light make-up finished the ensemble, and five minutes later, after navigating a dozen or so corridors, she was shown into a large dining room.

Zaid was already seated at the head of the table, with two butlers standing to attention next to a sideboard heaving with food. The room, like every one she'd seen so far, was stunning beyond words, every inch draped in breathtaking masterpieces.

She would never get used to the jaw-dropping beauty of Ja'ahr's Royal Palace, but her senses were over-saturated with it. So it was easy to focus on the man dressed in a different set of traditional clothes, this time a dark gold with black trim. Or so she told herself. Deep down, she was unwilling to admit that his presence in any room in the world would command immediate and complete attention.

The black *keffiyeh* secured with gold ropes framing his head threw his sharp, handsome features into stunning relief. But the eyes that swept over her body to meet her eyes were the cause of the dipping and diving in her belly as she made her way down the long banquet table towards him.

Just like the first time they'd met, he rose to his feet, the gallant greeting belying the primitive aura that surrounded his hard, lean body. She didn't want to admit that she found it sexy. Just as she didn't want to admit that the whole package that comprised Sultan Zaid Al-Ameen was so alluring it threatened to trigger another tongue-tied episode. Fear of that happening caused Esme to force out the words tripping on her tongue.

'I want to see my father. Before any further discussion happens between us, I want to see him,' she said the moment she reached him.

'Good morning, Esmeralda. I trust you slept well?' he drawled after a telling bubble of silence.

Embarrassment temporarily swamped every other emotion. She inwardly grimaced at her lack of grace. 'I'm sorry. Good morning, Your Highness.'

He stepped towards her and pulled out her chair. About to sink gratefully into it, she froze when she felt him lean towards her. 'Despite your questionable manners, since there is a great chance we'll be in each other's company for a while, you may drop the formalities when we are alone.'

Her head swivelled to his in surprise, and then other *urgent* sensations took over when she realised how close he was. Heat from his body buffeted hers, along with the lingering scent of soap and aftershave that punched a potent awareness straight into her bloodstream.

'I… What should I call you, then?' she murmured.

His gaze drifted over her face, lingering on her lips before rising to meet hers once more. 'My given name will suffice,' he replied.

Her mouth tingling, she attempted to nod. When she barely succeeded in moving her head, she swallowed and tried her voice instead. 'I… Okay.'

That damnable brow lifted. 'Okay? Perhaps you should try using my name. Let's be sure it is satisfactory to both of us. Perhaps in a morning greeting?'

'Good morning… Zaid.'

Brandy-coloured eyes turned a shade darker. He stared at her for a handful of seconds before his lids swept down, masking his gaze. This close, Esme couldn't help but appreciate the indecently long male beauty of his lashes. Too soon, he speared her with those piercing eyes, his mouth quirking when he caught her staring.

'Sit down, Esmeralda. Our breakfast is getting cold.'

She sat. She even managed to chew and swallow a few morsels of food. All in silence while several members of staff approached to speak to Zaid. Belatedly, she realised that for him this was a working breakfast. She was thankful for the chance to collect her scattered thoughts.

What she wasn't thankful for was the ominous approach of Fawzi as they were finishing their meal. The sixth sense she'd honed during her time with her father warned her that whatever news he was about to deliver wouldn't be welcome.

To give him his due, he didn't glance her way once. But even before he bent to murmur in his master's ear, even before Zaid's jaw clenched and he cast a glance at her, Esme's belly was rolling with dread.

'What is it? What's happened?' she demanded the moment Fawzi straightened.

'It looks like you'll get to see your father much sooner than planned. There's been another altercation at the prison.'

CHAPTER SIX

ESME HURRIED TO keep up with Zaid's strides, although she had no idea where they were headed. He'd merely risen from his chair and instructed her to come with him.

'How could there have been another altercation? He's still in the prison hospital,' she said.

'No, he's not. Apparently, he was moved back to his cell in the middle of the night.'

Her heart lurched. 'And he's been attacked again already?'

'The details are still sketchy. But I'll have answers within the hour.'

She believed him. The grim set of his jaw and the purpose to his stride told her so. What she didn't realise until they approached double doors manned by sentries who swung them open to reveal a walled terrace was that he intended on seeking the answers first-hand.

Stone steps led down to meticulously landscaped gardens that rolled for almost a quarter mile. In the middle of it all, on a patch of grass, a helipad the size of two tennis courts held three helicopters with the royal insignia emblazoned on their gleaming frames.

Time slowed, along with her feet. A loud buzzing sounded in her ears, her palms growing clammy as she stared at the helicopter that Zaid was heading towards. Dry-mouthed, she urged her feet to move, but it was like being stuck in treacle.

Zaid, noticing that she wasn't beside him, turned sharply. Esme sensed more than saw his frown. 'Is something the matter?' he demanded.

The sound of his voice brought time rushing back,

fast-forwarded in a kaleidoscope of shameful, cutting memories.

Vegas.

A thrilling helicopter ride over the Grand Canyon.

Hopeful smiles and a stumbling proposal of marriage. Bryan's haunting expression when he'd discovered the truth—

'What is wrong? Are you feeling unwell?' came the sharp query.

Esme jumped, blinking back into the present and the man whose towering shadow dwarfed her.

He was staring at her with a puzzled frown, one that grew darker with each second.

'I… I'm not a fan of helicopters.'

His eyes narrowed. 'You suffer from vertigo?'

It would have been so easy to lie and say yes. But the opposite was true. Her first and last ride on a helicopter had been an exhilarating experience. It was what had come after that shot raw pain through her. Her father had laid the trap, but she'd unwittingly led Bryan into it. For that she would never forgive herself. She'd known what her father was like. 'Not exactly.'

'Then what *exactly*?'

'I just don't like them.'

'Not even when they're the quickest means of getting you to your father?' His tone suggested he found her reluctance odd.

'How long will a car journey take?'

'Too long, considering the inmates are on the verge of a full-blown riot.'

Her breath caught. 'What?'

'Your father isn't the only person I'm concerned about, Esmeralda. So if you wish to get to him quickly, we need to go.'

She swallowed, glanced at the aircraft and nodded. ‘Okay, I’ll come.’

As if he didn’t totally believe her, he grasped her elbow. Her already frenzied senses spun even faster, a shiver coursing down her spine as they neared the helicopter.

If Zaid noticed, he didn’t react. His attention was focused on the sharply dressed pilot who gave a stiff salute and held the door open. One bodyguard climbed in beside the pilot and another four scrambled into the second aircraft.

Zaid helped her up and she slid to the far side of the chopper. The two bench seats facing one another were cut off from the pilot section, affording them complete privacy. And unlike her first ride, Esme noted the moment the door shut that they wouldn’t need headphones in order to communicate. The space was completely soundproof.

A fact confirmed when Zaid settled into the seat opposite her and instructed in a low, deep voice, ‘Put on your seat belt.’

She fumbled to comply, very much aware the eyes that rested on her remained inquisitive.

She glanced over at him, to find his unwavering gaze still pinned on her. ‘I’m fine now. You don’t need to be concerned that I’ll freak out again.’

‘Do you want to explain why you chose such a critical time to go into a trance?’ he asked.

She bit her inner lip. One of the many vows she’d made to herself when she’d walked away from her father eight years ago had been never to engage in the subterfuge Jeffrey Scott loved to indulge in. The truth, no matter how brutal, was always preferable to lies. If she’d confronted the truth eight years ago, seen her father for who he really was, Bryan might still be alive.

But telling Zaid the unvarnished truth right now would be opening not just herself but also her father up to total annihilation because Zaid was still the prosecutor intent on putting her father away. She could, however, offer an explanation without incriminating herself or her father.

'I had a bad experience after a helicopter ride a long time ago.'

'Where?' he fired back.

'Does it matter?'

He didn't answer. At least not with his lips anyway. His eyebrow, however, lifted in direct challenge of her defensive response.

She glanced out of the window, noted the severely dilapidated landscape abutting the desert in the distance. 'In… Las Vegas.'

'You were with a lover?' he asked.

Her gaze flew to his, her breath crushing in her lungs at the bold demand stamped across his face.

She wanted to tell him that it was none of his business.

But somehow, in that moment, denying Bryan's existence felt like dishonouring the man who'd been marked just by associating with her.

She prevaricated for a moment, then exhaled. 'I was with someone who cared about me.' Bryan hadn't been her lover. But he was the reason she'd never taken a lover. He was the reason that, at twenty-five, she was still a virgin.

'You were the reason the experience ended badly?'

His mildly condemning tone made her insides clench. 'Why would you assume that?'

'I wouldn't be good at my profession if simple deduction eluded me that easily, Esmeralda. Besides, a high percentage of couples who take such helicopter rides are already involved or about to be. You choose your words carefully, but correct me if I'm mistaken that things ended badly because you had a change of heart about advancing the relationship?'

He struck so close to the truth it robbed her of breath.

He took her slack-jawed look as confirmation, and his gaze hardened. 'Let me guess, he wanted to take things to the next level, and you suddenly decided you had somewhere else to be?'

'You make me sound so…calculating.' Which was such an apt description of Jeffrey Scott's annihilation of Bryan, she suppressed a shiver.

'Do I? If not that, then what? What was this bad experience that still makes you green at the gills with guilt?' His voice was harsher, his expression haughtily superior.

He'd seen her guilt. She had nowhere to hide. 'He… proposed to me…after the helicopter ride.'

Sharp, narrowed eyes darted to her bare left hand, then back to her face. 'And you said no, obviously.' Why was there such a thick vein of satisfaction in his voice? Was he that glad that he'd proved her as callous as she'd been forced to be with Bryan?

'Yes, I said no. I couldn't marry him.' For one thing, she'd been not quite eighteen to Bryan's twenty-one. For another, she hadn't been in love with him. And that was even before she'd discovered what her father had done to him.

'Why not?'

'I just couldn't.'

Although his gaze remained on her, he didn't probe further. Which was a relief, since everything that had occurred afterwards ate like acid in her belly, even after all this time. The pain of it would never go away. Someday it might lessen, enough for her to forge something of a life she could be proud of. Until then, her work would be her life.

The sudden dip of the helicopter had her gripping her seat, her heart tripping over itself. A quick look out the window showed they were approaching their destination. Like most prisons in the world, this one too consisted of large, interconnecting buildings ring-fenced by miles of menacing barbed wire, towers with guards armed to the teeth. Despite the awful things he'd done, the thought of her father spending the rest of his days there—

'Easy,' Zaid drawled from across her. 'You're in danger of ripping the seat to shreds.'

Esme looked down. Her knuckles were white from her death grip on the soft leather. With a deep breath, she released her hold on it, but her gaze returned to the looming structure. There were no outward signs of unrest. Which should have brought a little relief. Until her gaze flickered once more to Zaid.

'Should you be here?'

Dark brows clamped in a frown. 'Excuse me?'

'You're the Sultan. You're also the man who presumably put a lot of the criminals in there behind bars. Aren't you…won't you be exposing yourself to…um, danger at the prison?'

His brow slowly cleared. 'Are you concerned about my welfare, Esmeralda?' The softly voiced question rumbled between them, gaining an electric note that sent a jolt of awareness through her.

'I'm merely making a pertinent observation,' she replied.

The dangerous sensuality left his expression, replaced by the merciless resolution she was beginning to associate with the ruler of Ja'ahr. 'You expect me to cower behind the safety of my palace walls in times of crisis?'

It was the last thing she expected. His presence in her hotel room alone when he needn't have come to her aid at all was testament to the fact that Zaid Al-Ameen didn't back down from confrontations.

Letting his police chief take her would have been one less problem for him to contend with. Instead, he'd done the opposite. 'No, but that doesn't mean you should rush into danger either. What if…something happens to you?'

'So you *are* troubled by the idea of harm coming to me.' His voice held definite mockery, but it also held another ephemeral note. One that stroked her senses, and drew her gaze magnetically to his. The gold flecks that swirled through his eyes were almost hypnotic, transmitting a call that struck a curious hunger within her. When his gaze dropped to her lips, Esme's breath stuttered then died in her lungs. The need to slick her tongue over the tingling lower lip grew too strong to resist. She watched his eyes darken as he followed the slow glide.

'Being concerned about someone's safety is an act of common decency. Is that so bad?' Her voice was a husky murmur laden with emotions she didn't want to name.

A touch of hard cynicism fleeted over his face. 'In my experience, most acts of selflessness come at a price. I have learned that it's better to look a gift horse in the mouth. That way you know exactly what you're getting.'

The helicopter jostled gently as it rotated and landed with barely a bump on a designated platform near the outer perimeter of the prison. Zaid made no move to get out. Neither did she. The cocoon they were wrapped in felt too intimate, too powerful to break.

'You're entitled to your opinion, I suppose. But I assure you, my concern doesn't come with a price.'

'Perhaps not in this instance. Can you say the same for the future?' he queried.

'I can't predict the future, Zaid. Neither can you.'

His smile didn't touch his eyes, and his gaze flicked from her eyes to her mouth and back again, as if he couldn't look away. 'But it's in my interest to mitigate against it.'

'And that includes any emotional support offered to you? What kind of life is that?'

'One that grants me a high percentage of not being

surprised by the unexpected. I much prefer to see things coming than not.'

She shook her head, unable to come up with an appropriate response. Another handful of seconds passed, then he lifted his hand in a subtle, graceful command.

The doors slid back. Just like in the early hours of this morning, he alighted first, then turned to take her hand.

She attempted to guard herself against the pulse of erotic static she suspected would strike again when she touched him. But it was no use. The moment her palm brushed his, tiny volts of electricity shot over her skin. The short, sharp breath she sucked in was echoed by a more masculine sound from him.

Esme wasn't sure whether to be pleased or terrified that Zaid was just as affected as she was. Since Bryan she'd taken pains to avoid any form of emotional entanglement. The cost of her single mistake had been too much to ever risk letting her guard down. Nevertheless, the notion that she wasn't in this alone, that she wasn't imagining this powerful chemistry between them, was slightly easier to bear. Besides, from what he'd said only minutes ago, Zaid had no intention of letting any of this…disquieting reaction affect him. So her panic was unnecessary.

Satisfied with that conclusion, she stepped out beside him, even risked a glance at the dominant, patrician features of the King. To find his own gaze fixed on her with an intensity that made the hairs rise on her nape.

'Had we the time, I would be curious to know what machinations were being hatched behind that exquisite face,' he murmured.

Any response from her was forestalled by the swift arrival of a tall, lean man. He barely spared her a glance, his brisk bow and effusive greeting reserved for his Sultan.

But after a minute Zaid turned to her, no trace of the jittery sensation that still fizzed beneath her skin visible on his face. He was back to being the imperial overlord of his desert kingdom. 'This is the warden of the prison. He has arranged for you to see your father, while I attend to other matters.'

They sailed through three security checkpoints and arrived at a surprisingly well-appointed reception hall.

'Your father will be brought to you presently, Miss Scott,' the warden stiffly informed her, gesturing to one of the seats.

'Thank you,' she replied, then, as if drawn by a magnet, her gaze darted back to Zaid. He was clearly issuing instructions in Arabic to two of his bodyguards. She watched, stunned, as they approached and flanked her. Zaid's eyes met hers for an instant, then he turned and left the room with the warden.

The notion that she was under guard should have disturbed her. Except, again, the notion that Zaid was ensuring her safety assumed paramount proportions in her mind.

Or he's making sure you won't attempt to do anything else to embarrass him.

She was mulling that over when the doors opened.

Esme's heart jumped into her throat.

Despite the wheelchair he sat in, he was still restrained, the chains binding his hands connected to his ankles over the cuffs of his dark grey jumpsuit. But that wasn't the most shocking aspect of the prisoner rolling forward towards her.

The Jeffrey Scott she'd walked away from eight years ago had been the quintessential English gentleman, impeccable from the carefully groomed hair, slightly greying the temples, right down to the Oxford wingtip shoes he'd favoured.

The man in front of her was painfully thin, with severely dishevelled, shocking white hair and a full, unkempt beard. His skin was sallow, his cheeks and forehead grazed with signs of the fight he'd been involved in.

He saw her shock and gave a wry smile as the grim-faced guard applied the brakes to the wheelchair and retreated to a watchful distance.

They stared at each other for a long minute before he indicated his chains and gave a bitter laugh. 'I know I look a dreadful sight. Not like you, though.'

And just like that the faint tendrils of guilt that had always dwelled beneath the surface of her relationship with her father threatened to resurface.

Before Esme had come along, her parents had lived a high-octane lifestyle financed through fraud. Then Abigail Scott had got pregnant and decided to settle down. Her father had managed enforced domesticity for a few years, but had eventually succumbed to his old ways. Their disagreements and unhappiness had finally culminated in her mother walking out when Esme was fourteen. Abigail had moved to the Australian outback and was killed in a horse-riding accident barely a year later.

For months after her mother had left, she'd watched her father grapple with what to do with her. The ultimatum of boarding school with holidays spent with him or foster care had been delivered with the clear expectation that she would choose the latter option. He was all she had left in the world, for better or worse. It was why Esme had chosen to spend her holidays with him, even though she'd disapproved of his lifestyle. Better that than foster care.

It wasn't until it was too late that she'd realised just how unlovable she was to the man who should have loved and cared for her during her childhood. Perhaps being cast adrift in the foster care system would have been preferable.

She pushed the pain back now and returned her father's gaze as he continued, 'You look very well, Esmeralda. Even better than you did on TV.'

'You saw the broadcast?'

He smiled, eyes the same shade as hers twinkling wickedly. 'Only about a dozen times, until the warden banned it. Thanks for giving them hell.'

Esme winced. 'I may have caused more harm than good.'

He shrugged. 'Who cares?'

She frowned. 'I do.'

His smile dimmed, a harsher look entering his eyes. 'You have a soft heart. That's always been your downfall. But don't beat yourself up about it. You achieved what you wanted, didn't you?'

'At what price, though? Isn't there a riot brewing now because of it?'

His chains rattled as he waved away her concern. 'A riot is always brewing in this place.' After a quick glance at the guard, he leaned forward and said under his breath, 'But we can work all this to our advantage. The moment I saw you on TV, I knew things were looking up.'

'You couldn't possibly have predicted this?'

He sent her a droll look. 'How many times did you see me place the most unlikely bet and come out on top?'

Her unease grew, her heart picking up its beat as she stared at him. 'So you gambled with your health, with your *life*?'

He sat back with a huff. 'What life? I'd much rather throw a final dice than end up here for the long term. And I was right to do so, wasn't I? The rumours are true? You're living with Sultan Al-Ameen at the Royal Palace?'

'How do you—?' She stopped and shook her head. 'No, not in that way—'

'Don't lie to me!'

A knot of anger burst through her. 'I'm not lying! And I don't intend to, not for you, or for anyone.'

'That's a shame. You could have been so good at it if you hadn't been so pious and boring.'

The anger disappeared as quickly as it had arrived, leaving her sad and disappointed. 'I was a child, Dad. A child you manipulated and blackmailed to suit your own selfish gains.'

'Those selfish gains you're sneering at put you through boarding school, put food in your belly and gave you a front seat to a life most people dream of.'

'You were…*are* a con artist,' she whispered raggedly.

'And you benefitted from the fruits of my labour.' He grinned suddenly, as if the memory brought him paternal pride. 'So does the Sultan know what you did to that poor sucker in Vegas?'

Icy fingers crawled up her spine and latched onto her nape, along with a renewed dose of anger. 'That *man's* name was Bryan. And I didn't do anything to him. He was my friend before *you* ruined everything.'

'Still doesn't answer my question. Does the big man know?'

She blinked back tears, and pursed her lips. 'I haven't divulged every detail of my personal life to him, if that's what you're asking.'

All traces of laughter left his face. 'Because you don't plan on being here that long?'

'I'll be here for your trial.'

'And then what? You'll wait until they lock me up permanently and then wash your hands of me once and for all?' he sneered.

'I don't—'

His chains jangled again as his hand slashed through the air. 'Forget it. Maybe I'll die before any of this happens.'

She inhaled sharply. 'Don't say that!'

'Why not? Maybe expecting you to forget the past was too much to hope for—'

Whatever he'd been about to say was suddenly chopped off by the deep spate of coughing that racked him. The horrendous sound, accompanied by the sound of the rattling chains in jarring synchronicity, went on for almost a minute. And then he lowered his hand.

Three things happened almost simultaneously.

Esme's heart lurched at the bright red smear of blood coating her father's palm.

Her father's eyes caught hers for a moment then began to roll back in his head as his body listed sickeningly to the side.

Zaid walked back into the room, his eyes latching on her as she lunged for her father.

'Esmeralda.'

She barely heeded the taut command in his voice. Barely felt him arrive beside her as she dropped to her knees next to the wheelchair.

'Dad?'

'Step away from him, Esmeralda.'

'No!' Fear climbing into her throat, she placed her hand on his father's cheek. 'Dad!'

He didn't respond.

Zaid spoke sharply in Arabic, and she heard the sound of running feet. 'Esmeralda.'

She shook her head, her gaze fixed on the unmoving form of her father. 'Dad!'

Strong hands gripped her shoulders and pulled her up. Blindly she turned, fisted Zaid's lapels and stared into his grim face. 'I'll give you whatever you want. Please. Just help him!'

CHAPTER SEVEN

THE NEXT WEEK passed at times in a dizzying blur, at times in nerve-racking slow motion.

Her father had received the diagnosis of severe bronchitis and possible pneumonia with a shrug when he finally came round, and his fatalistic attitude seemed to deepen by the minute. Esme, her despair escalating, pleaded with Zaid again. His response after she'd been summoned to his office on her return from the hospital that first night had been bracing, to say the least.

'And what do you expect me to do about it?'

'Something. Anything! Please, Zaid. His lawyer isn't answering his phone calls. I know you're the prosecutor but surely you can make a recommendation for something to be done?'

'Something like what?' he enquired coldly. 'And don't be coy about what you want. I know many conversations have taken place between you and your father at the hospital.'

'I'm not asking for anything that's outside the law. Can't you offer him protective custody or something like that? And before you say he's a criminal, remember he hasn't been tried and found guilty yet. If the rule of law means so much to you, then prove it. Treat him like a human being and help me stop this from happening again.'

Despite the condemning emotions that swirled through his eyes at her outburst, he didn't respond immediately. She knew the tide was about to turn. So far his actions had been those of the ruler of a rich, if somewhat turbulent kingdom. But the ruthless lawyer whose skills had been honed in the glass and chrome power corridors of Washington DC was finally emerging.

He rounded his desk and placed himself squarely before her. 'You wish me to help your father?'

'Yes.'

'Is this where you suggest a *quid pro quo* arrangement? Reiterate your offer to do *anything*?'

The knot of apprehension didn't prevent her from responding. 'If it'll help my father, then yes.'

Again a contemplative silence greeted her question. Then he returned to his desk. 'Very well. You will be informed of the exact details in due course.'

In due course resulted in days of being left in suspense by his absolute silence until her summons today to the house two hours outside Ja'ahr City.

The trip to Jeddebah had been as rough and unforgiving as the terrain surrounding the stunning property in which she now stood, although Esme admitted some parts of it had been raw in their beauty and magnificent to witness.

The mountains, for instance. Green and majestic to the east, they formed a sharp contrast to the distant and endless roll of the desert to the west. Until they dramatically gave way to the turbulent waters of the Persian Gulf. She'd arrived three hours ago at the location on the southernmost point of Ja'ahr half an hour before a security escort had delivered her father.

Esme had been relieved to see his mood dramatically improved, despite the armed guards surrounding him and the menacing-looking security monitor attached to his left ankle. Despite his state, it didn't take long for the healthier-looking Jeffrey Scott to begin subtly owning the place.

A place she'd secured for him at a price she had yet to be fully cognisant of.

She'd been informed of her father's transfer to house arrest by Fawzi this morning, but the Sultan's private secretary had been mute about everything else, including when she would see Zaid again.

But she wasn't going to be kept in the dark for long.

She'd watched the helicopter land on the vast green lawn abutting the sheer cliffs of the house minutes ago. From the west-facing window she'd followed the tall, imposing figure silhouetted against the setting sun as he'd ducked beneath the rotor blades before striking a path for the house. His dark robes flowed dramatically around his head and body as he walked. He went out of sight, and her stomach hollowed. The sensation wasn't acute but it was real and astonishing enough to realise that she'd missed seeing Zaid.

Exhaling in a burst of unnerving disquiet, she frowned as her brain wrestled with the astounding revelation. She was still frozen in place when she sensed his presence. She didn't need to turn around to confirm that those penetrating eyes were on her body. Her spine was tingling, the skin between her shoulders twitching with an awareness she had no hope of suppressing. But still she fought what was happening to her. She had to try. Giving in to even a tiny bit of it would be risking emotions she'd sworn never to dally with again. Letting emotions get the better of her, letting herself be swept away with possibilities of a different life had ended badly the only time she'd allowed someone in.

So she stood at the window, fighting the sensations rampaging through her body with everything she had.

'Are you going to turn around and greet me, Esmeralda?' he drawled in a deep, low voice.

Her stomach dipped and tightened at the way he pronounced her name, the sensuality it evoked. Esme clenched her fists against the feeling, and turned.

'Hello, Za… Your Highness.' She changed her mind over using his given name. It was safer that way. Safer to maintain distance between them.

Keep this straightforward.

Keep it professional.

'Thank you for arranging all this for my father.' She indicated the room, and the house. 'And also for his care at the hospital. I don't know what would've happened if you hadn't been there. So…thank you.'

'Is this finally the frothing of gratitude you promised?' he asked as he stepped deeper into the room, his grace and elegance evoking images of a sleek jungle predator.

The reminder of her waspish words triggered a blush, one she was still fighting when he stopped in front of her. The disparity in their heights forced her head up. Again she was unable to quell the zap of heat that arrowed through her. 'If that is what you wish it to be.'

He remained silent for a stretch before he spoke. 'I would've preferred it not to have been triggered by your father,' he said, his voice containing a bite that produced a different reaction from her. She watched him cast a displeased glance around the room before returning his attention to her. 'I take it he's better pleased with his accommodations?' he drawled.

'Yes, he is.'

Esme wasn't surprised at all when his mouth flattened. 'He orchestrated everything to end up this way. You know this, don't you?' he bit out, his mood darkening further.

Her heart dropped because that same thought had occurred to her. 'Maybe. But the fact remains that his health, not to mention his personal safety, was at risk at the prison.'

The hand he lifted to trace her cheek was gentle but, in direct contrast, the look in his eyes was stark, resigned with more than a trace of bitterness.

Esme swallowed, instinctively shying away from knowing whatever was coming even as her skin heated and tingled at his touch.

'Be that as it may, you've proved me right after all. Nothing comes without a price.'

'But we're both getting what we want. Isn't that all that matters?' Her voice was barely a murmur, his continued caress and their opposing conversation ripping her concentration to shreds.

'Is that how you justify coming to a criminal's aid?' he accused.

Stung, she jerked away from his hand. 'I'm helping him because, criminal or not, he doesn't deserve to be attacked! I'd do the same for anyone else.'

'But you're going over and above for your father, despite knowing exactly what kind of man he is.'

The urge to fold her arms in the universal posture of defence was strong. But she managed to keep her hands at her sides. 'Did you come here merely to condemn me and my father?'

'I came to take you back to the palace. The next stage of our arrangement needs to be hammered out.'

A foreboding little shiver went through her. 'But my father—'

'Will be fine. One of his guards is an army medic. Besides, our agreement doesn't include you remaining here to play nursemaid.'

'What does it include exactly? You haven't yet told me.'

'We will discuss it back at the palace. If you wish to say goodbye to your father, do it now.'

'Did someone mention me?'

Zaid tensed at the intrusion. Then they both turned.

The eyes of a newly shaven, showered and dressed Jeffrey swung from her to Zaid. Then he executed a graceful bow worthy of an award-winning performance. 'Your

Highness, please allow me to express my gratitude for the kindness you have shown me.'

'You have your daughter to thank for this,' Zaid rasped.

Her father straightened and eyed her, the speculative gleam in his eyes intensifying. 'Do I? I hope the cost wasn't too dear. I don't know what I'd do without her.' His gaze returned to Zaid. 'She's the only family I have left, you see.'

Something passed between the two men. Something that made Esme's hackles rise. But then her father smiled and the sensation shifted. 'Are you staying for dinner, Esmeralda?' he asked. 'Your Highness, I would be honoured to have your company too, of course.'

'She's not staying,' Zaid answered for her. 'Neither am I. Remember, Mr Scott, that the only thing that has changed is the location of your incarceration. And this is only temporary. I'm sure you'll also have noticed that there isn't another dwelling for miles and no means of escape. There's a security drone watching the house at all times. Attempt anything foolish and steps will be taken to stop you. As for future dinners with your daughter, that won't be happening any time soon. After today, she will be permitted to visit you as per the usual regulations—once a week, in the middle of the day.'

Her father gave a curt nod. 'Understood, Your Highness.'

Zaid turned to her. 'We're leaving.' The command gave no room for refusal.

Even though a part of her was relieved not to have been forced into a lingering goodbye with her father, Esme was still bristling by the time she settled into the now-familiar seat of the helicopter and they took off.

He shifted in his seat and she jumped when his robe brushed her leg.

'Do you have something to say to me, Esmeralda, or

am I to be given the silent treatment for the whole of the journey?'

She turned her head, then wished she hadn't when she noted just how close he was. 'Did you have to talk to him like that?'

'Like what? A man who doesn't make his living from exploiting weakness in others? Tell me he wasn't seeking to take advantage of the situation and I will offer my regrets.'

She couldn't reply because she couldn't refute the accusation.

Silence fell between them for another ten minutes until she couldn't stand it any longer.

'Whatever he's done, he's still my father. Would you turn your back on yours in my shoes?'

'My father lived an exemplary life of honour and integrity. I would never have needed to make such a sacrifice,' he stated, overwhelming pride stamped in his voice.

But that wasn't what caught Esme's attention. It was his use of the past tense. 'Lived?' she asked, the thought occurring to her that although she knew he'd inherited the throne after his uncle's death from a heart attack, she hadn't come across any information about his parents in her brief research. Come to think of it, information on Zaid's own childhood and teenage years had been very sparse. Only his early professional life and later accomplishments had been documented.

She glanced at him at his continued silence and only then noticed the tension that gripped him. Even before he spoke, Esme knew something huge was coming. 'My father has been dead for a very long time,' he said.

Her chest tightened in sympathy. 'And your mother?'

His mouth compressed, dispersing the momentary flash of pain she glimpsed in his face. 'They perished together.'

Her earlier admonition to herself to stay away from personal subjects replayed in her mind, only to be ignored. 'How did they die?'

In the semi-darkness of the helicopter, his face settled into ragged, haunted lines. 'They were assassinated by my uncle as we drove home from my thirteenth birthday celebrations.'

Shock held her rigid for several seconds. 'Oh, Zaid… My God. I'm… I don't know what to say!'

'In such circumstances there rarely are adequate words,' he replied.

'I shouldn't have pried in the first place,' she returned, horrified at churning up bad memories for him.

He shrugged offhandedly, although the eyes that probed hers were an intense dark bronze. 'You have me wide open, Esmeralda. Ask your questions and I will answer them.'

The distinctive American term reminded her where he'd grown up. 'Did you go to the States after…after what happened to your parents?'

'I couldn't stay here. Not unless I wished to invite another attempt on my life.'

She gasped. 'You mean your uncle intended you to be killed too?'

'He had his eye on the throne. That meant doing away with everyone who stood in his way, including the boy who would grow to be the man with the rightful claim to the throne. He'd meant to have us all killed that night. My father shielded me with his body and his aides managed to raise the alarm before Khalid's men could finish the job properly.'

The matter-of-fact way he relayed the tale didn't stop her from seeing the pain in his eyes.

'What…what happened after that?'

'Khalid's hands were tied. He couldn't very well execute a child without incurring the wrath of his people, even though everyone knew how he'd become Sultan. Some things are unforgivable. I was delivered to my maternal grandmother and given safe passage out of Ja'ahr on condition that we would never return, and a murderer and despot took power and ruled Ja'ahr for twenty years. The rest, as they say, is history.'

For several minutes, she absorbed the stomach-turning news, a few pennies beginning to drop.

'That's why you became a lawyer, isn't it? To put criminals like your uncle behind bars? Perhaps to challenge his rule when the time came?'

A bitter smile cracked his lips, but it was gone in the next instant. 'I dedicated every day of my life after I was tossed out of the only home I'd ever known to honing judicial weapons that would right the wrongs done to my parents and to me. Except Khalid had the audacity to succumb to his excessive indulgences and die of a heart attack caused by a clogged artery before I got the chance to see justice done.'

The cold observation sent a shiver through her. So did the stark confirmation of why Zaid was a formidable opponent to have. The harrowing wrongs done to him as a child, and to his people in the years following, was the reason some viewed him as a ruthless ruler now. It was also the reason he didn't trust anyone.

But most of all, Esme knew, staring at him, that it was the reason he could never find out about her past. Those few weeks with Bryan and how everything had ended would never be struck from her copybook, no matter whose fault it had been. She didn't know what would happen to her father during his trial, but she instinctively knew that the reluctant concession Zaid had granted her father would be withdrawn the second he found out.

Unease whispered up her spine at the thought of discovery. And this time not even reminding herself that she was no longer that person could wash away that sensation.

But still she met his gaze, infused truth into her words. 'I'm sorry,' she said again. 'I didn't mean to drag all of this up for you.'

'Curiosity is a natural occurrence when swimming in the getting-to-know-you waters, at least on the part of women, is it not?'

The tiny mocking voice inside her head that irked her for wanting to know just how many women he'd *got to know* was smothered in favour of a much more persistent and powerful emotion. One that had her shifting sideways, the better to see his face, she told herself. What she didn't account for was her hand disobeying her brain to slide over the seat and come to rest on top of his. 'As is sympathy. I'm sorry for your loss.' Her voice was a husky murmur, reflecting her lingering regret at bringing up memories that must be hard for him to recall.

Zaid didn't answer. Instead his gaze dropped to the pale hand she'd placed over his brown one. To the fingers starting to tremble as that blasted, ever-present hyperawareness thickened in the space between them.

Still without speaking, he turned his hand over, splaying it open until his larger palm was pressed firmly against hers, dominating her small one. Heat singed their touching flesh as acutely as if a naked flame had been held against it. The sight of their clasped hands shouldn't have been so basely erotic. But it was.

He moved, sliding his skin more firmly against hers. Esme gasped as the sensation lodged low in her belly, then unfurled throughout her body, concentrating with shameless urgency between her thighs.

She dragged her gaze up a breathless second before she realised his intention. She had time to move, time to duck her head or vocalise her denial. But she didn't draw away. Because she didn't want to.

She stayed put, breath strangled to nothing, as Zaid slid his fingers through the loose knot of her hair and drew her firmly, inexorably, towards his kiss.

Just like the man, the kiss was unapologetically dominant, his mouth owning hers the moment they touched. He tasted of Ja'ahrian coffee and an elusive spice. He tasted like all the forbidden desires she'd sworn off years ago. But the formidable man who'd already taken up far too much room in her head was impossible to deny.

Hot, hungry, and intent on conquering her, Zaid pressed her back against the seat, angled his lips for a better fit and charged through her feeble defences.

Within seconds, her lips were parting beneath the possessive pressure of his, letting him in when he demanded entry. The slow, glorious slide of his tongue against her lower inner lip elicited a moan she couldn't have suppressed if she'd tried. As if the sound pleased him, he repeated it again and again, before catching her plump lip between his teeth. The nip of his teeth sent sparks racing through her system. She was chasing that unfamiliar strain of delight when he delved deeper between her lips. This time, his tongue slid boldly against hers. Pleasure arrowed straight between her legs, plumping up her most sensitive flesh, turning her slick with shockingly demanding need as the fingers in her hair drew her even closer.

On a desperate whimper that echoed through the enclosed space, Esme opened even wider for him, the hand lying against his on the seat shifting to grip him tighter. Zaid gave a thick groan, then meshed his fingers through hers. He brought their clasped hands up between them, then pressed his body against hers.

The feel of his heart beating against her hand, hers beating against his, caused something to lurch alarmingly inside her. Reluctant to explore why in that moment, she chose a different type of exploration. With her free hand, she slid her fingers over one strong bicep. Sleek muscles immediately rippled beneath her touch. Emboldened, she caressed upward, over the broad curve of his shoulder, to the neck opening of his robe. At the first brush of her fingers against his bare nape, Zaid muttered a thick, foreign imprecation. The sound was smashed between them as his kiss took on a frenzied, bone-melting intimacy. Something jolted inside her again. Only she realised a moment later that the movement wasn't just inside her.

The sound of the pilot's door sliding open announced their arrival back at the Royal Palace. She jerked back from Zaid, then pushed frantically at his muscled chest when he didn't budge. His fingers convulsed in her hair for a charged second before he drew back. But although he sat back in his seat, his hand held hers for another moment, his gaze tracking over her face with blatant hunger before he released her.

'Come. We will continue this inside,' he instructed in a rough, hoarse voice, then lifted his hand in a signal to his guards.

The notion that he just expected her to fall into his lap…or his bed, struck a fiery nerve, but, with the usual clutch of staff accompanying them, she had no choice but to swallow her irritation as she walked silently at his side.

Lost in her ire, Esme didn't realise where they were until the scents of mouth-watering spices and cooked meat hit her nostrils. Surprised and curiously out of sorts, she glanced around the dining room.

'We're having dinner?' she asked the moment his ever-present entourage were dismissed and they were alone.

Faint amusement drifted over his features, although his eyes retained a turbulent heat and his body a banked tension that suggested he was still caught in the throes of what had happened in the helicopter.

'Did you think that I intended to whisk you straight into my bed and have my way with you?' he drawled.

Heat flared up to stain her cheeks at his accurate reading of her thoughts. All the same, she raised her chin. 'You say that as if it would've been a foregone conclusion.'

He sauntered towards her, removing his *keffiyeh* and tossing it on a nearby surface. His outer robe followed, leaving him in only his muscle-skimming tunic and trousers. With his magnificent body on display, Esme couldn't fault his powerful animal grace, the lithe movement effortlessly trapping her attention, capturing both her mind and body.

She held her breath as he reached out, lazily, assuredly, and trailed his thumb over the mouth he'd kissed so thoroughly barely fifteen minutes ago. The mouth he eyed hungrily for a long moment, before his gaze met hers.

'I am not ashamed to admit that I desire you, Esmeralda. You captivate me. What took place a little earlier tells me the feeling is mutual. Where that captivation takes us is a destination I intend to thoroughly enjoy exploring.' His voice was full of erotic promise, of heady delights that had her body throbbing anew, setting off sensual fires that thrilled and terrified her.

It was the latter emotion that had her stepping back. 'It won't take us anywhere,' she blurted, as much out of the need to spell it out for herself as it was for him.

Pure male arrogance blazed from his eyes. When his gaze dropped to her lips again, it was all she could do not to tug the still tingling flesh into her mouth. 'Are you sure about that?' he challenged, his voice low, laced with sensual danger.

Alarm growing, Esme took another step back. 'Yes, I'm

sure. What happened tonight was a mistake. Rest assured, it won't happen again.'

It seemed almost superhuman, the way he concisely eradicated every vestige of arousal from his face. It didn't happen immediately, so she had time to wonder why her disappointment was so cutting, why she was already mourning something she'd rejected so definitively.

CHAPTER EIGHT

IT TOOK A considerable amount of effort to lock her knees to stay put as his hand dropped.

'Very well. But we still need to discuss the flip side of our arrangement,' he said, his tone brisk as he spun on his heel and walked to the head of the table. 'We'll do that while we eat. Unless you object to dinner too?' he threw over his shoulder.

'No, dinner is fine,' she said, scrambling to gather her wits.

She followed at a slower pace, properly taking in her surroundings for the first time. This dining room was different from where she'd shared breakfast with him a week ago. It was also different from where she herself had eaten her meals every day for the last week.

'Where are we? I mean, which part of the palace?' she asked when they were seated at the table.

'In my private wing.'

Which included his bedroom, she concluded on a dizzy, unwelcome thought. Were they, even now, a stone's throw from where Zaid slept? And did he sleep alone? It was the first time Esme had given herself permission to dwell on just who shared the enigmatic Sultan's bed. But now that she'd made it clear she had no intention of falling into his bed, her brain couldn't let go of wondering just who he would invite there instead.

She hadn't seen signs of it because she'd been preoccupied with other things, namely her father, but did the Ja'ahrian Royal Palace, as with most Sultanates, possess a harem?

The strong urge to ask hovered on her tongue. She bit

back the impulse and helped herself to the platter of fragrant couscous served with salad and an assortment of sliced meats. From previous meals, she knew the meats had been slow roasted for hours with honey, spices and nuts. The promise of the melt-in-your-mouth offering reminded her she hadn't eaten since breakfast.

'That isn't too much of an inconvenience for you, I hope?' he said blandly, and she realised he'd been watching her, waiting for a reaction to his answer.

'Not at all,' she offered boldly.

The twitch of his lips told her he didn't entirely believe her. But he didn't contradict her.

They ate the first course in silence, the uneasy tension building until chewing and swallowing each morsel of the delicious food became a chore.

'As of this afternoon, I have recused myself as your father's prosecutor.'

It was the last thing she'd expected him to say. But once absorbed, the statement should have brought relief. Instead, her senses tingled with a not so terrifying warning. 'Why?'

'I want there to be no conflict of interest arising from my association with you.'

'But…we have no association.'

Brandy-coloured eyes gleamed for a moment before his lashes swept his expression away. 'Not yet. But that is going to change soon, I think.'

For some reason, her breath strangled in her lungs. 'Even though our association will be strictly professional?'

He stared at her for a moment before his gaze dropped again, and Esme got the uncanny feeling he was keeping something from her. 'Even so.'

'Um, okay. Who will take your place?'

'That is for my attorney general to decide. He will present me with his recommendations at the end of this week.'

Before she could ask further questions, two butlers entered. She remained silent as their plates were whisked away, and just as efficiently dessert platters were set on the table before the servers were dismissed.

The creations were too exquisite to resist, even though Esme doubted she would be able to do them justice. Nevertheless, she helped herself to dates stuffed with goats' cheese and sprinkled with sugar, butter biscuits topped with Ja'ahrian yoghurt, and sweet dumplings topped with honey and ground pistachios.

'Touch Global have a base here in Ja'ahr,' he said without preamble the moment they were alone again.

Her nape tingled in premonition as she sampled a dumpling. 'I wasn't aware of that.'

'They weren't encouraged in their social work programme in my kingdom until recently,' he expanded.

He meant until after Khalid Al-Ameen's death and Zaid's ascension to the throne. The realisation that the dilapidated state of his kingdom was down to his uncle and not to Zaid hit home with brute force. Everything she'd accused him of during her TV interview came back to bite her hard. The fish had indeed rotted from the head down, but it had been a different head altogether.

'And that's what you want in repayment for what you did for my father? For me to work with Touch Global's branch here in Ja'ahr?' she asked.

He didn't answer immediately. Instead, he picked up a stuffed date and popped it into his mouth. The act of watching another person chew shouldn't have been so engrossing. And yet Esme couldn't look away from the tight jaw, the shadowed cheek or the sexy mouth that had possessed her own so expertly.

He swallowed and her breathing settled. Until she saw the brooding look in his eyes as he stared at her. 'No. I have decided to utilise your expertise in another way.'

The tingling on her nape increased. 'How?'

'You will be my personal liaison to the organisation.'

She tried not to dwell on the word *personal*. 'I… What does that mean?'

'In the next few weeks I'll be touring some of the more…out of the way parts of Ja'ahr. Touch Global are getting a handle on which communities are most needy here in Ja'ahr City and the surrounding areas. Much more help is needed in remote areas. You'll travel with me, assess the needs of the people, then report to Touch. Based on your recommendations, they'll ensure the necessary infrastructure is put in place.'

As positions went, it was an exciting one, even if a huge leap from what she did back in London. But the prospect of working that closely with Zaid made her go hot. And then cold. When the butterflies in her belly finally settled midway between the two points, she cleared her throat.

'I'm not sure that I can take the position for the whole length of time it will take for my father's trial to happen but I'll request an extension of my leave…' She trailed to a stop when his brooding eyes narrowed on her.

'This isn't a negotiation, Esmeralda. This is where I list my demands and you confirm in the vein of the "I'll give you whatever you want" you promised to me last week. Unless that was an empty promise?' he queried, his voice deceptively soft.

Esme had come to realise that was his most deadly tone.

Mouth dry, she hurried to speak. 'It wasn't empty, but I still have to ask—'

'Your employer has agreed to a transfer of your services, effective immediately, for as long as I want you,' he supplied in an authoritarian voice.

She froze in her chair. 'What? How…? You had no right to do that!'

'Why not?' he demanded haughtily.

'Because…because…'

'You wanted to do it in your own precious time?' he suggested when she sputtered. 'Did I not tell you I would inform you of the details in due course?'

'Details of what you wanted from me, not details of how you'd taken over my life!'

'I had no wish to waste time on unnecessary arguments like the one we're having right now. Besides, you forget I have experience in the corporate world. Asking your boss for an indefinable amount of leave wouldn't have gone down well. Not without divulging a more comprehensive reason as to why you were in Ja'ahr in the first place. I take it you didn't tell him about your father the first time around?' he asked, although his droll tone suggested he already knew the answer.

Esme's stomach dipped lower, her anger at his high-handedness taking a temporary back seat to his unerring reasoning. 'You…you didn't tell him, did you?'

'Since the call wasn't of a personal nature, no, I didn't.'

'So he agreed, just like that?' she pressed.

'Yes, Esmeralda. Just like that. But I dare say receiving a call from the Sultan of a notable kingdom isn't an everyday occurrence and he went the extra mile to treat it as such.'

'You mean you threw your weight around and got the results you wanted.'

'Of course,' he agreed smoothly. 'Although there wasn't much throwing needed. He will have the privilege of adding my kingdom to his portfolio of clients, and my promise of a personal recommendation should you do a good job was just the extra incentive he needed.' A hard, implacable look settled over his face, along with a trace of the hunger she thought he'd completely eradicated. 'So now your way has been cleared, do I have your agreement that you'll stay for as long as I need you?'

Esme fought against the distinct sensation that she'd

been well and truly cornered. And not for the purpose of serving as Zaid's liaison. There was stealth about him, a deeper purpose brewing behind his eyes that wouldn't allow the tightening in her stomach to ease. But how could she fight it when she didn't know what it was? Especially when in the face of what he'd said, what he'd done for her father, and what he was striving to do for his people, she could only give him one answer?

'Yes, I'll stay.'

In the moment before she answered, Zaid went through a half a dozen rebuttals in preparation for a negative response. Her inner battle had been plain to see on her face. So it took a moment or two before he realised she'd agreed. He absorbed her words with a relief he hadn't been expecting to feel. The punch of elation that followed on its heels was equally perturbing and irritating, considering he'd mentally slammed the door on the possibility of any future sexual interaction with her.

Zaid wasn't arrogant in thinking he could change her mind about her decision should he wish to. Esmeralda Scott was a desirable woman, and their brief interlude had spiked a hunger in his blood that he was still struggling with. He'd also seen her quickly hidden disappointment after his acceptance of her bold denial of their mutual chemistry.

But mixing business with pleasure rarely ended well. And he had enough people questioning his motives with her as it was, especially in light of the strings he'd pulled this week on behalf of her father.

No, he would be better off finding a discreet alternative avenue for slaking his lust. Except the thought of doing just that only increased his irritation. That and the reminder of why she was in his kingdom in the first place.

'Good.' His tone was much curter than necessary. The widening of her alluring eyes and the stiffening of her lush body told him so. But his patience was ebbing. 'Fawzi will provide you with an itinerary in the morning.'

She carried on staring at him for a moment before her gaze dropped. 'Okay. Um… I'll say goodnight, then.'

He rose and pulled back her chair, and noticed her faint surprise at the gesture. 'You have a problem with a little chivalry?'

She shook her head, and the already precarious knot of hair threatened to emancipate itself. The reminder of how soft and silky the tresses had felt between his fingers threatened another bout of hunger. Directing a silent, pithy curse at his libido did nothing to alleviate the growing ache.

'Not a problem, no, just a little surprised, that's all.'

He allowed himself a tiny smile. 'My grandmother, may she rest in peace, would turn in her grave if she thought for a moment that I'd abandoned my manners.'

Her answering smile was equally brief, but the transformation of her features from beautiful to enchanting made his grip tight on the back of her chair. 'Were you two very close?'

Zaid told himself all he would allow was a single breath of her cherry blossom and jasmine scent as she fell into step beside him and they left his dining room. But in the next breath he was sampling her alluring perfume again, wondering where the shampoo smell ended and the jasmine and feminine scent began. He pulled his focus back to what she'd asked him with aggravating effort.

'Despite our exile, she was determined to raise me as if I was a ruler in waiting. Besides my normal studies, I had to learn every single Ja'ahrian custom and law, excel in matters of diplomacy, and, of course, the correct table manners. She was a hard taskmistress, but she was also soft and maternal when it mattered.'

'I'm glad,' she murmured.

Something in her voice made him glance at her. He caught a trace of sadness before she attempted to reinstate that air of rigid control around herself. For some reason he couldn't fathom in that moment, he wanted to smash through it, leave the true Esmeralda Scott exposed. He was sure it was that notion that prompted his next question.

'When did you lose your mother?'

Wary tension stiffened her spine. 'How did you know?'

He steered her down another hallway, one he knew would be quieter at that time of night. 'Your father said you were the only family he had.'

The tiniest wave of relief washed over her face. 'Oh… yes.' She pretended an interest in a nearby sculpture of a warrior on a horse as she gathered herself. 'My mother died when I was fourteen. But she wasn't in my life by then. They divorced when I was thirteen and she moved to Australia.'

Zaid frowned. 'So then it was just your father and you?'

The wariness encroached again. 'Yes.'

'It won't come as a surprise to you that I did my homework on your father. He has been…active in a number of countries for a while now. Unless you were left in the care of others, I assume you were with him?'

Her laugh was a little strained. 'What is this, an interrogation? I thought you were no longer my father's prosecutor ?'

'You fault me for wishing to know better the woman who will be working for me?' Perhaps his tactics were unfair. Perhaps he needed to leave the subject alone. But, seeing her drag her lower lip between her teeth as she weighed up his question, Zaid felt that insanely strong urge to destroy her defences once more. He wanted to know her, wanted to find out what made her strong and wary and bold and vulnerable.

'I guess not.' He watched her consider her words carefully before responding. 'No, I wasn't left the in the care of others. I was in boarding school during term time, then I got a chance to see the world during school holidays with my father. It was a great adventure.'

The glossy veneer she tried to throw on her childhood sent a pulse of anger through him. 'If it was all so great, why have you been estranged from your father for the past eight years?'

He saw the shock his question brought. Then her stunning eyes narrowed. 'This feels awfully like an interrogation.'

'Perhaps you were ashamed of the man he was and wished to distance yourself from him?' he pressed.

'Or have you considered the possibility that we just came to a time in our lives where we needed to go our separate ways? Like most children do when they come of age, I wanted to spread my wings. I wanted a…career, so I returned home to England.'

She was lying. Or at the very least not telling the whole truth. Zaid frowned at the pang of unnerving disquiet at the revelation and wondered at it. He'd stopped being surprised by the actions of others a long time ago.

So why this woman's half-truths should disturb him so deeply, why it should tap into a well of disappointment he'd thought had dried up a long time ago, surprised him. Enough to make him quicken his footsteps towards her suite.

'Zaid…um… Your Highness?'

He whirled back, her reversion to using his title just one more irritant in the giant cluster of irritants she represented in his life.

He watched her stumble back from him and clawed back his control. 'What is it?' he asked.

In the lamplit softness of the corridor, her face was both

enthralling and wary, although she held his gaze boldly. 'I… I think I can find my way from here.'

He checked out his surroundings, noted they were a few corridors away from where she slept. 'I'll see you to your door,' he stated imperiously, then resumed walking.

She walked by his side in silence for the rest of the way. When they reached her suite, he pushed the double doors open.

Aisha and Nashwa turned at their entrance. At the sight of their Sultan both women dropped into low curtsies with softly lyrical greetings.

Zaid responded, and moments later both women were rushing away. When the doors closed behind them, Esme glanced at him.

'I know women in Ja'ahr aren't chaperoned as strictly as in other countries, but should I have been consulted as to whether I want to be gossiped about for having the Sultan in my bedroom at this time of night?'

'They will be back shortly. Had I harboured other motives, I would've dismissed them for the night,' he said, heat rising in his groin as thoughts of just such a scenario embedded themselves in his mind.

A blush crept into her cheeks. Zaid wanted to trace the creamy pink skin with his fingers. The memory of its softness bit into him with a savage hunger still puzzling to him.

'So what are your motives, besides triggering tongues to start wagging about me?'

'Tongues will not wag about you in that way. In Ja'ahr, a woman isn't punished for desiring a man, neither is she expected to have a chaperone guarding her virtue, unless she requests it. Women's rights are respected, and they are free to champion their own integrity once they come of age.'

'I'm pleased to hear that.'

'Good, so no one will condemn you for entertaining me in your suite.'

She inhaled sharply. 'But I'm not entertaining you here. And you could've said goodnight to me at the door.'

Her forthright manner, unlike everyone else who treated him deferentially, made the blood thrum faster through his veins. 'Perhaps it's that captivation I spoke about that keeps me here. Perhaps I wish to mark you as mine despite…'

Her eyes rounded, her breath growing visibly short. 'Despite?'

'Despite the instinctive warning that I should keep away from you.'

'Maybe you should heed the warning. Think of the gossip.'

'There will always be interest in what the King of Ja'ahr does and who he does it with. Will such attention bother you?'

Her tongue darted out to lick her lower lip. It took a considerable amount of willpower not to lower his head and taste her right then and there.

'Why are we talking about this?' she asked, her own gaze dropping to his mouth.

Lust and impatience prowled through him. 'You really need to ask? When you can hardly breathe for all the hunger threatening to consume us right now?'

Her breath audibly caught. The predator in him enjoyed that sound immensely. 'Zaid, I thought we agreed that there would be nothing—'

'Tell me you don't want me and I will leave,' he cut her off, unwilling to be reminded of what he'd so readily accepted earlier tonight.

'I…' She stopped, shook her head. 'This is a bad idea.'

He cupped her shoulders, felt her soft warm skin beneath the thin cotton of her dress. Hunger pounded harder. 'It's not the confirmation I requested. Admit how you feel and tell me you want me, Esmeralda. Or do you imagine a lie would be easier?'

A vein of hurt passed through her eyes. Despite her fixed stare, her mouth trembled for a telling second before she curbed the weakness. 'I don't lie.'

He brushed the hurt and the response aside, as he did with the reminder that even if she didn't lie, she still hadn't told him the complete truth about her past during their conversation earlier. 'Then tell me what I want to know.'

She looked cornered, defeated for a wild second. Then that defiant little chin rose. 'Fine! I want you. But I still think this is a bad—'

He slanted his mouth over hers, kissing the words that held undeniable truth in them from her delectable mouth. And just like that, the fuse of desire leapt high and became all-consuming. Zaid clasped her tighter to him, moulded her lissom body to his until her softness was pressed against his hardness. And still he wanted her closer. As if she felt the same, her hands rose to slide around his waist. Soft, velvety lips opened beneath his. He delved with an eagerness that bordered on the uncouth. But he didn't care. Her responsiveness, the little moans she gave at the back of her throat each time their tongues met, triggered the headiest sensation he'd ever experienced. But even as he deepened the kiss, Zaid knew there was more in store. He knew and he hungered for it.

It was what drew his fingers to tunnel through her hair, disposing of the handful of pins that secured the loose knot. Honey-gold strands tumbled over his fingers in a fall of glorious silk. Suffused in her wild feminine scent, he caressed her scalp, tightened his hold on her and pulled her even closer. The unmistakeable feeling of her belly cradling his erection was a thousand highs distilled into one glorious sensation.

The hands wrapped around his waist splayed over his

back, her fingers exploring, digging, sending him wild as she strained and whimpered against him. Mouths devouring each other, Zaid walked them backwards until the arm of the nearest sofa halted their progress. Expertly manoeuvring them, he sank down and pulled her into his lap without breaking the kiss. Still keeping her prisoner against him, he tasted her, deeper, longer, until their frantic breathing echoed lustily through the room. Zaid was aware he was getting carried away, that the servants he'd so cavalierly dismissed were hovering right outside the double doors.

But still he slid his hand from her hip and up her side to rest beneath the sweet curve of one full breast.

Her breath caught. He broke the kiss long enough to voice what he couldn't keep silent. 'You're like a lush oasis after a long exile in the desert, *jamila*,' before he sealed his lips to hers once more. Her long, helpless moan drove his hand up.

Firm, gorgeous, magnificent, he gloried in the weight of her full breast before sliding his thumb over the engorged peak. The beautiful little jerk she gave powered his arousal higher. Then, unable to resist the clarion call, he pulled down the elastic neckline of her dress. Zaid kissed her for a moment longer before the other temptation grew too much to resist. The straining pink tip of her nipple was visible through the delicate white lace covering her. With fingers that trembled with the force of his desire he tugged the material out of the way. The strangled sound she made in her throat drew his gaze up. Flushed. Breathless. Beautiful.

He deliberately kept their gazes locked as he lowered his head and drew her nipple into his mouth. Watched her lovely eyes darken with drowning desire before her eyelids began to flutter. Gripped with the need to witness even more of her pleasure, he flicked his tongue over her peak, again and again, then repeated it with the twin. Only when the heat coursing through his body threatened to rage completely out of control did he finally lift his head.

'Ambrosia, *habiba*,' he muttered roughly. 'You taste like pure, heavenly ambrosia.'

Her answer was to slide her hand over his nape and tug his head back down to her. With a ragged chuckle that spoke of his own unstoppable desire, he tossed himself headlong back into the drugging power of her body.

He was well and truly lost in it when she started to murmur something. With the scent of her arousal joining the maelstrom of powerful elixirs surrounding them, he didn't realise she was calling to him urgently until she began to push frantically at his shoulders.

'Zaid, stop!'

'Not yet,' he responded thickly. His other hand had left her hair a long time ago, and both hands now cupped the glorious globes of her breasts. He was nowhere near ready to relinquish his prize.

'Please!'

The frantic plea finally impinged on his senses. A deep but highly unsatisfying breath later, he drew back. And finally heard the sound of cautious knocking. He was glad she didn't understand his language as he issued a crude, pithy curse and reluctantly let her go.

She got the gist, though. Her face flamed as she hurriedly straightened her clothes and tumbled off his lap. She swayed slightly as she regained her feet. Zaid caught her hips and steadied her as he attempted to pin down his own runaway control.

Her shoes had come off at some point during their torrid interlude. In her bare feet, her face flushed and her hair in disarray, she was a deliciously petite morsel, one he knew he wouldn't be able to resist devouring in the very near future.

He couldn't stem the growl of anticipation that rose in his throat at the thought. She shifted beneath his hold, her agitated gaze darting to the door.

'Be calm. They will not come in until I give permission,' he reassured her gruffly.

Her teeth mangled her swollen bottom lip. 'Then give it,' she urged in a rushed whisper. 'Before they think you're…that we're…' She pressed her lips together as another blush deepened her colour.

'Making love? Get used to saying the words, Esmeralda, because it is going to happen. The next time I have you in my arms I won't stop at tasting those tempting lips and gorgeous breasts. When I have you in my bed, I won't stop until I possess you, thoroughly and completely.'

Her shaky inhalation drew his gaze back to her chest. Already he craved another taste. He rose to his feet, bent down and brushed her lips with his, gratified when she clung to him for a second. Then he forced himself to release her. Step back.

'Our journey begins early tomorrow. Be ready.'

CHAPTER NINE

THE NEXT TIME I have you in my arms…

For some stupid, sleep-depriving reason, Esme had assumed those words carried with them a very imminent time stamp.

She'd spent the next several nights after their departure from Ja'ahr City and the Royal Palace vacillating between the urge to give in and reiterating stern warnings of why she couldn't. Every night in the breath-taking beauty of her surroundings, be it in a camp made up of giant Bedouin tents or a hut in a desert village as they travelled north towards the oil fields that were the life blood of Ja'ahr, was spent wondering if that would be the night Zaid made his move.

Before she knew it, three weeks had passed.

Three weeks, when he'd treated her like a respected member of his travelling staff, each night reading the detailed reports she'd made on the social care needs of the communities they'd visited and peppering her with questions on points she'd made as they'd shared a simple dinner in the community tent or a mini-banquet in a chieftain's dining room, depending on which host they'd been blessed to spend the evening with.

Each night she'd retreated to her sleeping quarters with Nashwa and Aisha as her constant companions. The two had proved themselves invaluable sources of information, with Nashwa acting as an informal translator when needed. Esme had even learned to accept the presence of the two bodyguards who shadowed her at all times.

Had she not been thoroughly enjoying her new role, Esme was sure she would have gone completely out her mind. But the joy she'd gained from knowing she was making a difference went a long way towards helping her sleep at night, despite being dogged by thoughts of Zaid.

Because it wasn't as if Zaid had lost interest in her. Many times, she'd looked up from a conversation with a matriarch of a community, or a group of teenagers, to find his intense gaze on her. At those times, the depth of his hunger had been plain to see, although those long, lush eyelashes would all too soon sweep away the glimpse into his emotions as he returned to whatever conversation he was engrossed in.

The breathless yearning those looks left behind would leave her feeling needy and bereft for hours, a part of her hating him for eliciting such a devastating craving, and the other part admonishing herself for falling beneath his spell in the first place.

It wasn't surprising therefore then that she was feeling irritable as the sun set on another glorious day on their second night in Tujullah. The northernmost settlement of Ja'ahr was little more than a desert encampment, although the permanent tents were huge and contained an assortment of rooms.

As usual, she'd been allotted her own tent far from the one Zaid occupied—she knew that because she'd watched him disappear with Fawzi into his twenty minutes ago after he'd grilled her on her latest report. Her answers had grown increasingly short until he'd looked up from the document, his narrow-eyed gaze piercing hers before he'd dismissed her and conducted a terse conversation of his own with his personal secretary.

Normally, she would have lingered in the middle of the encampment where groups of men played musical instruments or engaged in heated discussions about the state of the world at large. Tonight, she'd chosen to take a long, relaxing bath in the privacy of her tent. Aisha had looked slightly put out after she'd filled the bath and Esme had dismissed her for the night but she hadn't thought it fair to visit her bad mood on the young girl.

So now she drew the soft sponge filled with jasmine-and-rosewater-scented water over her arm and absently watched the water sparkle in the light of the two dozen candles within the room. In four days they would be returning to Ja'ahr, remaining there for a fortnight before they made another trek east. Zaid had other matters of state to deal with, including a few court cases. Their return would also give her another chance to visit her father. She'd flown back by helicopter for her once weekly visit with him. Although their conversation had got increasingly terse after he'd tried to pry into her relationship with Zaid, she'd promised to return. All she had to do was remind herself that he no longer had any power over her.

She would also be able to liaise with Touch Global about her recommendations for the communities she'd assessed.

But tonight she couldn't concentrate on any of that. Her thoughts were fully centred on Zaid. On whether he'd changed his mind about having her, and why the thought that he might have made her gut clench with such keen disappointment. She was still grappling with those frustratingly divergent thoughts when she left the bath an hour later. Although she yearned for the oblivion of eventual sleep, it was too early to head to bed.

After spending mindless minutes brushing her hair, Esme tugged a lilac-coloured floor-length tunic over her head. Made of the softest silk with delicate gold embroidery at the wide cuffs and hem, the material whispered over her body with silken seduction, drawing a pleasured sigh from her before she grimaced at herself. It was true that she was falling in love with all things Ja'ahr, including the new wardrobe that Zaid had informed her via Nashwa was part of her welcome package. Esme didn't deny the new clothes helped her blend in better and gave her an extra boost of confidence in her new role.

She freed her hair from the collar, tying it into a loose knot at her nape before slipping her feet into matching Arabian slippers. A pair of simple gold chandelier earrings she'd bought at a bazaar two weeks ago and the glide of peach gloss over her lips rounded off her attire.

She was arranging a white scarf over her head when Aisha entered.

Surprised that she'd returned, Esme turned around, ready to gently dismiss her again. But the young girl curtsied shyly.

'Pardon me for the intrusion, Madam, but Fawzi Suleiman is here to see you.'

'Oh…okay.'

Aisha gave a quick nod and dashed back outside. A moment later Fawzi stepped into the tent. He hovered respectfully in the doorway, his fingers in a steeple in front of him.

'His Highness requests your presence, Miss Scott.'

Esme cursed the wild leap of her heart and bit back the strong urge to tell the unfortunate messenger where to tell His Highness to stick his request. She didn't think she could stand another roasting over her meticulous reports. Not to mention the prospect of her current heart rate soaring even higher in Zaid's presence.

'If you would be so kind.' He stepped back and made that elegant inviting gesture with his hand that was nevertheless subtly insistent.

She pursed her lips even as her feet moved towards the large black tent set apart from the rest of the dwellings. Unlike her own, the large opening was barred by a secondary wall of cured leather a few feet from the first, with the entrance to the tent on either side of that taut wall.

She followed Fawzi through the right entrance, and immediately stepped onto the first of a dozen priceless Persian rugs. The royal blue and gold theme of his palace was repeated in the immense cushions bordered by large cylindrical ones that served as a seating area, with dozens of smaller cushions tossed over the floor in sumptuous invitation.

Lit by a giant chandelier of candles hanging from the centre point in the ceiling, the living area was illuminated further by intricately carved Moroccan lanterns hung on various posts inside the tent. There was a smaller grouping of cushions in the centre of which was laid a large platter of fruits and nuts.

Esme took in all of this in seconds, before her senses and gaze zeroed in on the man rising lithely to his feet from the largest divan-like cushion.

A curt nod from him dismissed Fawzi. When his gaze returned to her, his eyes glowed an intense topaz in the light.

She hated the way her breath caught anew. So much she locked her knees to keep her in place. 'You wanted to see me?'

He advanced, a powerful being draped in a rich wine-red tunic, trousers and robe. He wasn't wearing his headgear, and his jet-black hair gleamed under the lamplight. 'You look…irritated,' he observed almost lazily.

But she wasn't fooled. There was a coiled tension within him that sent her pulse racing faster.

'Do I?' she replied. 'It must be because I was planning to go for an evening stroll before I was summoned here.'

A ghost of a smile whispered over his lips. Lips that had possessed hers with such bone-melting mastery. Lips she'd yearned for in her dreams and in her wakeful hours.

'Or perhaps you're feeling a little neglected?'

'Not at all. I'm doing the job I'm here to do. I've seen you every day to make my report. I'm constantly surrounded by Nashwa and Aisha. Oh, and my personal bodyguards. Let's not forget them,' she tagged on waspishly.

'The guards are here for your safety.'

'Are they? It's all a little OTT, if you ask me. I mean, each guest having a staff? What's that all about?'

A little of his indolence evaporated. 'There used to be five to a guest, half of whom were given three meals a day and nothing else in the form of a salary. The two members of staff assigned to you now earn enough to be able to feed and clothe their families.'

Contrition bit hard. 'Oh… I didn't know that. And the other three? Are they now on the unemployment line?'

He turned away and led her to the seat he'd just vacated. One of the things she'd learned in the past three weeks was how to sit on floor divans. She sank down sideways, and propped herself up with two cushions, noting too late that Zaid was doing the same. But in her direction.

Within one heartbeat and the next they were a mere foot apart. The slightly shaky breath she took infused her senses with his powerfully evocative scent.

Move.

But the voice of self-preservation was smothered beneath the mounting yearning that had dogged her for three long weeks. Her willpower was eroded in the face of the need to experience what had happened in her suite just one more time.

Although would it stop at one? Or was she deluding herself?

'They are in the process of being retrained in other skills,' he replied to the question she had already forgotten. She told herself to focus.

'And after that?'

'Brilliant people like you will guide them towards the right jobs,' he stated simply.

A warm glow fired up inside her. ‘So you do think I’m doing a good job?’

His gaze turned slightly mocking. ‘Are you fishing for compliments, Esmeralda?’

‘I’m seeking enlightenment as to why you grill me so hard every evening if you’re happy with the job I’m doing.’

‘Perhaps I give you a hard time because I don’t want you to rest on your laurels. Or…’ he drawled in an even deeper, lower voice, ‘perhaps giving you a hard time is my way of coping.’

She stopped breathing altogether. ‘Coping with what?’ Her voice was just above a husky murmur.

‘With the fact that I want you in my bed, beneath me, more than I want sustenance,’ he admitted gruffly.

The warm glow erupted into an inferno, but a large dose of confusion remained. ‘Then why haven’t you done anything…or said anything before now?’

He gave an elegant roll of one shoulder that was more an animalistic stretch than a shrug. ‘It was supposed to be a noble act. I wanted you to get embedded in your role without distractions. I was going to wait until we returned to my palace before making you mine.’

‘But…?’

‘But I find that there’s only so much altruism I can stomach before I’m driven insane by the need to have you,’ he growled.

Esme barely had time to brace herself against the wall of formidable man that came at her. Her scarf was tugged loose and disposed of, and the hair she’d pinned up minutes ago was freed within seconds, even as he bore her back against the cushions.

His large, muscular body covered hers, and his lips met hers in a hot, demanding kiss she felt all the way to her toes. She’d thought the first time they’d kissed that it couldn't get any better, that the need inside her couldn't get larger or hungrier.

But as her fingers tunnelled through his thick hair with urgency and greed, Esme was introduced to another level of need so great she actually whimpered with the thought of it going unsatisfied. Whether he sensed it or not, Zaid fed that need with renewed vigour, mouth and tongue and teeth ravaging hers in a relentless erotic dance that had her already dizzy senses spinning.

Strong muscled thighs parted hers, and he settled himself more firmly over her. As if he already owned the right to be there. Esme knew she'd given him that right, that with her silence these past three weeks she'd completely accepted that this was going to happen.

She would give her virginity to Sultan Zaid Al-Ameen.

A jet of alarm sprouted inside her, attempting to cool the blazing fires. She didn't need lessons in sex and sexuality to know twenty-five-year-old virgins were as rare as hen's teeth. But whereas the choice not to explore her sexuality had been solidly accepted and acceptable in her own mind, suddenly it occurred to her that it might not be the case from another's perspective.

The possibility of disappointing him suddenly loomed large in her mind, tossing another bucket of cold water over her frenzied senses.

The warm pads of his fingers drifted down her cheek, insisting on her attention and immediately receiving it. Brought back to the stunning desert oasis and the equally stunning, virile male whose eyes broadcast his ravenous hunger for her, she almost managed to convince herself her worries weren't warranted. A shaky sigh escaped her as he lowered his head, trailing kisses on her bottom lip and along her jaw. 'I'm attempting not to allow the fact that I've clearly lost your interest to dent my ego too much,' he drawled in her ear.

Short, shocked laughter barked out of her. To think he was remotely disturbed by the same worry that plagued her! 'Your ego has nothing to worry about from me.'

She sobered when he raised his head and she saw the speculative gleam swirling in his eyes. 'You want me,' he stated, a touch arrogantly, his hand leaving her cheek to chart a path of fire down her throat to the open neckline of her tunic.

She couldn't deny it, although the depth of it shocked her. 'Yes, I want you,' she gasped.

A rough inhalation expanded his chest as his lips continued to wreak havoc on her bare skin. 'Now we've got the most important detail out of the way, tell me the source of your second thoughts and I will deal with them.'

Esme bit her lip. Dared she risk telling him? Would he care? What if he stopped making love to her?

She held her breath as he raised his head again, the speculation much more intense this time. 'Esmeralda, what is it?' he demanded.

She slicked lips gone dry. 'I'm feeling a little bit out of my depth. I… I haven't done this before,' she stuttered.

He stared silently down at her for a full minute before he jumped lithely to his feet. The realisation that she'd lost him that quickly, that easily, stunned her so completely she stared mutely at him for endless seconds before she noticed the hand he was holding out to her. Warily, she placed her hand in his.

The moment she was upright, he swung her up into his arms. Esme's eyes widened.

'Zaid…'

He silenced her with a swift kiss before he strode out of the living room with long, purposeful strides. A short corridor later they walked through another opening and arrived in what could only be termed as the most masculine space she'd ever seen.

Animal-skin rugs graced the floor. Bold works of embroidered art hung on the walls. And in the middle of the floor a fire pit blazed with an intricate meshed metal dome that kept the flames contained.

But it was the bed that dominated her attention. Although it stood no higher than three feet off the floor, the emperor-sized bed, laid on exquisitely carved timber pallets, was enthralling in itself, even before the blinding-white satin sheets and the countless richly coloured pillows and cushions that graced the vast surface. Everything in the room screamed sensuality and endless luxury.

It also screamed that this place was reserved for those steeped in the art of lovemaking, and not for innocents such as herself.

The sensation of being out of her depth grew to stomach-churning proportions. She drew in another shaky breath as he lowered her to her feet.

Long, elegant fingers slid into her hair and angled her face up to his determined one. 'Your equivocation isn't unwarranted. This will be the first time I too will be mixing business with pleasure,' he confessed.

The drugging effect of his fingers on her scalp distracted her from his words for several moments. 'I… What?' she murmured faintly.

'That is what you're worried about, isn't it? That we risk compromising our professional relationship with a personal one?' he pressed, even as he stepped closer, brought his hips into singeing contact with hers and trailed his lips across hers once more. 'But the alternative is to deny ourselves this. And that, *habiba*, is not going to happen tonight,' he affirmed with deep, solid conviction.

Her mouth dropped open but coherent words failed to form. He thought she was reticent about sleeping with him because she was his employee!

The mouth hovering tantalisingly close returned to seal

over hers, his tongue breaching her lips with renewed sexual resolution that reinvigorated the fire inside her. With a helpless moan she clamped her hands around his shoulders, straining up to receive more of the drugging caress.

She needed to tell him. She *would* tell him. But not yet. After another kiss. Just in case all this came to an abrupt end the moment he found out she was so inexperienced.

They kissed until their breaths turned ragged, until touching over silk and satin was no longer enough. Until the need to feel skin on skin raged out of control. Somewhere along the line Zaid had shrugged off his robe. Her slippers had fallen off her feet, leaving her bare feet on soft rugs.

It was only when Zaid muttered urgently in Arabic against her lips that she started to heed the screaming voice in her head that told her she was running out of time to tell him. His hands were slowly drawing up her tunic, the soft breeze from a nearby opening sliding seductively over her skin.

She managed to free her tongue from the roof of her mouth. 'Zaid…'

'I need to see you,' he translated thickly. 'Touch you properly. Taste you.'

His hands brushed the side of her hips as he continued to tug up her dress, murmuring thick, sensual promises against her lips.

Her fingers convulsed against his sleek pectoral muscles as he worked to free her from the tunic. 'Zaid… I… have to tell you—'

'Shh, *jamila*, just give in to the pleasure.'

Before she could push the necessary words out, he was pulling the dress over her head. Her freed hair tumbled over her body in long tresses. He brushed the strands over her shoulders so he could better see her. Then he tossed

away the …
promised un…

One hand li… to trace her collar… rowed hot and hard t…

'I knew you were bea… my imagination, *habiba*,' h… gers drifted over the lace tha…

'Zaid…'

'Stay,' he commanded gruffly, … ur staining his haughty cheekbones as … hand and strolled lazily, imperiously around …

He stopped behind her, his breath catc… audibly. A second later a quick tug released the clasp of her bra. He didn't free her completely from it but, despite her self-consciousness, Esme had never felt so desired, so aware of her body. Her own breath caught as one finger stroked her first vertebra, then followed the line down in a languid caress that had liquid heat pooling at her feminine core. He stopped just above the cleft of her buttocks, his touch lingering as he stepped closer to plant a kiss on one bare shoulder. Then the other. A moment later his fingers were hooking into the sides of her lace panties, tugging them over her hips. They dropped to the floor and she heard his guttural sound of appreciation.

Tell him. Tell him now before it's too late.

With equal amounts of dread and desire she spun on her heel to face him. The quick movement dislodged the loose bra. In the next instant the scrap of lace fell free from her body to join her panties, leaving her completely naked, bare to his avid gaze. He traced her from head to toe, lingering at the shadowed place between her legs.

'You are truly exquisite, Esmeralda,' he praised.

At the sight of the ferocious hunger etched on his face,

d made a promise never to

understood me when I said I hadn't done

seemed to take a monumental effort for him to drag his gaze up from her tight-peaked breasts. A slow frown gathered on his dark brow. 'Then enlighten me, *habiba*, and do it quickly before my patience runs out,' he advised, his voice barely above a rough rumble.

'I mean that I'm…a virgin.'

He grew statue still, his eyes narrowing. Seconds ticked by, then his nostrils pinched on a sharp inhalation. 'That is impossible. You're twenty-five years old,' he said bluntly.

'I assure you it's not impossible. I've never slept with a man.'

Her statement seemed to trigger an emotion within him. One she breathlessly recognised as shockingly primal, stamped with a possessive fire that grew as he continued to stand there looking at her. But alongside that, as predicted, were questions that stormed through his eyes, even as his gaze rushed feverishly over her body.

She pre-empted them by placing a hand on his chest. 'It was my choice not to explore that side of my life.'

He nodded, but the speculation remained. 'And you choose to bestow such a gift on me now because…?'

It occurred to her that his power and position in life would have made him suspect such a gift. 'Not because of who you are, if that's what you're wondering. If I was that calculating I would've waited until…until you saw the evidence for yourself, not risked you rejecting me because you thought I was being untruthful. But… I want you, more than I want to keep my innocence. I told you because… I didn't want… I know my inexperience may be a turn-off for you—' She stopped, flushing as he made a gruff sound of disbelief.

He stepped closer, bringing his body heat, the very temptation of him into her personal space. 'You think what you've just told me makes you less desirable to me?' he demanded. He followed the statement with another singeing full-body appraisal.

Standing there, naked, while he was fully clothed and she was *dying* with need was suddenly too much. Her head dipped beneath the weight of her want, her arms rising to block the most private parts of her body from him.

He lunged forward, grabbing her hands as his breaths emerged in harsh pants. 'Don't hide yourself from me, *habiba*. I want to see you, all of you. I wish to commit every magnificent inch of the body that is about to become mine and mine alone to memory.'

Her breath caught, her head jerking up to meet his gaze. Pure fire blazed in the topaz depths, robbing her of words, of the fear of rejection she'd dreaded.

'I...' She would never know what she planned to say because the words shrivelled and died in her throat when he reached behind him and tugged his tunic off in one decisive move. His massive chest was a hairless, contoured landscape of honed muscles and bronze-skinned perfection. Her mouth dried up and the need to touch him flared wildly through her as he hurriedly toed off his loafers, then removed his trousers.

Zaid was by far the most superior male specimen she'd ever clapped eyes on. She reeled as her voracious gaze took in lean hips, powerful thighs and a body so magnificent she didn't think she could stand to look at him for much longer without screaming that he take her. But still she looked her fill, especially at the proud manhood, fully engorged and straining against his stomach. The thought of all that power directed at her, *inside* her, sent a wave of dizziness through her. But it was accompanied by an undeniable hunger.

As if he read her thoughts, he caught her hand, drew it to his body. 'Give in to your desire, Esmeralda. Touch me,' he ordered roughly.

She gladly gave in. And gasped in wonder and delight as her fingers met feverishly hot smooth skin layered over rock-hard muscle. A strong wish to circle his magnificent body, just as he'd done to her, assailed her. But she didn't think she could move from where she was rooted to the spot, such was the awesome power surging through her.

So she contented herself with learning the grooves of his abs, of skimming her fingers over his breastplate, grazing her nails over his flat nipples. At his harsh hiss, her fingers froze.

The next moment, he cupped her nape in a jerky movement, bringing her flush against his body before slamming his mouth on hers. The kiss was hard, and quick, and spoke of an edge riding him he was hanging onto with great difficulty.

Just as abruptly he ended the kiss and swept her into his arms.

'We need to move this to the bed, sweet one. Now. Before I reach the point of no return and take you here on the floor.'

CHAPTER TEN

THE TOUCH OF the cool sheets against her back sent a delicious shiver through Esme. That shiver turned into a warm shudder when Zaid's hot, virile body settled over hers. He didn't return to kissing her, but instead trailed his mouth over her cheeks, her forehead, the tip of her nose before journeying down her throat to the pulse that raced wildly there. Through it all, he murmured deep, lyrical words in his own language. She didn't care that she had no understanding of them, as they pulsed with meaning in her blood. Emotion that felt different from the physical magic happening to her tightened in her chest. She didn't have time to explore it because his lips were destroying her very sanity.

They deposited kisses between the valley of her breasts for an interminable age, before cresting her left breast to tug one tingling nipple into his mouth.

Just like last time, the sensation was beyond exquisite. Her fingers convulsed where they'd been trailing though his hair. 'Oh!'

Encouraged by her response, he repeated the caress, then graced her twin nipple with the same incredible attention. By the time he continued on his exploration, Esme was nearly incoherent with pleasure. So much so it took a moment to realise his next destination.

Her breath froze as he wrapped one hand around her slim thigh and parted her legs. Throughout her feverish imaginings of what making love with Zaid would feel like, she'd never factored in oral sex. The aggressive determination on his face, however, told her he'd very much factored it into his own process and was intent on fulfilling that wish.

Heat surged high and fiery beneath her skin as he bared her most intimate body part to his bold gaze. The hand that captured her thigh released her to caress a path of devastation up to her heated core. Sure fingers parted her, his gaze flickering up to meet hers for a charged second before dropping back down to her centre.

'You're beautiful, Esmeralda,' he stated throatily. Simple words. But their effect on her was nothing short of earth-shattering.

The last of her resolve melted away, leaving her with a bone-deep belief that whatever happened when the sun rose tomorrow, she was doing the right thing right now. As if he'd read her thoughts, his eyes met hers, the darker depths staying fixed on her face for a long spell before he lowered his head and tasted her in the most elemental of ways.

Newly freed from her self-doubt, she succumbed to the pleasure racing through her bloodstream. The warm satin sheets slid gloriously underneath her as she gave in to the instinct to roll her hips against Zaid's caress. He made a gravelly sound of approval in his throat. She moved again, meeting the expert flick of his tongue against the engorged nub that was the epicentre of her pleasure. Fireworks burst across her vision, and her breath emerged in harsh pants as an indescribable sensation began to take over. It gathered speed and power, catapulting her higher with each bold caress from Zaid. Her fingers clenched into the satin sheets as he spread her even wider, and deepened the intimate kiss.

The giant knot of pleasure burst wide open without warning, drawing a shocked scream from her lungs as she was flung high into a stratosphere of pure, incandescent bliss. The pleasure rolled in an endless loop, her body convulsing shamelessly as she drowned in it. When it finally released her from its vicious grip, her eyes fluttered open. To the sight of the man responsible for her incredible release.

His hands were clamped on her hip and in her hair, and the dark flush on his face spoke of his own savage need. The need to bestow on him a fraction of what he'd just given her urged her to raise a hand to his cheek, caress his taut skin, before raising her head to press her lips to his.

A pure animal sound ripped from his throat as he quickly donned a condom, levered his body over hers and resumed the kiss. His thighs parted hers and she felt the undeniable power of his arousal between her legs. She looked down at where they were about to join. Her heart caught, the reality of his impressive girth forcing an apprehensive swallow.

The fingers in her hair tightened a touch, directing her attention upward. 'It'll be all right, *habiba*. Don't fret. The pain will be fleeting… I've been told. Then I guarantee you untold pleasure.'

His promise settled her nerves, as did, astonishingly, his intimation that she was his first innocent. For some reason that knowledge made the already tight band of unrecognisable emotion in her chest tauten. She had no time to dwell on it, however. He was taking her mouth again, although this time the kiss was gentle. Or as gentle as a powerful man who rode the very edge of his control could be. One hand left her hair to retake control of her thigh.

'Esmeralda.' Her name was a hoarse command as he opened her even wider.

One she heeded by lifting her gaze to his. Eyes almost black with intense lust seared hers as the crown of his penis breached her core. Dizzy excitement warred with the unknown.

'Put your arms around me,' he ordered.

She obeyed. Her fingers slid around and latched onto the hot, smooth skin of his lower back.

Then, with a single, guttural oath, he pushed himself inside her.

The sharpest lance of pain arched through her, snatching a helpless scream from her throat. His mouth clamped on hers, devouring the sound as if it belonged to him. And right at that moment it did. They both stilled, breathing ragged, bodies clenched as they fought through pleasure and pain. The pain wasn't as fleeting as he'd said. It gripped her as if wanting her to remember this moment. To imprint on her psyche the awe and magnitude of sharing her body with Zaid Al-Ameen.

After a handful of heartbeats he lifted his head to look at her as he drew back and surged into her again.

Pain diminished, dissolved, then gave way to pleasure. A different, more potent pleasure than that she'd experienced a little while ago. On the third thrust, Zaid buried himself to the hilt inside her. They both groaned.

His thrusts gained pace, the strokes of possession masterful.

His hand left her thigh to clamp on her hip, holding her in place as he kept his promise to make her completely his. And through it all he watched her, his gaze intense as he absorbed every particle of her pleasure, fused it with his.

Her eyes rolled. Her fingers dug into his back. The scream that rose this time was one of awe and bliss she'd never dreamed possible.

'Zaid…' Her sigh of his name was meant to ground her in this room, on this plane of reality for a little while longer, but it was no use.

She was soaring once again, but this time towards a higher state of bliss she knew instinctively would change her for ever. His relentless pace told her he intended to make sure of it.

Sweat bathed her skin, bathed his as the intensity of their coupling grew to a breaking point. She clamped her legs around his waist in an instinctive move. One that pleased him enough to draw a hoarse moan from him. And then, between one moment and the next, she was caught in the grip of a wild, ecstatic fever.

'Zaid!'

'Yes,' he groaned above her. 'Give in to it. Take all of it.'

'Oh… God.' Surrender had never felt so right. Esme flew higher than before, but not before she felt him lower his head to whisper in her ear.

'*Habiba.*' Sweetheart. Darling. She'd heard many Ja'ahrians use that term of endearment. But coming from Zaid at that moment, Esme felt as if he'd showered her with a thousand priceless gems.

Tears prickled the back of her eyes, and finally, she let go completely.

Zaid couldn't tear his gaze from the beautiful woman writhing in ecstasy beneath him. Everything about her captivated him. It had from the first moment he'd seen her, but nothing had prepared him for this. For his total absorption in her pleasure or the reality that it triggered his own to an unconscionable level.

He never wanted it to end. Although he knew, like all things, that it would. It must. He didn't understand the part of him that already deeply mourned that future loss. Neither did he want to dwell on it right now. That would be a problem for when the sun rose.

For now…

Her back arched from the bed as bliss rolled over her. Presented with the perfection of her breasts, he lowered his head and fed his wild hunger. She felt exquisite. Her body was a magnificent prize he wanted to gorge on for a very long time.

As for the gift of her innocence she'd bestowed on him? The thrill of primitive pleasure that had stormed his blood at her confession had only intensified the moment he'd penetrated her. He hadn't needed the visual evidence he was sure was staining his sheets to know she'd spoken the truth. He'd felt it and revelled shamelessly in it.

She gave another cry beneath him, her nails scoring grooves in his back as her pleasure reached its zenith. He held out for as long as he could. Until, feeling the strong ripples of her flesh milking his own, he finally succumbed to the sublime ecstasy that beckoned.

The roar that ripped from his throat was as primal as the sexual act itself. Zaid wasn't ashamed to admit it was the most electric, intense climax he'd ever experienced. One that perhaps could be repeated, given that even as their bodies cooled in the aftermath, he was already anticipating their next coupling?

He gathered her close, exhaling in satisfaction when her hand stole up his body to rest on his chest. He smoothed her hair back from her face and pressed a kiss on her forehead. Watched her beautiful mouth curve in a tired post-coital smile and her stunning eyes begin to droop in slumber.

Reluctantly, he let her sleep because she needed to recover from her first sexual experience. And also because he wanted time to sift through the questions crowding his brain. Although one question that had gnawed at him had been answered.

Surely if she'd held onto her virginity in the hope of gaining the maximum prize for such a gift, she would have been better off staying in the high-rolling world her father favoured, where wealthy men paid a handsome price for such acquisitions, and not as a lowly social worker serving the less fortunate?

He didn't doubt that there was more to the estrangement between father and daughter than she let on, but in this Zaid was sure she was playing with a straight bat. It was the same honesty and integrity with which she'd gone about helping his people in the past weeks, many of whom she'd befriended in the process. According to Fawzi, Esmeralda Scott had gained, in such a short time, the respect and admiration of the people she'd met. Her daily reports had also shown an in-depth understanding of how to best serve each community. Zaid had known very quickly that he couldn't have picked a better candidate for the job of helping him to rebuild the Ja'ahrian communities his uncle had neglected so badly.

The only fly in the ointment was her father.

In the dimming firelight of his tent Zaid's jaw clenched. So far, her one weakness seemed to be Jeffrey Scott. Perhaps the sooner his fate was determined, the sooner she could focus properly on other matters.

Like on his kingdom? On him?

His arms tightened around her. Why not? The memorable interlude they'd shared in his bed would run its course eventually, as most things did. But there was no rational argument for that course not to be prolonged for as long as possible if they both wished it to. No reason at all.

So he would make that happen.

Satisfied, he pressed another kiss to her forehead, then let the blissful sleep that beckoned finally take him.

Even though the tent was still in darkness when she woke, Esme knew dawn was creeping very close. The coals in the fire pit no longer blazed high, although the room still held its sultry warmth. A cockerel's crow a moment later was accompanied by sounds of a rising camp.

She kept her eyes shut as memories of last night surged along with wave after wave of incredulity. She'd given her virginity to Zaid. The experience had been awe-inspiring both during, and afterwards, when she'd woken up more than once in the middle of the night to find his strong arms clamped around her as if he wouldn't let her go. Each time, she'd returned to sleep with her heart lifting with an emotion she was too scared to label.

That undefined emotion and the fact that she instinctively knew she was alone in bed right now kept her from opening her eyes just yet. Once she did, she'd have to face the day. Have to face the fact that she'd changed for ever.

So she listened to the camp sounds for a minute. Then, bracing herself, she opened her eyes. The confirmation that Zaid wasn't in the room made her stomach dip alarmingly. Esme firmed her lips and sat up in bed. She'd known this was a one-time thing. The quicker she learned to accept that fact the quicker she could get back to her assigned role in Zaid's life. Except that stern talking to brought nothing but a tightening in her chest and a yearning for that not to be the case.

Well, wishes weren't horses…

Determinedly, she pushed her tousled hair back from her face, and was looking around for her clothes when the tent flap to a previously unseen opening in the bedroom folded back to reveal the man dominating her thoughts.

Zaid was shirtless. His dark hair was ruffled as if fingers—her fingers—had tossed it into its sexily dishevelled state. Dark shadow graced his unshaven jaw, giving him a rakish look that sent a dozen sparks of renewed need firing through her belly. And the soft black pants that rode oh-so-low on his hips? She swallowed, unable to decide which part of the magnificent man to feast her eyes upon. Memories of all that power, all that majesty, devoted to her pleasure in the dark of night made her stomach flip in giddy excitement, despite the voice inside her head that screamed caution.

His steps slowed as his gaze fixed on her, his eyes growing a shade darker as his gaze roved over her body. Belatedly, she remembered she too was bare from the waist up. Self-consciously, she dragged the sheet up to cover her breasts.

His eyes narrowed a touch as he approached. 'Good morning, Esmeralda,' he rasped when he stopped beside the bed.

Suddenly tongue-tied, she dragged her gaze from his mouthwatering torso to his face. 'Um…hi.'

He moved as if to climb onto the bed, but then he froze. Her furtive glance showed his gaze fixed at a point on the bed. She followed his gaze, then blushed furiously at the sight of tell-tale stains on the white sheet.

Her hand dashed out, her intention to tuck the sheet away. He caught hold of her wrist, his grip implacable as his gaze returned to hers.

'No.' That was all he said. But he didn't need to say any more. The primitive look in his eyes, increased a hundredfold from last night, said it all. He'd been her first and he wanted the evidence on full display. Had this been a thousand years ago, she was certain he would have roared and beaten his male chest in arrogant triumph.

For some absurd reason, considering the fiercely charged moment, she had the strongest urge to smile. An urge she couldn't quite prevent.

His eyes gleamed as he caught her expression. 'Something amusing you, *habiba*?'

She blushed. Inhaled shakily as the fingers that held her caressed the pulse racing at her wrist. 'You should see your face. You look…'

'Tell me,' he invited as she hesitated.

'You look like you've savaged a dozen predators in order to win some sort of grand prize,' she said with an embarrassed smile.

His expression grew even more charged, his gaze slowly lowering to the sheet and then back up to hers. He let go of her wrist, prowling onto the bed until he was poised over her like the fierce marauder she'd likened him to. The kiss he slanted over her mouth was the last word in shameless, dominant claiming. The power of it bore her back onto the bed, even as she parted her lips to take everything he had to give.

The claiming was long and thorough, her senses swimming by the time he lifted his head. Topaz-dark eyes gleamed ferociously at her.

'I look like this because I *have* won a grand prize. Make no mistake,' he assured her. 'One I intend to keep.'

Esme was floundering to grasp the meaning of the last part of his statement when he rose off the bed again, drew the sheet away from her body and scooped her up in his arms.

Face flaming anew, she wrapped her arms around his neck and buried her face in his throat. 'Where are we going?' she mumbled when he began to stride across the room.

'You'll see,' he replied.

A little alarmed, she turned her head just as he stepped through the tent flap.

The high walls were made of the same hardened leather used to construct some of the sandstorm-proof shelters around the camp. This one was over ten feet high, built around a private oasis garden, in the middle of which stood a natural spring pool surrounded by a profusion of exotic shrubs and flowers.

The breath-taking sight made Esme temporarily forget she was naked in Zaid's arms, her gasp at the natural beauty surrounding her echoing in the dawn-encroaching space around them. 'Oh, my God, this place is amazing!'

A hint of a smile touched his lips as he strolled towards the pool. 'I'm glad you like it. My security team insisted on the walls to guard my privacy. I didn't want it at the time, but I am glad of it now,' he murmured in her ear as he slowly lowered her to her feet.

He glided his fingers down her side to rest on her hips as he took her mouth in another searing kiss. By the time he raised his head their bodies were plastered together, their breathing ragged. The strong hands clamped on her hips moved to cup her behind, long enough for Esme to become bracingly aware of his potent arousal against her belly before he drew her away.

'Take off my pants, *habiba*,' he ordered huskily. The combination of the American accent he'd never quite lost and the lyrical Arabic of the endearment was so sexy she couldn't stop the decadent shiver that raced through her.

She slowly disentangled her arms from around his neck, drifting her fingers down his naked shoulders. Last night she'd been too overawed to linger in her exploration of him.

She still was, to be honest. But having been granted this chance she thought might never come again, Esme seized it with both hands. She drew her fingers over his collarbone, past the steady pulse that beat beneath taut bronze skin, over the solid beauty of his pecs. This time she lingered over the flat male nipples that hungrily puckered beneath her touch. She yearned to press her mouth to them, but she hesitated, her gaze flicking up to his.

His eyes were at a watchful half-mast, his breath held as he waited to see her next move.

Something in his eyes lent her a confidence she hadn't thought herself capable of. Or it could have been the relentless hunger that pounded through her bloodstream. Whatever. Esme lowered her head and flicked her tongue over the tiny nub as he'd done to her so many times during their lovemaking last night.

The hot hiss that issued from his lips made her freeze. About to straighten, she jerked in surprise when he speared his fingers through her hair and held her to her task. She repeated it. Revelled in the fierce tremble that shook his powerful frame. Overjoyed at his reaction, she kissed her way across his massive chest to the twin peak, all the while exploring the rest of his glorious body with her fingers.

He allowed her to explore for countless minutes, his breath growing louder and rougher as her fingers drifted lower, and her mouth and teeth left fiery trails on his skin.

When she reached the waistband of his pants, Esme took a quick, steadying breath, then slipped her hand beneath the soft material.

The power and might of him sent her temperature soaring. Steel wrapped in velvet. Majestic. Potent. Insanely intoxicating. She was so intent on familiarising herself with that part of his body she didn't hear his tortured groan until he grasped her hand and drew it away.

'How quickly you recognise and seize your power, *jamila*.' His voice was strained. Gravel rough. He kissed her palm, then dropped her hand back to his waistband with an autocratic quirk of his brow.

Reminded of her initial task, she took hold of his trousers and tugged them down, unable to stop the renewed rush of heat to her face when he stepped out of them and stood naked, proud and ready before her.

He was so beautiful he robbed her of breath.

The deeply magical moment continued as he led her down natural steps hewn into the rock of the pool. Cool and silky, the water submerged them to chest level before Zaid stopped. His fingers returned to spike through her hair, drawing her into his arms to kiss her one more time. After that he swam next to her before grabbing a sponge on a nearby surface. He washed her with slow, languid strokes, then washed himself with brisker movements. She read the intent in his eyes long before he tugged her decisively to the edge of the pool.

'I only meant for us to bathe in case you were sore after

last night, but I've been wanting to do this again for hours, Esmeralda,' he murmured, drawing her down on top of him as he sat on the lowest step.

'I'm fine,' she managed to gasp out.

Kisses peppered the corners of her mouth, her throat, before he ravenously latched onto her nipples. Hunger, deep and unstoppable, stung to life between her legs. Legs that he arranged on either side of his hips even while he continued to ravage her breasts. Heart racing, she braced her hands on his shoulders, anticipation making her rock forward in blind search of the pleasure only he could bring. Her feminine core found the head of his penis.

Abruptly, he tore his mouth from her nipples, his face a taut mask of untamed need. With one hand he grasped himself, the other bracing her as he surged upward, seating himself inside her in one powerful thrust.

Her gasp mingled with his groan. Their lips fused for one charged second before they separated again, returning to stare at each other as if their union needed the connection of their gazes. Breathless, silent, he withdrew and powered back inside.

Her mouth parted on another soundless gasp. She met him halfway on the third thrust, earning her a grunt of approval that ramped up the pleasure stealing through her bloodstream.

Eyes still fused to hers, he nodded. 'Yes, that's it.'

Movement as old as time dictated the roll of her hips as she rose for a moment, then drove back down. The sensation of power and control and pleasure mingled in a heady potion, driving her to seek more and more of it.

As the water splashed around them, Zaid's hands left her to spread long arms on the rim of the pool, his head going back as he lounged, imperiously like the master and commander he was, against the rock. Then half-closed eyes the colour of polished topaz watched her with heated encouragement as she propelled them both to the edge of the glorious abyss.

Something in his expression drove her to take him deeper, increase the pace of her movements. His face grew tauter, twin swathes of colour staining his cheekbones as his breathing turned choppier. 'Yes,' he encouraged hoarsely. 'Take me, *habiba*, as I have taken you.'

Esme didn't need a second bidding. Fingers splaying on either side of his strong neck, she gave in to the siren song whispering through her body.

It wasn't long before the crescendo built to insane proportions, and Zaid's groans were turning guttural. Feeling even bolder than before, she stole another kiss from his sensual lips, then got lost in it when he took over. Connected in every possible way, they tumbled over the edge in unison, devouring each other's vocal expression of the nirvana they were drowning in.

They were still connected when his strong arms came around her and he rose from the pool and strode, dripping wet and not caring, back into the tent.

They were still fully connected when he lowered her onto the bed and then he froze for a split second, his eyes going wide with shock, before he disengaged and flung himself away from her with an ear-bleeding curse.

CHAPTER ELEVEN

SHE DIDN'T NEED a cipher to know something was wrong. Very wrong.

'Z-Zaid?' Hard on the heels of her earth-shattering climax, her voice was nowhere near steady as she watched him pace from one end of the tent to the other. For a mad instant she was jealous of his ability to do so while unashamedly naked. In contrast, Esme couldn't pull the sheet—the newly changed sheet, she absently observed—over her body fast enough.

'I cannot believe—' He stopped, went a little white, then turned his back on her one more time. He completed two more lengths of the room before he stopped at the foot of the bed, out of touching distance. 'We didn't use any protection just now…in the pool,' he stated in a grave voice steeped in dark regret.

She went cold despite her taking another few moments to fully grasp his meaning. When she did, her stomach hollowed out. Then, forcing herself to think, she blurted, 'I'm…on the Pill.'

The immense relief that crossed his face was almost comical. Almost. Because something severed any trace of laughter from her heart before she had time to absorb it.

And also because a frown was beginning to replace that relief. 'Why were you on the Pill if you weren't sexually active?' he whipped at her.

'Because my doctor recommended it to help regulate my periods,' she explained.

He exhaled. Nodded as relief returned, full blown. His fists started to unclench.

Just as memory began to poke holes in her hasty assurance.

He started to round the bed towards her. Then he froze again when he saw what must have been near horror on her face.

'But… I…'

'But what, Esmeralda?' he snapped.

'I ran out last week, when we were in Dishnaja. Nashwa managed to get a prescription filled for me yesterday, but I missed three doses…' Her voice trailed off as the enormity of the consequences hit her. Had she been standing, she was certain she would have lost the use of her legs. As it was, she felt the blood drain out of her head at the grim look that overcame Zaid's features.

'Three doses, so three days' worth?' he pressed, his face once again rigid with tension.

She nodded miserably.

'What are the repercussions of missing them?'

Dread steeped deeper. 'Anything more than one missed dose and… I have to use extra precautions,' she whispered raggedly.

He uttered another curse in his language, then sank heavily on the mattress. Still out of reach. Ominous silence ensued.

'Zaid, I didn't think…when you summoned me here last night, this…what happened wasn't what I was expecting.'

He rubbed a hard hand over his jaw. 'That is inconsequential in the circumstances. Once is all it takes. And if there is blame to be laid, I'm far more culpable in this than you. It was my responsibility, and while I have no excuse for my carelessness, I will say in my defence that you enchanted me to a degree that I forgot myself.'

At any other time, his words would have filled her heart with joy. Not now, though. Not when they were delivered in a clipped tone that told her he was berating himself a thousand different ways for the situation they now found themselves in.

'When will you know?' he asked after another sharp exhalation.

She made a quick calculation. 'I'm not expecting my period for another two weeks, but I can take an early pregnancy test in about nine or ten days' time. Or I can…the morning-after pill is an option if that's what you want—'

'No! It is not. You will not get rid of my child before we even know there is a possibility of one.'

A wave of relief hit her at his vehement rejection of the remedy that had disturbed her to even consider, despite reeling at the possibility that she might be pregnant. Last night had been monumental. But it was nothing compared to the realisation that there could be long-lasting consequences to what they'd done.

'Zaid… I don't know if I can—'

Strong hands seized her shoulders, cutting her off. But, unlike last time, there was no tenderness in his face, no promise of untold pleasure blazing from his eyes. 'Don't say it. Don't even think of uttering words that would deny my child's existence.'

'I wasn't. But I'm not prepared for any of this.'

Lips she'd kissed barely half an hour ago flattened before he sighed and released her. She sagged back into the bed as he trailed his fingers down her arm to capture her hand. But again there was no hint of warmth, and it felt more like a way of making sure she stayed where she was. In case she what? Bolted? Esme was sure her legs wouldn't carry her one single step, never mind to anywhere far enough away from this tent to give her some peace of mind.

'We will step back from the edge of any hasty decision. We will get dressed and start the day with something as mundane as breakfast.'

She contained the urge to break into hysterical laughter. Nothing about the everyday life of Zaid Al-Ameen would ever be considered mundane, even the food he ate. 'And then what?'

'Then we will consider our options. Ones that *don't* include taking drastic measures. Are we agreed?' The question was filled with purpose.

And because she needed time too to absorb everything that had happened since she'd followed Fawzi into this tent last night, she answered, 'Yes, we're agreed.'

And just like that the subject was shelved. He let go of her hand and rose from the bed, then left the room without a backward glance.

When she was sure her legs would keep her upright, Esme stood and dressed in the clothes from the night before, which had been folded and placed on the chair at the bottom of the bed. Then, unsure of whether to leave or wait for Zaid, she dawdled for another half an hour in the bedroom.

Eventually, it was one of the servants who came in and beckoned her out to where Zaid was already seated on floor cushions spread around the dining area.

Breakfast was a feast of fruit, nuts, yoghurt, pastries, an assortment of juices, tea and coffee, served in respectful silence by a clutch of servants who bowed and smiled at their noble ruler, and cast keenly speculative glances her way. If the notion lingered for a moment that the women's interest in her this morning was far greater than it had been yesterday, or the day before, Esme had no room to dwell on it. Not when the subject of a baby… Zaid's baby…had taken over every corner of her mind.

She declined all but a piece of tangerine, a slice of toast and a small helping of honeyed yoghurt. Although Zaid's lips firmed, he didn't comment, his brow clamped as he remained deep in his own thoughts.

The moment the meal was cleared away, she stood to retrieve her scarf in anticipation of returning to her own tent. Absently she noted that it too had been moved and neatly folded on a low armoire in the living room. About to pick it up, she froze.

Zaid might be the Sultan, but his life wasn't his own. It never would be. It was a life he'd been destined for from the moment of his birth, a life he'd been trained for and embraced even while he'd been exiled.

Whereas she…

Esme swallowed. On the wild chance that she'd fallen pregnant, her life, or at least a huge part of it as the mother of the future heir of Ja'ahr, would be lived in this same, exotic fishbowl, no matter where on earth she chose to reside. She would be scrutinised at every turn. And as the daughter of Jeffrey Scott, her past too would become a source of interest.

Her past would be exposed. Including her role in her father's life before she'd walked away from him. And what had happened in Vegas. With Bryan.

Her outstretched hand trembled so badly she clenched it into a fist.

'What's wrong?' Zaid demanded sharply.

She jumped and spun around to face him. Intelligent eyes were locked on her, examining her every breath, her every blink. The all-black traditional attire he'd changed into gave him an air of a merciless conqueror, despite the white trim bordering the material. 'I… I'm afraid shelving this isn't as easy as I thought it would be. Yesterday I was just a social worker, assigned to do a job I know and love. Today I'm…'

'You're the Sultan's lover, and the woman who could be carrying the next heir of Ja'ahr,' he intoned baldly, leaving no room for equivocation.

The tremble in her hand transmitted to her whole body.

For a single moment Esme found herself praying that his seed had not taken root inside her. If for no other reason than because of the shame she would bring on her child, its father, and the people of Ja'ahr should her secret be discovered. She clenched her gut against the guilt and pain that followed on the heels of that thought.

'Esmeralda?' His autocratic voice brought her mind back into focus.

She turned and snatched up her scarf. 'I'm going back to my tent. I expect you have…um…people waiting to meet with you.'

His frown intensified, but after a moment he nodded. 'I'll ensure you're not disturbed while you rest.'

Esme had very little doubt she would be doing any resting but, eager to escape his probing scrutiny, she nodded and murmured her thanks.

She passed Fawzi, who bowed suspiciously deeply the moment he spotted her. Walking through the camp, Esme also began to notice the marked difference in the greetings that came her way. Where they'd been open, carefree before, their greetings were now accompanied by respectful bows and almost deferential smiles.

They knew she'd spent the night in Zaid's bed. They probably knew she'd been sexually innocent. And now they were attempting to place her on a pedestal on which she didn't belong. The guilt congealing inside her had grown into an unbearable stone by the time she stumbled into her tent.

About to give in to the sobs that bubbled in her throat, she forced them back down when Aisha and Nashwa rushed in after her.

'His Highness says that you are to rest,' the older woman said. 'Aisha will make you some jasmine tea to—'

'No tea, thank you, Nashwa,' she said firmly. 'I just want to lie down for a bit, if that's okay.'

'Of course, Madam.'

She glided past her, heading for the bedroom, while Aisha stepped up and gently tugged the scarf from her hand. Aware that the women wouldn't rest until they felt they'd been of service, Esme succumbed to being attended to, then sighed in relief the moment they retreated.

But the relief didn't last against the thoughts tearing her mind apart. Her secret wasn't the kind she could keep to herself, but it also wasn't the kind she would wish for Zaid to be blindsided by. And then there was the inescapable truth that publicly admitting what she knew about her father's past would hammer another, possibly irredeemable, nail in his coffin.

She grabbed the nearest pillow and buried her face in it. But as much as her head wanted to wind the clock back to this time yesterday, where the extent of her problems was whether Zaid wanted her or not, her heart wouldn't allow that wish to remain. Because then she wouldn't have experienced the most magical hours of her life. And if there was a baby growing inside her… Her breath caught.

She had a little time before she found out one way or the other. Maybe, Zaid too, with time to think, wouldn't feel so strongly about claiming a child whose mother was a nobody and whose grandfather was a criminal. For all she knew, he might prefer her and her child to exist far away from his kingdom. Then all she would have to worry about was how to protect her baby from the shaky legacy of her past.

The effort it took to block out the mocking voice that ridiculed her thinking that Zaid wouldn't claim her child finally wore her out. She was staring blankly at the wall of the tent when she heard excited voices, followed by the unmistakeable sound of rotors approaching.

A glance at her phone showed she'd been lying in bed for two hours. Although she wasn't due to meet with the teachers of the community for another hour, Esme rose, slid off the tunic and went into the bathroom to splash water on her face. She changed into another tunic, this one in a deep blue. She added the accompanying accessories and walked out into the living room, just as Zaid walked in.

His eyes raked her from head to toe, his face unsmiling. 'You're dressed to travel. Very good.'

'Why? Are we going somewhere?' she asked.

'Yes, we're retuning to the Royal Palace.'

She frowned. 'But we still have a day's work to finish here. I'm meeting the teachers in an hour.'

'The report you drew up yesterday was more than sufficient. Any further assessments can be done by other means.'

'What other means?'

He gestured impatiently. 'Phone calls. Video conferences. A dozen other different ways. We're not a backwater tribe, you know.'

'Of course I know. I wasn't suggesting that at all.'

'Then let's go,' he commanded, holding out his hand in imperious emphasis when she hesitated.

'Why do I feel that there's more going on here than you're telling me?'

A muscle rippled in his jaw. 'Because there is. I suggested that we take some time to absorb the possibility that you may be carrying my child. I was wrong to do so. If you are truly carrying my child—'

'A fact that is *still* only a possibility…

'Then we need to put certain arrangements in place,' he finished as if she hadn't spoken.

'What kinds of arrangements?' she demanded.

'The kind that you will be apprised of in due course.'

'So I will be the last one to know?'

'No, you will be one of the first to know when final decisions have been made.'

She wasn't going to get any more out of him. She knew it from the way he angled his body determinedly towards the door and expected her to fall in line. She knew it from the way Fawzi guided her towards the helicopter the moment she stepped out while Zaid said his goodbyes to the Tujullah elders. She knew it when he took his seat beside her and immediately activated his satellite phone.

As they soared into the air and the pilot pointed the aircraft towards the capital, Esme became blindingly aware of one thing. Whether her pregnancy had been confirmed or not didn't matter to Zaid. While his heir was even a possibility, he was going all out to lay his claim on it.

Zaid observed his small council of advisors as the monthly meeting came to an end. He knew the last un-itemised point of the meeting was about to be brought up because it had been broached, sometimes subtly, sometimes boldly, at each meeting for the last six months.

This time, though, he wasn't as disinterested by or dismissive of the subject as he'd been on previous occasions. In fact, there was a hum of anticipation within him that had been present ever since he'd walked into the room.

It had been ten days since he'd returned to the Royal Palace with Esmeralda. Ten days during which he'd tried to get to grips with the possibility that he might be a father. He hadn't sought confirmation yet, since his initial research had advised that it might still be too early. But, like he'd told Esmeralda, decisions needed to be made. And the more he'd weighed up all his options, the more he'd realised he had only one. More than that, though, was the realisation he couldn't keep avoiding the decision he'd been putting off. Whether Esmeralda was pregnant or not, he would have to marry some time in the near future.

He couldn't deny that marriage to a woman from an allied kingdom would bring another layer of stability to

Ja'ahr. But marriage and the announcement of an heir would be even more welcomed by his people.

Either way, it was a decision that needed to be addressed. So why not now?

And why not Esmeralda and the possible child she might be carrying?

Two birds…one stone…

He tented his fingers and focused on the oldest member of his group of advisors, an ageing man in his seventies who'd been a good friend and aide to his own father. Zaid trusted him because, aside from the sound counsel he'd given him, Anwar Hanuf was also the man who'd risked his life to save him the night his parents had been assassinated.

Anwar cleared his throat, and the room fell silent. 'At the risk of repeating myself for the umpteenth time, I think it's time you solidified your position as Sultan and married, Zaid.'

Zaid kept silent, an action that surprised Anwar since this was usually the time Zaid waved him away, stood up and brought the meeting to an abrupt end.

Anwar, seeing his opportunity, ploughed ahead. 'Our neighbouring states are dying to form firmer alliances through commerce, but one or two are also hoping for a much stronger alliance through marriage.' He stopped, and eyed Zaid. When Zaid nodded for him to continue, he hastily opened a dossier and reeled off a list of possible candidates.

Zaid shook his head after the fourth one. 'No. As much as I accept that arranged marriages forged in the name of stronger alliances have a good success rate among our people, that isn't going to work for me. I won't marry a woman I don't know, neither do I have the time to date and get to know one well enough to propose. But I do accept your argument that marriage will help stabilise our country.'

Anwar sat up straighter, keen black eyes probing Zaid. 'Do you also accept that it needs to happen sooner rather than later?'

'Yes. And I may already have a candidate,' he supplied.

The group exchanged glances. Anwar voiced the question blazing through their minds. 'The English woman?' he asked, a little deflated.

Zaid's eyes narrowed. 'Do you have a problem with her?'

'Of course not. Her suitability isn't the issue. But we are concerned about her father, your potential father-in-law.'

Zaid's jaw tightened. 'His fate lies with a jury of his peers, not with me. Whatever the verdict, we will deal with it.'

The men fell silent, absorbing his resolute reply. Anwar cleared his throat. 'There's concern that our enemies might use her father's situation to stir up trouble.'

He stiffened, recalling his conversation with the chief of police. 'Then they will be dealt with the same way we deal with criminals—using the letter of the law.'

Anwar nodded. 'Very well, Your Highness. We look forward to your instruction on when we can make a formal announcement.'

Zaid remained in the room after the men had departed. Had he jumped the gun a little where Esmeralda was concerned?

No.

Whether she was pregnant or not, his argument for marriage was a sound one. They were compatible both in bed and out of it. She'd proved in a short time that she could be very good for his people, her ability to adapt to his country and it customs stunningly impressive.

She was intelligent enough to know what was at stake. He was confident she would see that saying no to him wasn't an option.

* * *

'No.'

For the first time since she'd known him, Zaid looked lost for words. So was she, to be honest, since the last question she'd expected to hear from his lips were the ones he'd uttered a minute ago.

'Marry me?'

But the answer that powered from her soul stemmed from the knowledge that, even though her heart had leapt for a single moment, this was wrong. Perhaps it had also stemmed from the fact that the previous time she'd received a proposal, it had also been the under wrong circumstances. Plus she'd spent the last ten days in near isolation, Zaid's terse words that she remain in the palace when they'd returned from Tujullah ringing in her ears. He'd offered very little explanation save to say she'd earned a break after throwing herself into her work for three weeks. But she'd known there was more to the command.

Marry me.

The words weren't delivered with flowery sentiment or devotion, but with the gravity of a thousand drums behind them. Wherever he'd been these last few days, this conclusion had been well thought out and finalised. Without her input or approval.

'What did you say?' he finally demanded.

'I said no. I won't marry you. And before you narrow your eyes at me, we both know this proposal is based solely on the possibility that I might be pregnant.'

His eyes did narrow. And his body tensed too as he strolled to where she'd been admiring the garden in one of the many private courtyards that peppered the palace. She'd had a lot of time on her hands to explore over the past ten days. Each new discovery had been more breathtaking than the last. Esme didn't know whether she loved the Royal Palace more because she'd discovered that Zaid's parents had chosen to live in a hotel for three years while they'd built this palace from the ground up after they'd donated their old palace to an orphanage in desperate need of housing, or because each stone contained a rich history that spoke of the love and devotion Ja'ahrians held for Zaid's parents.

The knowledge that she was falling in love with the culture and people of Ja'ahr had crept up on her. The knowledge that she'd roamed the palace secretly, looking out for its ruler and wishing they were still out on the road when he'd been more accessible was a more disturbing discovery.

Her leaping senses absorbed his face, his voice, now even as she accepted that what he was asking of her was impossible.

'Of course it is,' he confirmed, his expression puzzled at her response. 'It's the right thing to do to legitimise my heir.'

Esme almost laughed. Only the peculiar ache lodged in her chest kept the sound from escaping. 'And how would waiting a few more days make a difference?' she asked, even though she knew marriage would be an impossible choice for her then, too. 'Or, better still, we can clear this up right now if you'll allow me to take an early pregnancy test.'

His frown deepened. 'Why are you convinced you're not carrying my child?'

'I'm not convinced. It's just I don't understand why you're waiting to find out. And I don't understand why you're proposing marriage. Like you said, your people are forward-thinking. Will they really question the legitimacy of your baby, *if* there is one, based on when exactly he or she is born?'

His jaw clenched. 'The general advice is to wait until two weeks have passed or better still once the date of your next cycle is exceeded to be definite. As for the timing of the marriage, I don't care what other people think. *I* would prefer that we move as quickly as possible. A wedding, especially one to a sovereign, takes time to plan and execute.'

She shook her head. 'But that's not everything, is it? What aren't you telling me, Zaid?'

He kept silent for so long she thought he wouldn't respond. He paced to the edge of the bubbling fountain, looking at it for a long moment.

'There's been a push for me to marry for a while now. A push I've resisted even though it's my destiny and duty to marry and produce heirs. But the time has come and I don't wish to wait any longer.'

Esme conjured up an image of a future Zaid, married to a faceless woman, one who would happily wear his ring and bear his children. The certainty it wouldn't be her sent a large dose of disquiet ringing through her, escalating her fear that her growing attachment to all things Ja'ahr extended to its ruler too.

Sternly, she pushed the suggestion away. She had too much baggage to ever contemplate such a thing.

'All the better reason for you to rule out a pregnancy quickly. Then once we discover that I'm not pregnant, you can find someone more appropriate to marry.'

He whirled to face her. *'Appropriate?'*

The laughter that finally emerged scraped her throat. 'Come on, Zaid. Would you have even considered me as a suitable bride had we not had a mishap with contraception?'

He had the grace to hesitate, to not insult them both by rushing to deny what she'd said. His lids veiled his expression for a moment before he looked back up at her. 'We are where we are. The only way is to be pragmatic about our situation.'

'This is absurd. An early pregnancy test will clear all

of this up. They're very reliable now. Then we can both go back to living our lives.'

For some reason that made his expression darker. 'You say that as if it's a separate thing. Have you forgotten that you've committed to living under my roof, under my protection, for as long as I require?' he asked.

'I haven't forgotten. But neither have I forgotten that it won't be for ever.' Again that punch of disquiet unnerved her at the thought of her future departure from Ja'ahr. From Zaid.

The observation displeased him even more. He stared at her for an age, before he reached out and caught her wrist in a firm hold, then began to lead her out of the courtyard. 'Very well, let's get this over and done with,' he rasped.

'Where are we going?' Esme demanded as she hurried to keep up with his longer strides.

'You're not prepared to wait another few days for a more accurate confirmation so we'll try things your way. But I'm agreeing on the basis that we will follow it up with more precise blood tests when the time comes.'

She'd had time to grow more familiar with the intricate layout of the Royal Palace in the last week and a half, so within a minute she knew they were headed for Zaid's private chambers.

'We're going to do the pregnancy test now?' she blurted, suddenly unsure whether she was prepared for it. Whether she was prepared for her future, her possible departure, to be made finite.

He slanted her a narrow-eyed look. 'Isn't that what you've been angling for?'

'But we… I don't have any kits.' She'd been unwilling to ask Nashwa to buy any for her because she hadn't wanted the speculation she knew was brewing to overflow.

She watched Zaid calmly extract his phone and hit dial.

After a few terse words were exchanged he hung up. 'Problem solved.'

She'd got what she wanted. And yet apprehension clawed up her spine the closer they got to his private wing. In minutes she'd know if her fate would be sealed with Zaid's for ever, or whether the clock would be starting a wind-down of her time in his life.

Esme wasn't surprised to see Fawzi waiting inside Zaid's lush, private living room with a rectangular box that looked like it had been dug straight out of Aladdin's treasure chest. With a deep bow and a cryptic look at her he handed the box over and left the room.

Zaid released her, then lifted the lid of the box. Inside, on a bed of red velvet, lay two early pregnancy test kits still sealed in their containers. He picked them up and held them out to her.

Her breath stalled in her lungs. The moment of truth.

Her fingers trembled as she took the items from him. A look at his face showed he too was in the throes of a deep, earth-shattering emotion. He set the box down and silently walked her through a set of white double doors that led to a bathroom.

The space was as jaw dropping as the rest of the palace, if not even more so. But all Esme could concentrate on was the fate that awaited her minutes from now.

And fate rammed home, loud and terrifying, in two sets of thick blue lines.

She had no recollection of walking back to the bathroom doors or opening them. Only of Zaid, tall and proud, breath held and immovable before her.

Waiting for the words she couldn't keep inside any more. 'I'm pregnant.'

CHAPTER TWELVE

SHE DIDN'T RECALL much of the moments following her announcement. It was as if those two words, once uttered, had expanded to fill every atom of her life. But, somehow, between one moment and the next, she was lying on a long velvet sofa with a grim, slightly pale Zaid crouched over her.

'What…what happened?' she ventured.

Eyes turned a dark bronze pierced almost accusingly into her. 'It seems I was wrong in thinking rationality would prevail once you had your answer. Instead, the knowledge that you're pregnant with my child seems to have adversely overcome you. You delivered the news and then promptly collapsed,' he stated sombrely.

Esme felt the room sway as the reality of it kicked her hard. She was pregnant. With Zaid's child.

Oh, God.

She shut her eyes. Took a shallow breath, then another when the first didn't quite make it to her lungs. When that didn't work, she gulped some more.

'It would please me greatly if you would stop hyperventilating.'

Because it wasn't good for the baby? She forced herself to take the next breath more slowly.

'Open your eyes, Esmeralda. We need to face this together,' he instructed heavily.

She obeyed only because he was right, no matter how much she wanted to slip into oblivion. He looked graver than before. 'Zaid…' Her voice was a choked noise that sounded worse lying down. She started to sit, only to find herself being pressed firmly back.

'Don't get up. The doctor is on his way.'

She started. 'What? I don't need a doctor!'

'That's a matter of opinion. Unfortunately for you, fainting into my arms takes the decision out of your hands.'

She sagged against the plump cushions, unwilling to acknowledge the weakness dredging through her at the feel of his hand through the thin cotton of her yellow sundress. In the next moment she realised his hand was splayed directly over their baby. Her heart jumped as she watched the same thought occur to him.

His eyelashes swept down to veil his gaze. Esme didn't know whether to rejoice or mourn when he removed his hand a moment later.

He crossed to a nearby drinks cabinet and returned with a glass of water and a conveniently placed straw. She took a few sips under his intense scrutiny before he set the glass down.

Esme cleared her throat and tried again. 'I think you were right. We need to wait for the proper time to do the test again. Maybe this was a false positive…' She trailed off when a bleak, shuttered look entered his eyes.

'Does it fill you with that much horror, the idea of carrying my child?'

Shock froze the blood in her veins. *'What?'*

'First you wanted to take the test immediately, but now we have the results, you want to deny the truth? A more paranoid man would think the idea of marrying me, of having my child, is abhorrent to you, *habiba*,' he said chillingly.

A single shake of her head was all she could manage in denial. 'No. You misunderstand. It's not you.' She stopped and took a breath, struggling to calm her racing mind. 'I just… I don't want you to make a mistake you'll regret,' she finished weakly.

Her explanation tugged a mirthless smile from him.

'You seem bent on saving me from myself. Do you think I didn't weigh all the options before arriving at my decision?'

How could he have, when he didn't have the whole truth?

Tell him!

'No, I don't think you have.'

'Then enlighten me.'

'I have too much baggage, Zaid. My father—'

One autocratic hand slashed through the air. 'You're nothing like your father,' he dismissed. 'If you were, I wouldn't have given you the position you hold. My people are already beginning to embrace you. My council of advisors has approved you as my bride. And for those still swayed by that sort of thing, it's already known that you were an innocent when I took you to my bed.'

The sharp left turn in the conversation jumbled her thoughts. 'What? How would they have…? Oh, the *sheets*?'

He shrugged, not in the least bit embarrassed by referring to a subject that made her face flame. 'The hard-core traditionalists will just have to be content with the wedding night coming after the deed.'

'Oh, my God,' she murmured incredulously, her head still spinning. A swipe of her tongue over lips turned dry, and she attempted again. 'Zaid, listen to me—'

'My grandmother was a second wife, did you know that?' he cut across her again. Was he doing it deliberately to stop her from telling him what she needed to?

'Um…no, I didn't know.'

'My grandfather's first wife was an American,' he continued. 'She was fully accepted, even loved by the people until her unfortunate, premature death. So, you see, Ja'ahrians aren't complete traditionalists when it comes to the wives their rulers take.'

'But there are other factions that won't welcome this,

aren't there?' she countered. 'Like whoever was pushing the chief of police's buttons?'

His jaw flexed. 'If he and they need reminding, I will merely reconfirm what I said to him the night I came for you.'

'Which was?'

'That you belong to me and I have taken you under my protection.'

Despite the foolish weakness threatening to overcome common sense, she grimaced. 'You make me sound like a chattel.'

'*He* was the one who intended to use you as a pawn. I needed to communicate with him in a language that he understood. I believe the message got through to him. If that's all you're worried about, rest easy.'

'It's not—' She was interrupted for the third time, but this time by a firm knock on the door. At Zaid's command, Fawzi entered with a tall, lean man with rimless glasses, greying hair and a brisk air of confidence.

After a hurried exchange of greetings, Fawzi departed, and the man approached her. 'I'm Dr Aziz. I understand you fainted?' The question was posed in a distinct American accent.

Surprised to hear it, she glanced at Zaid.

'Dr Aziz has been my personal doctor since I was a boy. He left Ja'ahr with me and I brought him back from the States when I returned. I trust him implicitly.' Simple words, but delivered with a thread of emotion that spoke of a bond between the two men.

The doctor cracked a smile as he opened his case. 'He means he trusts me not to tell you he's not as invincible as he likes everyone to think.'

His easy charm drew a smile from her. And a deep scowl from Zaid. 'Perhaps you would like to get on with seeing to your patient?'

'I'm fine, really—'

'She's pregnant.' Zaid calmly dropped the bombshell.

Dr Aziz hid his shock well as he looked from her to Zaid. 'This is great news, son. Congratulations.'

'Offer felicitations *after* examining her, Joseph,' Zaid clipped out.

The other man nodded. 'How far along are you?' he asked.

'I'm…um…we just did the tests,' Esme said.

'The relevant date you require is ten days ago,' Zaid added, naming the exact date.

Joseph Aziz frowned. 'It's too soon to be feeling faint.'

'Stop stating the obvious and fix her.'

'Zaid!'

The doctor smiled. 'Don't worry, I'm used to it. He gets cranky when he's worried.'

Zaid swung away, muttering under his breath. Joseph carried on unperturbed, asking her questions and taking notes on his tablet. He frowned again as she guiltily confessed to her recent loss of appetite. Five minutes later, he snapped his case shut.

'Well?' Zaid had returned, looming over them like a dark cloud.

'Nothing serious. Miss Scott is a little low on blood sugar. I'm guessing that, coupled with the momentous news that she's carrying our next Sultan, would throw anyone. She just needs to avoid skipping meals, and she'll be fine.' He offered her a reassuring smile, while Zaid stared at her with narrowed eyes as she finally sat up.

'I told you I was fine.'

'You and I have different definitions of fine, *habiba*, especially when you're not eating,' he rasped, before turning to Joseph. They exchanged a few words in Arabic before the doctor departed. And Fawzi re-entered moments later.

'Your Highness, your conference call is about to begin.'

Zaid nodded curtly and his assistant moved to a respectful but expectant distance. Her heart dipped.

'Zaid, we need to talk,' she murmured.

He faced her. 'You're carrying my child, Esmeralda,' he whispered fiercely. 'Nothing you have to say will shift the importance of that fact and our need to focus on it and it alone. From the moment you walked out of the bathroom, your arguments have become null and void.'

Her insides trembled as she shook her head. 'But you don't know—'

'Don't I? You're about to confess a less than stellar past association with your father.' He barely blinked as she gasped. 'But you forget that I know the sort of man he is. He's a gifted con artist in whose web you were caught at a vulnerable age.'

'There's more, Zaid,' she insisted.

He stepped close, clasped her shoulders. 'There's always more. But what matters is that you wised up and walked away eventually. The estrangement was your doing, was it not?' he pressed.

Lips pursed, she nodded. 'Yes.'

A hint of a genuine smile cracked his lips, before his face grew serious again. 'So you turned your life around. I don't need any more proof that my decision is sound.'

The sensation of sinking further into quicksand, despite the rope he was throwing her, escalated. 'Please, Zaid. Hear me out.'

'Your Highness?' Fawzi prompted.

Zaid sighed. 'You will marry me, Esmeralda. For the sake of our child you will marry me and we will make this work.'

A spurt of frustrated anger rose. 'Just like that?'

The fierce eyes that raked her face held a banked hunger that turned her anger into something equally primal. 'Trust me, *jamila*, nothing that happens between us will ever be *just like that*. But for now you'll stay here. Fawzi will summon Nashwa and Aisha. They'll bring you a late lunch. You'll nourish yourself. Nourish our child. And when I return, if you still insist on talking, then we'll talk.'

He left after that. As promised, her staff appeared, their barely suppressed chatter a marked indication that they were even more excited to be serving her in the Sultan's private chamber. Their complete lack of judgement as they darted between the living room and the private kitchen, where Zaid's personal chef was preparing what sounded like a feast fit for an army, forced Esme to examine Zaid's words.

By assuming the throne after his uncle's long tyrannical rule and giving so much of himself to his people without asking for anything in return, he'd laid down a path of trust and dependability and set up the cornerstone for change.

The protests, which had died down in the last few weeks, were a sign that Zaid was winning even those disgruntled citizens over. She knew through her own studies and experience with social work that marriage was almost always a better stability provider than single parenthood. And when that provider was the ruler of a kingdom…?

Esme believed in her heart she could make it work. But should the truth ever come out, would Zaid forgive what she'd done?

By the time she finished sampling a little bit of each dish set before her, she knew she needed to lay her cards on the table the moment Zaid returned.

Except, when he walked through the doors five hours later, a single look was all it took to realise something was badly wrong.

'I need to leave for Paris immediately,' he announced.

She struggled to her feet, and although he frowned when she stumbled slightly, he carried on walking towards his bedroom. Given no choice but to follow or shout the conversation, she trailed behind him.

Two butlers were already packing suitcases, and Zaid was shrugging off his outer robe.

She dragged her gaze from the ripple of muscle beneath his tunic. Already her chest was tightening at the thought of him being absent again much like he'd been for the past ten days. The possible reason for that feeling was a little terrifying but not enough to prevent her from asking, 'Why?'

'A deal I was supposed to finalise at the trade summit next week is in jeopardy. It's been six months in the making. It can't fall apart now.'

Esme wasn't prepared to feel so bereft at the thought of his absence. 'Oh…right. How long will you be away?'

His whole frame brimmed with majestic confidence as he shrugged. 'For as long as it takes to salvage it. I don't intend that to be long at all.'

'Okay. I'll…see you when you get back, then.'

He paused in the process of removing his *keffiyeh*. 'No, you'll see me every day while I'm away because you're coming with me, Esmeralda.'

Her eyes widened. 'I'm… Why?'

His air of determination intensified. 'Because for one thing we haven't finished our conversation. And I'm hoping that once we do agree that marriage is the only course of action, you'll spend the rest of the time consulting with the Royal Palace's designated designers to pick your wedding trousseau.'

A neat, efficiently presented argument. There was no way she could say no unless she was prepared to wait for days, maybe even longer, for Zaid to return from his trip. The thought of having that unfinished conversation hanging over her head, disturbing her sleep, didn't fill her with joy.

'Okay, I'll go and get packed.'

He slanted a very masculine smile her way as he reefed his tunic over his head and headed for his vast dressing room. 'No need. It's being taken care of as we speak.'

It was the sight of his bare torso that robbed her of the heated response she'd planned. Esme was sure of it. Or perhaps the fact that she was still in his bedroom when he re-emerged five minutes later wearing a pair of grey chinos and a pristine white polo shirt.

The casual clothes should have made him less intimidating. Instead, the power of his magnetic attraction seemed to expand even further, encompassing everything in its way. Her included. She watched him glide his fingers hurriedly through his glossy hair and found herself wishing they were hers. Her breath caught when he stopped before her.

'Did you have lunch?' he asked, his face pinched in serious lines.

She nodded, a touch breathlessly, as her senses filled with his scent.

'Good. We should be wheels up in an hour. If you wish to supervise your staff, I suggest you go and do so now.'

Time seemed to trip into fast forward from then. A quick, refreshing shower and a change of clothes into white palazzo linen pants, matching wide-sleeved top and gold wedge sandals, and she was heading out to join Zaid in his motorcade.

The jumbo-sized royal jet, its wings and tail painted in the same signature colours, stood waiting on the tarmac, its crew courteous and efficient as they readied their King for his journey. But, contrary to thinking she would get a chance to speak to Zaid, she was promptly installed in a sumptuous living suite with Nashwa and Aisha keeping her company, while Zaid cloistered himself with his financial advisors in a separate part of the plane.

That theme continued when they reached Paris. Only with more people thrown into the mix. The royal party had hired the whole upper floor of the hotel on Avenue Montaigne, with she and Zaid occupying two separate bedrooms in the Royal Suite. Decorated with typical Parisian glamour, the hotel nevertheless held hints of eastern exoticism that made Esme feel at home the moment she walked in, although the thought that she was beginning to think of Ja'ahr as home struck and stayed with her.

Despite the jaw-dropping elegance of their hotel, Esme felt as if she was on pins and needles as the days rolled by and every opportunity to talk to Zaid was thwarted. In her uncharitable moments, she suspected it was by design. But then she would catch a glimpse of him through an open conference room door, see the haggard expressions of his advisors reflected a hundredfold on his face, and feel regretful. On one of those occasions his gaze caught hers as she hesitated in the doorway. Then his intense eyes dropped to her flat belly for a long moment before he resumed his conversation.

The wordless indication that she and their baby were also on his mind only doubled her guilt.

It was that emotion that stopped her from sending away the designers when they started to arrive on their sixth day in Paris. That and the undeniable fact that her period hadn't made its prompt appearance on her due date. She'd found herself alone with Zaid for a rare minute in the living room a few hours after absorbing that reality.

He'd taken one look at her and frowned. 'What's wrong?'

'I… My period didn't come.'

The brush of knuckles on her cheek was at variance with the almost reproachful look in his eyes as he nodded. 'I know,' was all he said before yet another group of business-suited men walked into the room.

With the confirmation that she was well and truly impregnated fixed in her mind, Esme sat in the designated throne-like chair in her suite and watched row after row of exquisite gowns being wheeled into the room.

Apparently, His Highness had requested a full trousseau and new set of clothes for her honeymoon. For the Ja'ahrian wedding, her traditional wedding gown was being prepared in a secret location she wasn't to be privy to.

Esme went through a cycle of frustration, anxiety and anger as she inspected the beautiful gowns. But her mind kept returning to one kernel of hope that wouldn't disappear.

Zaid had arranged for all of this despite knowing that her past was less than exemplary. If he was prepared to take a risk for the sake of their child, was she not doing it a disservice by attempting to stand in the way of her child's rightful inheritance?

The only thing holding her back was her secret.

She would tell him. She had to before anything irreversible happened. But in the meantime she squashed down her churning feelings and carried on choosing the clothes that were to her taste.

Nashwa and Aisha's enthusiastic applause the moment she tried the clothes on confirmed her choices. With that out of the way, a knot of anxiety eased and Esme allowed herself to relax a little.

Zaid walked in as the stylists were transporting the clothes to her bedroom. He took one look around, then his eyes zeroed in on her.

'You've chosen your trousseau.' It wasn't a question, but confirmation of what he'd willed her to do all along.

Her breath emerged shakily as she replied. 'Yes.'

'So you will marry me?' This time it was a question, but one he knew the answer to already.

On a silent prayer, Esme swallowed. 'Yes.'

* * *

If she'd thought the events since their arrival in Paris were hurried, the momentum once she'd given her consent was nothing short of warp speed. The morning after, Zaid presented her with a staggeringly beautiful yellow diamond set in Arabian gold. Tears were already prickling her eyes at the sheer beauty of the stone when he informed her solemnly that the ring had belonged to his mother.

The moment would have been perfect, magical even, had it not all been witnessed by his twenty-strong staff and captured on camera by a professional photographer drafted in for the sole purpose of documenting Zaid's formal proposal. After that, a formal announcement was made in Ja'ahr.

Zaid stood in the centre of the room, his hand holding hers, surrounded by his staff as they watched a televised version of the announcement.

The rock of anxiety that sat in her belly doubled in size as the camera panned over the crowds gathered in parks and stadiums to await the news. At the replay of Zaid's proposal, they erupted in deafening cheers.

Inside the hotel suite, his staff also applauded as Zaid leaned down and murmured in her ear, 'I told you they would welcome you with open arms.'

Almost instantly, Esme's popularity exploded.

But then so did the delicate trade talks Zaid had been painstakingly stitching together.

Meetings went on late into the night, tempers frayed and were lost. When he emerged from a conference room three days after their engagement, still looking haggard and frustrated, Esme's heart lurched. Then it dipped even further when he approached her with a grim, resolute look.

'Fawzi is instructing your staff to pack for you. You're returning to Ja'ahr this afternoon.'

It was the last thing she was expecting. The last thing her heart seemed to be prepared for. 'Why?' she blurted, knowing she was in deep trouble where her feelings for Zaid were concerned.

'I'm going to be here for a little longer. And you need to return and ensure the wedding preparations are under way.'

She didn't want to leave, but now she'd agreed to marry him, any objection would be seen as dragging her feet. But there was still an issue between them.

'Zaid, we still need to talk about my past.'

His hand slashed through the air. 'Enough with this need to talk!'

Frustration and anger welled inside her. 'This is important—'

'So is this wedding. Perhaps you ought to concentrate on the future and stop dwelling on the past?' he bit out.

'All I need is ten minutes,' she insisted.

He clawed his fingers through his hair. 'That's ten more than I have right now, Esmeralda. I merely came out here to say goodbye.'

'If all you wanted was to tell me I was being shipped out, perhaps you should've sent Fawzi. Or a text message.'

He growled under his breath. 'I do not wish to fight with you.'

'You don't wish to do anything with me, except throw directives and expect me to jump when you say so!'

His gaze dropped to her stomach. 'In your state, I would prefer less jumping and more co-operation,' he suggested, with a possessive throb in his voice that was directed solely at his heir.

Pain struck somewhere in the region of her heart. 'I'm well aware that I'm merely a vessel for your heir, Zaid, but perhaps you might spare a thought for my state of mind, too?'

He looked puzzled for a moment. That moment passed

almost instantly when Fawzi appeared like an unwanted apparition.

'Your Highness, your presence is needed.'

Zaid exhaled noisily. 'I'll be right there.'

Esme couldn't stop her mouth twisted in bitterness. 'Of course you will.'

His eyes narrowed. 'Esmeralda—'

She waved him away, her gesture carefree despite the pain and anxiety twisting her insides. 'It's fine, Zaid. I understand completely where I stand in the pecking order. So I guess I'll see you when I see you.'

Then she did what he'd done to her many times since their arrival. She left *him* standing there, staring after her.

The return journey to Ja'ahr was uneventful, probably because she retired to the master suite the moment she boarded the jet and spent the whole trip curled up with her pillow for company.

Zaid couldn't have spelled it out more conclusively if he'd tried that she was merely a means to an end. He'd brought her to Paris to apply pressure on her to marry him. The moment she'd agreed her place on the chessboard had become redundant.

And it wasn't as if he'd hidden his motives. Zaid had been upfront about this marriage being for the sole benefit of his people and his heir.

So why did it hurt so much? The answer mocked her in the dull thudding of her heart. Zaid's feelings might be purposefully basic, but along the line hers had gained strings and bows and hopes for a happy ever after with no basis in reality. And even now she feared it was too late.

Melancholy born of that realisation stayed with her long after they landed back in Ja'ahr and into the days that followed. Lost in her gloomy world that not even the joy of the child growing in her womb could shake, it took a while to realise the mood of the people had shifted slightly.

When she started to pay attention, she saw TV reports and debates that questioned her suitability as the daughter of a criminal to be the first lady of Ja'ahr. When further questions arose about her father and her past, her anxiety grew. But then so did her sense of finality. Maybe it was all for the best. Maybe the decision would be taken out of her hands by the people who mattered. Ja'ahr's citizens.

Ironically, her thoughts manifested into reality the very next day, a full week after her return from Paris with almost zero contact from Zaid.

Nashwa's announcement that she had a visitor came as a surprise. An unpleasant one when she realised just who her visitor was.

The chief of police, Ahmed Haruni, was pacing her private office as if he owned the place. Black, beady eyes fixed on her as he lazily replaced the paperweight he'd been examining when Esme entered. Unlike most people did since her betrothal announcement, he didn't bow to her.

Esme didn't care about that as much as she cared to know why he was there. 'Can I help you, sir?'

He didn't leave her hanging for long. 'I'll come straight to the point, Miss Scott. There are a growing number of concerned Ja'ahrians who believe this proposed marriage is a mistake.'

Despite her own growing feelings in that regard, her heart lurched. 'And let me guess, you're one of them?'

The small man shrugged. 'I love my country. It would be remiss of me not to speak up before it's too late.'

'Why are you bringing this to me? Why not take it up with your Sultan?'

He spread his arms wide, a mildly contemptuous look on his face. 'Because he's not here. He's chasing flimsy deals when he should be here, looking after the welfare of his people.'

Anger spiked through her pain. 'The reason for his absence is not flimsy, I assure you.'

'I did not come to debate that with you.'

'Then tell me what you *did* come for.'

His gave a snake-like smile. 'You may have pulled the wool over our leader's eyes, but I know exactly who you are, Miss Scott. I know what happened in Las Vegas with a certain young man named Bryan Atkins.'

Shock lanced through her. He witnessed her reaction and his smile widened. 'Do I have your attention now, Miss Scott?'

She nodded numbly. 'What do you want?'

His eyes hardened. 'For you to do the right thing, of course. If Zaid Al-Ameen isn't fit to rule this country, then *you* are even less fit to be our Sultana.'

She gasped. 'You don't think Zaid is fit to be Sultan?'

'There are others more qualified than he.'

She raised her chin. 'You mean others you can bend to your will?'

Black eyes narrowed. 'You'd be wise to watch your tongue, Miss Scott. The Sultan isn't here to protect you now.'

Icy fingers crawled down her spine. 'Is that all you came to say?'

He reached into his pocket and brought out a rectangular envelope. 'This is a first-class ticket back to your country. I will be pleased to provide you with a police escort to the airport if you wish it.'

'I don't wish it, thank you. *If* I decide to leave, I'll do so under my own steam.'

He placed the envelope on her desk anyway and walked towards her. Esme fought the urge to step back from his oily, menacing presence. 'Get out of the country while you still have the chance, Miss Scott. This regime will not thrive for much longer.'

With that ominous threat, he walked out.

Esme expelled the breath she'd been holding, then immediately gulped in another. Her mind darted back and forth, debating which action to take first. She needed to warn Zaid. But she also needed to put into action the thoughts she'd been skirting before the chief of police's noxious visit.

She couldn't marry Zaid.

Not now she knew the depths of her feelings for him. Not now she knew her presence would cause nothing but dissension among his people.

The walk to her desk felt like a walk to the gallows. But surprisingly the letter was easy to compose. As was the packing of her things three hours later. She thought of calling her father but discarded the idea. His phone calls were being monitored, and the last thing she needed was for her quiet exit to be announced. But what surprised her most was how easy her request to be driven to the airport was granted.

The ticket attendant smiled widely and nodded when she requested a seat on the next available flight out of Ja'ahr. Esme didn't care that it was headed to Rome instead of England. It was close enough.

It was only as she began the two-hour wait for her flight that Esme got an inkling that something was going on. First the attendant came to inform her that her flight was delayed for a further two hours. Then the area around where she sat slowly started to empty of people. When she realised they were being herded away from her, Esme looked around and caught a few phone cameras pointed her way. Next she realised the bodyguards she thought she'd dismissed were still very much present. And a few more were fanned out close by.

Esme rose from her seat as a hum built in the gathering crowd. When someone pointed at the window behind her, she turned. And swallowed hard at the sight of the royal jet parked on the tarmac.

In the next instant she saw Zaid, robes flowing, ruthless intent stamped on his face as he stalked towards her.

When he reached her he said nothing. Not with his lips anyway. His eyes however, blazed with fury, censure and disappointment.

'Zaid—'

'We are in public, *jamila*, and that is the only thing saving you from being placed over my knee and spanked to within an inch of your life,' he growled, nostrils flared. 'Now you will smile and take my hand and we will walk out of here and return to the palace.'

Her heart leapt wildly. Then plummeted just as hard.

'I can't.'

The tendons in his neck stood out as he struggled to control himself. 'You can and you will. I'm not letting you go, Esmeralda.'

'But, Zaid, the chief of police—'

'Has been thoroughly and conclusively dealt with.' He held up the letter she'd written to him, his eyes as cold as chips, although she caught something in there too. Something that made her heart lurch wildly. 'This changes nothing, Esmeralda. You're not leaving me. This wedding is going to happen, so get used to the idea.'

CHAPTER THIRTEEN

THE JA'AHRIAN MARRIAGE ceremony was like nothing she'd ever witnessed. Celebrated over a seven-day period, each evening at sunset, she and Zaid met before a different set of marriage elders to repeat vows of faithfulness, honour and devotion, after which they hosted a banquet for the thousand-strong guests and dignitaries who'd accepted their invitation.

Had she been in a different state of mind, sheer awe would have rolled through her, each moment steeped in vivid Technicolor. But the pain and bewilderment lodged in her heart made names and faces blur into one, even as she pasted on a fake smile until she was sure her face would split in two.

She was gazing entranced at fireworks that marked the official end to the celebrations when she felt Zaid's eyes on her.

His refusal to accept her backing out of the wedding had been absolute, his fury at her going back on her word catastrophic.

Esme would have fought and rejected both had she not realised, at the moment she'd seen him walking towards her at the airport, that she was irrevocably, for better or worse, requited or not, head over heels in love with Zaid Al-Ameen.

He'd made the right decision. His wife, his Queen, and the future mother of his children was beautiful, poised, and a natural with his people. Many had come to the gates of the palace to offer her flowers. After the ceremony, before they departed for their honeymoon, she would take her place next to his and thank his people for their support in a live broadcast.

All this could easily not have come to pass. He should have acted sooner to deal with Ahmed Haruni but he'd needed that final piece of evidence that the man had been inciting others to overthrow Zaid's rule. He could so easily have lost Esmeralda. The knowledge still had the power to shake him. Even now, watching her, he knew how close it had all been.

But no matter. They were married now. And Zaid couldn't wait to show her off to the world. More than that, he couldn't wait to be alone with her. To reacquaint himself with the delights of her body. And then perhaps the infernal hunger that dogged him would ease. He mentally shrugged. But who cared if it didn't? She was his wife. His partner in life. They would always have each other.

So why did he feel a kernel of unease gnawing at him each time he saw a shadow cross her face?

He shook off the bad feeling. The doctor had declared her healthy and strong, her pregnancy thriving. And if the feelings swirling through him grew into something else…why not?

He firmly broke off the conversation with the talkative minister and returned to his wife's side. Taking her hand, he pressed a kiss to the back of it, grimacing inwardly when he felt her stiffen slightly. His behaviour at the airport had left a lot to be desired, he knew. But he intended to work on it. 'It's time to say our goodbyes.'

Her eyes widened. 'Already?'

'They've had seven days of you. It's my turn to spend time *alone* with you.'

He made sure their goodbyes were quick, and the prepared speech was gratifying but brief.

Then, finally done, he instructed his driver to deliver them to his jet. It was time to make Esmeralda his wife in every sense of the word.

* * *

They flew to the Bahamas before boarding the royal yacht moored in Nassau. Although travelling in extreme luxury had its perks, Esme was still tired when they finally arrived on board. Turned out keeping her emotions under constant guard did that to a woman. She may have admitted her feelings to herself, but she didn't intend to admit them to Zaid. Not when it was clear he wouldn't welcome them.

They set sail immediately, the idea being to island-hop for the next two weeks.

Nashwa and Aisha had remained behind this time, and although Esme found herself missing their effervescent presence, she welcomed the peace and quiet and the chance to bathe and clothe herself without their well-intentioned interference.

She was still fighting the emotions that seemed to bubble just below her skin when the door to the opulent shower cubicle opened and a very naked and aroused Zaid stepped in.

She had a mere second to school her features, but the weeks since they had first made love had done nothing but sharpen the edge of her desire, and by the time he prowled over to where the water cascaded over her body, every atom of her being was on fire for him.

'Is it irrational that I am jealous of the water caressing your body?' he enquired huskily as he lowered his head to trail a kiss across one shoulder.

She jerked back, bumped her shoulder on the wall. 'What…what are you doing in here?'

His eyes narrowed. 'If you have to ask then something's seriously wrong.' He prowled closer.

She had nowhere to go, so she held out a warding hand. 'I know we're on our honeymoon, but…'

'But?'

'I… Zaid, you don't really want me—'

'Take a very good look, *habiba*. The evidence speaks for itself, I believe.'

Her hungry gaze swept over him, her face flaming when it lingered on the proud, rigid parts of his anatomy.

'I…don't mean that.'

He sighed. 'We got off to a rocky start, I admit. But whatever problems we need to iron out, let's not make this one of them. Okay?'

She knew she was weak when it came to him. Esme discovered just how weak when her body, independent of her mind, lunged into his arms.

He made a rough sound in his throat, then took her mouth in a hot, carnal, demanding kiss. Like the first and second time, he set her aflame with just his mouth. But now she knew what else was coming. And she could barely contain herself. Boldly, she caressed him, driving him to the same fever pitch he'd inspired in her.

On a wild whim, she grabbed the gel she'd just used, squeezing a few drops into her palm. The moment he broke the kiss, she stepped back and glided her hands over his torso. The surprise on his face was followed instantaneously by encouragement. Hard on the heels of that came a rough, thick curse before he was bundling her out of the shower and drying them off.

When they reached the bed, he lifted her high, his gaze upturned to hers. 'Now I truly make you my wife.'

'And you my husband.'

The arms that laid her reverently on the bed shook a little. The kiss he bestowed on her lacked a little of his usual smooth finesse. But she didn't care.

The magnificent man she'd fallen in love with was making love to her. Yes, there was pain in her heart, but for now there was bliss too. And she intended to hold onto that for as long as possible.

That was her last thought before Zaid kissed his way

down her body. Before he lingered on the flat plane of her belly where their child grew.

Before, after praising her through her first climax, he rose above her and took her body with his.

Unhurried, exquisite, their union brought tears to her eyes and a gruff shout from Zaid when he reached his own peak. Then, arms wrapped around each other, they slid into sleep.

It set the tone for their honeymoon.

By day they ate, sunbathed and explored the islands. And by night they made love after sharing mouth-watering meals on the top deck and talking long into the night.

Besides his bodyguards, only Fawzi and another member of his staff accompanied them. Their presence barely registered, although Fawzi had taken to bowing from the waist when he walked into her presence.

When she commented on it, Zaid laughed.

'And why does he look disconcerted whenever I speak to him?'

'Because he's there solely for my benefit. And also because he sees it as a sign of disrespect to me to be brought into a private conversation.'

'But I mean no disrespect! Surely he knows that?'

'Whether you do or not doesn't alter his belief.'

'Really?'

Zaid sobered. 'Yes. There was a time when he would've been severely punished for being addressed directly in the presence of his ruler.'

'What? That's preposterous! It's not his fault if he's spoken to while he's in the room.'

'He's supposed to be unobtrusive. Being made to feel self-conscious doesn't sit right with him.'

'Okay. Thanks for telling me that. I'll make sure he's not uncomfortable in my presence.'

She gasped when he caught her hand and linked their

fingers. 'You're a true gem, Esmeralda Al-Ameen. I'm a very blessed man.'

Esme allowed her heart to take the leap it wanted. Although it soon fell with the knowledge that with each day that passed, and the more she fell under her husband's spell, the more heartache she was inviting.

As for her rush to tell Zaid her sordid secret, he'd said her past didn't matter. She'd decided to take his word for it.

For now.

One day he would need to know. And when that day came, she would tell him.

Except the day came much, much sooner than she anticipated. Eleven days into their two-week honeymoon, to be exact. It didn't matter that the day was perfect, cloudless and the happiest day of her life.

The moment Fawzi walked onto the sunny middle deck, where she and Zaid were having post-swimming drinks, she knew her days in paradise were over. His bow to her was brusque, and when he spoke it wasn't in the deferential English he'd taken to speaking to both of them but in his master's language.

Slowly, she watched Zaid's whole body turn deathly still, then he started to fire questions at his private secretary. Questions Fawzi answered without once looking her way. But Zaid was looking straight at her, with cold eyes that froze her to the marrow. He spoke again to his assistant, and this time Fawzi's gaze darted to her. Esme wished he'd kept ignoring her. That way she wouldn't have seen the pity in his eyes.

He started to walk away. Zaid issued one last instruction. The younger man actually swallowed before he bowed and left the deck.

Thick silence ensued. Despite the blazing temperatures, she shivered.

'You know about Bryan, don't you?' Her voice was as weak as she felt.

His nostrils flared for a wild instant before he spoke. 'Is it true? He killed himself because you fleeced him out of one hundred thousand dollars then rejected him?'

Her heart shook with misery. 'No, it was my father. But he wouldn't have gone after Bryan if I hadn't made friends with him. My interest in him was what triggered my father's attention.' Like every time she thought about Bryan, she wished she'd walked away the day he'd approached her in that restaurant in Vegas.

'This is the guy who took you in his helicopter?' he pressed. 'He's the reason you're racked with guilt whenever you approach a helicopter?'

She nodded, her throat clogged with a boulder of dreadful pain. Not just because of the memory but the certain knowledge that she was about to lose Zaid.

'When did he take his own life?'

'The day after I refused his proposal. It was a few days before my eighteenth birthday. He wanted us to get married on my birthday. I said no. I was too young. God, so was he. We rowed after the helicopter ride and I never saw him again. A few days later his letter arrived. My father had emptied his bank account. Bryan thought I'd helped Dad to do it, but I didn't. I hadn't known anything about it. I tried to get my father to return the money. But…'

'But?' Zaid demanded harshly.

'It was too late. Bryan threw himself off a bridge that morning.'

His face hardened. 'Did you know he loved you? Did *you* love him?'

'No, I didn't love him. He was just my friend. But I love you, Zaid,' she confessed desperately.

Wrong time. Wrong place. She knew it before his head

went back and his eyes went black as if her words had physically assaulted him.

'You *love* me? What a curious time to admit it. Do you think it'll distract me from the fact that this news could rip apart the fragile foundations I've built in Ja'ahr?'

The tears choking her finally fell free. 'I didn't say it because of that. I said it because it's true.' She stopped, her heart bleeding. 'I'm sorry.'

He rose from the lounger and paced away from her. 'Sorry? A man lost his life because of your father's greed! Several newspapers are poised to print that you and your father lured him in with lies and falsehoods, knowing all the time he was nothing but a pawn to you. My people have fallen in love with you. *I…*' he stopped and gritted his jaw.

Her heart shredded into a tiny million pieces. She pulled her knees to her chest, wrapped her arms around her cold body. 'I promise I didn't know about what my father did to Bryan, Zaid, not until it was too late. But I should have known what my father was up to. I blame myself for bringing Bryan into my life.'

When he didn't say anything, she ventured a glance. His face was an ashen landscape of anger and condemnation.

'I've tried to become a better person. By doing whatever good I can wherever I can,' she pleaded.

But he was gone.

He may have been physically on the deck with her but she'd lost her husband. The man she really shouldn't have married in the first place. And when he turned and walked away without uttering another word to her, all she could do was bury her face in her arms and sob her heart out.

Needless to say, the honeymoon was over. Within a few hours the yacht was back in its moorings, their bags were packed and they were headed towards Nassau airport.

At first she was confused by the sight of two identical

planes on the tarmac. When the penny dropped, her already shredded heart dropped along with it.

'I'm going home alone, aren't I?' she asked Zaid the moment he stepped out of the SUV.

'Yes, it's for the best.'

The harsh laughter that escaped scraped her throat. 'Is it?' she asked, mostly self-mockingly.

To her surprise, he nodded. 'It's best if we don't travel together.'

'But why?'

'It's protocol when you're carrying my future heir. We shouldn't have travelled here together.'

'Then why did we?'

'I needed… I chose to bend the rules a little.'

'And now you're back to being Mr Responsible?'

His jaw flexed. 'Your crew is waiting, Esmeralda. And I need to do what I can to prevent this from ruining everything.' He strode off and boarded the first aircraft.

And when the pilot of the second jet summoned her, she walked with leaden legs, boarded the plane and flew to Ja'ahr alone.

Only to find out on her arrival at the palace that Zaid wasn't in residence. According to the staff left manning his office when she visited each morning, they had no clue when His Highness would be available.

Esme discovered very quickly that she was being held prisoner in her own palace. Without Zaid she had no authorisation to leave the palace grounds, not even with an armed escort. But she discovered that whatever damage control he was exerting seemed to be working. At least on an international level. No news outlet carried the story.

But within Ja'ahr, protests that had started to die down rose up again, with one in particular staged close to the palace gates.

Three weeks after her return, she was standing at the

viewing window that circled the palace's giant dome when Nashwa approached her.

'Am I imagining it or has the crowd grown since yesterday?' Esme asked worriedly.

'You're not imagining it, Your Highness. Those are Ahmed Haruni's people, protesting his arrest.'

She winced at the title, her heart tearing as it did each time she heard the reminder of who she was now.

She also knew that on some level Ahmed Haruni had spoken the truth. She would never be completely accepted here.

After a minute of watching the group of angry youths waving their placards, she turned to Nashwa. 'I'm sorry. Did you want something?'

'No, Your Highness. But there's someone here to see you.'

Her heart leapt for a wild minute, then she mocked herself for her foolishness. If Zaid had returned the whole palace would have been abuzz by now. It wouldn't be the soulless place it felt like now.

That too was her fault.

She swallowed her sigh and followed Nashwa down to the office she'd been designated but had never used as Sultana. The man waiting for her was vaguely familiar. He came forward and offered a shallow bow.

'Forgive the intrusion, Your Highness. My name is Anwar Hanuf, a surrogate uncle to His Highness.'

Esme nodded. 'Yes, you're one of his advisors. I remember you from the wedding.'

He smiled. 'It's kind of you to recall our brief meeting.'

Nodding again, she indicated a chair. 'What can I do for you?' she said after they'd sat down and he'd declined refreshments.

'I'm afraid I'm going to be blunt.'

Her stomach dipped but she kept her composure. 'I can do blunt.'

'You've seen the crowd gathered outside the palace gate, I'm sure.'

'Yes, I have.'

'In my experience situations like this only escalate unless they're dealt with.'

'I would gladly talk to them, but sadly I've been forbidden from leaving the palace.'

He nodded. 'For your safety and that of our future ruler, that is the right decision.'

'Is it? Only I would've liked to have been consulted before those decisions were made regarding my safety. Sadly, my husband seems to have fallen off the face of the earth.'

A look crossed his face and her breath caught. 'You know where Zaid is, don't you?'

'That is not why I'm here—'

'Is he planning on coming back here anytime soon?' she blurted.

He sighed. 'It's time to do the right thing, Miss Scott.'

She wanted to tell him her name was Esme Al-Ameen, but the cold tingling at her nape pushed the words back down.

'The people's hearts and their trust have been broken. You need to cauterise the wounds so they can heal. Or we'll only be going backwards.'

'What exactly are you asking of me?'

He stared fixedly at her. 'I think you know.' He rose and bowed. 'Good day to you, Miss Scott.'

Sorrow scraped at her insides as her heart dropped to her feet. Two emissaries, bearing the same message. She couldn't bury her head in the sand any more. She placed the calls she needed to make, then dialled the number of the palace security team.

'This is Sultana Al-Ameen. I'm expecting guests at

the palace gates within the hour. Make sure they're admitted and shown every courtesy, then let me know when they're ready.'

'Yes, Your Highness.'

She put the phone down, feeling like a complete fraud. But she reassured herself that she'd never have to use her power and title again.

The vans started to arrive after half an hour.

When the call came, she rose and headed to the conference room. Lights mounted on powerful cameras and TV lenses erupted when she entered the room, and for the first time, she was glad of the bodyguards standing on alert nearby.

Tears threatened again but she swallowed hard and unfolded her piece of paper.

'Thank you for coming. And thank you to every single Ja'ahrian who has made me feel welcome since my arrival. I've fallen in love with this beautiful country and been proud to call it my home.' She cleared her throat. 'But I also realise that I've been very unfair to you. My father's and my less than stellar pasts should not be the burden of the people. My mistakes should not be the cause of your unhappiness. So from this moment, I renounce my position as your Sultana. I should not have taken the position in the first place, not without baring my heart and showing you the whole truth. But I hope you will still accept your Sultan's child when he or she is born. Our baby is innocent in all this. Please don't let him or her pay for my mistakes. The same goes for your Sultan, Zaid Al-Ameen. He deserves better than me. But most of all he deserves your love, your respect and your understanding. I leave him in your tender care. *Shukraan*, Ja'ahr.'

She stepped off the podium and let the bodyguards steer her away from the barrage of questions that exploded through the room. She managed to hold it together until she was safely behind closed doors. Then she hugged her arms around her body and sobbed. When there were no more tears left, she trudged to her dressing room. She was folding her black dress into the small pile on the centre island when a white-faced Nashwa rushed in.

Esme smiled sadly. 'Can you find a suitcase for me? I can't seem to find one anywhere. An overnight bag will do.' She'd never got round to giving up her flat in London. She could slot back into being Esme Scott as if she'd never left.

'But…where are you going, Your Highness?' Nashwa shrieked. 'And what you said on the TV…'

'I'm sorry you had to find out that way. But I really need the bag. Please?'

Nashwa stared at her for long seconds before she plugged her fist in her mouth and fled the room. On automatic, Esme resumed gathering her things. Half an hour later, when it was clear Nashwa wasn't going to return, Esme looked through her shelves and took down the biggest handbag she could find. She was stuffing the meagre belongings into it when the bedroom door slammed back on its hinges.

A moment later, Zaid stood framed in the door of her dressing room.

'What did you do, *habiba*?' he breathed raggedly. 'What the *hell* did you do?'

The sight of him. Oh, God. He looked terrible, thick stubble bracing his jaw. He'd suffered. Because of her. And still she trembled from head to toe with the purely selfish need to rush into his arms, clasp herself to his wonderful strength. But she held herself still. 'It was the right thing to do,' she murmured.

Fists clenched tight, he crossed the room in five quick strides. 'No, it wasn't, you fool! Are you going to try and leave me every time my back is turned?'

'Don't shout at me. Not after pulling another disappearing act on me.'

He took another step closer, bringing his bristling, glorious body within touching distance. 'I'll do whatever I want when you act like…like…' He clawed a hand through his hair. 'Like the noblest sacrificial lamb to an undeserving bastard.'

Her mouth dropped open. 'What?'

'What you said on TV was—'

'All true.'

He cupped her jaw oh-so-gently. 'No, *jamila*, not all true. What happened was unfortunate and wrong. But your father was the one who took his money. Not you. You were still a child, caught on the end of her father's puppet strings. A father who, I'm guessing, liked to dangle the threat of leaving you very often?'

Pain ripped through her as she nodded. 'I only spent the school holidays with him but even then he threatened me with foster care if I didn't toe his line.'

'And the fear of losing what is right in front of you is even worse than missing what you no longer have, isn't it?'

'Yes. So much more.' Her voice broke and a sob ripped free.

His thumbs caressed her cheeks. 'Shh, *habiba*. Don't cry. It pains me to see your tears.'

'Why? You walked away from me. You were furious with me.'

'Yes, but I was never far away from you. I can never be. I started off being angry with you because a loss of life is personal to me. I also lost sight of the fact that I was a child once too. I know what the pain of losing a parent feels like. After losing your mother, you lived in constant threat of losing your remaining parent, even if you'd have been better off without him.'

She nodded. 'One time, when I was sixteen, I woke up

one morning in our hotel, and Jeffrey was gone. No note, nothing. I'd refused to help him land a mark the night before. He was livid. I was in a strange country and terrified. He capitalised on that. I promised myself the moment I turned eighteen that I would walk away from him. I wish I'd stayed away from Bryan too.'

He nodded, his face set. 'I know. But there's something you don't know. I had Atkins investigated.'

She frowned. 'And?'

'He suffered from severe depression and had attempted suicide more than once.'

Her heart squeezed. 'That doesn't make it any better.'

'No, but he went to Vegas with the aim of blowing all his inheritance and then ending his life that weekend.'

'Oh, God.'

'It's cold comfort, I know, *habiba*, but his mind was made up. But you have people who need you, who love you. Do you know that since your press conference there's been an online petition for you to stay?'

'What?'

'If you renounce your title I'll renounce mine too.'

She gasped. 'You can't. Your people need you. Anwar said—'

'To hell with what Anwar said. He thinks he was acting in my best interests. I'll talk to him later. And anyone else who thinks they know my heart. The only thing they need to know is that it won't beat without you. So where you go, I go.'

'No, Zaid, you're better off—'

'Without my heart? Without my soul? Without the very air I need to live? No, *jamila*. I might as well be dead then.'

'Oh, Zaid…'

His fingers slid into her hair, and he leaned down to brush her lips with his. 'I was going to tell you I loved you that afternoon on the deck. You know that?'

Her gasp whispered over his lips. 'You love me?'

'Oh, yes, my love. So very much. Fawzi couldn't have picked a worse time to deliver his news. I think it's partly why I behaved like a wounded bear. I'm sorry, Esmeralda. Can you forgive me?'

'I forgive you, because I love you too. I managed to tell you, though, remember?'

He grimaced, although his face transformed at her confession. 'I remember, and I'm ashamed to have rejected it then. I would be honoured if you would tell me again.'

'I love you, Zaid Al-Ameen.'

He sealed her lips in a kiss that lifted her heart and her soul. Her heart grew bigger when his hand dropped to caress her belly. 'And you'll remain the wife of my heart? The mother of this beautiful blessing bestowed on us and the many more to come?'

'Yes, Zaid.'

He exhaled shakily, kissed her one more time, before sweeping her off her feet.

A long while later, they lay, blissful, content and gloriously naked on her bed.

With a smile, she caressed his hard chest. 'So did I cause a lot of trouble renouncing my title?'

He chuckled richly. 'It takes a hell of a lot more than a speech to give me up, *habiba*. But attempt it again and I will have you jump through a lifetime of hoops. Even then you won't be free.'

'And why not?'

He rolled her over in one smooth move and braced her hands above her head. 'Because Al-Ameens marry for life. I'm never letting you go. Not even in the afterlife,' he growled.

She leaned up and kissed his beautiful mouth, her heart brimming with happiness. 'That's good, because your Sultana is happy exactly where she is. By your side. For ever.'

EPILOGUE

One year later

'ARE YOU GOING to re-create our honeymoon *exactly* the way it happened last year?' Esme laughed as her husband rolled towards her and trailed a kiss over her shoulder.

'Right up to the point where I ruined it, yes. And then I intend to make it all better from then on. I want the memory erased from your mind for ever.'

'It's already better for me, Zaid. I promise,' she murmured, gliding her fingers through his thick black hair when he levered himself over her.

He placed a lingering kiss on her lips before he raised his head. 'Shhh, don't spoil my plans.' He glanced at his phone nearby. 'It's almost three fifteen. One more minute,' he murmured.

Esme's eyebrows rose. 'You remember the exact time?'

'It was supposed to be a momentous occasion, *jamila*. It's imprinted in my memory.'

The phone beeped softly. Zaid's gaze shifted from it to her face, his features settling into the same mask of love and devotion she'd witnessed so many times in the past year.

'I love you, Esmeralda. So much more than I ever thought I could love anyone. I thank Allah every day that he brought you to me. That you found space in your heart for me. Everything that I am is devoted to you. I will love you even after the breath leaves my body.'

'Oh, Zaid... I love you, too. So much it hurts sometimes.'

He lowered his head and they sealed their love with a

kiss. Then he raised his head and elevated a brow. 'So, are you happy you stayed?'

She laughed. 'Ecstatic. Not that I had a choice after my renunciation of my title was so thoroughly rejected.'

They both laughed, then her joy dimmed a little.

Zaid caressed a thumb down her cheek. 'You're thinking about your father again.'

She nodded. 'Being a mother myself now, feeling the way I do about Amir, it hurts to think that I was so unlovable that he couldn't—'

'No, *habiba*. It wasn't you who was unlovable. It was your father. Not everyone is cut out to be a father. He failed in his duty to you and to your mother. You have nothing to blame yourself for.'

Although she nodded, her heart shook with sadness as she thought of all the opportunities she would never have.

Jeffrey Scott's death in prison from a heart attack two months into his eight-year prison sentence had come as a shock. Despite everything, Esme mourned the fact that they would never have a normal loving relationship and that he'd never get to meet her beloved son, Amir. But that too was something she would eventually put behind her.

Especially when she had more love than she could ever dream of from the husband of her wildest dreams and the son who made her heart burst with gratitude and joy every day.

As if summoned, Aisha mounted the steps to the deck with her precious bundle cradled in her arms.

'Ah, a much better interruption this time round,' Zaid observed with immense satisfaction. 'Although I was hoping to follow that declaration of love with a very physical demonstration.'

Esme smiled and dropped a kiss on his mouth. 'You'll get your chance later, I promise.'

'I'll hold you to that,' he drawled. Then sat up to hold out his arms for his son.

She watched him cradle their son in his strong arms, his face a picture of utter bliss. And then, just because she couldn't help herself, Esme rose too, and put her arms around both her men.

The man of her heart glanced up and smiled, deep abiding love blazing in eyes. 'I love you, Esmeralda.'

The last of her sadness evaporated. 'I love you, too, my Sultan.'

In the brilliant sunlight, the son of her soul gurgled happily as he watched his parents seal their love with one more kiss.

* * * * *